MW00795500

FINAL EDITION
Volume 2

STORY
Rick Remender

THE
LAST GOODBYE

PENCILS
Tony Moore

INKS, CH. 1-2
ANDE PARKS

INKS, CH. 3-4
RICK REMENDER

COLORS
LEE LOUGHRIDGE

HATCHET JOB

PENCILS & INKS, FINISHES CH. 4 & 5
Jerome Opeña

PENCILS CH. 4 & 5
Kieron Dwyer

COLORS
MICHELLE MADSEN

LETTERS
RUS WOOTON

COVER BY
TONY MOORE

FEAR AGENT CREATED BY **RICK REMENDER**,
TONY MOORE AND **JEROME OPEÑA**

FEAR AGENT LOGO BY **RICK REMENDER**

COLLECTION DESIGN BY **JEFF POWELL**

IMAGE COMICS, INC.

Robert Kirkman: Chief Operating Officer
Erik Larsen: Chief Financial Officer
Todd McFarlane: President
Marc Silvestri: Chief Executive Officer
Jim Valentino: Vice President
Eric Stephenson: Publisher / Chief Creative Officer
Corey Hart: Director of Sales
Jeff Boison: Director of Publishing Planning & Book Trade Sales
Chris Ross: Director of Digital Sales
Jeff Stang: Director of Specialty Sales
Kat Salazar: Director of PR & Marketing
Drew Gill: Art Director
Heather Doornink: Production Director
Nicole Lapalme: Controller
IMAGECOMICS.COM

FEAR AGENT: FINAL EDITION, VOLUME 2. First printing. July 2018. Published by Image Comics, Inc. Office of publication: 2701 NW Vaughn St., Suite 780, Portland, OR 97210. Copyright © 2018 Rick Remender and Tony Moore. All rights reserved. Contains material originally published in single magazine form as FEAR AGENT #12-15 and 17-21. "Fear Agent," its logos, and the likenesses of all characters herein are trademarks of Rick Remender and Tony Moore, unless otherwise noted. "Image" and the Image Comics logos are registered trademarks of Image Comics, Inc. No part of this publication may be reproduced or transmitted, in any form or by any means (except for short excerpts for journalistic or review purposes), without the express written permission of Rick Remender, or Image Comics, Inc. All names, characters, events, and locales in this publication are entirely fictional. Any resemblance to actual persons (living or dead), events, or places, without satirical intent, is coincidental. Printed in the USA. For information regarding the CPSIA on this printed material call: 203-595-3636 and provide reference #RICH-801005. For international rights, contact: foreignlicensing@imagecomics.com. ISBN: 978-1-5343-0824-4

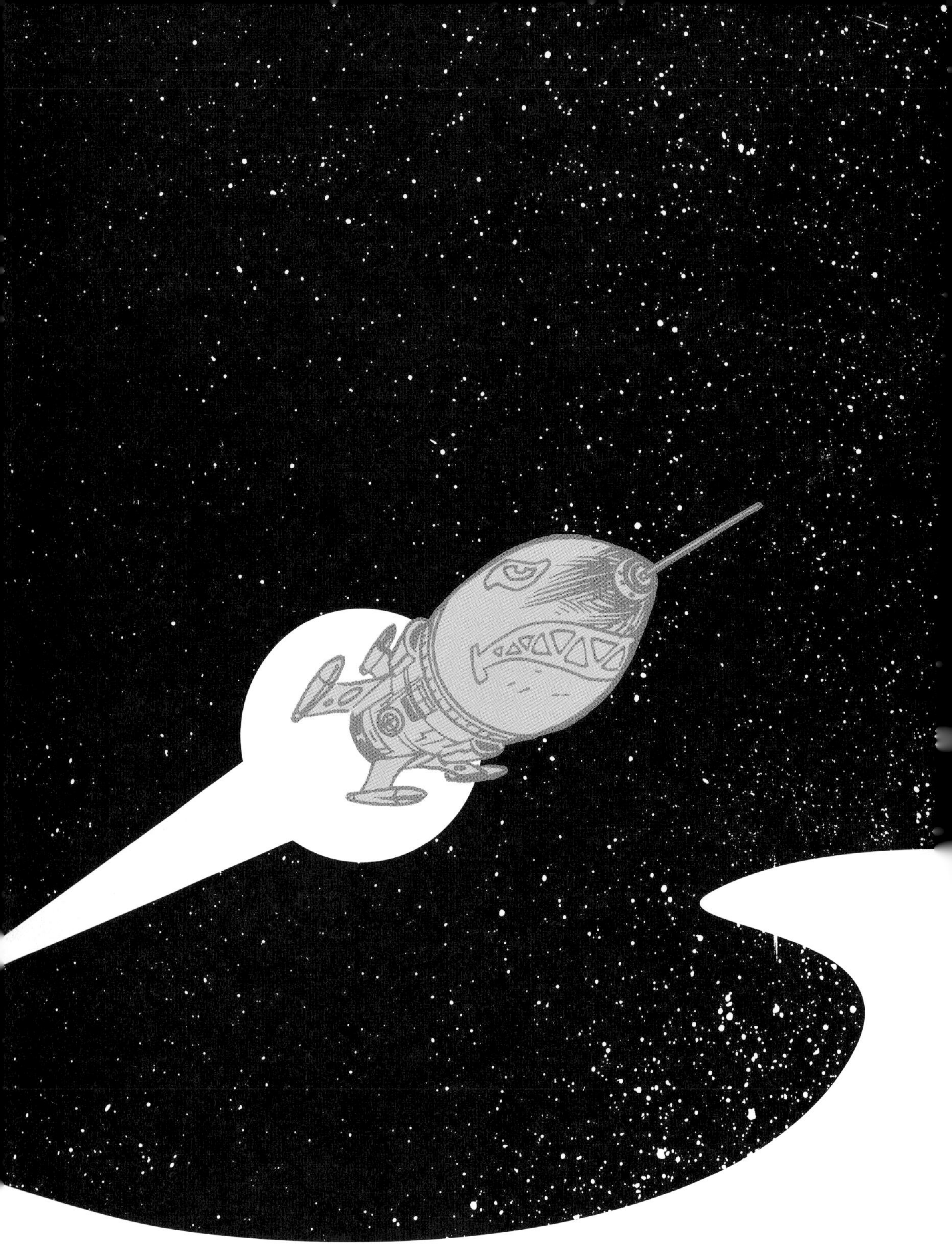

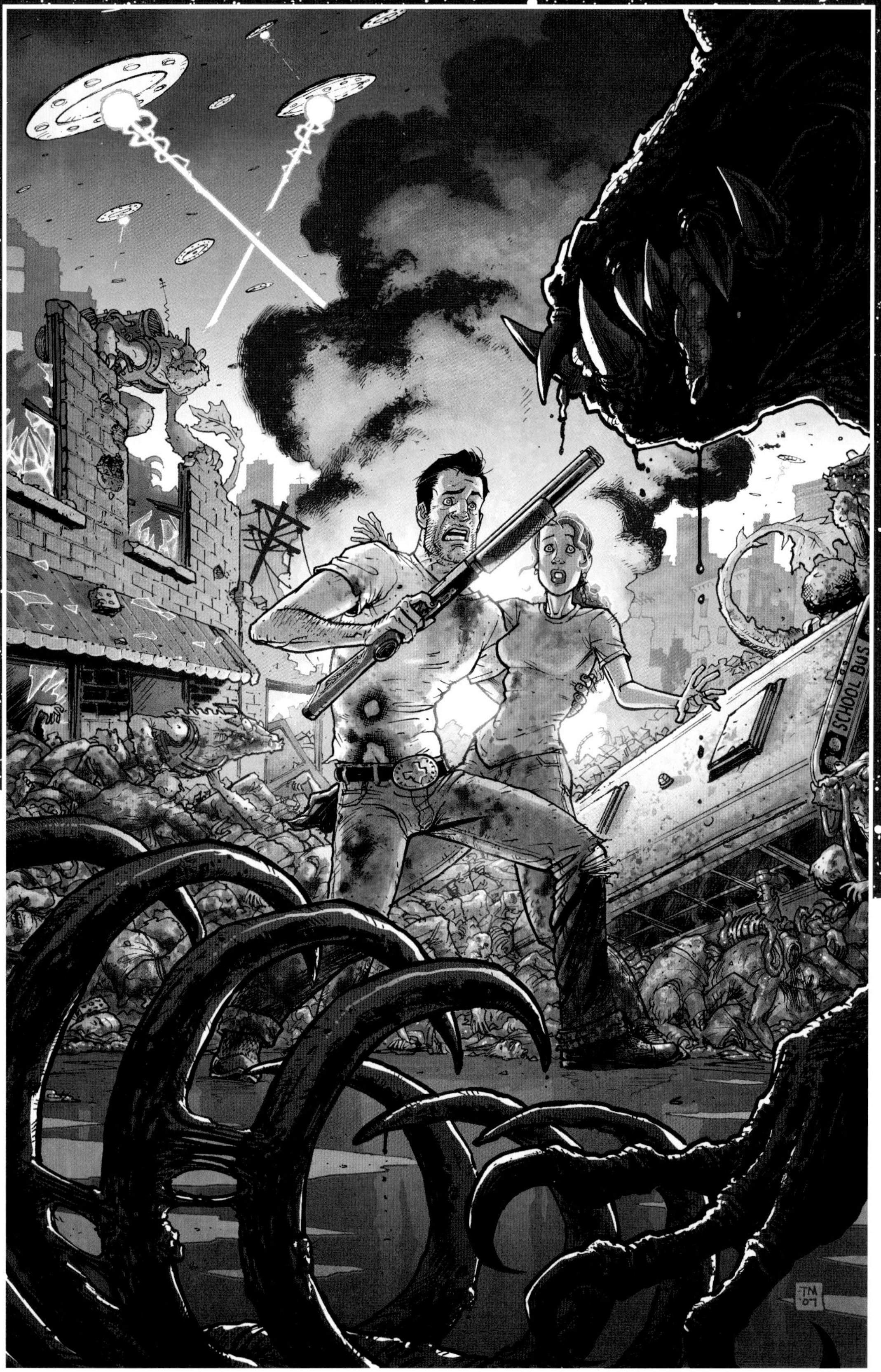
SCHOOL BUS

FEAR AGENT #12

ART BY **TONY MOORE**

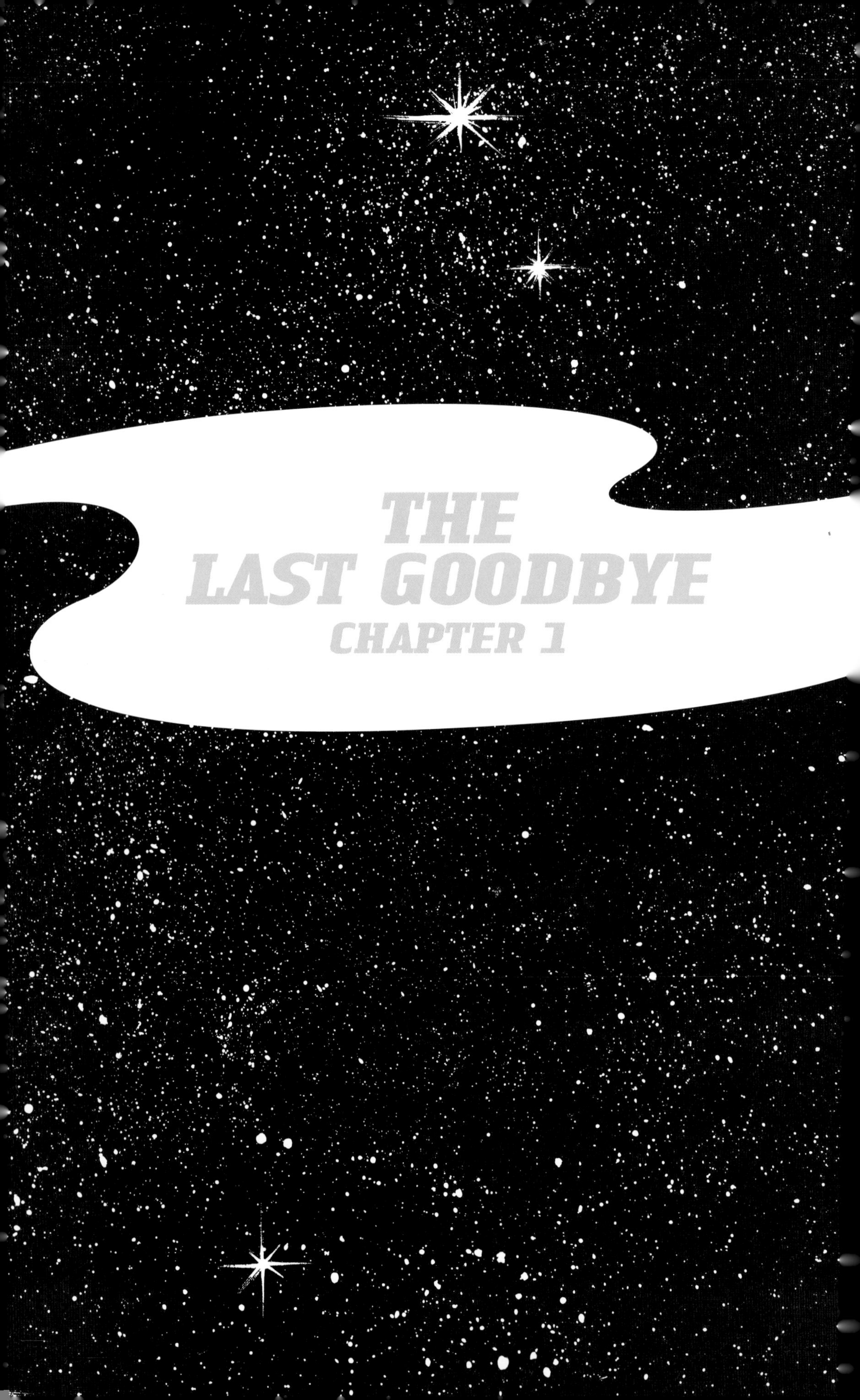
THE
LAST GOODBYE
CHAPTER 1

FEAR AGENT

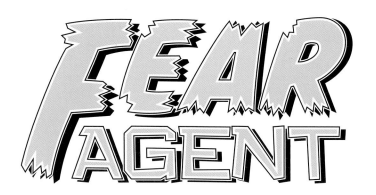

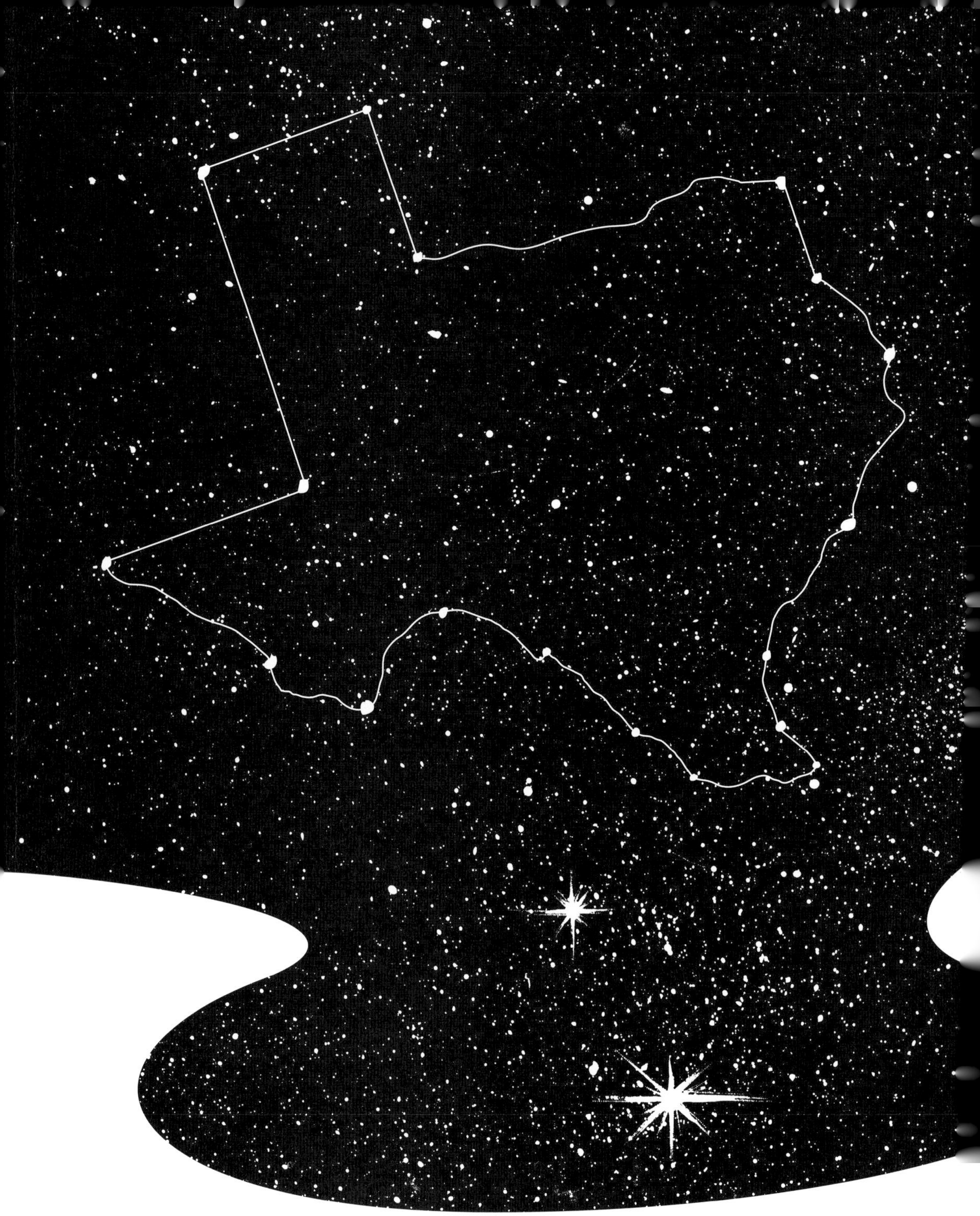

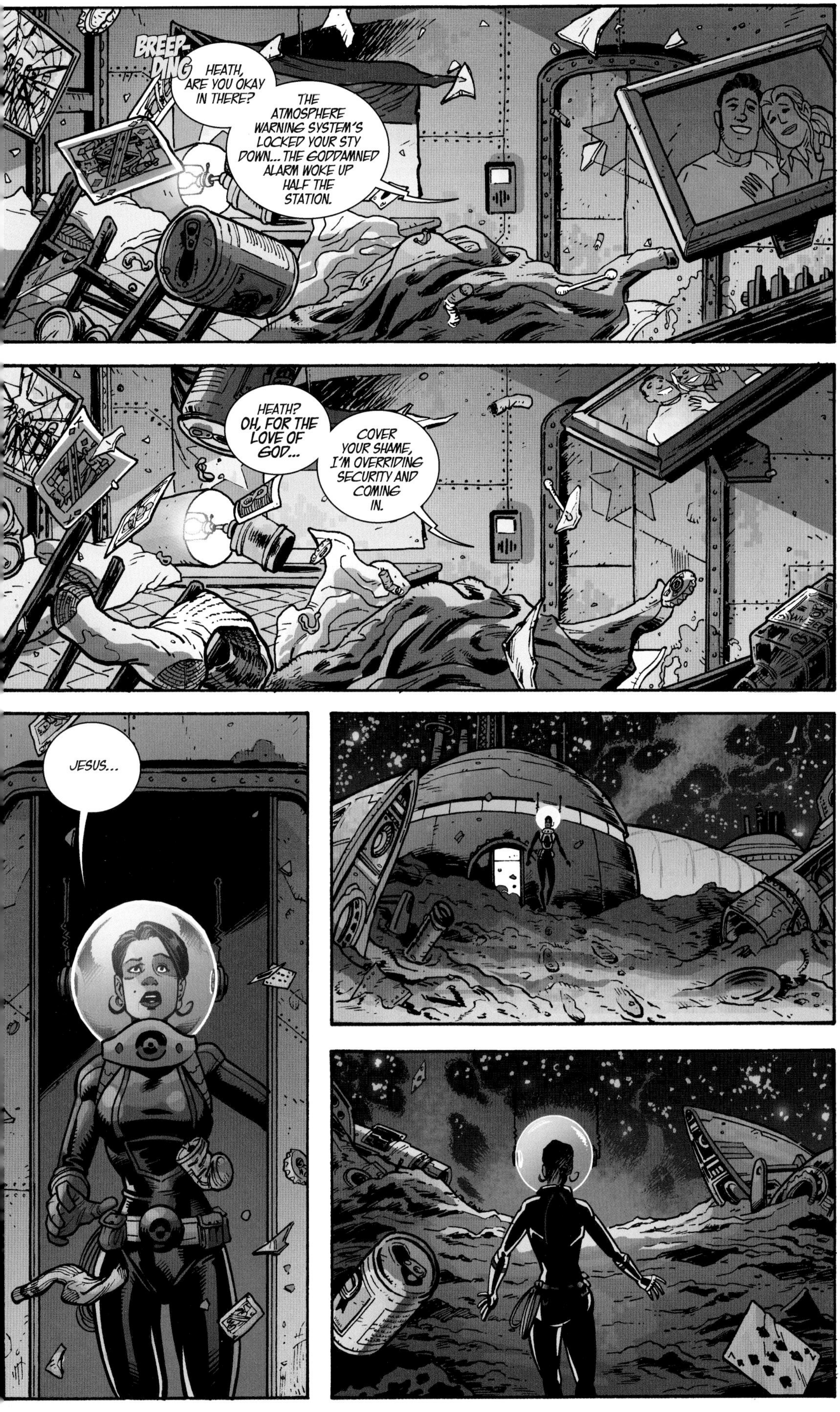
BREEP-DING
HEATH, ARE YOU OKAY IN THERE?
THE ATMOSPHERE WARNING SYSTEM'S LOCKED YOUR STY DOWN... THE GODDAMNED ALARM WOKE UP HALF THE STATION.
HEATH? OH, FOR THE LOVE OF GOD...
COVER YOUR SHAME, I'M OVERRIDING SECURITY AND COMING IN.
JESUS...

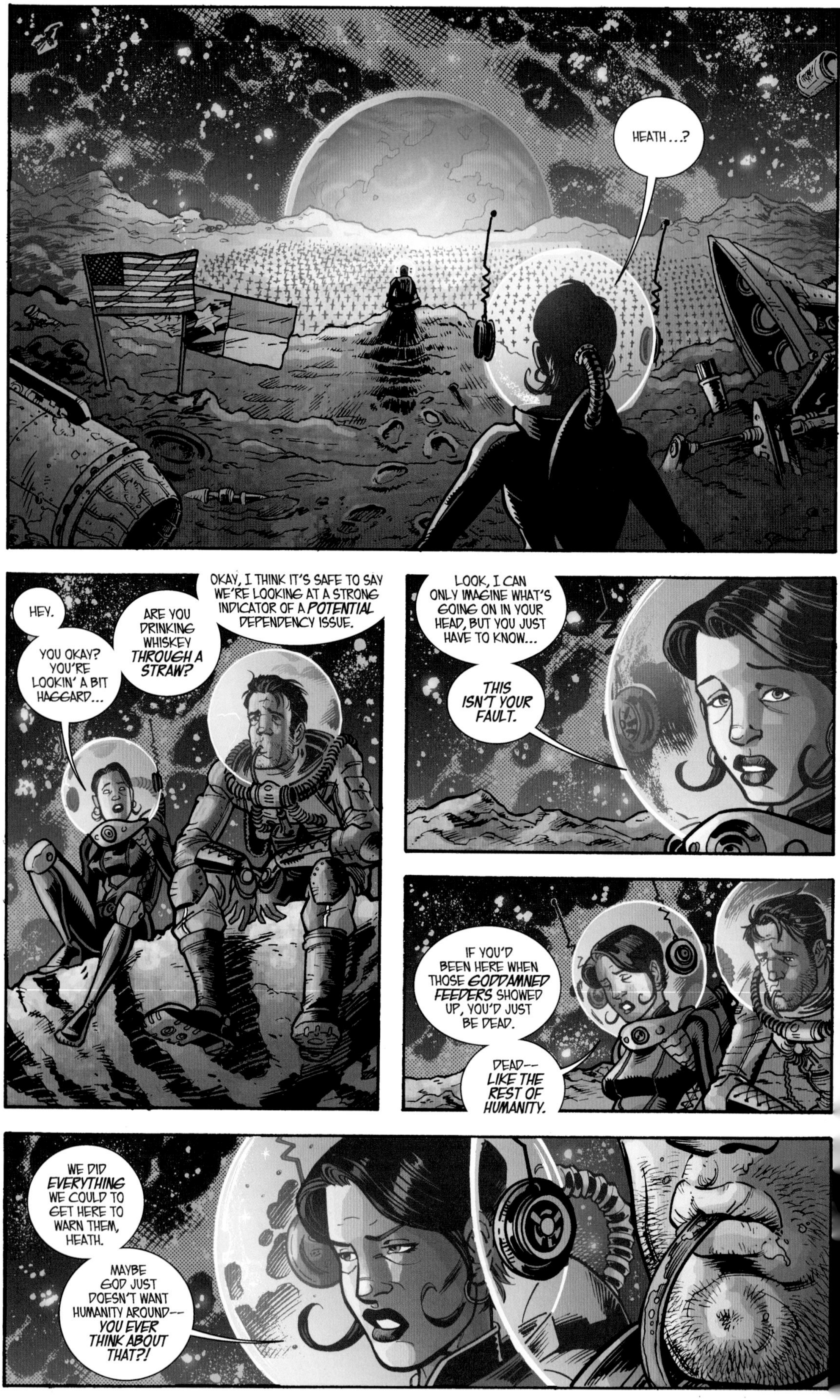
HEATH...?
HEY.
YOU OKAY? YOU'RE LOOKIN' A BIT HAGGARD...
ARE YOU DRINKING WHISKEY THROUGH A STRAW?
OKAY, I THINK IT'S SAFE TO SAY WE'RE LOOKING AT A STRONG INDICATOR OF A POTENTIAL DEPENDENCY ISSUE.
LOOK, I CAN ONLY IMAGINE WHAT'S GOING ON IN YOUR HEAD, BUT YOU JUST HAVE TO KNOW...
THIS ISN'T YOUR FAULT.
IF YOU'D BEEN HERE WHEN THOSE GODDAMNED FEEDERS SHOWED UP, YOU'D JUST BE DEAD.
DEAD-- LIKE THE REST OF HUMANITY.
WE DID EVERYTHING WE COULD TO GET HERE TO WARN THEM, HEATH.
MAYBE GOD JUST DOESN'T WANT HUMANITY AROUND-- YOU EVER THINK ABOUT THAT?!

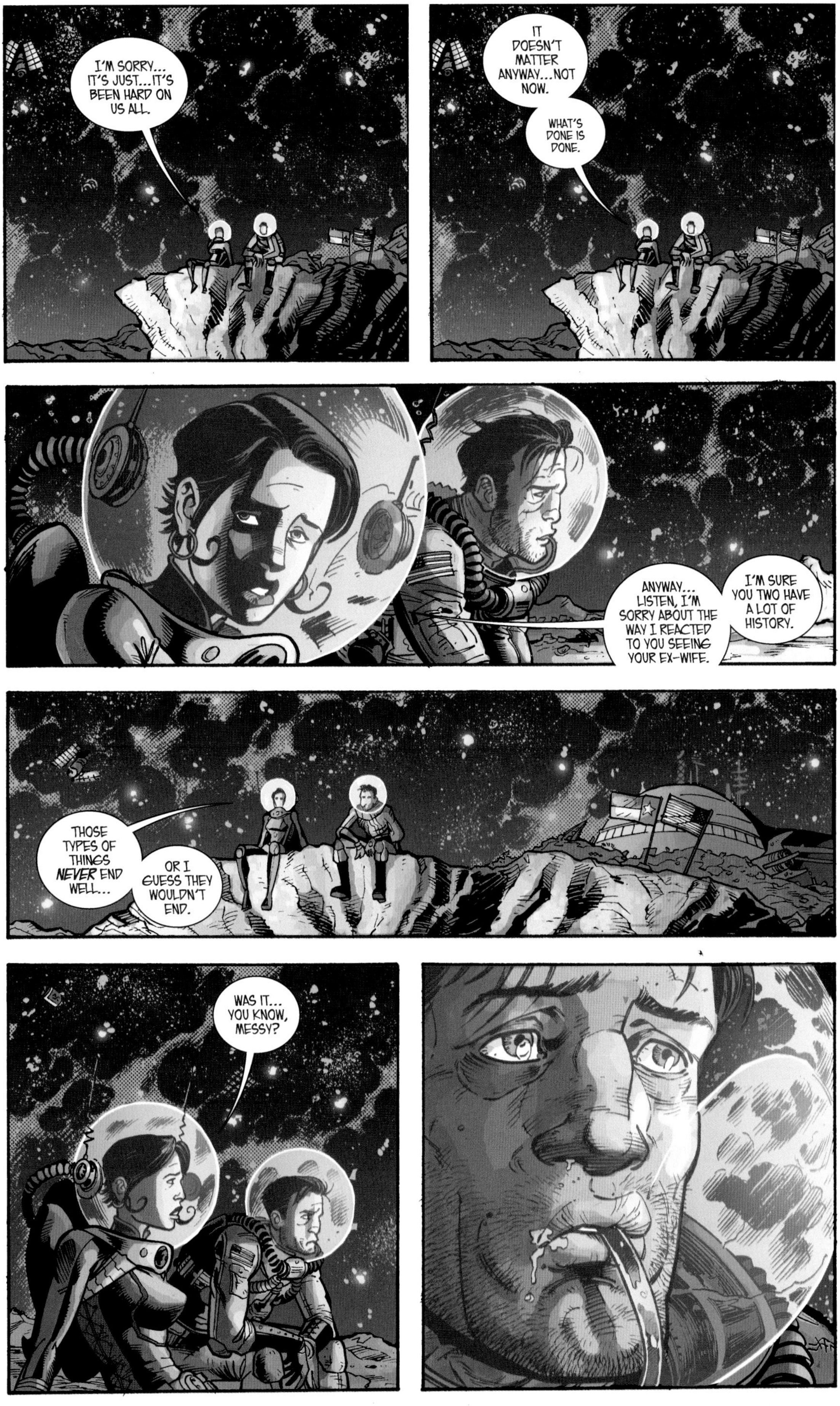
I'M SORRY... IT'S JUST...IT'S BEEN HARD ON US ALL.
IT DOESN'T MATTER ANYWAY...NOT NOW.
WHAT'S DONE IS DONE.
ANYWAY... LISTEN, I'M SORRY ABOUT THE WAY I REACTED TO YOU SEEING YOUR EX-WIFE.
I'M SURE YOU TWO HAVE A LOT OF HISTORY.
THOSE TYPES OF THINGS *NEVER* END WELL...
OR I GUESS THEY WOULDN'T END.
WAS IT... YOU KNOW, MESSY?

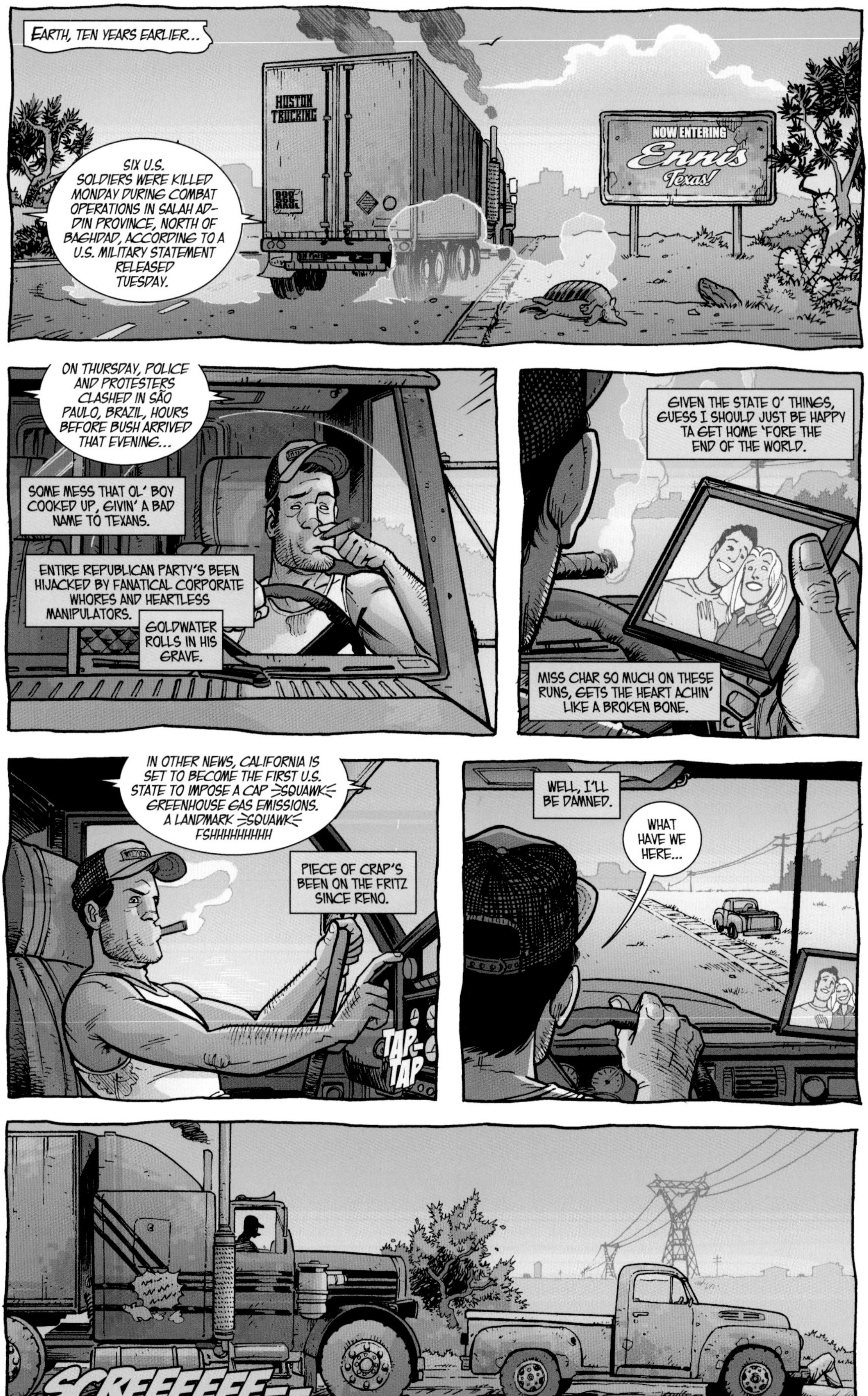
EARTH, TEN YEARS EARLIER...
HUSTON TRUCKING
NOW ENTERING Ennis Texas!
SIX U.S. SOLDIERS WERE KILLED MONDAY DURING COMBAT OPERATIONS IN SALAH AD-DIN PROVINCE, NORTH OF BAGHDAD, ACCORDING TO A U.S. MILITARY STATEMENT RELEASED TUESDAY.
ON THURSDAY, POLICE AND PROTESTERS CLASHED IN SÃO PAULO, BRAZIL, HOURS BEFORE BUSH ARRIVED THAT EVENING...
SOME MESS THAT OL' BOY COOKED UP, GIVIN' A BAD NAME TO TEXANS.
ENTIRE REPUBLICAN PARTY'S BEEN HIJACKED BY FANATICAL CORPORATE WHORES AND HEARTLESS MANIPULATORS.
GOLDWATER ROLLS IN HIS GRAVE.
GIVEN THE STATE O' THINGS, GUESS I SHOULD JUST BE HAPPY TA GET HOME 'FORE THE END OF THE WORLD.
MISS CHAR SO MUCH ON THESE RUNS, GETS THE HEART ACHIN' LIKE A BROKEN BONE.
IN OTHER NEWS, CALIFORNIA IS SET TO BECOME THE FIRST U.S. STATE TO IMPOSE A CAP =SQUAWK= GREENHOUSE GAS EMISSIONS. A LANDMARK =SQUAWK= FSHHHHHHHHH
PIECE OF CRAP'S BEEN ON THE FRITZ SINCE RENO.
TAP-TAP
WELL, I'LL BE DAMNED.
WHAT HAVE WE HERE...
SCREEEEEEE--

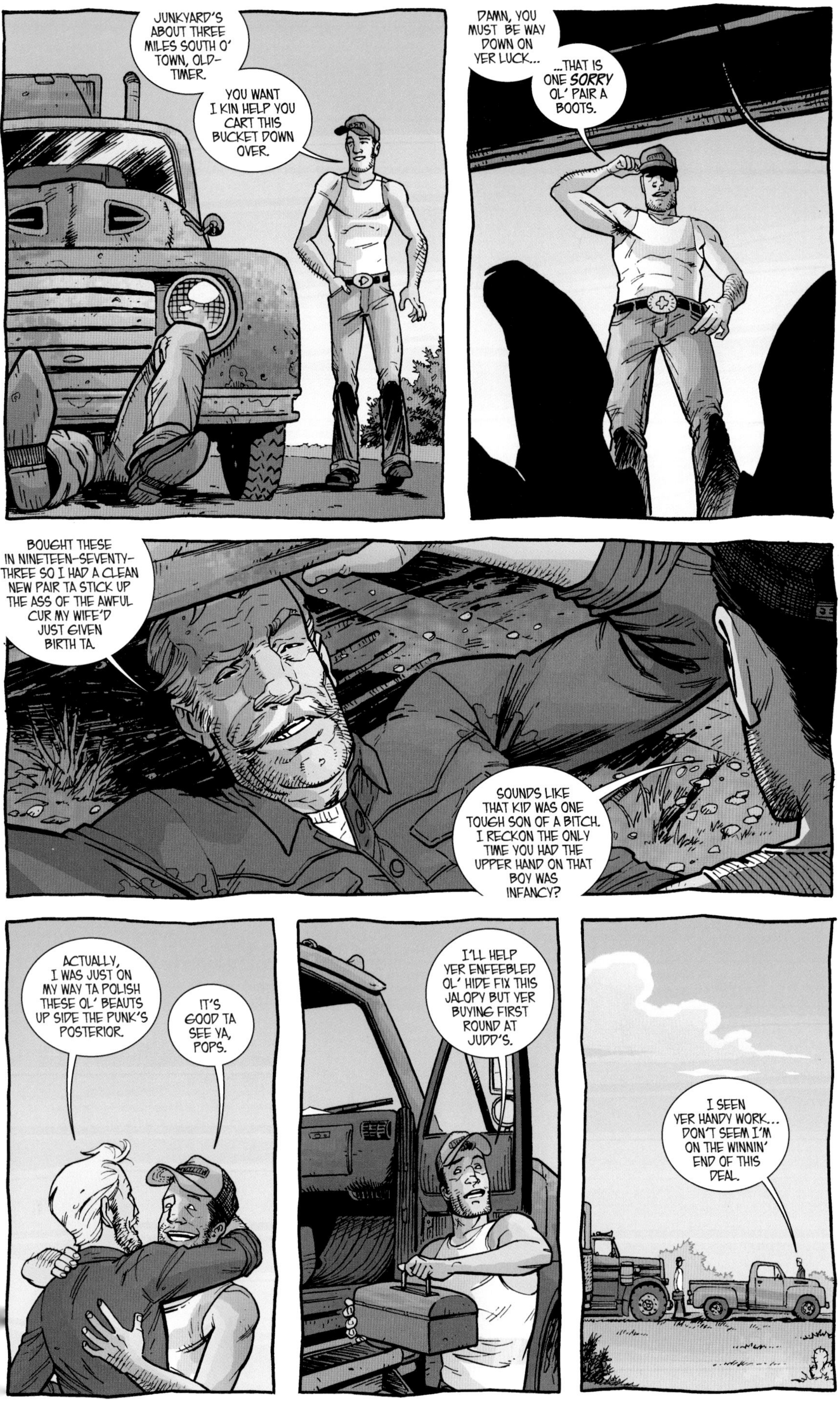
JUNKYARD'S ABOUT THREE MILES SOUTH O' TOWN, OLD-TIMER.
YOU WANT I KIN HELP YOU CART THIS BUCKET DOWN OVER.
DAMN, YOU MUST BE WAY DOWN ON YER LUCK...
...THAT IS ONE SORRY OL' PAIR A BOOTS.
BOUGHT THESE IN NINETEEN-SEVENTY-THREE SO I HAD A CLEAN NEW PAIR TA STICK UP THE ASS OF THE AWFUL CUR MY WIFE'D JUST GIVEN BIRTH TA.
SOUNDS LIKE THAT KID WAS ONE TOUGH SON OF A BITCH. I RECKON THE ONLY TIME YOU HAD THE UPPER HAND ON THAT BOY WAS INFANCY?
ACTUALLY, I WAS JUST ON MY WAY TA POLISH THESE OL' BEAUTS UP SIDE THE PUNK'S POSTERIOR.
IT'S GOOD TA SEE YA, POPS.
I'LL HELP YER ENFEEBLED OL' HIDE FIX THIS JALOPY BUT YER BUYING FIRST ROUND AT JUDD'S.
I SEEN YER HANDY WORK... DON'T SEEM I'M ON THE WINNIN' END OF THIS DEAL.

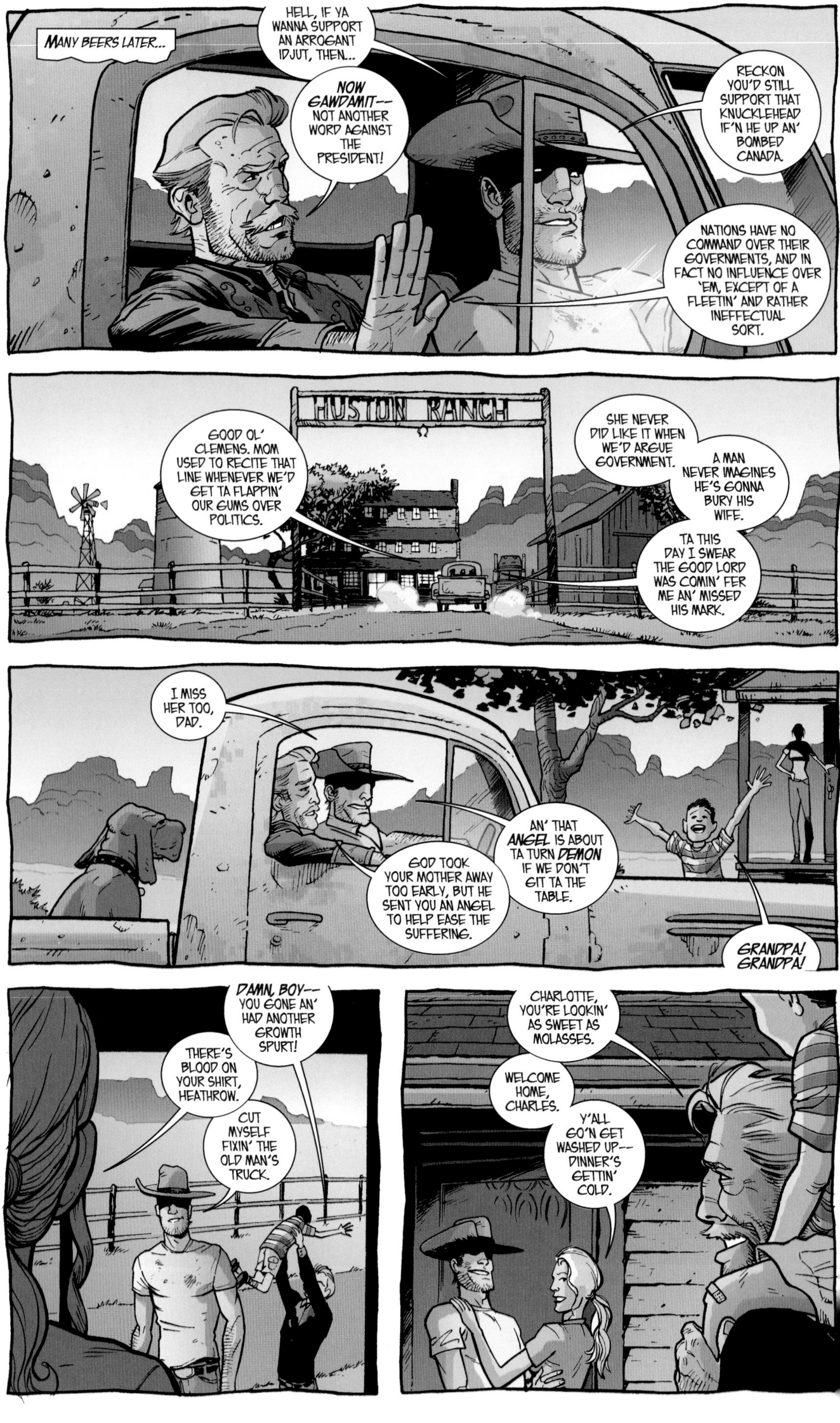
MANY BEERS LATER...
HELL, IF YA WANNA SUPPORT AN ARROGANT IDJUT, THEN...
NOW GAWDAMIT-- NOT ANOTHER WORD AGAINST THE PRESIDENT!
RECKON YOU'D STILL SUPPORT THAT KNUCKLEHEAD IF'N HE UP AN' BOMBED CANADA.
NATIONS HAVE NO COMMAND OVER THEIR GOVERNMENTS, AND IN FACT NO INFLUENCE OVER 'EM, EXCEPT OF A FLEETIN' AND RATHER INEFFECTUAL SORT.
HUSTON RANCH
GOOD OL' CLEMENS. MOM USED TO RECITE THAT LINE WHENEVER WE'D GET TA FLAPPIN' OUR GUMS OVER POLITICS.
SHE NEVER DID LIKE IT WHEN WE'D ARGUE GOVERNMENT.
A MAN NEVER IMAGINES HE'S GONNA BURY HIS WIFE.
TA THIS DAY I SWEAR THE GOOD LORD WAS COMIN' FER ME AN' MISSED HIS MARK.
I MISS HER TOO, DAD.
GOD TOOK YOUR MOTHER AWAY TOO EARLY, BUT HE SENT YOU AN ANGEL TO HELP EASE THE SUFFERING.
AN' THAT ANGEL IS ABOUT TA TURN DEMON IF WE DON'T GIT TA THE TABLE.
GRANDPA! GRANDPA!
DAMN, BOY-- YOU GONE AN' HAD ANOTHER GROWTH SPURT!
THERE'S BLOOD ON YOUR SHIRT, HEATHROW.
CUT MYSELF FIXIN' THE OLD MAN'S TRUCK.
CHARLOTTE, YOU'RE LOOKIN' AS SWEET AS MOLASSES.
WELCOME HOME, CHARLES.
Y'ALL GO'N GET WASHED UP-- DINNER'S GETTIN' COLD.

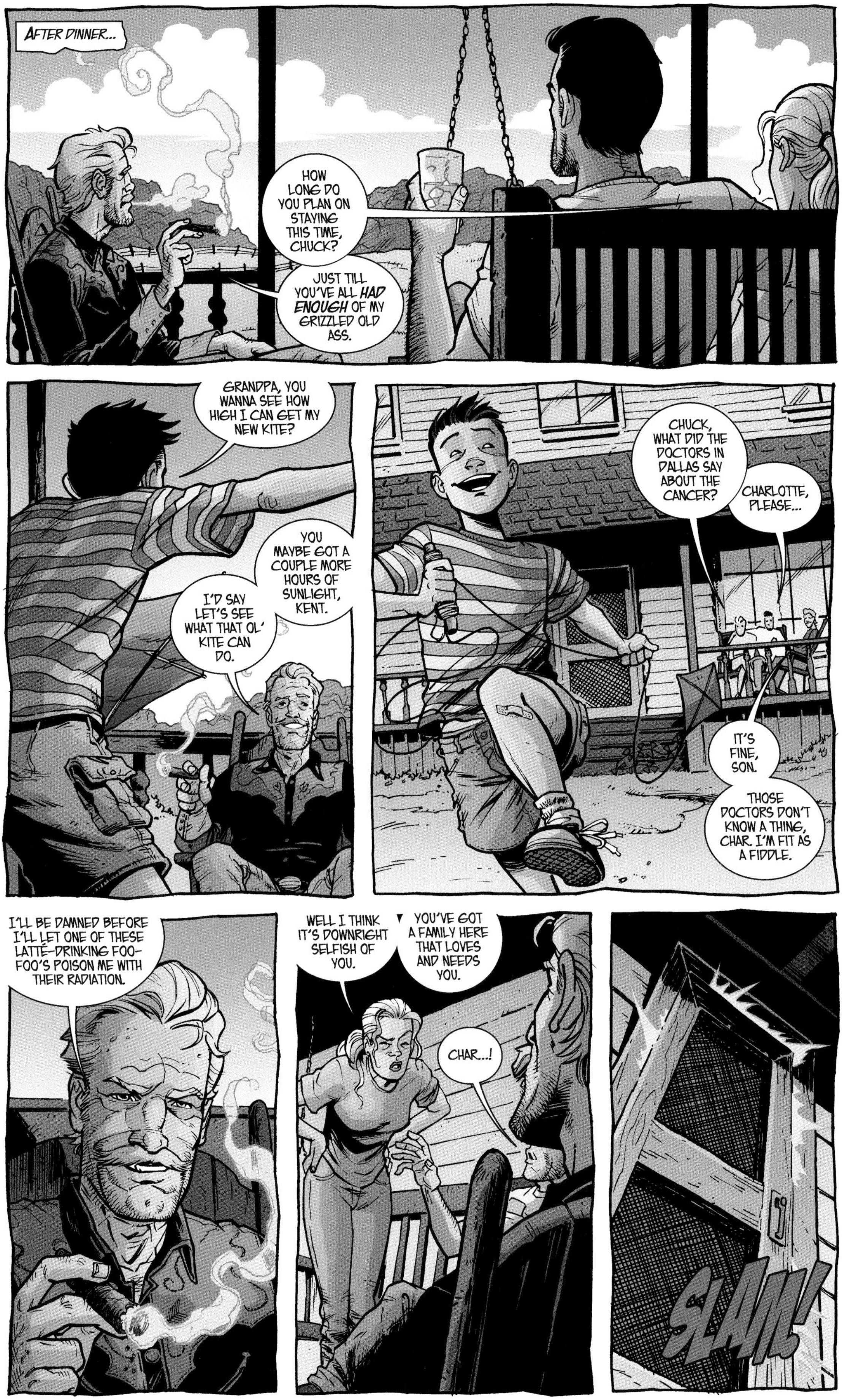
AFTER DINNER...
HOW LONG DO YOU PLAN ON STAYING THIS TIME, CHUCK?
JUST TILL YOU'VE ALL HAD ENOUGH OF MY GRIZZLED OLD ASS.
GRANDPA, YOU WANNA SEE HOW HIGH I CAN GET MY NEW KITE?
YOU MAYBE GOT A COUPLE MORE HOURS OF SUNLIGHT, KENT.
I'D SAY LET'S SEE WHAT THAT OL' KITE CAN DO.
CHUCK, WHAT DID THE DOCTORS IN DALLAS SAY ABOUT THE CANCER?
CHARLOTTE, PLEASE...
IT'S FINE, SON.
THOSE DOCTORS DON'T KNOW A THING, CHAR. I'M FIT AS A FIDDLE.
I'LL BE DAMNED BEFORE I'LL LET ONE OF THESE LATTÉ-DRINKING FOO-FOO'S POISON ME WITH THEIR RADIATION.
WELL I THINK IT'S DOWNRIGHT SELFISH OF YOU.
YOU'VE GOT A FAMILY HERE THAT LOVES AND NEEDS YOU.
CHAR...!
SLAM!

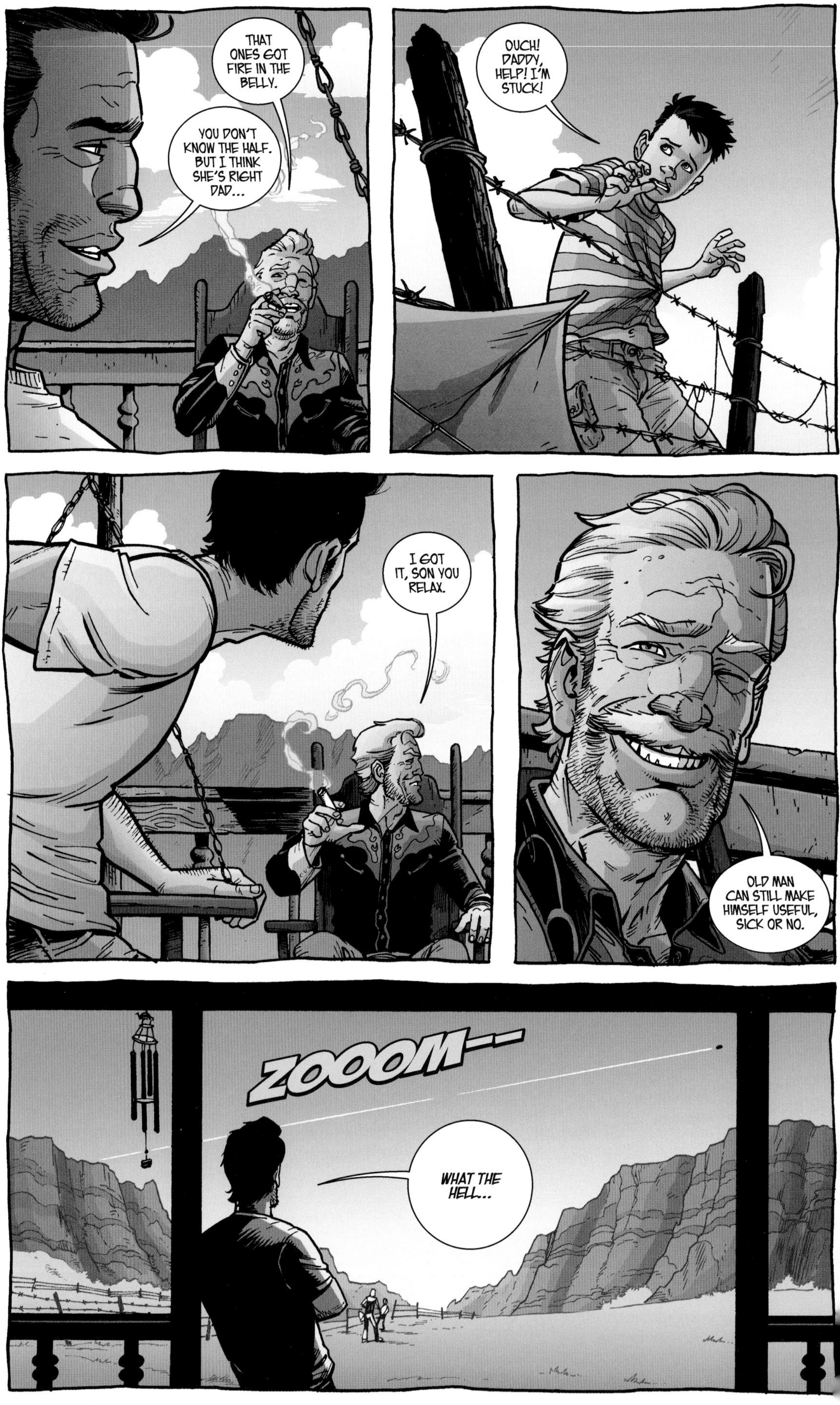
THAT ONES GOT FIRE IN THE BELLY.
YOU DON'T KNOW THE HALF. BUT I THINK SHE'S RIGHT DAD...
OUCH! DADDY, HELP! I'M STUCK!
I GOT IT, SON YOU RELAX.
OLD MAN CAN STILL MAKE HIMSELF USEFUL, SICK OR NO.
ZOOOM--
WHAT THE HELL...

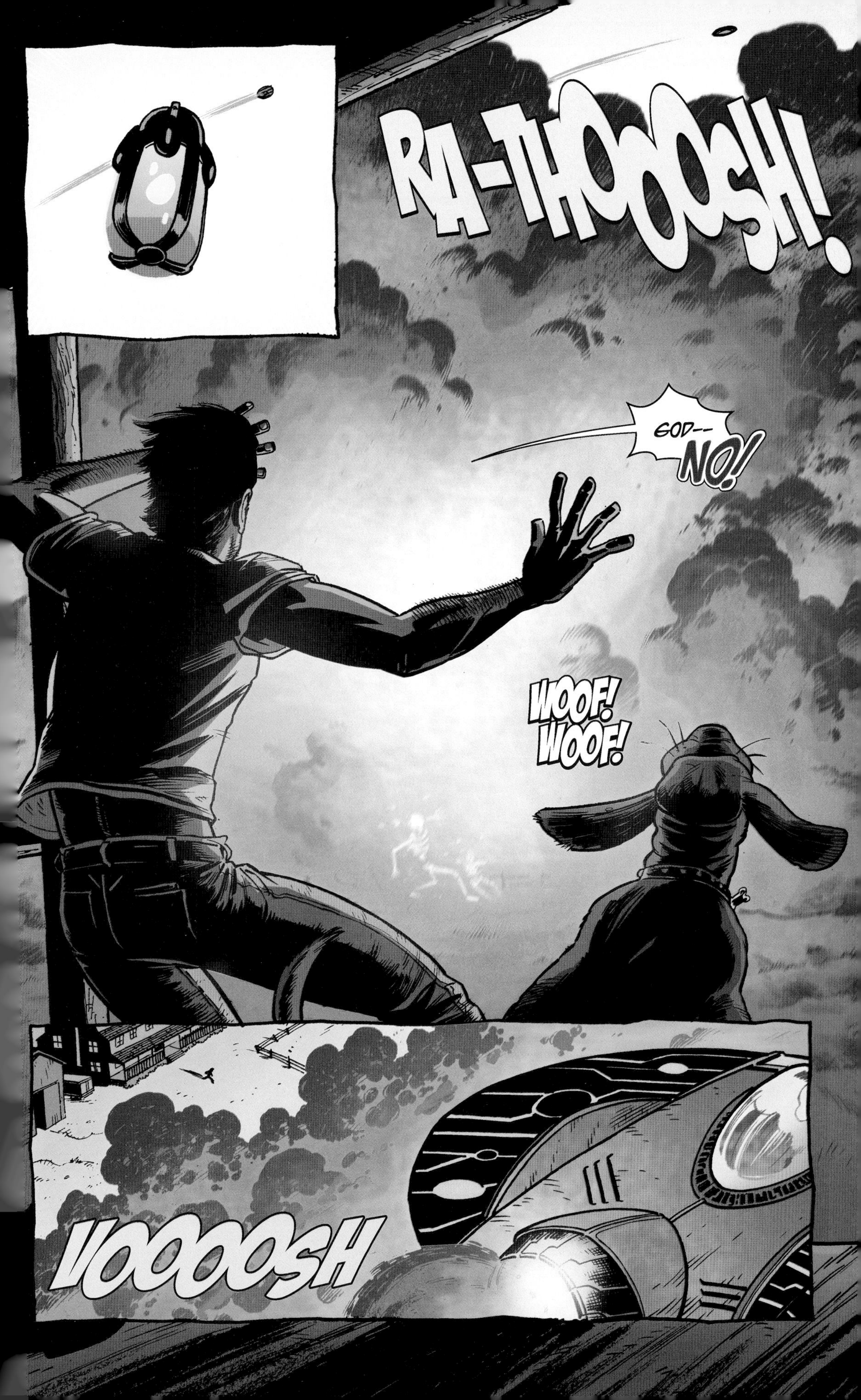
RA-THOOOOSH!
GOD--
NO!
WOOF! WOOF!
VOOOOSH

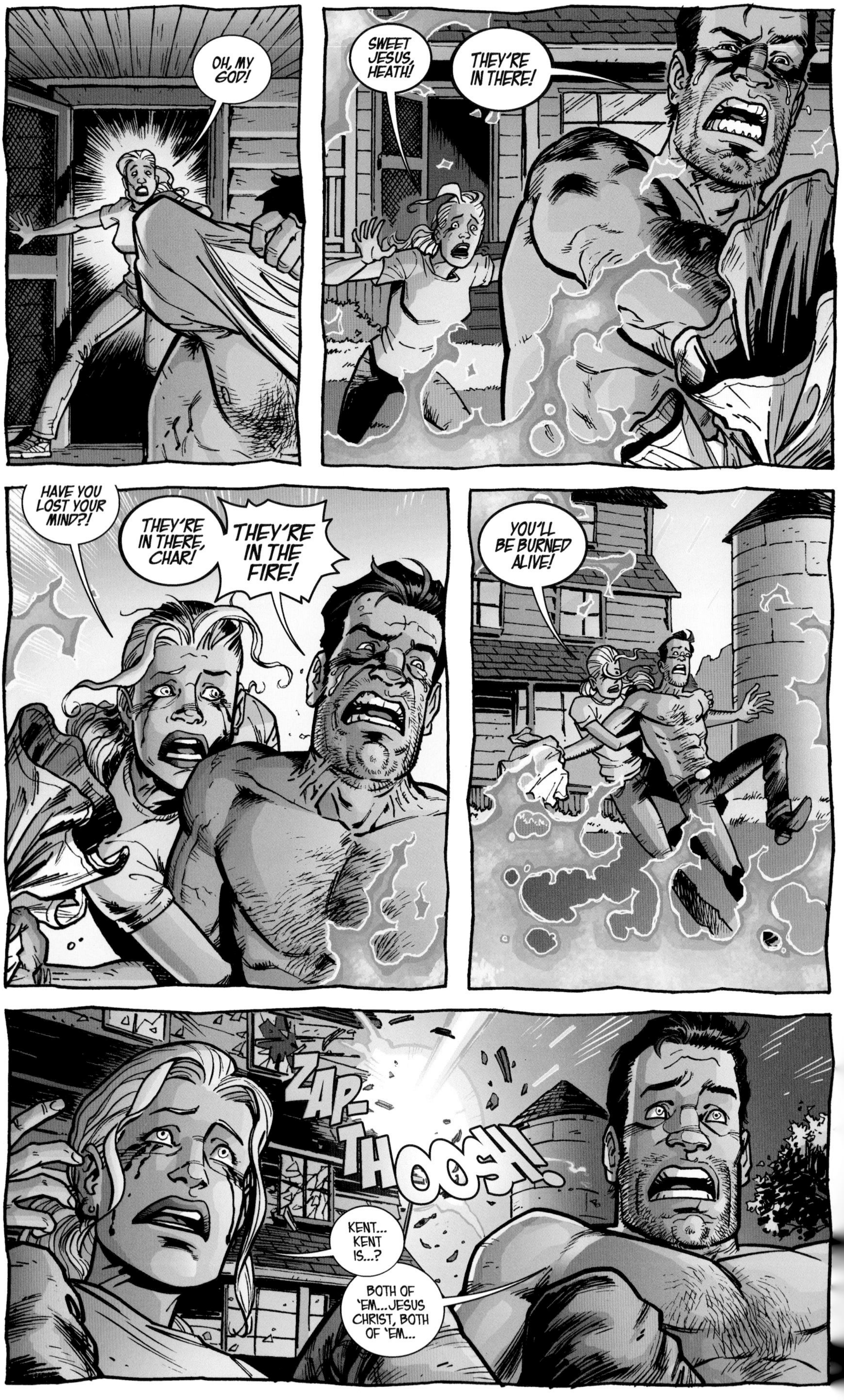
OH, MY GOD!
SWEET JESUS, HEATH!
THEY'RE IN THERE!
HAVE YOU LOST YOUR MIND?!
THEY'RE IN THERE, CHAR!
THEY'RE IN THE FIRE!
YOU'LL BE BURNED ALIVE!
ZAP-THOOSH!
KENT... KENT IS...?
BOTH OF 'EM...JESUS CHRIST, BOTH OF 'EM...

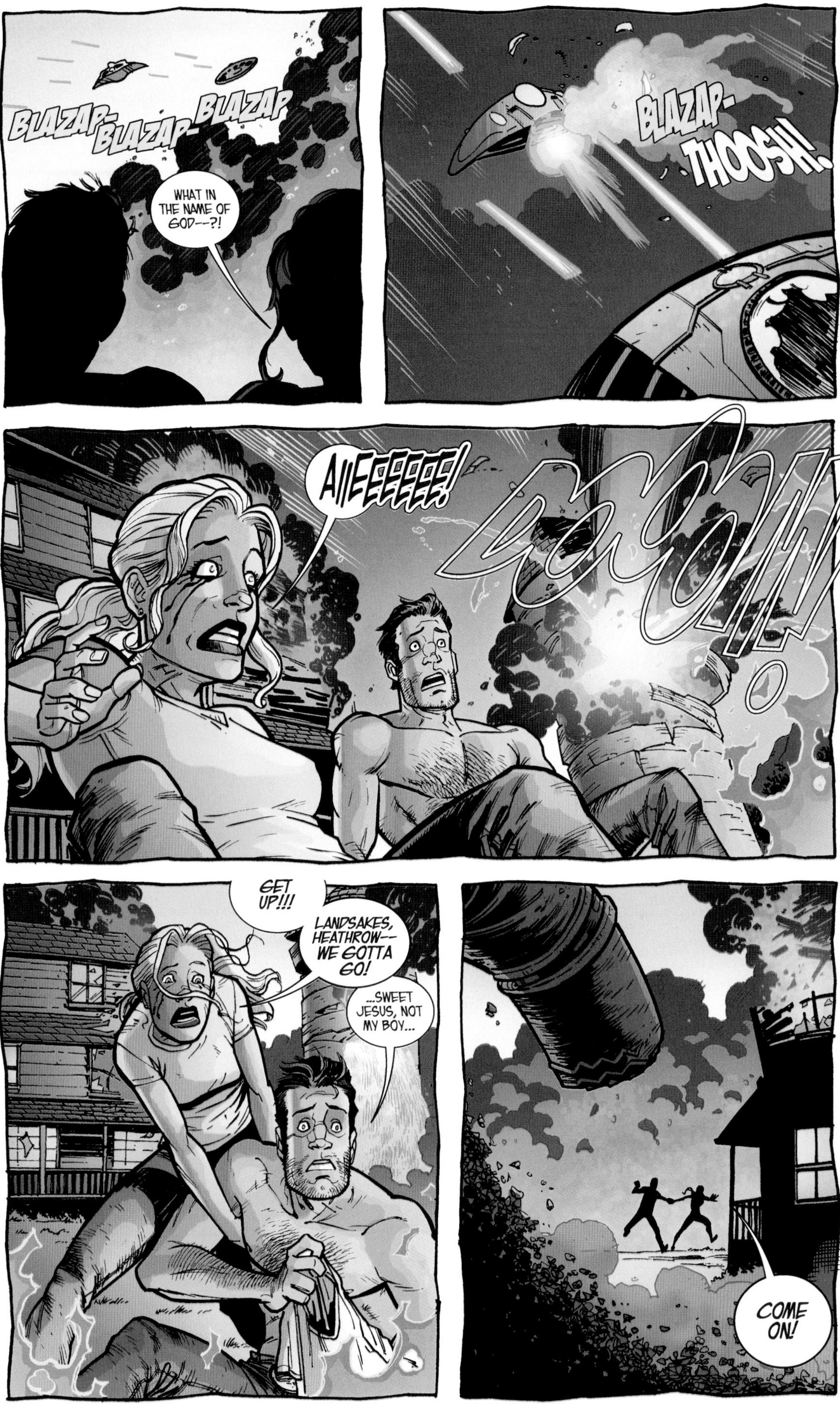
BLAZAP-
BLAZAP-
BLAZAP
WHAT IN THE NAME OF GOD--?!
BLAZAP-
THOOSH!
AIIEEEEEE!
GET UP!!!
LANDSAKES, HEATHROW-- WE GOTTA GO!
...SWEET JESUS, NOT MY BOY...
COME ON!

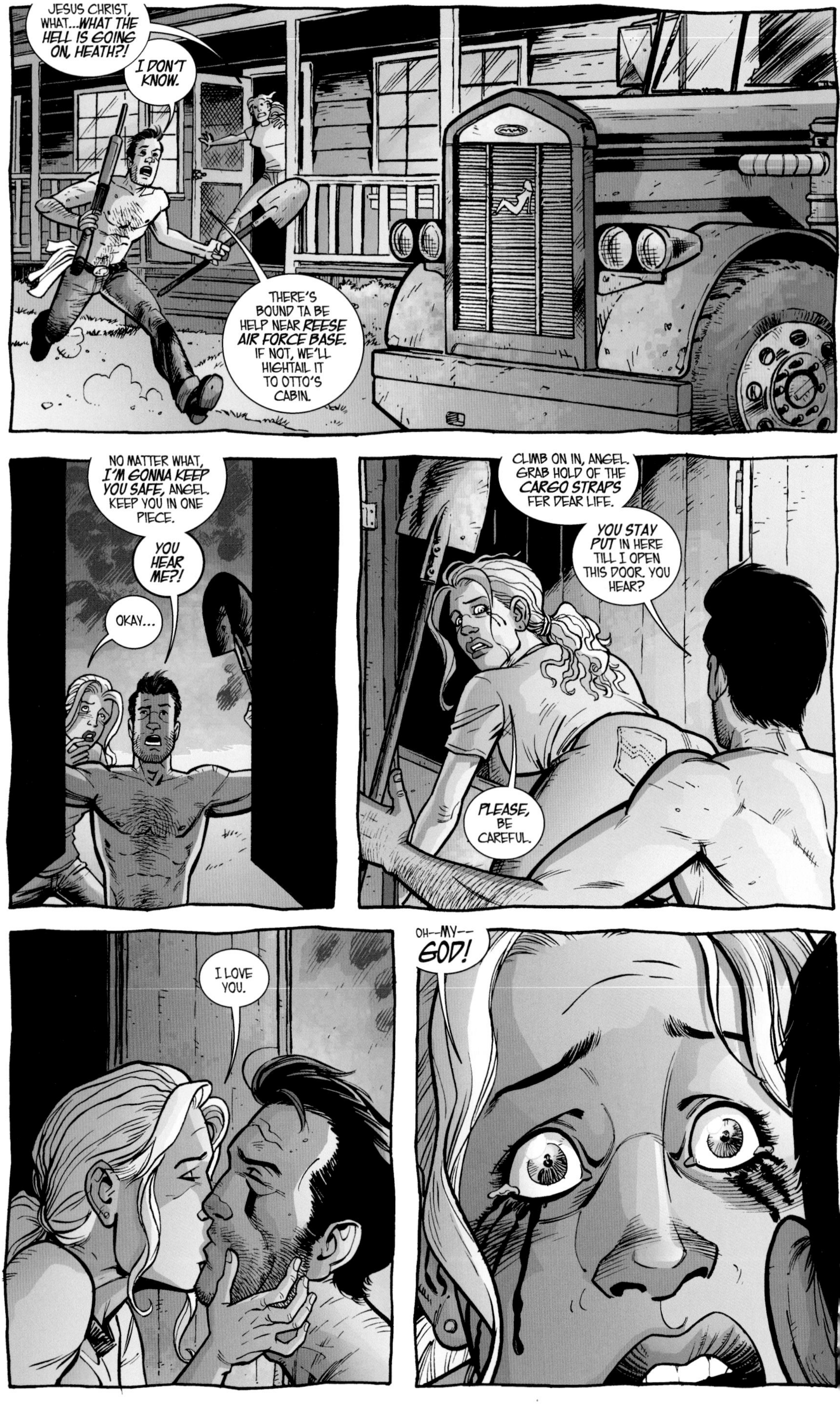
JESUS CHRIST, WHAT...WHAT THE HELL IS GOING ON, HEATH?!
I DON'T KNOW.
THERE'S BOUND TA BE HELP NEAR REESE AIR FORCE BASE. IF NOT, WE'LL HIGHTAIL IT TO OTTO'S CABIN.
NO MATTER WHAT, I'M GONNA KEEP YOU SAFE, ANGEL. KEEP YOU IN ONE PIECE.
YOU HEAR ME?!
OKAY...
CLIMB ON IN, ANGEL. GRAB HOLD OF THE CARGO STRAPS FER DEAR LIFE.
YOU STAY PUT IN HERE TILL I OPEN THIS DOOR. YOU HEAR?
PLEASE, BE CAREFUL.
I LOVE YOU.
OH--MY--
GOD!

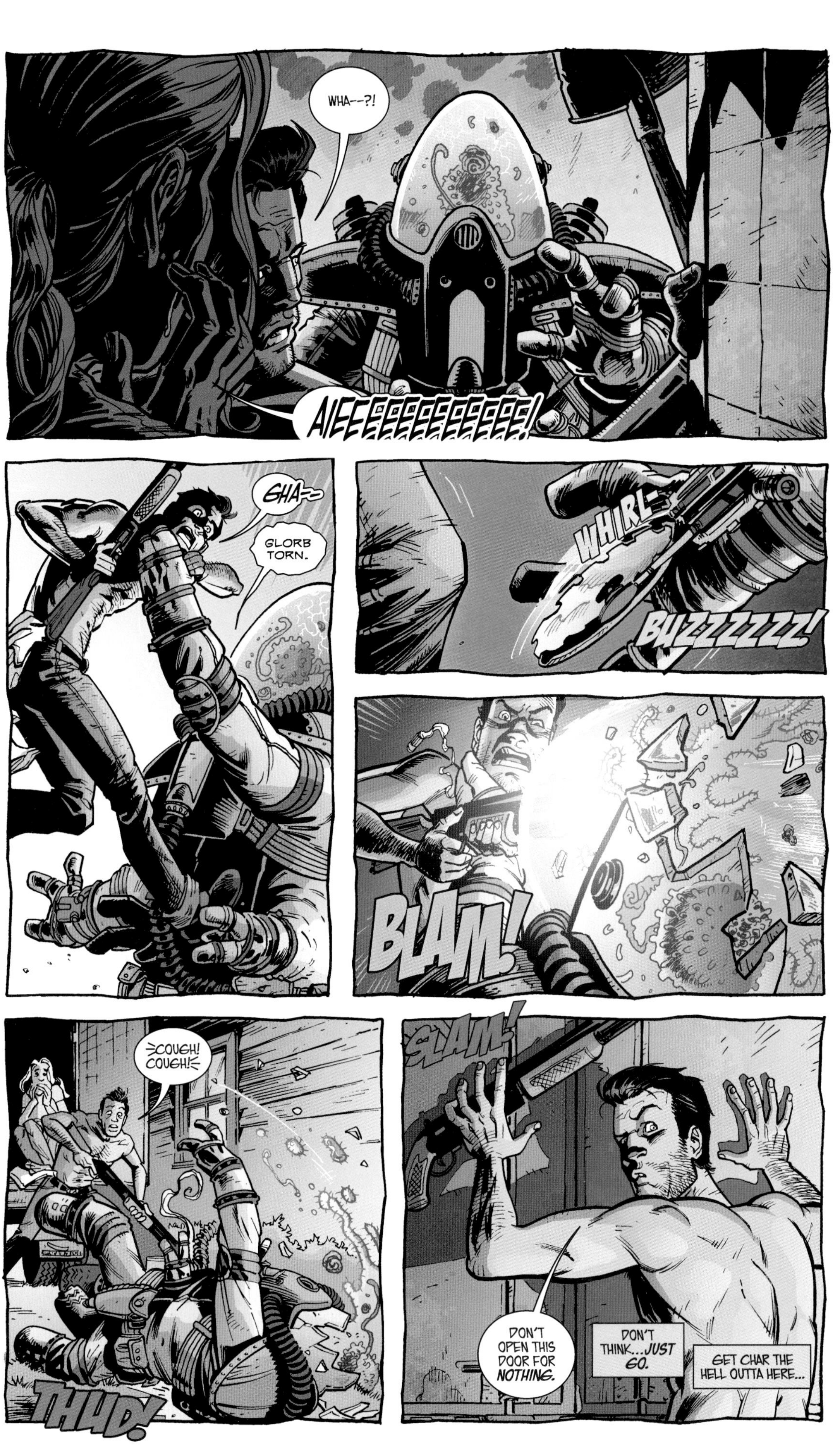
WHA--?!
AIEEEEEEEEEEEEEE!
GHA--
GLORB TORN.
WHIRL-
BUZZZZZZ!
BLAM!
COUGH! COUGH!
THUD!
SLAM!
DON'T OPEN THIS DOOR FOR NOTHING.
DON'T THINK...JUST GO.
GET CHAR THE HELL OUTTA HERE...

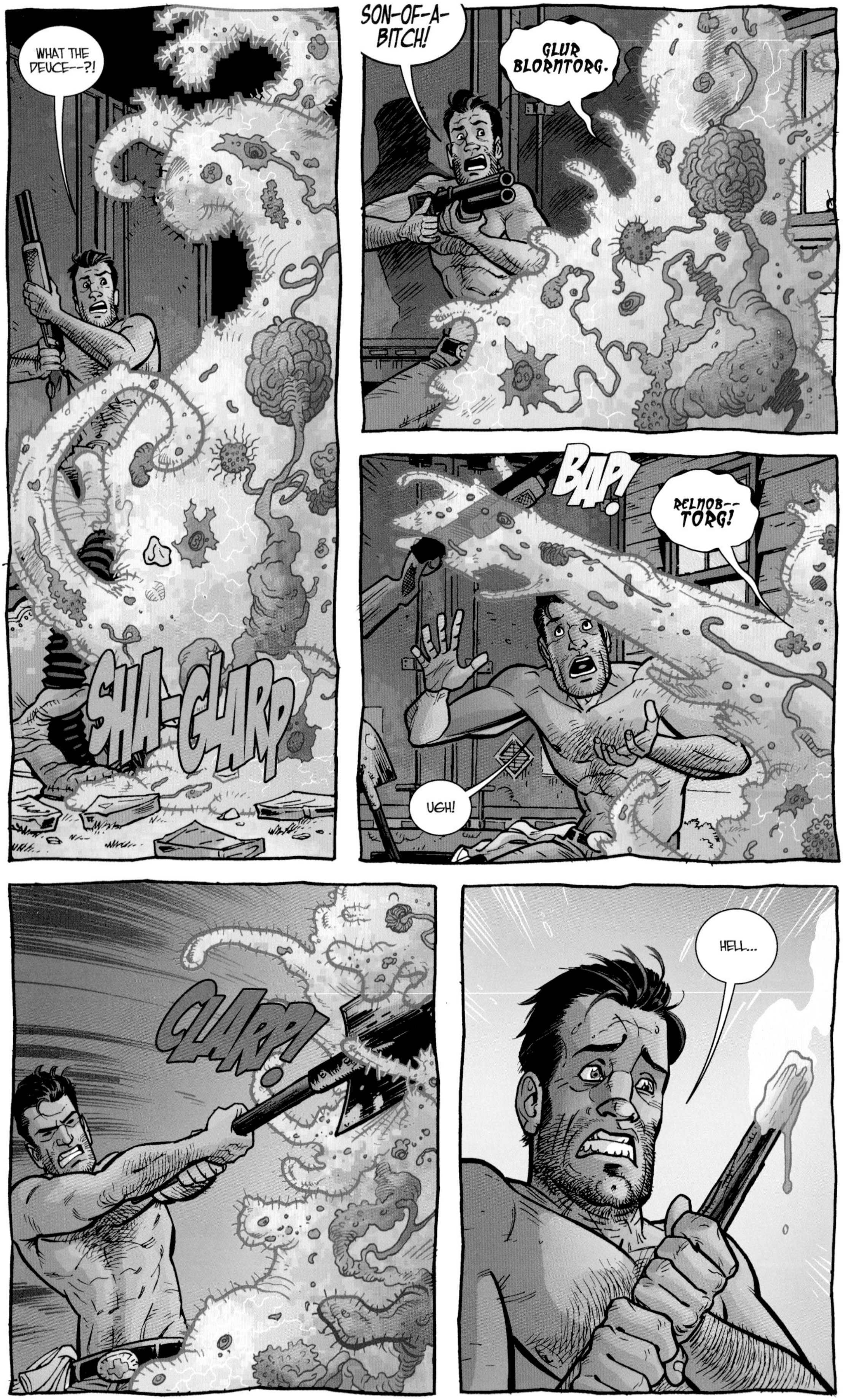
WHAT THE DEUCE--?!
SHA-GLARP
SON-OF-A-BITCH!
GLUR BLORNTORG.
BAP!
RELNOB--TORG!
UGH!
CLARP!
HELL...

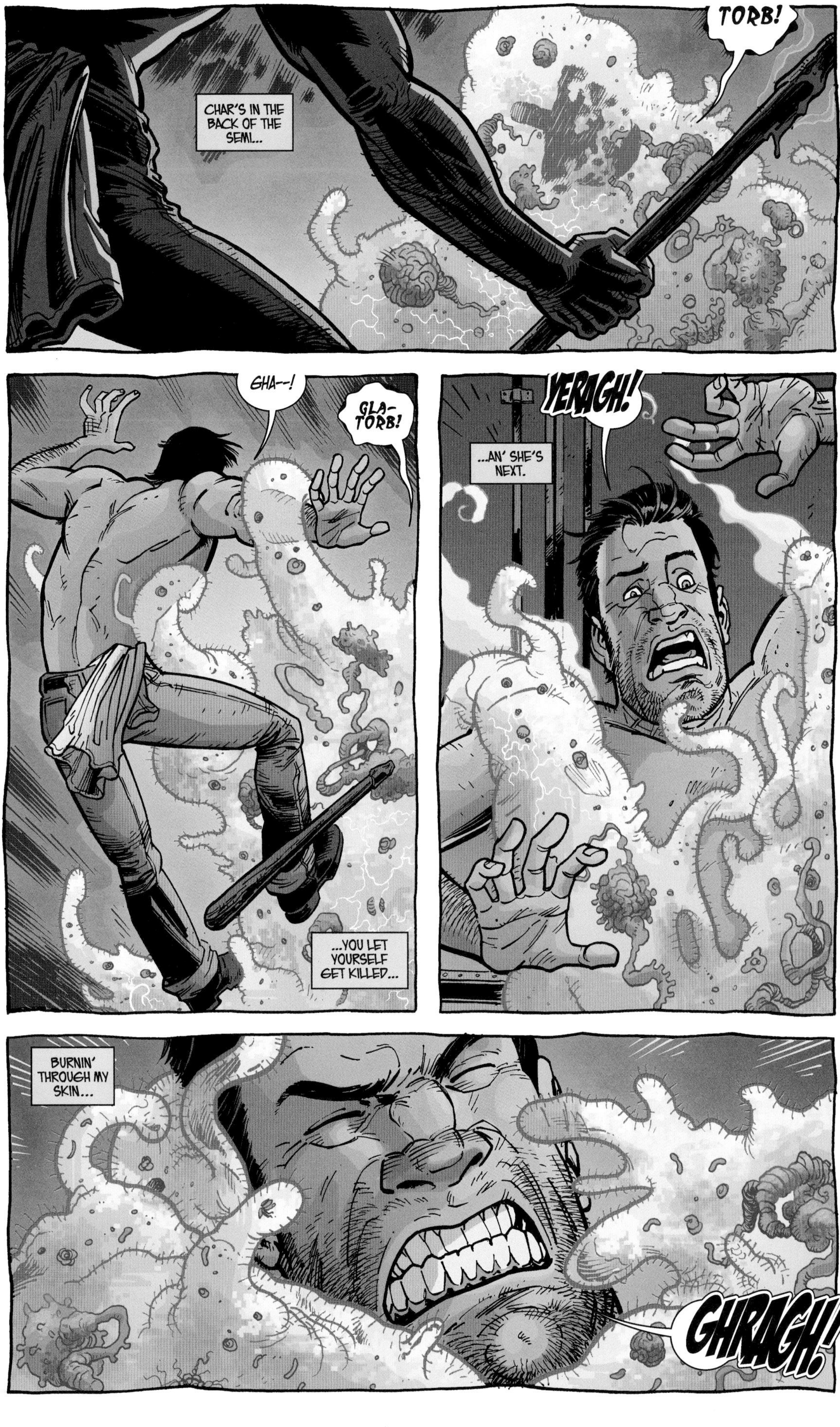
TORB!
CHAR'S IN THE BACK OF THE SEMI...
GHA--!
GLA-TORB!
...YOU LET YOURSELF GET KILLED...
YERAGH!
...AN' SHE'S NEXT.
BURNIN' THROUGH MY SKIN...
GHRAGH!

YERASH!

...I'M SORRY, ANGEL...

BLOGOOSH!!

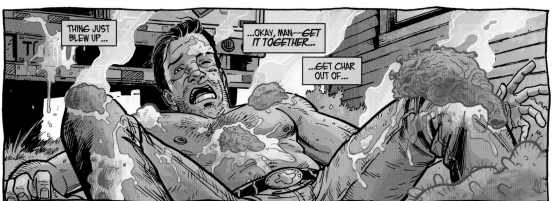

THING JUST BLEW UP...

...OKAY, MAN—GET IT TOGETHER...

...GET CHAR OUT OF...

...DEAR MOTHER OF GOD.

ZERTEEB-THUM.

RUN...

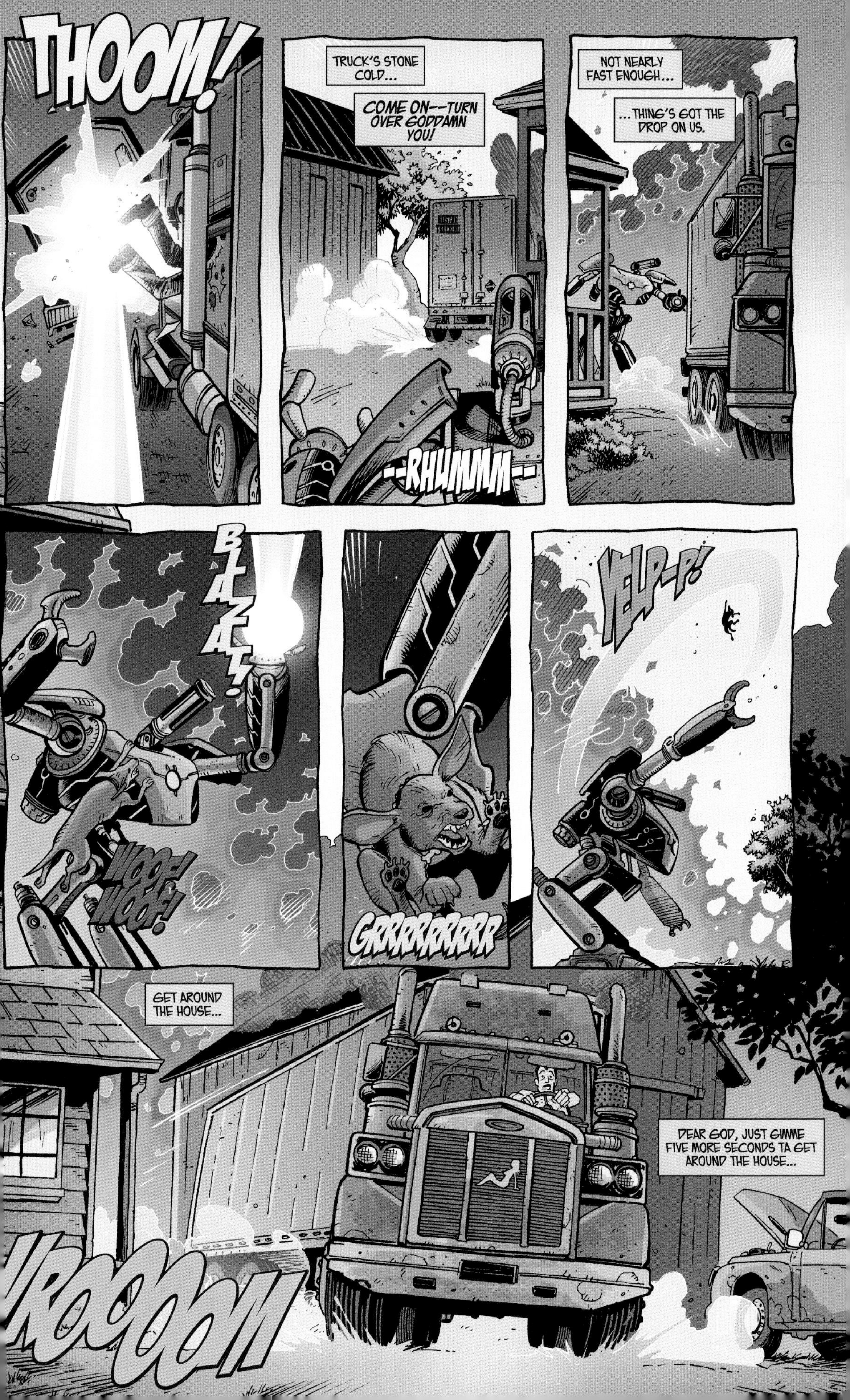
THOOM!
TRUCK'S STONE COLD...
COME ON--TURN OVER GODDAMN YOU!
--RHUMMM--
NOT NEARLY FAST ENOUGH...
...THING'S GOT THE DROP ON US.
BLAZAT!
WOOF! WOOF!
GRRRRRRRR
YELP-P!
GET AROUND THE HOUSE...
DEAR GOD, JUST GIMME FIVE MORE SECONDS TA GET AROUND THE HOUSE...
VROOOOM

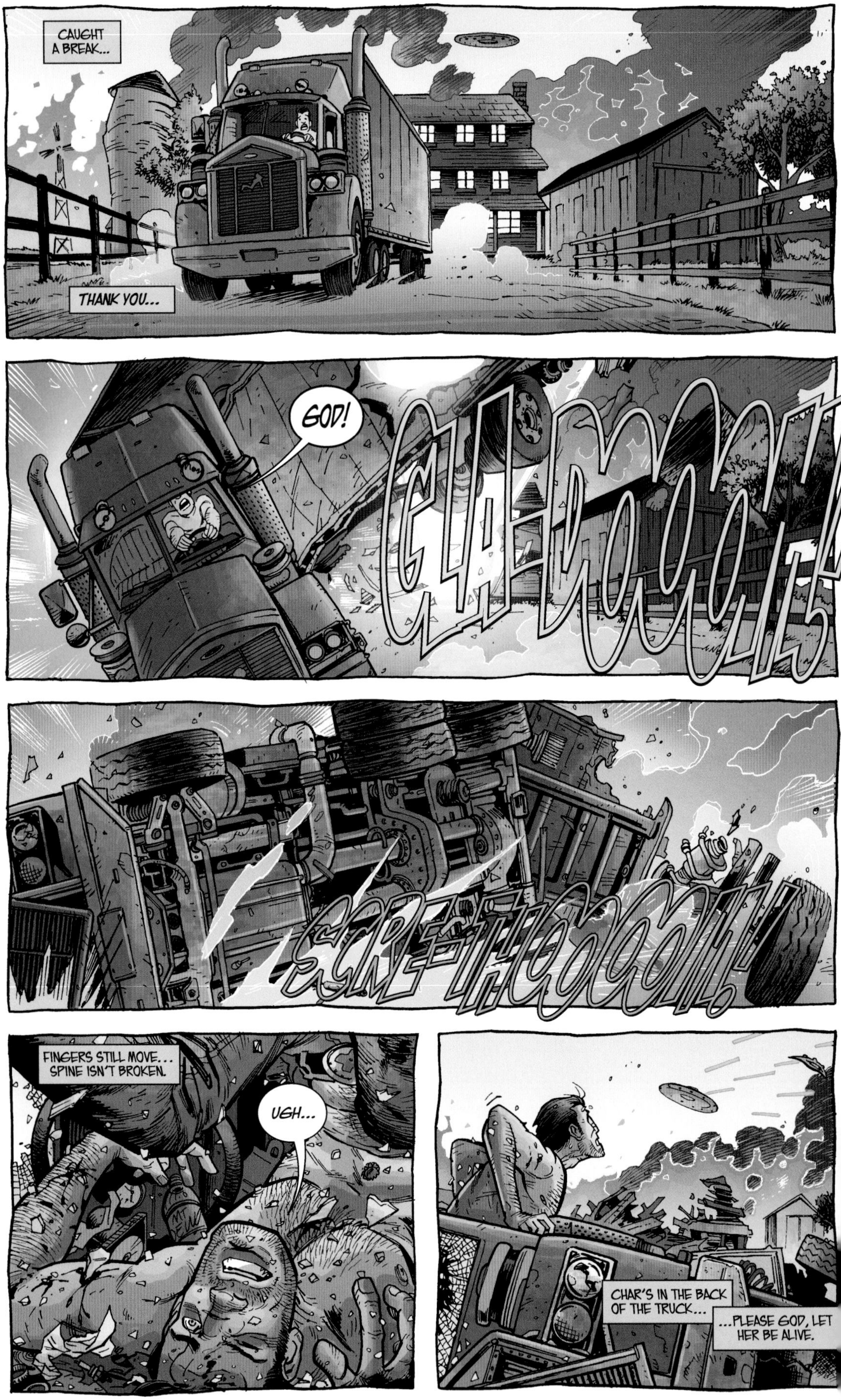
CAUGHT A BREAK...
THANK YOU...
GOD!
FINGERS STILL MOVE... SPINE ISN'T BROKEN.
UGH...
CHAR'S IN THE BACK OF THE TRUCK...
...PLEASE GOD, LET HER BE ALIVE.

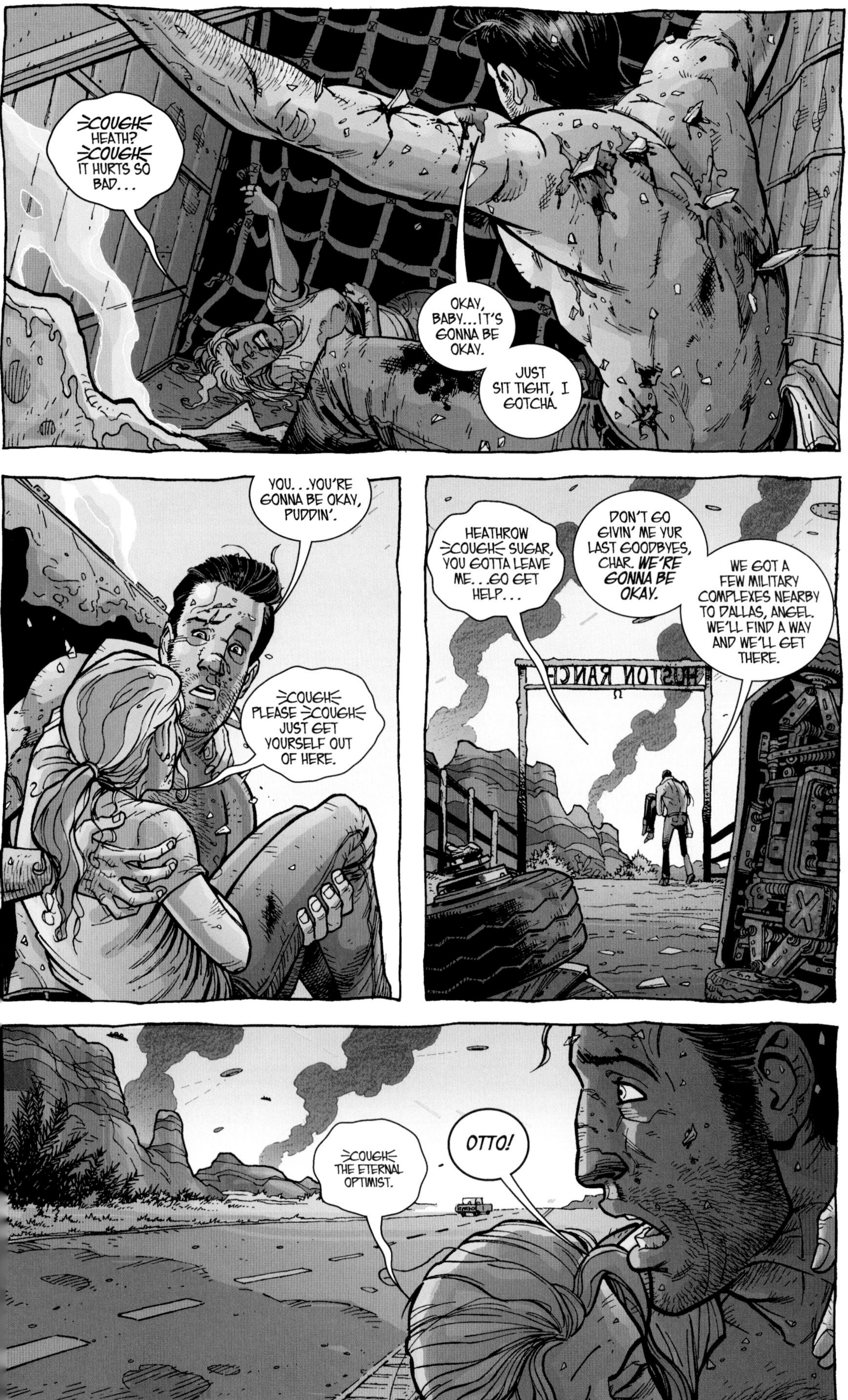

≥COUGH≤ HEATH? ≥COUGH≤ IT HURTS SO BAD...
OKAY, BABY...IT'S GONNA BE OKAY.
JUST SIT TIGHT, I GOTCHA.
YOU...YOU'RE GONNA BE OKAY, PUDDIN'.
≥COUGH≤ PLEASE ≥COUGH≤ JUST GET YOURSELF OUT OF HERE.
HEATHROW ≥COUGH≤ SUGAR, YOU GOTTA LEAVE ME...GO GET HELP...
DON'T GO GIVIN' ME YUR LAST GOODBYES, CHAR. WE'RE GONNA BE OKAY.
WE GOT A FEW MILITARY COMPLEXES NEARBY TO DALLAS, ANGEL. WE'LL FIND A WAY AND WE'LL GET THERE.
HUSTON RANCH
≥COUGH≤ THE ETERNAL OPTIMIST.
OTTO!

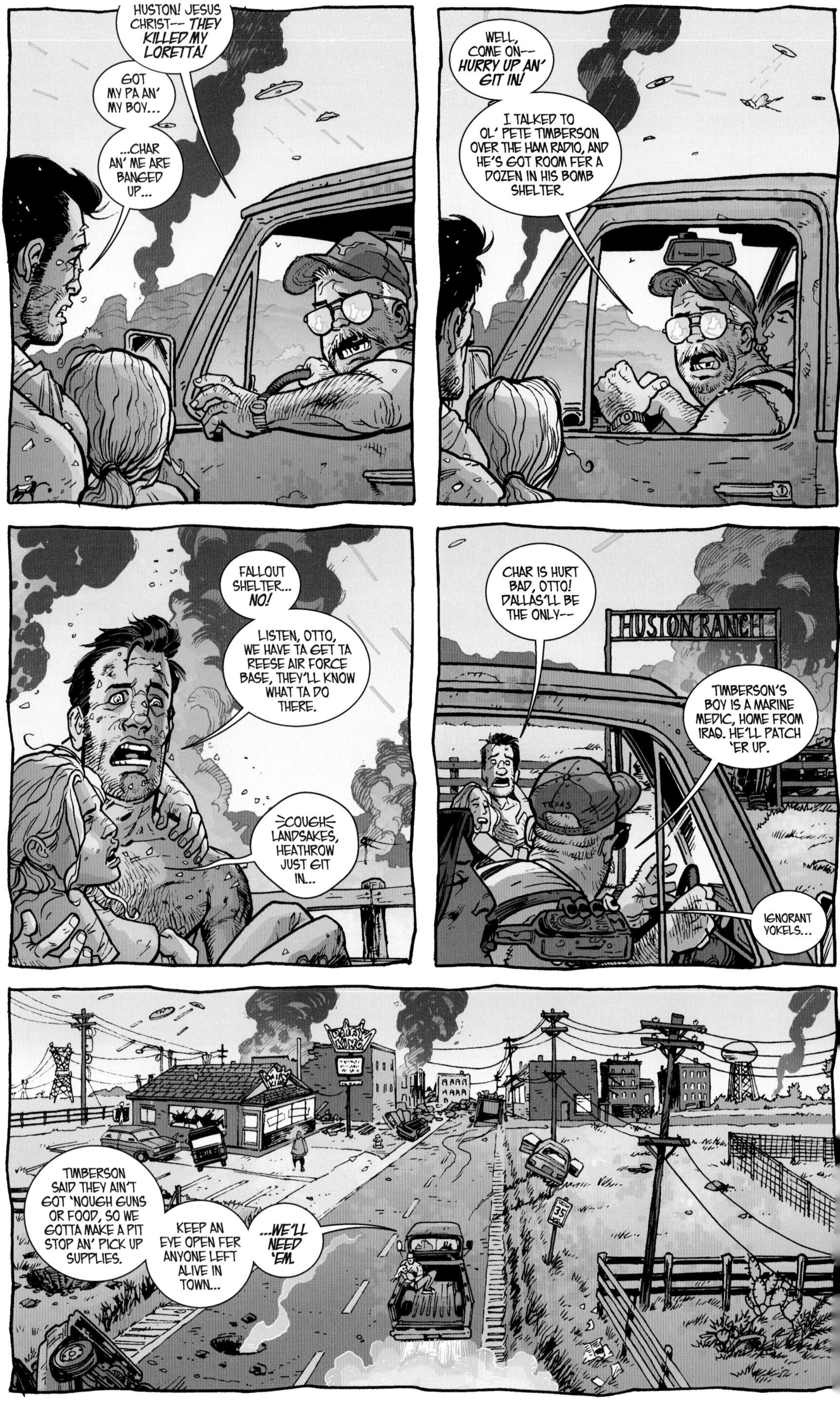
HUSTON! JESUS CHRIST-- THEY KILLED MY LORETTA!
GOT MY PA AN' MY BOY...
...CHAR AN' ME ARE BANGED UP...
WELL, COME ON-- HURRY UP AN' GIT IN!
I TALKED TO OL' PETE TIMBERSON OVER THE HAM RADIO, AND HE'S GOT ROOM FER A DOZEN IN HIS BOMB SHELTER.
FALLOUT SHELTER... NO!
LISTEN, OTTO, WE HAVE TA GET TA REESE AIR FORCE BASE, THEY'LL KNOW WHAT TA DO THERE.
COUGH LANDSAKES, HEATHROW JUST GIT IN...
CHAR IS HURT BAD, OTTO! DALLAS'LL BE THE ONLY--
HUSTON RANCH
TIMBERSON'S BOY IS A MARINE MEDIC, HOME FROM IRAQ. HE'LL PATCH 'ER UP.
IGNORANT YOKELS...
TIMBERSON SAID THEY AIN'T GOT 'NOUGH GUNS OR FOOD, SO WE GOTTA MAKE A PIT STOP AN' PICK UP SUPPLIES.
KEEP AN EYE OPEN FER ANYONE LEFT ALIVE IN TOWN...
...WE'LL NEED 'EM.

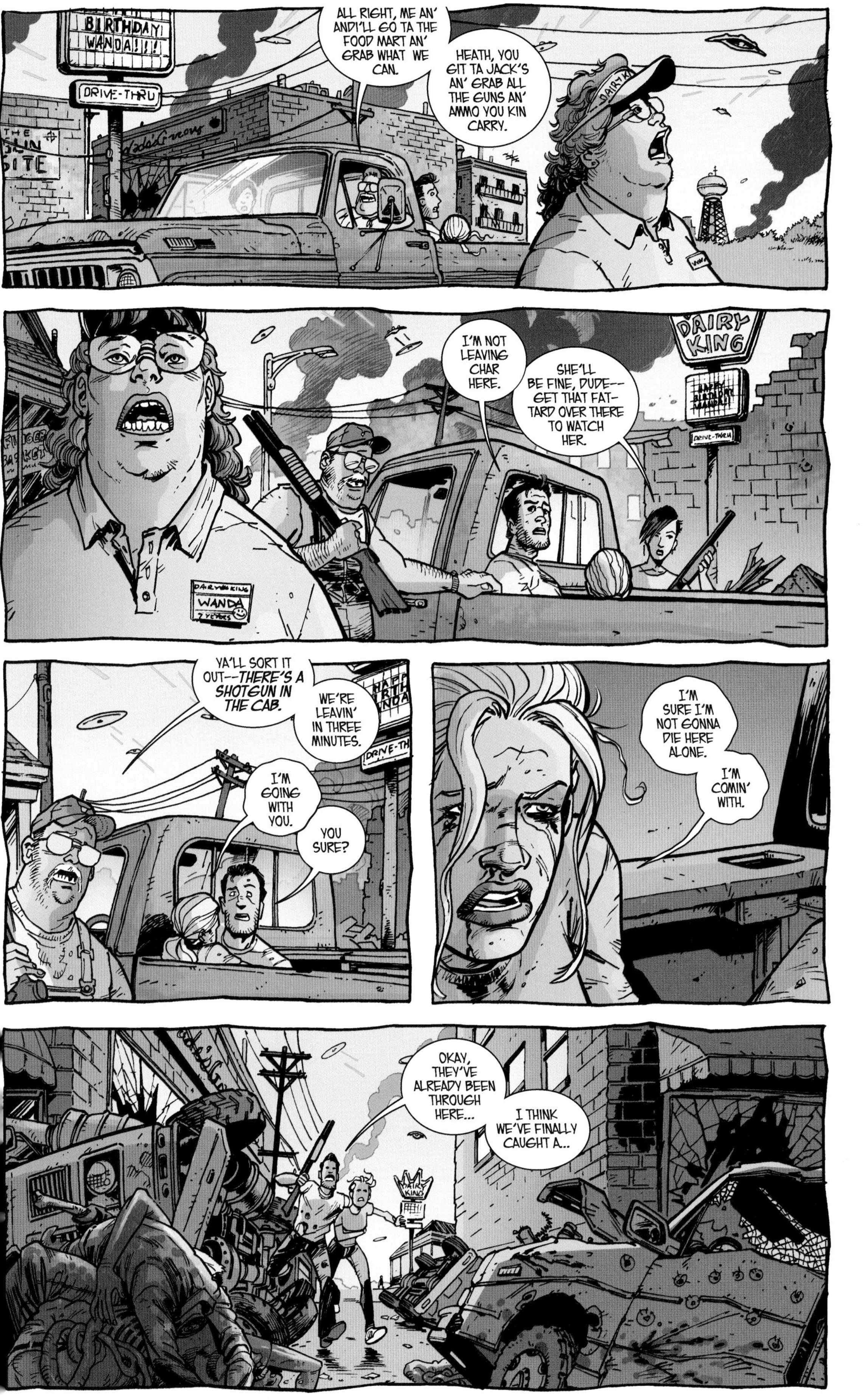
BIRTHDAY WANDA!!!
DRIVE-THRU
ALL RIGHT, ME AN' ANDI'LL GO TA THE FOOD MART AN' GRAB WHAT WE CAN.
HEATH, YOU GIT TA JACK'S AN' GRAB ALL THE GUNS AN' AMMO YOU KIN CARRY.
DAIRY KING
I'M NOT LEAVING CHAR HERE.
SHE'LL BE FINE, DUDE--GET THAT FAT-TARD OVER THERE TO WATCH HER.
DRIVE-THRU
WANDA
YA'LL SORT IT OUT--THERE'S A SHOTGUN IN THE CAB.
WE'RE LEAVIN' IN THREE MINUTES.
I'M GOING WITH YOU.
YOU SURE?
I'M SURE I'M NOT GONNA DIE HERE ALONE.
I'M COMIN' WITH.
OKAY, THEY'VE ALREADY BEEN THROUGH HERE...
I THINK WE'VE FINALLY CAUGHT A...

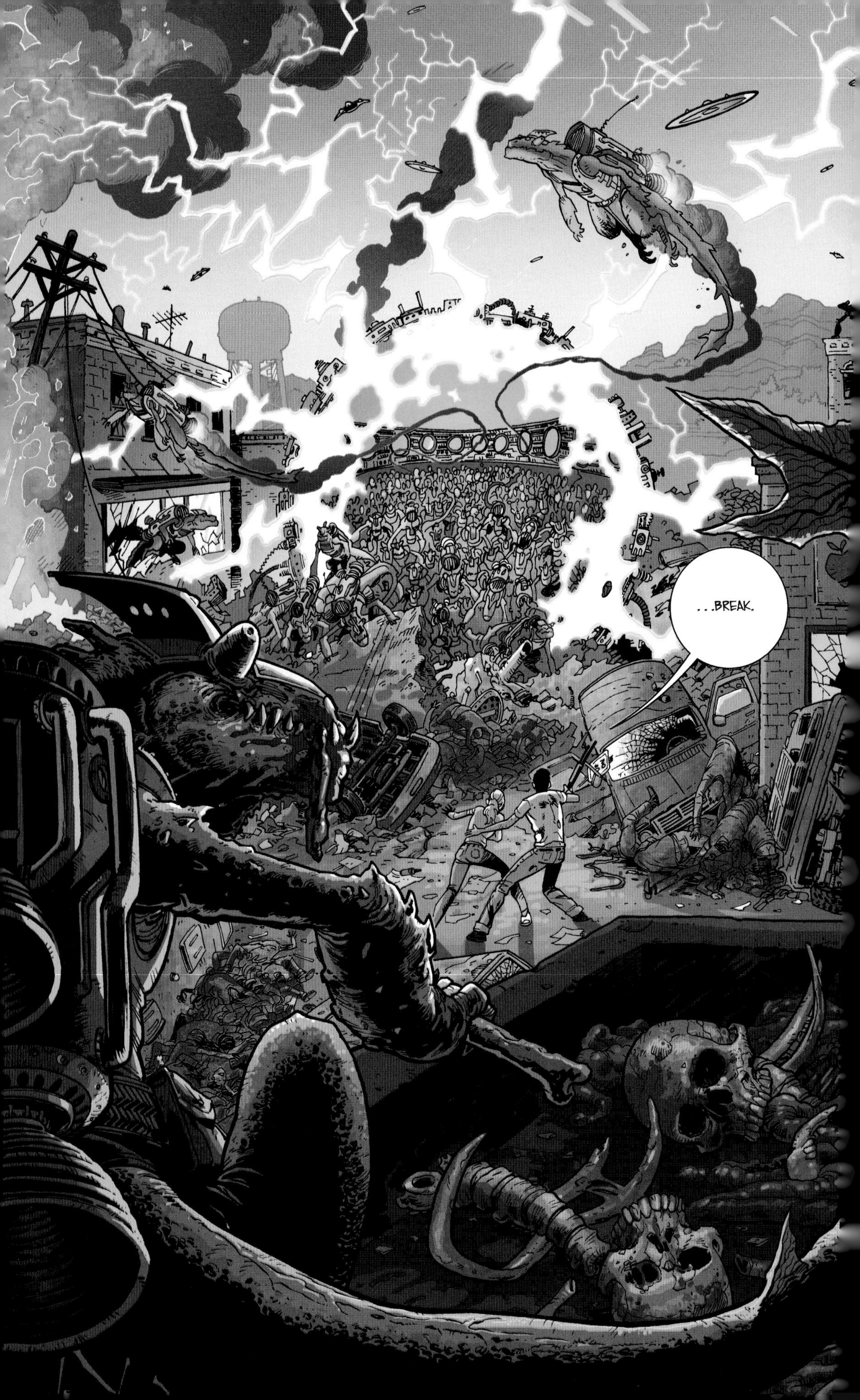
...BREAK.

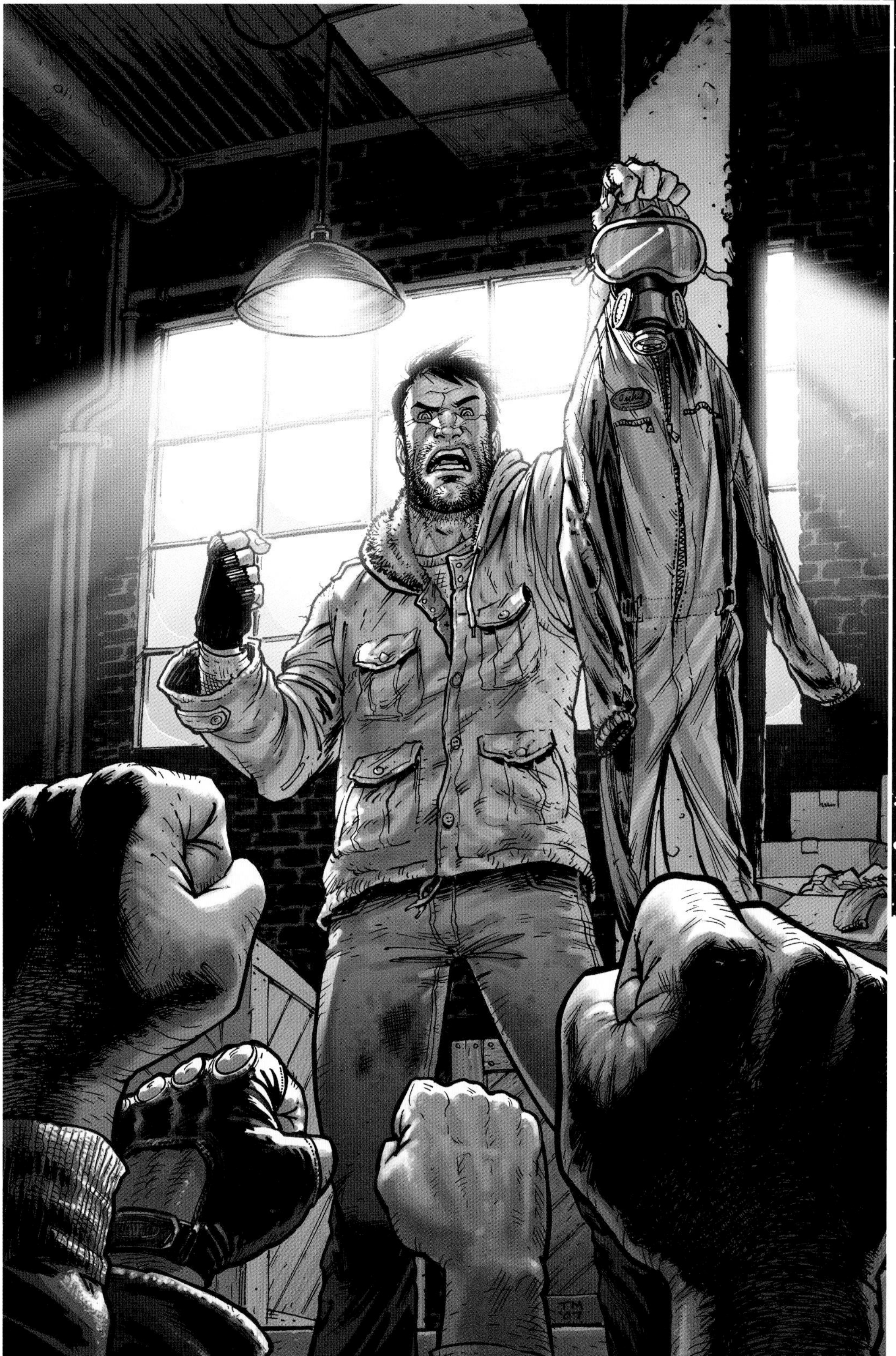

FEAR AGENT #13
ART BY **TONY MOORE**

THE LAST GOODBYE

CHAPTER 2

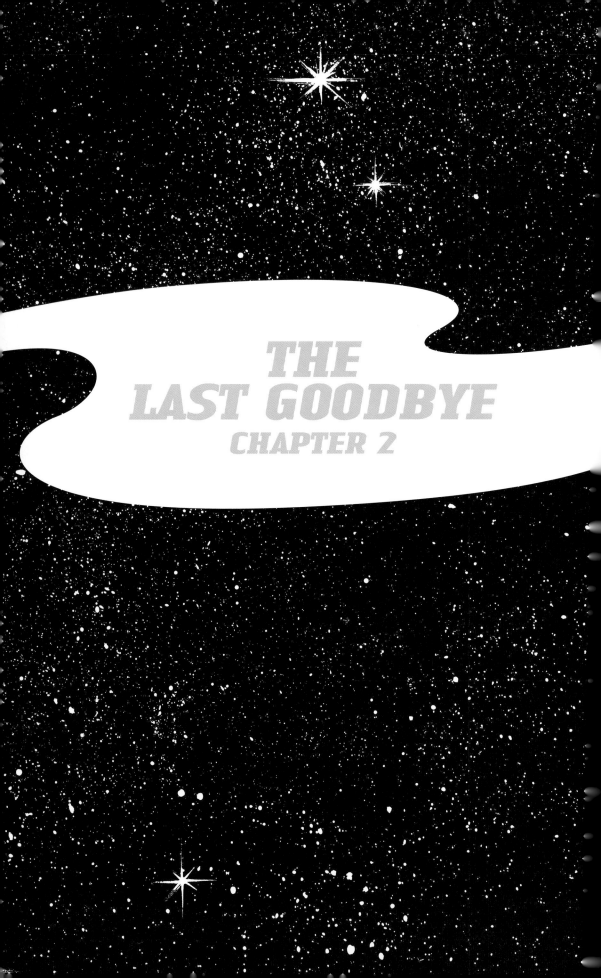

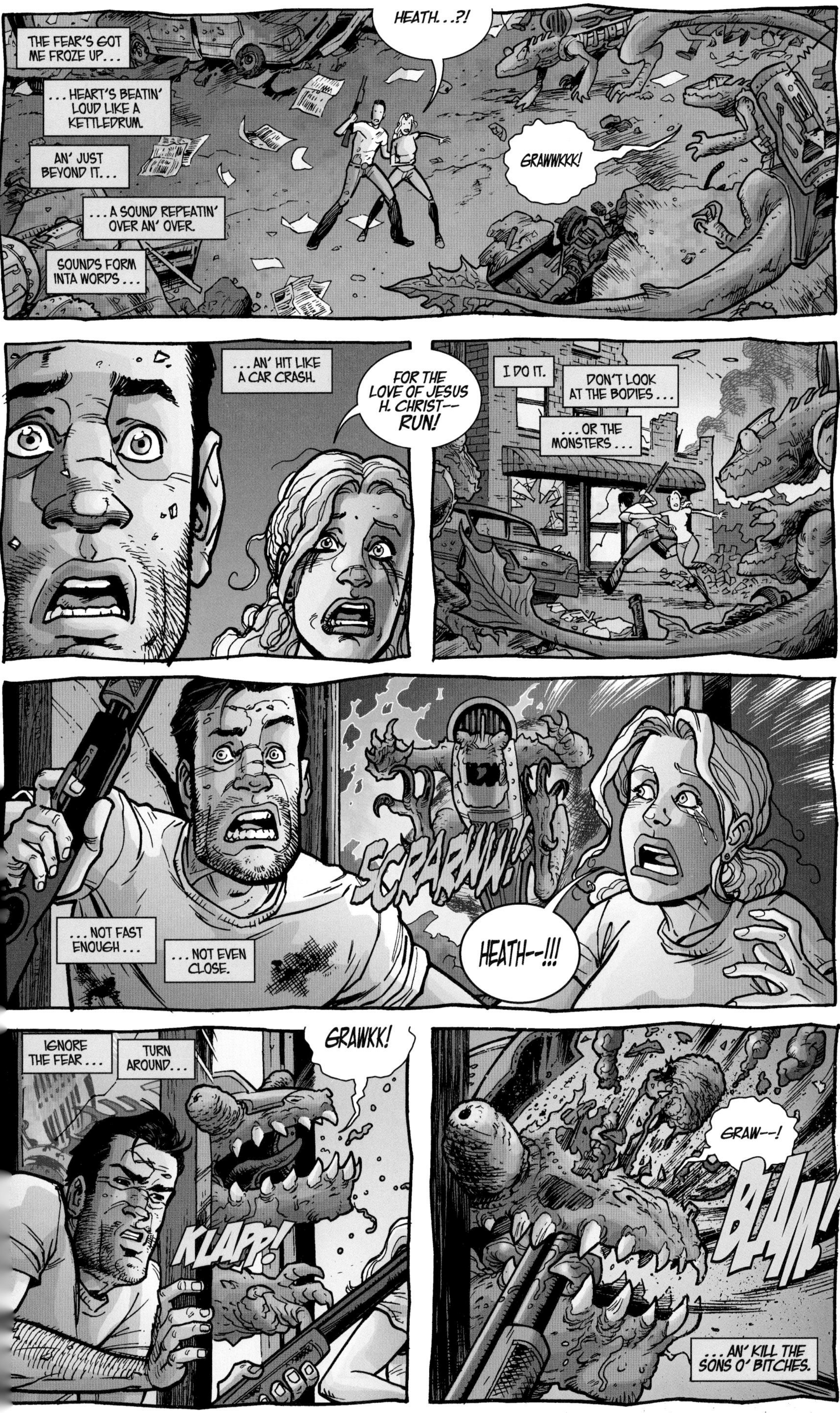
THE FEAR'S GOT ME FROZE UP...
HEATH...?!
...HEART'S BEATIN' LOUD LIKE A KETTLEDRUM.
AN' JUST BEYOND IT...
GRAWWKKK!
...A SOUND REPEATIN' OVER AN' OVER.
SOUNDS FORM INTA WORDS...
...AN' HIT LIKE A CAR CRASH.
FOR THE LOVE OF JESUS H. CHRIST-- RUN!
I DO IT.
DON'T LOOK AT THE BODIES...
...OR THE MONSTERS...
SCRAAW!
...NOT FAST ENOUGH...
...NOT EVEN CLOSE.
HEATH--!!!
IGNORE THE FEAR...
TURN AROUND...
GRAWKK!
KLAPP!
GRAW--!
BLAM!
...AN' KILL THE SONS O' BITCHES.

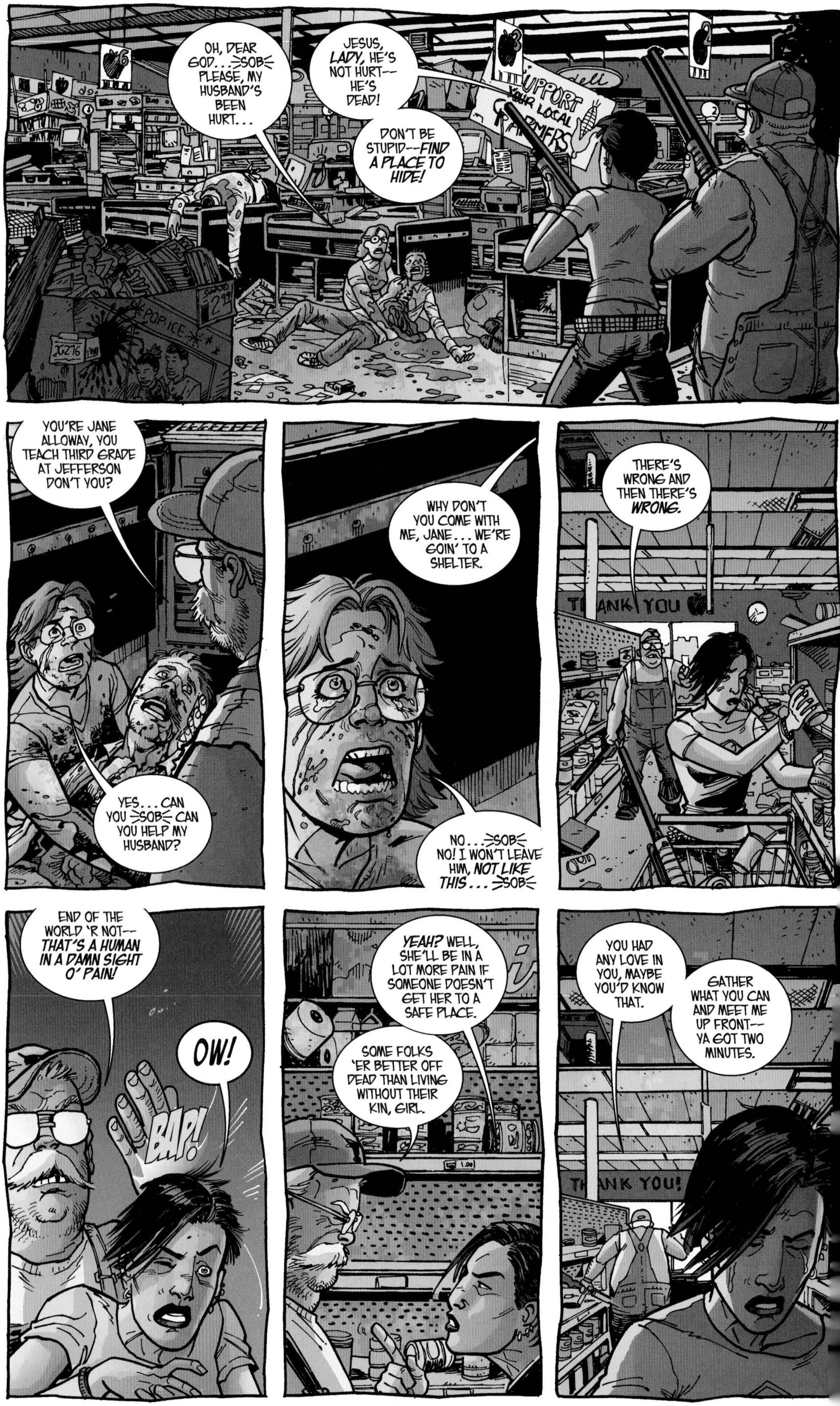
OH, DEAR GOD... SOB PLEASE, MY HUSBAND'S BEEN HURT...
JESUS, LADY, HE'S NOT HURT-- HE'S DEAD!
DON'T BE STUPID--FIND A PLACE TO HIDE!
SUPPORT YOUR LOCAL FARMERS
YOU'RE JANE ALLOWAY, YOU TEACH THIRD GRADE AT JEFFERSON DON'T YOU?
YES... CAN YOU SOB CAN YOU HELP MY HUSBAND?
WHY DON'T YOU COME WITH ME, JANE... WE'RE GOIN' TO A SHELTER.
NO... SOB NO! I WON'T LEAVE HIM, NOT LIKE THIS... SOB
THERE'S WRONG AND THEN THERE'S WRONG.
THANK YOU
END OF THE WORLD 'R NOT-- THAT'S A HUMAN IN A DAMN SIGHT O' PAIN!
OW!
BAP!
YEAH? WELL, SHE'LL BE IN A LOT MORE PAIN IF SOMEONE DOESN'T GET HER TO A SAFE PLACE.
SOME FOLKS 'ER BETTER OFF DEAD THAN LIVING WITHOUT THEIR KIN, GIRL.
YOU HAD ANY LOVE IN YOU, MAYBE YOU'D KNOW THAT.
GATHER WHAT YOU CAN AND MEET ME UP FRONT-- YA GOT TWO MINUTES.
THANK YOU!

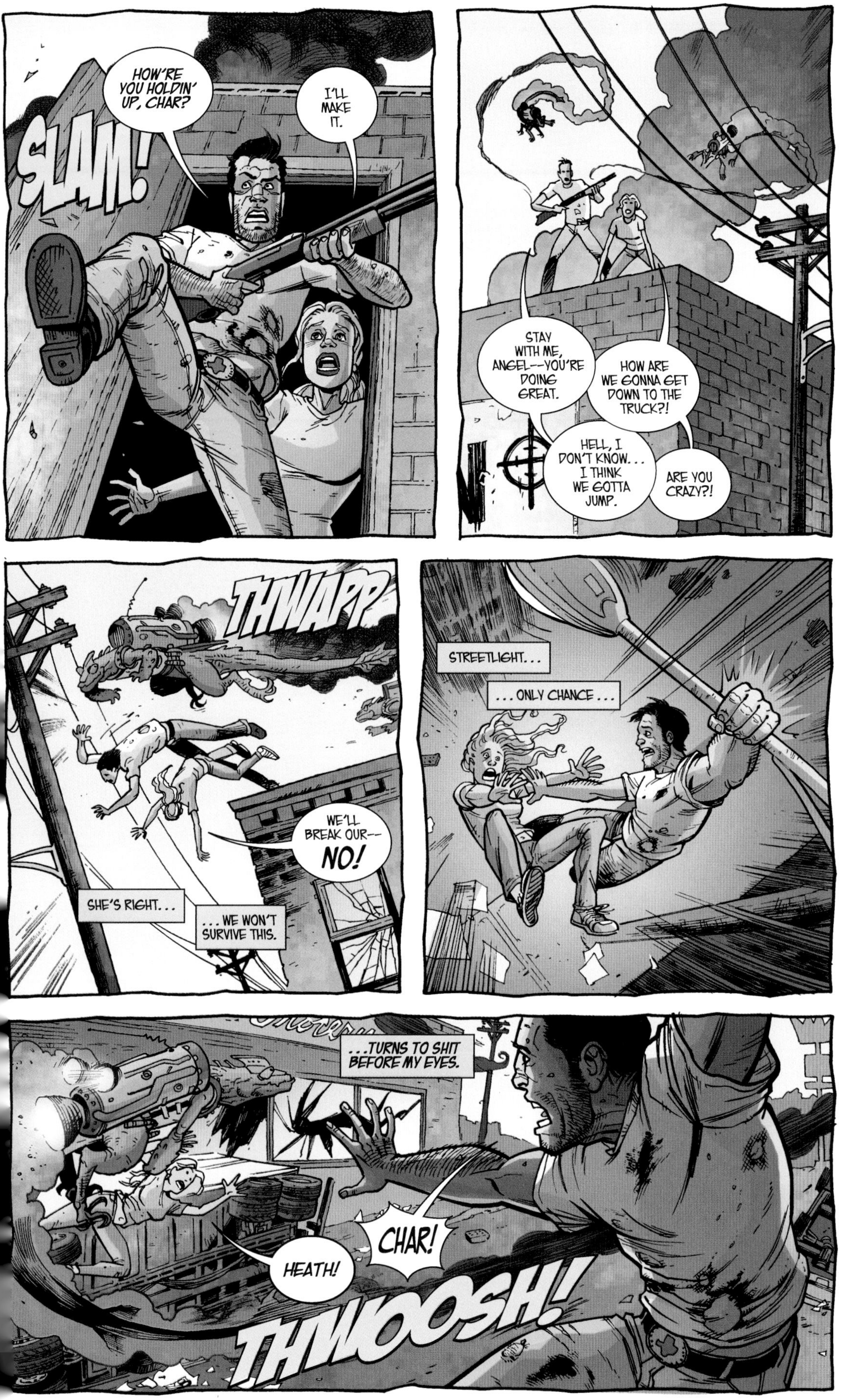

SLAM!
HOW'RE YOU HOLDIN' UP, CHAR?
I'LL MAKE IT.
STAY WITH ME, ANGEL--YOU'RE DOING GREAT.
HOW ARE WE GONNA GET DOWN TO THE TRUCK?!
HELL, I DON'T KNOW... I THINK WE GOTTA JUMP.
ARE YOU CRAZY?!
THWAPP.
WE'LL BREAK OUR-- NO!
SHE'S RIGHT...
...WE WON'T SURVIVE THIS.
STREETLIGHT...
...ONLY CHANCE...
...TURNS TO SHIT BEFORE MY EYES.
CHAR!
HEATH!
THWOOSH!

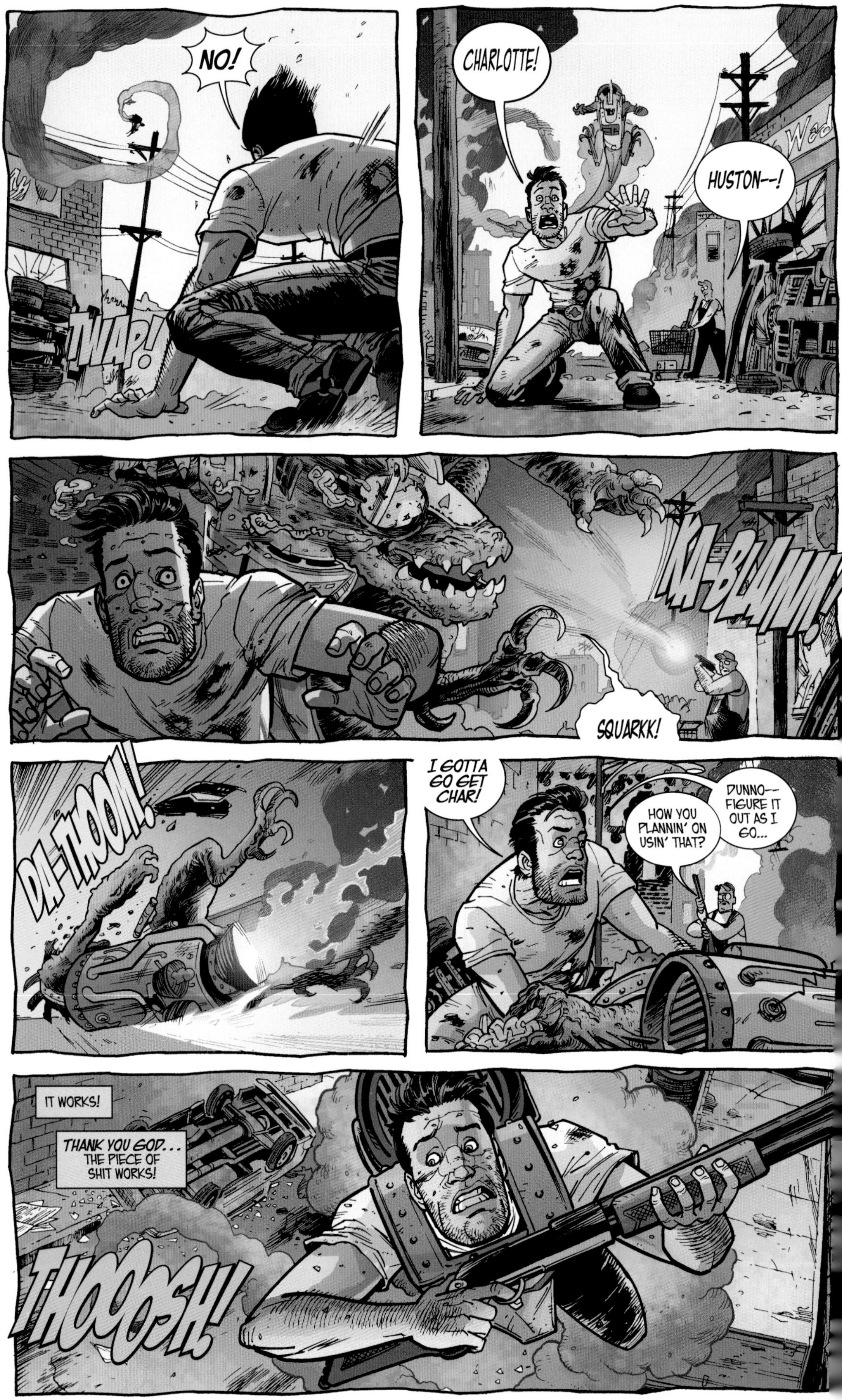
NO!
TWAP!
CHARLOTTE!
HUSTON--!
KA-BLAMM!
SQUARKK!
DA-THOOM!
I GOTTA GO GET CHAR!
HOW YOU PLANNIN' ON USIN' THAT?
DUNNO-- FIGURE IT OUT AS I GO...
IT WORKS!
THANK YOU GOD... THE PIECE OF SHIT WORKS!
THOOOSH!

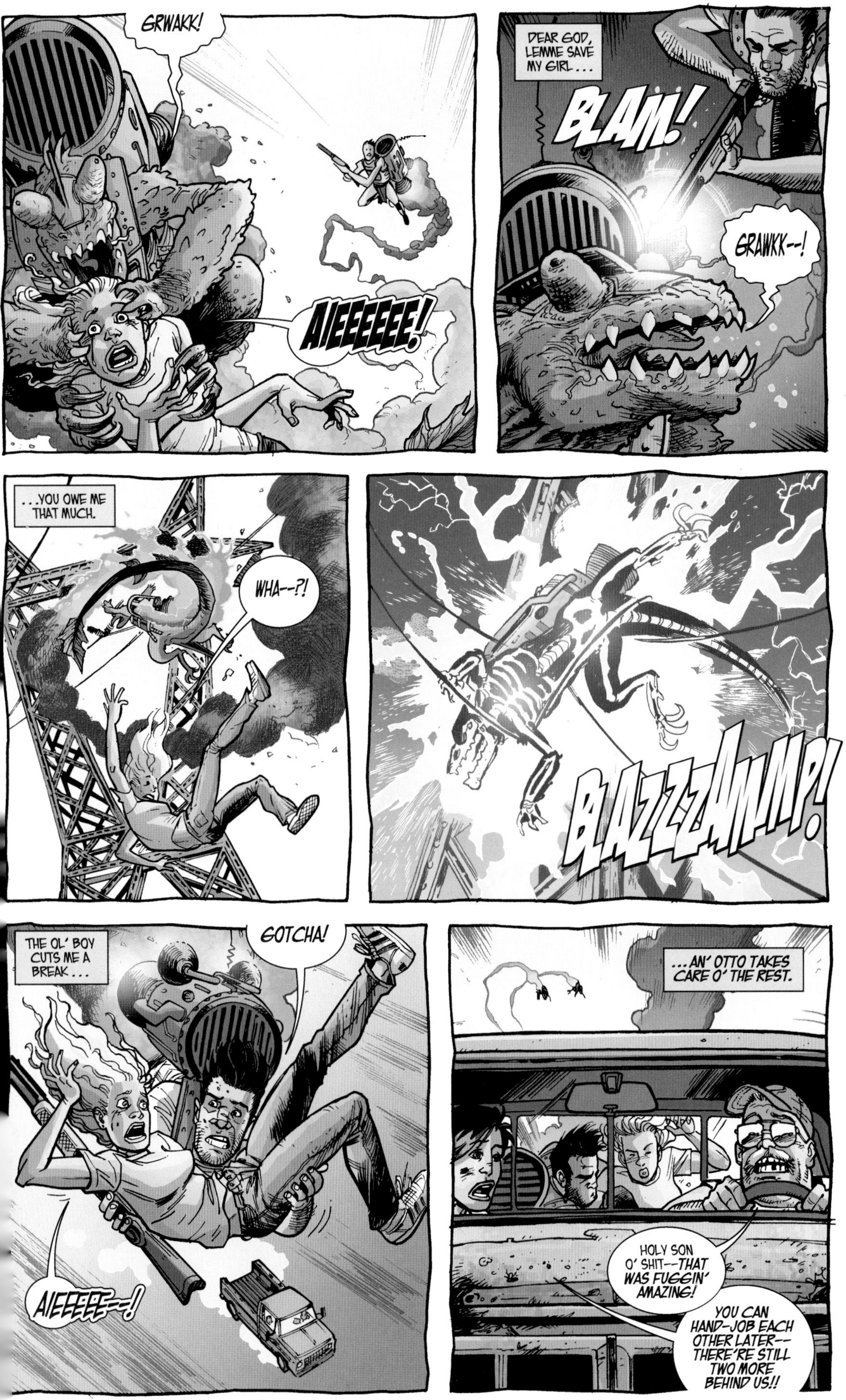
GRWAKK!
AIEEEEEE!
DEAR GOD, LEMME SAVE MY GIRL...
BLAM!
GRAWKK--!
...YOU OWE ME THAT MUCH.
WHA--?!
BLAZZZAMMP!
THE OL' BOY CUTS ME A BREAK...
GOTCHA!
AIEEEEE--!
...AN' OTTO TAKES CARE O' THE REST.
HOLY SON O' SHIT--THAT WAS FUGGIN' AMAZING!
YOU CAN HAND-JOB EACH OTHER LATER--THERE'RE STILL TWO MORE BEHIND US!!

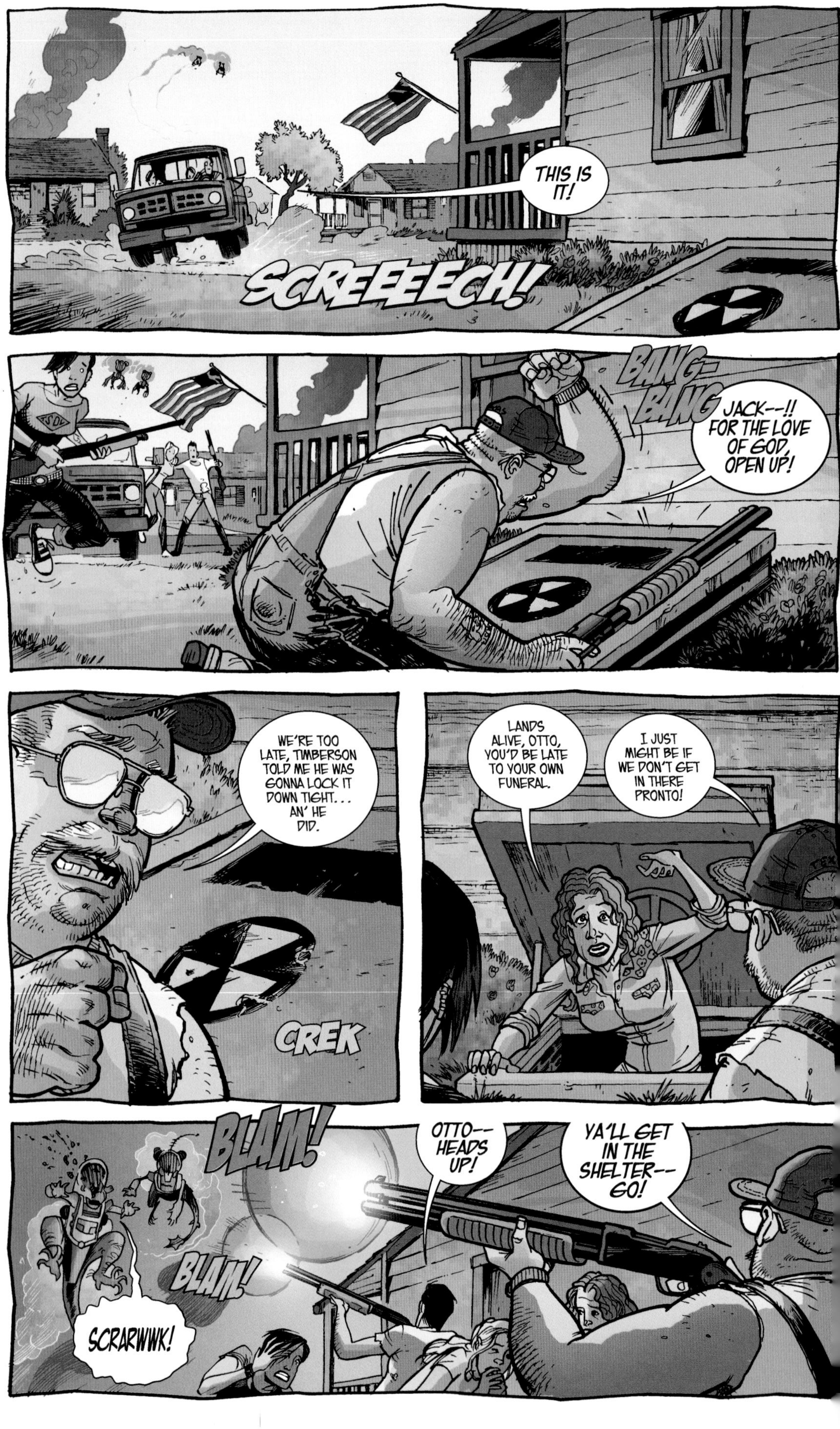
THIS IS IT!
SCREEEEECH!
BANG-BANG
JACK--!! FOR THE LOVE OF GOD, OPEN UP!
WE'RE TOO LATE, TIMBERSON TOLD ME HE WAS GONNA LOCK IT DOWN TIGHT... AN' HE DID.
CREK
LANDS ALIVE, OTTO, YOU'D BE LATE TO YOUR OWN FUNERAL.
I JUST MIGHT BE IF WE DON'T GET IN THERE PRONTO!
BLAM!
OTTO--HEADS UP!
YA'LL GET IN THE SHELTER--GO!
BLAM!
SCRARWWK!

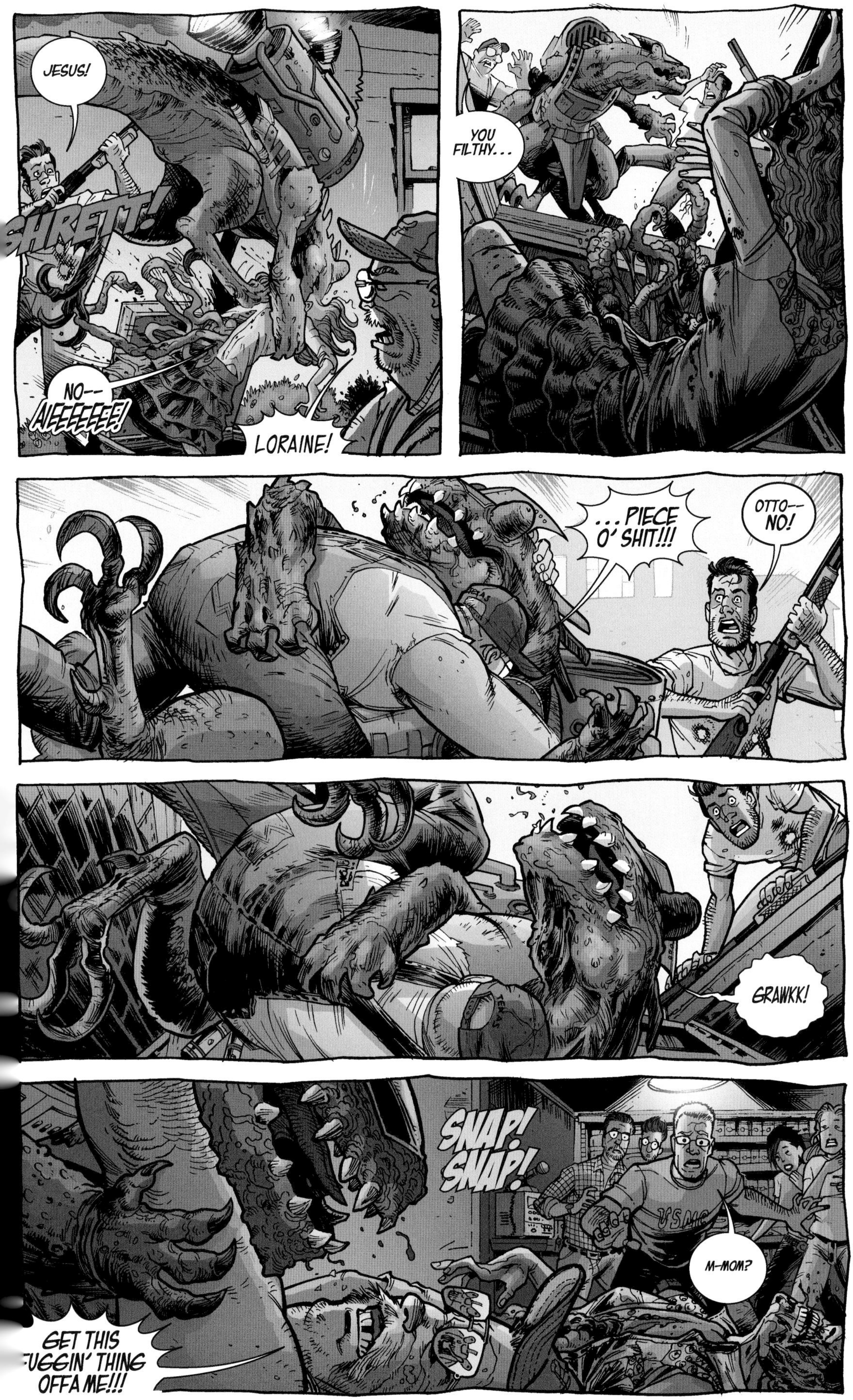
JESUS!
SHRETT!
NO--
AIEEEEEEE!
LORAINE!
YOU FILTHY...
...PIECE O' SHIT!!!
OTTO--
NO!
GRAWKK!
SNAP! SNAP!
M-MOM?
GET THIS FUGGIN' THING OFFA ME!!!

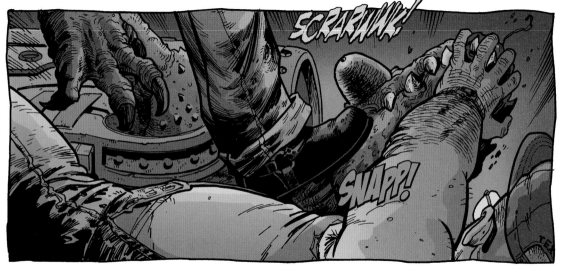

SCRARNNN!

SNAPP!

M-MOM? NO, OH, JESUS, NO . . .

LORAINE?

LORAINE?!

SHE'S . . . SHE'S DEAD . . .

SONOFABITCH!

THIS IS YOUR FAULT! WE TOLD YOU TO BE HERE AN HOUR AGO!!

I'M SORRY, JACK.

JESUS CHRIST, I'M SO SORRY.

SHOVE YOUR APOLOGIES UP YOUR ASS!

I SHOULD KILL YOU!

TWAPP!

YOUR MOTHER . . . SHE ALWAYS WANTED TO HELP PEOPLE . . . SHE'S A HERO, SON.

OH, GOD, GLEN . . . I'M SO SORRY . . .

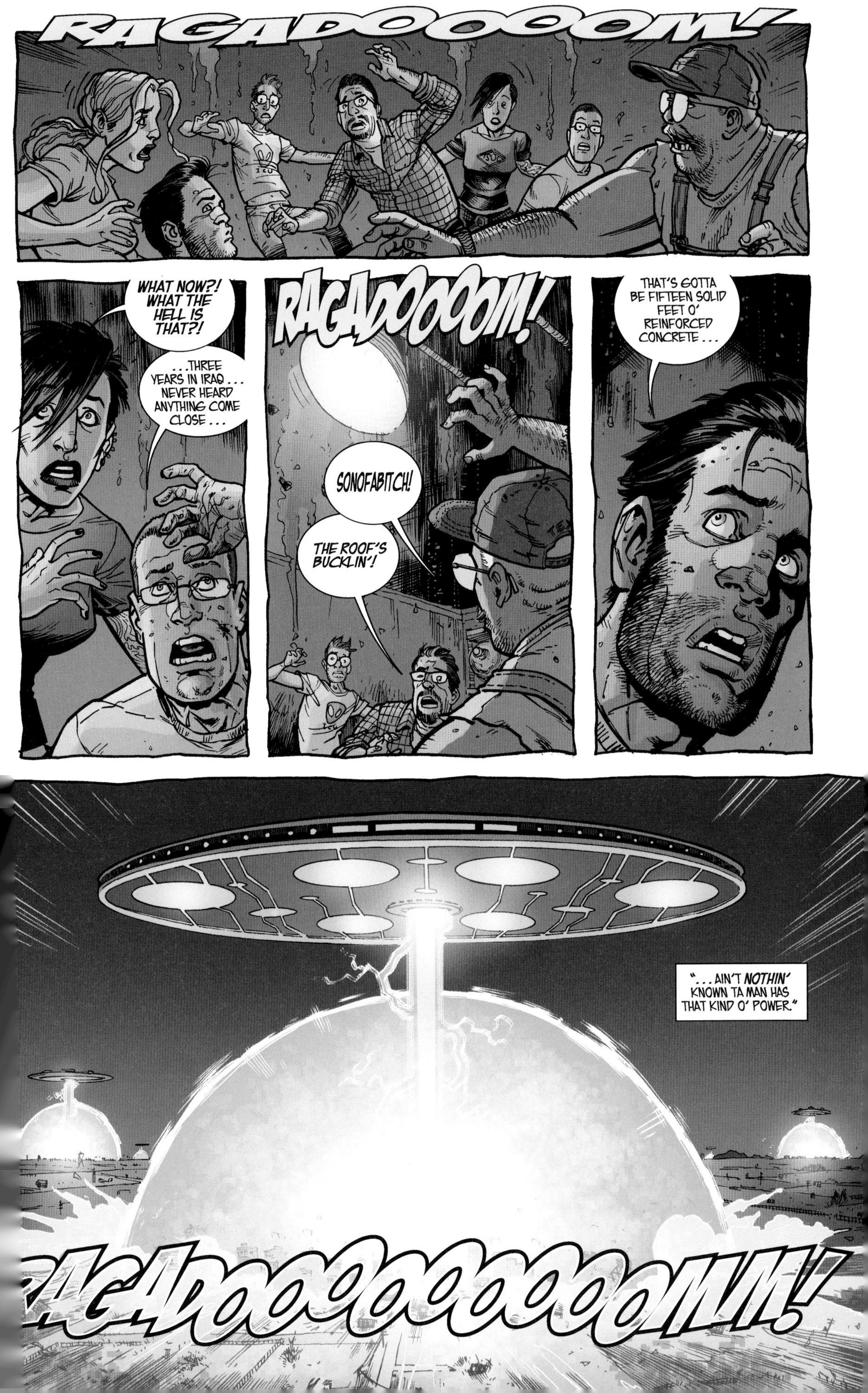
RAGADOOOOOM!
WHAT NOW?! WHAT THE HELL IS THAT?!
. . . THREE YEARS IN IRAQ . . . NEVER HEARD ANYTHING COME CLOSE . . .
RAGADOOOOOM!
SONOFABITCH!
THE ROOF'S BUCKLIN'!
THAT'S GOTTA BE FIFTEEN SOLID FEET O' REINFORCED CONCRETE . . .
". . . AIN'T NOTHIN' KNOWN TA MAN HAS THAT KIND O' POWER."
RAGADOOOOOOOOMM!

THREE MONTHS PASS . . .

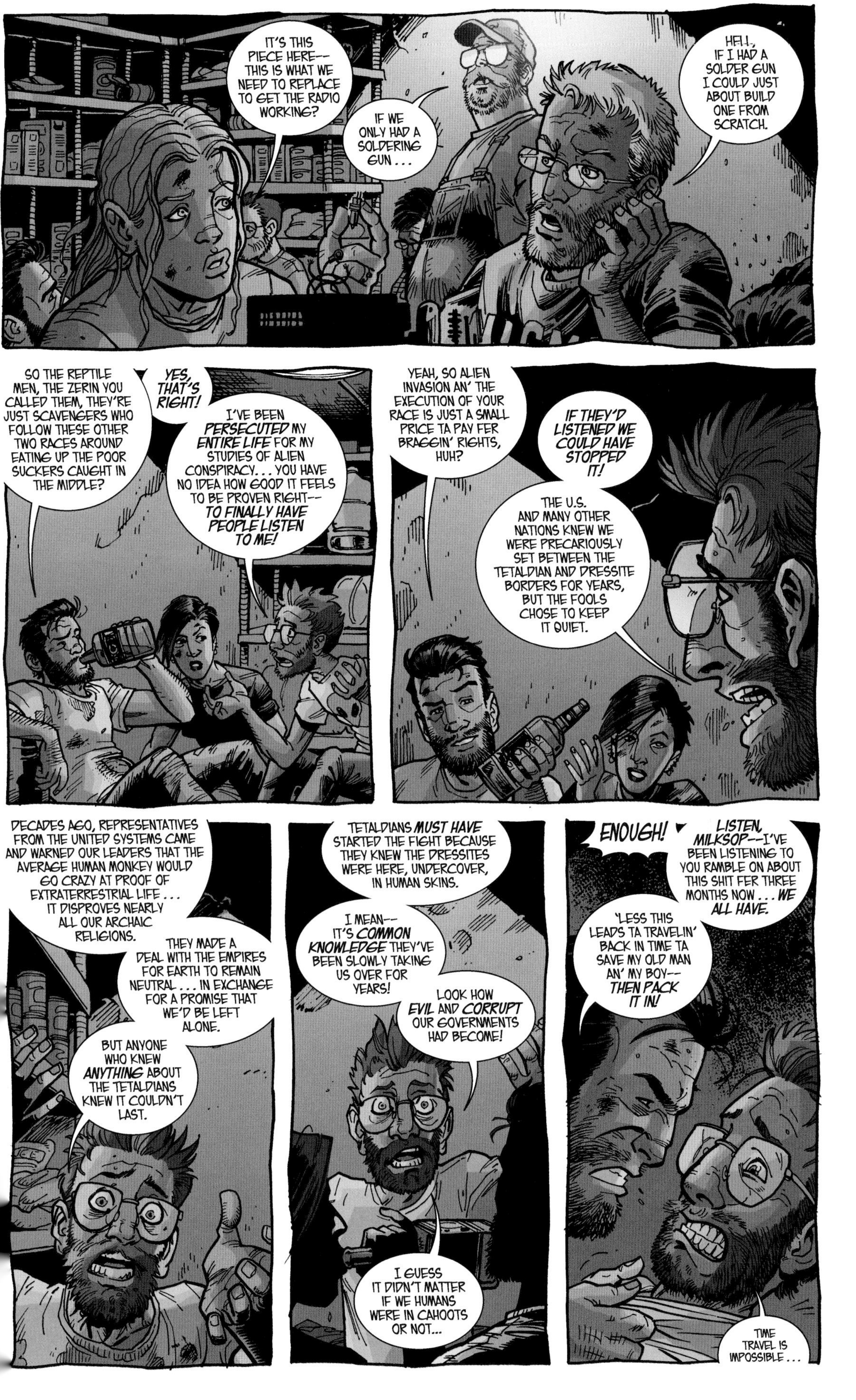
IT'S THIS PIECE HERE-- THIS IS WHAT WE NEED TO REPLACE TO GET THE RADIO WORKING?
IF WE ONLY HAD A SOLDERING GUN . . .
HELL, IF I HAD A SOLDER GUN I COULD JUST ABOUT BUILD ONE FROM SCRATCH.
SO THE REPTILE MEN, THE ZERIN YOU CALLED THEM, THEY'RE JUST SCAVENGERS WHO FOLLOW THESE OTHER TWO RACES AROUND EATING UP THE POOR SUCKERS CAUGHT IN THE MIDDLE?
YES, THAT'S RIGHT!
I'VE BEEN PERSECUTED MY ENTIRE LIFE FOR MY STUDIES OF ALIEN CONSPIRACY. . . YOU HAVE NO IDEA HOW GOOD IT FEELS TO BE PROVEN RIGHT-- TO FINALLY HAVE PEOPLE LISTEN TO ME!
YEAH, SO ALIEN INVASION AN' THE EXECUTION OF YOUR RACE IS JUST A SMALL PRICE TA PAY FER BRAGGIN' RIGHTS, HUH?
IF THEY'D LISTENED WE COULD HAVE STOPPED IT!
THE U.S. AND MANY OTHER NATIONS KNEW WE WERE PRECARIOUSLY SET BETWEEN THE TETALDIAN AND DRESSITE BORDERS FOR YEARS, BUT THE FOOLS CHOSE TO KEEP IT QUIET.
DECADES AGO, REPRESENTATIVES FROM THE UNITED SYSTEMS CAME AND WARNED OUR LEADERS THAT THE AVERAGE HUMAN MONKEY WOULD GO CRAZY AT PROOF OF EXTRATERRESTRIAL LIFE . . . IT DISPROVES NEARLY ALL OUR ARCHAIC RELIGIONS.
THEY MADE A DEAL WITH THE EMPIRES FOR EARTH TO REMAIN NEUTRAL . . . IN EXCHANGE FOR A PROMISE THAT WE'D BE LEFT ALONE.
BUT ANYONE WHO KNEW ANYTHING ABOUT THE TETALDIANS KNEW IT COULDN'T LAST.
TETALDIANS MUST HAVE STARTED THE FIGHT BECAUSE THEY KNEW THE DRESSITES WERE HERE, UNDERCOVER, IN HUMAN SKINS.
I MEAN-- IT'S COMMON KNOWLEDGE THEY'VE BEEN SLOWLY TAKING US OVER FOR YEARS!
LOOK HOW EVIL AND CORRUPT OUR GOVERNMENTS HAD BECOME!
I GUESS IT DIDN'T MATTER IF WE HUMANS WERE IN CAHOOTS OR NOT...
ENOUGH!
LISTEN, MILKSOP--I'VE BEEN LISTENING TO YOU RAMBLE ON ABOUT THIS SHIT FER THREE MONTHS NOW . . . WE ALL HAVE.
'LESS THIS LEADS TA TRAVELIN' BACK IN TIME TA SAVE MY OLD MAN AN' MY BOY-- THEN PACK IT IN!
TIME TRAVEL IS IMPOSSIBLE . . .

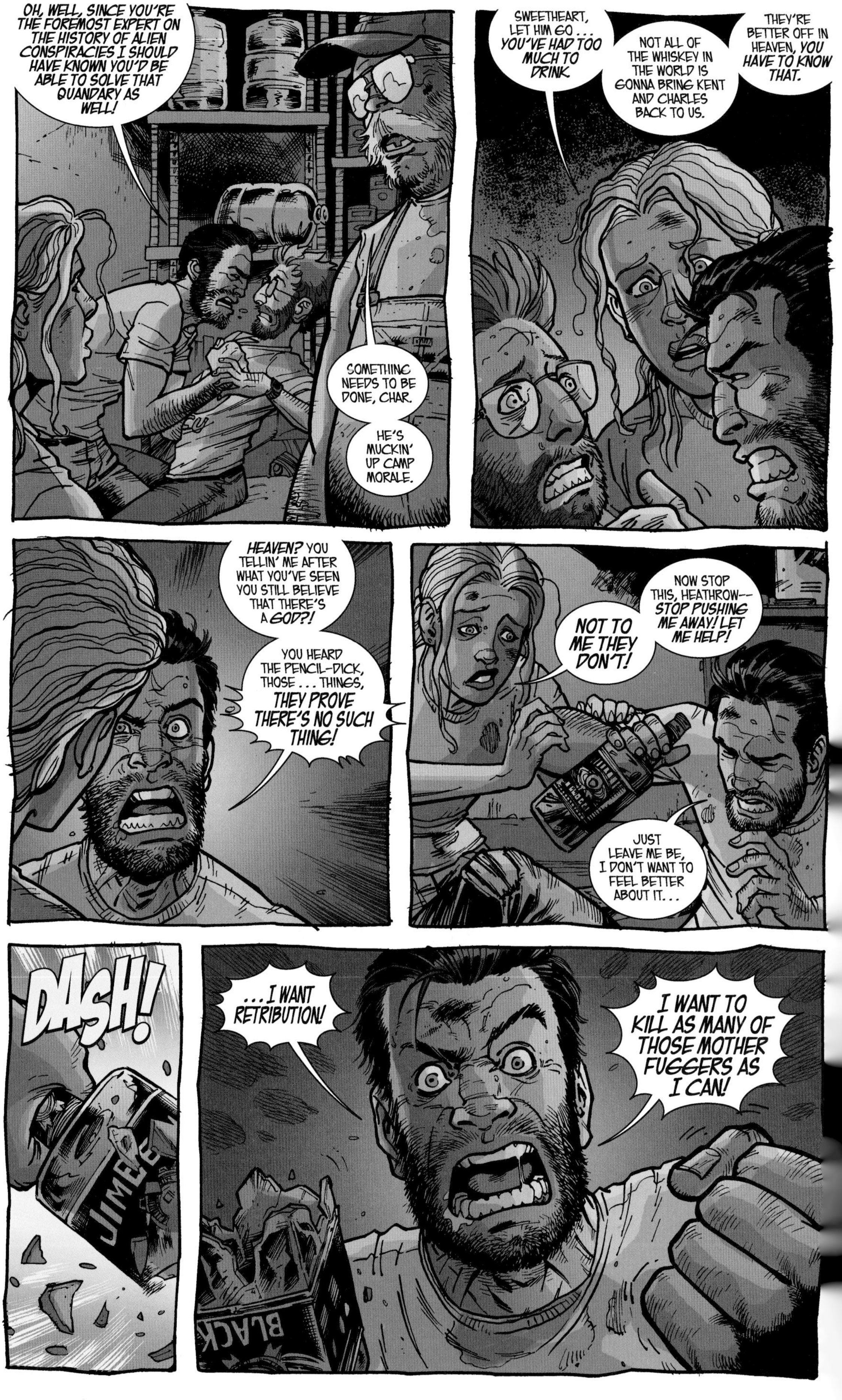
OH, WELL, SINCE YOU'RE THE FOREMOST EXPERT ON THE HISTORY OF ALIEN CONSPIRACIES I SHOULD HAVE KNOWN YOU'D BE ABLE TO SOLVE THAT QUANDARY AS WELL!
SOMETHING NEEDS TO BE DONE, CHAR.
HE'S MUCKIN' UP CAMP MORALE.
SWEETHEART, LET HIM GO . . . YOU'VE HAD TOO MUCH TO DRINK.
NOT ALL OF THE WHISKEY IN THE WORLD IS GONNA BRING KENT AND CHARLES BACK TO US.
THEY'RE BETTER OFF IN HEAVEN, YOU HAVE TO KNOW THAT.
HEAVEN? YOU TELLIN' ME AFTER WHAT YOU'VE SEEN YOU STILL BELIEVE THAT THERE'S A GOD?!
YOU HEARD THE PENCIL-DICK, THOSE . . . THINGS, THEY PROVE THERE'S NO SUCH THING!
NOT TO ME THEY DON'T!
NOW STOP THIS, HEATHROW-- STOP PUSHING ME AWAY! LET ME HELP!
JUST LEAVE ME BE, I DON'T WANT TO FEEL BETTER ABOUT IT . . .
DASH!
JIMBE
. . . I WANT RETRIBUTION!
I WANT TO KILL AS MANY OF THOSE MOTHER FUGGERS AS I CAN!
BLACK

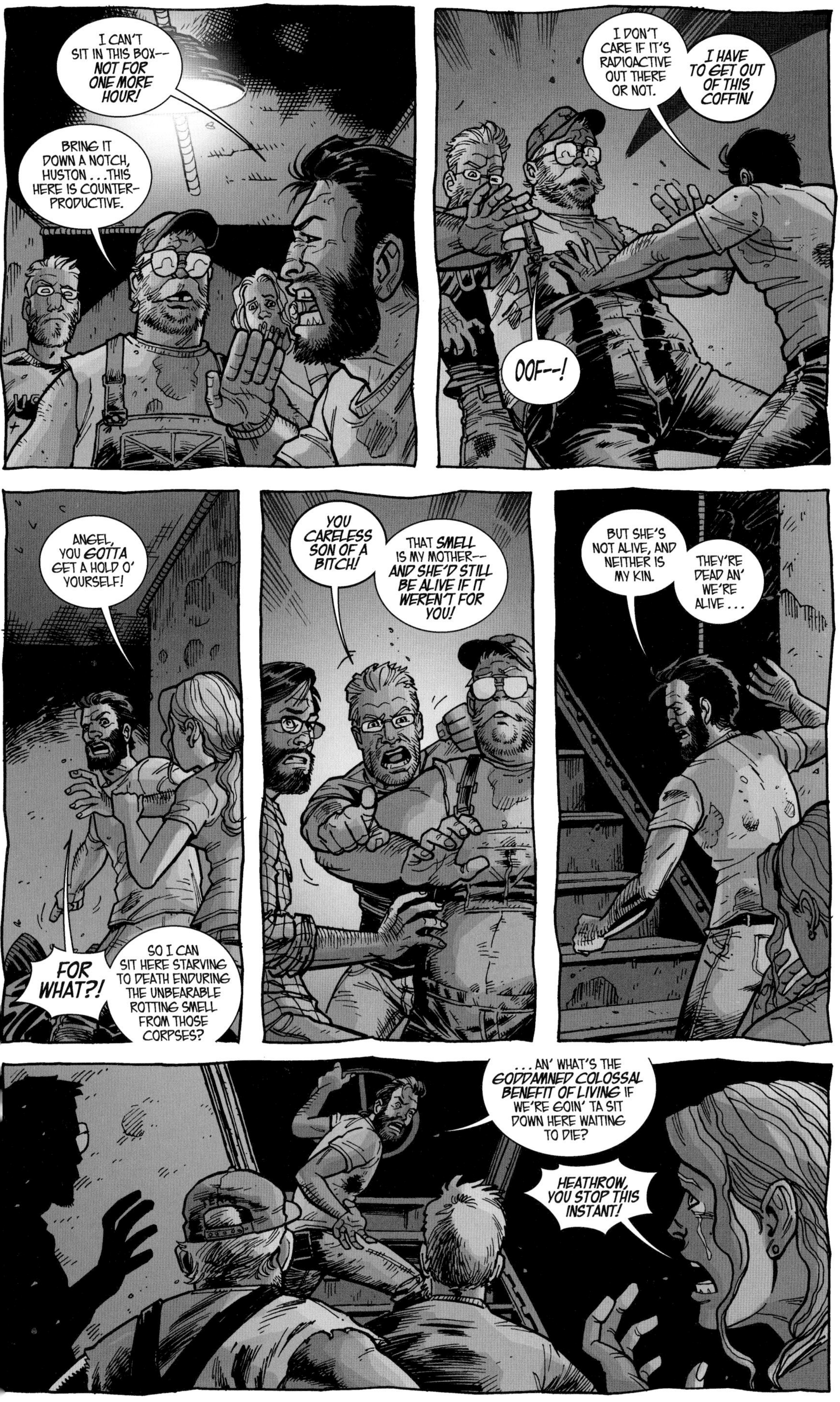
I CAN'T SIT IN THIS BOX-- NOT FOR ONE MORE HOUR!
BRING IT DOWN A NOTCH, HUSTON . . . THIS HERE IS COUNTER-PRODUCTIVE.
I DON'T CARE IF IT'S RADIOACTIVE OUT THERE OR NOT.
I HAVE TO GET OUT OF THIS COFFIN!
OOF--!
ANGEL, YOU GOTTA GET A HOLD O' YOURSELF!
FOR WHAT?!
SO I CAN SIT HERE STARVING TO DEATH ENDURING THE UNBEARABLE ROTTING SMELL FROM THOSE CORPSES?
YOU CARELESS SON OF A BITCH!
THAT SMELL IS MY MOTHER-- AND SHE'D STILL BE ALIVE IF IT WEREN'T FOR YOU!
BUT SHE'S NOT ALIVE, AND NEITHER IS MY KIN.
THEY'RE DEAD AN' WE'RE ALIVE . . .
. . . AN' WHAT'S THE GODDAMNED COLOSSAL BENEFIT OF LIVING IF WE'RE GOIN' TA SIT DOWN HERE WAITING TO DIE?
HEATHROW, YOU STOP THIS INSTANT!

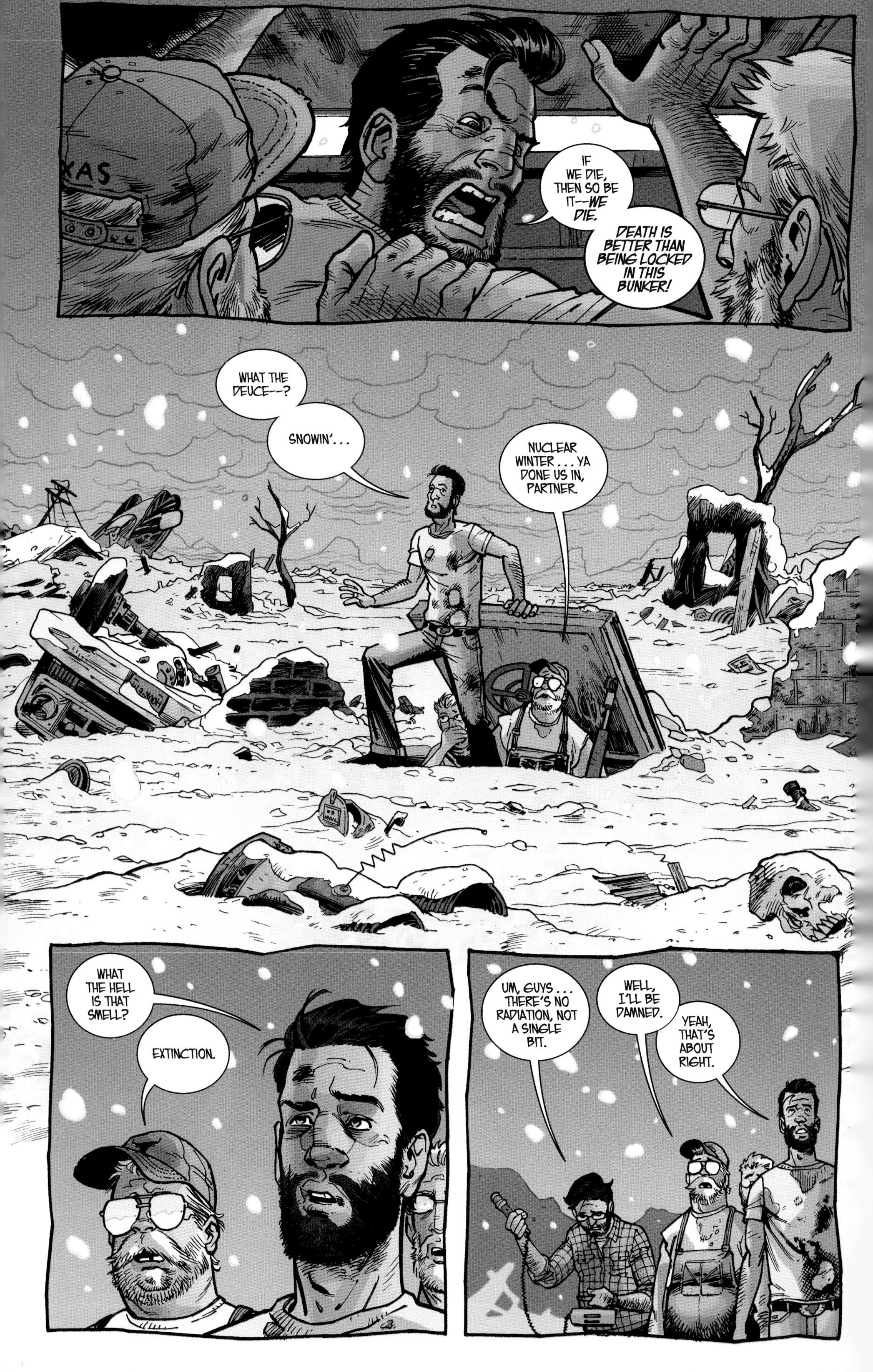
IF WE DIE, THEN SO BE IT--WE DIE.
DEATH IS BETTER THAN BEING LOCKED IN THIS BUNKER!
WHAT THE DEUCE--?
SNOWIN'...
NUCLEAR WINTER . . . YA DONE US IN, PARTNER.
WHAT THE HELL IS THAT SMELL?
EXTINCTION.
UM, GUYS . . . THERE'S NO RADIATION, NOT A SINGLE BIT.
WELL, I'LL BE DAMNED.
YEAH, THAT'S ABOUT RIGHT.

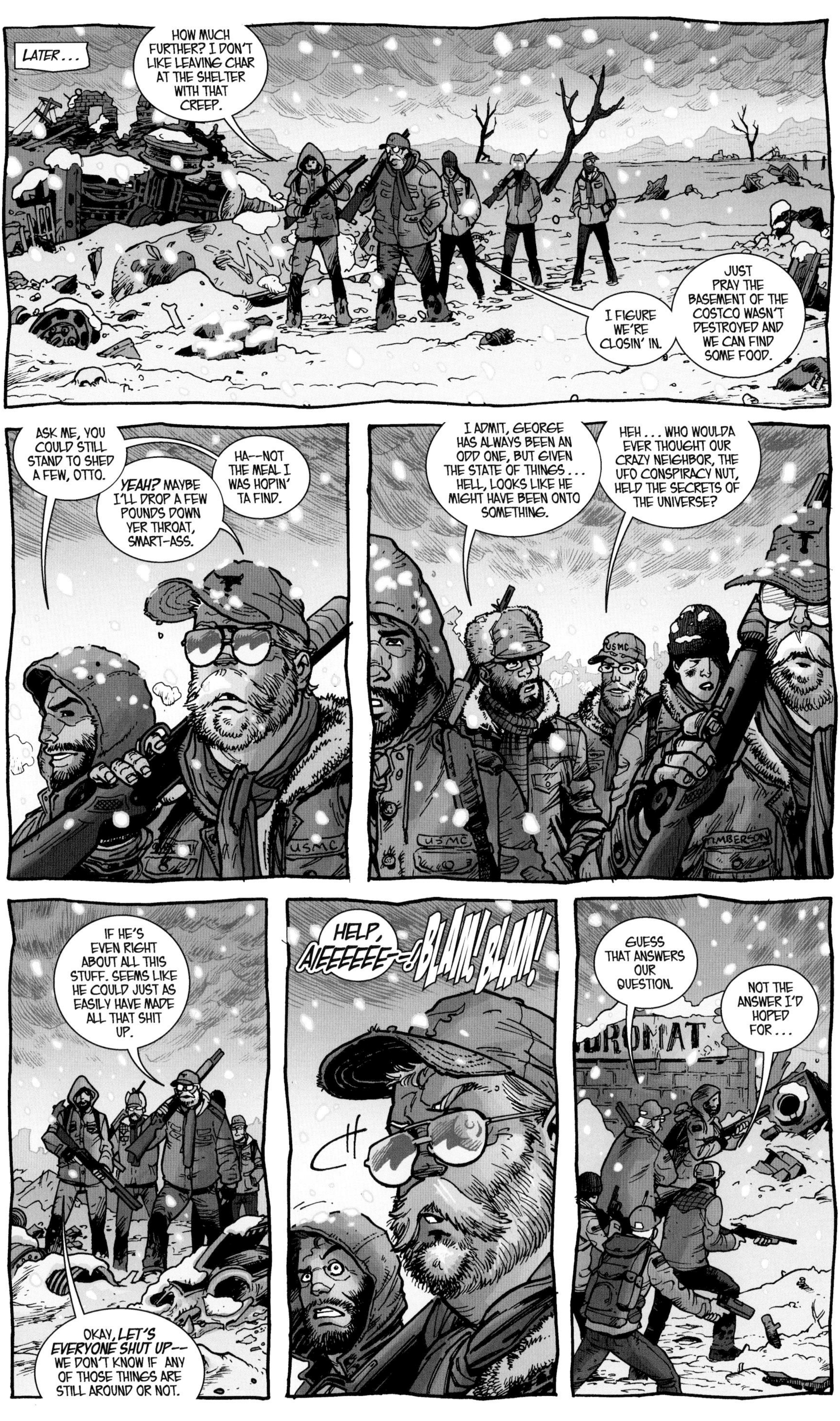
LATER . . .
HOW MUCH FURTHER? I DON'T LIKE LEAVING CHAR AT THE SHELTER WITH THAT CREEP.
I FIGURE WE'RE CLOSIN' IN.
JUST PRAY THE BASEMENT OF THE COSTCO WASN'T DESTROYED AND WE CAN FIND SOME FOOD.
ASK ME, YOU COULD STILL STAND TO SHED A FEW, OTTO.
YEAH? MAYBE I'LL DROP A FEW POUNDS DOWN YER THROAT, SMART-ASS.
HA--NOT THE MEAL I WAS HOPIN' TA FIND.
USMC
I ADMIT, GEORGE HAS ALWAYS BEEN AN ODD ONE, BUT GIVEN THE STATE OF THINGS . . . HELL, LOOKS LIKE HE MIGHT HAVE BEEN ONTO SOMETHING.
HEH . . . WHO WOULDA EVER THOUGHT OUR CRAZY NEIGHBOR, THE UFO CONSPIRACY NUT, HELD THE SECRETS OF THE UNIVERSE?
USMC
USMC
TIMBERSON
IF HE'S EVEN RIGHT ABOUT ALL THIS STUFF. SEEMS LIKE HE COULD JUST AS EASILY HAVE MADE ALL THAT SHIT UP.
OKAY, LET'S EVERYONE SHUT UP-- WE DON'T KNOW IF ANY OF THOSE THINGS ARE STILL AROUND OR NOT.
HELP, AIEEEEEE--!
BLAM! BLAM!
GUESS THAT ANSWERS OUR QUESTION.
NOT THE ANSWER I'D HOPED FOR . . .
UROMAT

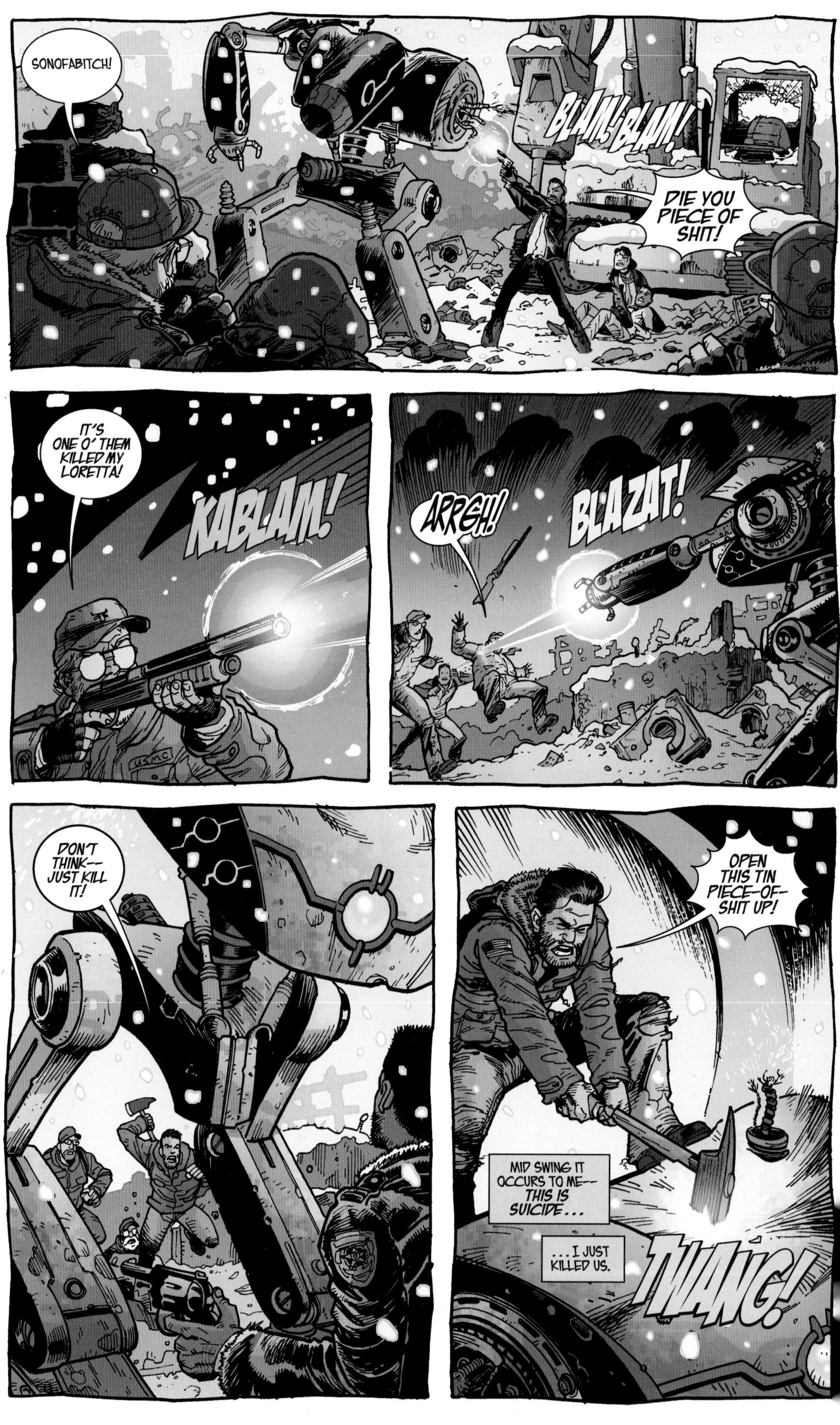
SONOFABITCH!
BLAM! BLAM!
DIE YOU PIECE OF SHIT!
IT'S ONE O' THEM KILLED MY LORETTA!
KABLAM!
ARRGH!
BLAZAT!
DON'T THINK-- JUST KILL IT!
OPEN THIS TIN PIECE-OF-SHIT UP!
MID SWING IT OCCURS TO ME-- THIS IS SUICIDE...
...I JUST KILLED US.
TWANG!

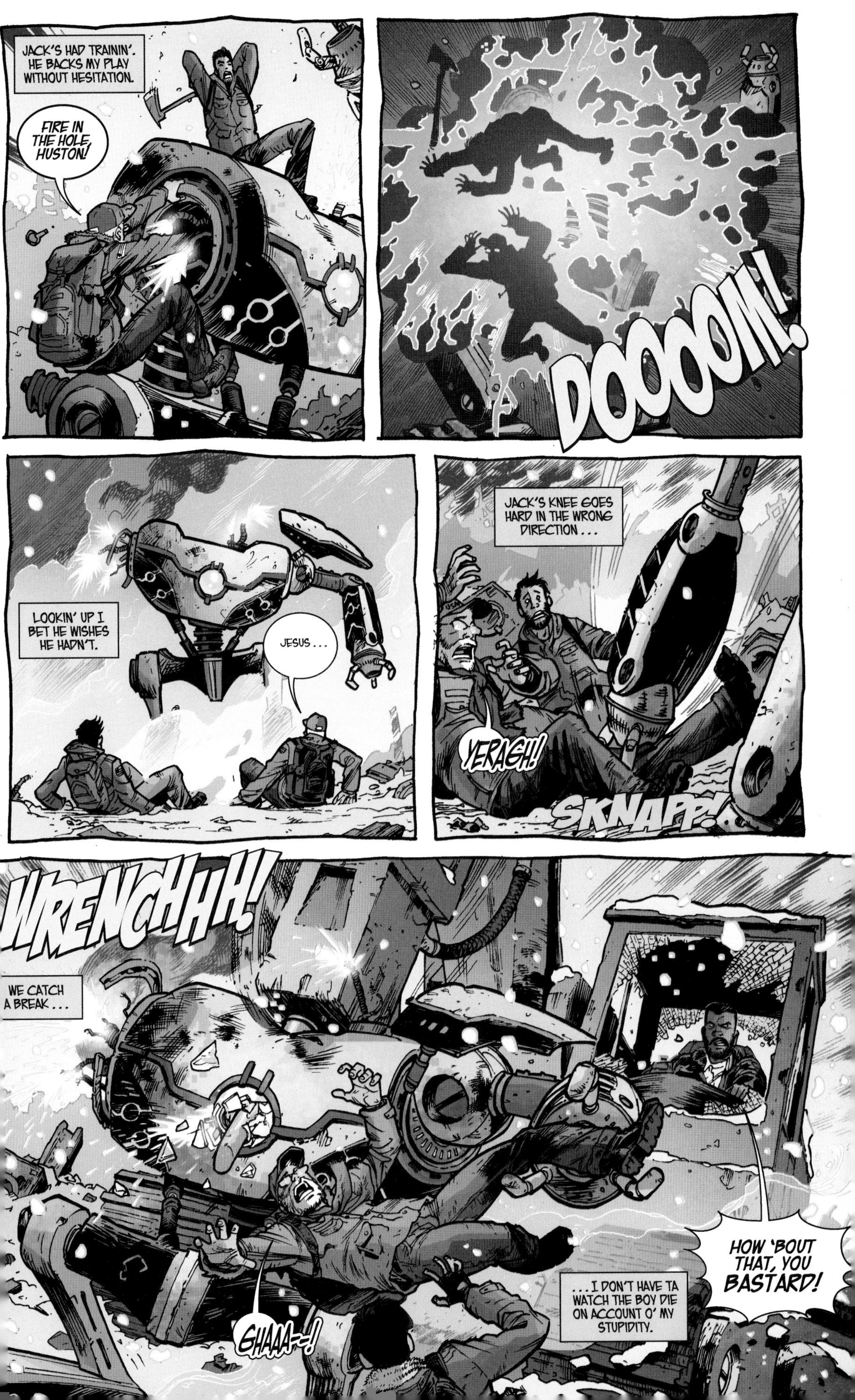
JACK'S HAD TRAININ'. HE BACKS MY PLAY WITHOUT HESITATION.
FIRE IN THE HOLE, HUSTON!
DOOOOOM!
LOOKIN' UP I BET HE WISHES HE HADN'T.
JESUS . . .
JACK'S KNEE GOES HARD IN THE WRONG DIRECTION . . .
YERAGH!
SKNAPP!
WRENCHHH!
WE CATCH A BREAK . . .
. . . I DON'T HAVE TA WATCH THE BOY DIE ON ACCOUNT O' MY STUPIDITY.
HOW 'BOUT THAT, YOU BASTARD!
GHAAA--!

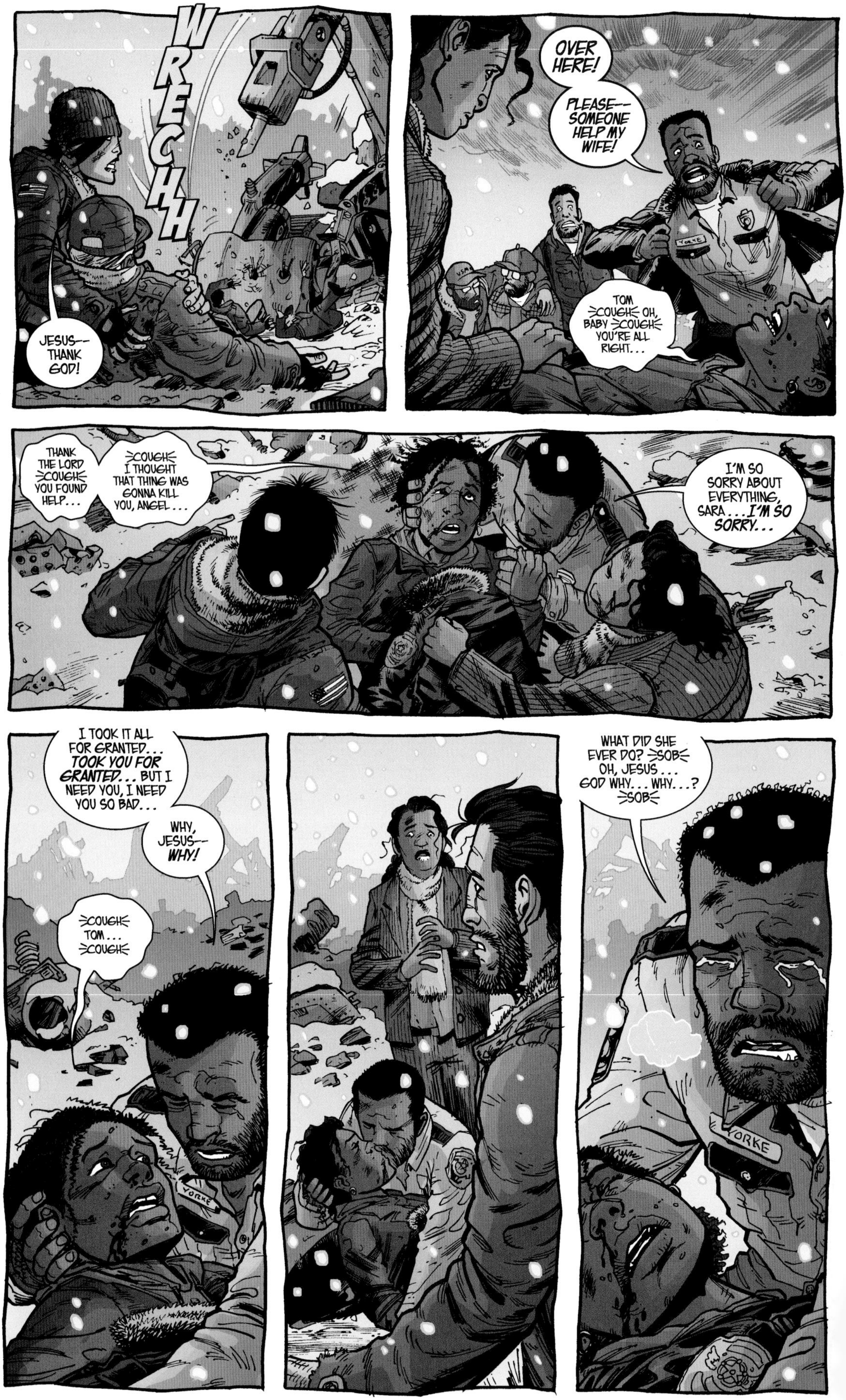
WRECHHH
JESUS-- THANK GOD!
OVER HERE!
PLEASE-- SOMEONE HELP MY WIFE!
TOM ≶COUGH≷ OH, BABY ≶COUGH≷ YOU'RE ALL RIGHT...
THANK THE LORD ≶COUGH≷ YOU FOUND HELP...
≶COUGH≷ I THOUGHT THAT THING WAS GONNA KILL YOU, ANGEL...
I'M SO SORRY ABOUT EVERYTHING, SARA... I'M SO SORRY...
I TOOK IT ALL FOR GRANTED... TOOK YOU FOR GRANTED... BUT I NEED YOU, I NEED YOU SO BAD...
WHY, JESUS-- WHY!
≶COUGH≷ TOM... ≶COUGH≷
WHAT DID SHE EVER DO? ≶SOB≷ OH, JESUS... GOD WHY... WHY...? ≶SOB≷
YORKE

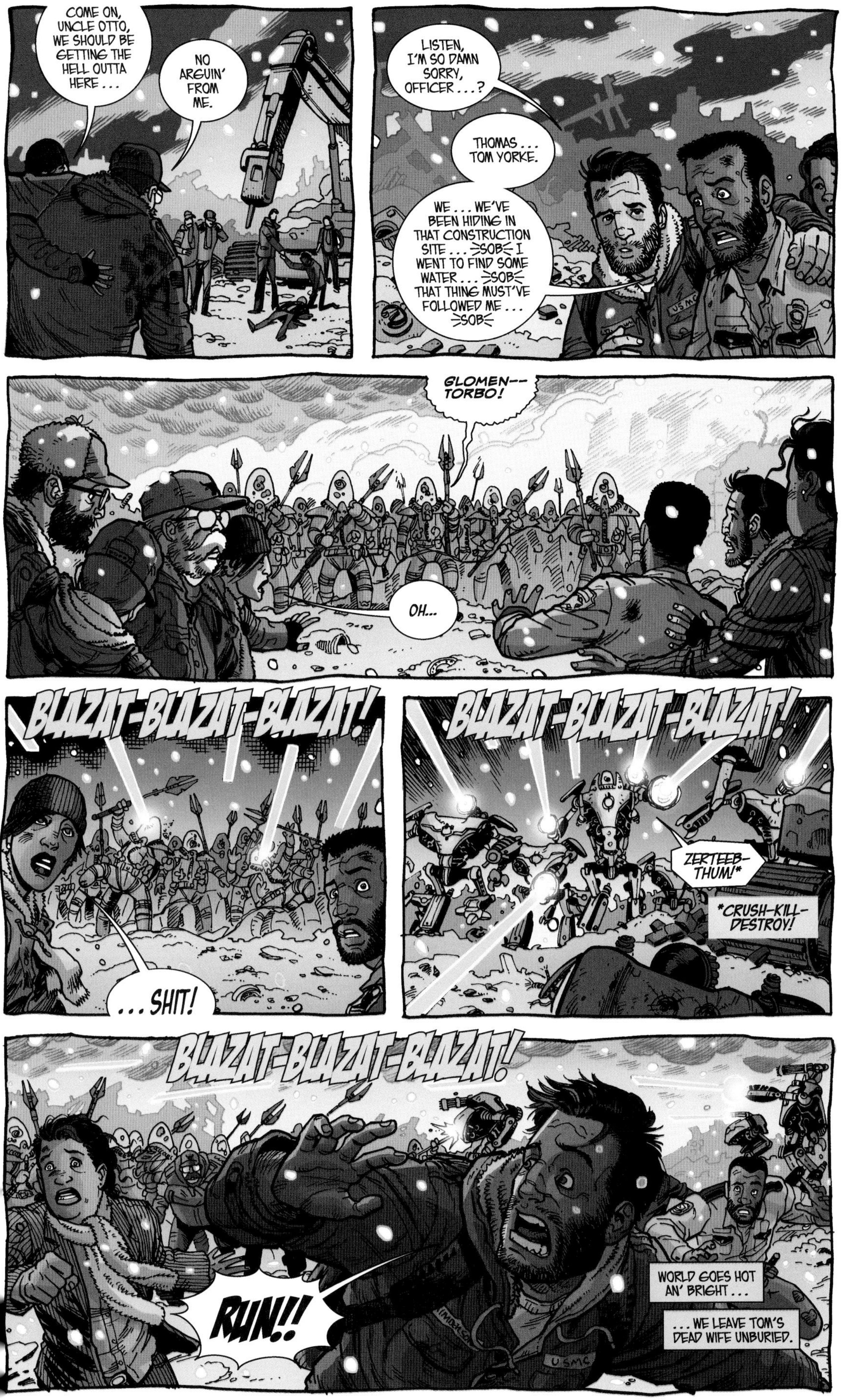
COME ON, UNCLE OTTO, WE SHOULD BE GETTING THE HELL OUTTA HERE . . .
NO ARGUIN' FROM ME.
LISTEN, I'M SO DAMN SORRY, OFFICER . . . ?
THOMAS . . . TOM YORKE.
WE . . . WE'VE BEEN HIDING IN THAT CONSTRUCTION SITE . . . SOB I WENT TO FIND SOME WATER . . . SOB THAT THING MUST'VE FOLLOWED ME . . . SOB
GLOMEN--TORBO!
OH...
BLAZAT-BLAZAT-BLAZAT!
. . . SHIT!
BLAZAT-BLAZAT-BLAZAT!
ZERTEEB-THUM!*
*CRUSH-KILL-DESTROY!
BLAZAT-BLAZAT-BLAZAT!
RUN!!
WORLD GOES HOT AN' BRIGHT . . .
. . . WE LEAVE TOM'S DEAD WIFE UNBURIED.

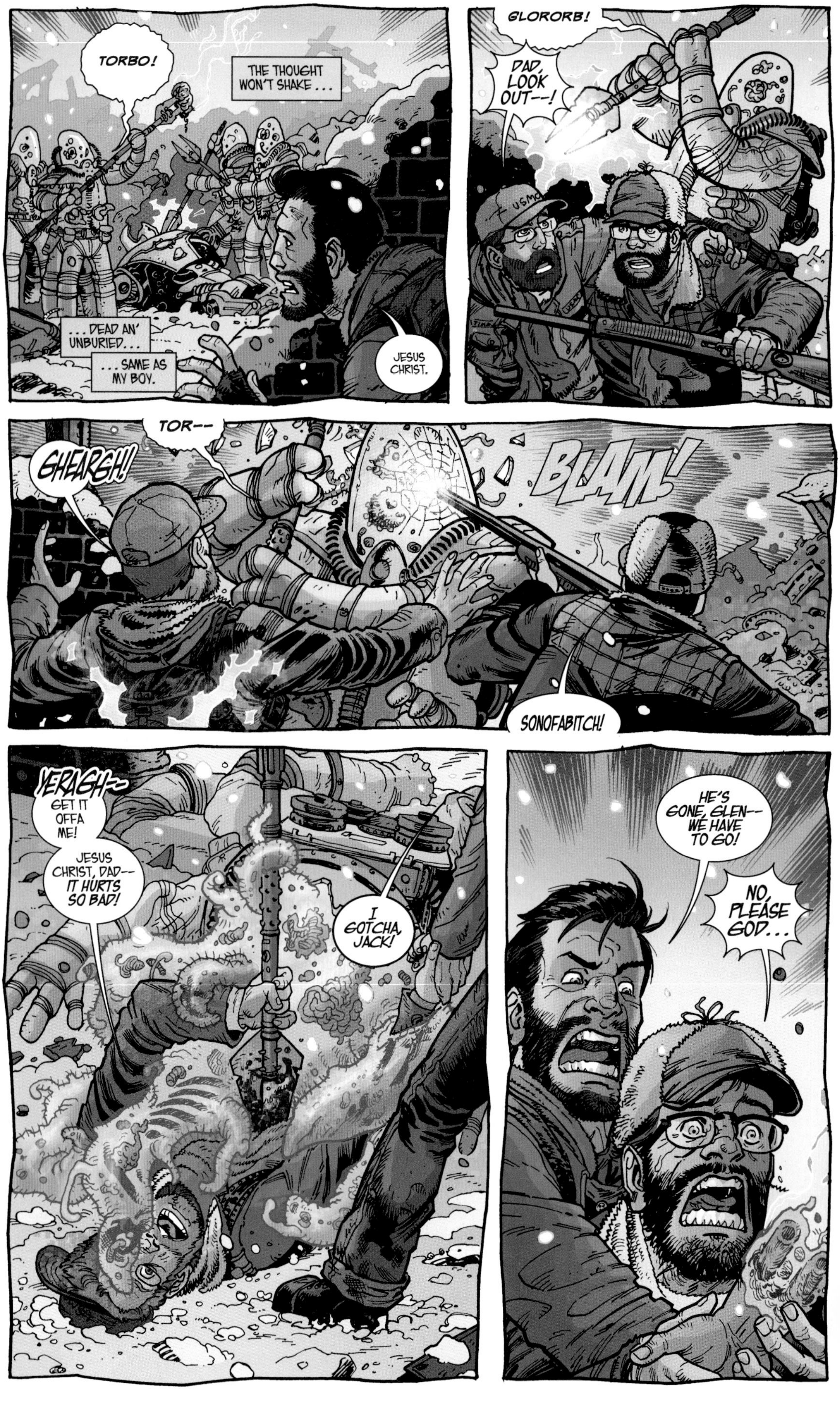

TORBO!
THE THOUGHT WON'T SHAKE...
...DEAD AN' UNBURIED...
...SAME AS MY BOY.
JESUS CHRIST.
GLORORB!
DAD, LOOK OUT--!
TOR--
GHEARGH!
BLAM!
SONOFABITCH!
YERAGH--
GET IT OFFA ME!
JESUS CHRIST, DAD-- IT HURTS SO BAD!
I GOTCHA, JACK!
HE'S GONE, GLEN-- WE HAVE TO GO!
NO, PLEASE GOD...

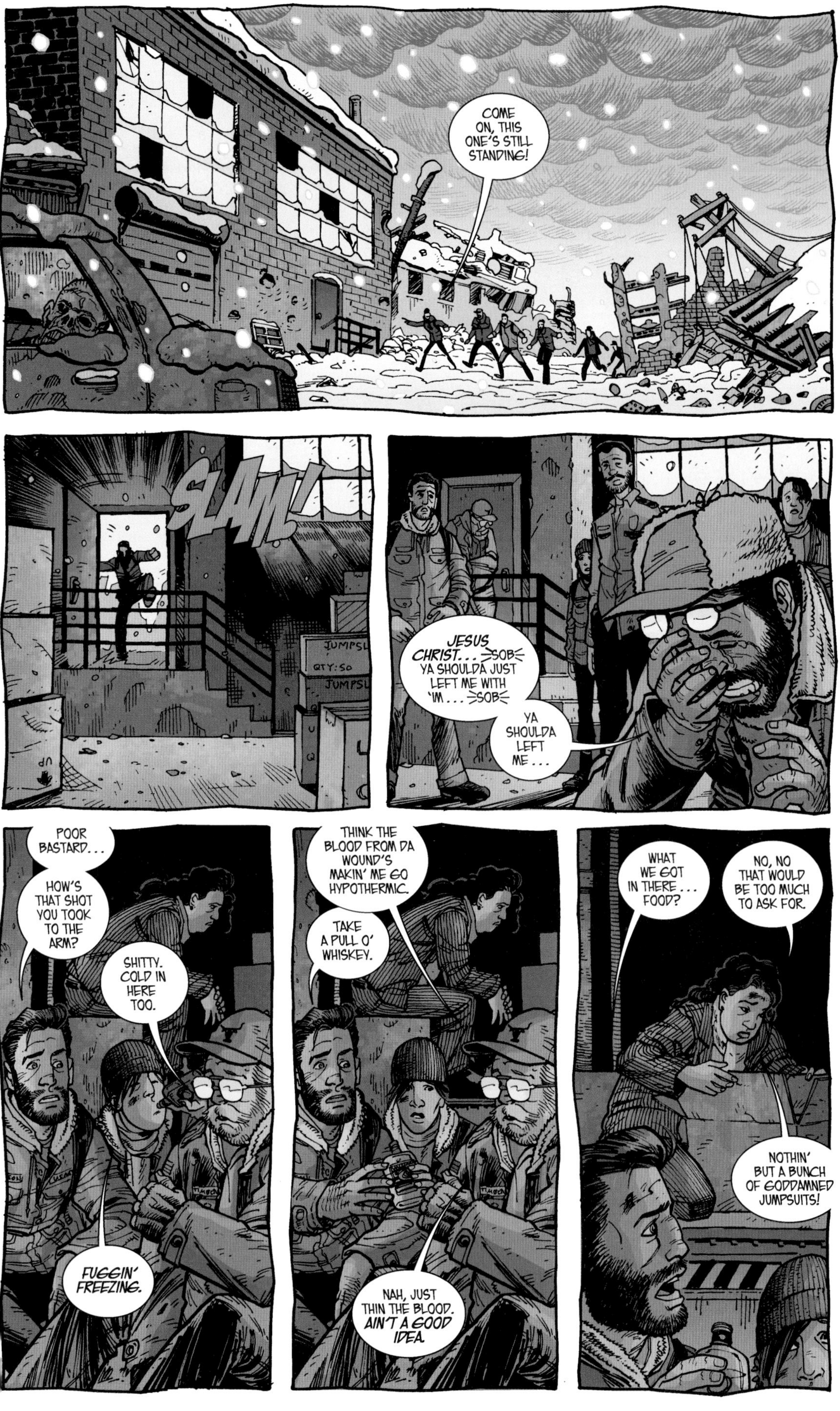
COME ON, THIS ONE'S STILL STANDING!
SLAM!
JUMPSU
QTY: 50
JUMPSU
UP
JESUS CHRIST... SOB YA SHOULDA JUST LEFT ME WITH 'IM... SOB
YA SHOULDA LEFT ME...
POOR BASTARD...
HOW'S THAT SHOT YOU TOOK TO THE ARM?
SHITTY. COLD IN HERE TOO.
FUGGIN' FREEZING.
THINK THE BLOOD FROM DA WOUND'S MAKIN' ME GO HYPOTHERMIC.
TAKE A PULL O' WHISKEY.
NAH, JUST THIN THE BLOOD. AIN'T A GOOD IDEA.
WHAT WE GOT IN THERE... FOOD?
NO, NO THAT WOULD BE TOO MUCH TO ASK FOR.
NOTHIN' BUT A BUNCH OF GODDAMNED JUMPSUITS!

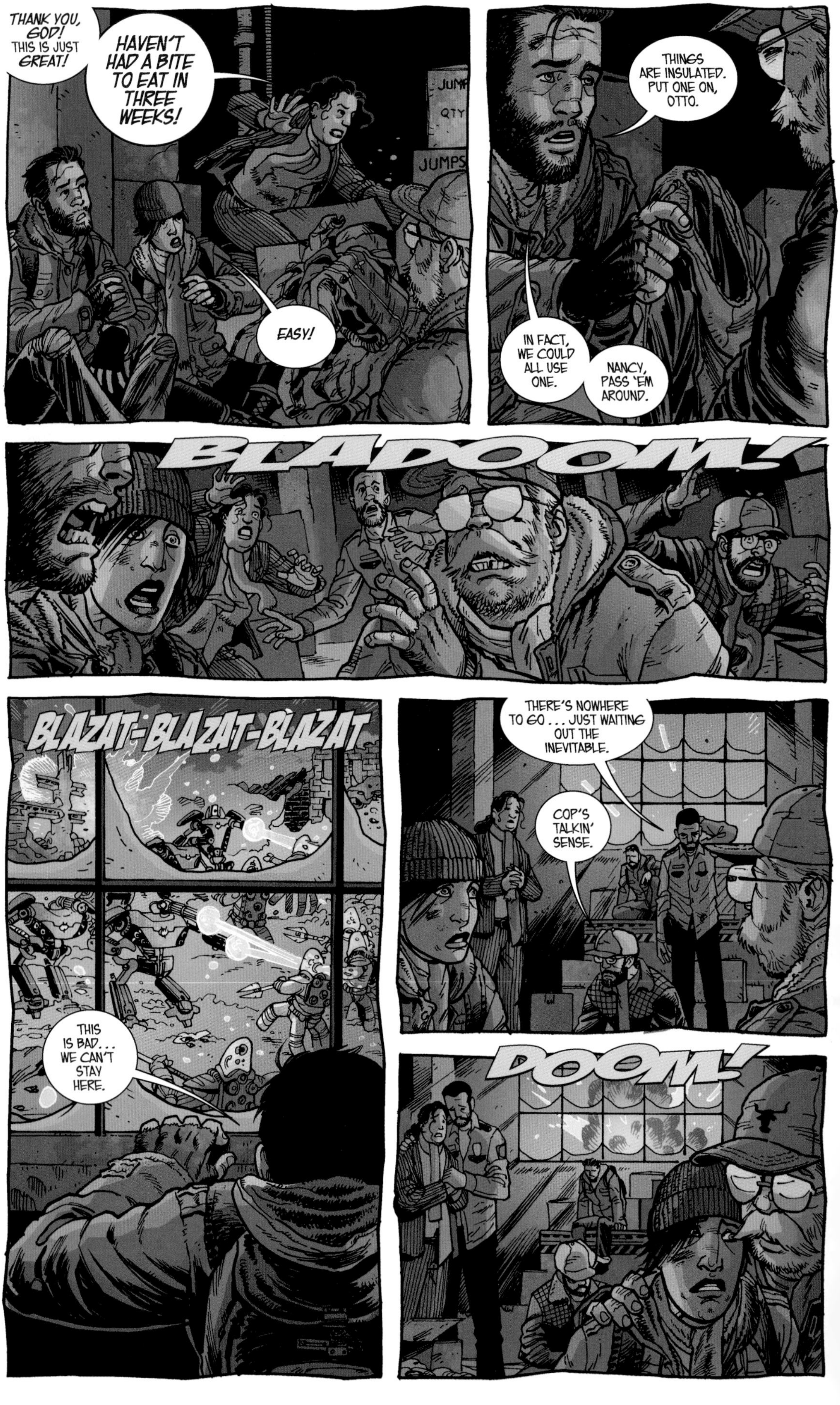
THANK YOU, GOD! THIS IS JUST GREAT!
HAVEN'T HAD A BITE TO EAT IN THREE WEEKS!
EASY!
THINGS ARE INSULATED. PUT ONE ON, OTTO.
IN FACT, WE COULD ALL USE ONE.
NANCY, PASS 'EM AROUND.
BLADOOM!
BLAZAT-BLAZAT-BLAZAT
THIS IS BAD... WE CAN'T STAY HERE.
THERE'S NOWHERE TO GO... JUST WAITING OUT THE INEVITABLE.
COP'S TALKIN' SENSE.
DOOM!

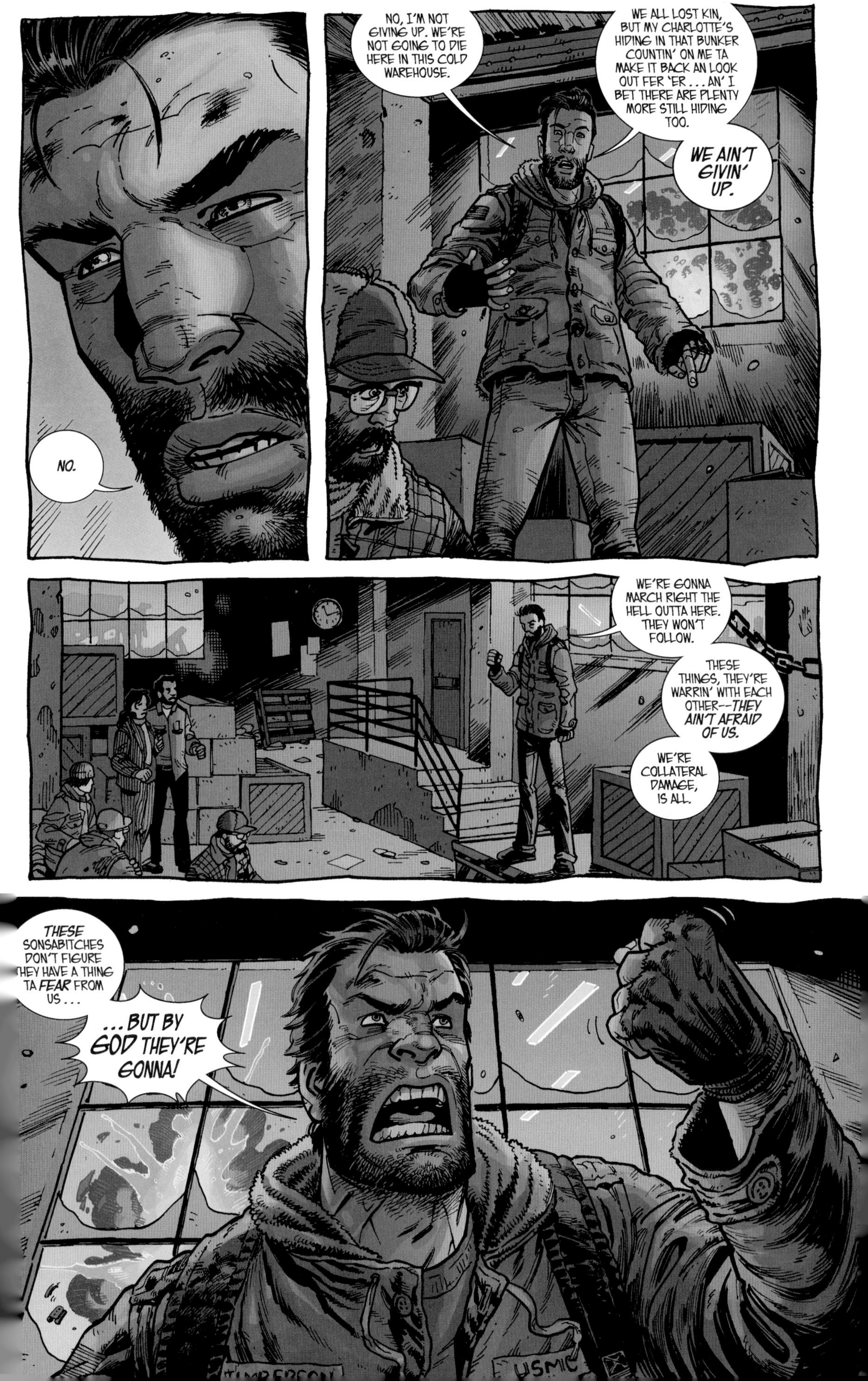
NO.
NO, I'M NOT GIVING UP. WE'RE NOT GOING TO DIE HERE IN THIS COLD WAREHOUSE.
WE ALL LOST KIN, BUT MY CHARLOTTE'S HIDING IN THAT BUNKER COUNTIN' ON ME TA MAKE IT BACK AN' LOOK OUT FER 'ER . . . AN' I BET THERE ARE PLENTY MORE STILL HIDING TOO.
WE AIN'T GIVIN' UP.
WE'RE GONNA MARCH RIGHT THE HELL OUTTA HERE. THEY WON'T FOLLOW.
THESE THINGS, THEY'RE WARRIN' WITH EACH OTHER--THEY AIN'T AFRAID OF US.
WE'RE COLLATERAL DAMAGE, IS ALL.
THESE SONSABITCHES DON'T FIGURE THEY HAVE A THING TA FEAR FROM US . . .
. . . BUT BY GOD THEY'RE GONNA!
USMC

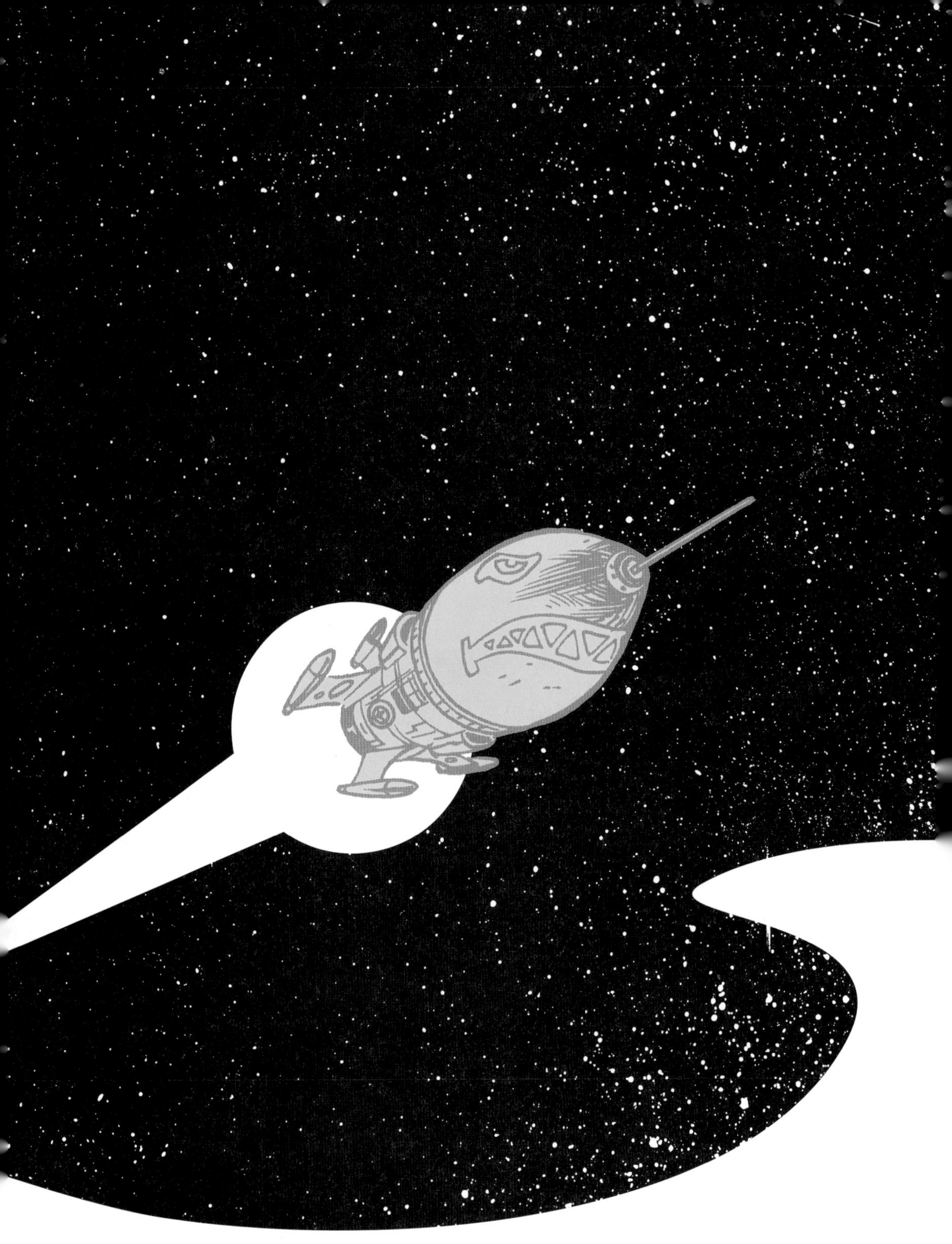

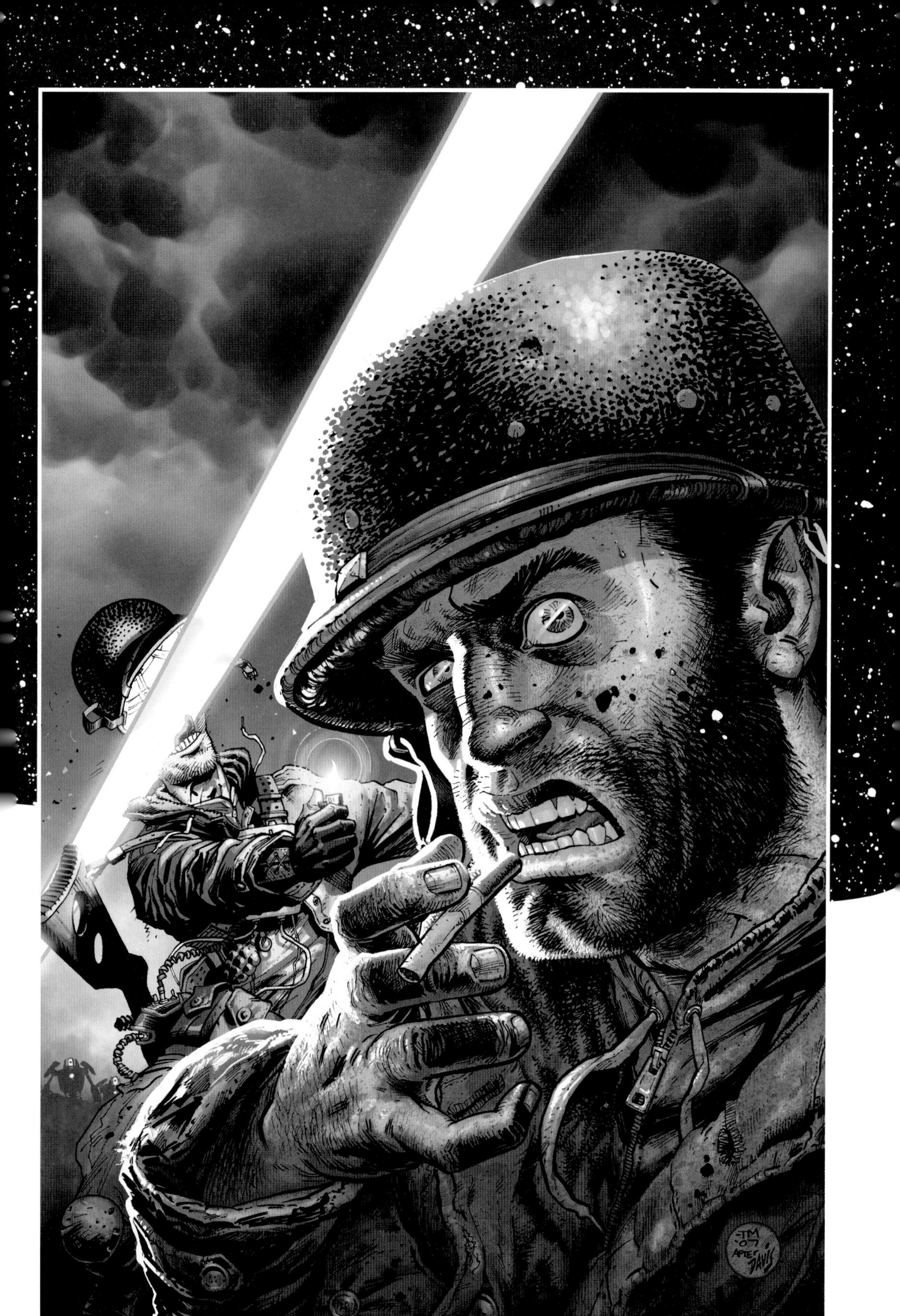

FEAR AGENT #14
ART BY **TONY MOORE**

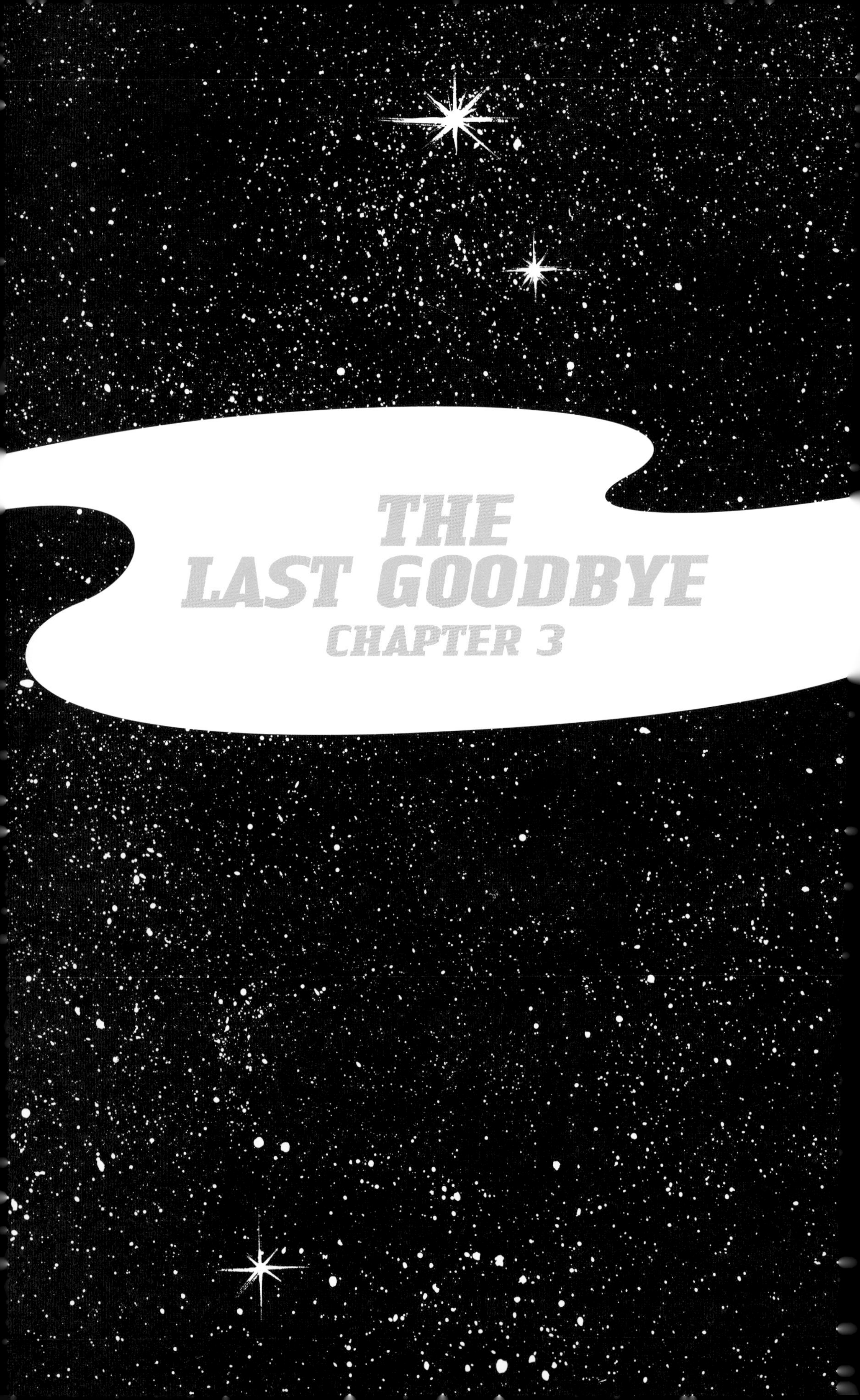
THE
LAST GOODBYE
CHAPTER 3

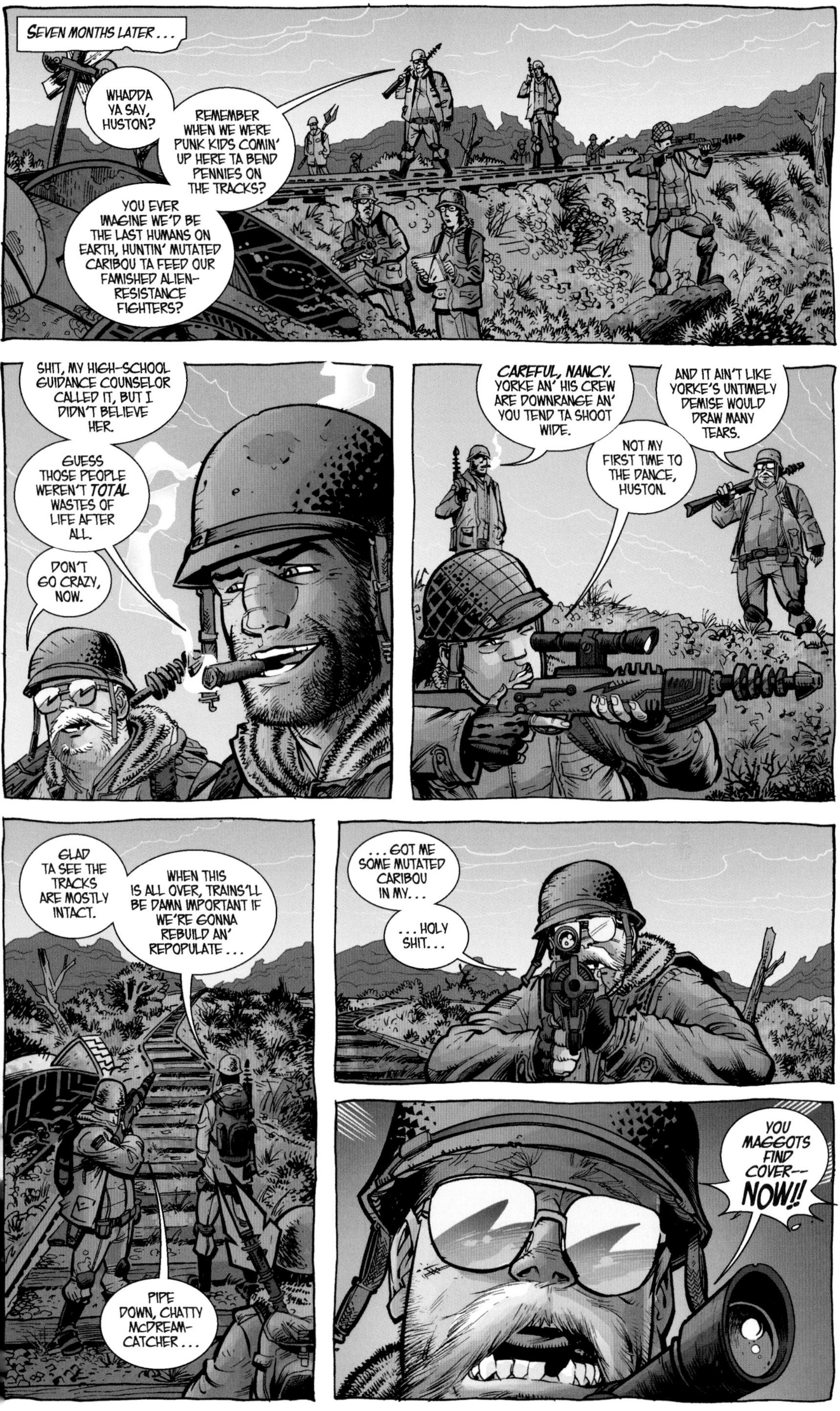
SEVEN MONTHS LATER . . .
WHADDA YA SAY, HUSTON?
REMEMBER WHEN WE WERE PUNK KIDS COMIN' UP HERE TA BEND PENNIES ON THE TRACKS?
YOU EVER IMAGINE WE'D BE THE LAST HUMANS ON EARTH, HUNTIN' MUTATED CARIBOU TA FEED OUR FAMISHED ALIEN-RESISTANCE FIGHTERS?
SHIT, MY HIGH-SCHOOL GUIDANCE COUNSELOR CALLED IT, BUT I DIDN'T BELIEVE HER.
GUESS THOSE PEOPLE WEREN'T TOTAL WASTES OF LIFE AFTER ALL.
DON'T GO CRAZY, NOW.
CAREFUL, NANCY. YORKE AN' HIS CREW ARE DOWNRANGE AN' YOU TEND TA SHOOT WIDE.
AND IT AIN'T LIKE YORKE'S UNTIMELY DEMISE WOULD DRAW MANY TEARS.
NOT MY FIRST TIME TO THE DANCE, HUSTON.
GLAD TA SEE THE TRACKS ARE MOSTLY INTACT.
WHEN THIS IS ALL OVER, TRAINS'LL BE DAMN IMPORTANT IF WE'RE GONNA REBUILD AN' REPOPULATE . . .
PIPE DOWN, CHATTY McDREAM-CATCHER . . .
. . . GOT ME SOME MUTATED CARIBOU IN MY . . .
. . . HOLY SHIT . . .
YOU MAGGOTS FIND COVER-- NOW!!

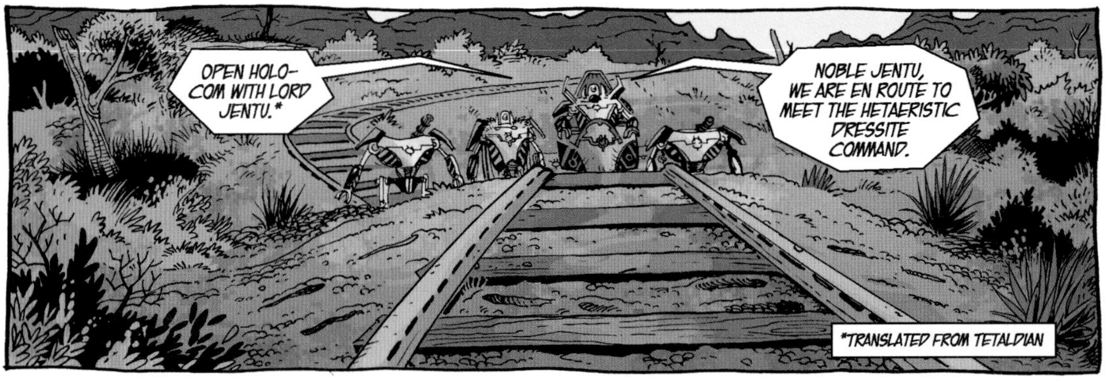
OPEN HOLO-COM WITH LORD JENTU.*
NOBLE JENTU, WE ARE EN ROUTE TO MEET THE HETAERISTIC DRESSITE COMMAND.
*TRANSLATED FROM TETALDIAN

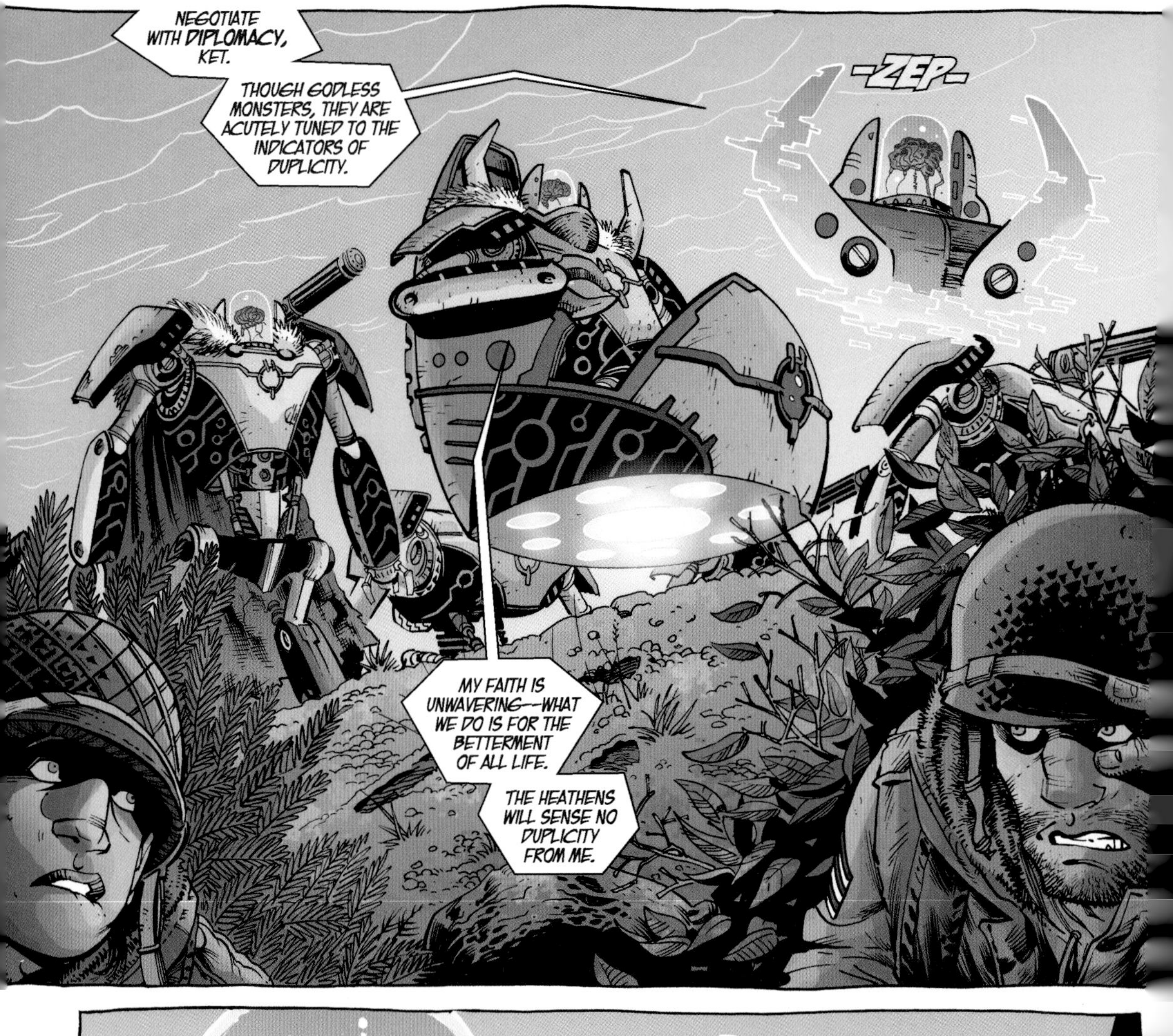
NEGOTIATE WITH DIPLOMACY, KET.
THOUGH GODLESS MONSTERS, THEY ARE ACUTELY TUNED TO THE INDICATORS OF DUPLICITY.
-ZEP-
MY FAITH IS UNWAVERING--WHAT WE DO IS FOR THE BETTERMENT OF ALL LIFE.
THE HEATHENS WILL SENSE NO DUPLICITY FROM ME.

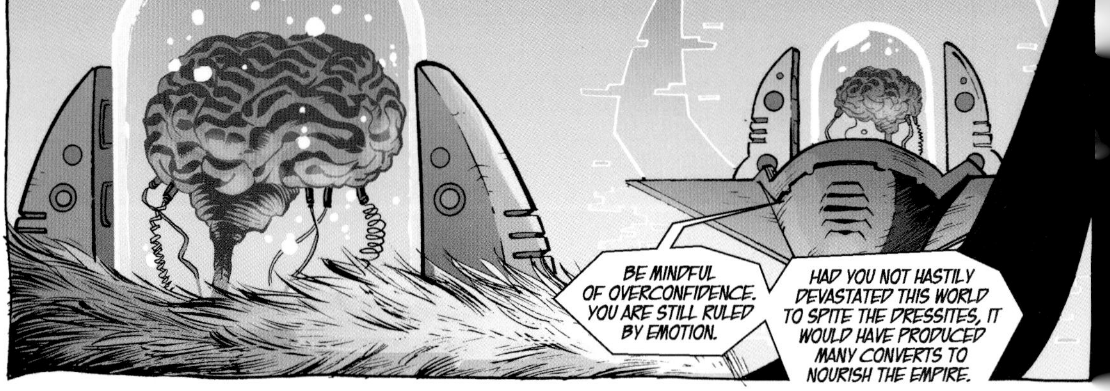
BE MINDFUL OF OVERCONFIDENCE. YOU ARE STILL RULED BY EMOTION.
HAD YOU NOT HASTILY DEVASTATED THIS WORLD TO SPITE THE DRESSITES, IT WOULD HAVE PRODUCED MANY CONVERTS TO NOURISH THE EMPIRE.

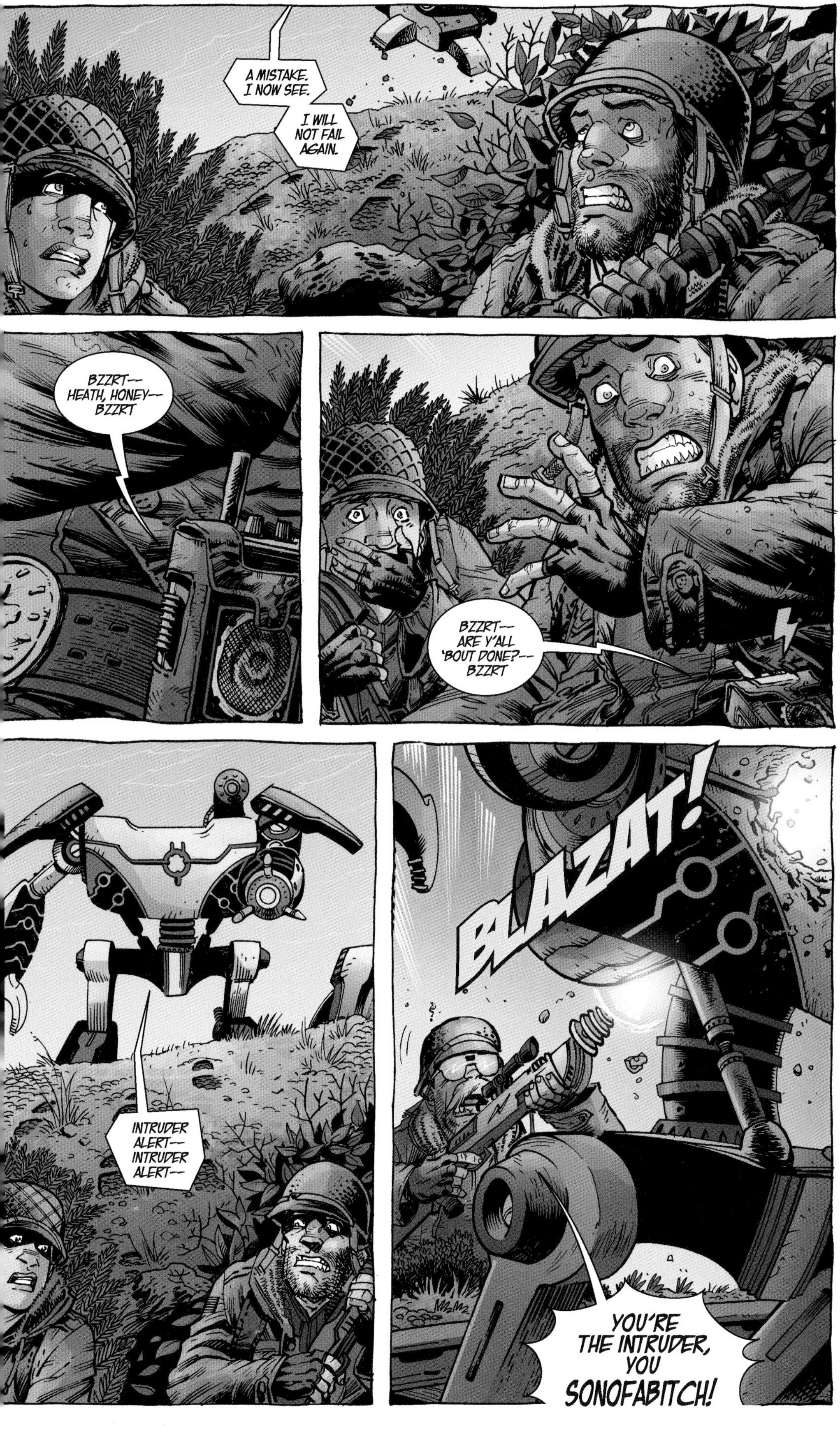
A MISTAKE. I NOW SEE.
I WILL NOT FAIL AGAIN.
BZZRT-- HEATH, HONEY-- BZZRT
BZZRT-- ARE Y'ALL 'BOUT DONE?-- BZZRT
INTRUDER ALERT-- INTRUDER ALERT--
BLAZAT!
YOU'RE THE INTRUDER, YOU SONOFABITCH!

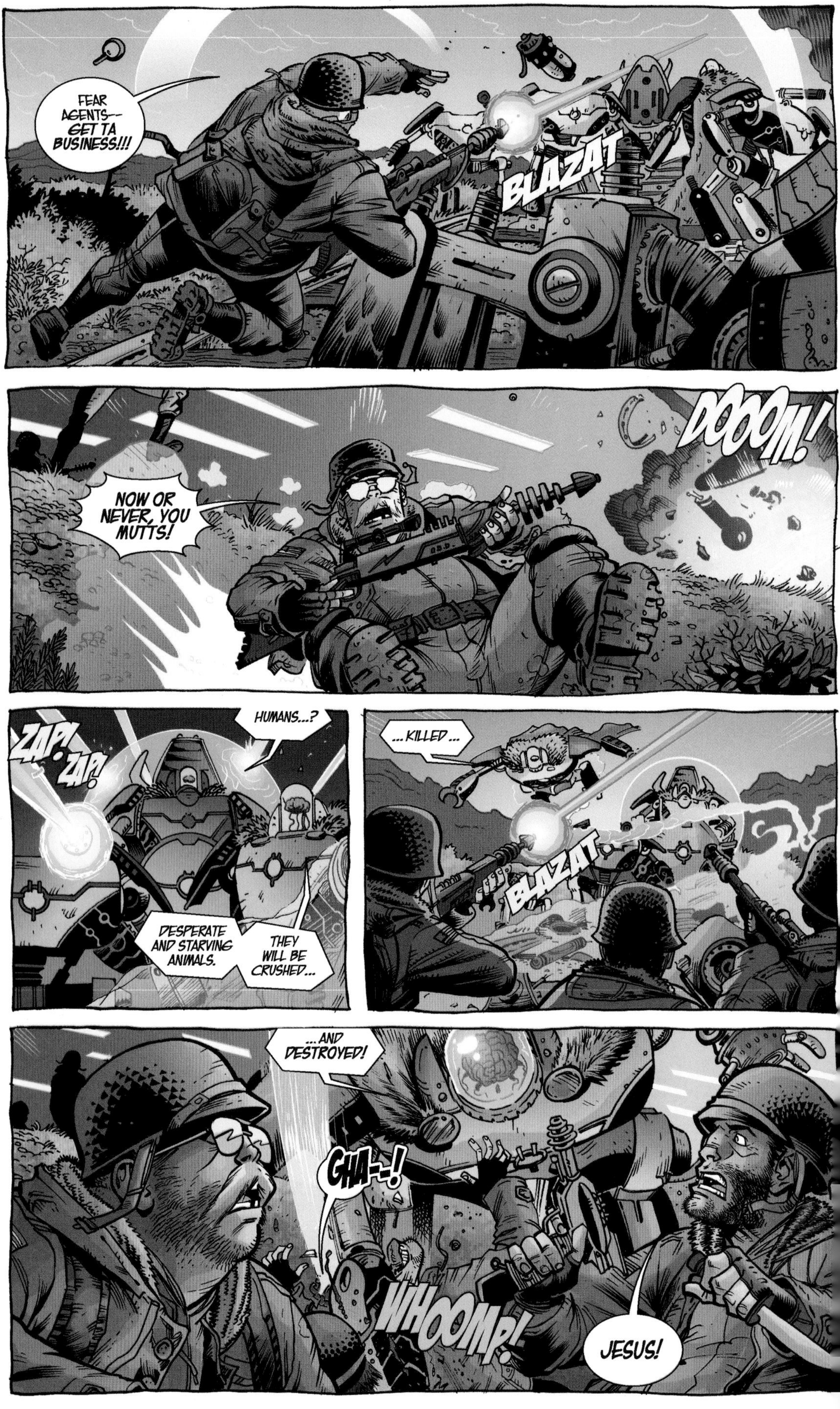
FEAR AGENTS-- GET TA BUSINESS!!!
BLAZAT
NOW OR NEVER, YOU MUTTS!
DOOOM!
ZAP! ZAP!
HUMANS...?
DESPERATE AND STARVING ANIMALS.
THEY WILL BE CRUSHED...
...KILLED...
BLAZAT
...AND DESTROYED!
GHA--!
WHOOMP!
JESUS!

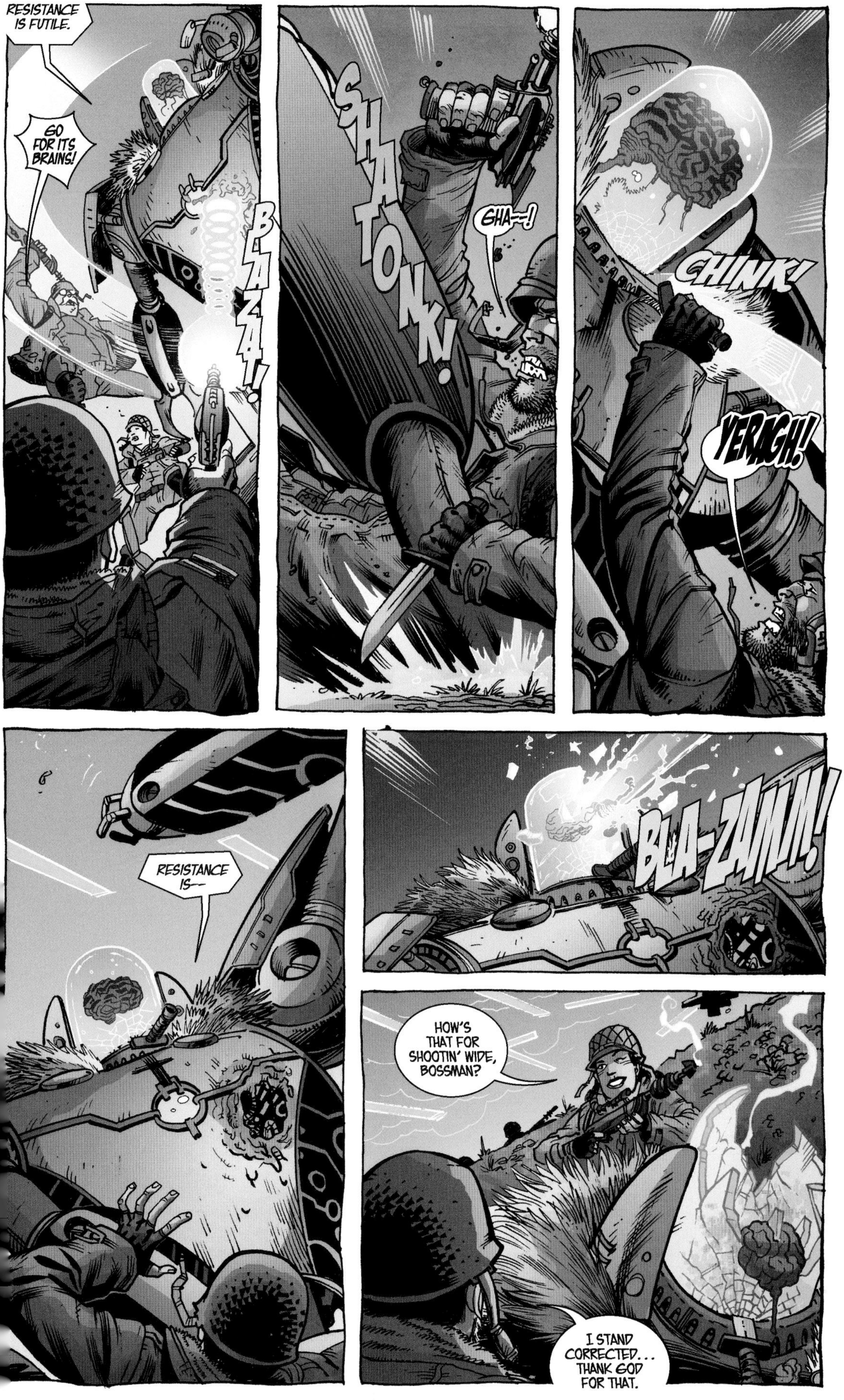

RESISTANCE IS FUTILE.
GO FOR ITS BRAINS!
BLAZAT!
SHATONK!
GHA--!
CHINK!
YERAGH!
RESISTANCE IS--
BLA-ZAMM!
HOW'S THAT FOR SHOOTIN' WIDE, BOSSMAN?
I STAND CORRECTED... THANK GOD FOR THAT.

AIEEEEEE!!!
NANCY!
BLAZAT!
ZAP!
GET WITH THE GAME, SOLDIER. WHAT WE JUST SAW--SHAKE IT OFF.
DON'T YOU THINK ABOUT IT... NOT NOW.
YOU WITH ME? CAN YOU FIGHT?
IT'S THE ONLY THING I KNOW I CAN DO.
BLAZAT!
IT HURTS... IT HURTS SO BAD...
BLAZAT!
WE AIN'T HOWDIED.
NAME'S TIMBERSON...
BLAZAT!
BLAZAT!

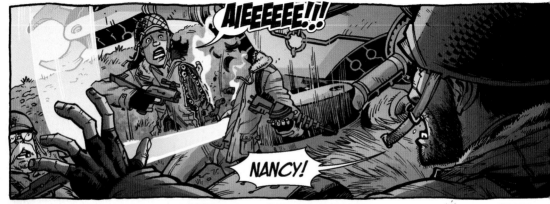

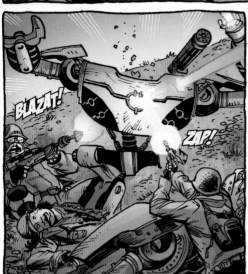

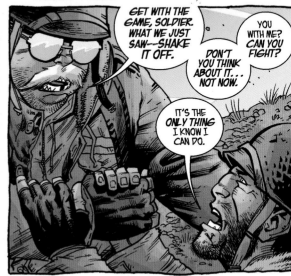

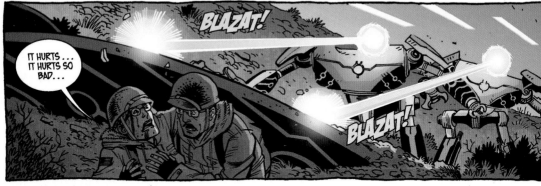

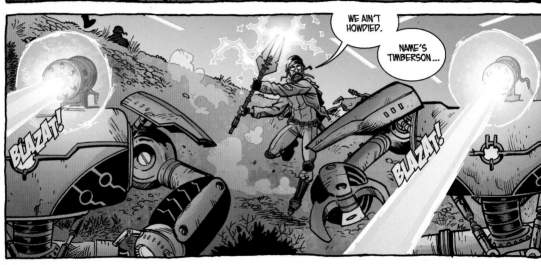

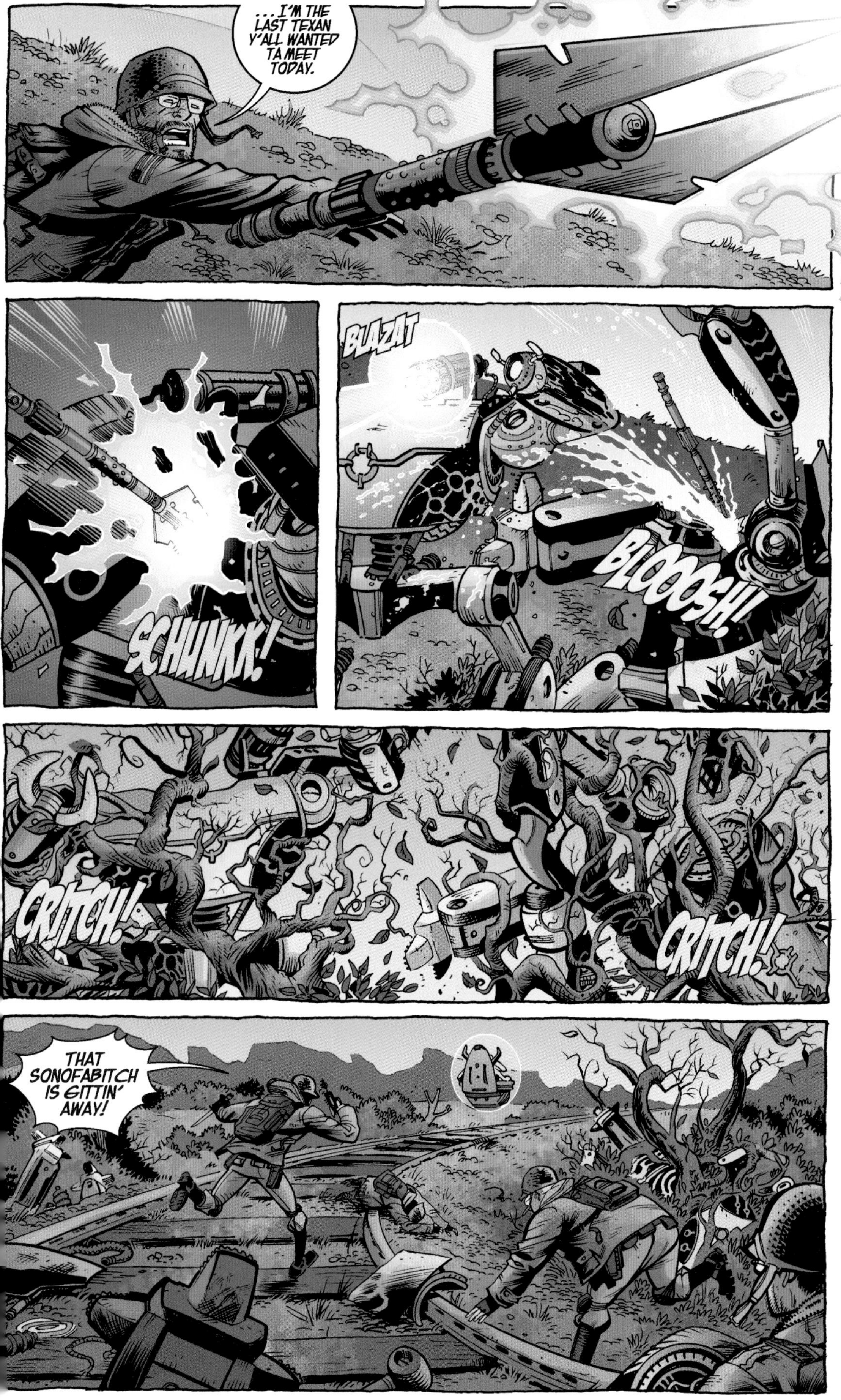
...I'M THE LAST TEXAN Y'ALL WANTED TA MEET TODAY.
BLAZAT
SCHUNKK!
BLOOOSH!
CRITCH!
CRITCH!
THAT SONOFABITCH IS GITTIN' AWAY!

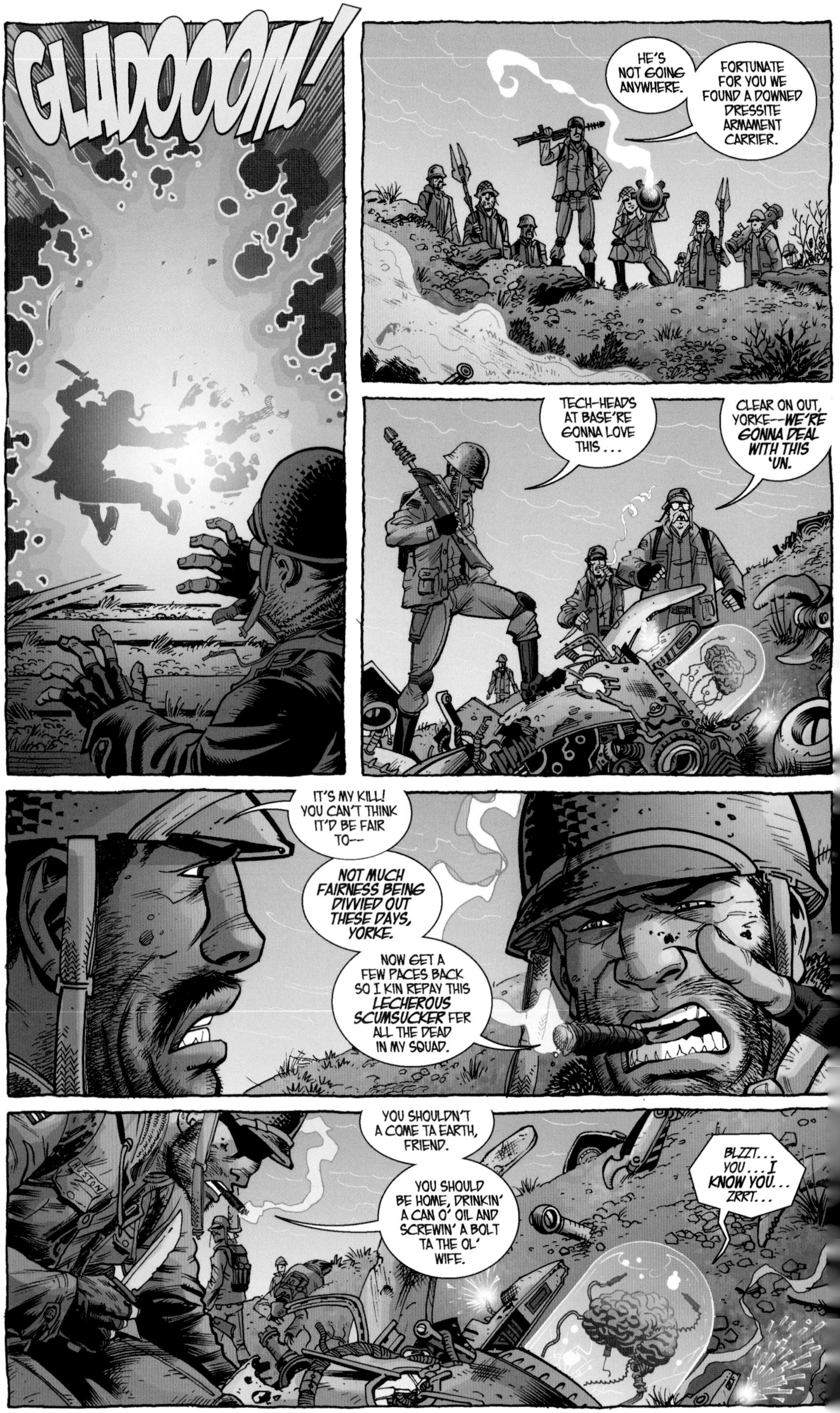

GLADOOOM!
HE'S NOT GOING ANYWHERE.
FORTUNATE FOR YOU WE FOUND A DOWNED DRESSITE ARMAMENT CARRIER.
TECH-HEADS AT BASE'RE GONNA LOVE THIS . . .
CLEAR ON OUT, YORKE--WE'RE GONNA DEAL WITH THIS 'UN.
IT'S MY KILL! YOU CAN'T THINK IT'D BE FAIR TO--
NOT MUCH FAIRNESS BEING DIVVIED OUT THESE DAYS, YORKE.
NOW GET A FEW PACES BACK SO I KIN REPAY THIS LECHEROUS SCUMSUCKER FER ALL THE DEAD IN MY SQUAD.
YOU SHOULDN'T A COME TA EARTH, FRIEND.
YOU SHOULD BE HOME, DRINKIN' A CAN O' OIL AND SCREWIN' A BOLT TA THE OL' WIFE.
BLZZT. . . YOU . . . I KNOW YOU. . . ZRRT. . .
HUSTON

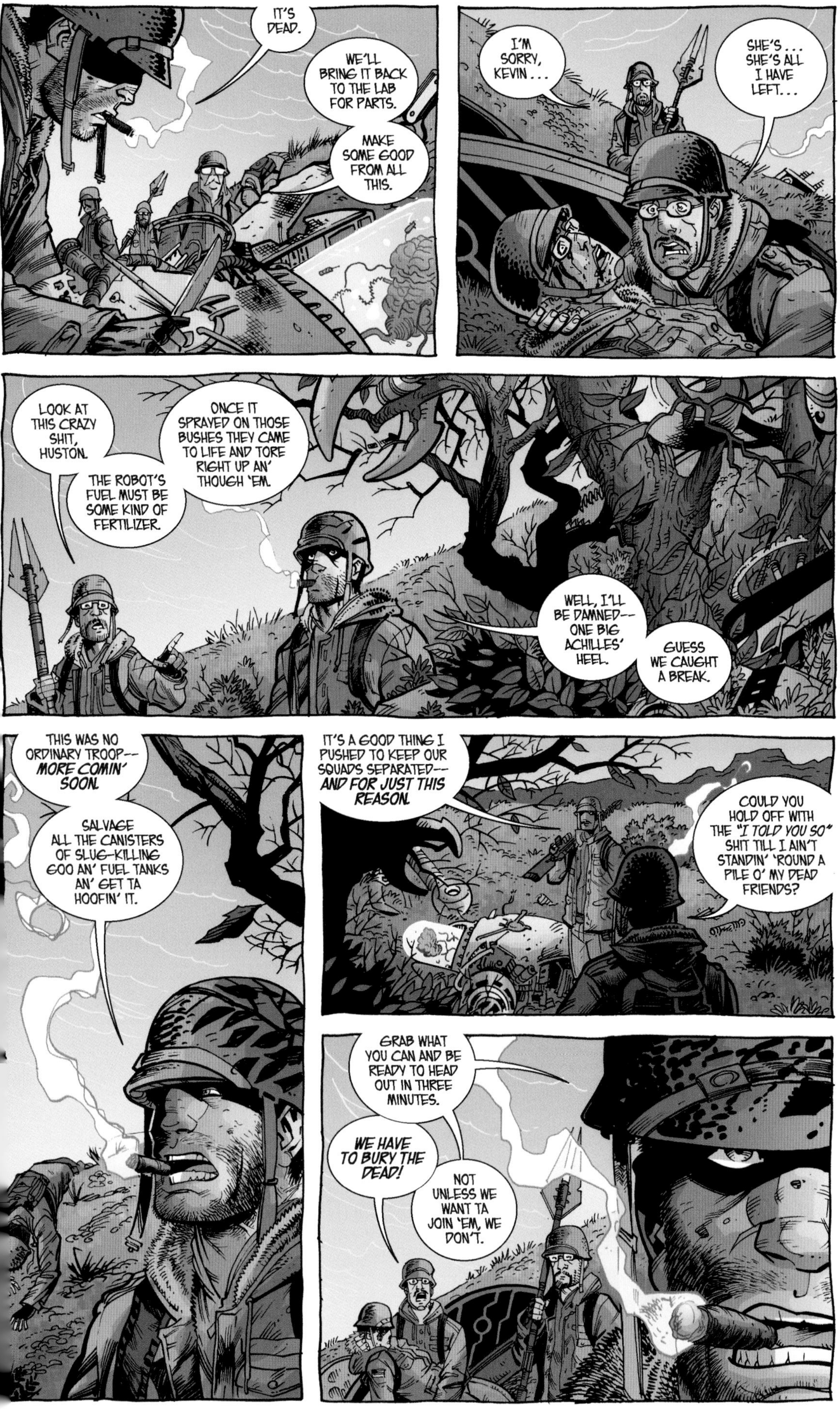
IT'S DEAD.
WE'LL BRING IT BACK TO THE LAB FOR PARTS.
MAKE SOME GOOD FROM ALL THIS.
I'M SORRY, KEVIN...
SHE'S... SHE'S ALL I HAVE LEFT...
LOOK AT THIS CRAZY SHIT, HUSTON.
THE ROBOT'S FUEL MUST BE SOME KIND OF FERTILIZER.
ONCE IT SPRAYED ON THOSE BUSHES THEY CAME TO LIFE AND TORE RIGHT UP AN' THOUGH 'EM.
WELL, I'LL BE DAMNED-- ONE BIG ACHILLES' HEEL.
GUESS WE CAUGHT A BREAK.
THIS WAS NO ORDINARY TROOP-- *MORE COMIN' SOON.*
SALVAGE ALL THE CANISTERS OF SLUG-KILLING GOO AN' FUEL TANKS AN' GET TA HOOFIN' IT.
IT'S A GOOD THING I PUSHED TO KEEP OUR SQUADS SEPARATED-- *AND FOR JUST THIS REASON.*
COULD YOU HOLD OFF WITH THE *"I TOLD YOU SO"* SHIT TILL I AIN'T STANDIN' 'ROUND A PILE O' MY DEAD FRIENDS?
GRAB WHAT YOU CAN AND BE READY TO HEAD OUT IN THREE MINUTES.
WE HAVE TO BURY THE DEAD!
NOT UNLESS WE WANT TA JOIN 'EM, WE DON'T.

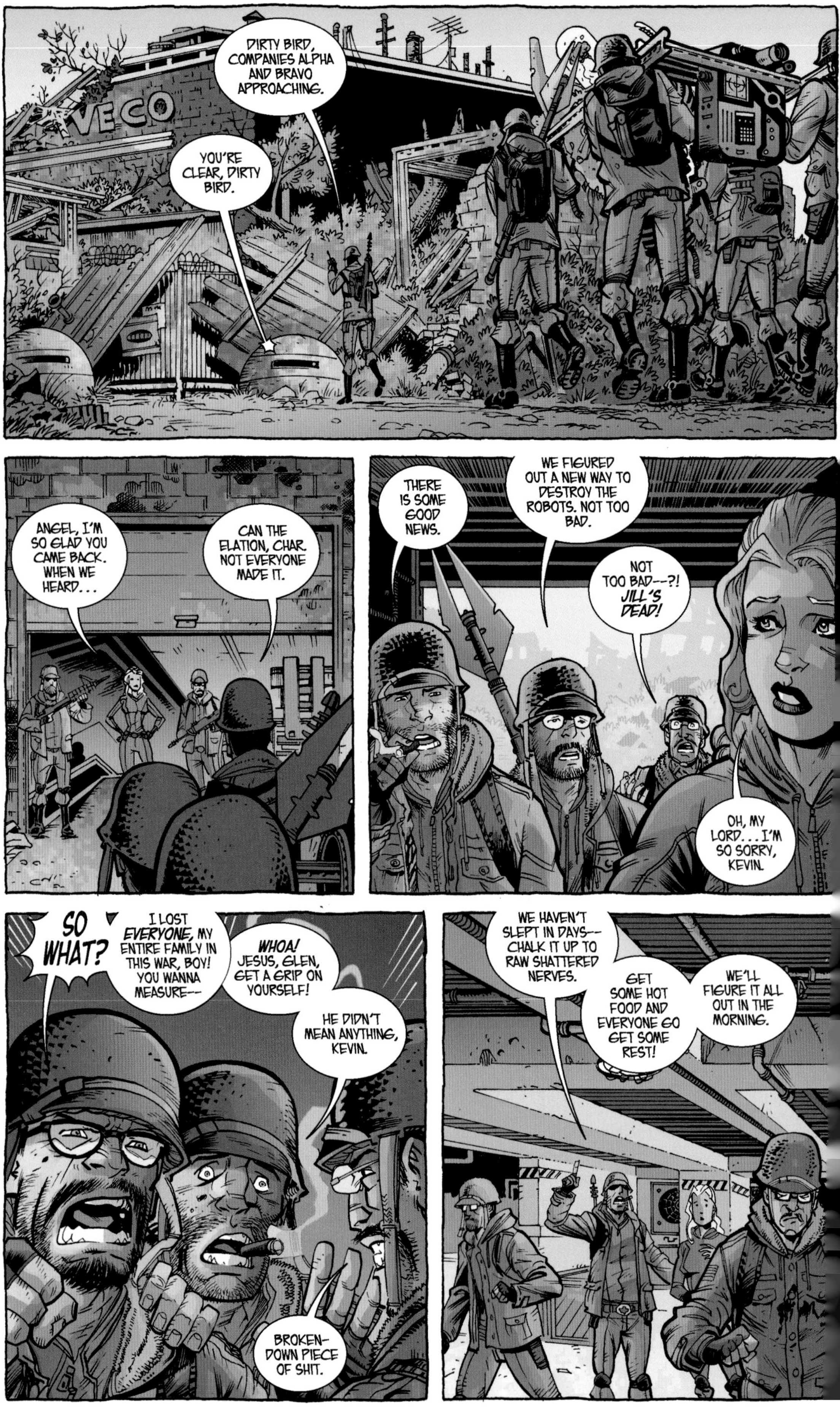
VECO
DIRTY BIRD, COMPANIES ALPHA AND BRAVO APPROACHING.
YOU'RE CLEAR, DIRTY BIRD.
ANGEL, I'M SO GLAD YOU CAME BACK. WHEN WE HEARD...
CAN THE ELATION, CHAR. NOT EVERYONE MADE IT.
THERE IS SOME GOOD NEWS.
WE FIGURED OUT A NEW WAY TO DESTROY THE ROBOTS. NOT TOO BAD.
NOT TOO BAD--?! JILL'S DEAD!
OH, MY LORD... I'M SO SORRY, KEVIN.
SO WHAT?
I LOST EVERYONE, MY ENTIRE FAMILY IN THIS WAR, BOY! YOU WANNA MEASURE--
WHOA! JESUS, GLEN, GET A GRIP ON YOURSELF!
HE DIDN'T MEAN ANYTHING, KEVIN.
BROKEN-DOWN PIECE OF SHIT.
WE HAVEN'T SLEPT IN DAYS-- CHALK IT UP TO RAW SHATTERED NERVES.
GET SOME HOT FOOD AND EVERYONE GO GET SOME REST!
WE'LL FIGURE IT ALL OUT IN THE MORNING.

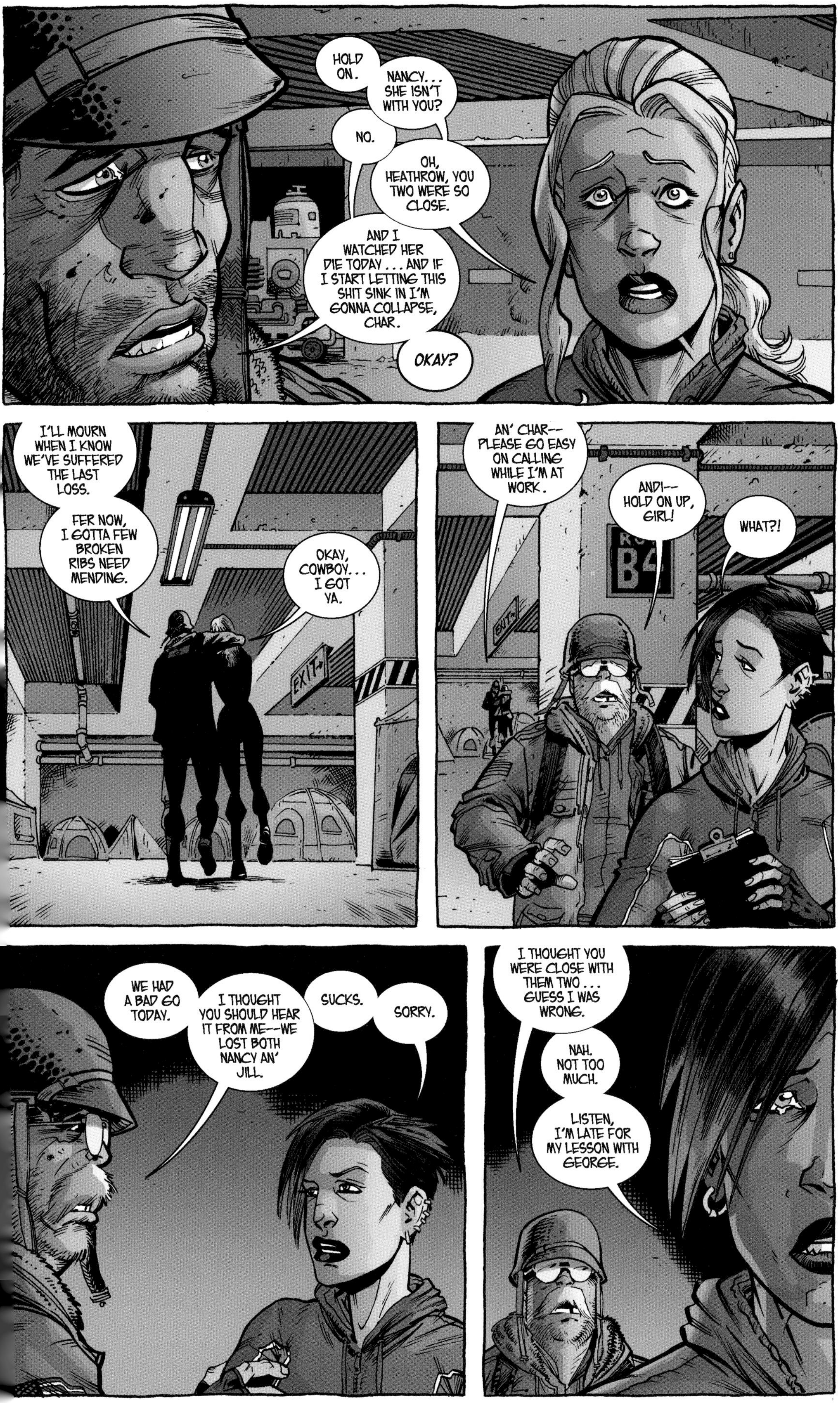
HOLD ON.
NANCY... SHE ISN'T WITH YOU?
NO.
OH, HEATHROW, YOU TWO WERE SO CLOSE.
AND I WATCHED HER DIE TODAY... AND IF I START LETTING THIS SHIT SINK IN I'M GONNA COLLAPSE, CHAR.
OKAY?
I'LL MOURN WHEN I KNOW WE'VE SUFFERED THE LAST LOSS.
FER NOW, I GOTTA FEW BROKEN RIBS NEED MENDING.
OKAY, COWBOY... I GOT YA.
EXIT
AN' CHAR-- PLEASE GO EASY ON CALLING WHILE I'M AT WORK.
ANDI-- HOLD ON UP, GIRL!
WHAT?!
B4
WE HAD A BAD GO TODAY.
I THOUGHT YOU SHOULD HEAR IT FROM ME--WE LOST BOTH NANCY AN' JILL.
SUCKS.
SORRY.
I THOUGHT YOU WERE CLOSE WITH THEM TWO... GUESS I WAS WRONG.
NAH. NOT TOO MUCH.
LISTEN, I'M LATE FOR MY LESSON WITH GEORGE.

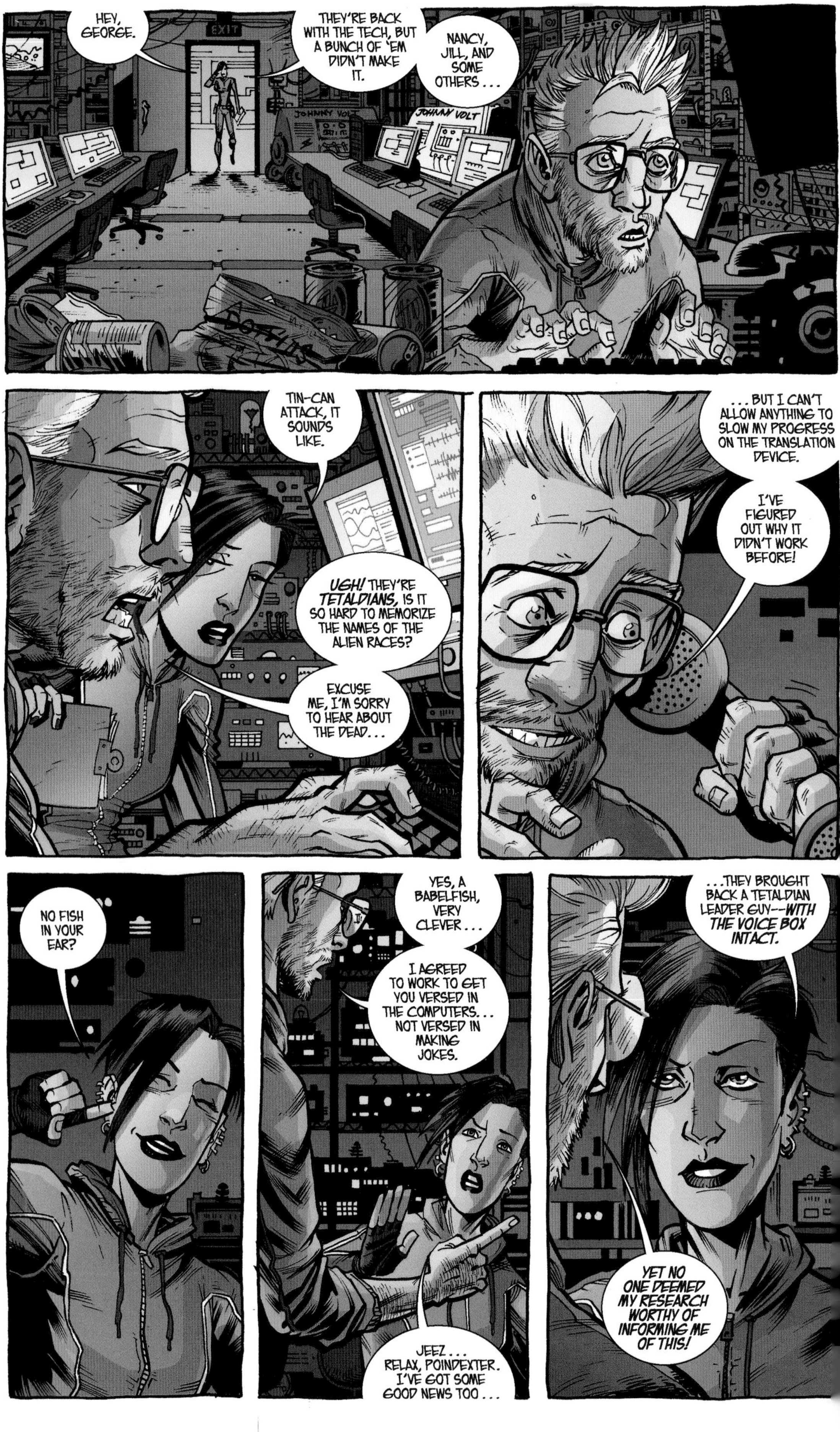
HEY, GEORGE.
THEY'RE BACK WITH THE TECH, BUT A BUNCH OF 'EM DIDN'T MAKE IT.
NANCY, JILL, AND SOME OTHERS . . .
EXIT
JOHNNY VOLT
JOHNNY VOLT
TIN-CAN ATTACK, IT SOUNDS LIKE.
UGH! THEY'RE TETALDIANS, IS IT SO HARD TO MEMORIZE THE NAMES OF THE ALIEN RACES?
EXCUSE ME, I'M SORRY TO HEAR ABOUT THE DEAD . . .
. . . BUT I CAN'T ALLOW ANYTHING TO SLOW MY PROGRESS ON THE TRANSLATION DEVICE.
I'VE FIGURED OUT WHY IT DIDN'T WORK BEFORE!
NO FISH IN YOUR EAR?
YES, A BABELFISH, VERY CLEVER . . .
I AGREED TO WORK TO GET YOU VERSED IN THE COMPUTERS. . . NOT VERSED IN MAKING JOKES.
JEEZ . . . RELAX, POINDEXTER. I'VE GOT SOME GOOD NEWS TOO . . .
. . .THEY BROUGHT BACK A TETALDIAN LEADER GUY--WITH THE VOICE BOX INTACT.
YET NO ONE DEEMED MY RESEARCH WORTHY OF INFORMING ME OF THIS!

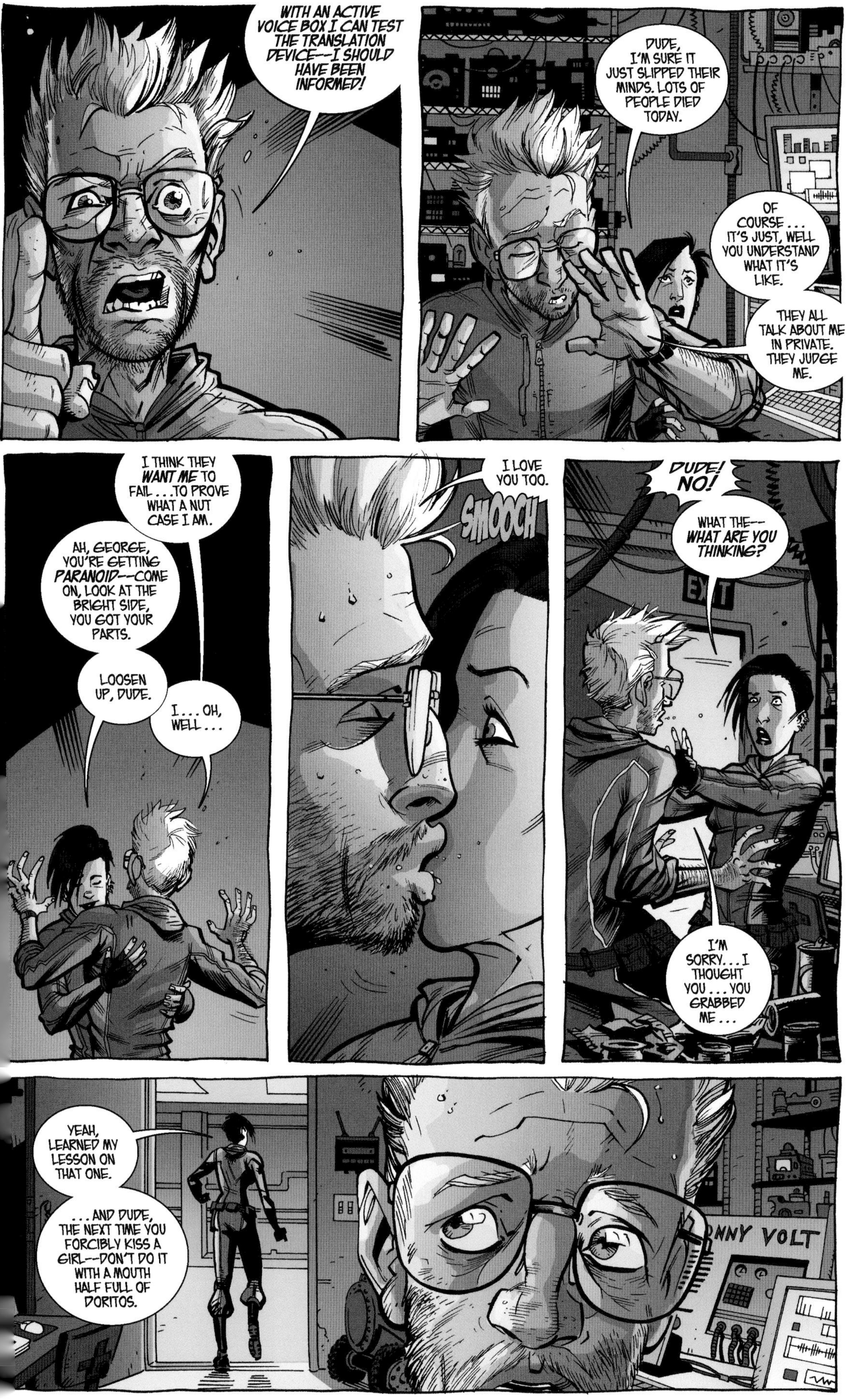
WITH AN ACTIVE VOICE BOX I CAN TEST THE TRANSLATION DEVICE--I SHOULD HAVE BEEN INFORMED!
DUDE, I'M SURE IT JUST SLIPPED THEIR MINDS. LOTS OF PEOPLE DIED TODAY.
OF COURSE . . . IT'S JUST, WELL YOU UNDERSTAND WHAT IT'S LIKE.
THEY ALL TALK ABOUT ME IN PRIVATE. THEY JUDGE ME.
I THINK THEY WANT ME TO FAIL . . . TO PROVE WHAT A NUT CASE I AM.
AH, GEORGE, YOU'RE GETTING PARANOID--COME ON, LOOK AT THE BRIGHT SIDE, YOU GOT YOUR PARTS.
LOOSEN UP, DUDE.
I . . . OH, WELL . . .
I LOVE YOU TOO.
SMOOCH
DUDE! NO!
WHAT THE-- WHAT ARE YOU THINKING?
EXIT
I'M SORRY . . . I THOUGHT YOU . . . YOU GRABBED ME . . .
YEAH, LEARNED MY LESSON ON THAT ONE.
. . . AND DUDE, THE NEXT TIME YOU FORCIBLY KISS A GIRL--DON'T DO IT WITH A MOUTH HALF FULL OF DORITOS.
NNY VOLT

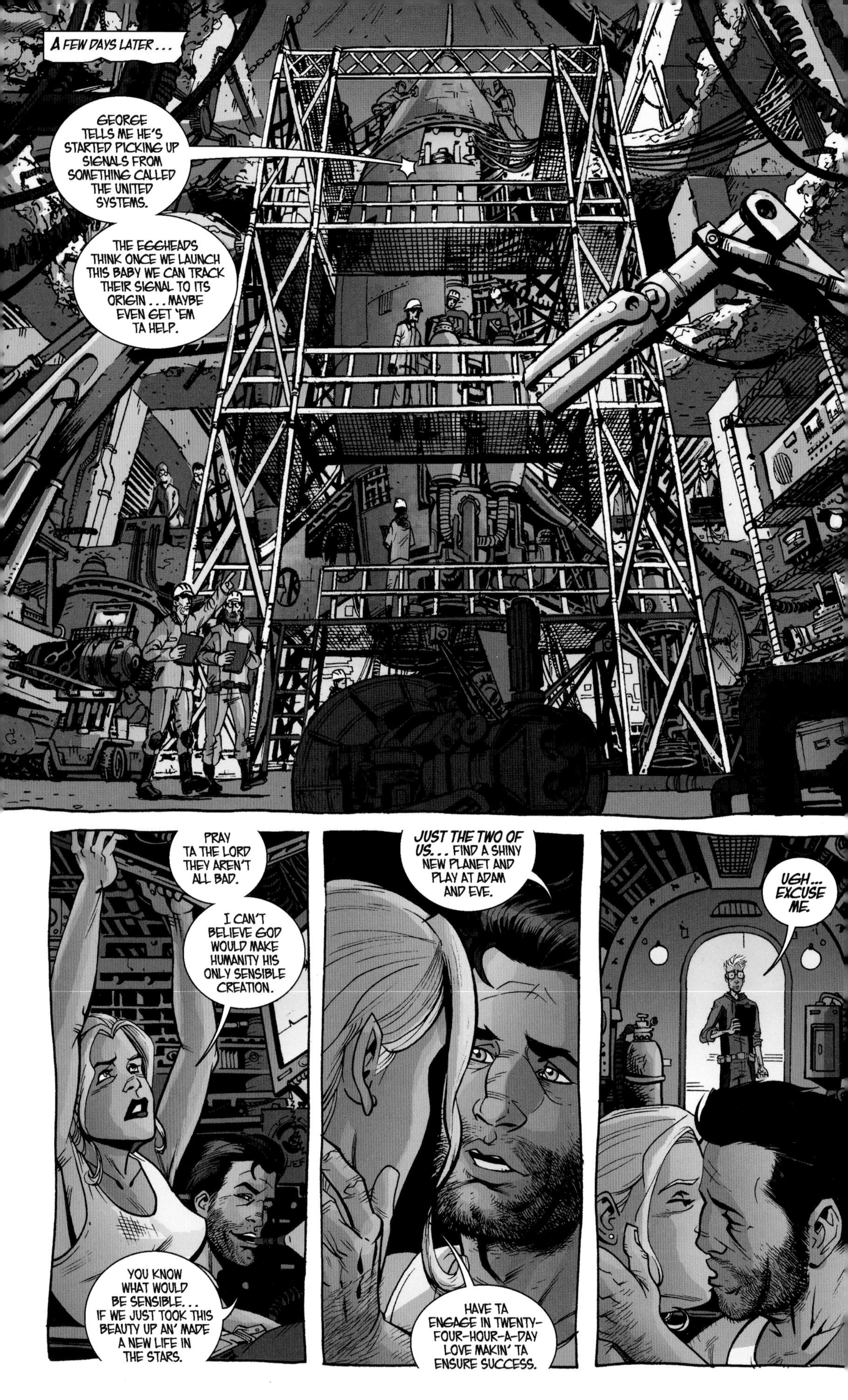
A FEW DAYS LATER . . .
GEORGE TELLS ME HE'S STARTED PICKING UP SIGNALS FROM SOMETHING CALLED THE UNITED SYSTEMS.
THE EGGHEADS THINK ONCE WE LAUNCH THIS BABY WE CAN TRACK THEIR SIGNAL TO ITS ORIGIN . . . MAYBE EVEN GET 'EM TA HELP.
PRAY TA THE LORD THEY AREN'T ALL BAD.
I CAN'T BELIEVE GOD WOULD MAKE HUMANITY HIS ONLY SENSIBLE CREATION.
YOU KNOW WHAT WOULD BE SENSIBLE. . . IF WE JUST TOOK THIS BEAUTY UP AN' MADE A NEW LIFE IN THE STARS.
JUST THE TWO OF US. . . FIND A SHINY NEW PLANET AND PLAY AT ADAM AND EVE.
HAVE TA ENGAGE IN TWENTY-FOUR-HOUR-A-DAY LOVE MAKIN' TA ENSURE SUCCESS.
UGH... EXCUSE ME.

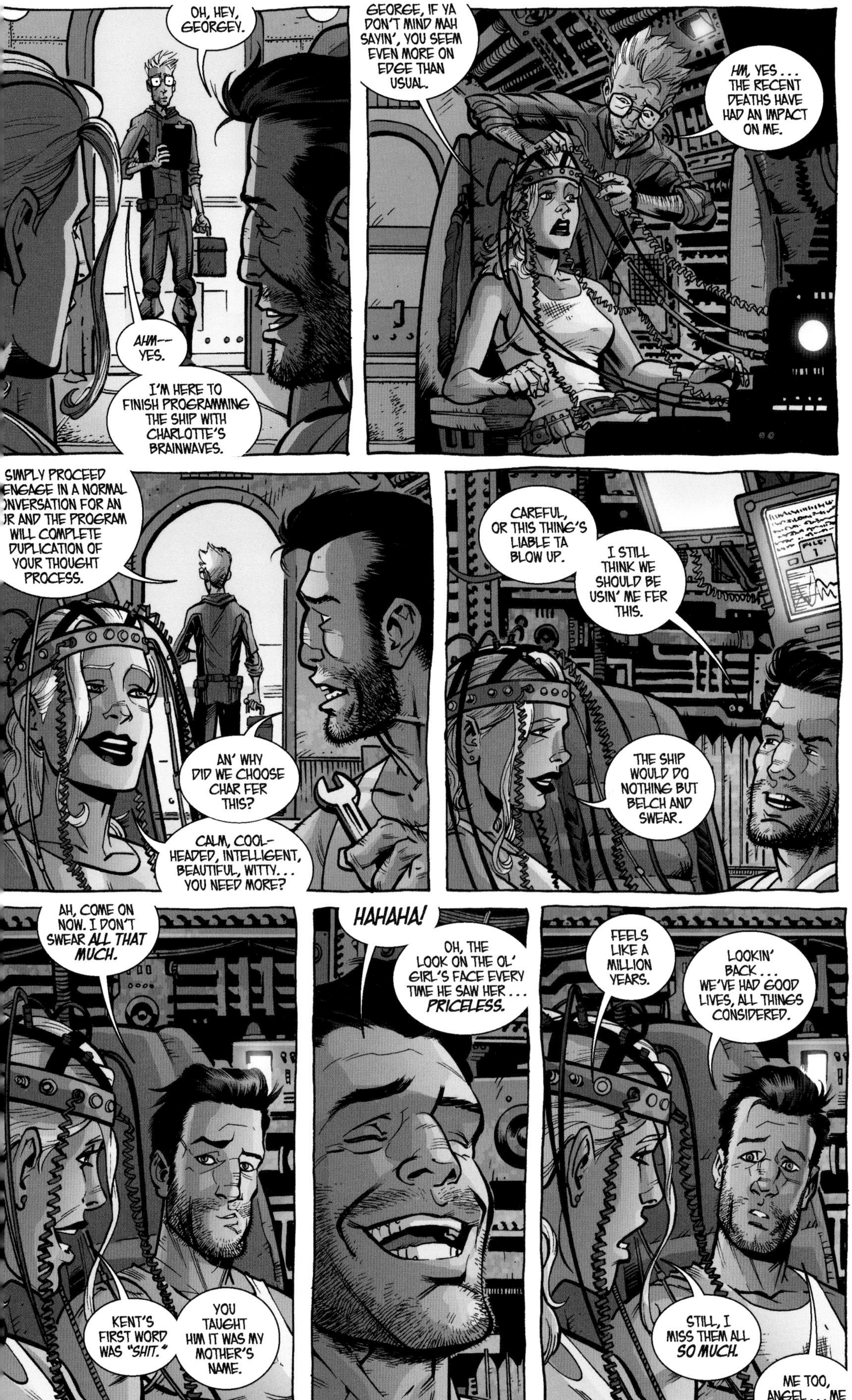
OH, HEY, GEORGEY.
AHM-- YES.
I'M HERE TO FINISH PROGRAMMING THE SHIP WITH CHARLOTTE'S BRAINWAVES.
GEORGE, IF YA DON'T MIND MAH SAYIN', YOU SEEM EVEN MORE ON EDGE THAN USUAL.
HM, YES... THE RECENT DEATHS HAVE HAD AN IMPACT ON ME.
SIMPLY PROCEED ENGAGE IN A NORMAL ONVERSATION FOR AN R AND THE PROGRAM WILL COMPLETE DUPLICATION OF YOUR THOUGHT PROCESS.
AN' WHY DID WE CHOOSE CHAR FER THIS?
CALM, COOL-HEADED, INTELLIGENT, BEAUTIFUL, WITTY... YOU NEED MORE?
CAREFUL, OR THIS THING'S LIABLE TA BLOW UP.
I STILL THINK WE SHOULD BE USIN' ME FER THIS.
THE SHIP WOULD DO NOTHING BUT BELCH AND SWEAR.
AH, COME ON NOW. I DON'T SWEAR ALL THAT MUCH.
KENT'S FIRST WORD WAS "SHIT."
YOU TAUGHT HIM IT WAS MY MOTHER'S NAME.
HAHAHA!
OH, THE LOOK ON THE OL' GIRL'S FACE EVERY TIME HE SAW HER... PRICELESS.
FEELS LIKE A MILLION YEARS.
LOOKIN' BACK... WE'VE HAD GOOD LIVES, ALL THINGS CONSIDERED.
STILL, I MISS THEM ALL SO MUCH.
ME TOO, ANGEL... ME TOO.

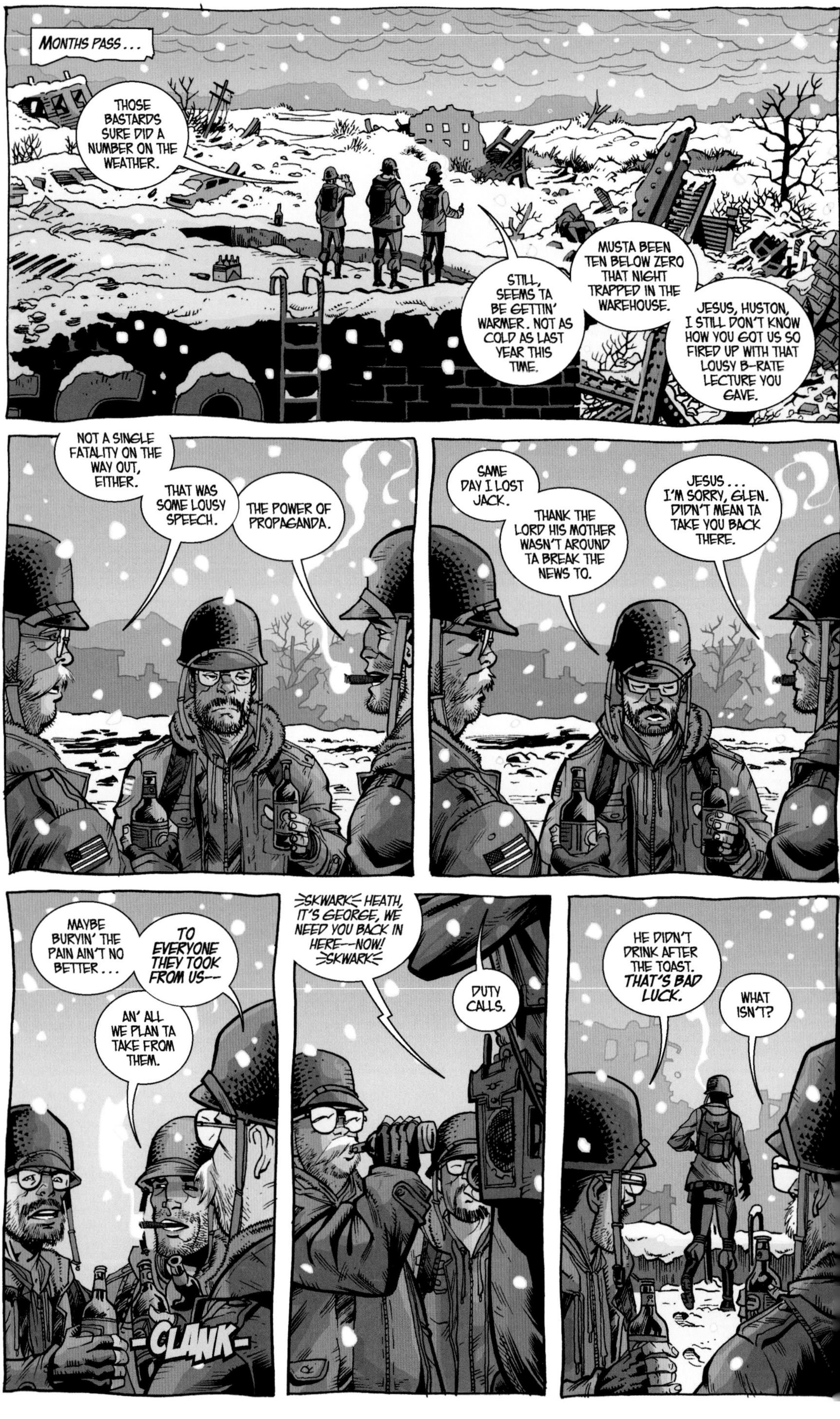
MONTHS PASS . . .
THOSE BASTARDS SURE DID A NUMBER ON THE WEATHER.
STILL, SEEMS TA BE GETTIN' WARMER. NOT AS COLD AS LAST YEAR THIS TIME.
MUSTA BEEN TEN BELOW ZERO THAT NIGHT TRAPPED IN THE WAREHOUSE.
JESUS, HUSTON, I STILL DON'T KNOW HOW YOU GOT US SO FIRED UP WITH THAT LOUSY B-RATE LECTURE YOU GAVE.
NOT A SINGLE FATALITY ON THE WAY OUT, EITHER.
THAT WAS SOME LOUSY SPEECH.
THE POWER OF PROPAGANDA.
SAME DAY I LOST JACK.
THANK THE LORD HIS MOTHER WASN'T AROUND TA BREAK THE NEWS TO.
JESUS . . . I'M SORRY, GLEN. DIDN'T MEAN TA TAKE YOU BACK THERE.
MAYBE BURYIN' THE PAIN AIN'T NO BETTER . . .
TO EVERYONE THEY TOOK FROM US--
AN' ALL WE PLAN TA TAKE FROM THEM.
-CLANK-
=SKWARK= HEATH, IT'S GEORGE, WE NEED YOU BACK IN HERE--NOW! =SKWARK=
DUTY CALLS.
HE DIDN'T DRINK AFTER THE TOAST. THAT'S BAD LUCK.
WHAT ISN'T?

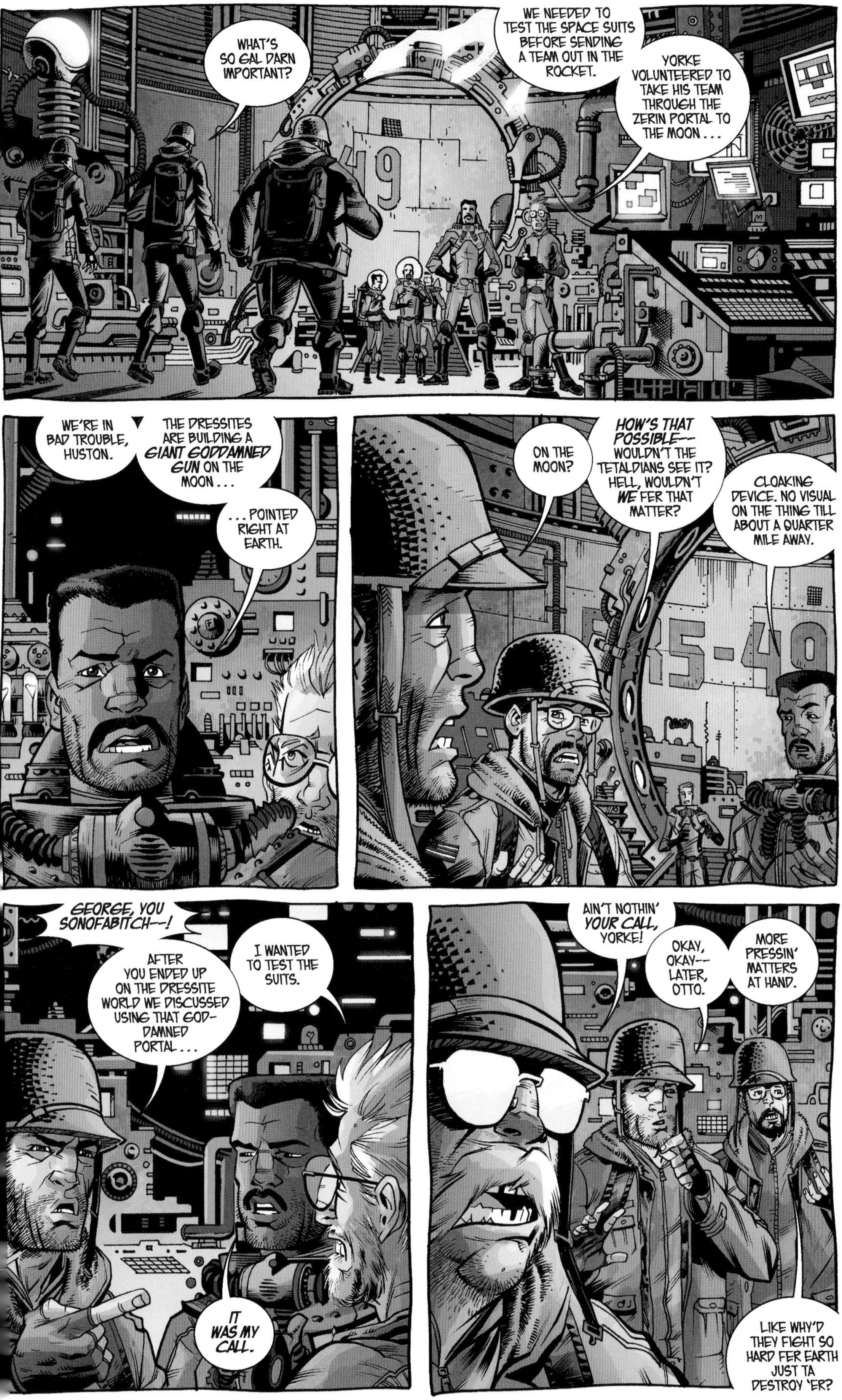
WHAT'S SO GAL DARN IMPORTANT?
WE NEEDED TO TEST THE SPACE SUITS BEFORE SENDING A TEAM OUT IN THE ROCKET.
YORKE VOLUNTEERED TO TAKE HIS TEAM THROUGH THE ZERIN PORTAL TO THE MOON . . .
49
WE'RE IN BAD TROUBLE, HUSTON.
THE DRESSITES ARE BUILDING A GIANT GODDAMNED GUN ON THE MOON . . .
. . . POINTED RIGHT AT EARTH.
ON THE MOON?
HOW'S THAT POSSIBLE-- WOULDN'T THE TETALDIANS SEE IT? HELL, WOULDN'T WE FER THAT MATTER?
CLOAKING DEVICE. NO VISUAL ON THE THING TILL ABOUT A QUARTER MILE AWAY.
R5-49
GEORGE, YOU SONOFABITCH--!
AFTER YOU ENDED UP ON THE DRESSITE WORLD WE DISCUSSED USING THAT GOD-DAMNED PORTAL . . .
I WANTED TO TEST THE SUITS.
IT WAS MY CALL.
AIN'T NOTHIN' YOUR CALL, YORKE!
OKAY, OKAY-- LATER, OTTO.
MORE PRESSIN' MATTERS AT HAND.
LIKE WHY'D THEY FIGHT SO HARD FER EARTH JUST TA DESTROY 'ER?

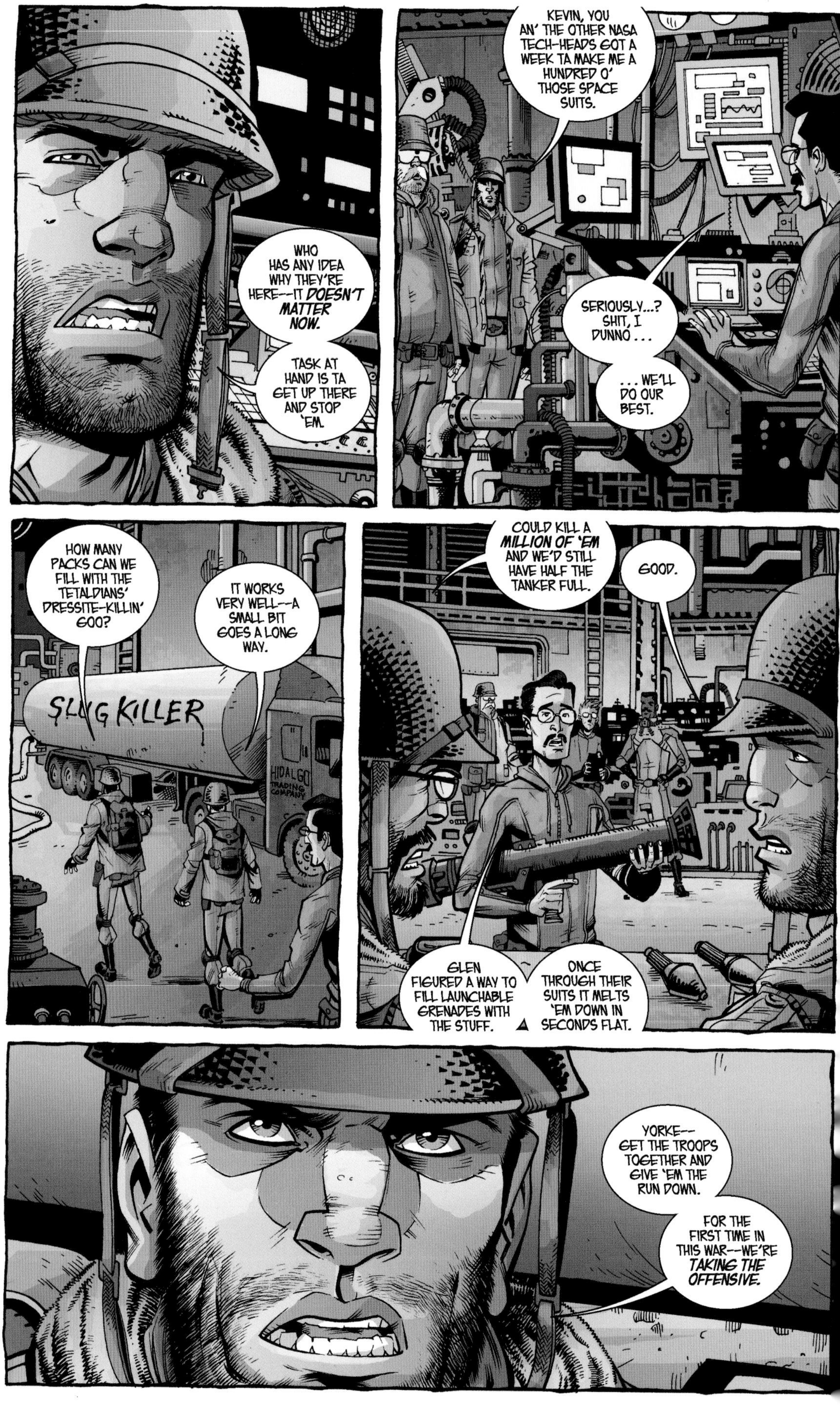
WHO HAS ANY IDEA WHY THEY'RE HERE--IT DOESN'T MATTER NOW.
TASK AT HAND IS TA GET UP THERE AND STOP 'EM.
KEVIN, YOU AN' THE OTHER NASA TECH-HEADS GOT A WEEK TA MAKE ME A HUNDRED O' THOSE SPACE SUITS.
SERIOUSLY...? SHIT, I DUNNO . . .
. . . WE'LL DO OUR BEST.
HOW MANY PACKS CAN WE FILL WITH THE TETALDIANS' DRESSITE-KILLIN' GOO?
IT WORKS VERY WELL--A SMALL BIT GOES A LONG WAY.
SLUG KILLER
HIDALGO TRADING COMPANY
COULD KILL A MILLION OF 'EM AND WE'D STILL HAVE HALF THE TANKER FULL.
GOOD.
GLEN FIGURED A WAY TO FILL LAUNCHABLE GRENADES WITH THE STUFF.
ONCE THROUGH THEIR SUITS IT MELTS 'EM DOWN IN SECONDS FLAT.
YORKE--GET THE TROOPS TOGETHER AND GIVE 'EM THE RUN DOWN.
FOR THE FIRST TIME IN THIS WAR--WE'RE TAKING THE OFFENSIVE.

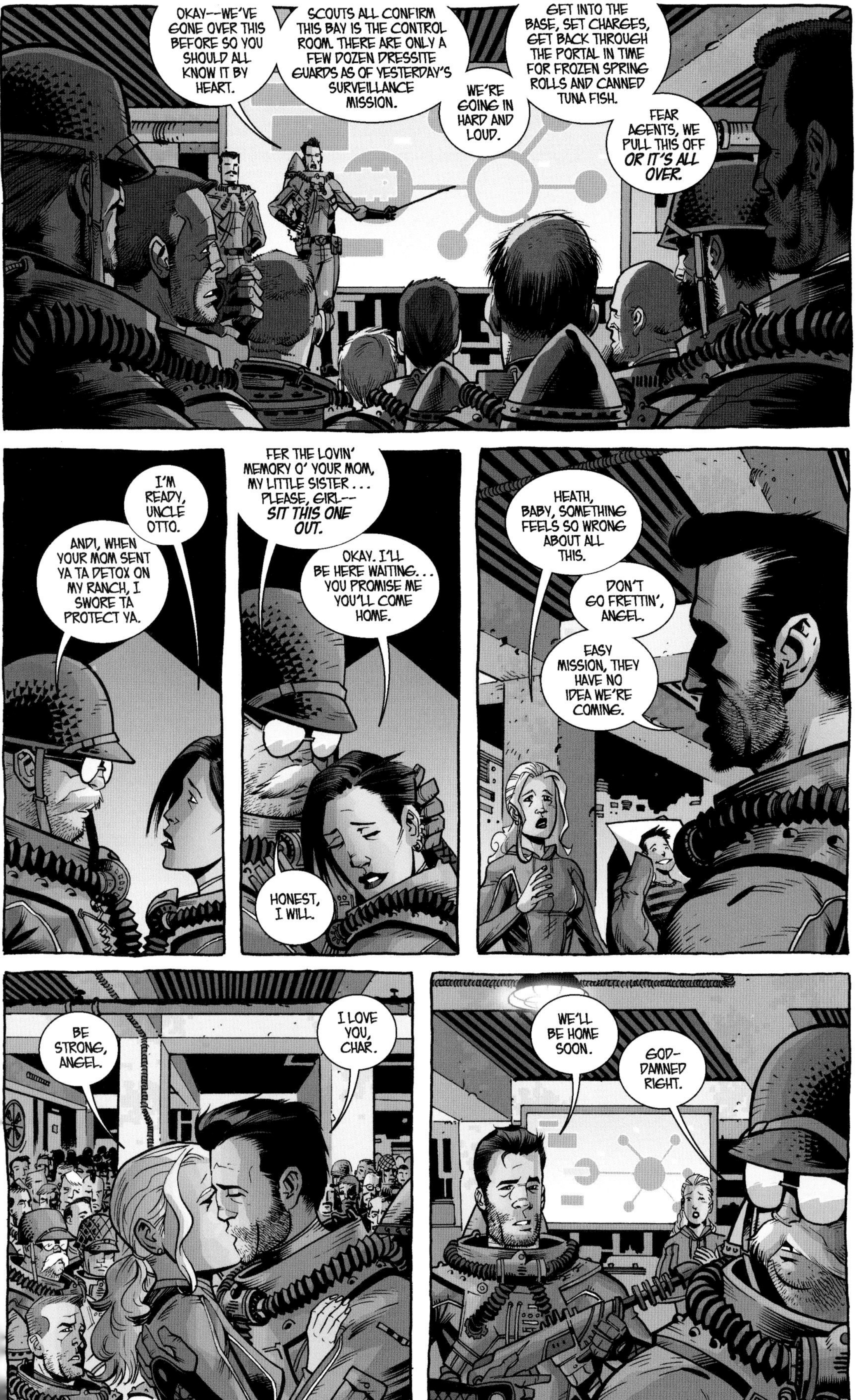
OKAY--WE'VE GONE OVER THIS BEFORE SO YOU SHOULD ALL KNOW IT BY HEART.
SCOUTS ALL CONFIRM THIS BAY IS THE CONTROL ROOM. THERE ARE ONLY A FEW DOZEN DRESSITE GUARDS AS OF YESTERDAY'S SURVEILLANCE MISSION.
WE'RE GOING IN HARD AND LOUD.
GET INTO THE BASE, SET CHARGES, GET BACK THROUGH THE PORTAL IN TIME FOR FROZEN SPRING ROLLS AND CANNED TUNA FISH.
FEAR AGENTS, WE PULL THIS OFF *OR IT'S ALL OVER.*
I'M READY, UNCLE OTTO.
ANDI, WHEN YOUR MOM SENT YA TA DETOX ON MY RANCH, I SWORE TA PROTECT YA.
FER THE LOVIN' MEMORY O' YOUR MOM, MY LITTLE SISTER . . . PLEASE, GIRL-- *SIT THIS ONE OUT.*
OKAY. I'LL BE HERE WAITING. . . YOU PROMISE ME YOU'LL COME HOME.
HONEST, I WILL.
HEATH, BABY, SOMETHING FEELS SO WRONG ABOUT ALL THIS.
DON'T GO FRETTIN', ANGEL.
EASY MISSION, THEY HAVE NO IDEA WE'RE COMING.
BE STRONG, ANGEL.
I LOVE YOU, CHAR.
WE'LL BE HOME SOON.
GOD-DAMNED RIGHT.

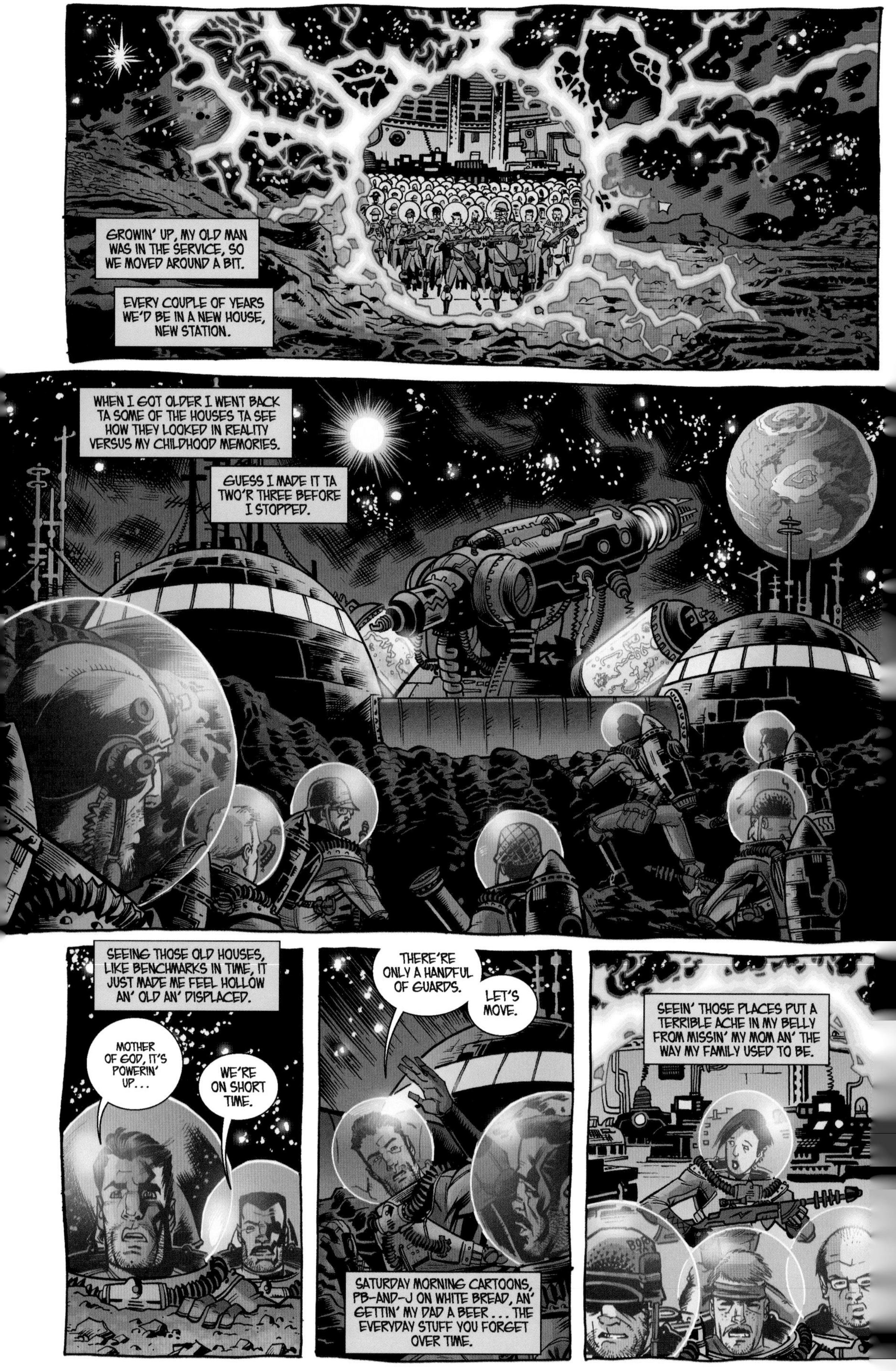
GROWIN' UP, MY OLD MAN WAS IN THE SERVICE, SO WE MOVED AROUND A BIT.
EVERY COUPLE OF YEARS WE'D BE IN A NEW HOUSE, NEW STATION.
WHEN I GOT OLDER I WENT BACK TA SOME OF THE HOUSES TA SEE HOW THEY LOOKED IN REALITY VERSUS MY CHILDHOOD MEMORIES.
GUESS I MADE IT TA TWO'R THREE BEFORE I STOPPED.
SEEING THOSE OLD HOUSES, LIKE BENCHMARKS IN TIME, IT JUST MADE ME FEEL HOLLOW AN' OLD AN' DISPLACED.
MOTHER OF GOD, IT'S POWERIN' UP...
WE'RE ON SHORT TIME.
THERE'RE ONLY A HANDFUL OF GUARDS.
LET'S MOVE.
SATURDAY MORNING CARTOONS, PB-AND-J ON WHITE BREAD, AN' GETTIN' MY DAD A BEER... THE EVERYDAY STUFF YOU FORGET OVER TIME.
SEEIN' THOSE PLACES PUT A TERRIBLE ACHE IN MY BELLY FROM MISSIN' MY MOM AN' THE WAY MY FAMILY USED TO BE.

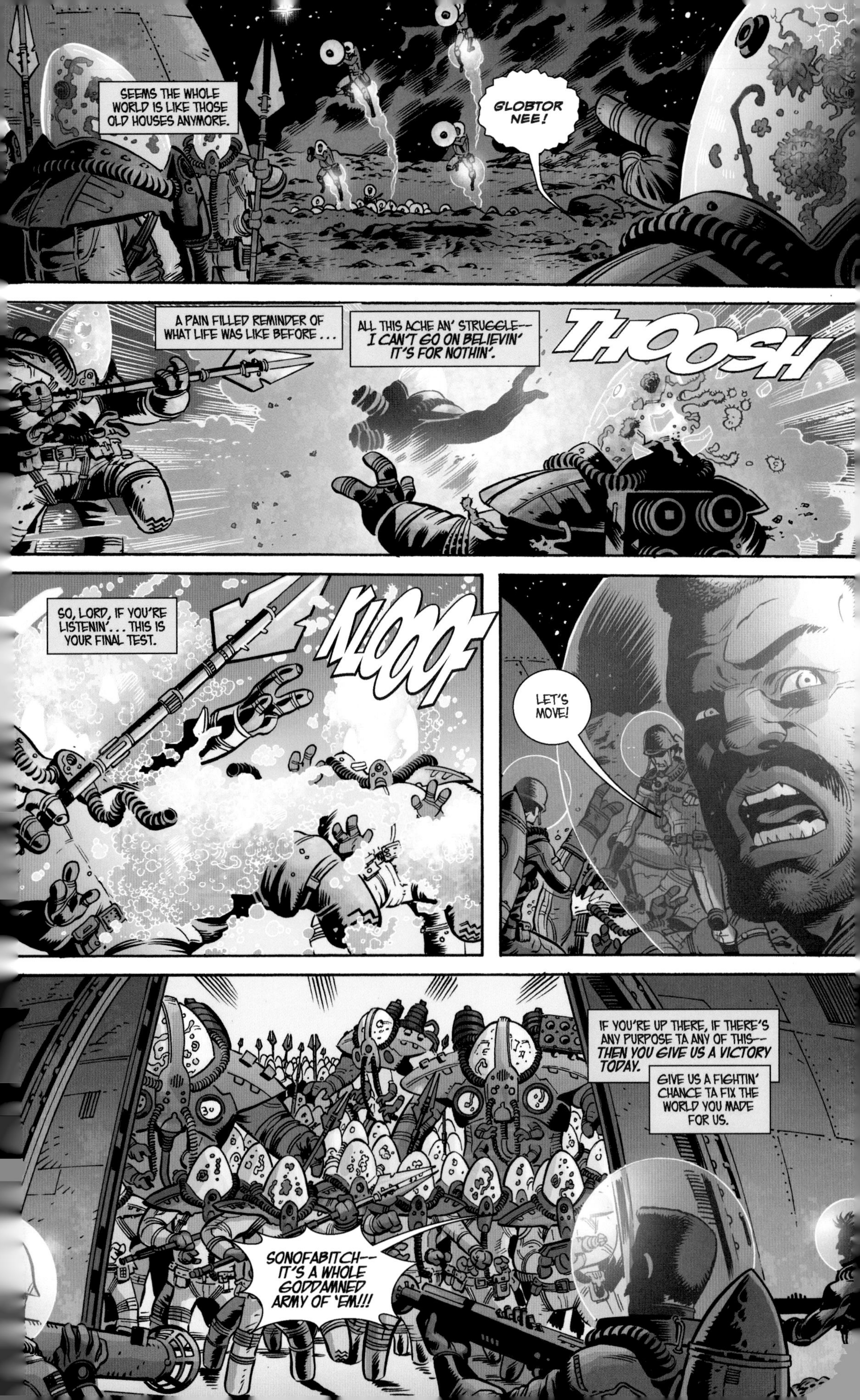
SEEMS THE WHOLE WORLD IS LIKE THOSE OLD HOUSES ANYMORE.
GLOBTOR NEE!
A PAIN FILLED REMINDER OF WHAT LIFE WAS LIKE BEFORE . . .
ALL THIS ACHE AN' STRUGGLE-- I CAN'T GO ON BELIEVIN' IT'S FOR NOTHIN'.
THOOSH
SO, LORD, IF YOU'RE LISTENIN'. . . THIS IS YOUR FINAL TEST.
KLOOOF
LET'S MOVE!
IF YOU'RE UP THERE, IF THERE'S ANY PURPOSE TA ANY OF THIS-- THEN YOU GIVE US A VICTORY TODAY.
GIVE US A FIGHTIN' CHANCE TA FIX THE WORLD YOU MADE FOR US.
SONOFABITCH-- IT'S A WHOLE GODDAMNED ARMY OF 'EM!!!

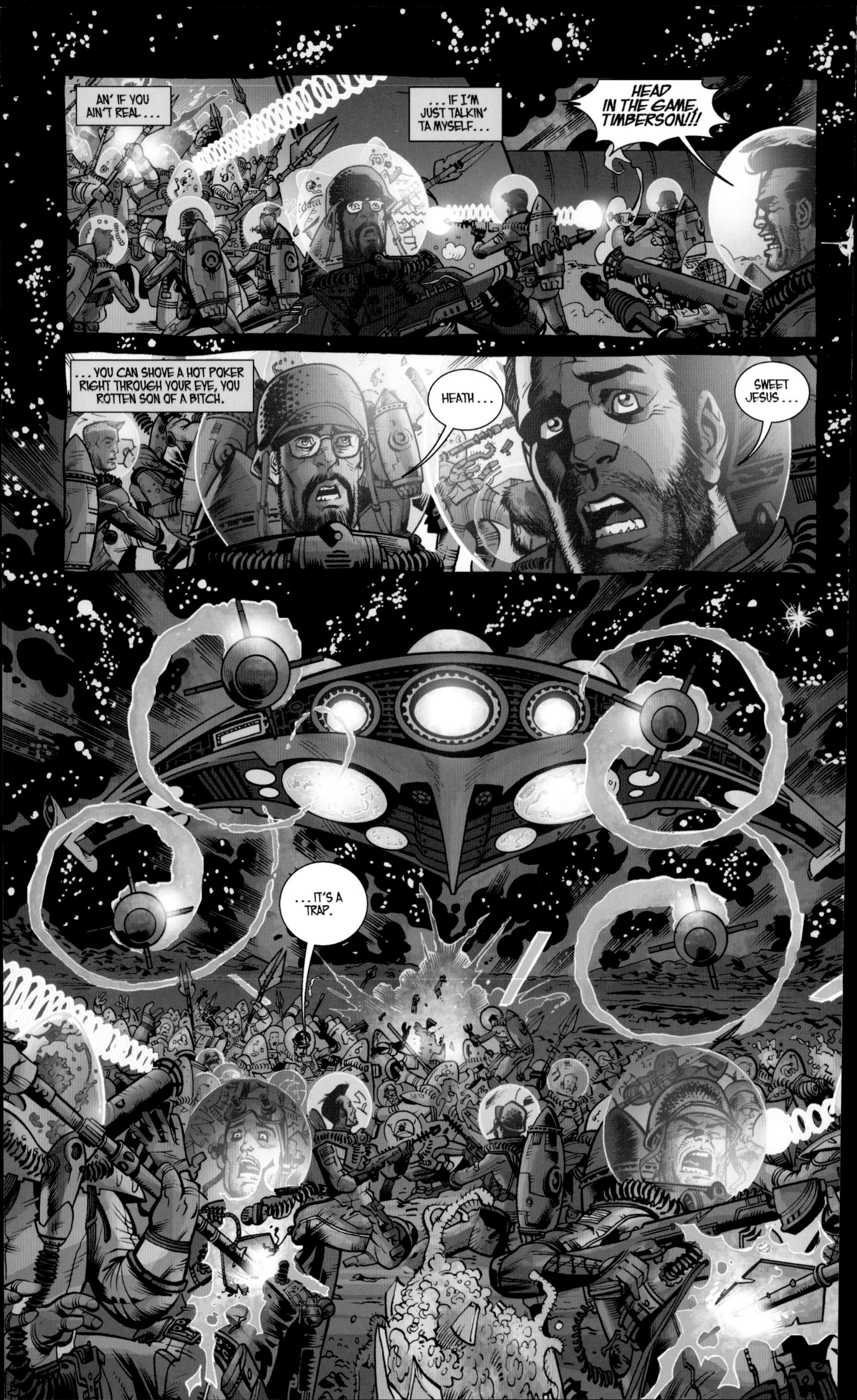
AN' IF YOU AIN'T REAL...
...IF I'M JUST TALKIN' TA MYSELF...
HEAD IN THE GAME, TIMBERSON!!!
...YOU CAN SHOVE A HOT POKER RIGHT THROUGH YOUR EYE, YOU ROTTEN SON OF A BITCH.
HEATH...
SWEET JESUS...
...IT'S A TRAP.

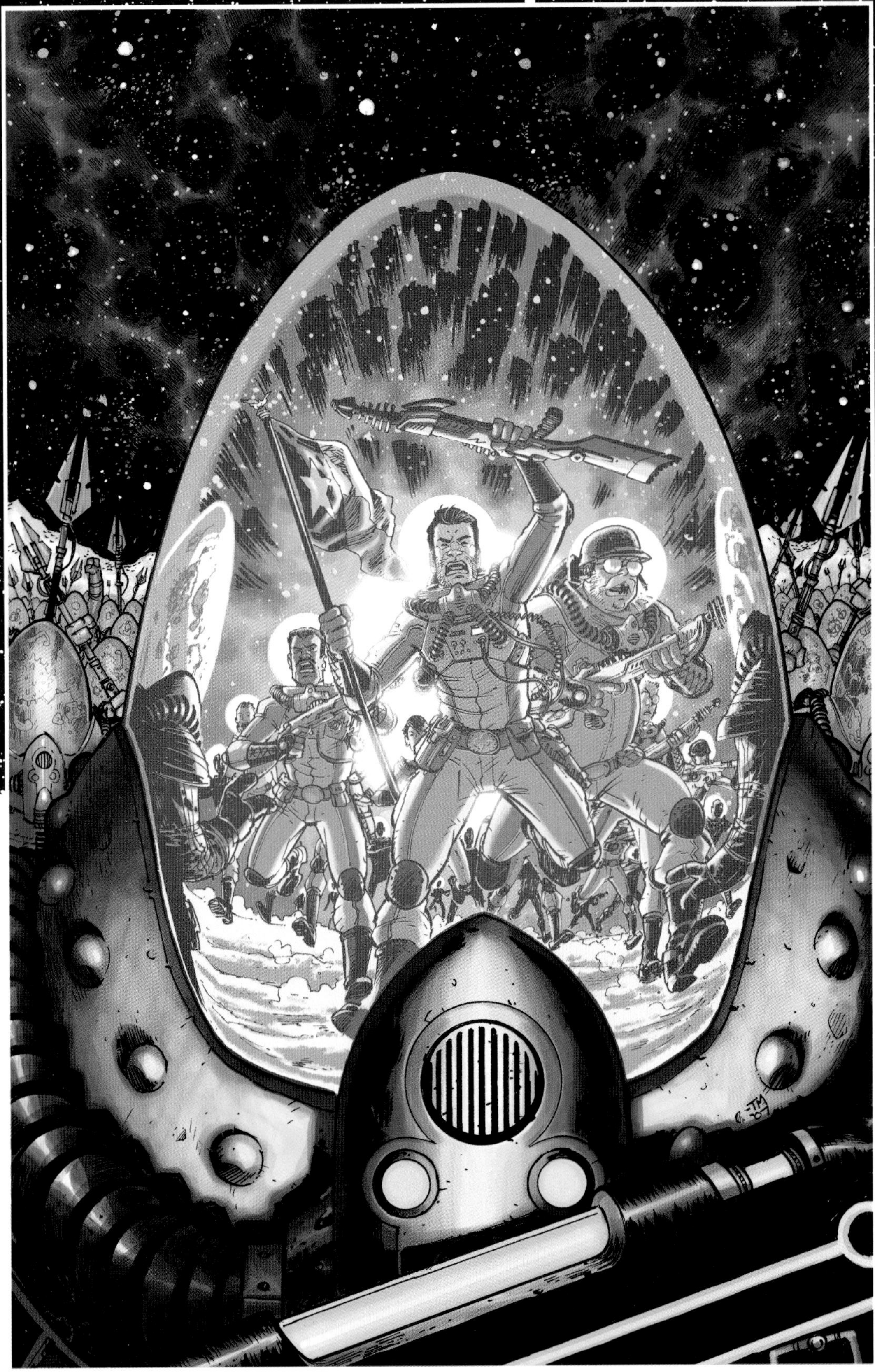
TM
'07

FEAR AGENT #15
ART BY **TONY MOORE**

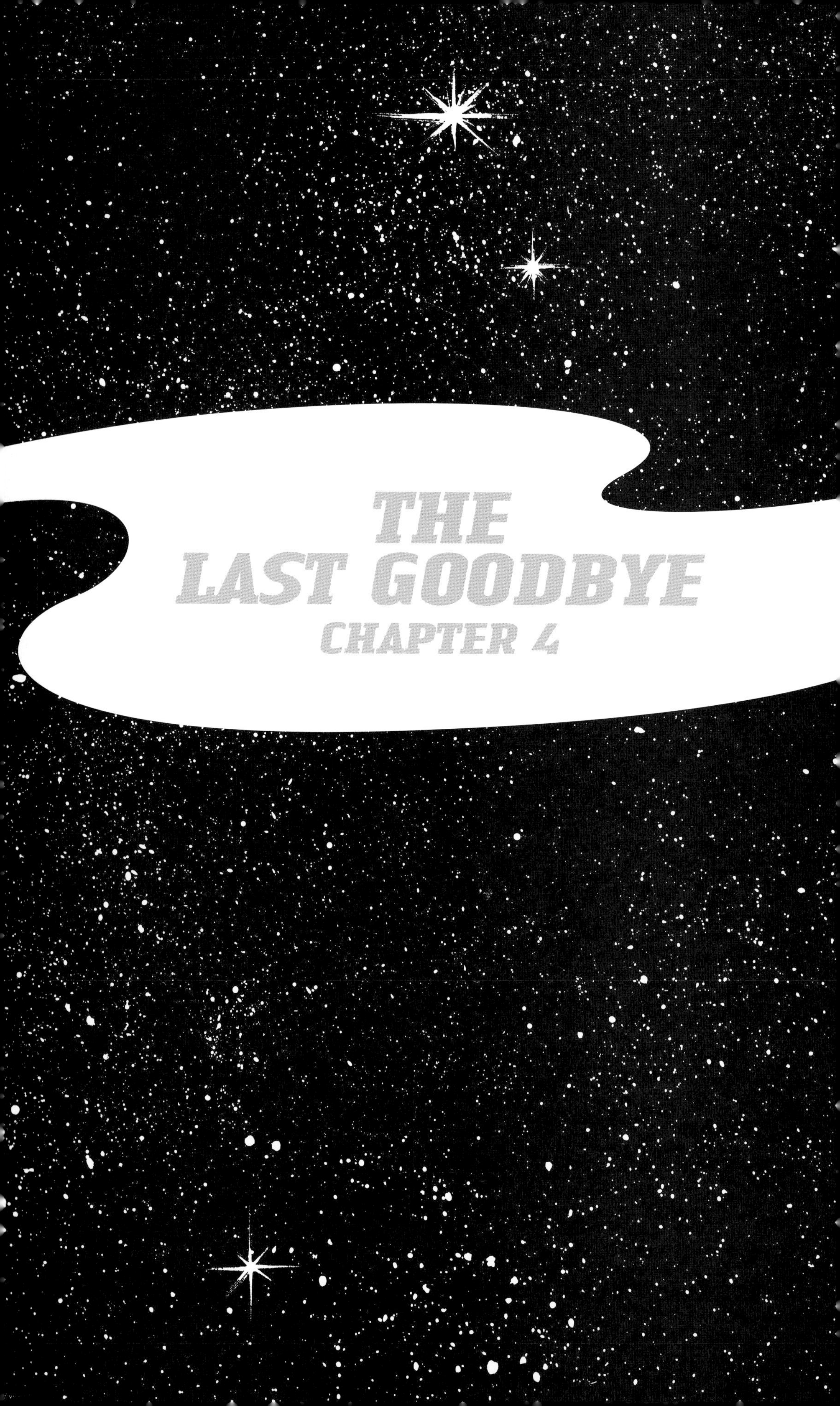
THE
LAST GOODBYE
CHAPTER 4

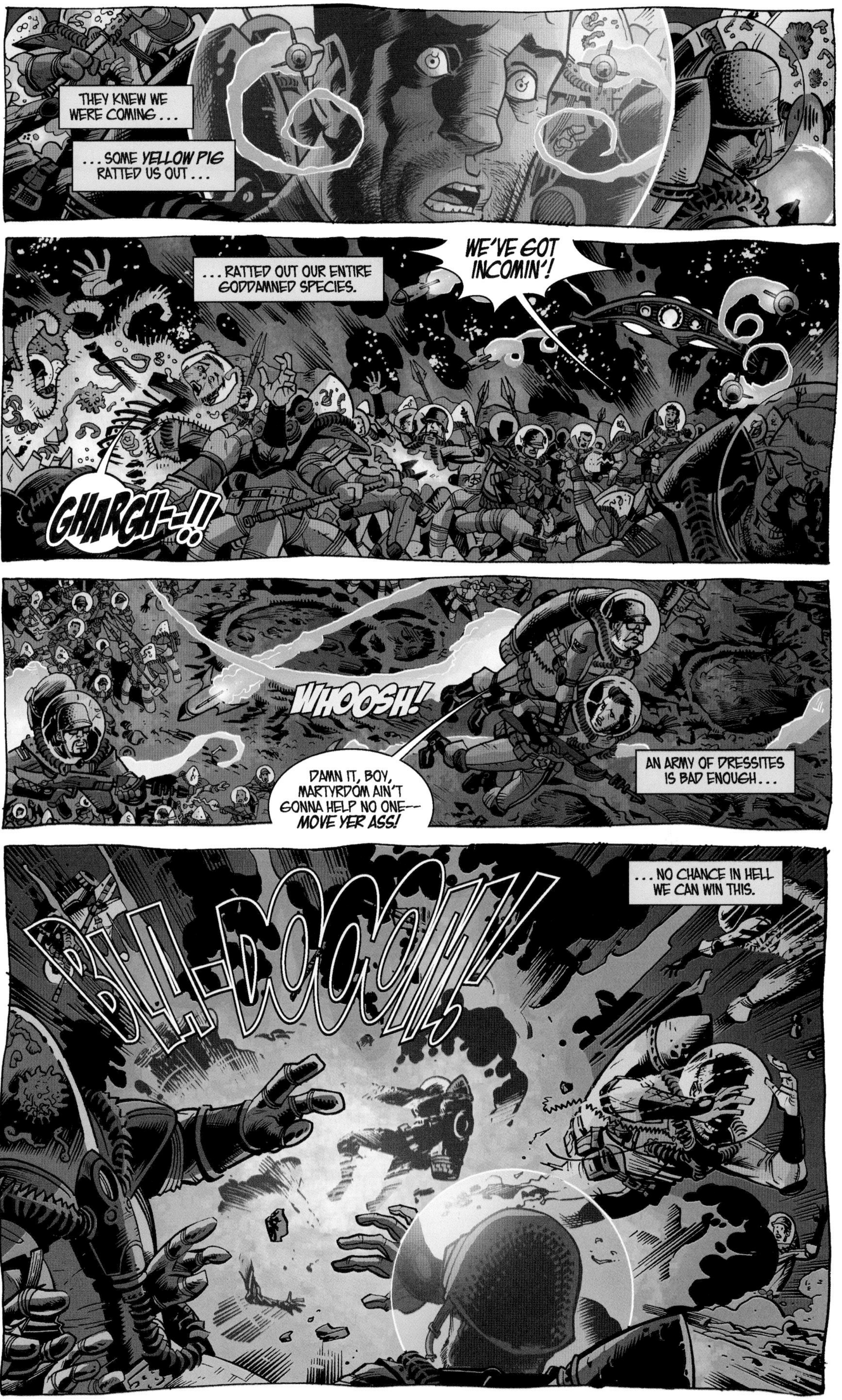
THEY KNEW WE WERE COMING . . .
. . . SOME YELLOW PIG RATTED US OUT . . .
. . . RATTED OUT OUR ENTIRE GODDAMNED SPECIES.
WE'VE GOT INCOMIN'!
GHARGH--!!
WHOOSH!
DAMN IT, BOY, MARTYRDOM AIN'T GONNA HELP NO ONE-- MOVE YER ASS!
AN ARMY OF DRESSITES IS BAD ENOUGH . . .
. . . NO CHANCE IN HELL WE CAN WIN THIS.
BLU-DOOOOM!

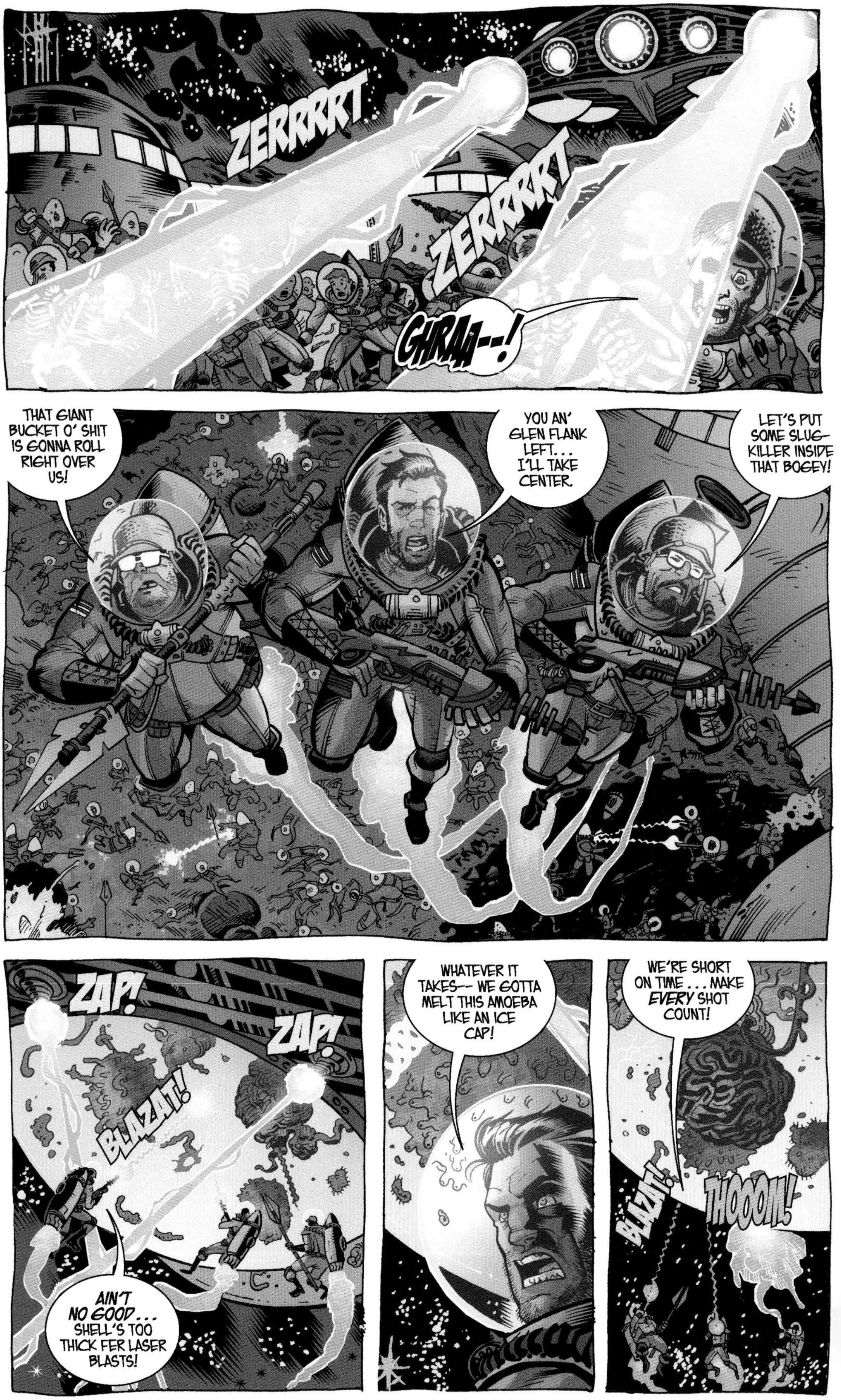
ZERRRRT
ZERRRRT
GHRAA--!
THAT GIANT BUCKET O' SHIT IS GONNA ROLL RIGHT OVER US!
YOU AN' GLEN FLANK LEFT... I'LL TAKE CENTER.
LET'S PUT SOME SLUG-KILLER INSIDE THAT BOGEY!
ZAP!
ZAP!
BLAZAT!
AIN'T NO GOOD... SHELL'S TOO THICK FER LASER BLASTS!
WHATEVER IT TAKES-- WE GOTTA MELT THIS AMOEBA LIKE AN ICE CAP!
WE'RE SHORT ON TIME... MAKE EVERY SHOT COUNT!
BLAZAT!
THOOOM!

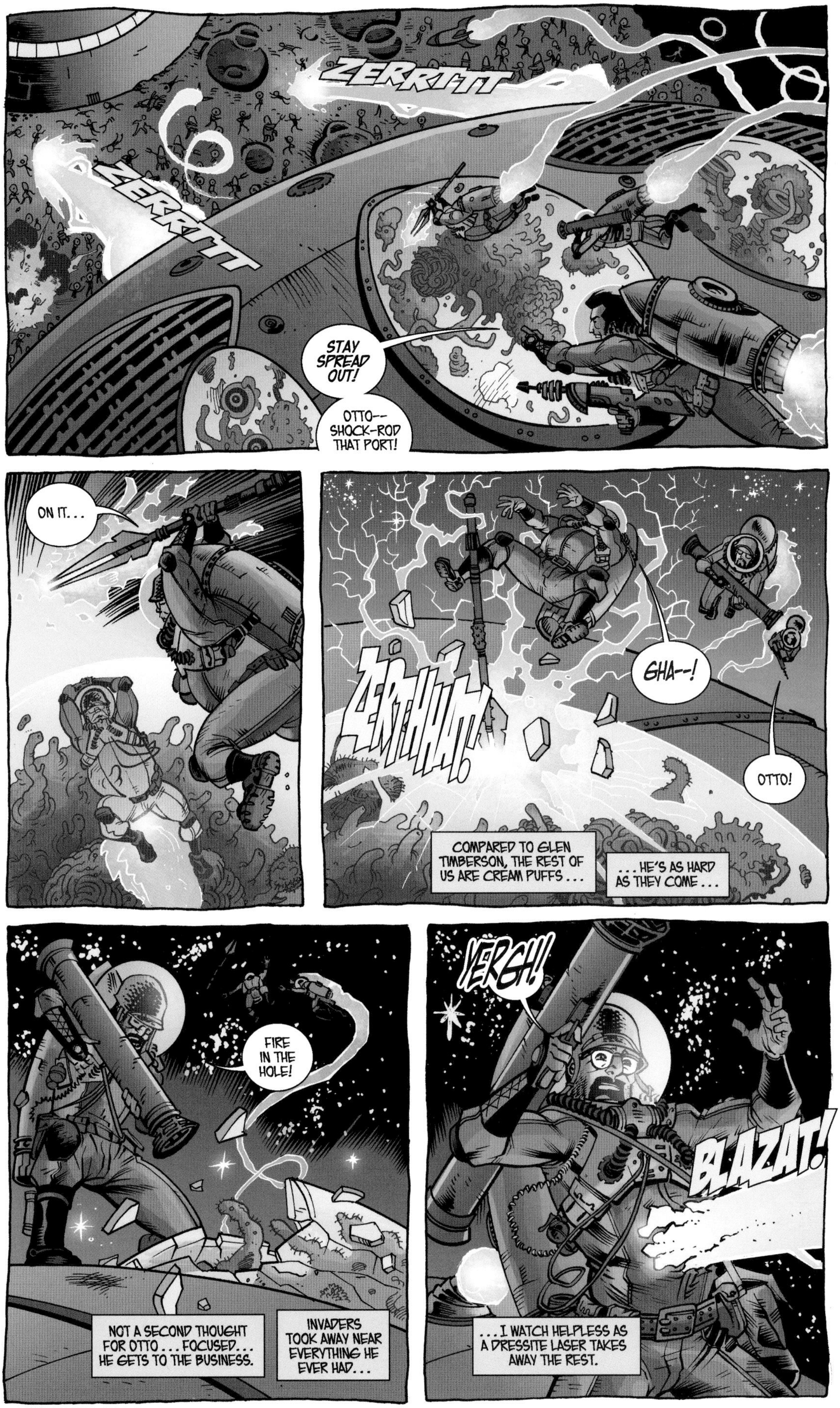
ZERRTTT
ZERRTTT
STAY SPREAD OUT!
OTTO-- SHOCK-ROD THAT PORT!
ON IT. . .
ZERTHHAT!
GHA--!
OTTO!
COMPARED TO GLEN TIMBERSON, THE REST OF US ARE CREAM PUFFS . . .
. . . HE'S AS HARD AS THEY COME . . .
FIRE IN THE HOLE!
NOT A SECOND THOUGHT FOR OTTO . . . FOCUSED . . . HE GETS TO THE BUSINESS.
INVADERS TOOK AWAY NEAR EVERYTHING HE EVER HAD . . .
YERGH!
BLAZAT!
. . . I WATCH HELPLESS AS A DRESSITE LASER TAKES AWAY THE REST.

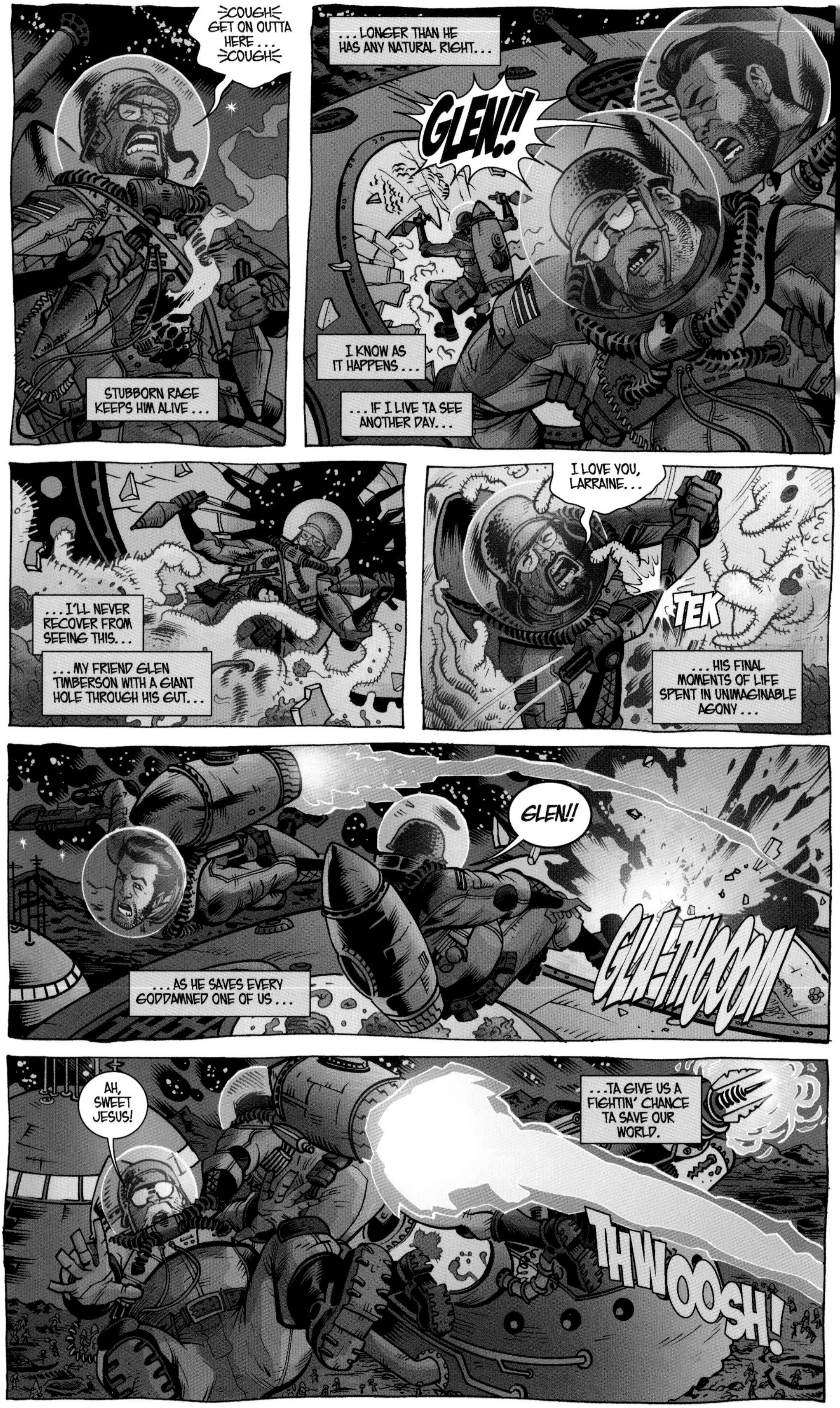

≡COUGH≡ GET ON OUTTA HERE . . . ≡COUGH≡
STUBBORN RAGE KEEPS HIM ALIVE . . .
. . . LONGER THAN HE HAS ANY NATURAL RIGHT. . .
GLEN!!
I KNOW AS IT HAPPENS . . .
. . . IF I LIVE TA SEE ANOTHER DAY. . .
. . . I'LL NEVER RECOVER FROM SEEING THIS. . .
. . . MY FRIEND GLEN TIMBERSON WITH A GIANT HOLE THROUGH HIS GUT. . .
I LOVE YOU, LARRAINE. . .
TEK
. . . HIS FINAL MOMENTS OF LIFE SPENT IN UNIMAGINABLE AGONY . . .
GLEN!!
GLA-THOOOM
. . . AS HE SAVES EVERY GODDAMNED ONE OF US . . .
AH, SWEET JESUS!
. . . TA GIVE US A FIGHTIN' CHANCE TA SAVE OUR WORLD.
THWOOSH!

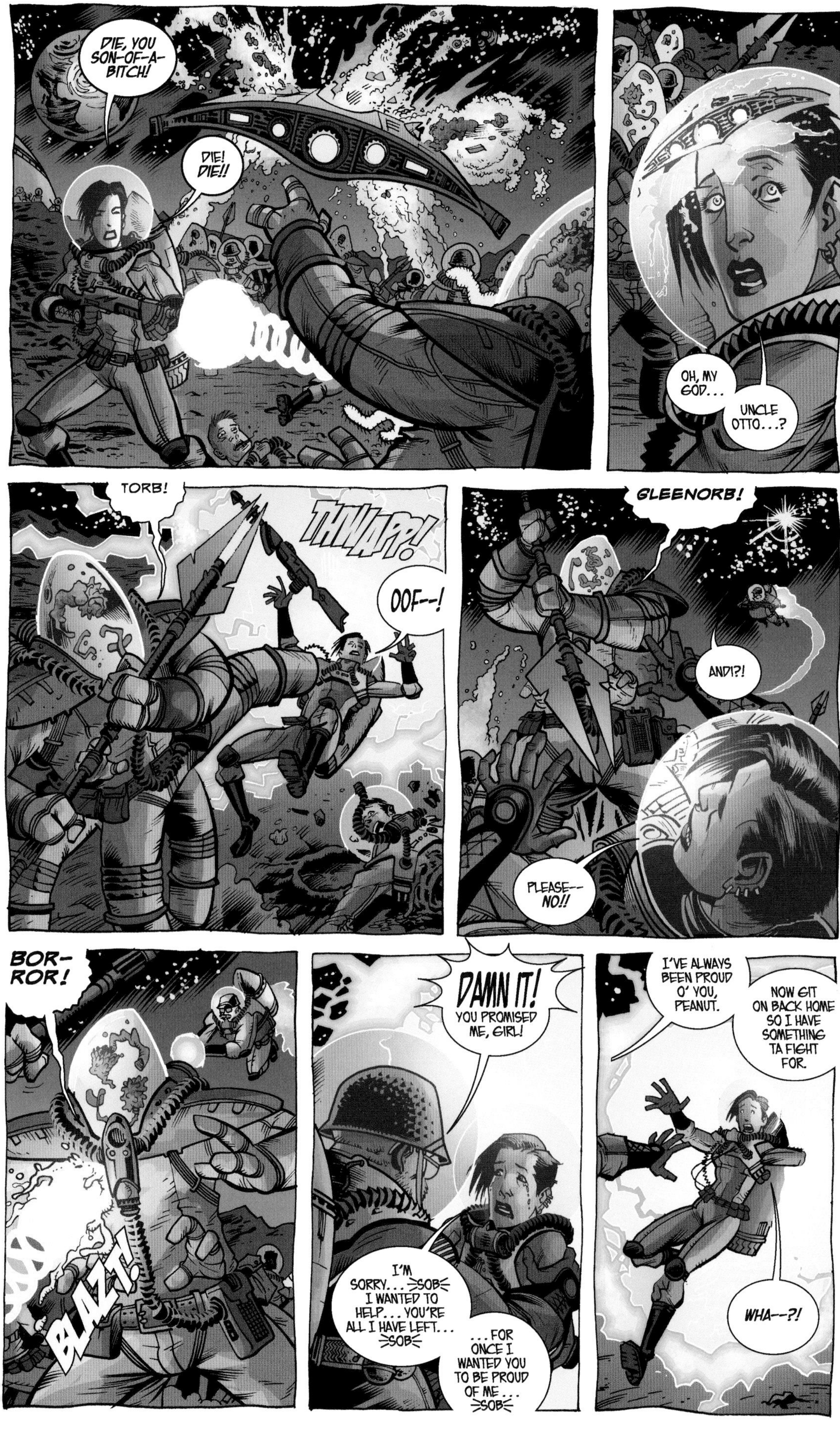
DIE, YOU SON-OF-A-BITCH!
DIE! DIE!!
OH, MY GOD...
UNCLE OTTO...?
TORB!
THWAPP!
OOF--!
GLEENORB!
ANDI?!
PLEASE-- NO!!
BOR-ROR!
BLAZT!
DAMN IT! YOU PROMISED ME, GIRL!
I'M SORRY... =SOB= I WANTED TO HELP... YOU'RE ALL I HAVE LEFT... =SOB=
...FOR ONCE I WANTED YOU TO BE PROUD OF ME... =SOB=
I'VE ALWAYS BEEN PROUD O' YOU, PEANUT.
NOW GIT ON BACK HOME SO I HAVE SOMETHING TA FIGHT FOR.
WHA--?!

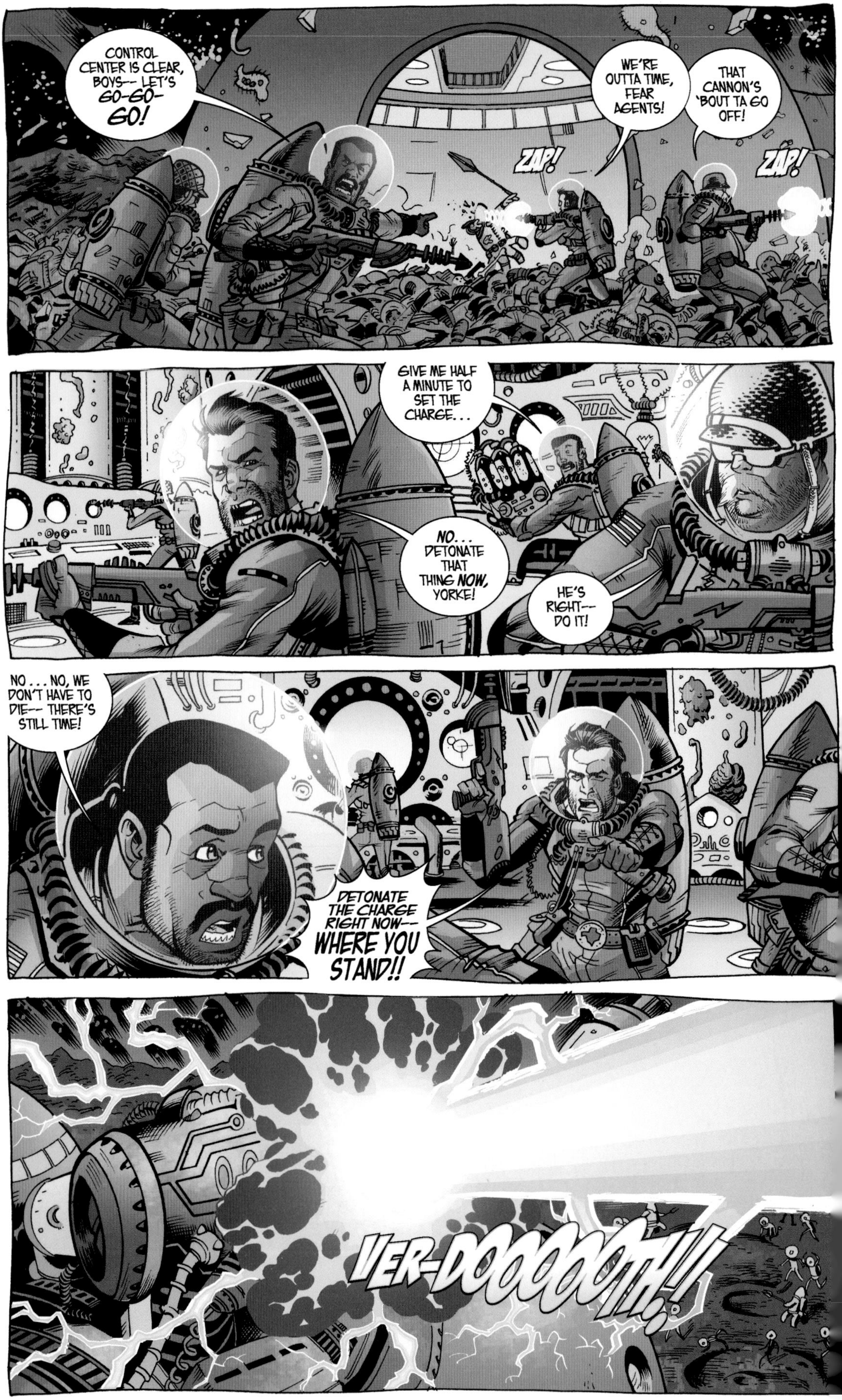
CONTROL CENTER IS CLEAR, BOYS-- LET'S GO-GO-GO!
WE'RE OUTTA TIME, FEAR AGENTS!
THAT CANNON'S 'BOUT TA GO OFF!
ZAP!
ZAP!
GIVE ME HALF A MINUTE TO SET THE CHARGE...
NO... DETONATE THAT THING NOW, YORKE!
HE'S RIGHT--- DO IT!
NO... NO, WE DON'T HAVE TO DIE-- THERE'S STILL TIME!
DETONATE THE CHARGE RIGHT NOW-- WHERE YOU STAND!!
VER-DOOOOOOTH!!

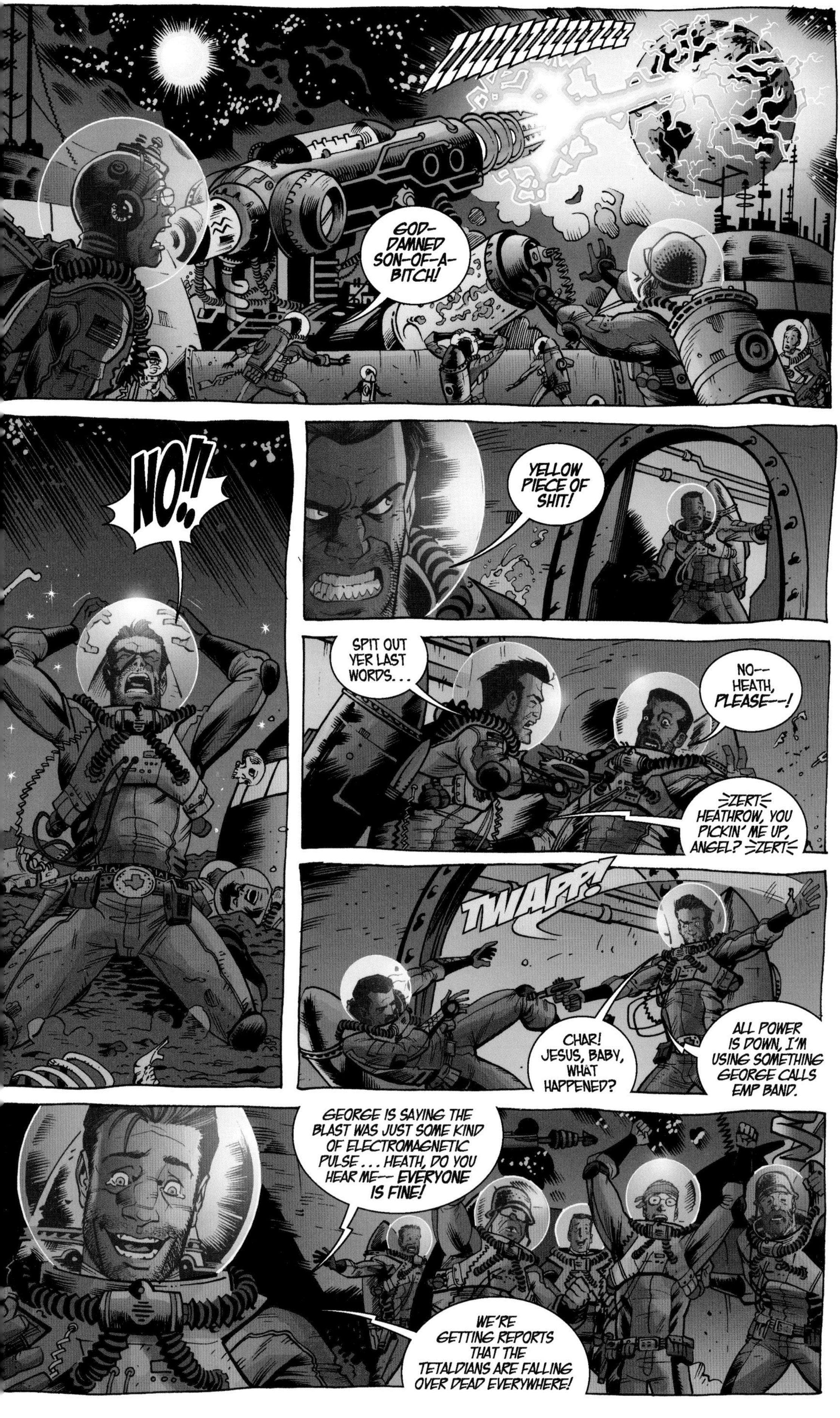
ZZZZZZZZZZZZZZZZ
GOD-DAMNED SON-OF-A-BITCH!
NO!!
YELLOW PIECE OF SHIT!
SPIT OUT YER LAST WORDS...
NO-- HEATH, PLEASE--!
ZERT HEATHROW, YOU PICKIN' ME UP, ANGEL? ZERT
TWAPP!
CHAR! JESUS, BABY, WHAT HAPPENED?
ALL POWER IS DOWN, I'M USING SOMETHING GEORGE CALLS EMP BAND.
GEORGE IS SAYING THE BLAST WAS JUST SOME KIND OF ELECTROMAGNETIC PULSE... HEATH, DO YOU HEAR ME-- EVERYONE IS FINE!
WE'RE GETTING REPORTS THAT THE TETALDIANS ARE FALLING OVER DEAD EVERYWHERE!

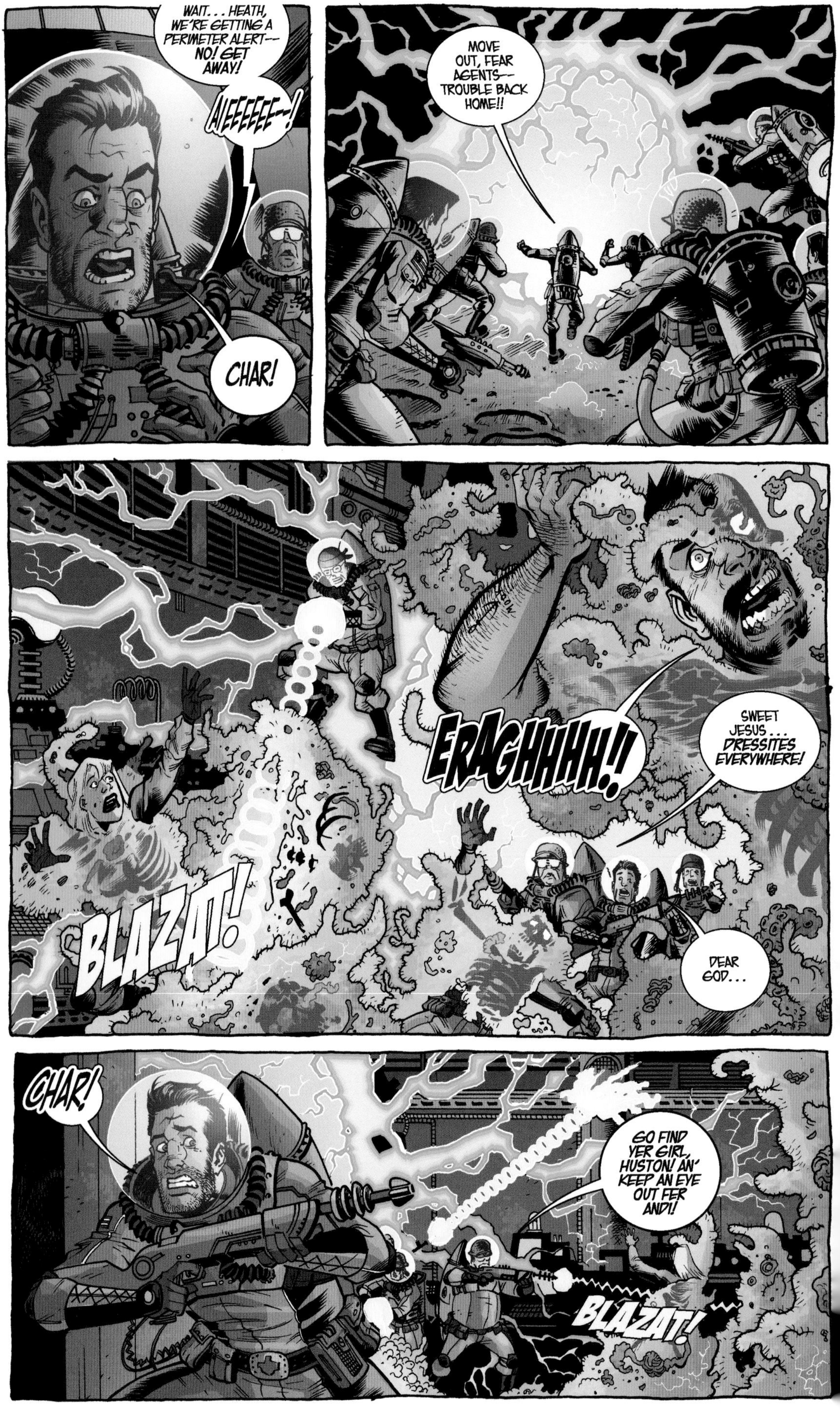
WAIT. . . HEATH, WE'RE GETTING A PERIMETER ALERT-- NO! GET AWAY!
AIEEEEEE--!
CHAR!
MOVE OUT, FEAR AGENTS-- TROUBLE BACK HOME!!
ERAGHHHH!!
SWEET JESUS . . . DRESSITES EVERYWHERE!
BLAZAT!
DEAR GOD. . .
CHAR!
GO FIND YER GIRL, HUSTON! AN' KEEP AN EYE OUT FER ANDI!
BLAZAT!

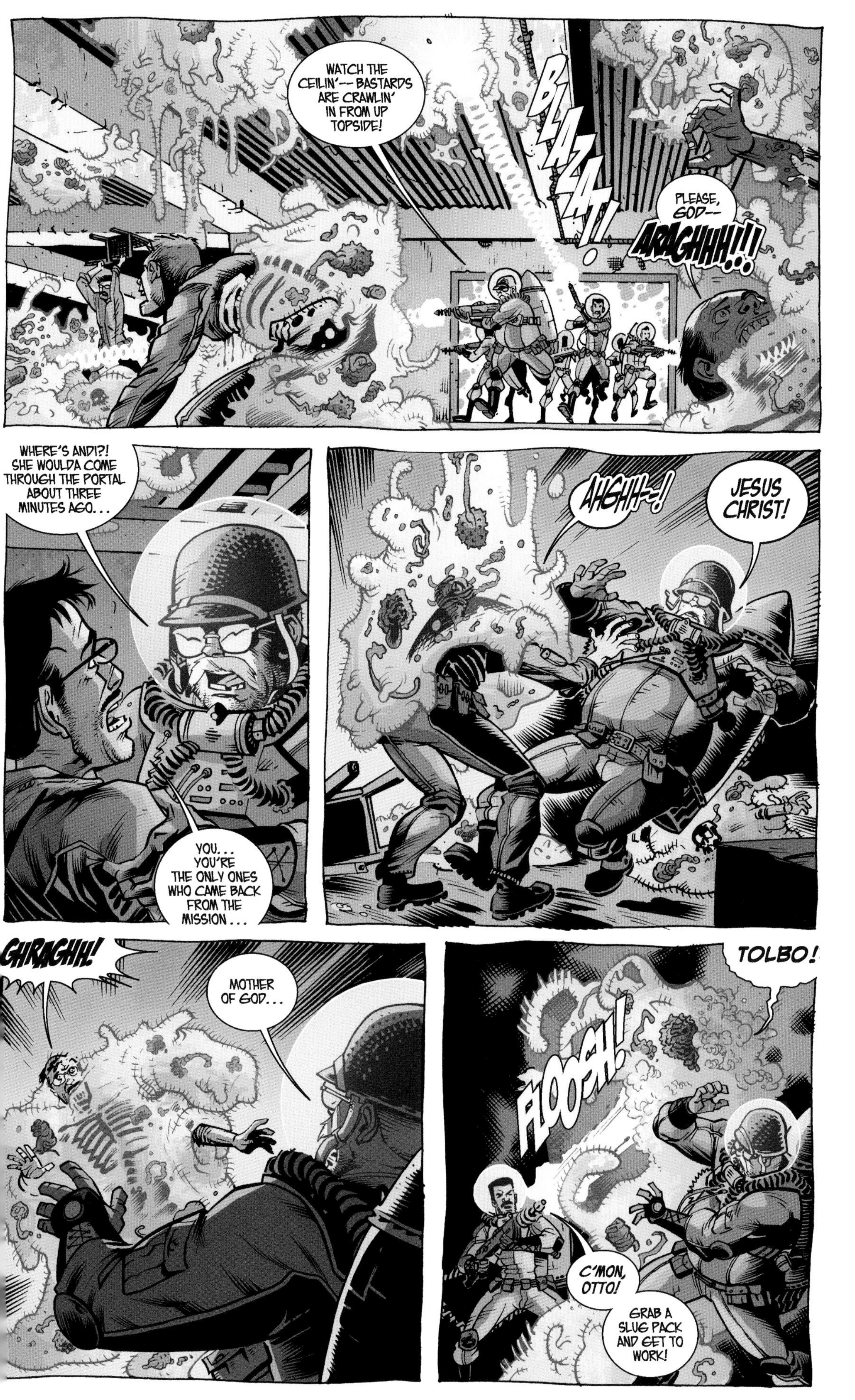
WATCH THE CEILIN'-- BASTARDS ARE CRAWLIN' IN FROM UP TOPSIDE!
BLAZAT!!
PLEASE, GOD--
ARAGHHH!!!
WHERE'S ANDI?! SHE WOULDA COME THROUGH THE PORTAL ABOUT THREE MINUTES AGO...
YOU... YOU'RE THE ONLY ONES WHO CAME BACK FROM THE MISSION...
AHGHH--!
JESUS CHRIST!
GHRAGHH!
MOTHER OF GOD...
TOLBO!
FLOOSH!
C'MON, OTTO!
GRAB A SLUG PACK AND GET TO WORK!

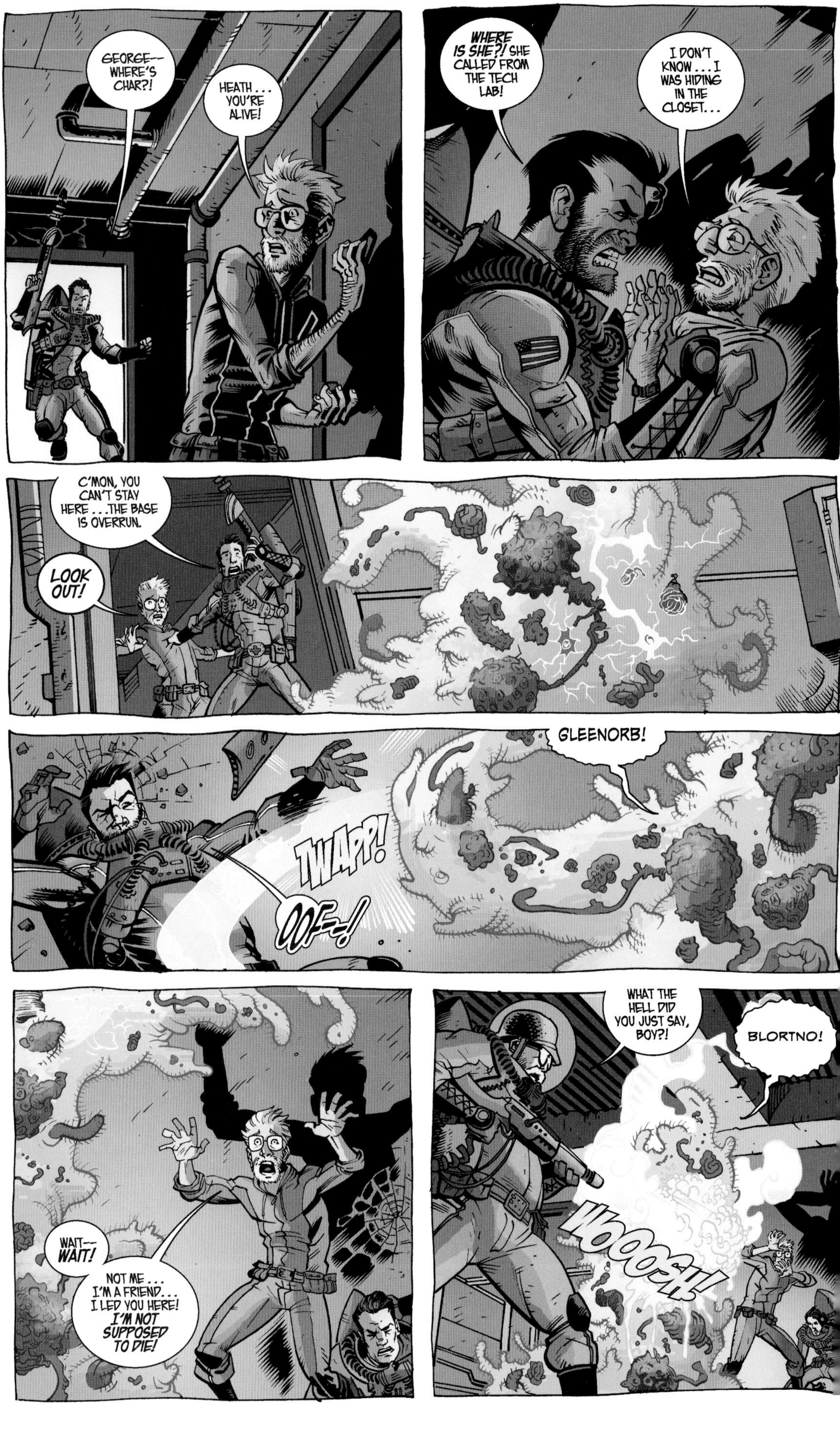
GEORGE--
WHERE'S
CHAR?!
HEATH . . .
YOU'RE
ALIVE!
WHERE
IS SHE?! SHE
CALLED FROM
THE TECH
LAB!
I DON'T
KNOW . . . I
WAS HIDING
IN THE
CLOSET . . .
C'MON, YOU
CAN'T STAY
HERE . . . THE BASE
IS OVERRUN.
LOOK
OUT!
GLEENORB!
TWAPP!
OOF--!
WAIT--
WAIT!
NOT ME . . .
I'M A FRIEND . . .
I LED YOU HERE!
I'M NOT
SUPPOSED
TO DIE!
WHAT THE
HELL DID
YOU JUST SAY,
BOY?!
BLORTNO!
WOOOOSH!

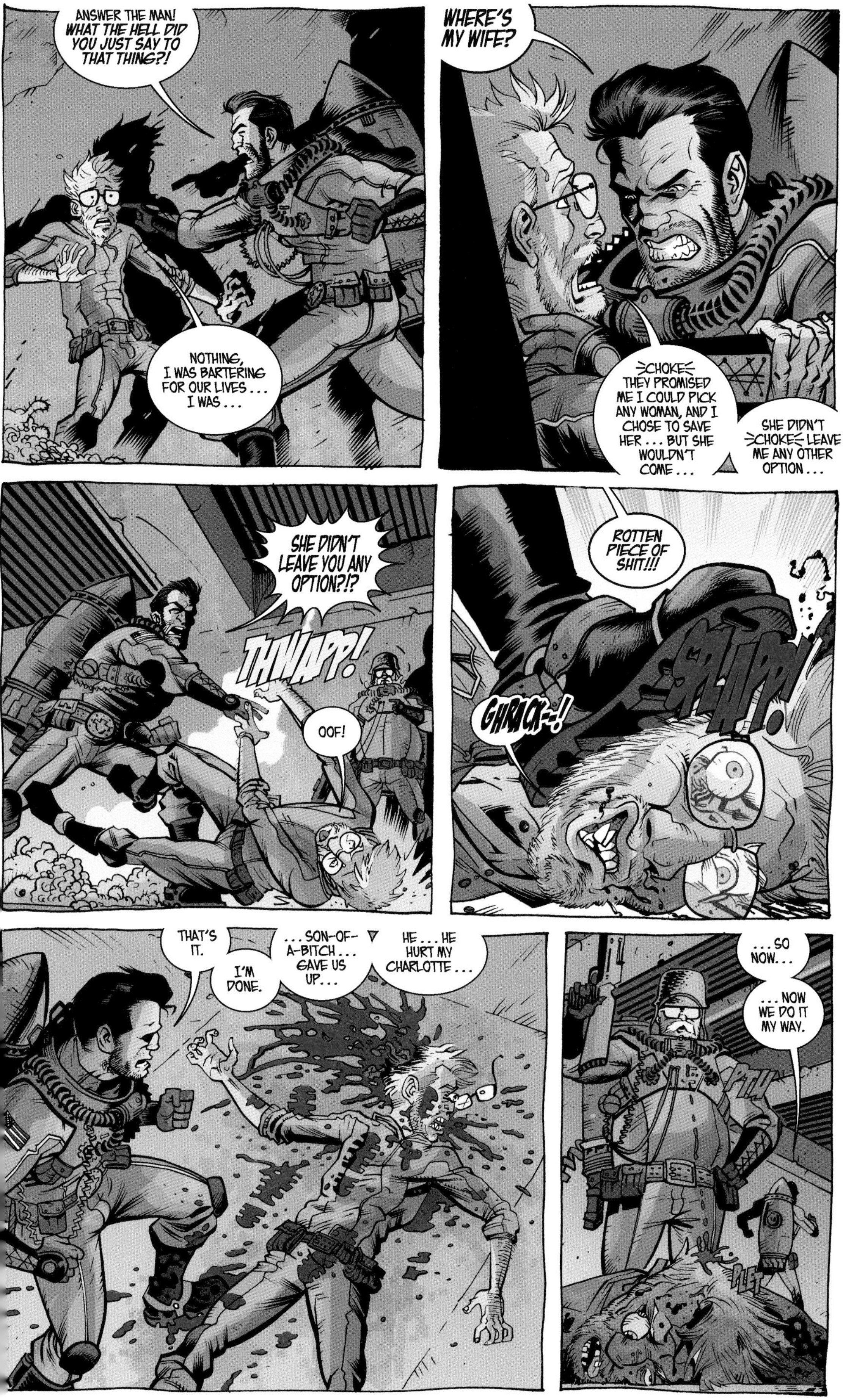

ANSWER THE MAN! WHAT THE HELL DID YOU JUST SAY TO THAT THING?!
NOTHING, I WAS BARTERING FOR OUR LIVES . . . I WAS . . .
WHERE'S MY WIFE?
≡CHOKE≡ THEY PROMISED ME I COULD PICK ANY WOMAN, AND I CHOSE TO SAVE HER . . . BUT SHE WOULDN'T COME . . .
SHE DIDN'T ≡CHOKE≡ LEAVE ME ANY OTHER OPTION . . .
SHE DIDN'T LEAVE YOU ANY OPTION?!?
THWAPP!
OOF!
ROTTEN PIECE OF SHIT!!!
GHRACK-!
THAT'S IT.
I'M DONE.
. . . SON-OF-A-BITCH . . . GAVE US UP . . .
HE . . . HE HURT MY CHARLOTTE . . .
. . . SO NOW. . .
. . . NOW WE DO IT MY WAY.

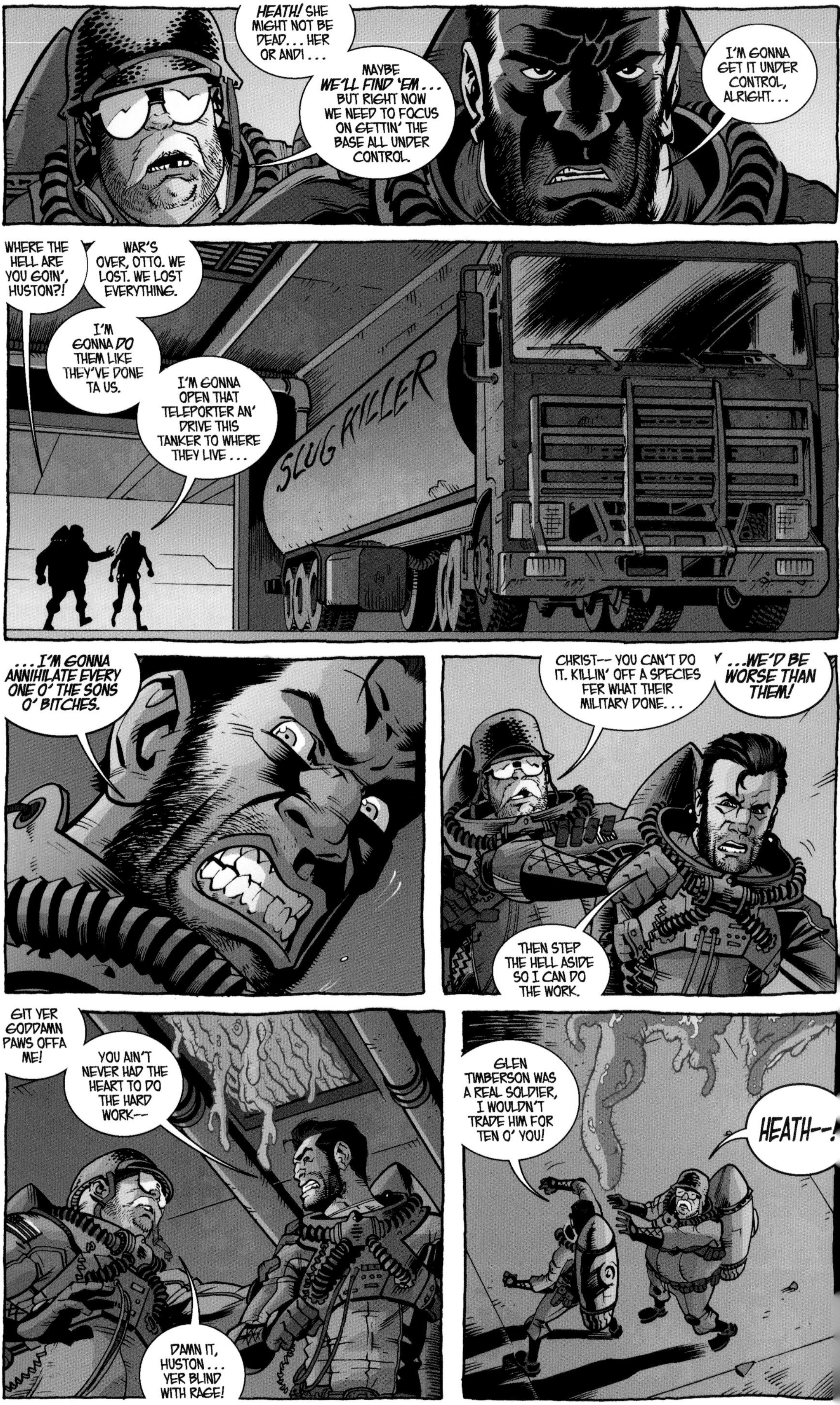
HEATH! SHE MIGHT NOT BE DEAD... HER OR ANDI...
MAYBE WE'LL FIND 'EM... BUT RIGHT NOW WE NEED TO FOCUS ON GETTIN' THE BASE ALL UNDER CONTROL.
I'M GONNA GET IT UNDER CONTROL, ALRIGHT...
WHERE THE HELL ARE YOU GOIN', HUSTON?!
WAR'S OVER, OTTO. WE LOST. WE LOST EVERYTHING.
I'M GONNA DO THEM LIKE THEY'VE DONE TA US.
I'M GONNA OPEN THAT TELEPORTER AN' DRIVE THIS TANKER TO WHERE THEY LIVE...
SLUG KILLER
...I'M GONNA ANNIHILATE EVERY ONE O' THE SONS O' BITCHES.
CHRIST-- YOU CAN'T DO IT. KILLIN' OFF A SPECIES FER WHAT THEIR MILITARY DONE...
...WE'D BE WORSE THAN THEM!
THEN STEP THE HELL ASIDE SO I CAN DO THE WORK.
GIT YER GODDAMN PAWS OFFA ME!
YOU AIN'T NEVER HAD THE HEART TO DO THE HARD WORK--
DAMN IT, HUSTON... YER BLIND WITH RAGE!
GLEN TIMBERSON WAS A REAL SOLDIER, I WOULDN'T TRADE HIM FOR TEN O' YOU!
HEATH--!

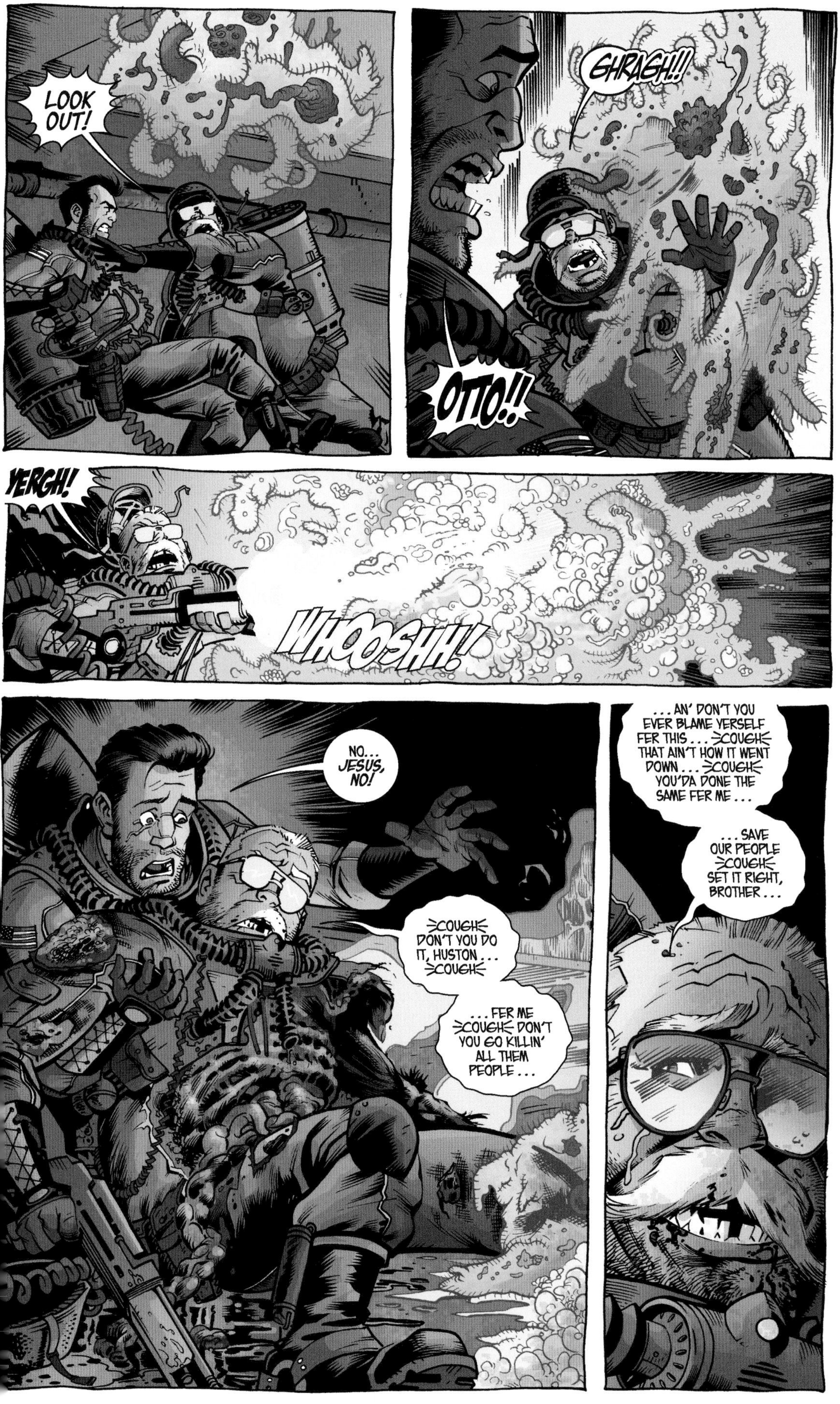
LOOK OUT!
GHRAGH!!
OTTO!!
YERGH!
WHOOSHH!
NO... JESUS, NO!
⋛COUGH⋚ DON'T YOU DO IT, HUSTON... ⋛COUGH⋚
...FER ME ⋛COUGH⋚ DON'T YOU GO KILLIN' ALL THEM PEOPLE...
...AN' DON'T YOU EVER BLAME YERSELF FER THIS... ⋛COUGH⋚ THAT AIN'T HOW IT WENT DOWN... ⋛COUGH⋚ YOU'DA DONE THE SAME FER ME...
...SAVE OUR PEOPLE ⋛COUGH⋚ SET IT RIGHT, BROTHER...

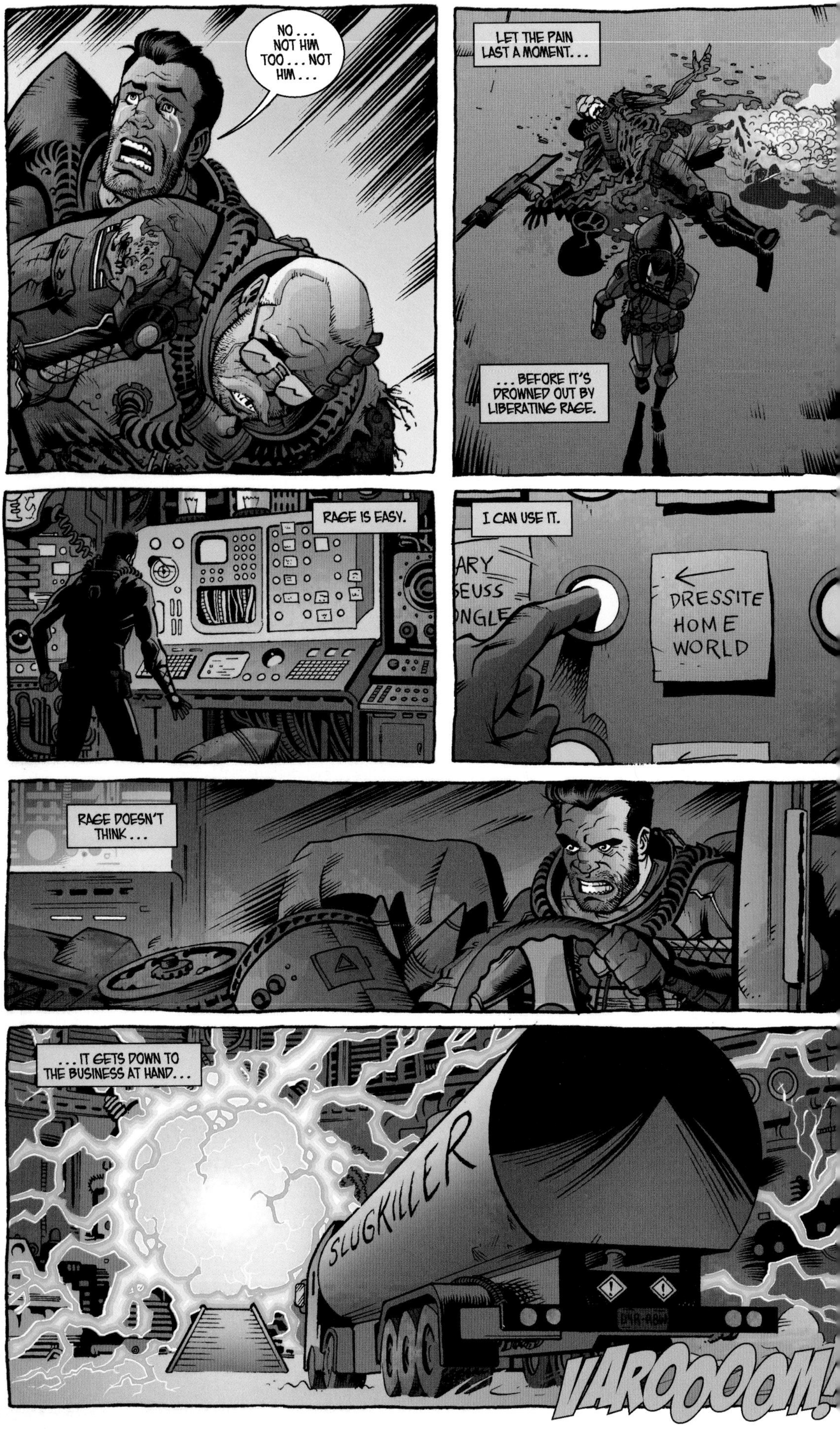
NO . . . NOT HIM TOO . . . NOT HIM . . .
LET THE PAIN LAST A MOMENT . . .
. . . BEFORE IT'S DROWNED OUT BY LIBERATING RAGE.
RAGE IS EASY.
I CAN USE IT.
DRESSITE HOME WORLD
RAGE DOESN'T THINK . . .
. . . IT GETS DOWN TO THE BUSINESS AT HAND . . .
SLUGKILLER
VAROOOOM!

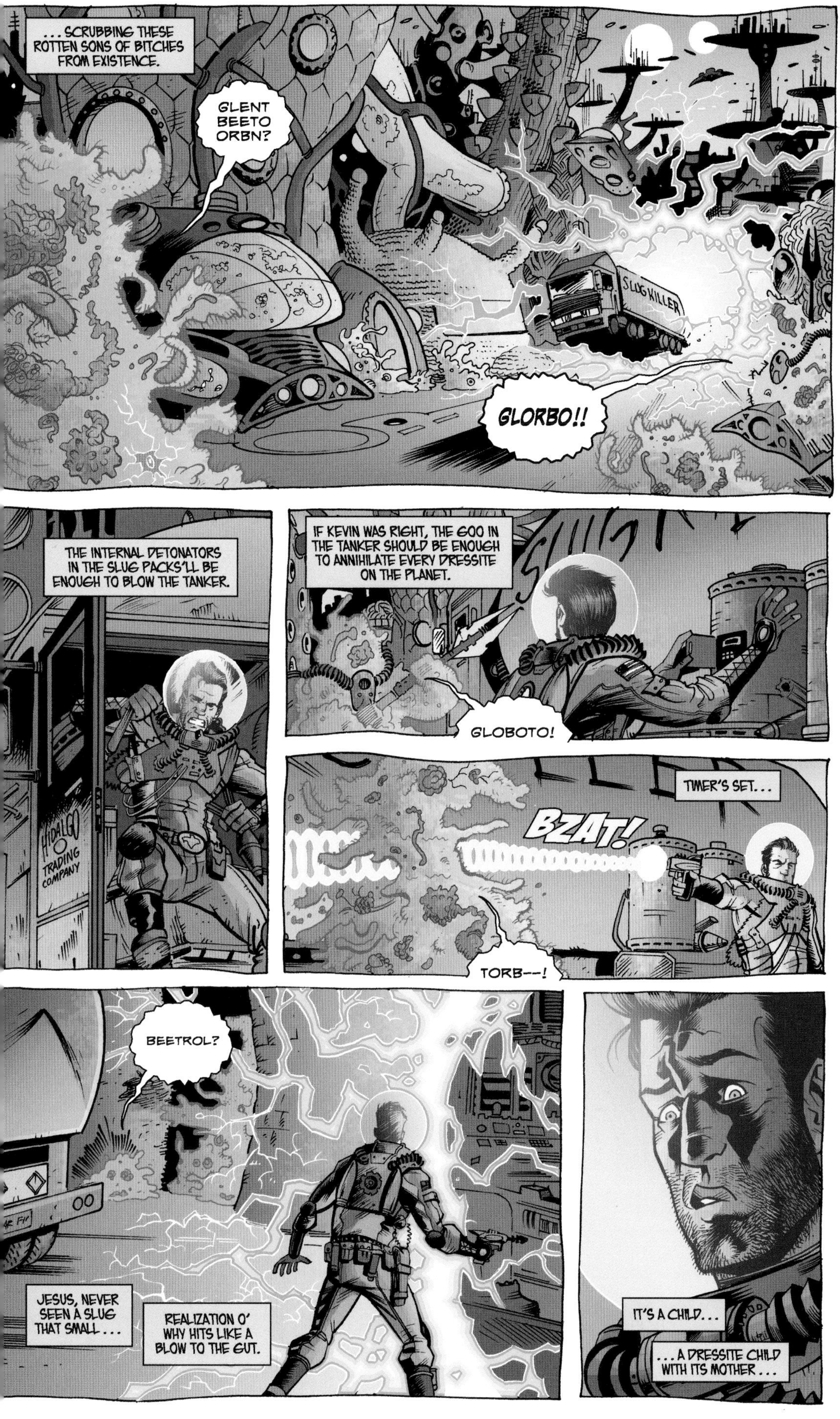
...SCRUBBING THESE ROTTEN SONS OF BITCHES FROM EXISTENCE.
GLENT BEETO ORBN?
SLUG KILLER
GLORBO!!
THE INTERNAL DETONATORS IN THE SLUG PACKS'LL BE ENOUGH TO BLOW THE TANKER.
HIDALGO TRADING COMPANY
IF KEVIN WAS RIGHT, THE GOO IN THE TANKER SHOULD BE ENOUGH TO ANNIHILATE EVERY DRESSITE ON THE PLANET.
GLOBOTO!
TIMER'S SET...
BZAT!
TORB--!
BEETROL?
JESUS, NEVER SEEN A SLUG THAT SMALL...
REALIZATION O' WHY HITS LIKE A BLOW TO THE GUT.
IT'S A CHILD...
...A DRESSITE CHILD WITH ITS MOTHER...

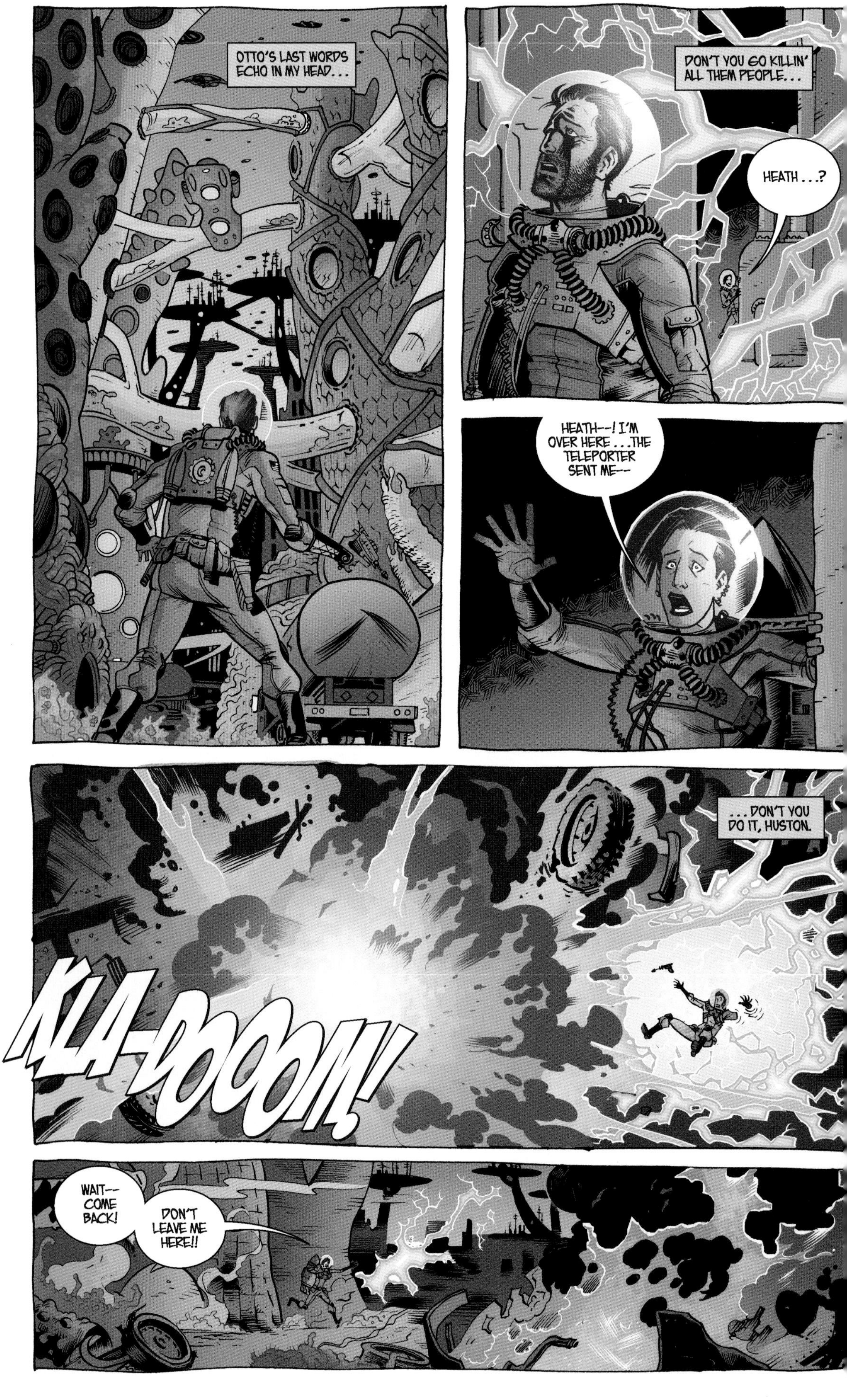
OTTO'S LAST WORDS ECHO IN MY HEAD...
DON'T YOU GO KILLIN' ALL THEM PEOPLE...
HEATH...?
HEATH--! I'M OVER HERE...THE TELEPORTER SENT ME--
...DON'T YOU DO IT, HUSTON.
KLA-DOOOM!
WAIT-- COME BACK!
DON'T LEAVE ME HERE!!

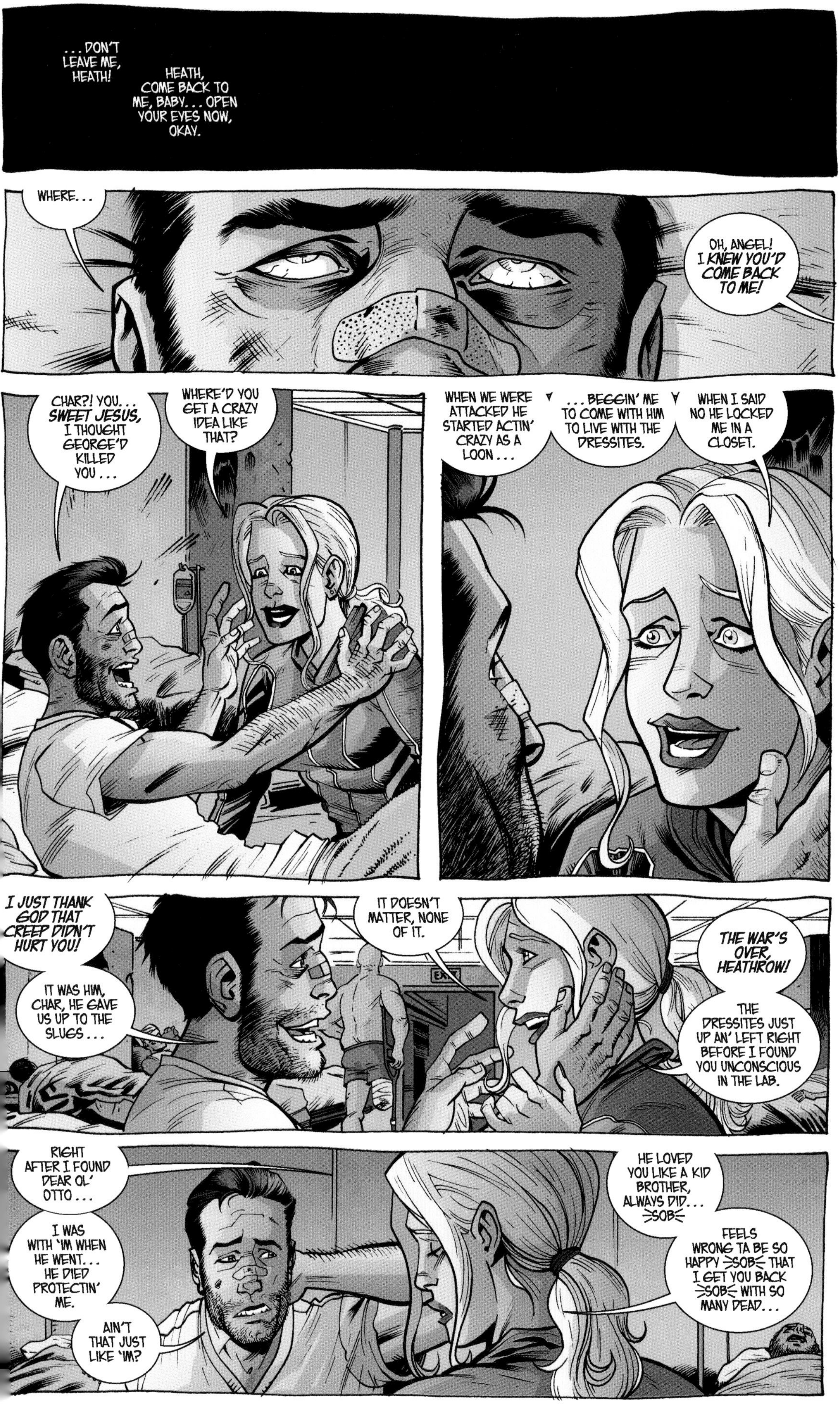

. . . DON'T LEAVE ME, HEATH!
HEATH, COME BACK TO ME, BABY. . . OPEN YOUR EYES NOW, OKAY.
WHERE. . .
OH, ANGEL! I *KNEW YOU'D COME BACK TO ME!*
CHAR?! YOU. . . ***SWEET JESUS,*** I THOUGHT GEORGE'D KILLED YOU . . .
WHERE'D YOU GET A CRAZY IDEA LIKE THAT?
WHEN WE WERE ATTACKED HE STARTED ACTIN' CRAZY AS A LOON . . .
. . . BEGGIN' ME TO COME WITH HIM TO LIVE WITH THE DRESSITES.
WHEN I SAID NO HE LOCKED ME IN A CLOSET.
I JUST THANK GOD THAT CREEP DIDN'T HURT YOU!
IT DOESN'T MATTER, NONE OF IT.
IT WAS HIM, CHAR, HE GAVE US UP TO THE SLUGS . . .
THE WAR'S OVER, HEATHROW!
THE DRESSITES JUST UP AN' LEFT RIGHT BEFORE I FOUND YOU UNCONSCIOUS IN THE LAB.
RIGHT AFTER I FOUND DEAR OL' OTTO . . .
I WAS WITH 'IM WHEN HE WENT. . . HE DIED PROTECTIN' ME.
AIN'T THAT JUST LIKE 'IM?
HE LOVED YOU LIKE A KID BROTHER, ALWAYS DID. . . SOB
FEELS WRONG TA BE SO HAPPY SOB THAT I GET YOU BACK SOB WITH SO MANY DEAD. . .

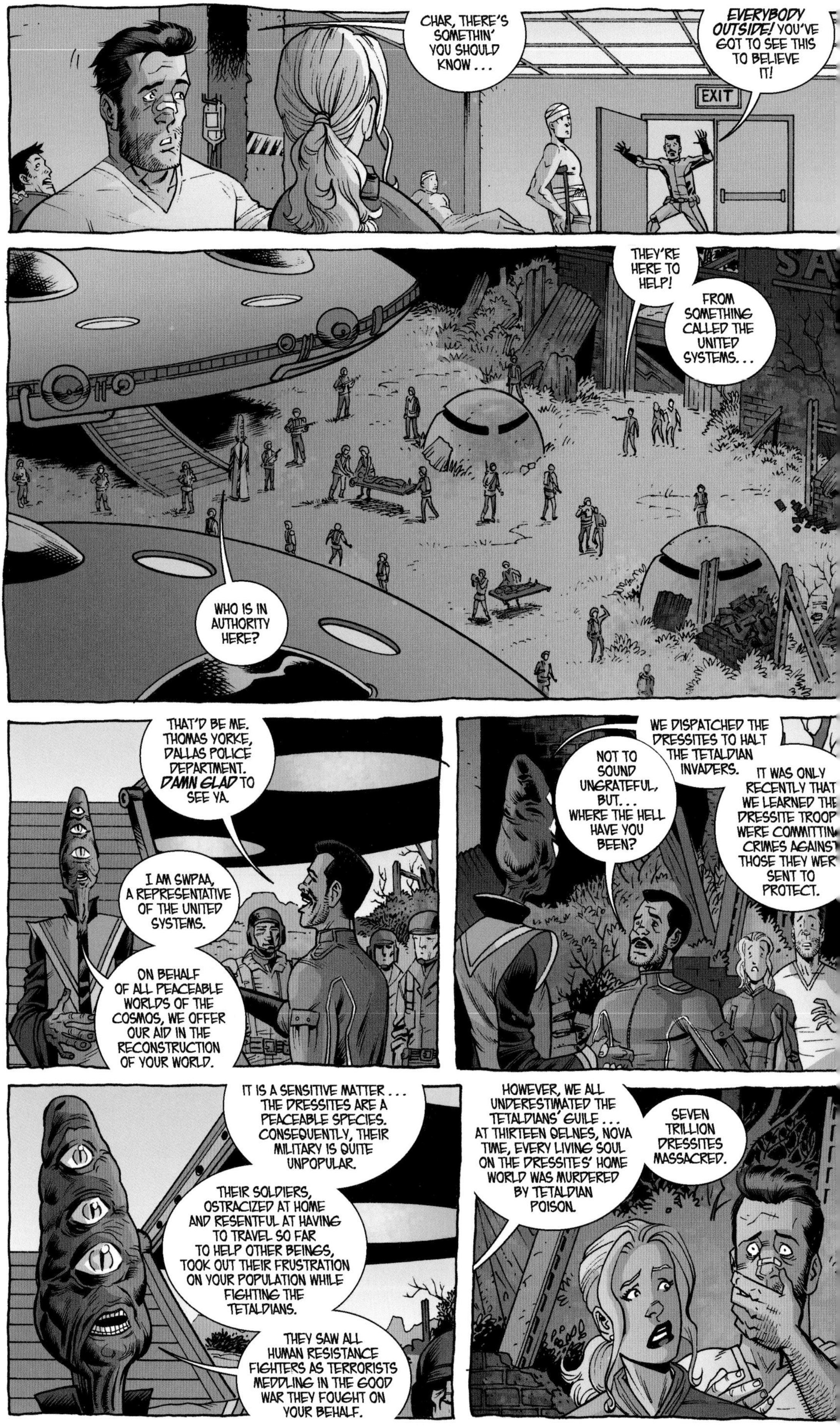
CHAR, THERE'S SOMETHIN' YOU SHOULD KNOW . . .
EVERYBODY OUTSIDE! YOU'VE GOT TO SEE THIS TO BELIEVE IT!
EXIT
THEY'RE HERE TO HELP!
FROM SOMETHING CALLED THE UNITED SYSTEMS. . .
WHO IS IN AUTHORITY HERE?
THAT'D BE ME. THOMAS YORKE, DALLAS POLICE DEPARTMENT. DAMN GLAD TO SEE YA.
I AM SWPAA, A REPRESENTATIVE OF THE UNITED SYSTEMS.
ON BEHALF OF ALL PEACEABLE WORLDS OF THE COSMOS, WE OFFER OUR AID IN THE RECONSTRUCTION OF YOUR WORLD.
NOT TO SOUND UNGRATEFUL, BUT. . . WHERE THE HELL HAVE YOU BEEN?
WE DISPATCHED THE DRESSITES TO HALT THE TETALDIAN INVADERS.
IT WAS ONLY RECENTLY THAT WE LEARNED THE DRESSITE TROOP WERE COMMITTIN CRIMES AGAINST THOSE THEY WER SENT TO PROTECT.
IT IS A SENSITIVE MATTER . . . THE DRESSITES ARE A PEACEABLE SPECIES. CONSEQUENTLY, THEIR MILITARY IS QUITE UNPOPULAR.
THEIR SOLDIERS, OSTRACIZED AT HOME AND RESENTFUL AT HAVING TO TRAVEL SO FAR TO HELP OTHER BEINGS, TOOK OUT THEIR FRUSTRATION ON YOUR POPULATION WHILE FIGHTING THE TETALDIANS.
THEY SAW ALL HUMAN RESISTANCE FIGHTERS AS TERRORISTS MEDDLING IN THE GOOD WAR THEY FOUGHT ON YOUR BEHALF.
HOWEVER, WE ALL UNDERESTIMATED THE TETALDIANS' GUILE . . . AT THIRTEEN QELNES, NOVA TIME, EVERY LIVING SOUL ON THE DRESSITES' HOME WORLD WAS MURDERED BY TETALDIAN POISON.
SEVEN TRILLION DRESSITES MASSACRED.

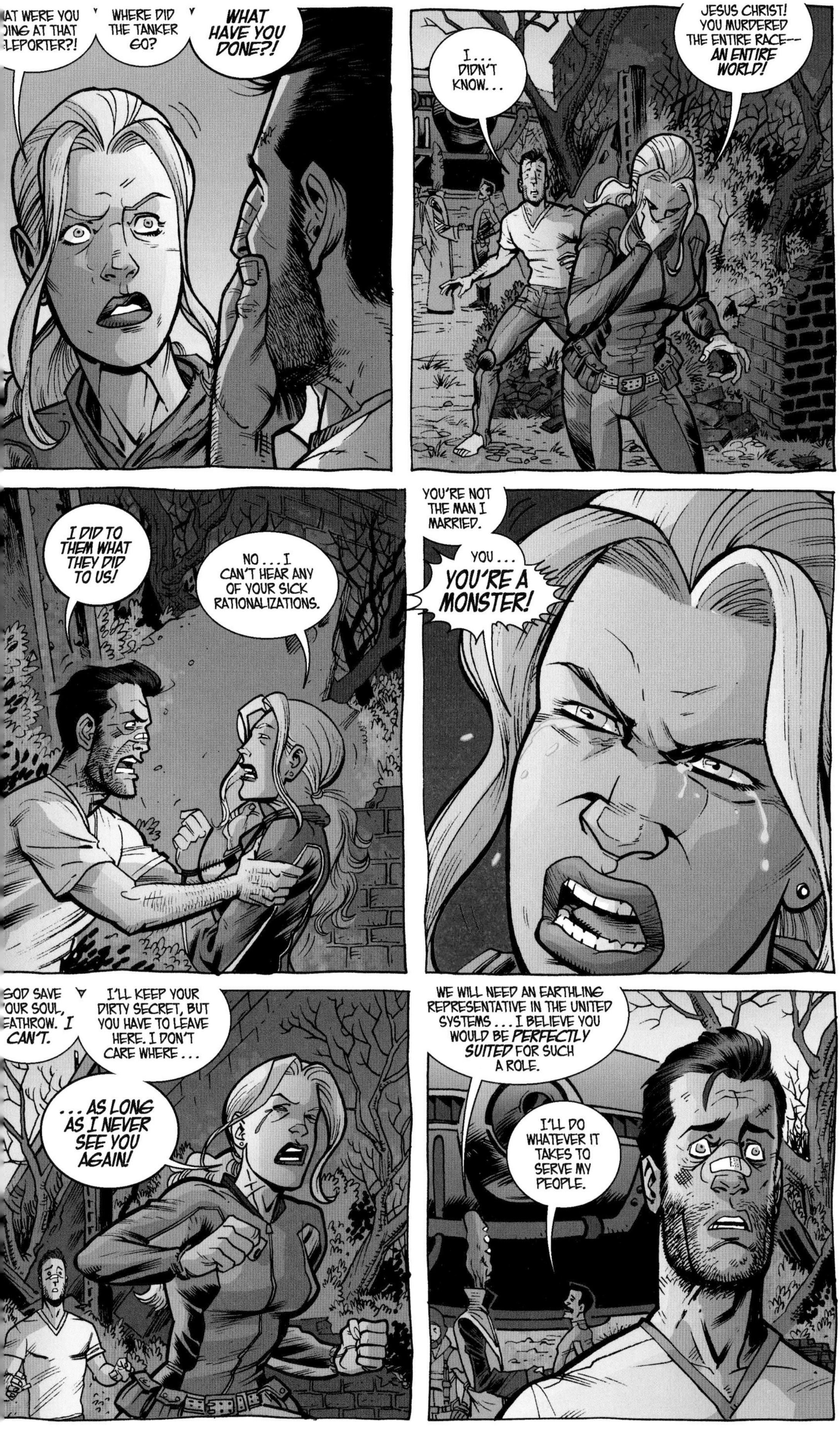

AT WERE YOU OING AT THAT ELEPORTER?!
WHERE DID THE TANKER GO?
WHAT HAVE YOU DONE?!
I . . . DIDN'T KNOW. . .
JESUS CHRIST! YOU MURDERED THE ENTIRE RACE-- AN ENTIRE WORLD!
I DID TO THEM WHAT THEY DID TO US!
NO . . . I CAN'T HEAR ANY OF YOUR SICK RATIONALIZATIONS.
YOU'RE NOT THE MAN I MARRIED.
YOU . . . YOU'RE A MONSTER!
OD SAVE OUR SOUL, EATHROW. I CAN'T.
I'LL KEEP YOUR DIRTY SECRET, BUT YOU HAVE TO LEAVE HERE. I DON'T CARE WHERE . . .
. . . AS LONG AS I NEVER SEE YOU AGAIN!
WE WILL NEED AN EARTHLING REPRESENTATIVE IN THE UNITED SYSTEMS . . . I BELIEVE YOU WOULD BE PERFECTLY SUITED FOR SUCH A ROLE.
I'LL DO WHATEVER IT TAKES TO SERVE MY PEOPLE.

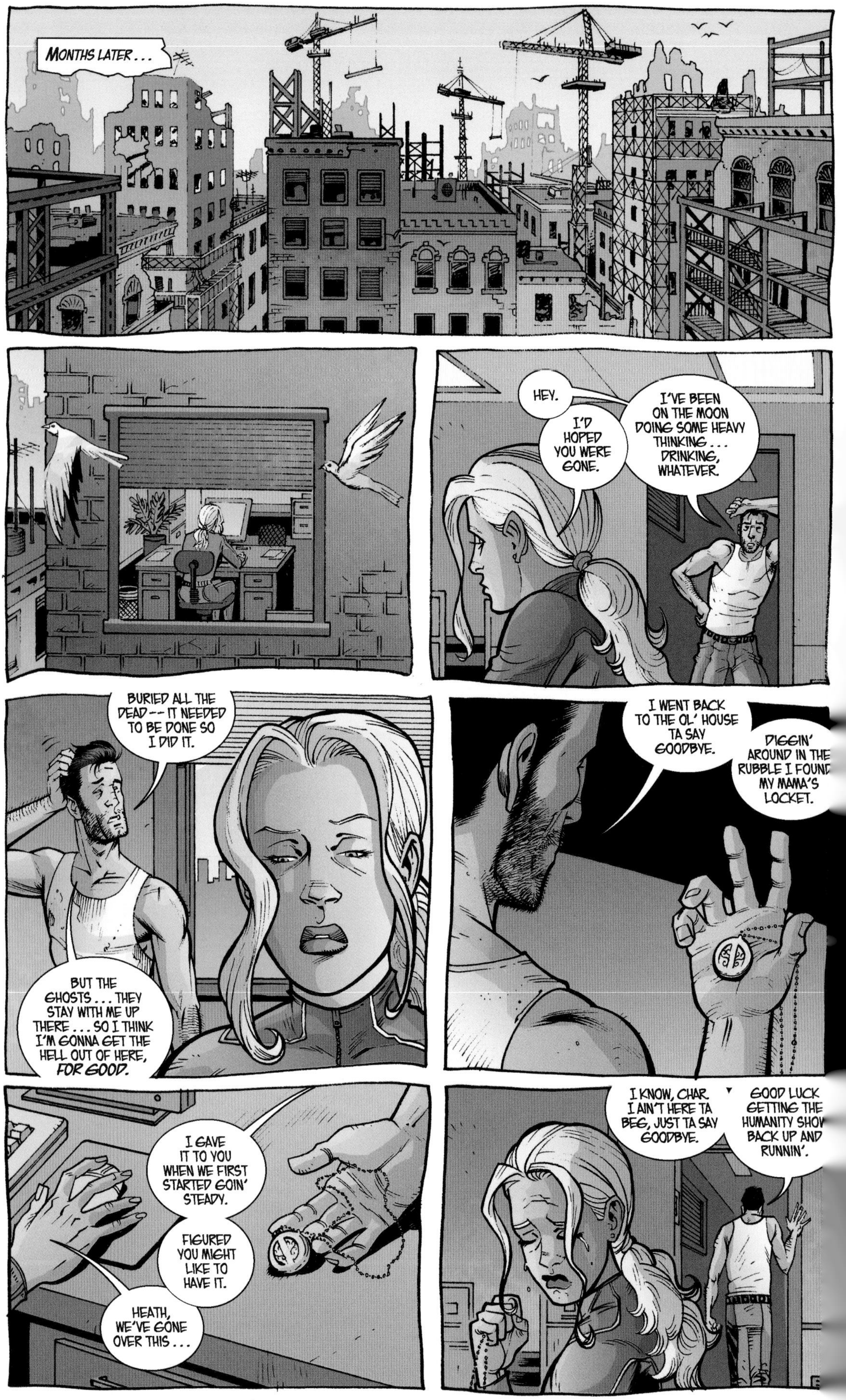
MONTHS LATER . . .
HEY.
I'D HOPED YOU WERE GONE.
I'VE BEEN ON THE MOON DOING SOME HEAVY THINKING . . . DRINKING, WHATEVER.
BURIED ALL THE DEAD -- IT NEEDED TO BE DONE SO I DID IT.
BUT THE GHOSTS . . . THEY STAY WITH ME UP THERE . . . SO I THINK I'M GONNA GET THE HELL OUT OF HERE, FOR GOOD.
I WENT BACK TO THE OL' HOUSE TA SAY GOODBYE.
DIGGIN' AROUND IN THE RUBBLE I FOUND MY MAMA'S LOCKET.
I GAVE IT TO YOU WHEN WE FIRST STARTED GOIN' STEADY.
FIGURED YOU MIGHT LIKE TO HAVE IT.
HEATH, WE'VE GONE OVER THIS . . .
I KNOW, CHAR. I AIN'T HERE TA BEG, JUST TA SAY GOODBYE.
GOOD LUCK GETTING THE HUMANITY SHOW BACK UP AND RUNNIN'.

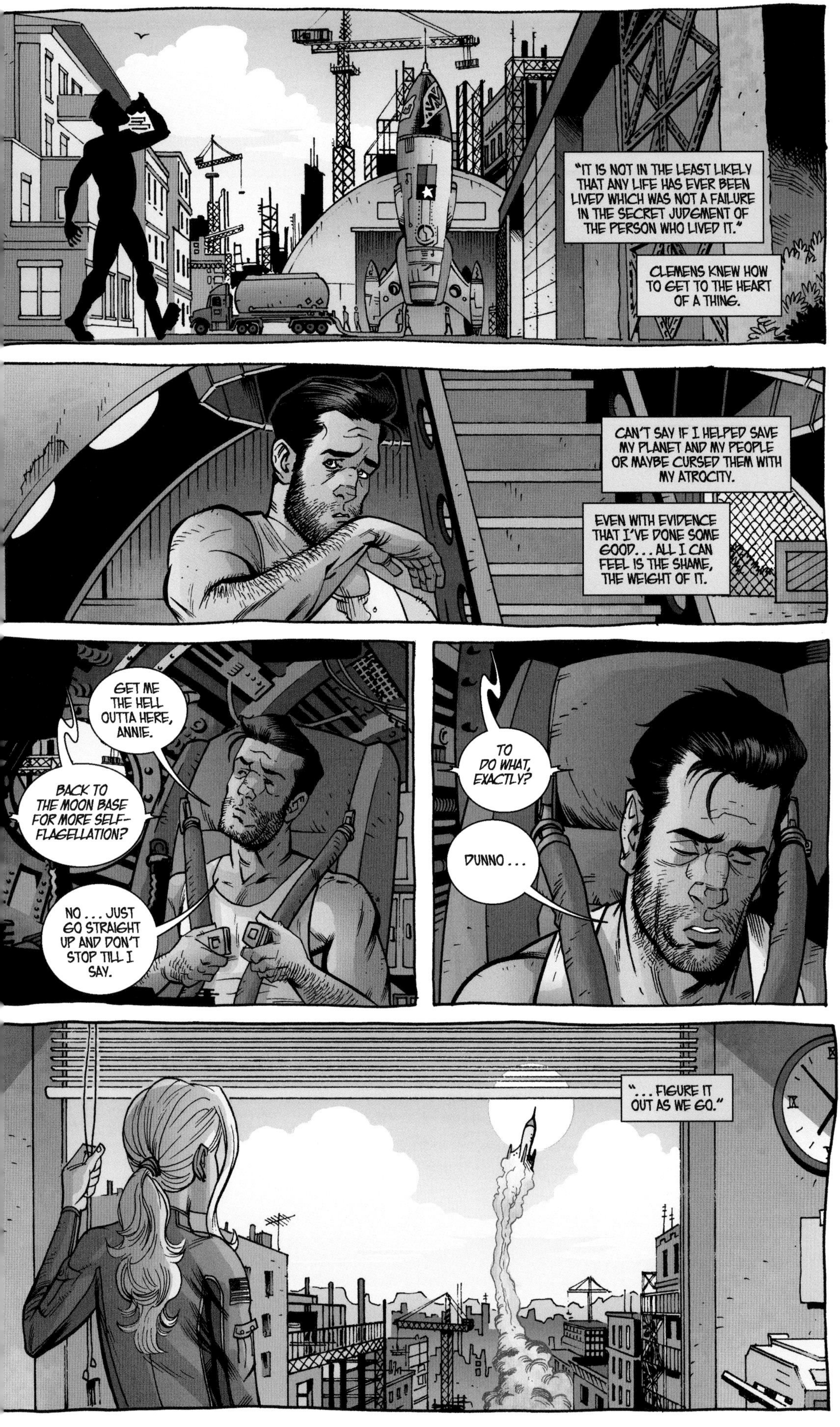
"IT IS NOT IN THE LEAST LIKELY THAT ANY LIFE HAS EVER BEEN LIVED WHICH WAS NOT A FAILURE IN THE SECRET JUDGMENT OF THE PERSON WHO LIVED IT."
CLEMENS KNEW HOW TO GET TO THE HEART OF A THING.
CAN'T SAY IF I HELPED SAVE MY PLANET AND MY PEOPLE OR MAYBE CURSED THEM WITH MY ATROCITY.
EVEN WITH EVIDENCE THAT I'VE DONE SOME GOOD... ALL I CAN FEEL IS THE SHAME, THE WEIGHT OF IT.
GET ME THE HELL OUTTA HERE, ANNIE.
BACK TO THE MOON BASE FOR MORE SELF-FLAGELLATION?
NO... JUST GO STRAIGHT UP AND DON'T STOP TILL I SAY.
TO DO WHAT, EXACTLY?
DUNNO...
"...FIGURE IT OUT AS WE GO."

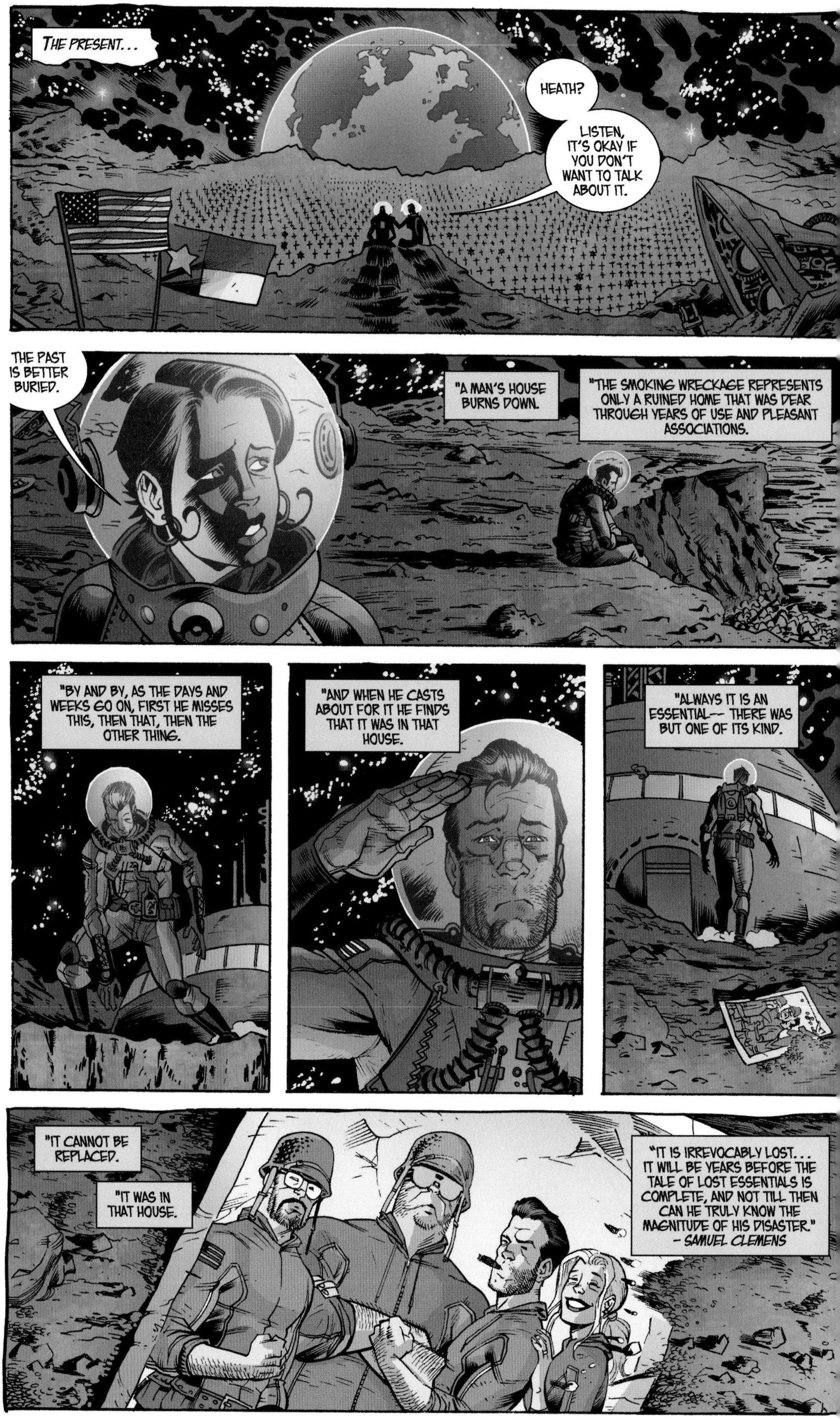
THE PRESENT...
HEATH?
LISTEN, IT'S OKAY IF YOU DON'T WANT TO TALK ABOUT IT.
THE PAST IS BETTER BURIED.
"A MAN'S HOUSE BURNS DOWN.
"THE SMOKING WRECKAGE REPRESENTS ONLY A RUINED HOME THAT WAS DEAR THROUGH YEARS OF USE AND PLEASANT ASSOCIATIONS.
"BY AND BY, AS THE DAYS AND WEEKS GO ON, FIRST HE MISSES THIS, THEN THAT, THEN THE OTHER THING.
"AND WHEN HE CASTS ABOUT FOR IT HE FINDS THAT IT WAS IN THAT HOUSE.
"ALWAYS IT IS AN ESSENTIAL-- THERE WAS BUT ONE OF ITS KIND.
"IT CANNOT BE REPLACED.
"IT WAS IN THAT HOUSE.
"IT IS IRREVOCABLY LOST... IT WILL BE YEARS BEFORE THE TALE OF LOST ESSENTIALS IS COMPLETE, AND NOT TILL THEN CAN HE TRULY KNOW THE MAGNITUDE OF HIS DISASTER."
- SAMUEL CLEMENS

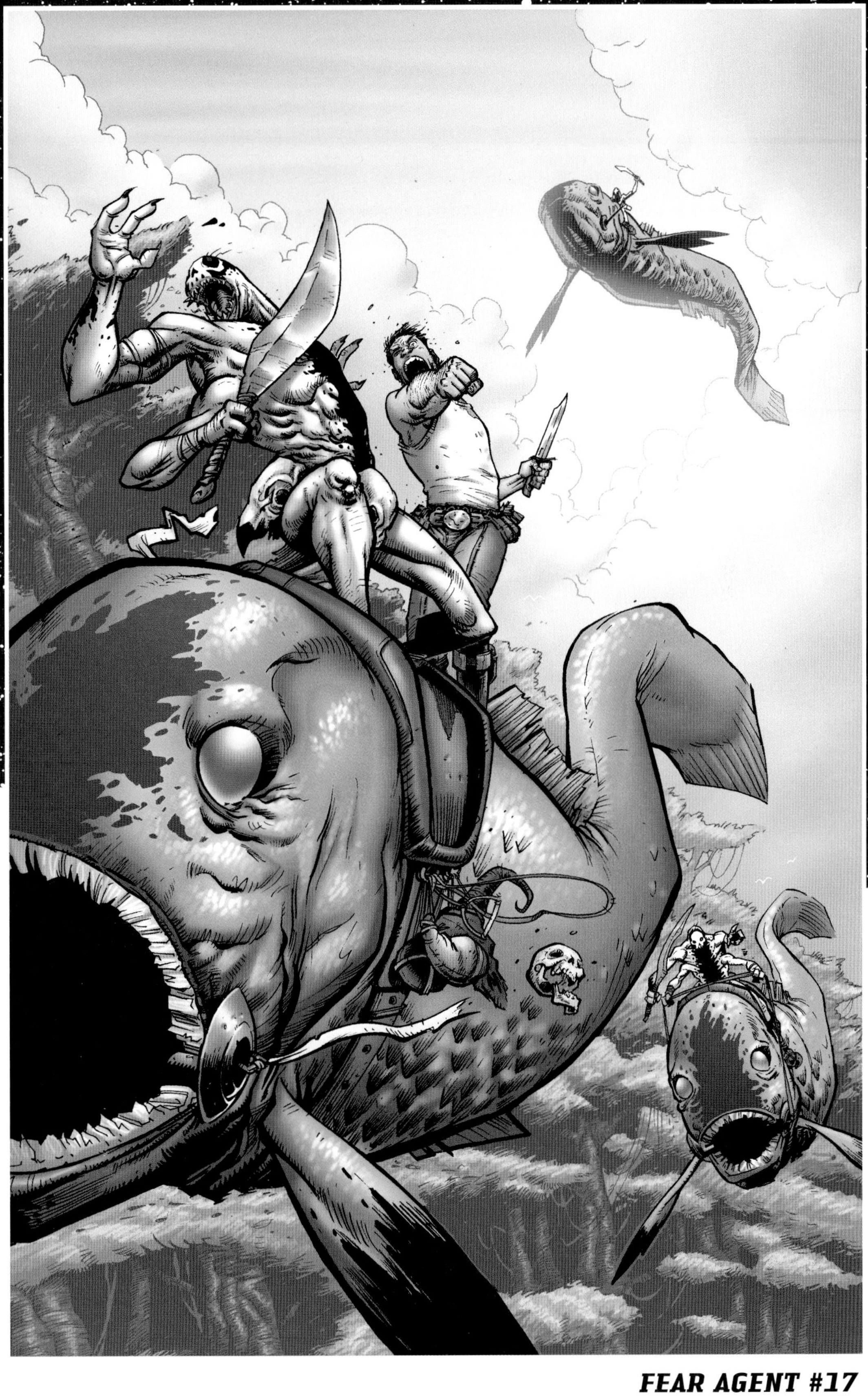

FEAR AGENT #17
ART BY **JEROME OPEÑA**

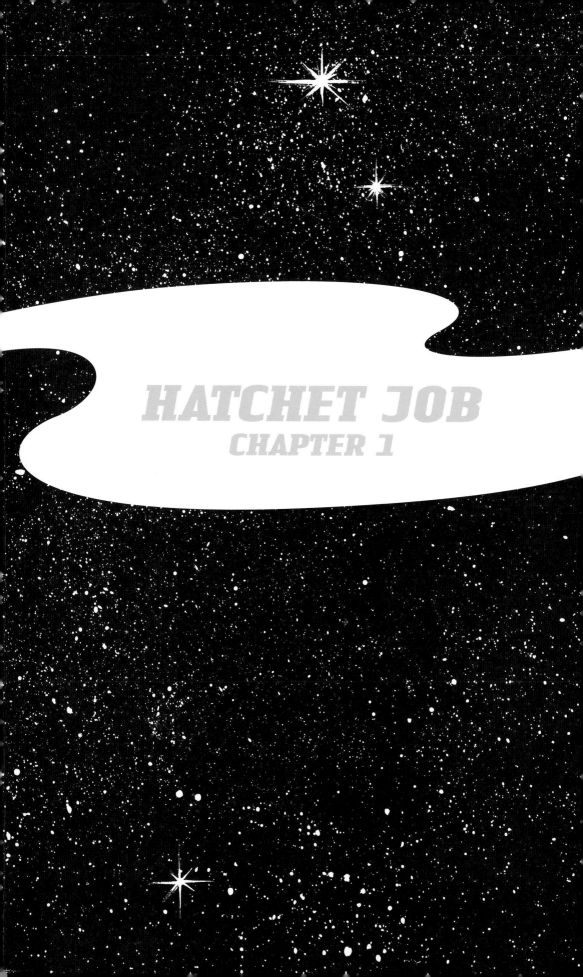

HATCHET JOB
CHAPTER 1

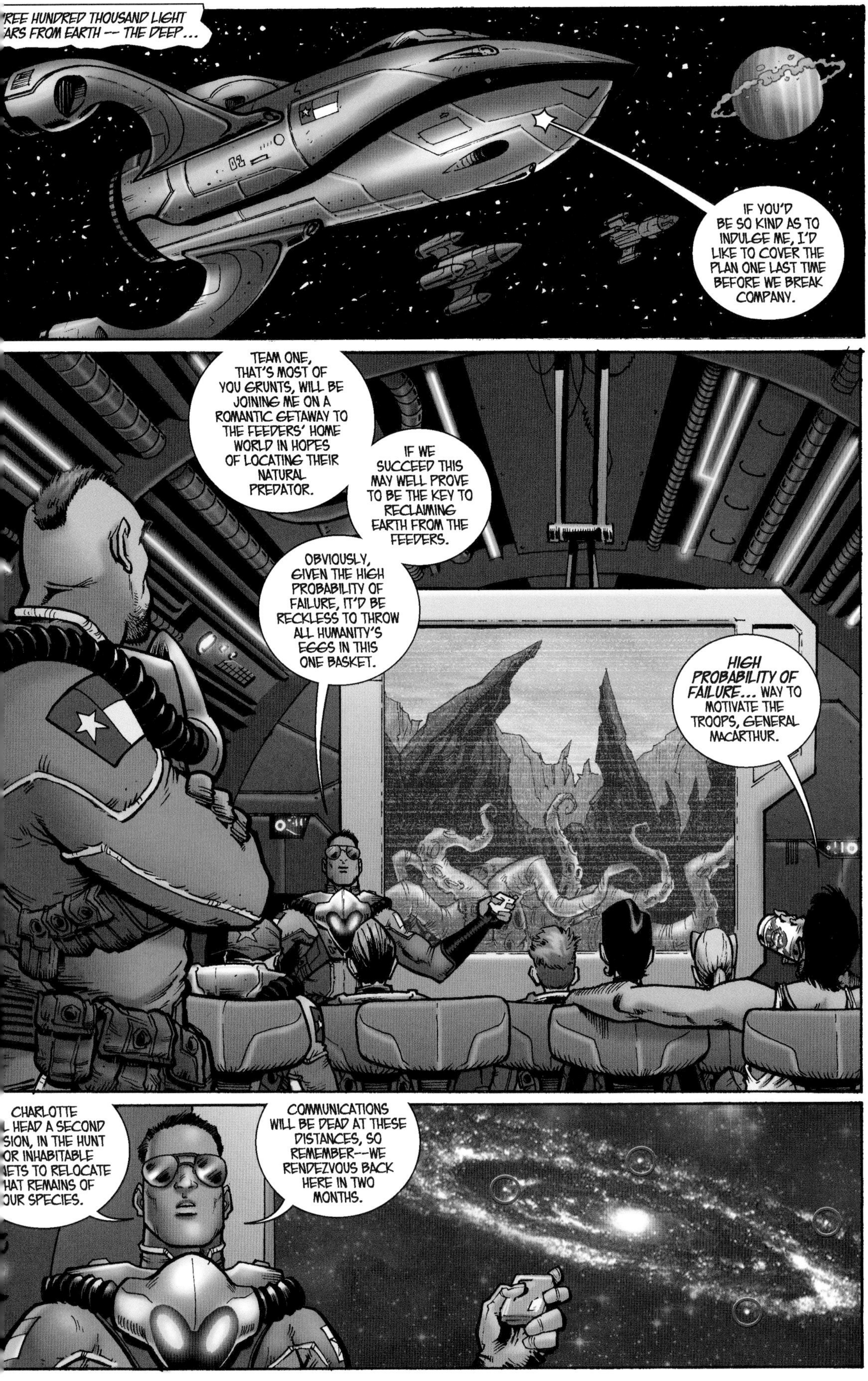
REE HUNDRED THOUSAND LIGHT ARS FROM EARTH -- THE DEEP...
IF YOU'D BE SO KIND AS TO INDULGE ME, I'D LIKE TO COVER THE PLAN ONE LAST TIME BEFORE WE BREAK COMPANY.
TEAM ONE, THAT'S MOST OF YOU GRUNTS, WILL BE JOINING ME ON A ROMANTIC GETAWAY TO THE FEEDERS' HOME WORLD IN HOPES OF LOCATING THEIR NATURAL PREDATOR.
IF WE SUCCEED THIS MAY WELL PROVE TO BE THE KEY TO RECLAIMING EARTH FROM THE FEEDERS.
OBVIOUSLY, GIVEN THE HIGH PROBABILITY OF FAILURE, IT'D BE RECKLESS TO THROW ALL HUMANITY'S EGGS IN THIS ONE BASKET.
HIGH PROBABILITY OF FAILURE... WAY TO MOTIVATE THE TROOPS, GENERAL MACARTHUR.
CHARLOTTE L HEAD A SECOND SION, IN THE HUNT OR INHABITABLE NETS TO RELOCATE HAT REMAINS OF OUR SPECIES.
COMMUNICATIONS WILL BE DEAD AT THESE DISTANCES, SO REMEMBER--WE RENDEZVOUS BACK HERE IN TWO MONTHS.

DUE TO HER TRAVELS AND KNOWLEDGE OF THESE AREAS, MARA HAS REQUESTED TO SERVE AS CHIEF NAVIGATION OFFICER FOR TEAM TWO.

WHAT?

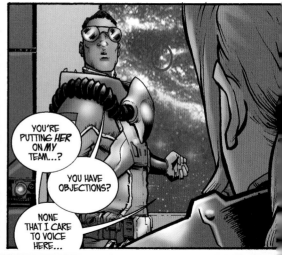

YOU'RE PUTTING *HER* ON *MY* TEAM...?

YOU HAVE OBJECTIONS?

NONE THAT I CARE TO VOICE HERE...

YOU STILL COMIN' WITH US, HUSTON?

I RECKON SO.

GUESS THAT LEAVES ME AS THE ONLY GAL YOU'LL NEED TA KEEP CONTENTED.

THEN SISTER, I HOPE YOU CAN OBTAIN CONTENTMENT FROM A HALF-SAIL WHISKEY DICK.

AH, *COME ON!* I'M SITTIN' RIGHT HERE.

HAH!

OKAY, SAY YOUR GOODBYES, PEOPLE.

WE SPLIT COMPANIES AT FOURTEEN HUNDRED HOURS.

HEATH, YOU STILL UP FOR A FOOD RUN ONCE WE SPLIT?

NOT MUCH CHOICE IN THE MATTER--ANNIE'S THE ONLY SHIP BUILT FOR A FAST LAND.

PERFECT, SO YOU DON'T MIND IF I TAG ALONG?

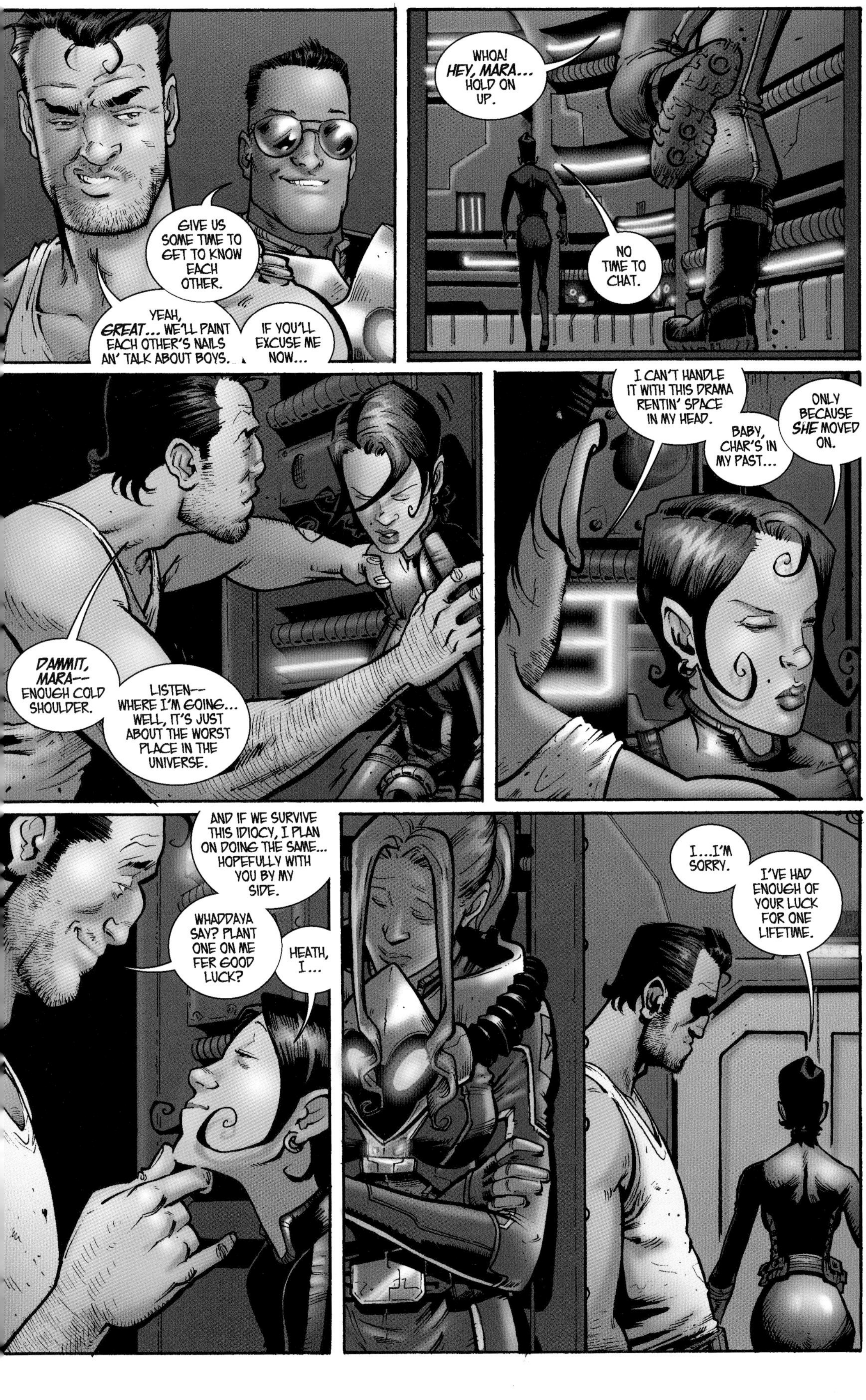
GIVE US SOME TIME TO GET TO KNOW EACH OTHER.
YEAH, GREAT... WE'LL PAINT EACH OTHER'S NAILS AN' TALK ABOUT BOYS.
IF YOU'LL EXCUSE ME NOW...
WHOA! HEY, MARA... HOLD ON UP.
NO TIME TO CHAT.
DAMMIT, MARA-- ENOUGH COLD SHOULDER.
LISTEN-- WHERE I'M GOING... WELL, IT'S JUST ABOUT THE WORST PLACE IN THE UNIVERSE.
I CAN'T HANDLE IT WITH THIS DRAMA RENTIN' SPACE IN MY HEAD.
BABY, CHAR'S IN MY PAST...
ONLY BECAUSE SHE MOVED ON.
AND IF WE SURVIVE THIS IDIOCY, I PLAN ON DOING THE SAME... HOPEFULLY WITH YOU BY MY SIDE.
WHADDAYA SAY? PLANT ONE ON ME FER GOOD LUCK?
HEATH, I...
I...I'M SORRY.
I'VE HAD ENOUGH OF YOUR LUCK FOR ONE LIFETIME.

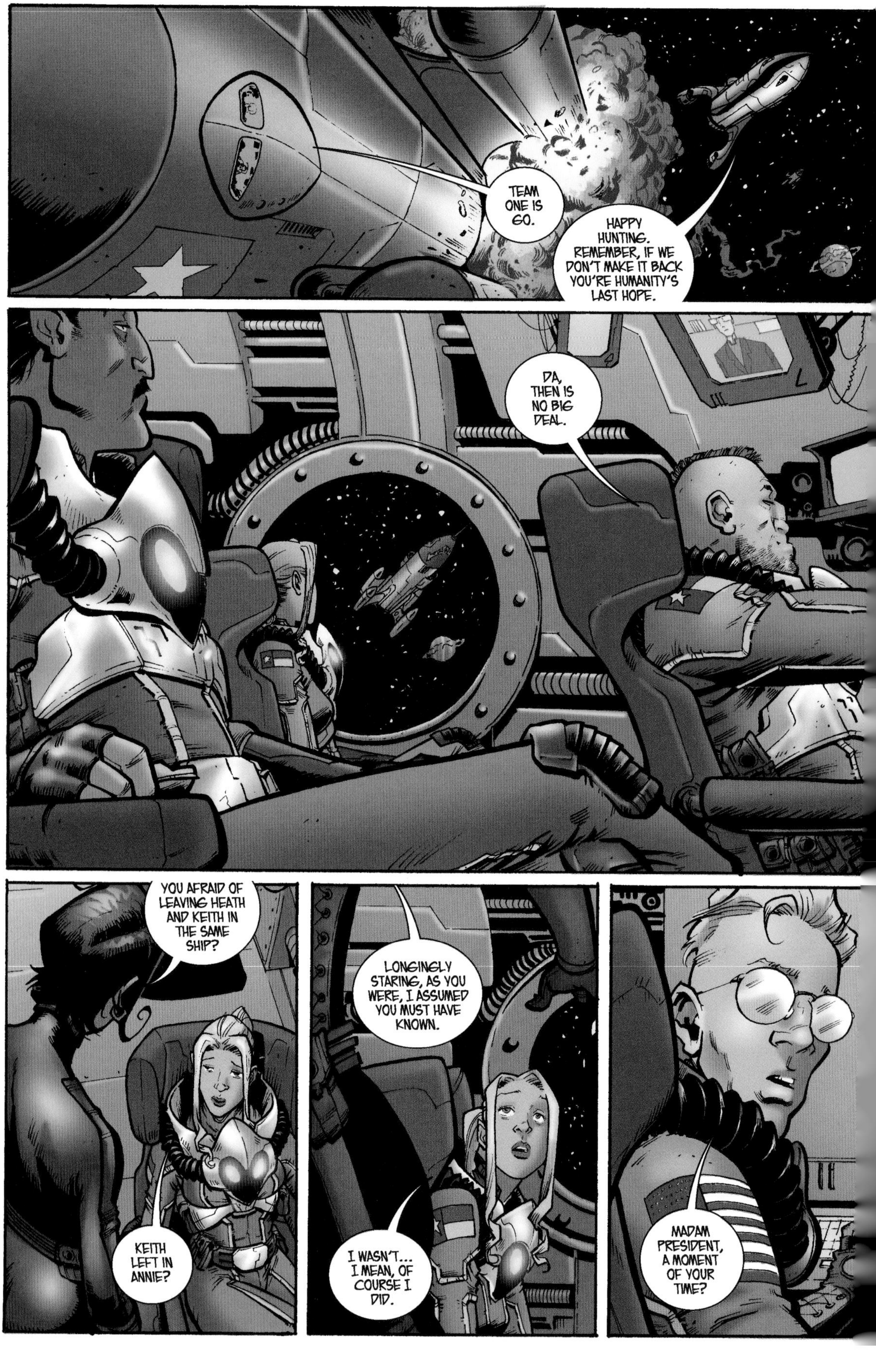
TEAM ONE IS GO.
HAPPY HUNTING. REMEMBER, IF WE DON'T MAKE IT BACK YOU'RE HUMANITY'S LAST HOPE.
DA, THEN IS NO BIG DEAL.
YOU AFRAID OF LEAVING HEATH AND KEITH IN THE SAME SHIP?
KEITH LEFT IN ANNIE?
LONGINGLY STARING, AS YOU WERE, I ASSUMED YOU MUST HAVE KNOWN.
I WASN'T... I MEAN, OF COURSE I DID.
MADAM PRESIDENT, A MOMENT OF YOUR TIME?

WE'VE GOT A FEW OPTIONS NEARBY. OLIVER AND HIS PEOPLE WERE HEADED HERE TO FLIN.
ACCORDIN' TA HEATHROW, AIN'T NOT BUT FLY-PEOPLE AND GIANT SPIDERS THERE.
THIS GREENISH PLANET HERE ISN'T LISTED ON THE UNITED SYSTEMS LOGS, SO IT'S NOT A MEMBER AND COULD BE UNINHABITED.
WHOA--! SCOTT, PULL IN ON IT.
IS THAT...? WELL I'LL BE A MONKEY'S UNCLE, IT SURE IS.
WHAT YOU'RE LOOKING AT IS A WORLD KNOWN AS THE BOG.
THE BOG...?
THAT PLACE IS PACKED TO THE GILLS WITH VICIOUS AMPHIBIAN CREATURES, BAD JUJU.
OVER HERE, NEAVSIVIA... THIS IS THE ONE WE WANT.
WELL, WE'LL HAVE TA START SOMEWHERE.
ANDI, SET A COURSE TO NEAVSIVIA.
IMMEDIATELY, MADAM PRESIDENT.
SNIFF-SNIFF...

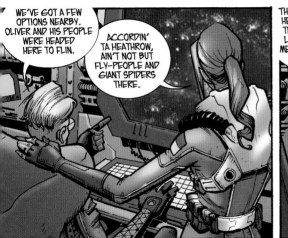

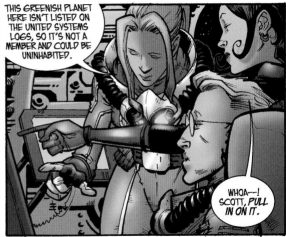

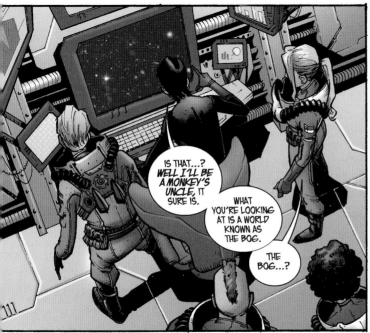

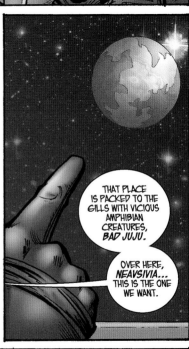

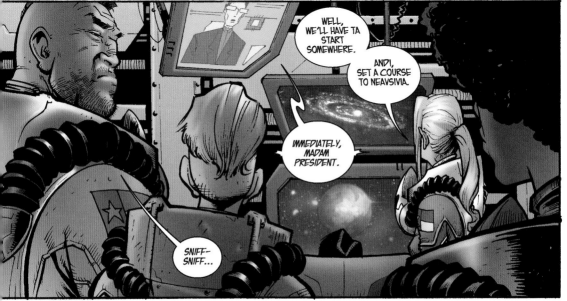

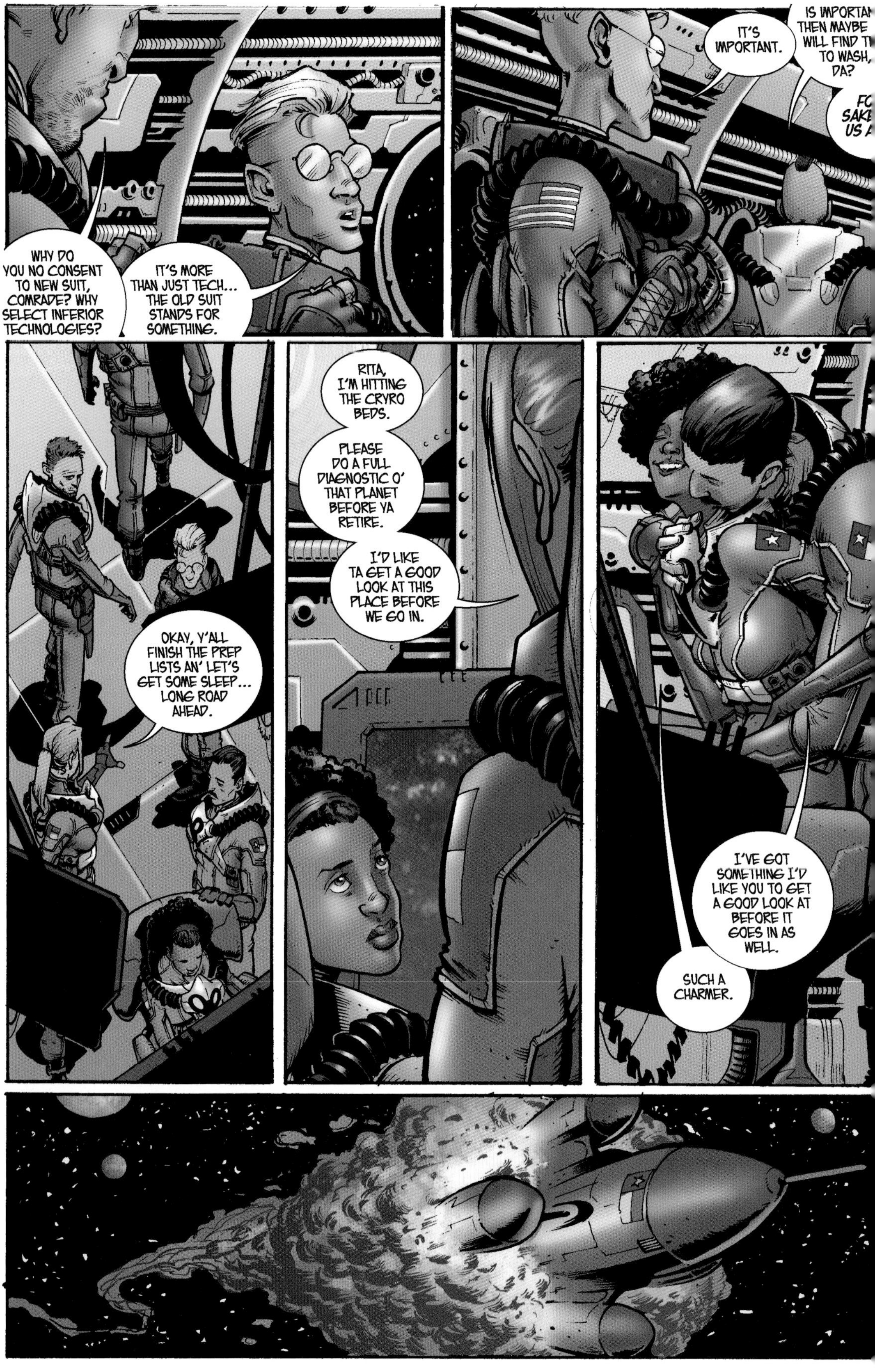
WHY DO YOU NO CONSENT TO NEW SUIT, COMRADE? WHY SELECT INFERIOR TECHNOLOGIES?
IT'S MORE THAN JUST TECH... THE OLD SUIT STANDS FOR SOMETHING.
IT'S IMPORTANT.
IS IMPORTAN THEN MAYBE WILL FIND T TO WASH, DA?
OKAY, Y'ALL FINISH THE PREP LISTS AN' LET'S GET SOME SLEEP... LONG ROAD AHEAD.
RITA, I'M HITTING THE CRYRO BEDS.
PLEASE DO A FULL DIAGNOSTIC O' THAT PLANET BEFORE YA RETIRE.
I'D LIKE TA GET A GOOD LOOK AT THIS PLACE BEFORE WE GO IN.
I'VE GOT SOMETHING I'D LIKE YOU TO GET A GOOD LOOK AT BEFORE IT GOES IN AS WELL.
SUCH A CHARMER.

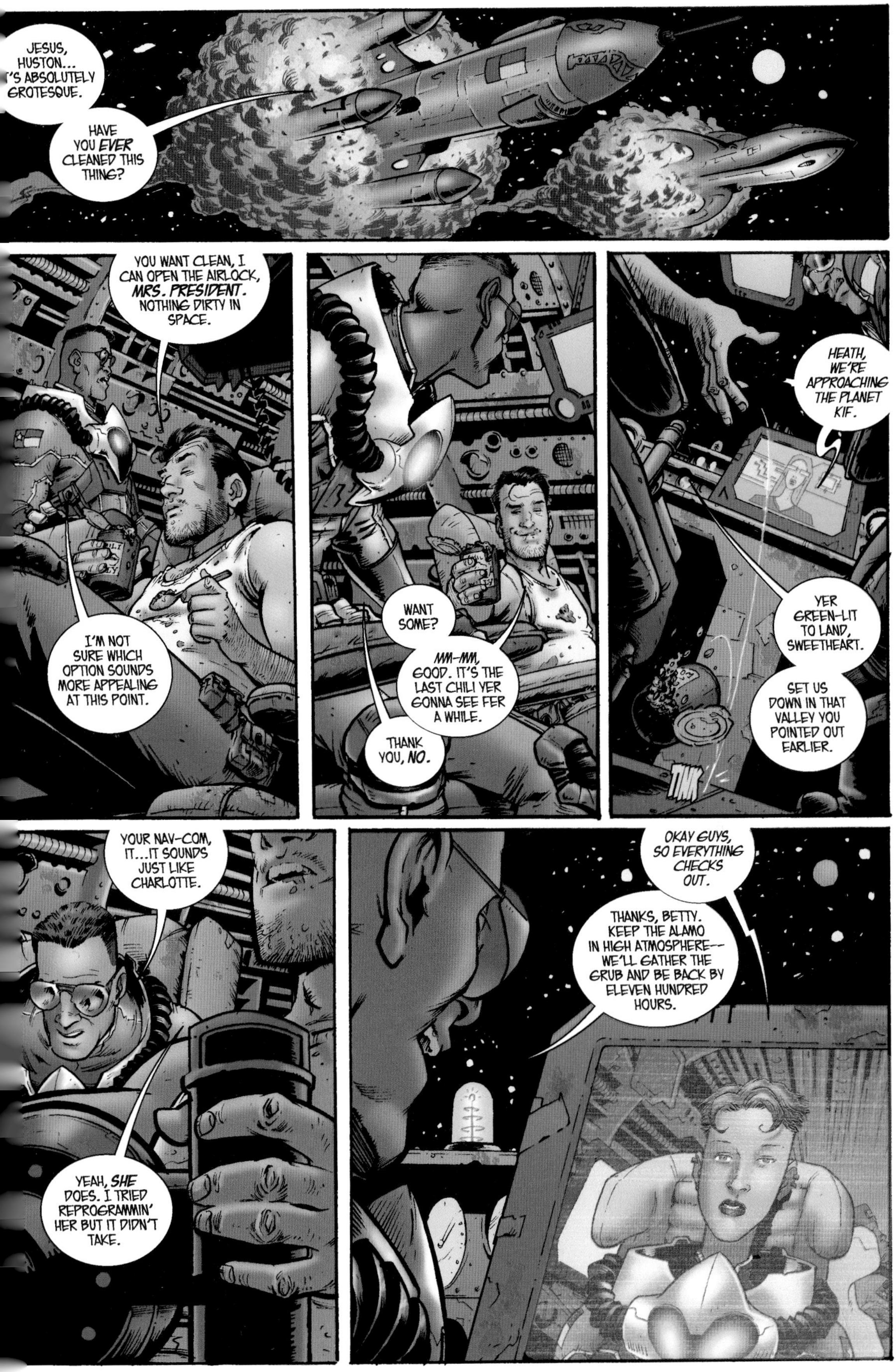
JESUS, HUSTON... IT'S ABSOLUTELY GROTESQUE.
HAVE YOU EVER CLEANED THIS THING?
YOU WANT CLEAN, I CAN OPEN THE AIRLOCK, MRS. PRESIDENT. NOTHING DIRTY IN SPACE.
I'M NOT SURE WHICH OPTION SOUNDS MORE APPEALING AT THIS POINT.
WANT SOME?
MM-MM, GOOD. IT'S THE LAST CHILI YER GONNA SEE FER A WHILE.
THANK YOU, NO.
HEATH, WE'RE APPROACHING THE PLANET KIF.
YER GREEN-LIT TO LAND, SWEETHEART.
SET US DOWN IN THAT VALLEY YOU POINTED OUT EARLIER.
TINK
YOUR NAV-COM, IT...IT SOUNDS JUST LIKE CHARLOTTE.
YEAH, SHE DOES. I TRIED REPROGRAMMIN' HER BUT IT DIDN'T TAKE.
OKAY GUYS, SO EVERYTHING CHECKS OUT.
THANKS, BETTY. KEEP THE ALAMO IN HIGH ATMOSPHERE-- WE'LL GATHER THE GRUB AND BE BACK BY ELEVEN HUNDRED HOURS.

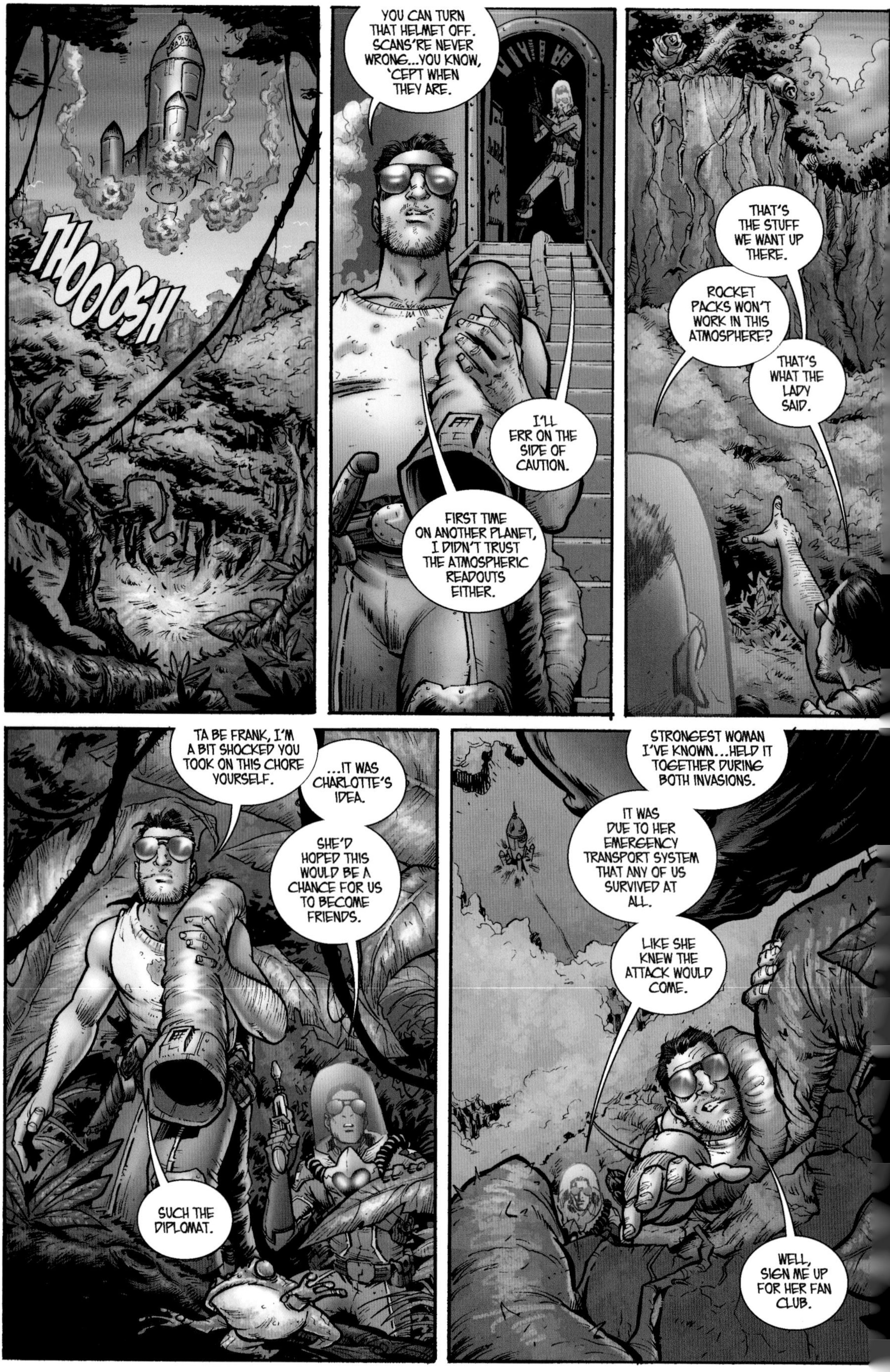
THOOOSH
YOU CAN TURN THAT HELMET OFF. SCANS'RE NEVER WRONG...YOU KNOW, 'CEPT WHEN THEY ARE.
I'LL ERR ON THE SIDE OF CAUTION.
FIRST TIME ON ANOTHER PLANET, I DIDN'T TRUST THE ATMOSPHERIC READOUTS EITHER.
THAT'S THE STUFF WE WANT UP THERE.
ROCKET PACKS WON'T WORK IN THIS ATMOSPHERE?
THAT'S WHAT THE LADY SAID.
TA BE FRANK, I'M A BIT SHOCKED YOU TOOK ON THIS CHORE YOURSELF.
...IT WAS CHARLOTTE'S IDEA.
SHE'D HOPED THIS WOULD BE A CHANCE FOR US TO BECOME FRIENDS.
SUCH THE DIPLOMAT.
STRONGEST WOMAN I'VE KNOWN...HELD IT TOGETHER DURING BOTH INVASIONS.
IT WAS DUE TO HER EMERGENCY TRANSPORT SYSTEM THAT ANY OF US SURVIVED AT ALL.
LIKE SHE KNEW THE ATTACK WOULD COME.
WELL, SIGN ME UP FOR HER FAN CLUB.

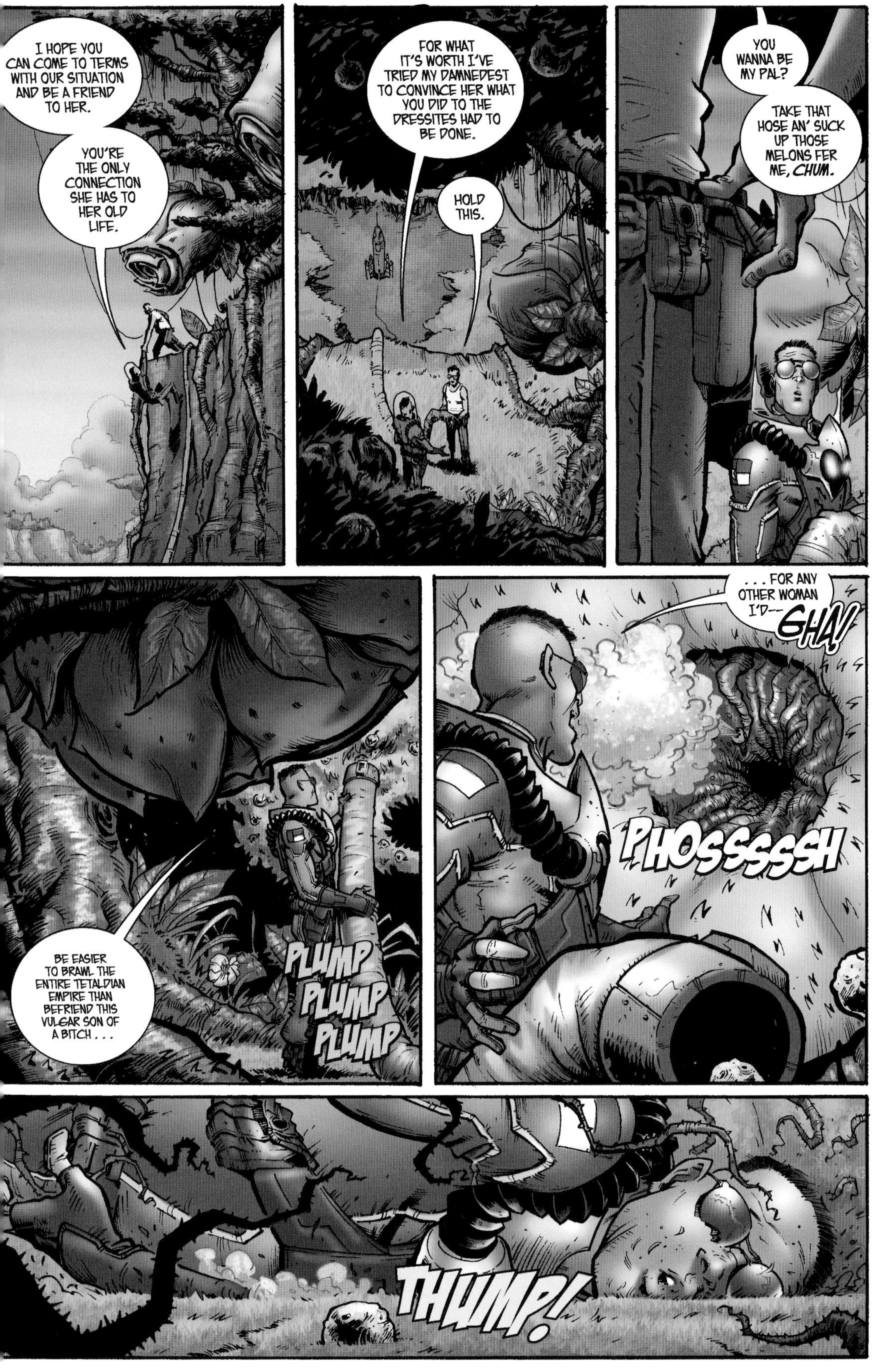

I HOPE YOU CAN COME TO TERMS WITH OUR SITUATION AND BE A FRIEND TO HER.
YOU'RE THE ONLY CONNECTION SHE HAS TO HER OLD LIFE.
FOR WHAT IT'S WORTH I'VE TRIED MY DAMNEDEST TO CONVINCE HER WHAT YOU DID TO THE DRESSITES HAD TO BE DONE.
HOLD THIS.
YOU WANNA BE MY PAL?
TAKE THAT HOSE AN' SUCK UP THOSE MELONS FER ME, *CHUM*.
BE EASIER TO BRAWL THE ENTIRE TETALDIAN EMPIRE THAN BEFRIEND THIS VULGAR SON OF A BITCH . . .
PLUMP
PLUMP
PLUMP
. . . FOR ANY OTHER WOMAN I'D-- GHA!
PHOSSSSSH
THUMP!

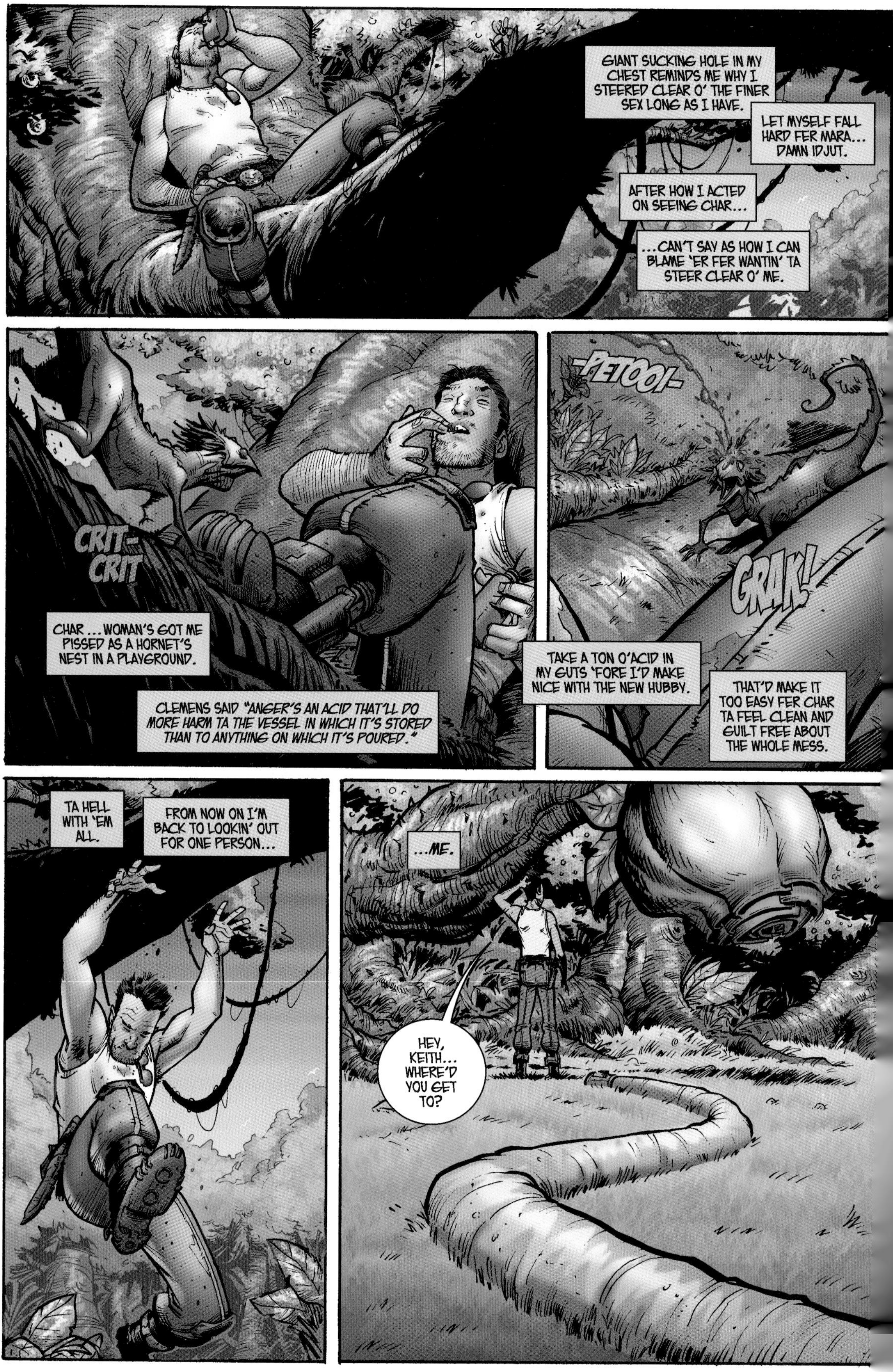
GIANT SUCKING HOLE IN MY CHEST REMINDS ME WHY I STEERED CLEAR O' THE FINER SEX LONG AS I HAVE.
LET MYSELF FALL HARD FER MARA... DAMN IDJUT.
AFTER HOW I ACTED ON SEEING CHAR...
...CAN'T SAY AS HOW I CAN BLAME 'ER FER WANTIN' TA STEER CLEAR O' ME.
CRIT-CRIT
CHAR ...WOMAN'S GOT ME PISSED AS A HORNET'S NEST IN A PLAYGROUND.
CLEMENS SAID "ANGER'S AN ACID THAT'LL DO MORE HARM TA THE VESSEL IN WHICH IT'S STORED THAN TO ANYTHING ON WHICH IT'S POURED."
-PETOOI-
GRAK!
TAKE A TON O'ACID IN MY GUTS 'FORE I'D MAKE NICE WITH THE NEW HUBBY.
THAT'D MAKE IT TOO EASY FER CHAR TA FEEL CLEAN AND GUILT FREE ABOUT THE WHOLE MESS.
TA HELL WITH 'EM ALL.
FROM NOW ON I'M BACK TO LOOKIN' OUT FOR ONE PERSON...
...ME.
HEY, KEITH... WHERE'D YOU GET TO?

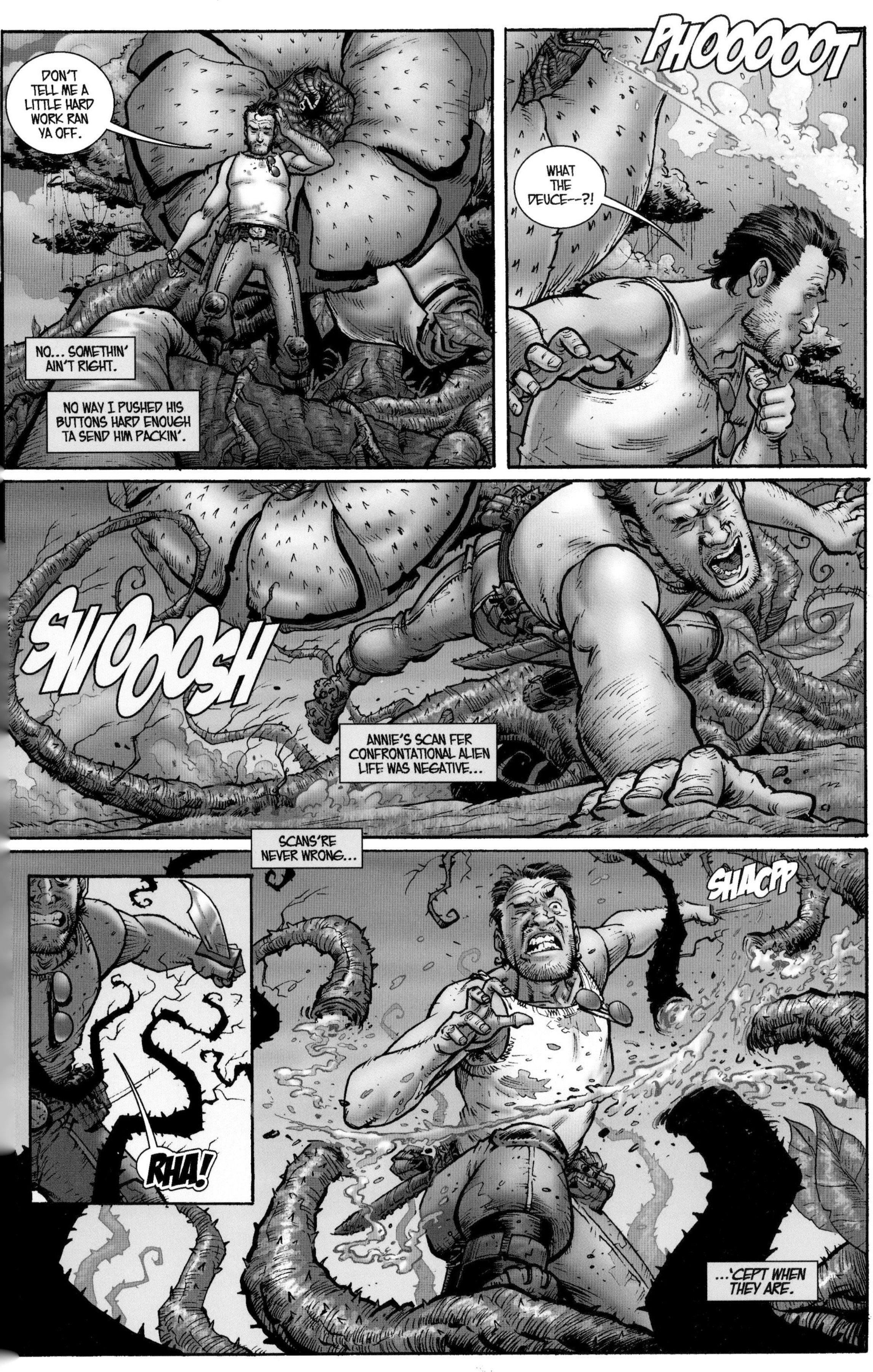
DON'T TELL ME A LITTLE HARD WORK RAN YA OFF.
NO... SOMETHIN' AIN'T RIGHT.
NO WAY I PUSHED HIS BUTTONS HARD ENOUGH TA SEND HIM PACKIN'.
PHOOOOOOT
WHAT THE DEUCE--?!
SWOOOSH
ANNIE'S SCAN FER CONFRONTATIONAL ALIEN LIFE WAS NEGATIVE...
SCANS'RE NEVER WRONG...
RHA!
SHACPP
...'CEPT WHEN THEY ARE.

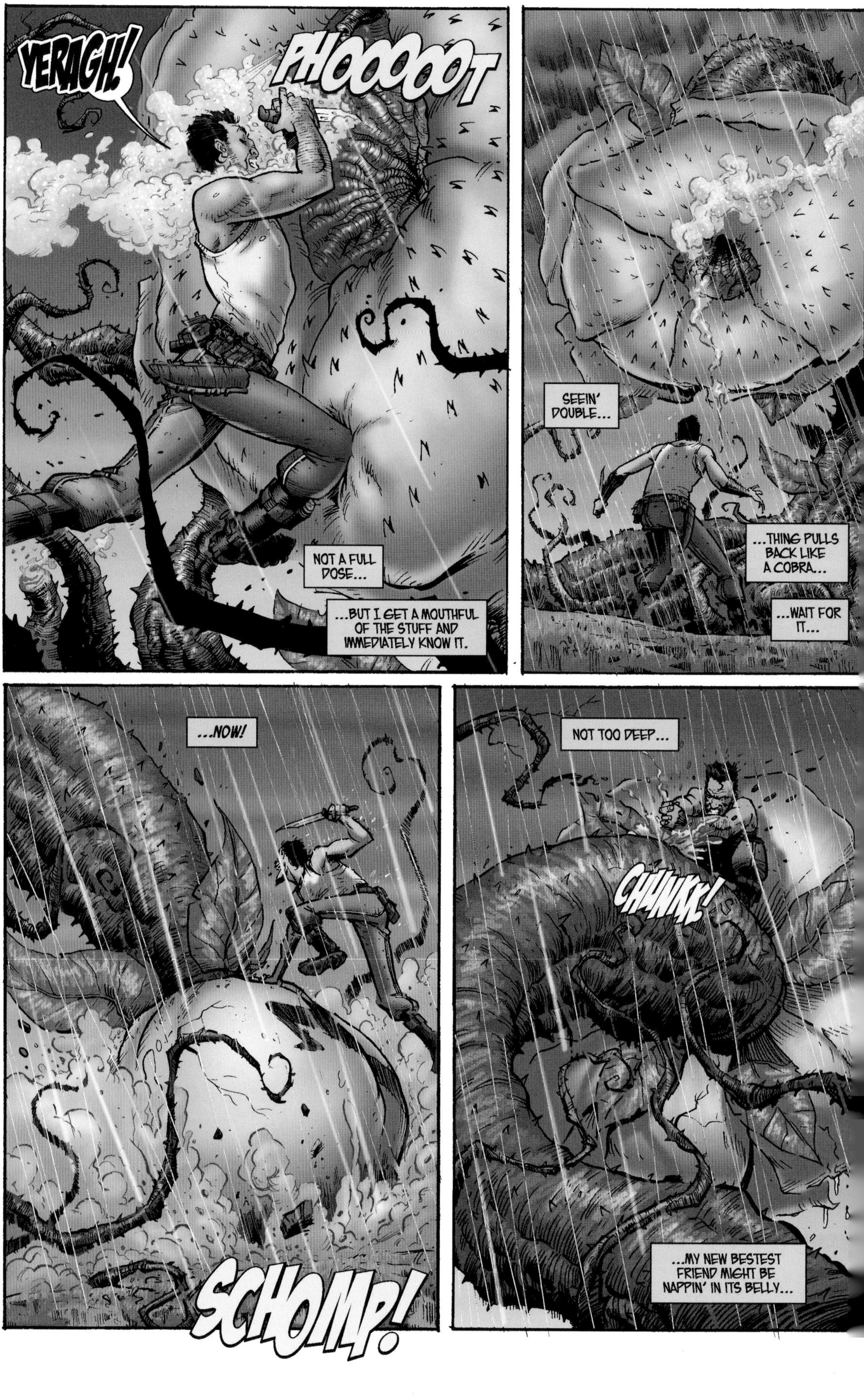
YERAGH!
PHOOOOOOT
NOT A FULL DOSE...
...BUT I GET A MOUTHFUL OF THE STUFF AND IMMEDIATELY KNOW IT.
SEEIN' DOUBLE...
...THING PULLS BACK LIKE A COBRA...
...WAIT FOR IT...
...NOW!
SCHOMP!
NOT TOO DEEP...
CHUNKK!
...MY NEW BESTEST FRIEND MIGHT BE NAPPIN' IN ITS BELLY...

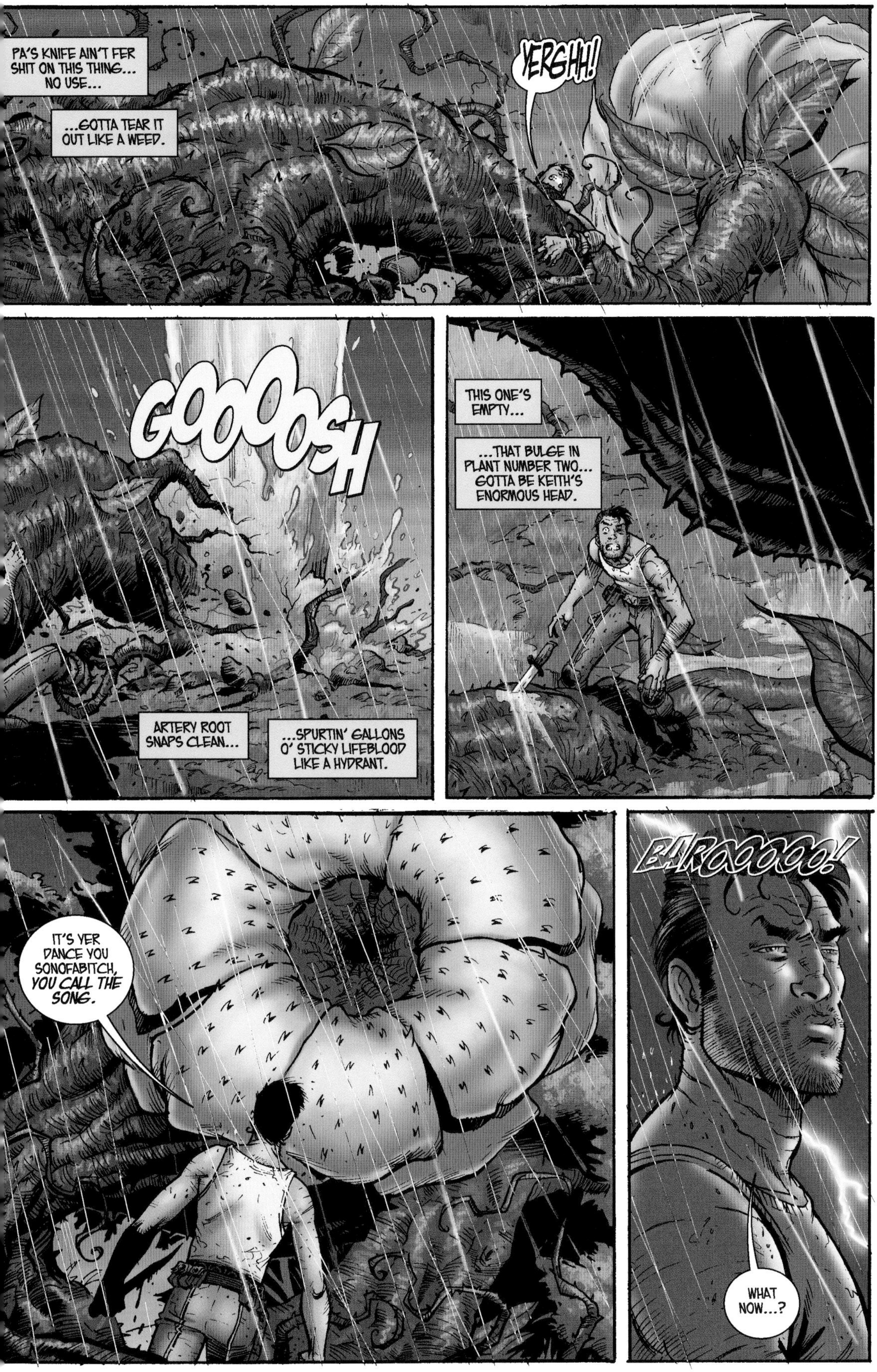
PA'S KNIFE AIN'T FER SHIT ON THIS THING... NO USE...
...GOTTA TEAR IT OUT LIKE A WEED.
YERGHH!
GOOOOSH
ARTERY ROOT SNAPS CLEAN...
...SPURTIN' GALLONS O' STICKY LIFEBLOOD LIKE A HYDRANT.
THIS ONE'S EMPTY...
...THAT BULGE IN PLANT NUMBER TWO... GOTTA BE KEITH'S ENORMOUS HEAD.
IT'S YER DANCE YOU SONOFABITCH, *YOU CALL THE SONG.*
BHROOOOOO!
WHAT NOW...?

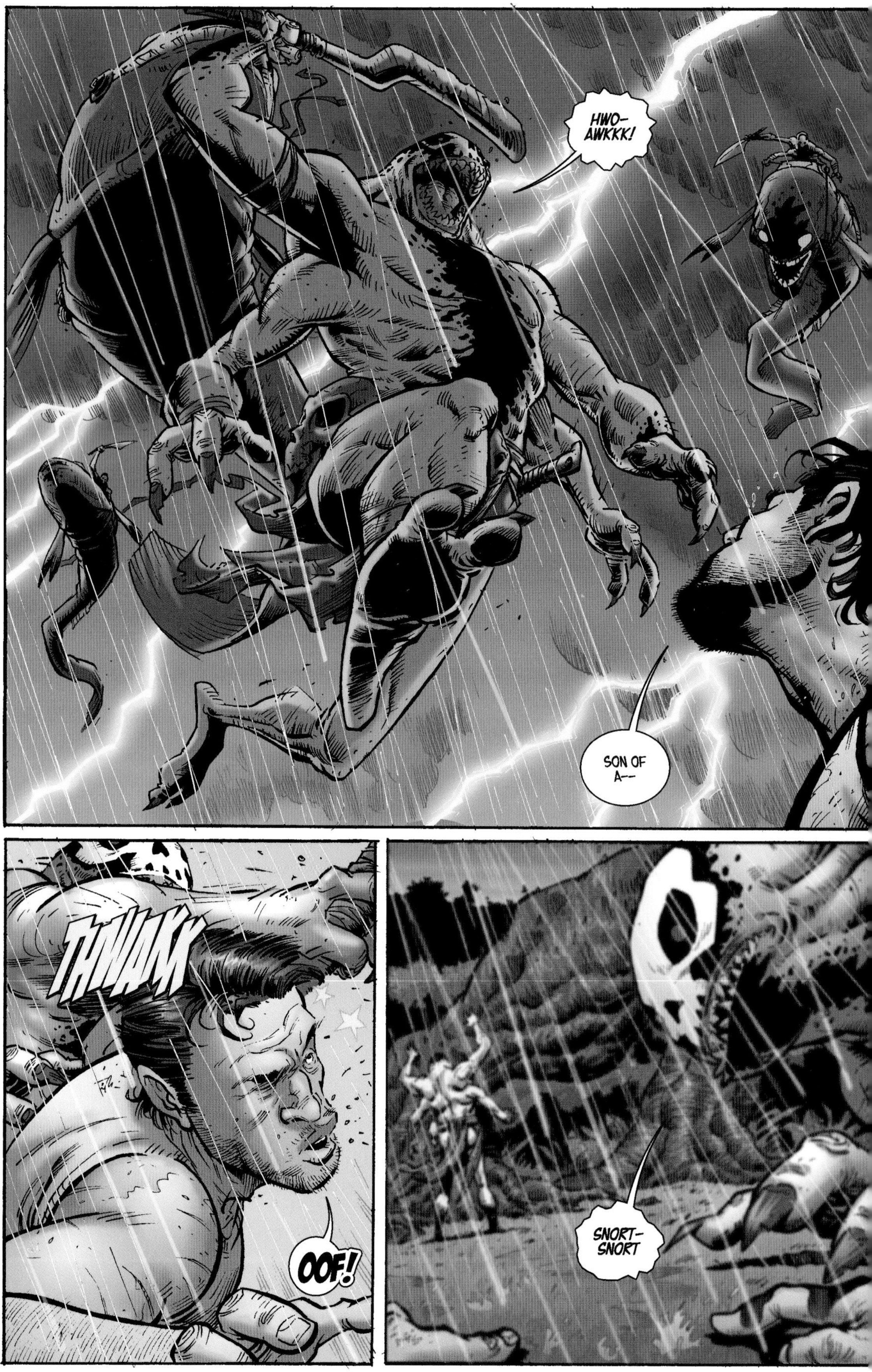
HWO-
AWKKK!
SON OF
A--
THWAKK
OOF!
SNORT-
SNORT

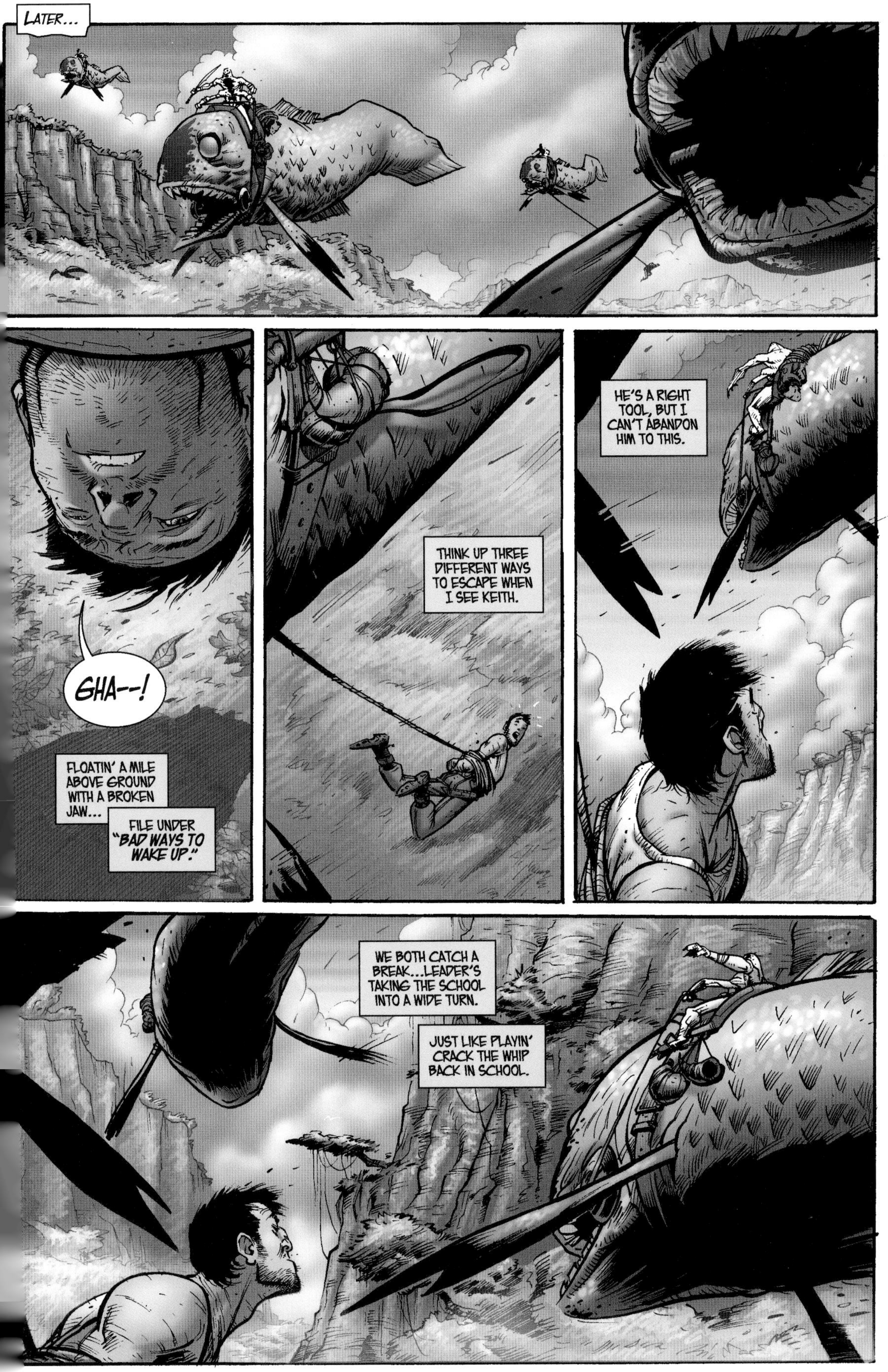
LATER...
GHA--!
FLOATIN' A MILE ABOVE GROUND WITH A BROKEN JAW...
FILE UNDER "BAD WAYS TO WAKE UP."
THINK UP THREE DIFFERENT WAYS TO ESCAPE WHEN I SEE KEITH.
HE'S A RIGHT TOOL, BUT I CAN'T ABANDON HIM TO THIS.
WE BOTH CATCH A BREAK...LEADER'S TAKING THE SCHOOL INTO A WIDE TURN.
JUST LIKE PLAYIN' CRACK THE WHIP BACK IN SCHOOL.

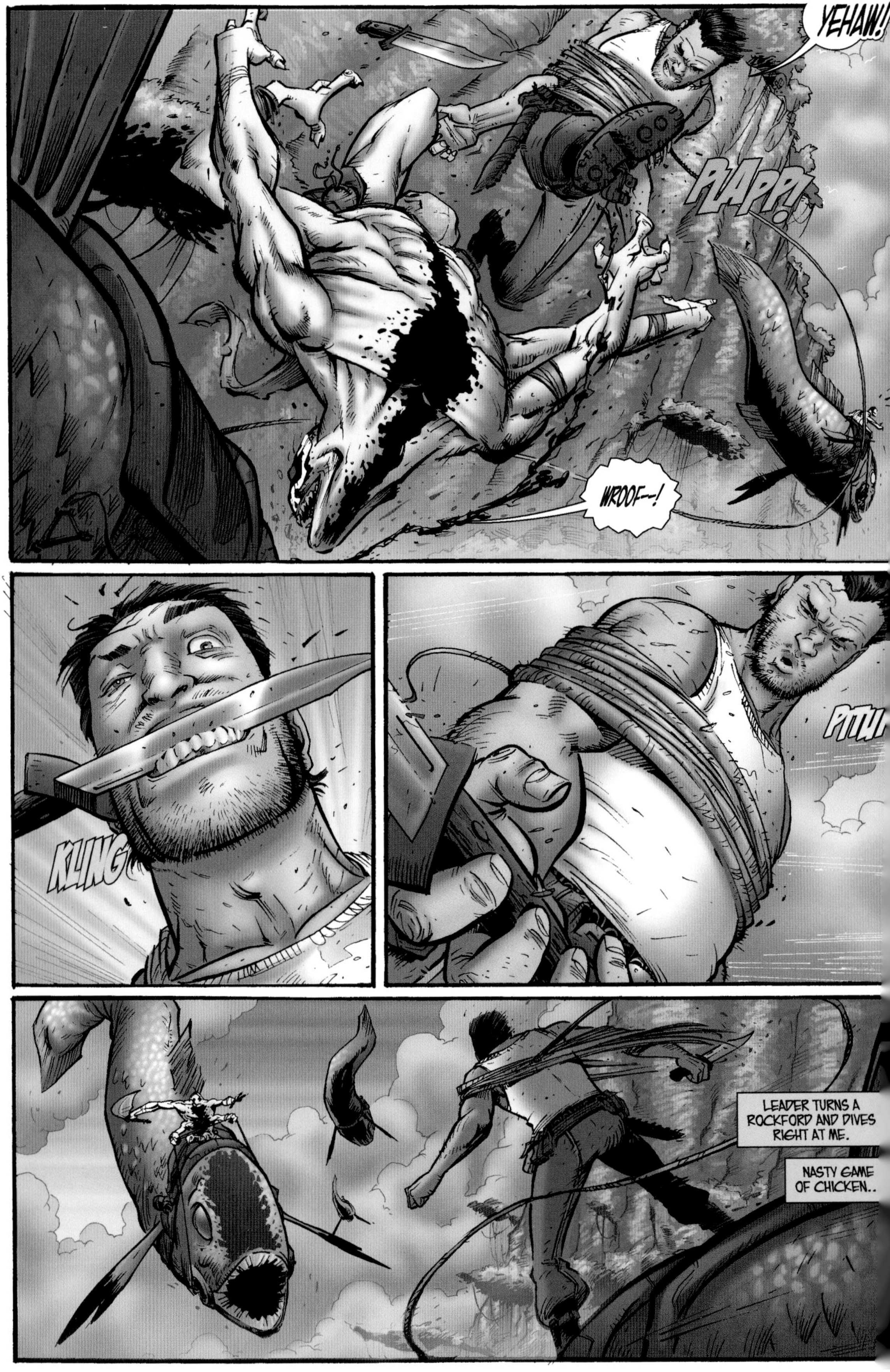
YEHAW!
PLAPP!
WROOF--!
KLING
PTUI
LEADER TURNS A ROCKFORD AND DIVES RIGHT AT ME.
NASTY GAME OF CHICKEN..

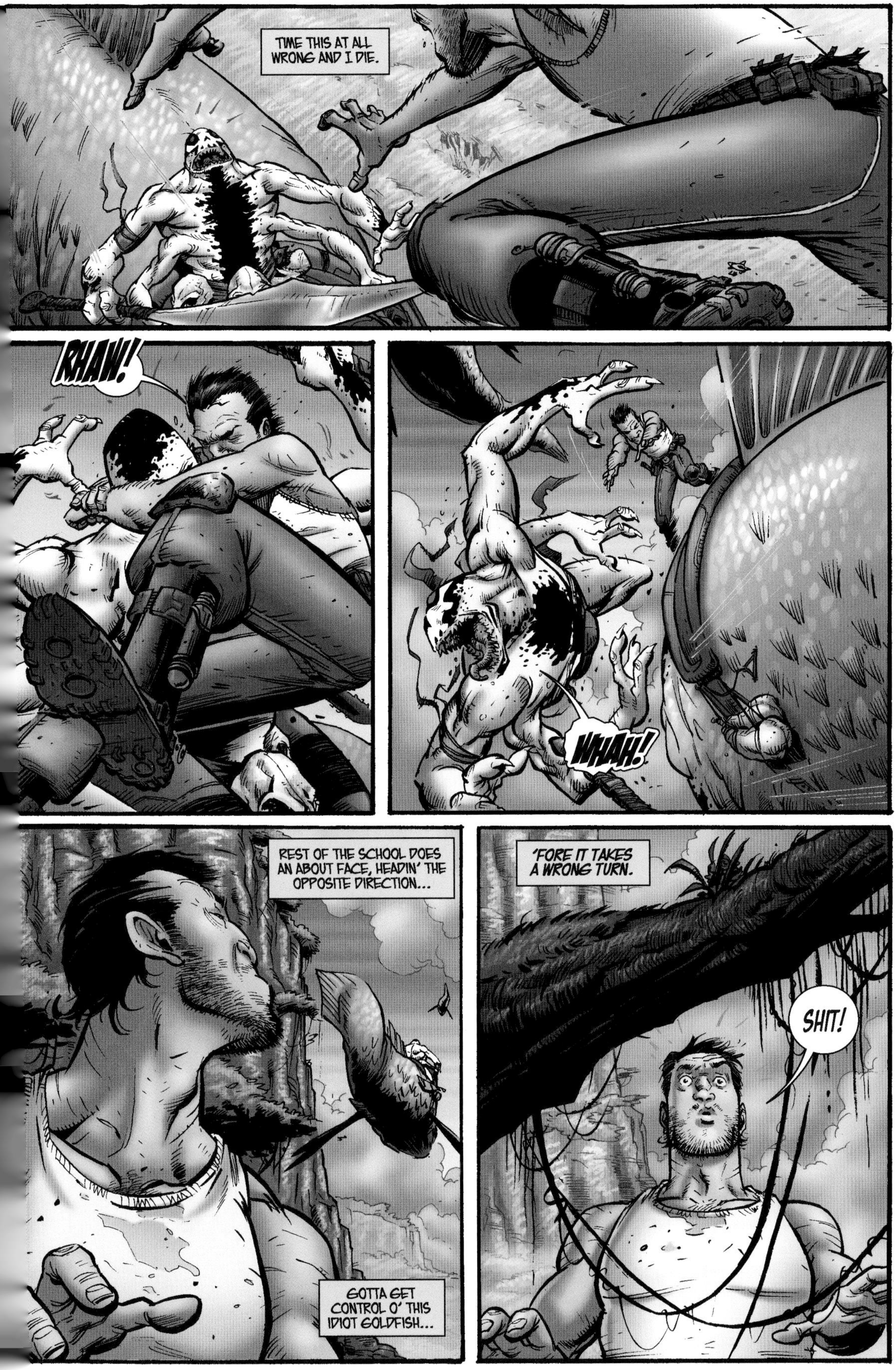
TIME THIS AT ALL WRONG AND I DIE.
RHAW!
WHAH!
REST OF THE SCHOOL DOES AN ABOUT FACE, HEADIN' THE OPPOSITE DIRECTION...
GOTTA GET CONTROL O' THIS IDIOT GOLDFISH...
'FORE IT TAKES A WRONG TURN.
SHIT!

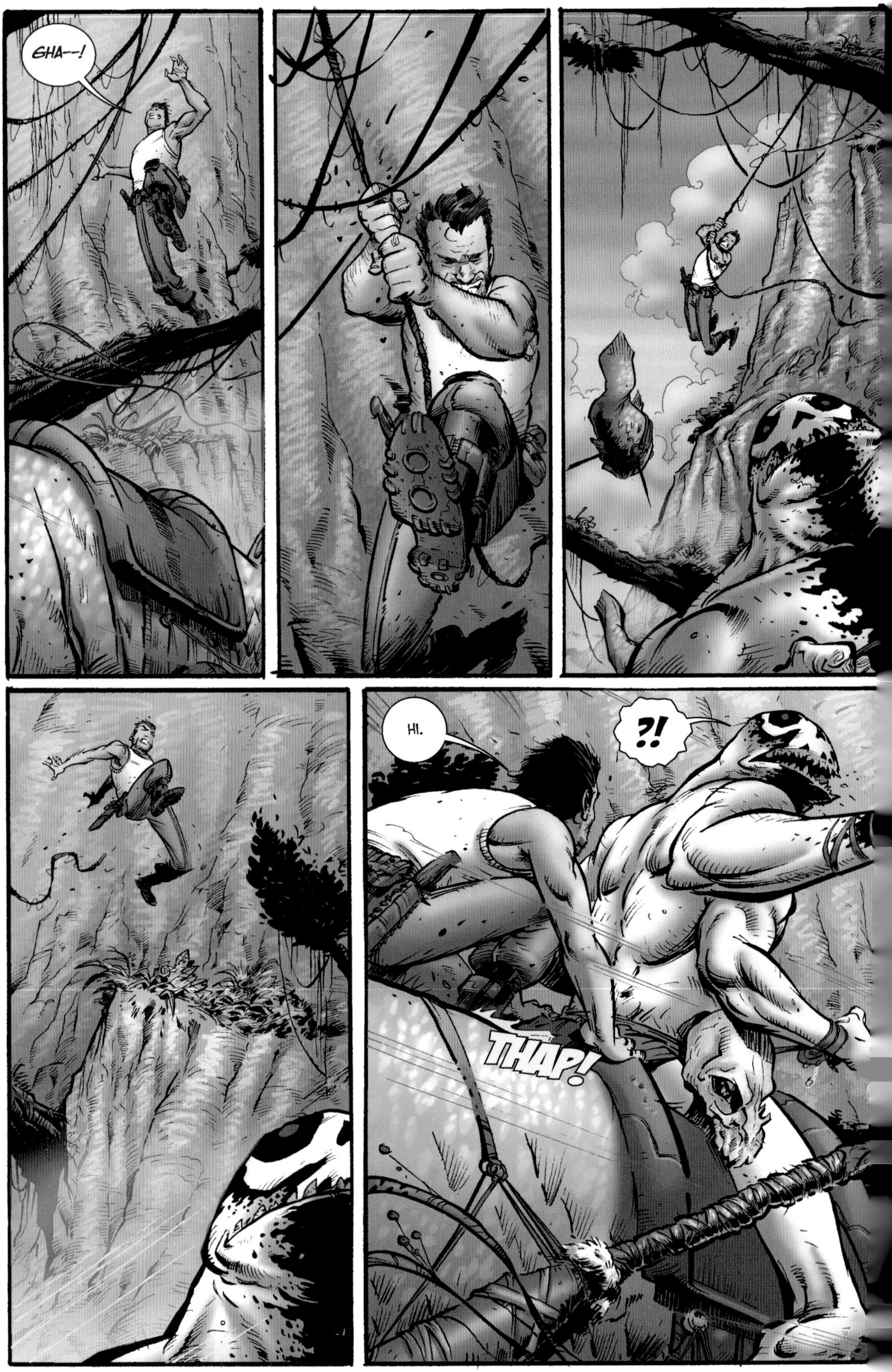
GHA--!
HI.
?!
THAP!

BASTARD AIN'T GOIN' EASY...
...TAKES US INTO A HARD DIVE.
SON-OF-A-BITCH!
STALACTITE NEARLY KNOCKS ME GALLEY WEST...
...FILE UNDER "BAD TIME TO FALL."
BAPP
OOF!
HOT AS HADES... OXYGEN LEVELS'RE FALLING FASTER THAN WE ARE.
YERGHH!
WRRACKK!
...TWO FEET CLOSER AN' BREATHIN' WON'T BE A CONCERN O' MINE...

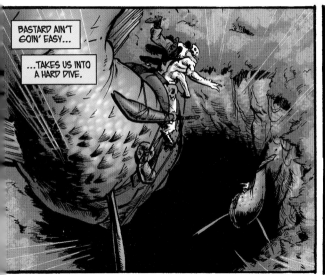

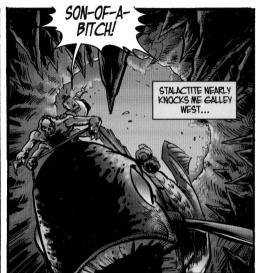

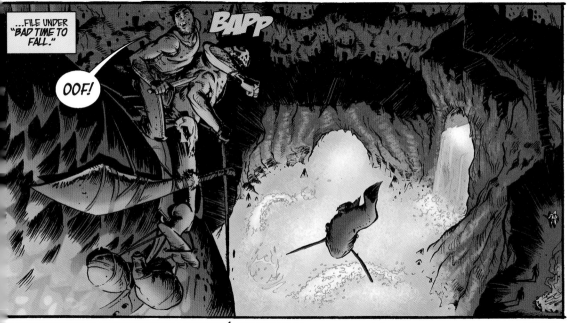

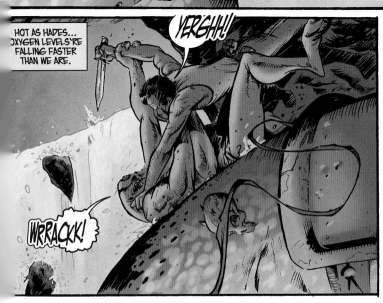

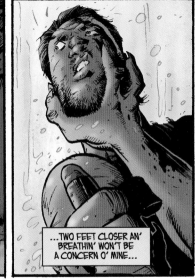

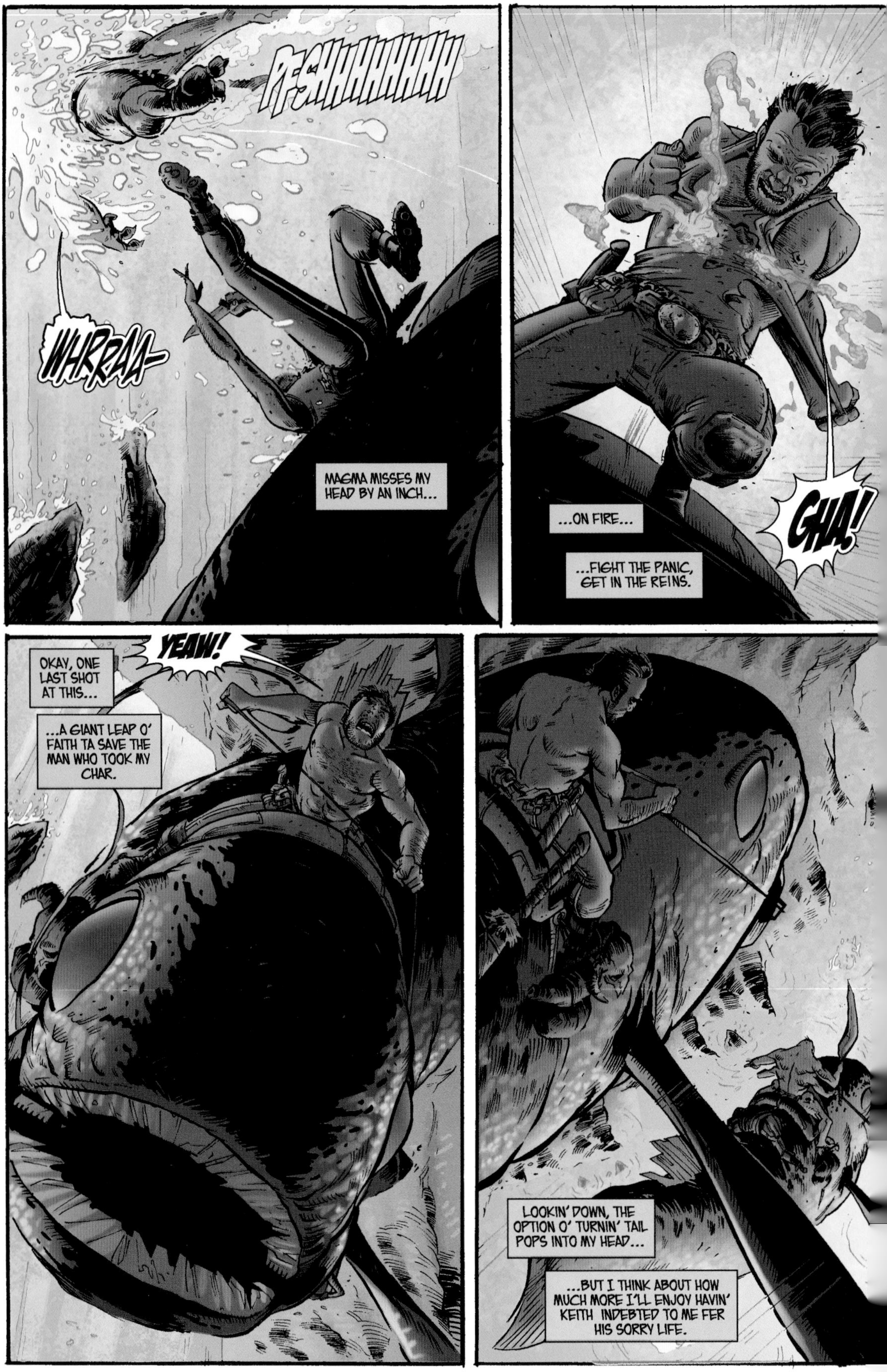
PFSHHHHHHHH
WHRRAA
MAGMA MISSES MY HEAD BY AN INCH...
...ON FIRE...
...FIGHT THE PANIC, GET IN THE REINS.
GHA!
OKAY, ONE LAST SHOT AT THIS...
...A GIANT LEAP O' FAITH TA SAVE THE MAN WHO TOOK MY CHAR.
YEAW!
LOOKIN' DOWN, THE OPTION O' TURNIN' TAIL POPS INTO MY HEAD...
...BUT I THINK ABOUT HOW MUCH MORE I'LL ENJOY HAVIN' KEITH INDEBTED TO ME FER HIS SORRY LIFE.

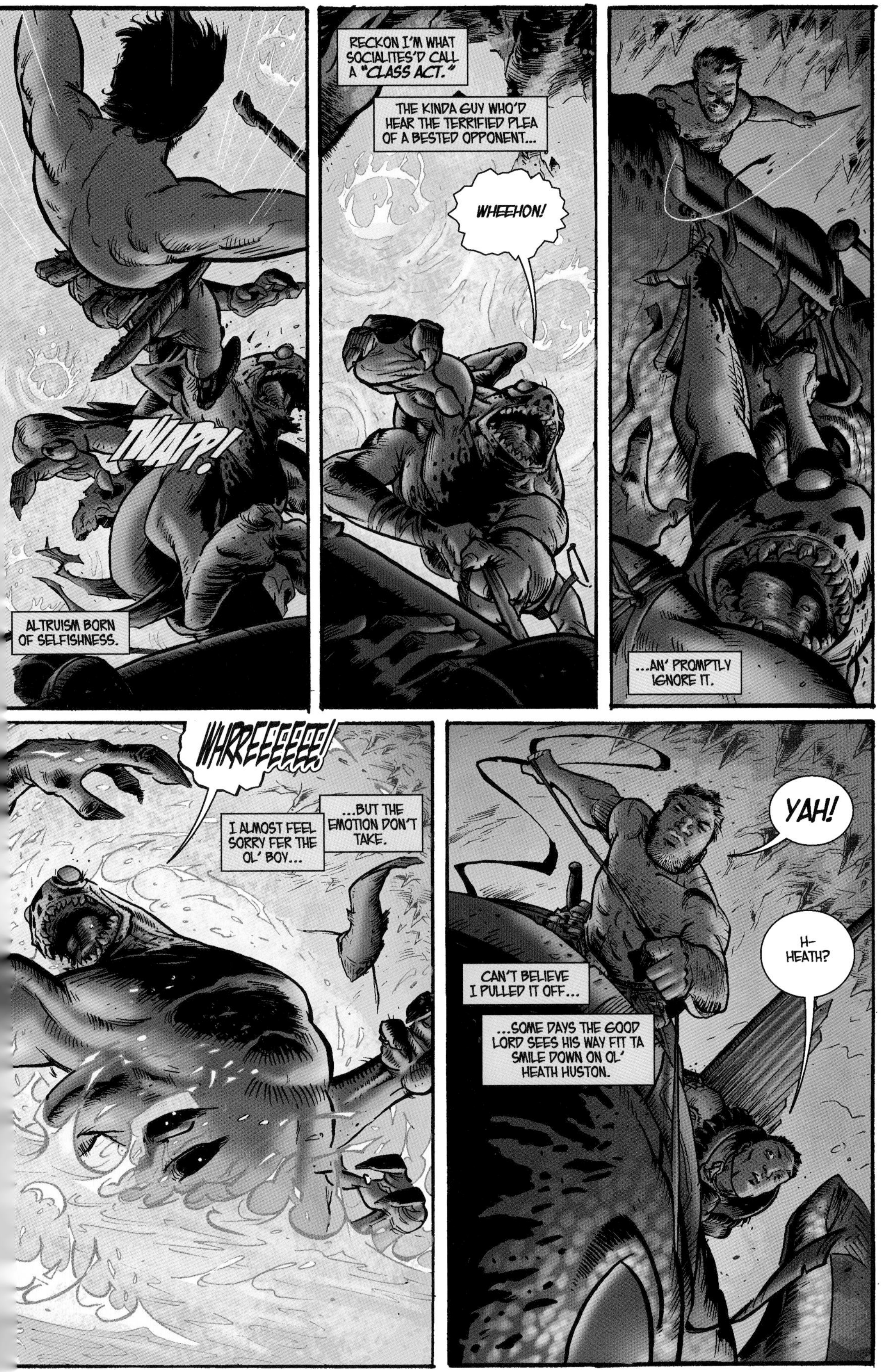
THWAPP!
ALTRUISM BORN OF SELFISHNESS.
RECKON I'M WHAT SOCIALITES'D CALL A "CLASS ACT."
THE KINDA GUY WHO'D HEAR THE TERRIFIED PLEA OF A BESTED OPPONENT...
WHEEHON!
...AN' PROMPTLY IGNORE IT.
WHRREEEEEEE!
I ALMOST FEEL SORRY FER THE OL' BOY...
...BUT THE EMOTION DON'T TAKE.
YAH!
CAN'T BELIEVE I PULLED IT OFF...
...SOME DAYS THE GOOD LORD SEES HIS WAY FIT TA SMILE DOWN ON OL' HEATH HUSTON.
H-HEATH?

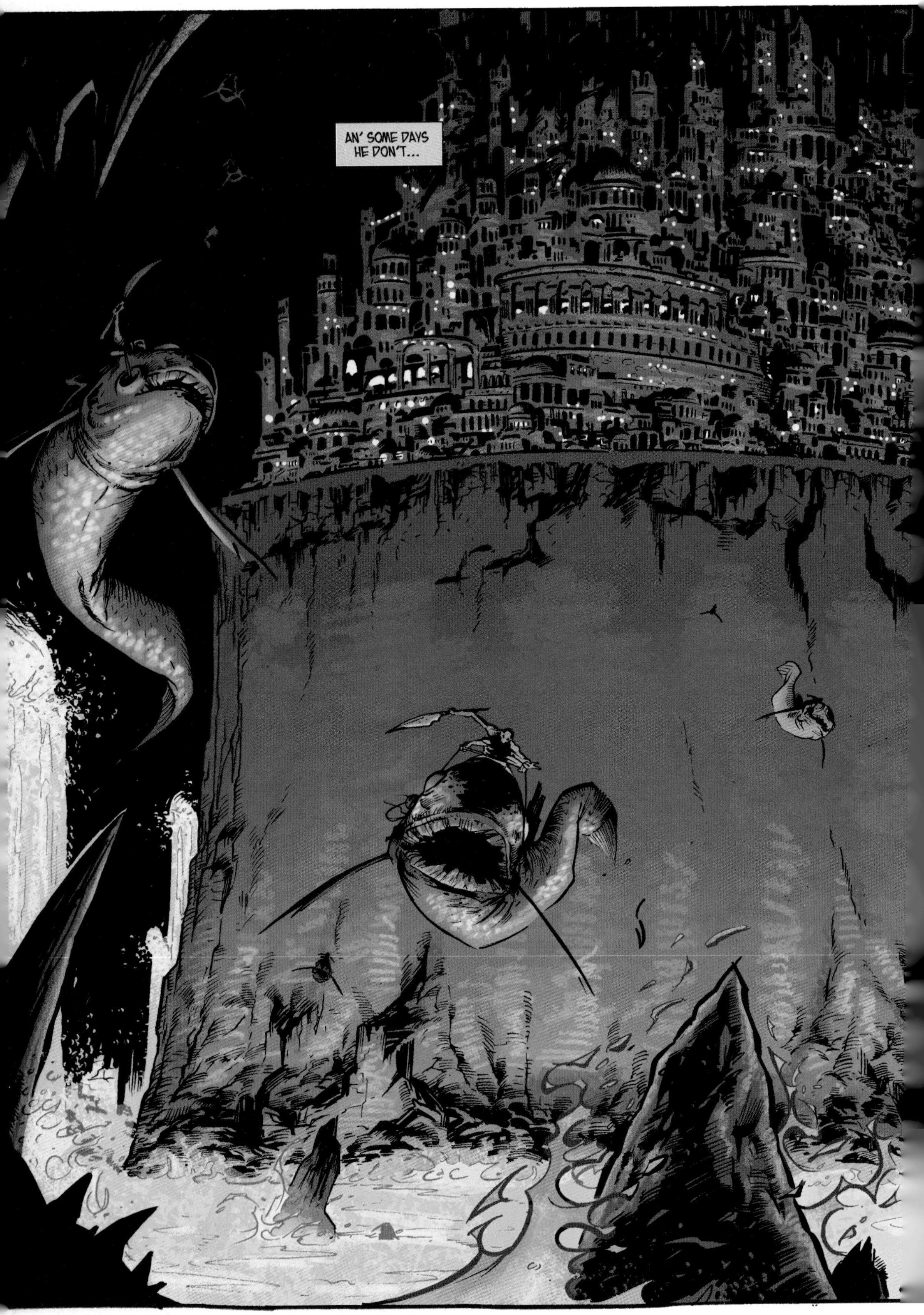
AN' SOME DAYS
HE DON'T...

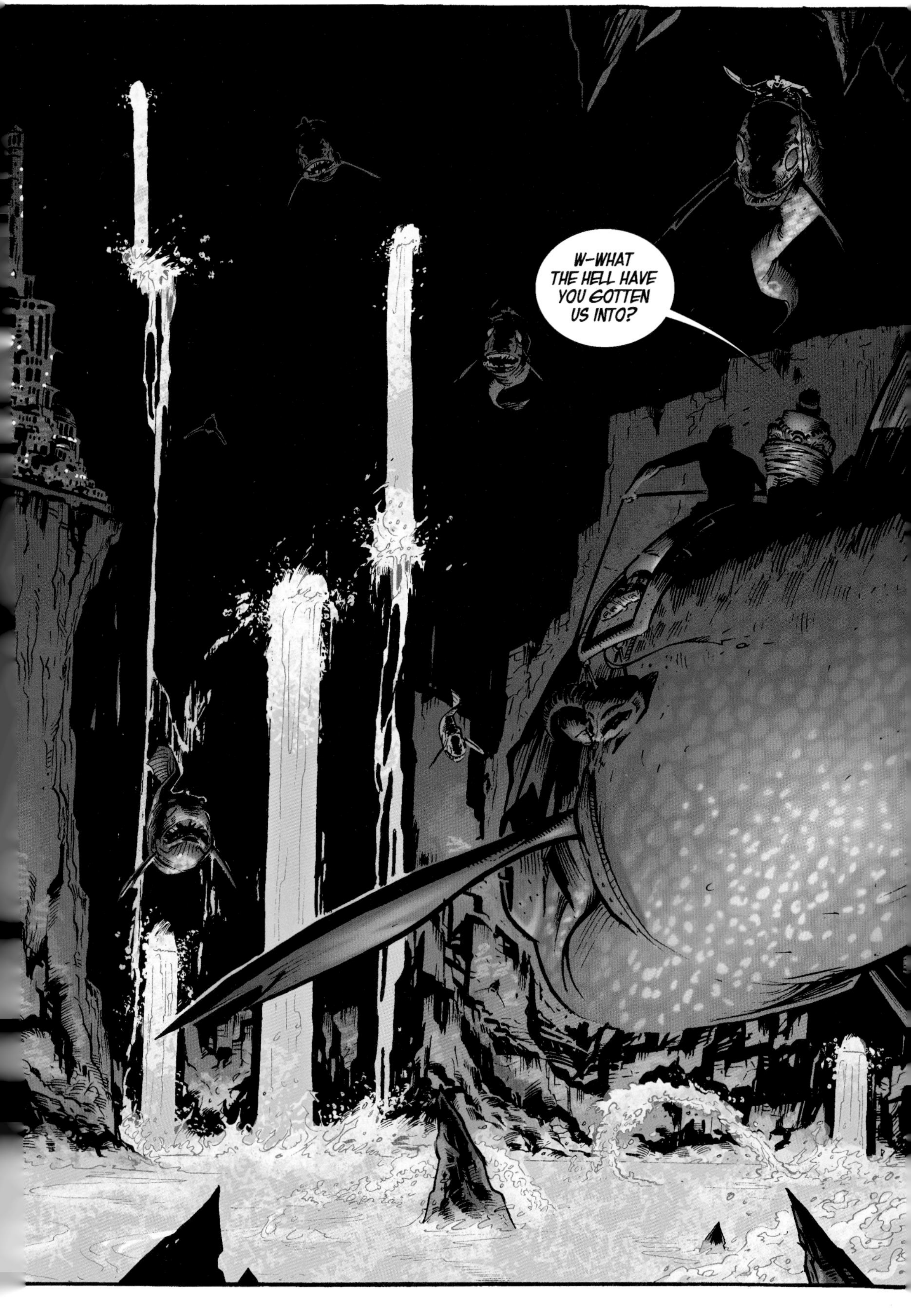
W-WHAT THE HELL HAVE YOU GOTTEN US INTO?

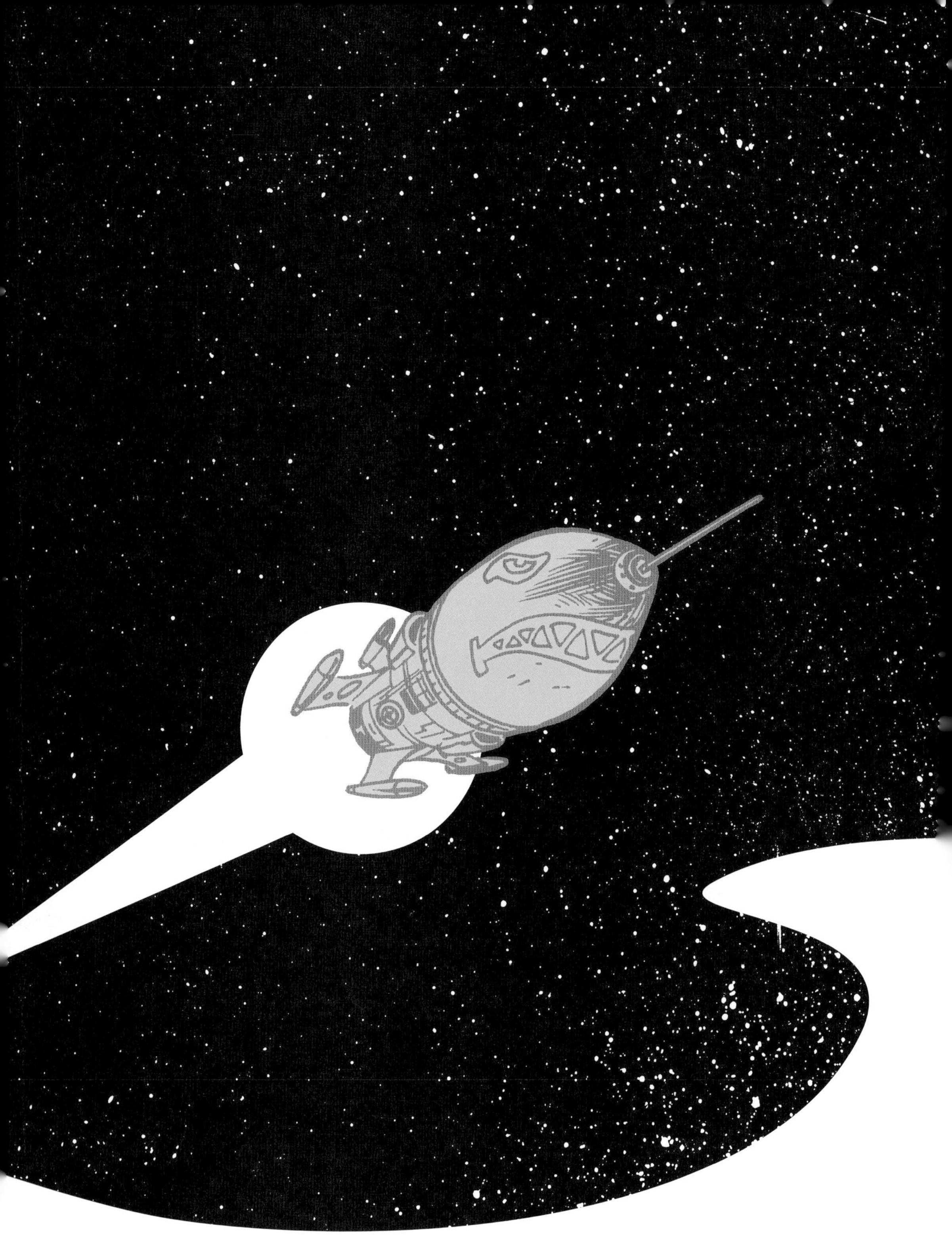

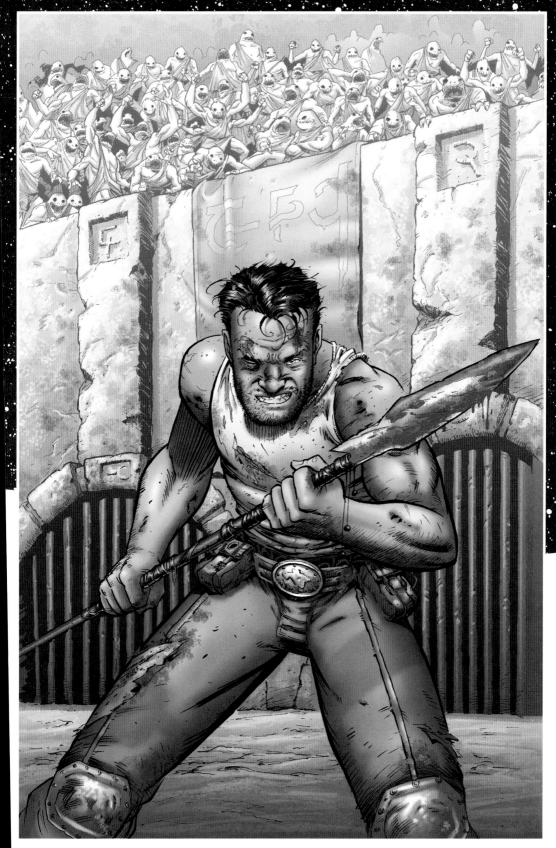

FEAR AGENT #18
ART BY JEROME OPEÑA

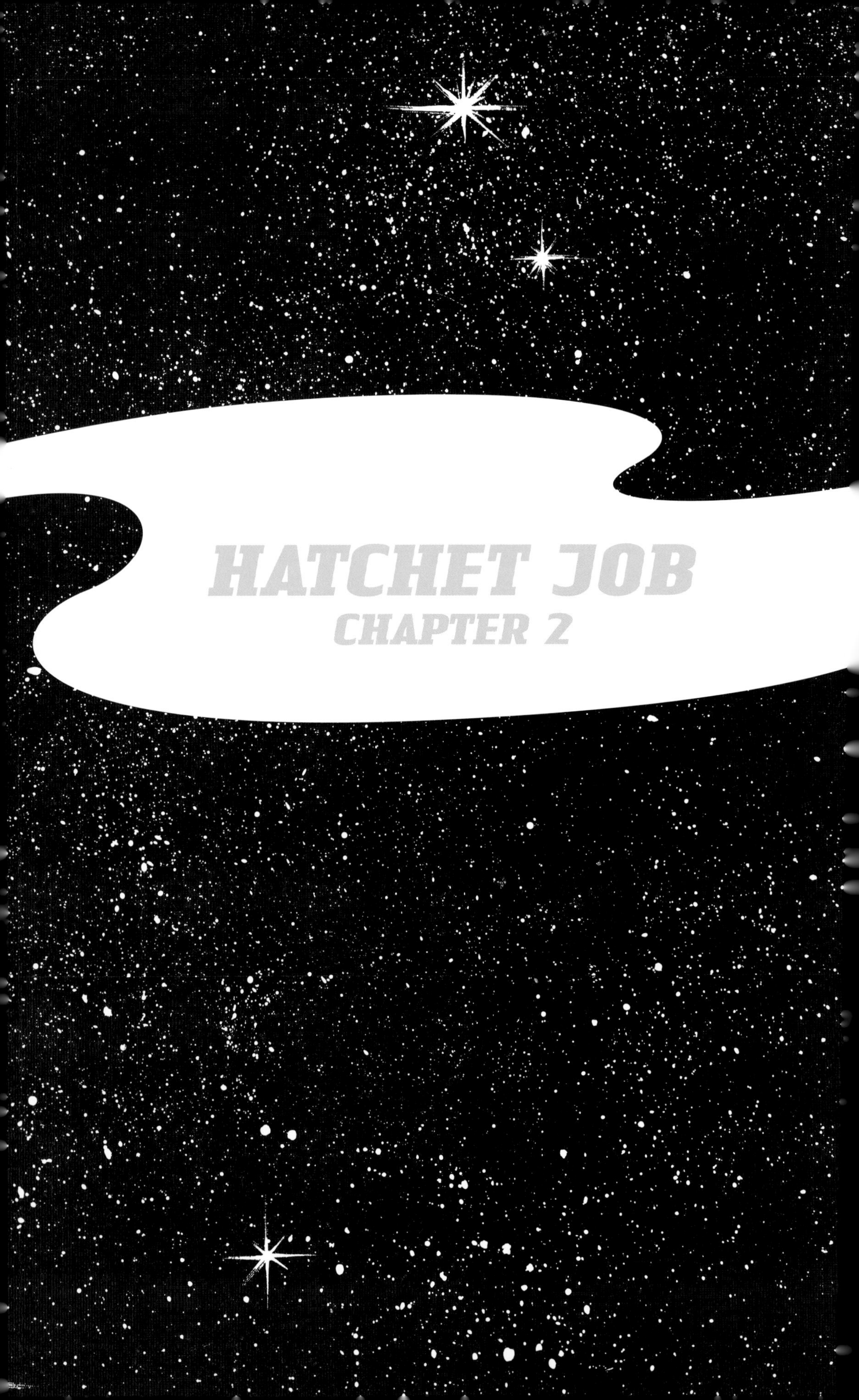
HATCHET JOB
CHAPTER 2

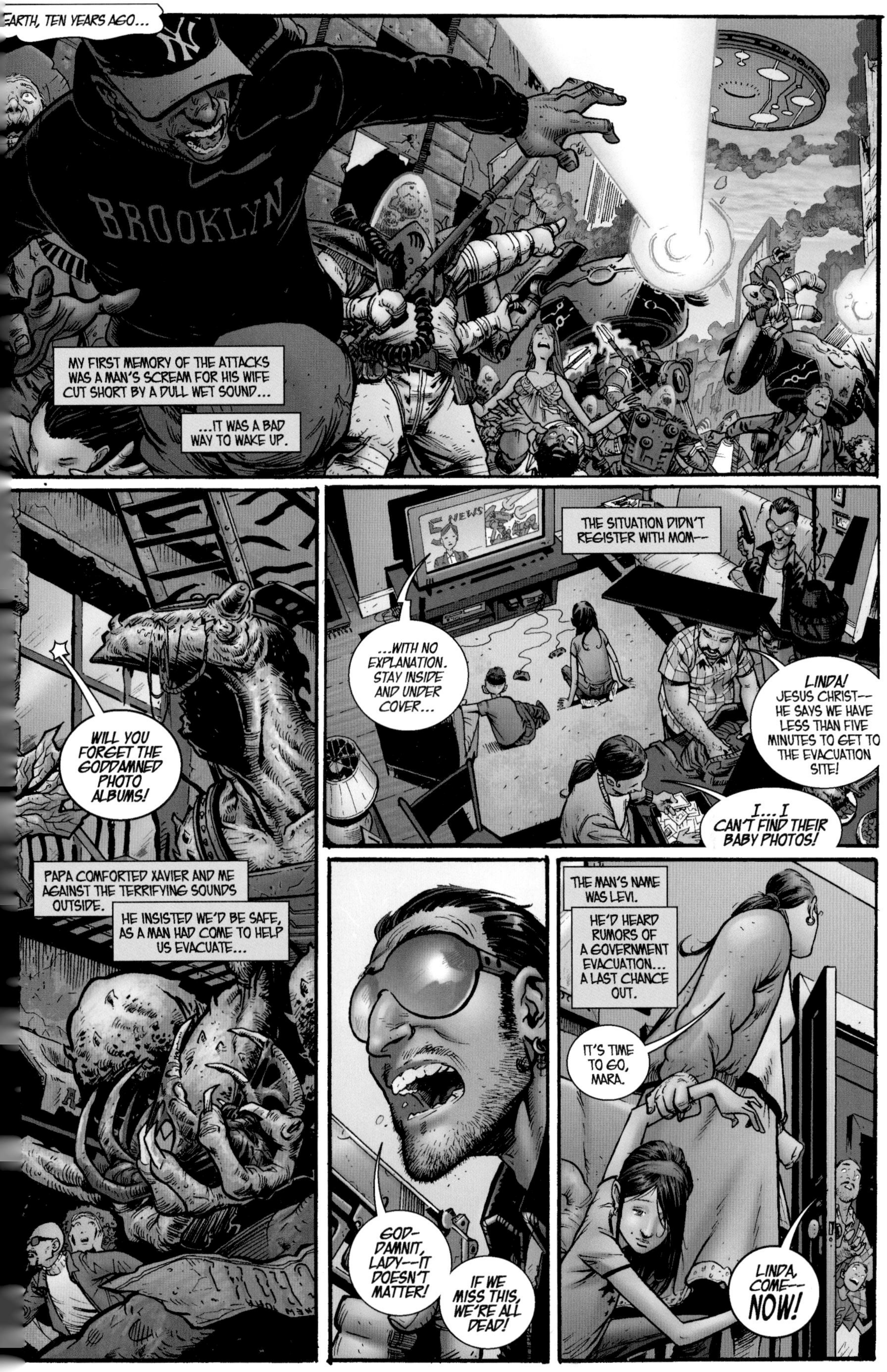
EARTH, TEN YEARS AGO...
BROOKLYN
MY FIRST MEMORY OF THE ATTACKS WAS A MAN'S SCREAM FOR HIS WIFE CUT SHORT BY A DULL WET SOUND...
...IT WAS A BAD WAY TO WAKE UP.
WILL YOU FORGET THE GODDAMNED PHOTO ALBUMS!
PAPA COMFORTED XAVIER AND ME AGAINST THE TERRIFYING SOUNDS OUTSIDE.
HE INSISTED WE'D BE SAFE, AS A MAN HAD COME TO HELP US EVACUATE...
NEWS
THE SITUATION DIDN'T REGISTER WITH MOM--
...WITH NO EXPLANATION. STAY INSIDE AND UNDER COVER...
LINDA! JESUS CHRIST-- HE SAYS WE HAVE LESS THAN FIVE MINUTES TO GET TO THE EVACUATION SITE!
I... I CAN'T FIND THEIR BABY PHOTOS!
GOD-DAMNIT, LADY--IT DOESN'T MATTER!
IF WE MISS THIS, WE'RE ALL DEAD!
THE MAN'S NAME WAS LEVI.
HE'D HEARD RUMORS OF A GOVERNMENT EVACUATION... A LAST CHANCE OUT.
IT'S TIME TO GO, MARA.
LINDA, COME-- NOW!

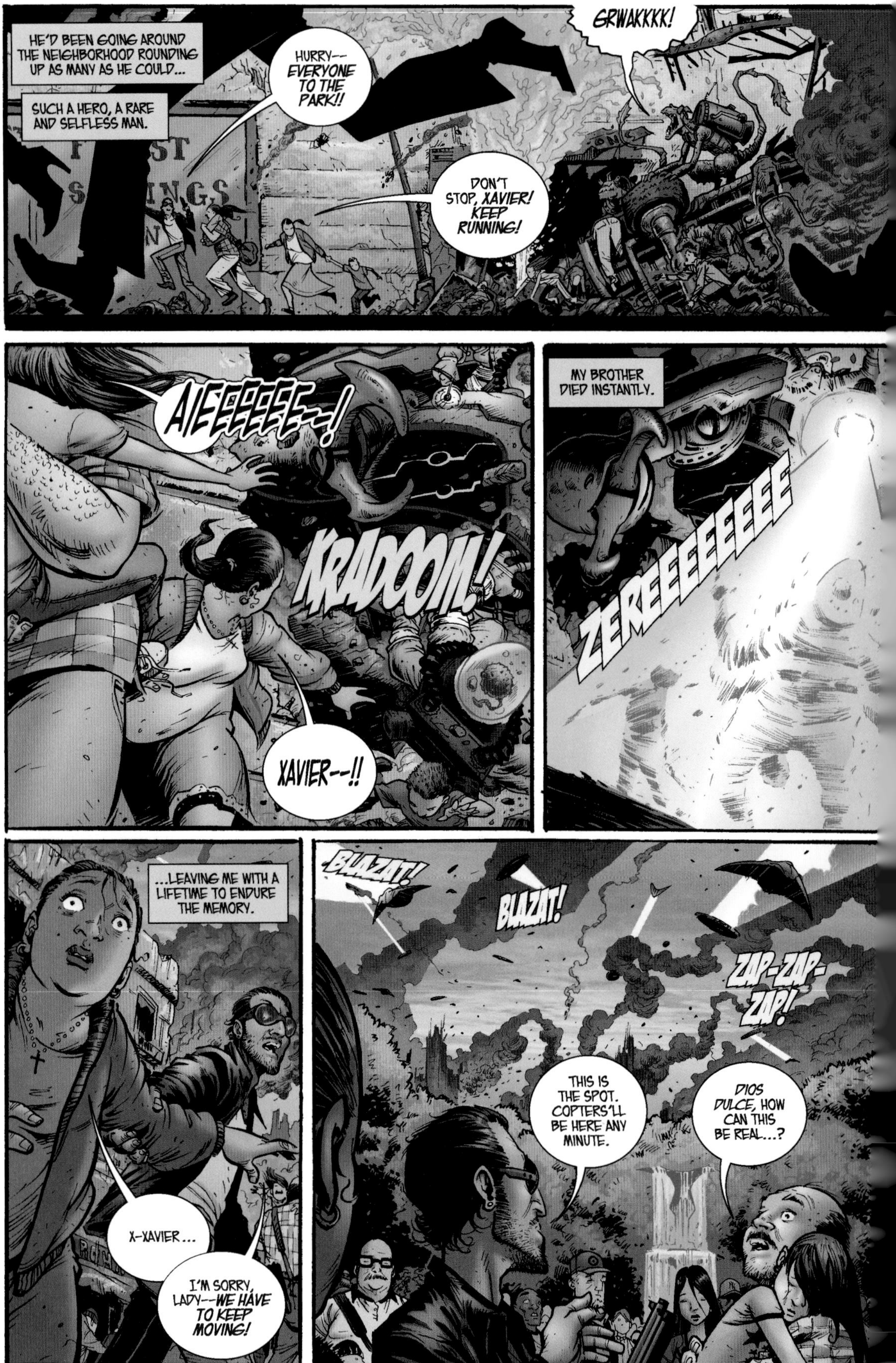
HE'D BEEN GOING AROUND THE NEIGHBORHOOD ROUNDING UP AS MANY AS HE COULD...
SUCH A HERO, A RARE AND SELFLESS MAN.
HURRY-- EVERYONE TO THE PARK!!
DON'T STOP, XAVIER! KEEP RUNNING!
GRWAKKKK!
AIEEEEEEE--!
KRADOOM!
XAVIER--!!
MY BROTHER DIED INSTANTLY.
ZEREEEEEEEE
...LEAVING ME WITH A LIFETIME TO ENDURE THE MEMORY.
X-XAVIER...
I'M SORRY, LADY--WE HAVE TO KEEP MOVING!
BLAZAT!
BLAZAT!
ZAP-ZAP-ZAP!
THIS IS THE SPOT. COPTERS'LL BE HERE ANY MINUTE.
DIOS DULCE, HOW CAN THIS BE REAL...?

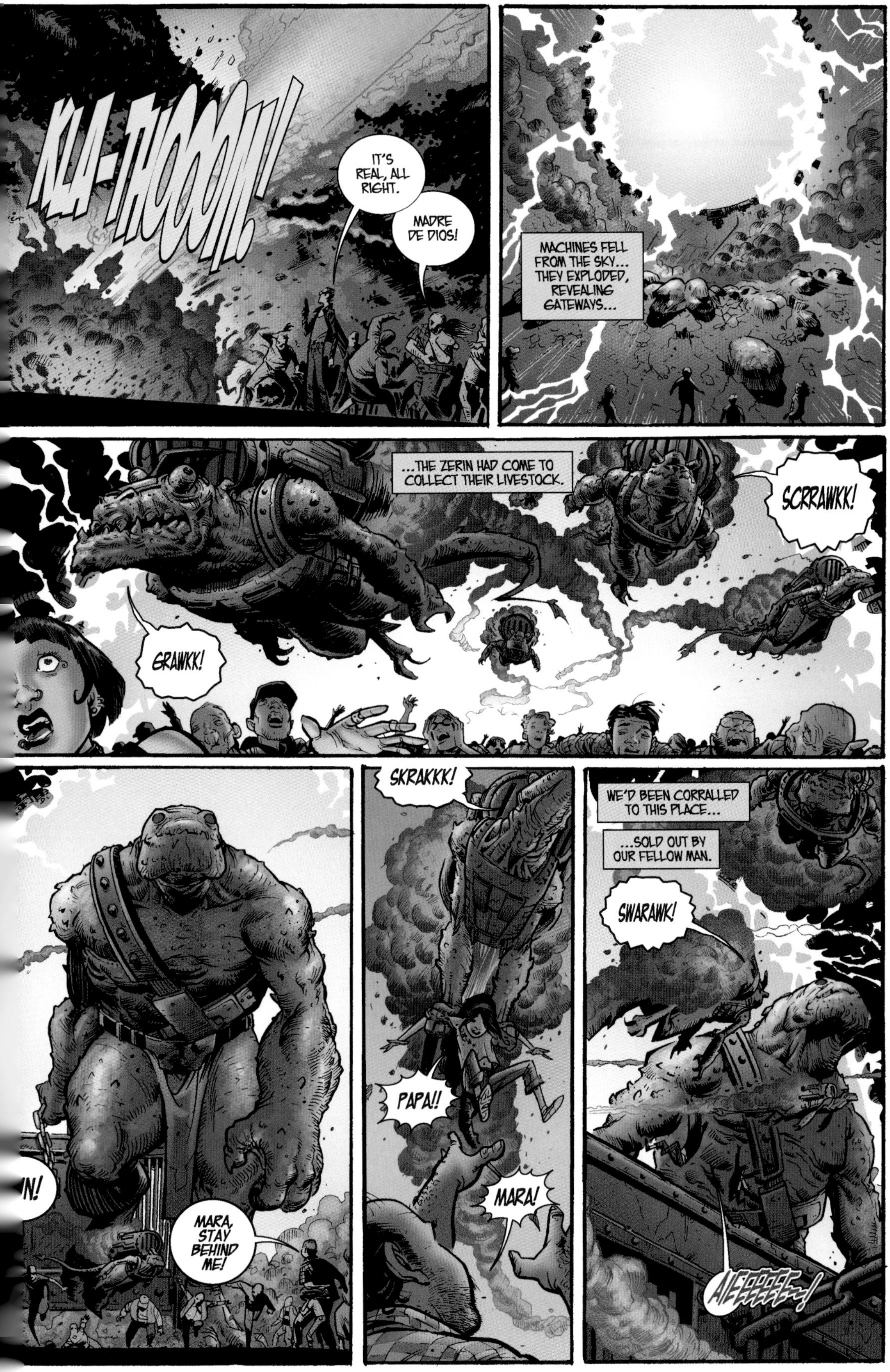
KLA-THOOOM!!
IT'S REAL, ALL RIGHT.
MADRE DE DIOS!
MACHINES FELL FROM THE SKY... THEY EXPLODED, REVEALING GATEWAYS...
...THE ZERIN HAD COME TO COLLECT THEIR LIVESTOCK.
SCRRAWKK!
GRAWKK!
N!
MARA, STAY BEHIND ME!
SKRAKKK!
PAPA!!
MARA!
WE'D BEEN CORRALLED TO THIS PLACE...
...SOLD OUT BY OUR FELLOW MAN.
SWARAWK!
AIEEEEEEE--!

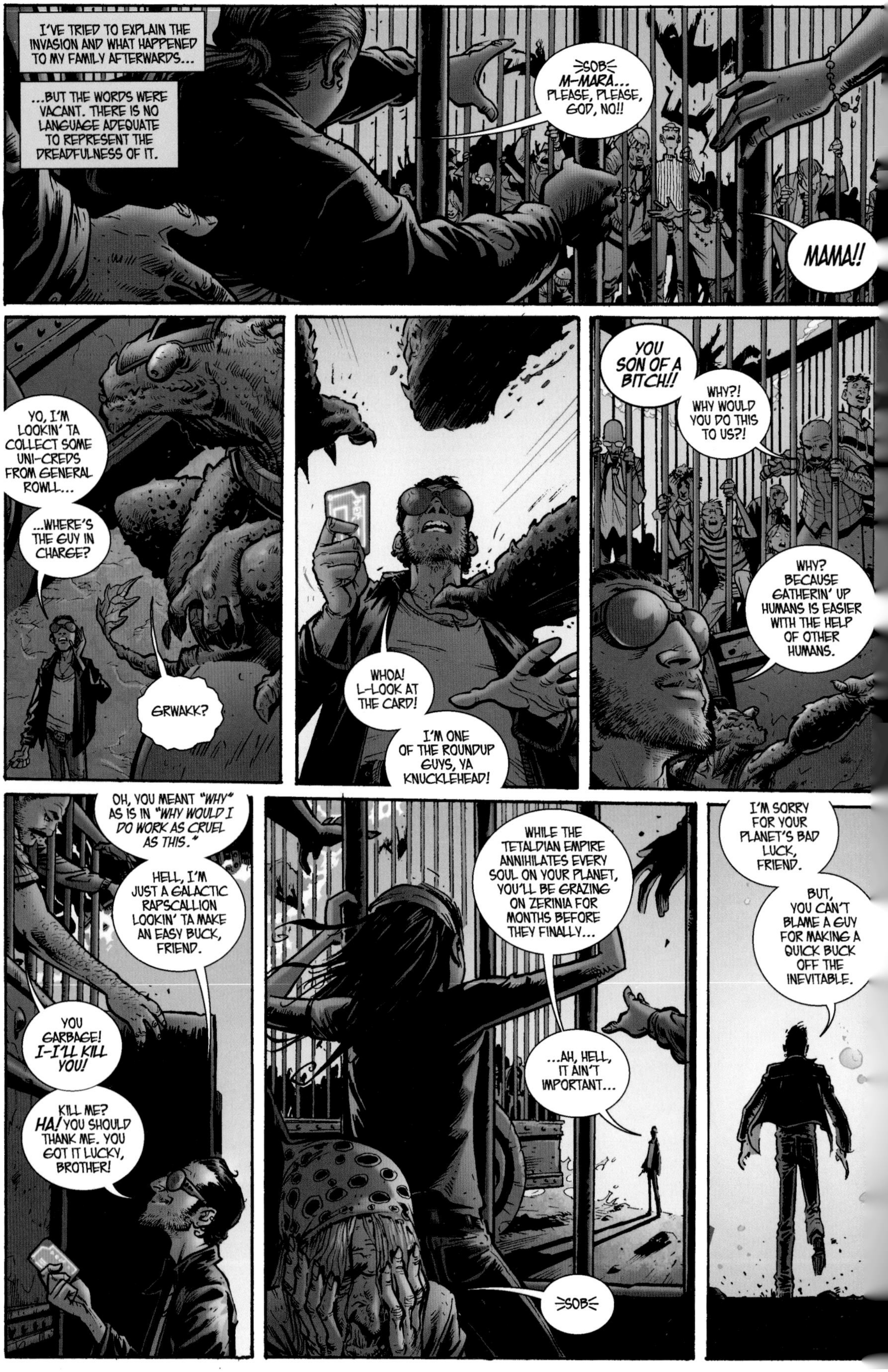
I'VE TRIED TO EXPLAIN THE INVASION AND WHAT HAPPENED TO MY FAMILY AFTERWARDS...
...BUT THE WORDS WERE VACANT. THERE IS NO LANGUAGE ADEQUATE TO REPRESENT THE DREADFULNESS OF IT.
SOB M-MARA... PLEASE, PLEASE, GOD, NO!!
MAMA!!
YO, I'M LOOKIN' TA COLLECT SOME UNI-CREDS FROM GENERAL ROWLL...
...WHERE'S THE GUY IN CHARGE?
GRWAKK?
WHOA! L-LOOK AT THE CARD!
I'M ONE OF THE ROUNDUP GUYS, YA KNUCKLEHEAD!
YOU SON OF A BITCH!!
WHY?! WHY WOULD YOU DO THIS TO US?!
WHY? BECAUSE GATHERIN' UP HUMANS IS EASIER WITH THE HELP OF OTHER HUMANS.
OH, YOU MEANT "WHY" AS IS IN "WHY WOULD I DO WORK AS CRUEL AS THIS."
HELL, I'M JUST A GALACTIC RAPSCALLION LOOKIN' TA MAKE AN EASY BUCK, FRIEND.
YOU GARBAGE! I-I'LL KILL YOU!
KILL ME? HA! YOU SHOULD THANK ME. YOU GOT IT LUCKY, BROTHER!
WHILE THE TETALDIAN EMPIRE ANNIHILATES EVERY SOUL ON YOUR PLANET, YOU'LL BE GRAZING ON ZERINIA FOR MONTHS BEFORE THEY FINALLY...
...AH, HELL, IT AIN'T IMPORTANT...
SOB
I'M SORRY FOR YOUR PLANET'S BAD LUCK, FRIEND.
BUT, YOU CAN'T BLAME A GUY FOR MAKING A QUICK BUCK OFF THE INEVITABLE.

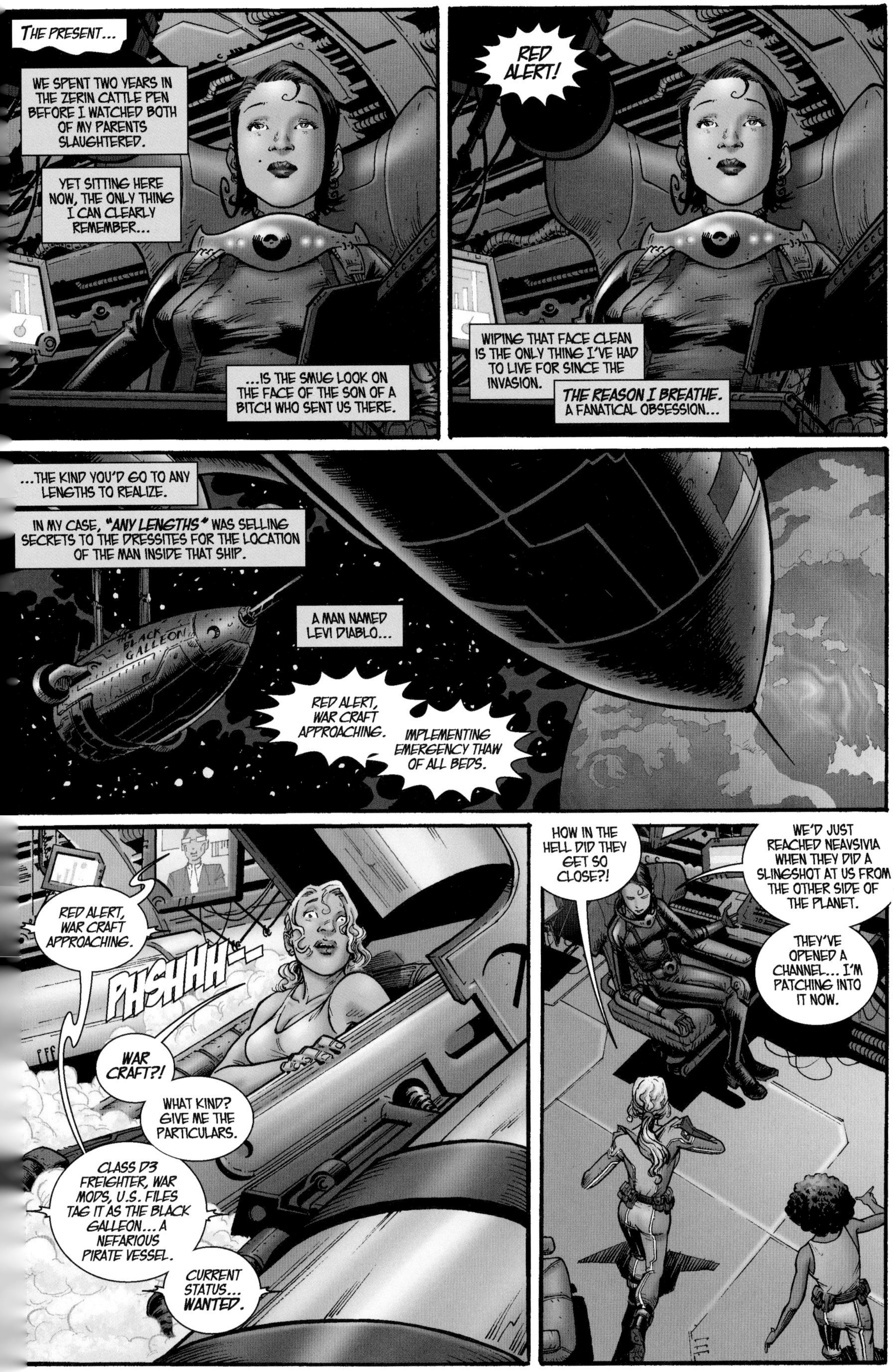
THE PRESENT...
WE SPENT TWO YEARS IN THE ZERIN CATTLE PEN BEFORE I WATCHED BOTH OF MY PARENTS SLAUGHTERED.
YET SITTING HERE NOW, THE ONLY THING I CAN CLEARLY REMEMBER...
...IS THE SMUG LOOK ON THE FACE OF THE SON OF A BITCH WHO SENT US THERE.
RED ALERT!
WIPING THAT FACE CLEAN IS THE ONLY THING I'VE HAD TO LIVE FOR SINCE THE INVASION.
THE REASON I BREATHE. A FANATICAL OBSESSION...
...THE KIND YOU'D GO TO ANY LENGTHS TO REALIZE.
IN MY CASE, "ANY LENGTHS" WAS SELLING SECRETS TO THE DRESSITES FOR THE LOCATION OF THE MAN INSIDE THAT SHIP.
THE BLACK GALLEON
A MAN NAMED LEVI DIABLO...
RED ALERT, WAR CRAFT APPROACHING.
IMPLEMENTING EMERGENCY THAW OF ALL BEDS.
RED ALERT, WAR CRAFT APPROACHING.
PHSHHH--
WAR CRAFT?!
WHAT KIND? GIVE ME THE PARTICULARS.
CLASS D3 FREIGHTER, WAR MODS, U.S. FILES TAG IT AS THE BLACK GALLEON... A NEFARIOUS PIRATE VESSEL.
CURRENT STATUS... WANTED.
HOW IN THE HELL DID THEY GET SO CLOSE?!
WE'D JUST REACHED NEAVSIVIA WHEN THEY DID A SLINGSHOT AT US FROM THE OTHER SIDE OF THE PLANET.
THEY'VE OPENED A CHANNEL... I'M PATCHING INTO IT NOW.

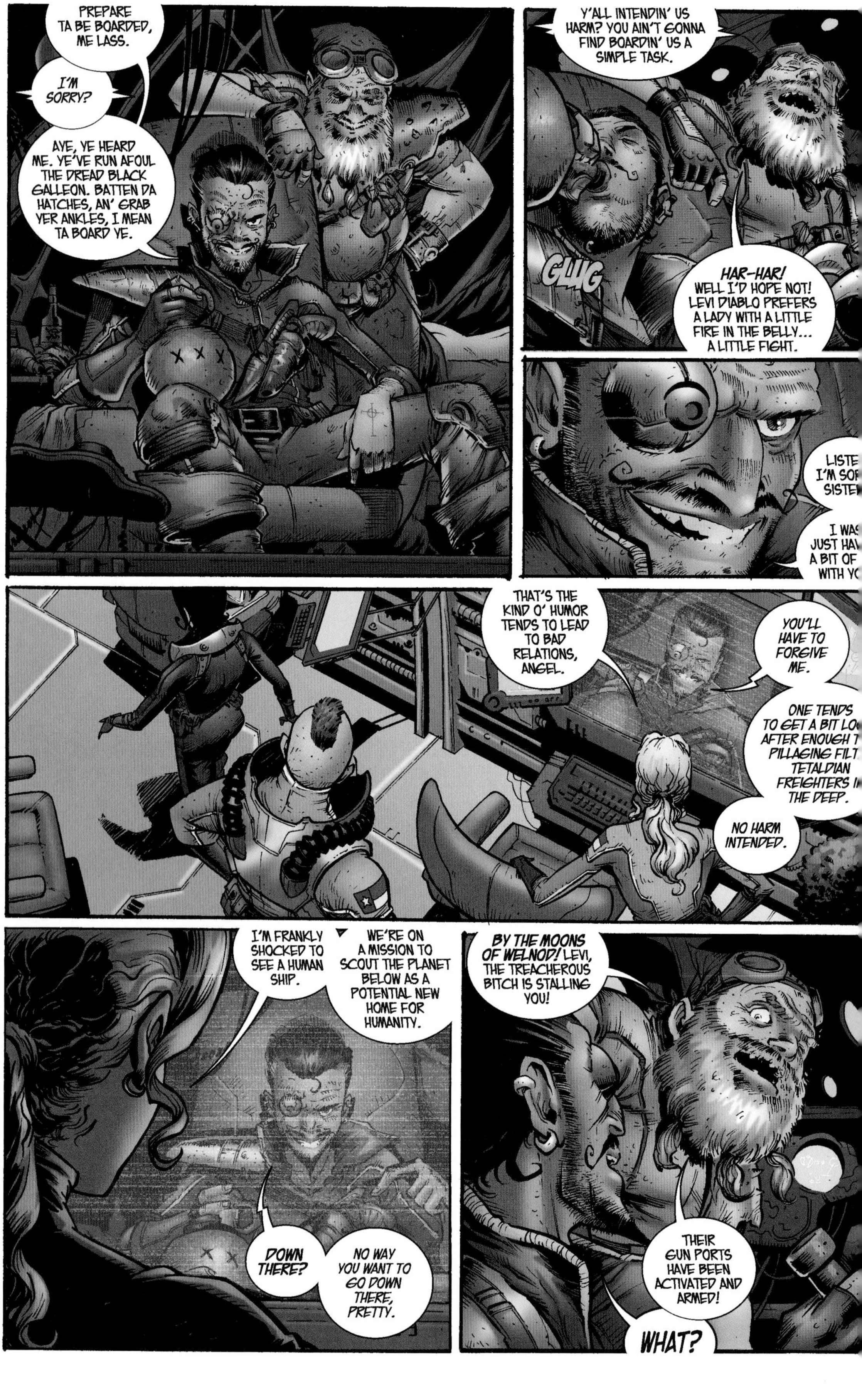

PREPARE TA BE BOARDED, ME LASS.
I'M SORRY?
AYE, YE HEARD ME. YE'VE RUN AFOUL THE DREAD BLACK GALLEON. BATTEN DA HATCHES, AN' GRAB YER ANKLES, I MEAN TA BOARD YE.
Y'ALL INTENDIN' US HARM? YOU AIN'T GONNA FIND BOARDIN' US A SIMPLE TASK.
GLUG
HAR-HAR! WELL I'D HOPE NOT! LEVI DIABLO PREFERS A LADY WITH A LITTLE FIRE IN THE BELLY... A LITTLE FIGHT.
THAT'S THE KIND O' HUMOR TENDS TO LEAD TO BAD RELATIONS, ANGEL.
YOU'LL HAVE TO FORGIVE ME.
NO HARM INTENDED.
I'M FRANKLY SHOCKED TO SEE A HUMAN SHIP.
WE'RE ON A MISSION TO SCOUT THE PLANET BELOW AS A POTENTIAL NEW HOME FOR HUMANITY.
DOWN THERE?
NO WAY YOU WANT TO GO DOWN THERE, PRETTY.
BY THE MOONS OF WELNOD! LEVI, THE TREACHEROUS BITCH IS STALLING YOU!
THEIR GUN PORTS HAVE BEEN ACTIVATED AND ARMED!
WHAT?

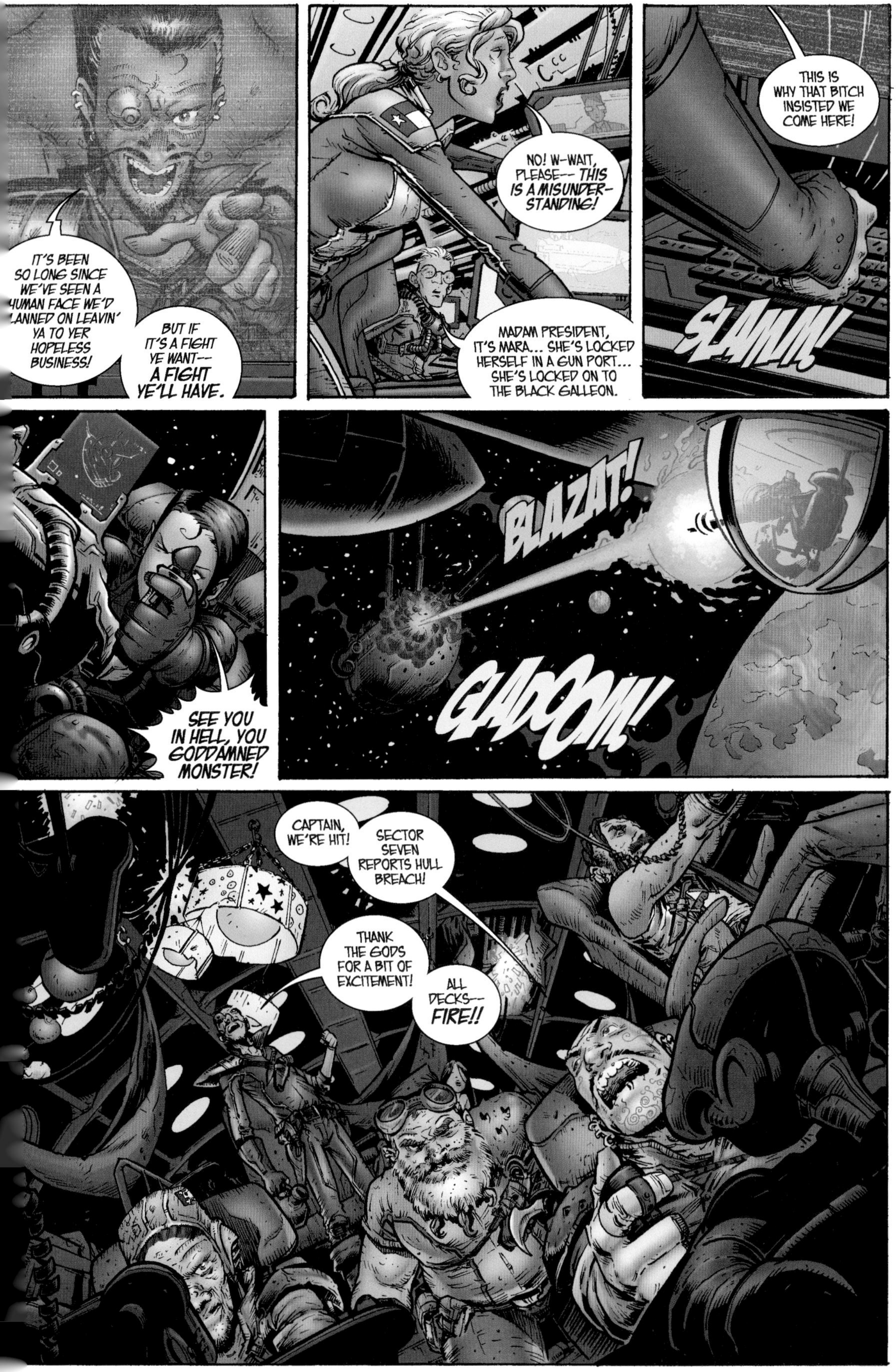
IT'S BEEN SO LONG SINCE WE'VE SEEN A HUMAN FACE WE'D PLANNED ON LEAVIN' YA TO YER HOPELESS BUSINESS!
BUT IF IT'S A FIGHT YE WANT-- A FIGHT YE'LL HAVE.
NO! W-WAIT, PLEASE-- THIS IS A MISUNDER-STANDING!
MADAM PRESIDENT, IT'S MARA... SHE'S LOCKED HERSELF IN A GUN PORT... SHE'S LOCKED ON TO THE BLACK GALLEON.
THIS IS WHY THAT BITCH INSISTED WE COME HERE!
SLAMM!
SEE YOU IN HELL, YOU GODDAMNED MONSTER!
BLAZAT!
GLADOOM!
CAPTAIN, WE'RE HIT!
SECTOR SEVEN REPORTS HULL BREACH!
THANK THE GODS FOR A BIT OF EXCITEMENT!
ALL DECKS-- FIRE!!

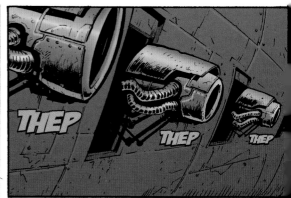

THEP THEP THEP

GA-DOOM GA-DOOM GA-DOOM GA-DOOM GA-DOOM

NICHOLAS, STOP THAT HORRIBLE GODDAMNED WOMAN FROM FIRING AGAIN!

INCOMING!!

THRAGGOOOM!

NICHOLAS, TIE HER DOWN! EVERYONE INTO CRASH POSITIONS!

LET ME GO!

LUCKY I NOT SNAP NECK!

ALL SYSTEMS OFFLINE!

SEND AN EMERGENCY DISTRESS SIGNAL TO KEITH AND THE OTHERS. WE'RE GOING DOWN!

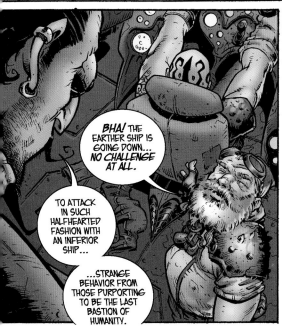

BHA! THE EARTHER SHIP IS GOING DOWN... NO CHALLENGE AT ALL.

TO ATTACK IN SUCH HALFHEARTED FASHION WITH AN INFERIOR SHIP...

...STRANGE BEHAVIOR FROM THOSE PURPORTING TO BE THE LAST BASTION OF HUMANITY.

I ACTED ON EMOTION--DIDN'T EVEN CONSIDER THEY'D HAVE SUCH HIGH-GRADE ARMOR.

AFTER ALL I'VE GONE THROUGH TO GET HERE, TO GET TO THIS MOMENT...

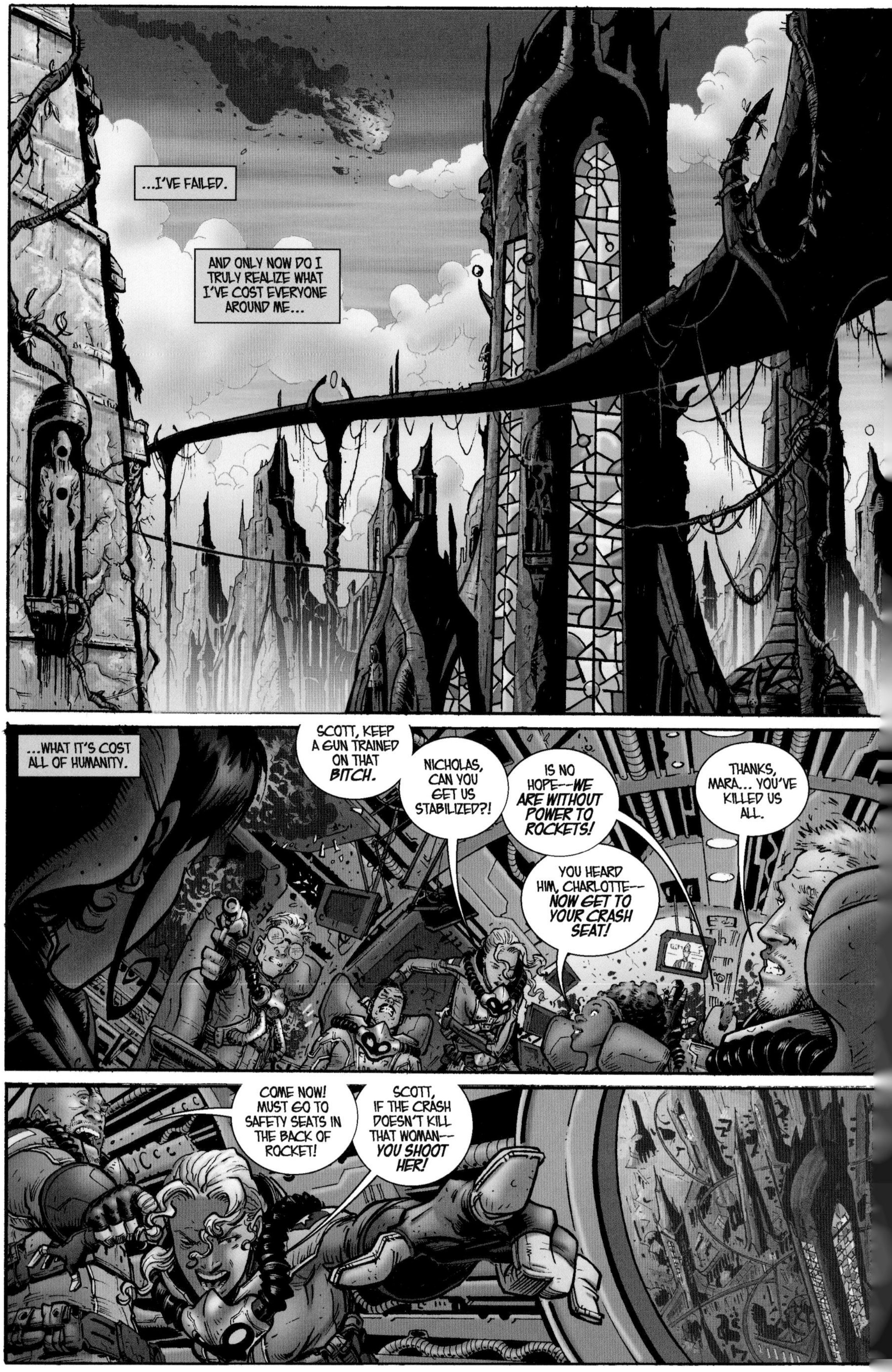
...I'VE FAILED.
AND ONLY NOW DO I TRULY REALIZE WHAT I'VE COST EVERYONE AROUND ME...
...WHAT IT'S COST ALL OF HUMANITY.
SCOTT, KEEP A GUN TRAINED ON THAT BITCH.
NICHOLAS, CAN YOU GET US STABILIZED?!
IS NO HOPE--WE ARE WITHOUT POWER TO ROCKETS!
YOU HEARD HIM, CHARLOTTE--NOW GET TO YOUR CRASH SEAT!
THANKS, MARA... YOU'VE KILLED US ALL.
COME NOW! MUST GO TO SAFETY SEATS IN THE BACK OF ROCKET!
SCOTT, IF THE CRASH DOESN'T KILL THAT WOMAN--YOU SHOOT HER!

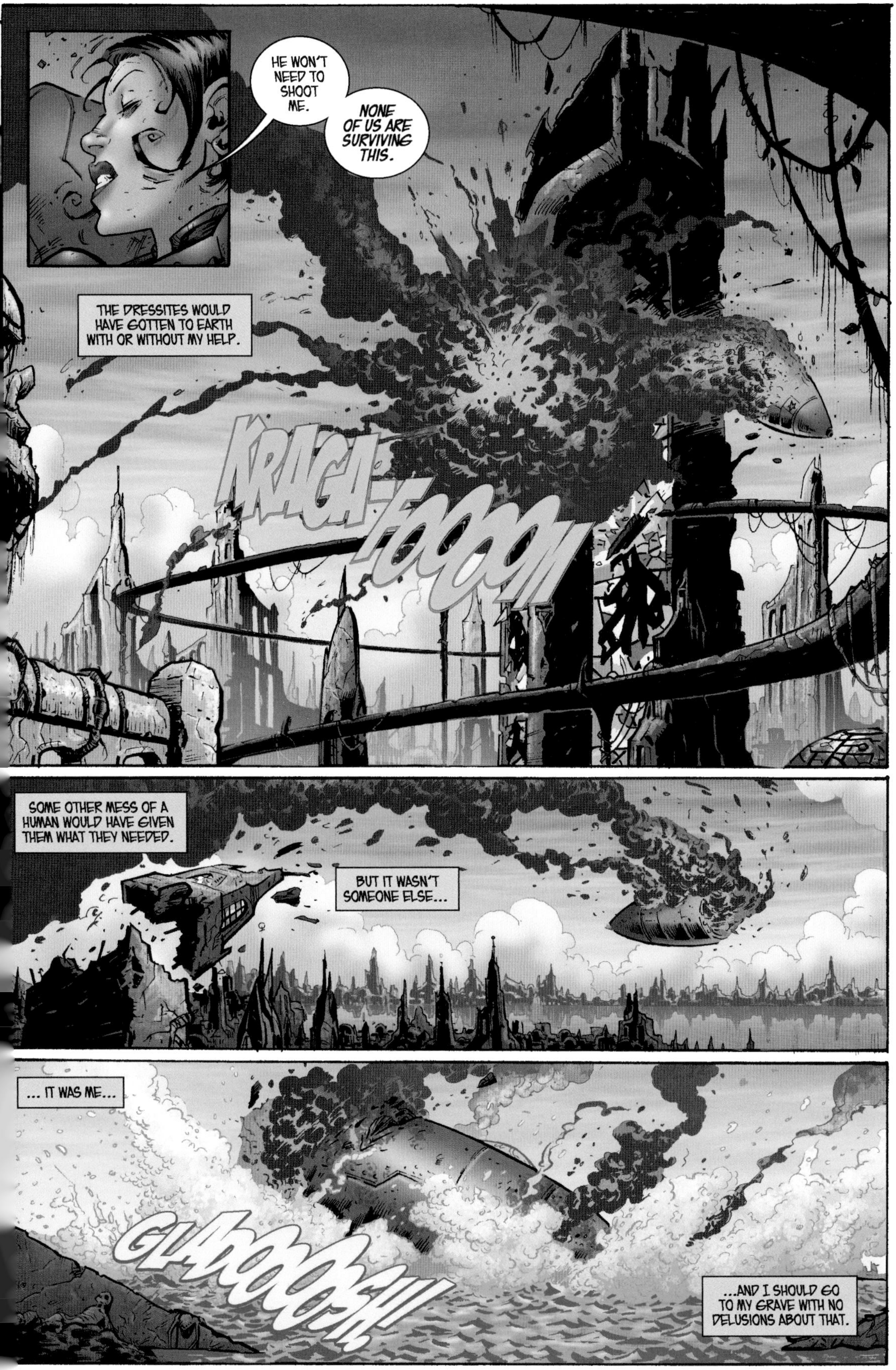
HE WON'T NEED TO SHOOT ME.
NONE OF US ARE SURVIVING THIS.
THE DRESSITES WOULD HAVE GOTTEN TO EARTH WITH OR WITHOUT MY HELP.
KRAGA-FOOOOM
SOME OTHER MESS OF A HUMAN WOULD HAVE GIVEN THEM WHAT THEY NEEDED.
BUT IT WASN'T SOMEONE ELSE...
... IT WAS ME...
GLADOOOSH!!
...AND I SHOULD GO TO MY GRAVE WITH NO DELUSIONS ABOUT THAT.

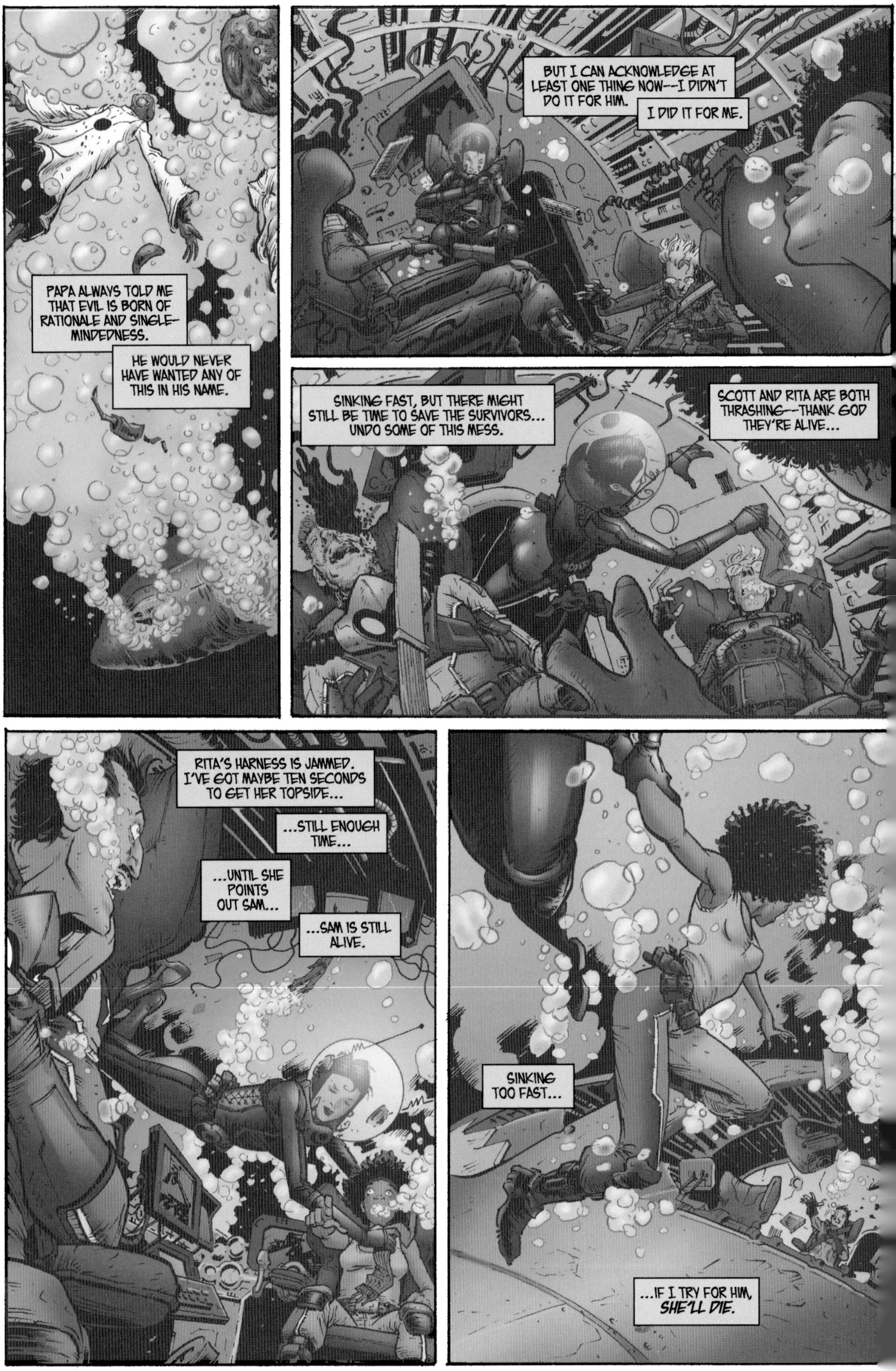
PAPA ALWAYS TOLD ME THAT EVIL IS BORN OF RATIONALE AND SINGLE-MINDEDNESS.
HE WOULD NEVER HAVE WANTED ANY OF THIS IN HIS NAME.
BUT I CAN ACKNOWLEDGE AT LEAST ONE THING NOW--I DIDN'T DO IT FOR HIM.
I DID IT FOR ME.
SINKING FAST, BUT THERE MIGHT STILL BE TIME TO SAVE THE SURVIVORS... UNDO SOME OF THIS MESS.
SCOTT AND RITA ARE BOTH THRASHING--THANK GOD THEY'RE ALIVE...
RITA'S HARNESS IS JAMMED. I'VE GOT MAYBE TEN SECONDS TO GET HER TOPSIDE...
...STILL ENOUGH TIME...
...UNTIL SHE POINTS OUT SAM...
...SAM IS STILL ALIVE.
SINKING TOO FAST...
...IF I TRY FOR HIM, ***SHE'LL DIE.***

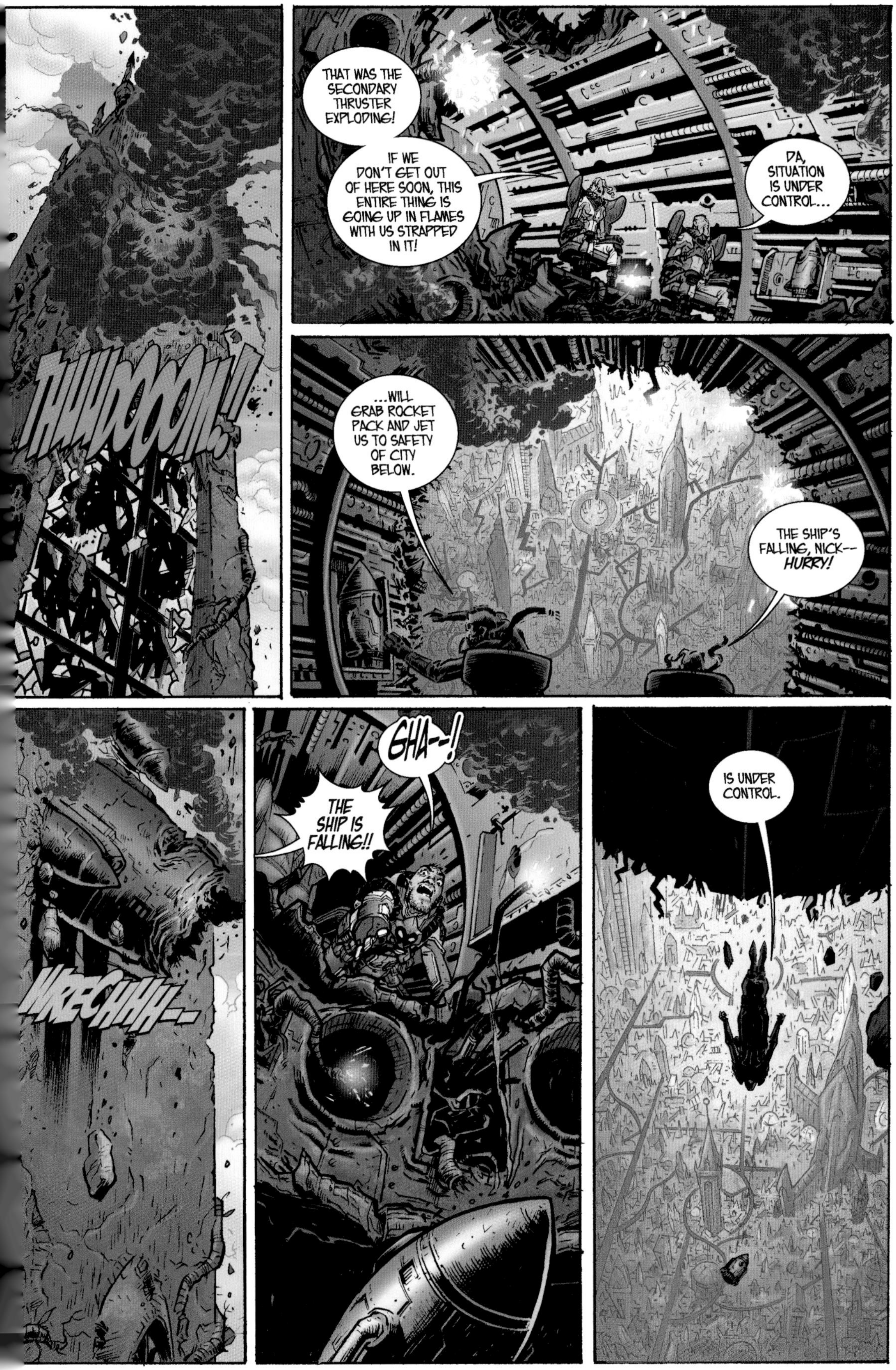
THUDOOOM!!
THAT WAS THE SECONDARY THRUSTER EXPLODING!
IF WE DON'T GET OUT OF HERE SOON, THIS ENTIRE THING IS GOING UP IN FLAMES WITH US STRAPPED IN IT!
DA, SITUATION IS UNDER CONTROL...
...WILL GRAB ROCKET PACK AND JET US TO SAFETY OF CITY BELOW.
THE SHIP'S FALLING, NICK-- HURRY!
KRE-CHHH--
GHA--!
THE SHIP IS FALLING!!
IS UNDER CONTROL.

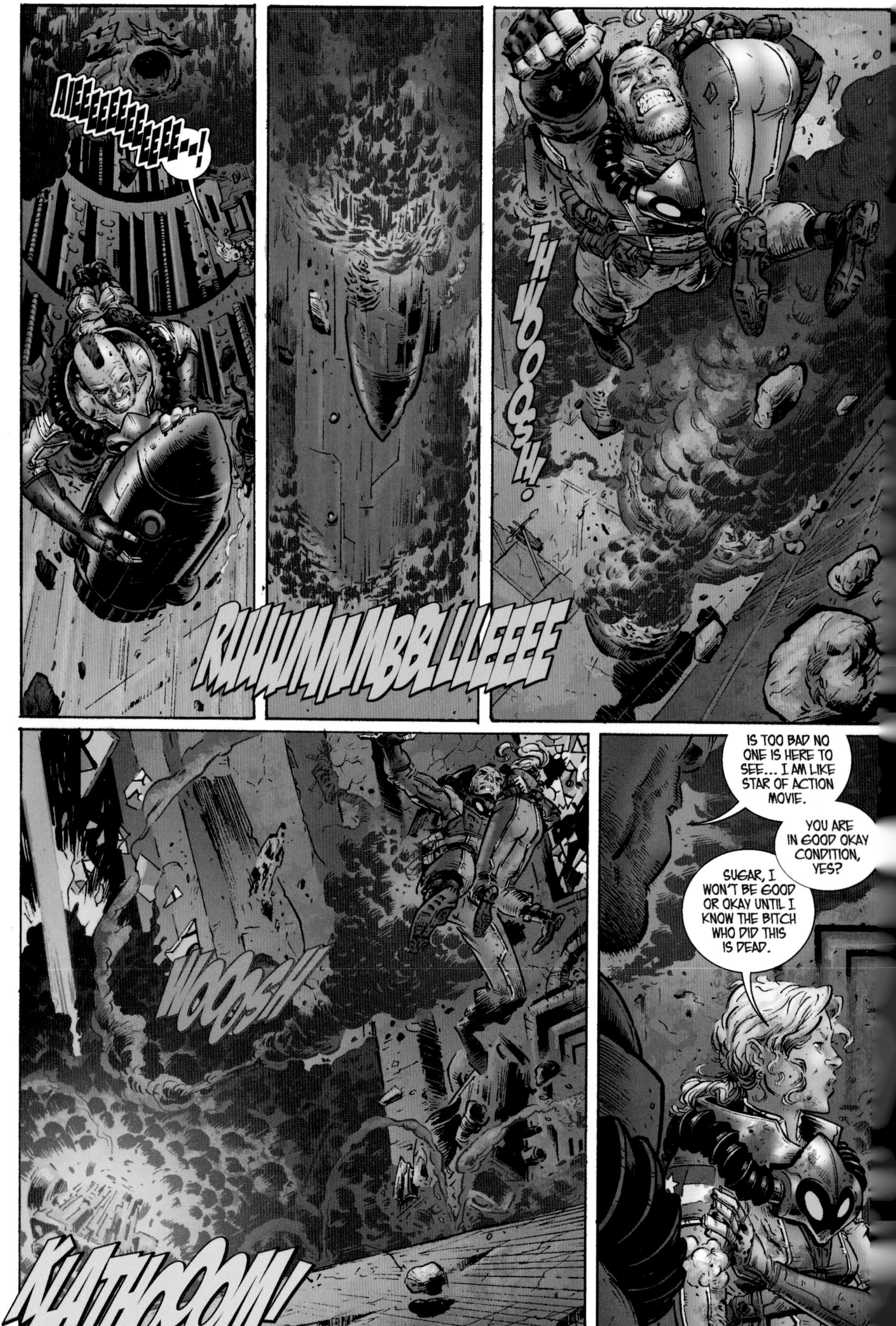
AIEEEEEEEEEEEEE--!
RUUUMMMBBLLLEEEE
THWOOOOSH!
WOOOSH
KLATHOOOM!
IS TOO BAD NO ONE IS HERE TO SEE... I AM LIKE STAR OF ACTION MOVIE.
YOU ARE IN GOOD OKAY CONDITION, YES?
SUGAR, I WON'T BE GOOD OR OKAY UNTIL I KNOW THE BITCH WHO DID THIS IS DEAD.

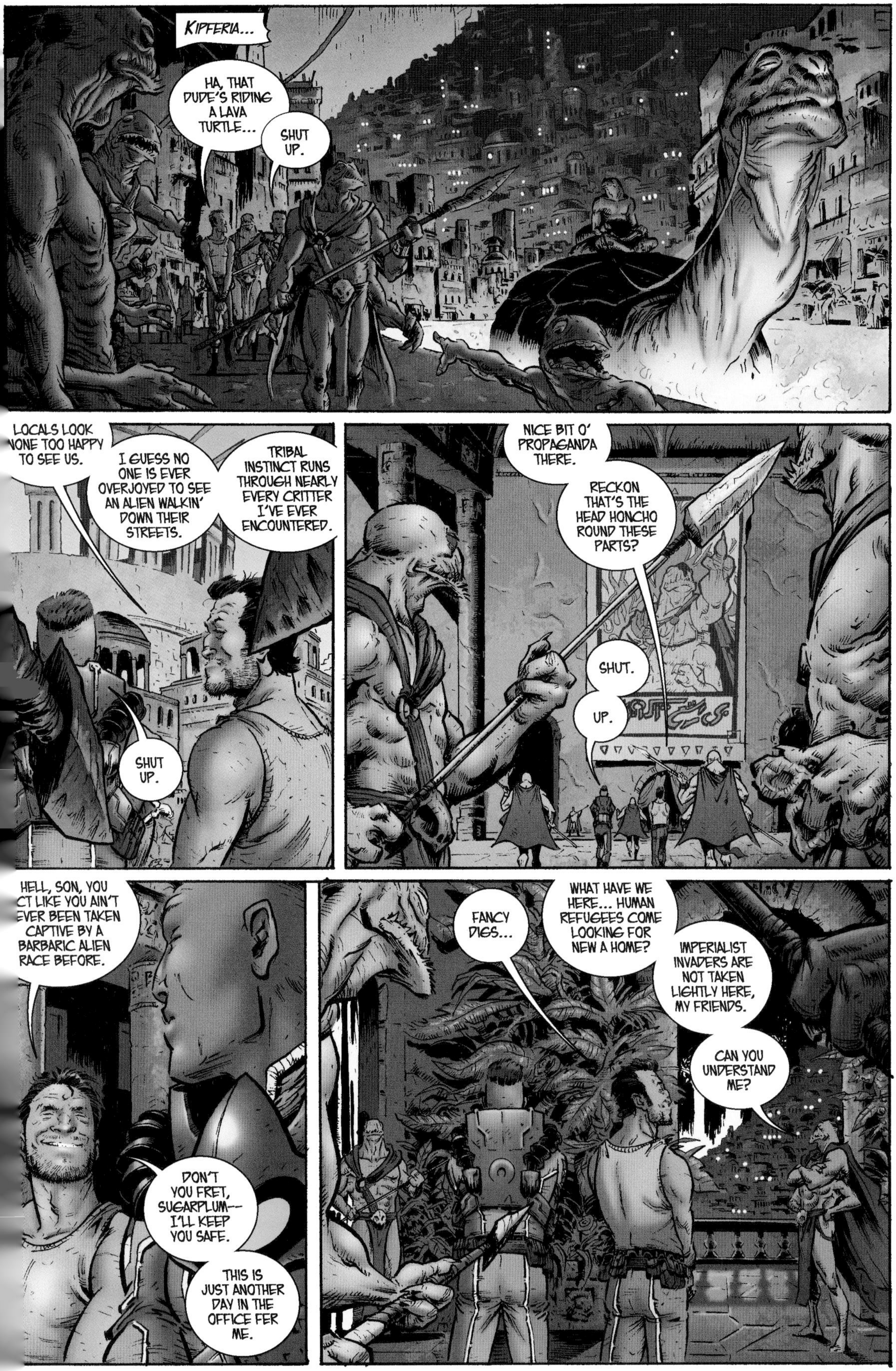
KIPFERIA...
HA, THAT DUDE'S RIDING A LAVA TURTLE...
SHUT UP.
LOCALS LOOK NONE TOO HAPPY TO SEE US.
I GUESS NO ONE IS EVER OVERJOYED TO SEE AN ALIEN WALKIN' DOWN THEIR STREETS.
TRIBAL INSTINCT RUNS THROUGH NEARLY EVERY CRITTER I'VE EVER ENCOUNTERED.
SHUT UP.
NICE BIT O' PROPAGANDA THERE.
RECKON THAT'S THE HEAD HONCHO ROUND THESE PARTS?
SHUT.
UP.
HELL, SON, YOU ACT LIKE YOU AIN'T EVER BEEN TAKEN CAPTIVE BY A BARBARIC ALIEN RACE BEFORE.
DON'T YOU FRET, SUGARPLUM-- I'LL KEEP YOU SAFE.
THIS IS JUST ANOTHER DAY IN THE OFFICE FER ME.
FANCY DIGS...
WHAT HAVE WE HERE... HUMAN REFUGEES COME LOOKING FOR NEW A HOME?
IMPERIALIST INVADERS ARE NOT TAKEN LIGHTLY HERE, MY FRIENDS.
CAN YOU UNDERSTAND ME?

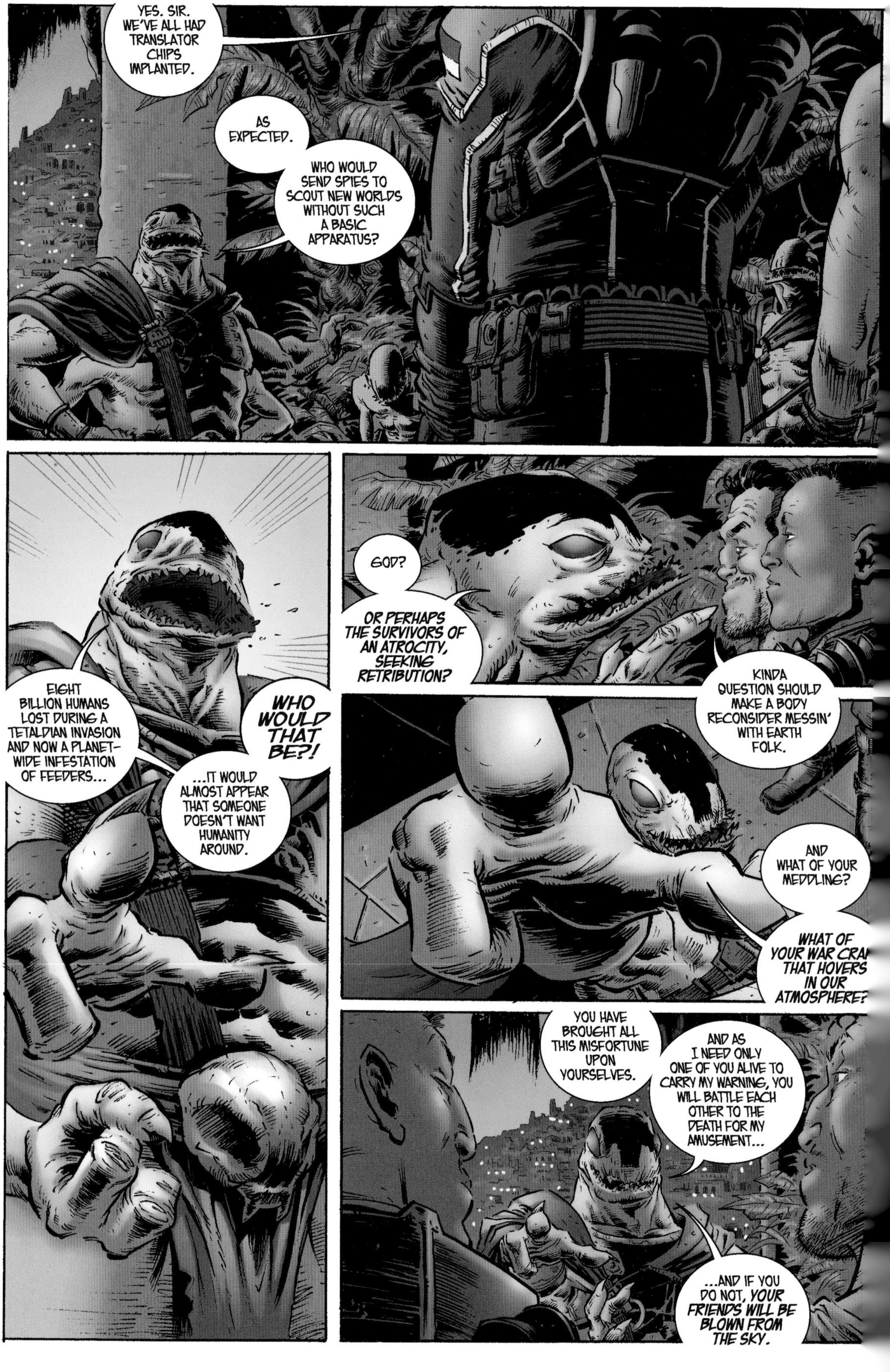
YES. SIR. WE'VE ALL HAD TRANSLATOR CHIPS IMPLANTED.
AS EXPECTED.
WHO WOULD SEND SPIES TO SCOUT NEW WORLDS WITHOUT SUCH A BASIC APPARATUS?
EIGHT BILLION HUMANS LOST DURING A TETALDIAN INVASION AND NOW A PLANET-WIDE INFESTATION OF FEEDERS...
...IT WOULD ALMOST APPEAR THAT SOMEONE DOESN'T WANT HUMANITY AROUND.
WHO WOULD THAT BE?!
GOD?
OR PERHAPS THE SURVIVORS OF AN ATROCITY, SEEKING RETRIBUTION?
KINDA QUESTION SHOULD MAKE A BODY RECONSIDER MESSIN' WITH EARTH FOLK.
AND WHAT OF YOUR MEDDLING?
WHAT OF YOUR WAR CRA THAT HOVERS IN OUR ATMOSPHERE?
YOU HAVE BROUGHT ALL THIS MISFORTUNE UPON YOURSELVES.
AND AS I NEED ONLY ONE OF YOU ALIVE TO CARRY MY WARNING, YOU WILL BATTLE EACH OTHER TO THE DEATH FOR MY AMUSEMENT...
...AND IF YOU DO NOT, YOUR FRIENDS WILL BE BLOWN FROM THE SKY.

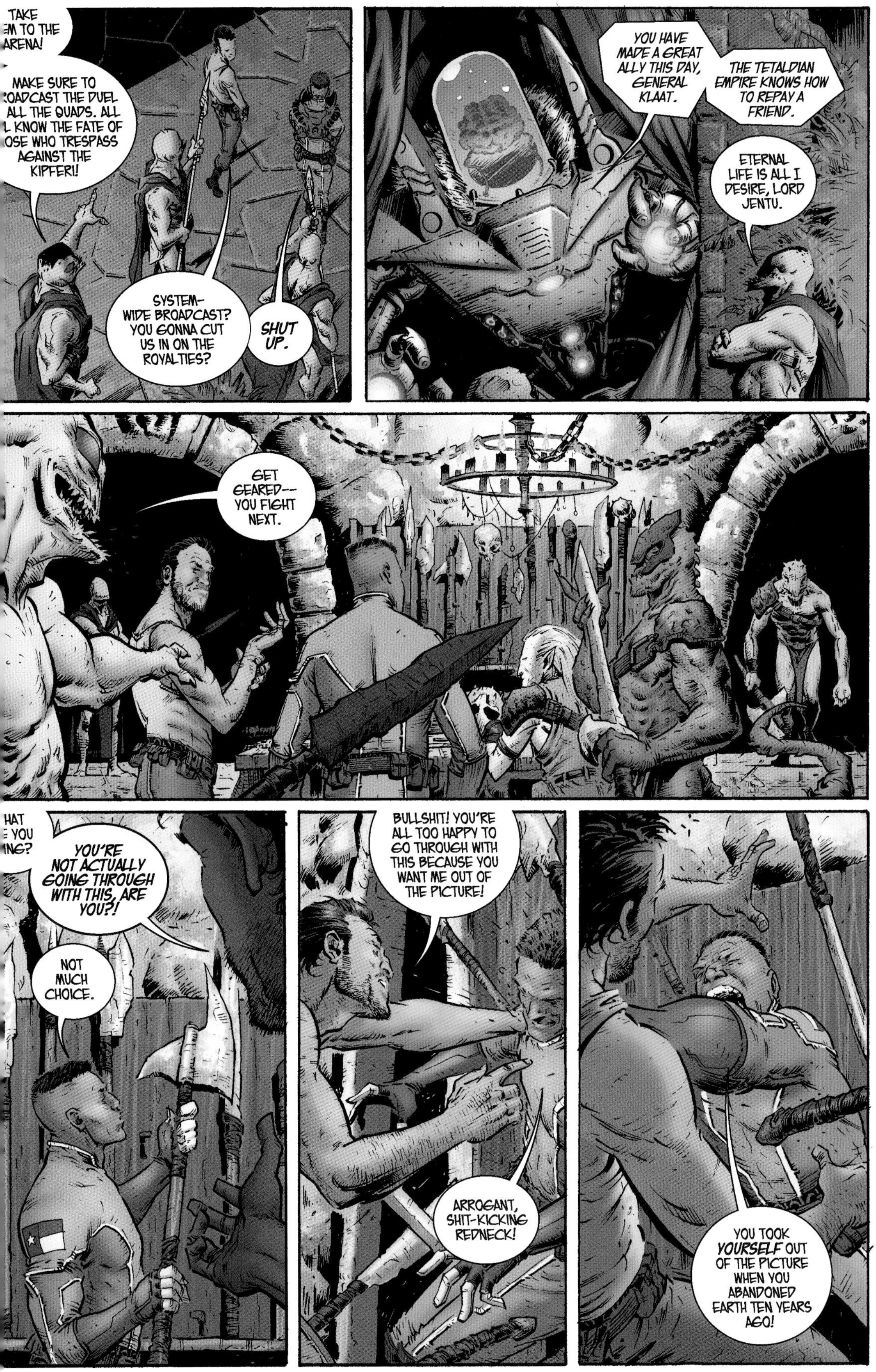
TAKE ...EM TO THE ARENA!
MAKE SURE TO ...OADCAST THE DUEL ... ALL THE QUADS. ALL ...L KNOW THE FATE OF ...OSE WHO TRESPASS AGAINST THE KIPFERI!
SYSTEM-WIDE BROADCAST? YOU GONNA CUT US IN ON THE ROYALTIES?
SHUT UP.
YOU HAVE MADE A GREAT ALLY THIS DAY, GENERAL KLAAT.
THE TETALDIAN EMPIRE KNOWS HOW TO REPAY A FRIEND.
ETERNAL LIFE IS ALL I DESIRE, LORD JENTU.
GET GEARED-- YOU FIGHT NEXT.
...HAT ...E YOU ...NG?
YOU'RE NOT ACTUALLY GOING THROUGH WITH THIS, ARE YOU?!
NOT MUCH CHOICE.
BULLSHIT! YOU'RE ALL TOO HAPPY TO GO THROUGH WITH THIS BECAUSE YOU WANT ME OUT OF THE PICTURE!
ARROGANT, SHIT-KICKING REDNECK!
YOU TOOK YOURSELF OUT OF THE PICTURE WHEN YOU ABANDONED EARTH TEN YEARS AGO!

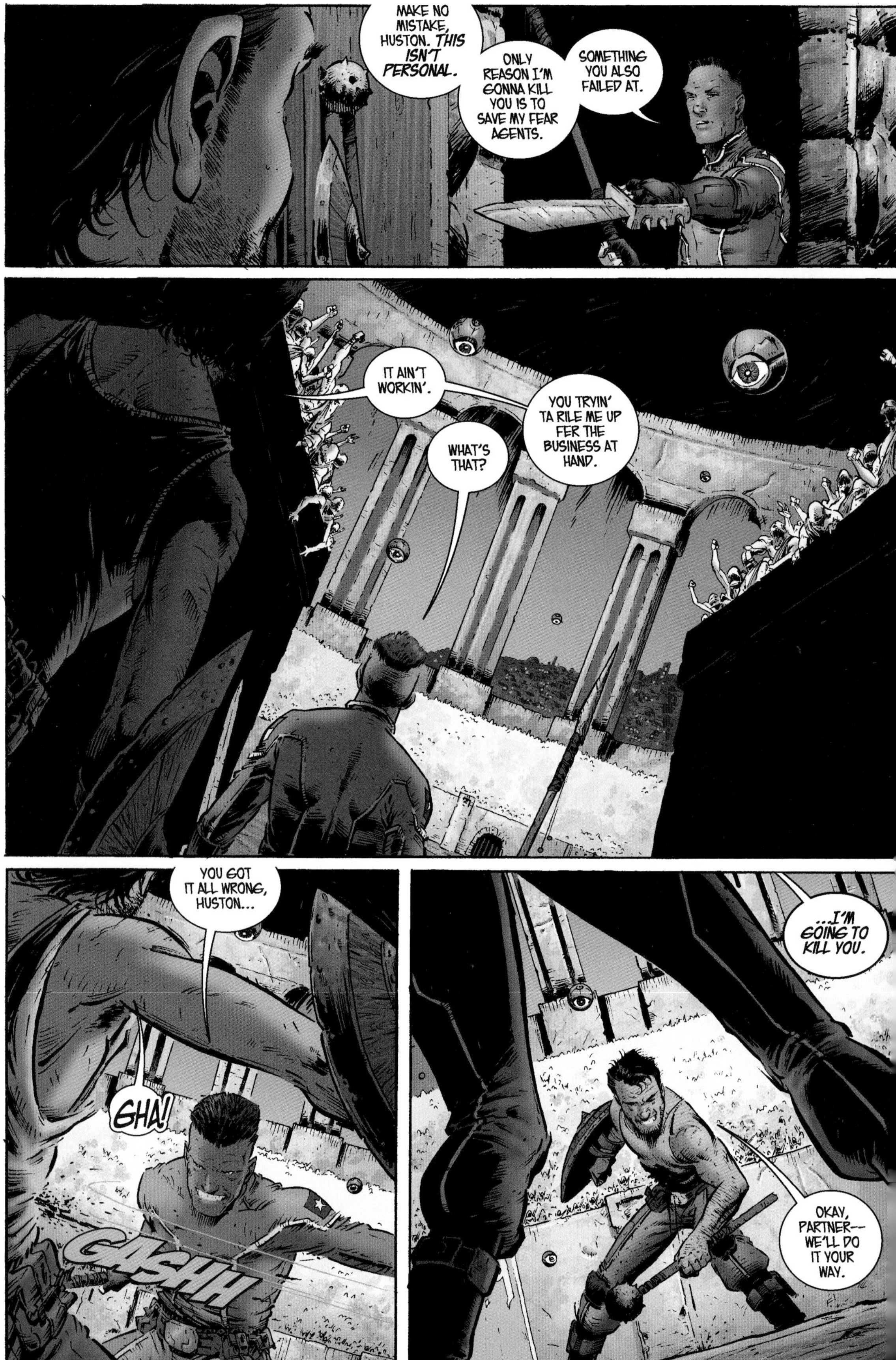
MAKE NO MISTAKE, HUSTON. *THIS ISN'T PERSONAL.*
ONLY REASON I'M GONNA KILL YOU IS TO SAVE MY FEAR AGENTS.
SOMETHING YOU ALSO FAILED AT.
IT AIN'T WORKIN'.
WHAT'S THAT?
YOU TRYIN' TA RILE ME UP FER THE BUSINESS AT HAND.
YOU GOT IT ALL WRONG, HUSTON...
GHA!
GASHH
...*I'M GOING TO KILL YOU.*
OKAY, PARTNER-- WE'LL DO IT YOUR WAY.

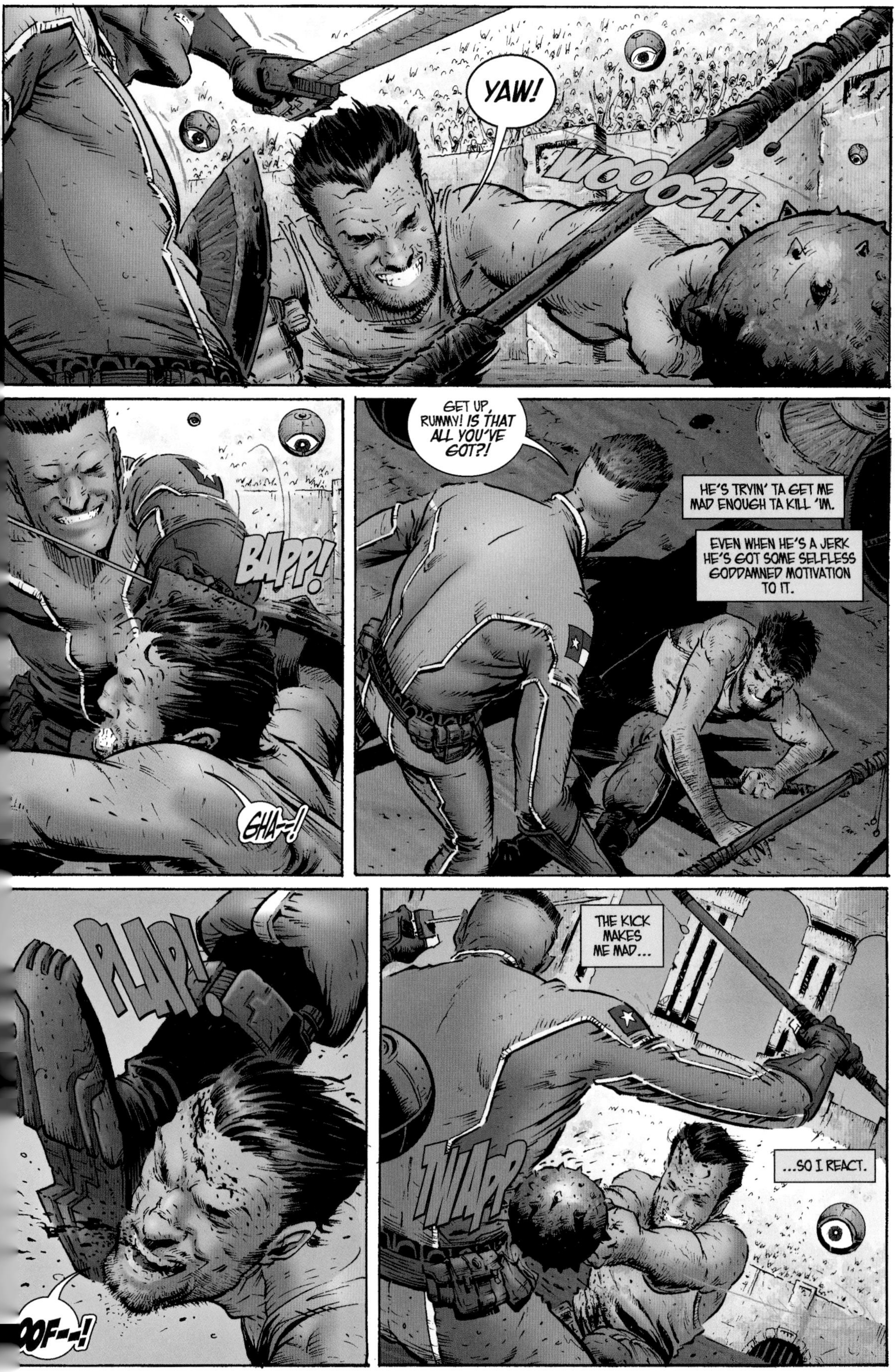
YAW!
WOOOSH
BAPP!
GHA--!
GET UP, RUMMY! IS THAT ALL YOU'VE GOT?!
HE'S TRYIN' TA GET ME MAD ENOUGH TA KILL 'IM.
EVEN WHEN HE'S A JERK HE'S GOT SOME SELFLESS GODDAMNED MOTIVATION TO IT.
PLAP!
OOF--!
THE KICK MAKES ME MAD...
TWAPP
...SO I REACT.

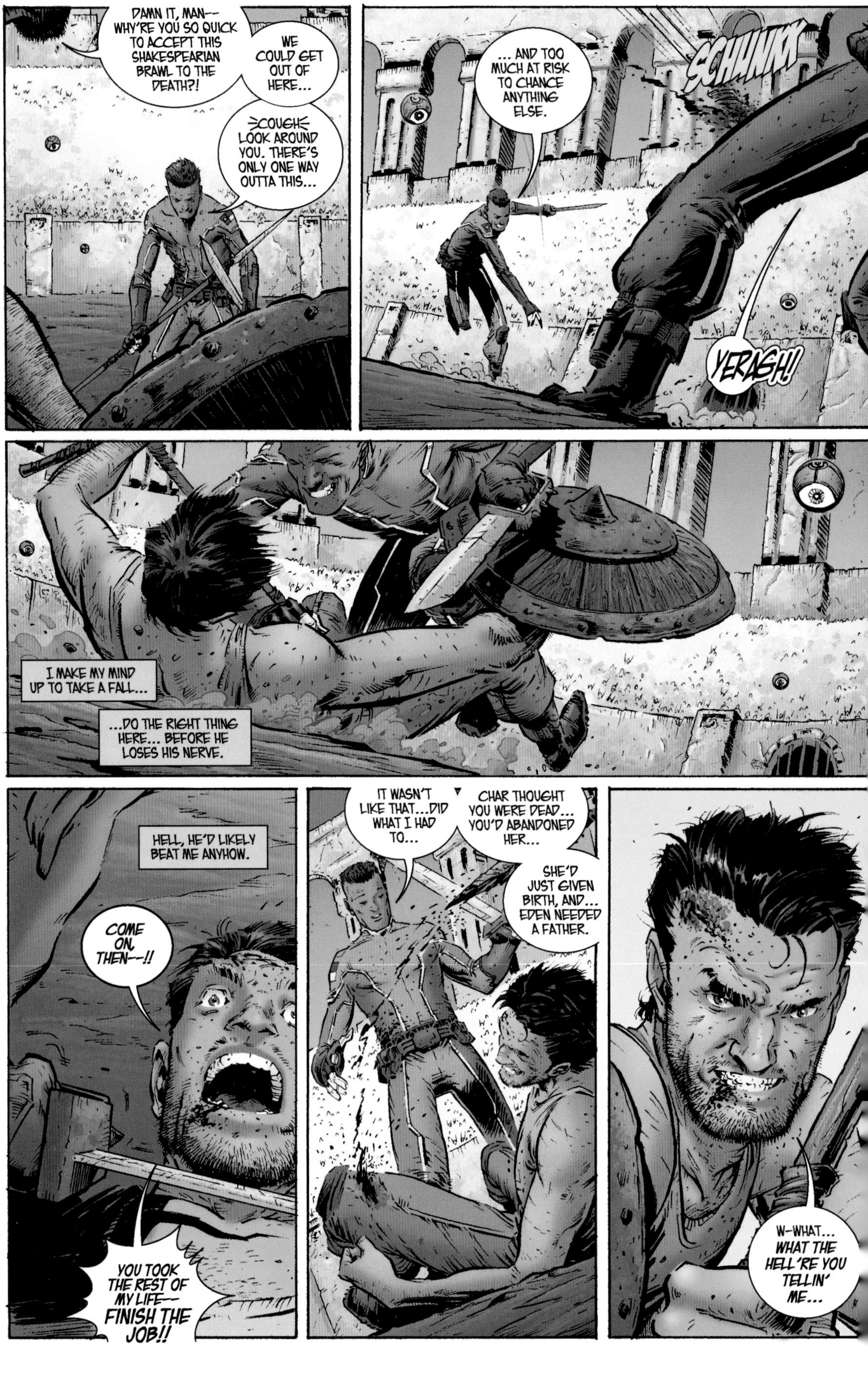
DAMN IT, MAN-- WHY'RE YOU SO QUICK TO ACCEPT THIS SHAKESPEARIAN BRAWL TO THE DEATH?!
WE COULD GET OUT OF HERE...
=COUGH= LOOK AROUND YOU. THERE'S ONLY ONE WAY OUTTA THIS...
...AND TOO MUCH AT RISK TO CHANCE ANYTHING ELSE.
SCHUNKK
YERASH!
I MAKE MY MIND UP TO TAKE A FALL...
...DO THE RIGHT THING HERE... BEFORE HE LOSES HIS NERVE.
HELL, HE'D LIKELY BEAT ME ANYHOW.
COME ON, THEN--!!
YOU TOOK THE REST OF MY LIFE-- FINISH THE JOB!!
IT WASN'T LIKE THAT...DID WHAT I HAD TO...
CHAR THOUGHT YOU WERE DEAD... YOU'D ABANDONED HER...
SHE'D JUST GIVEN BIRTH, AND... EDEN NEEDED A FATHER.
W-WHAT... WHAT THE HELL'RE YOU TELLIN' ME...

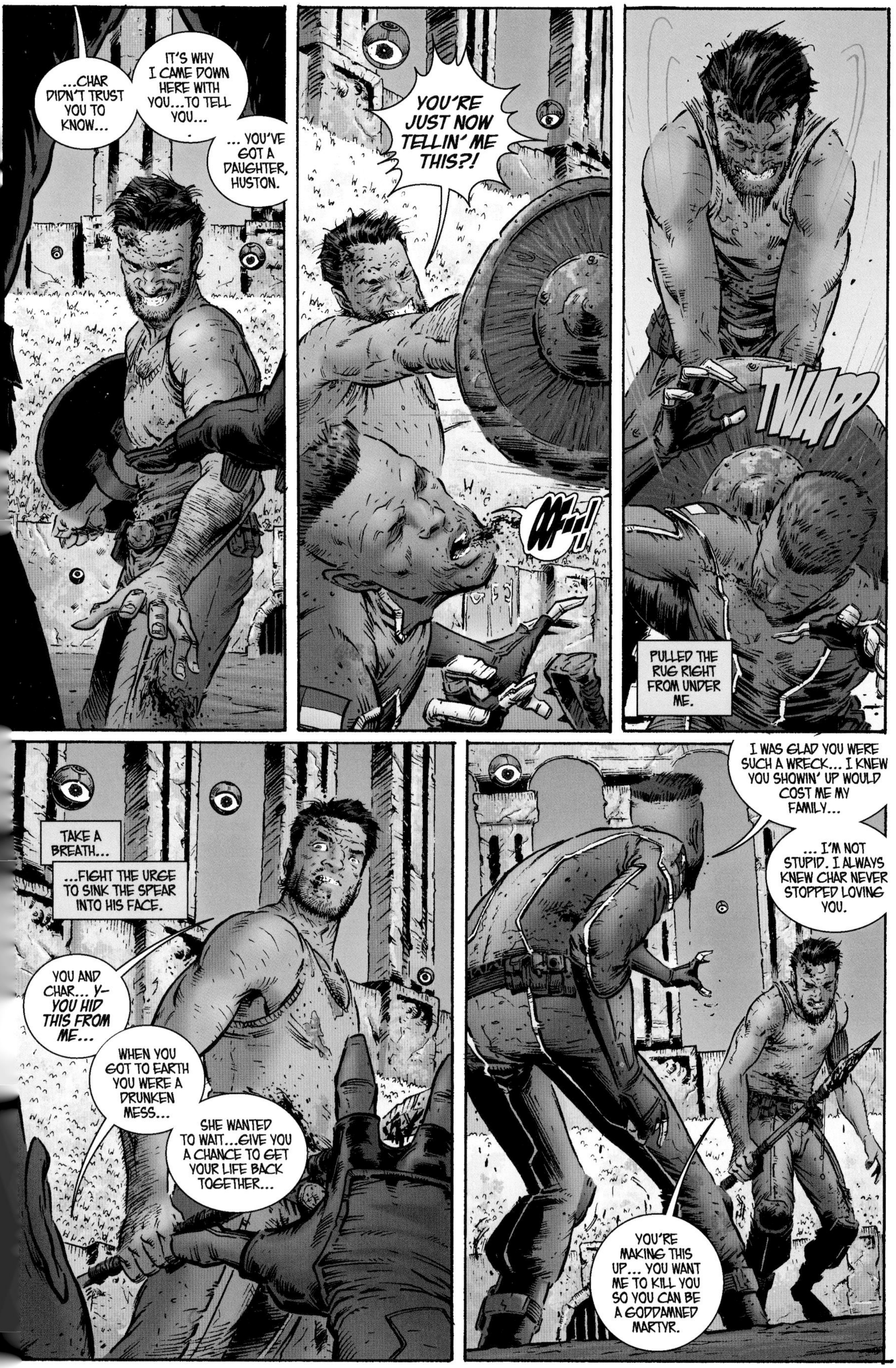
...CHAR DIDN'T TRUST YOU TO KNOW...
IT'S WHY I CAME DOWN HERE WITH YOU...TO TELL YOU...
... YOU'VE GOT A DAUGHTER, HUSTON.
YOU'RE JUST NOW TELLIN' ME THIS?!
OOF
TWAPP
PULLED THE RUG RIGHT FROM UNDER ME.
TAKE A BREATH...
...FIGHT THE URGE TO SINK THE SPEAR INTO HIS FACE.
YOU AND CHAR... Y-YOU HID THIS FROM ME...
WHEN YOU GOT TO EARTH YOU WERE A DRUNKEN MESS...
SHE WANTED TO WAIT...GIVE YOU A CHANCE TO GET YOUR LIFE BACK TOGETHER...
I WAS GLAD YOU WERE SUCH A WRECK... I KNEW YOU SHOWIN' UP WOULD COST ME MY FAMILY...
... I'M NOT STUPID. I ALWAYS KNEW CHAR NEVER STOPPED LOVING YOU.
YOU'RE MAKING THIS UP... YOU WANT ME TO KILL YOU SO YOU CAN BE A GODDAMNED MARTYR.

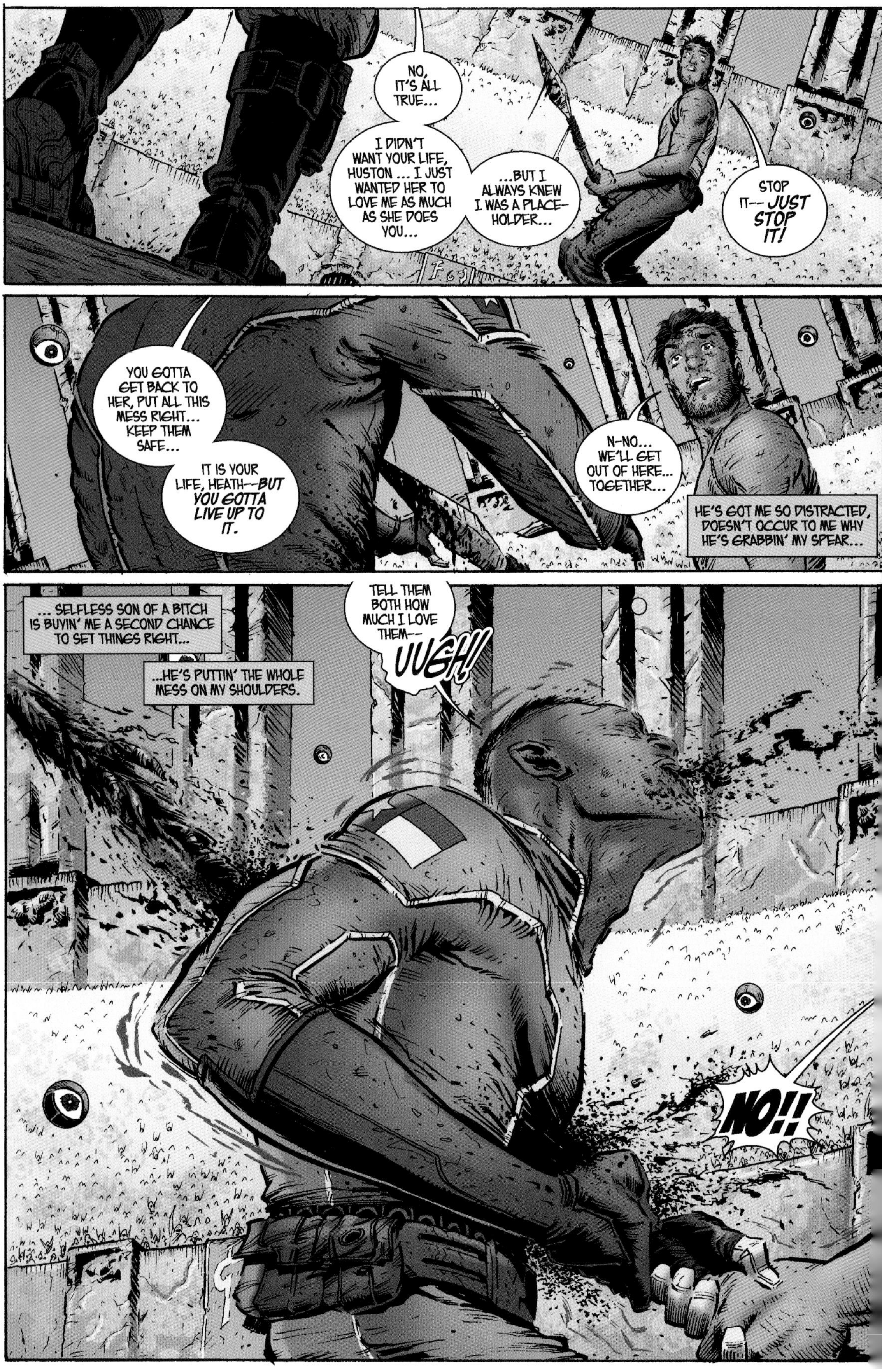
NO, IT'S ALL TRUE...
I DIDN'T WANT YOUR LIFE, HUSTON ... I JUST WANTED HER TO LOVE ME AS MUCH AS SHE DOES YOU...
...BUT I ALWAYS KNEW I WAS A PLACE-HOLDER...
STOP IT-- JUST STOP IT!
YOU GOTTA GET BACK TO HER, PUT ALL THIS MESS RIGHT... KEEP THEM SAFE...
IT IS YOUR LIFE, HEATH--BUT YOU GOTTA LIVE UP TO IT.
N-NO... WE'LL GET OUT OF HERE... TOGETHER...
HE'S GOT ME SO DISTRACTED, DOESN'T OCCUR TO ME WHY HE'S GRABBIN' MY SPEAR...
... SELFLESS SON OF A BITCH IS BUYIN' ME A SECOND CHANCE TO SET THINGS RIGHT...
TELL THEM BOTH HOW MUCH I LOVE THEM--
UUGH!
...HE'S PUTTIN' THE WHOLE MESS ON MY SHOULDERS.
NO!!

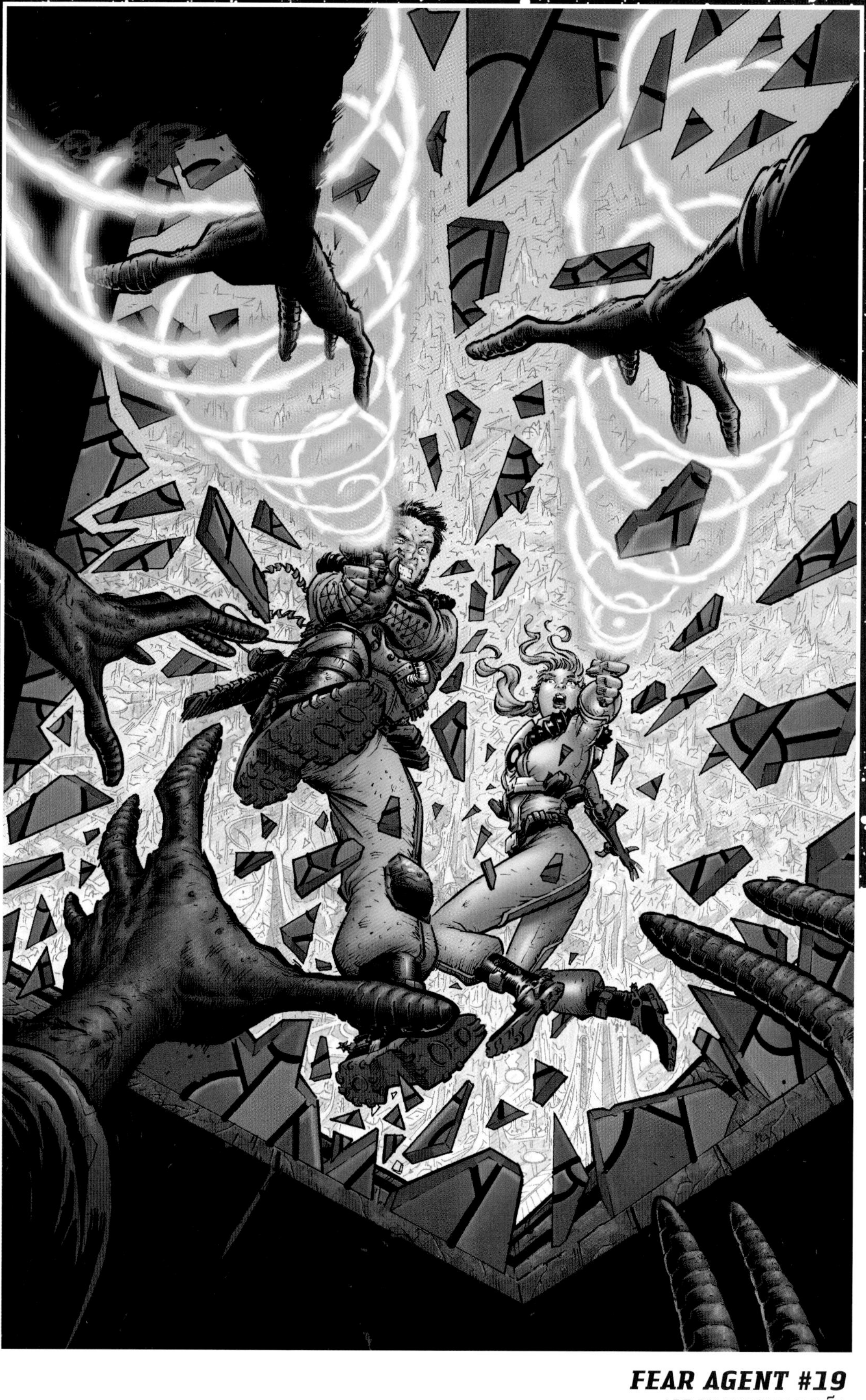

FEAR AGENT #19
ART BY JEROME OPEÑA

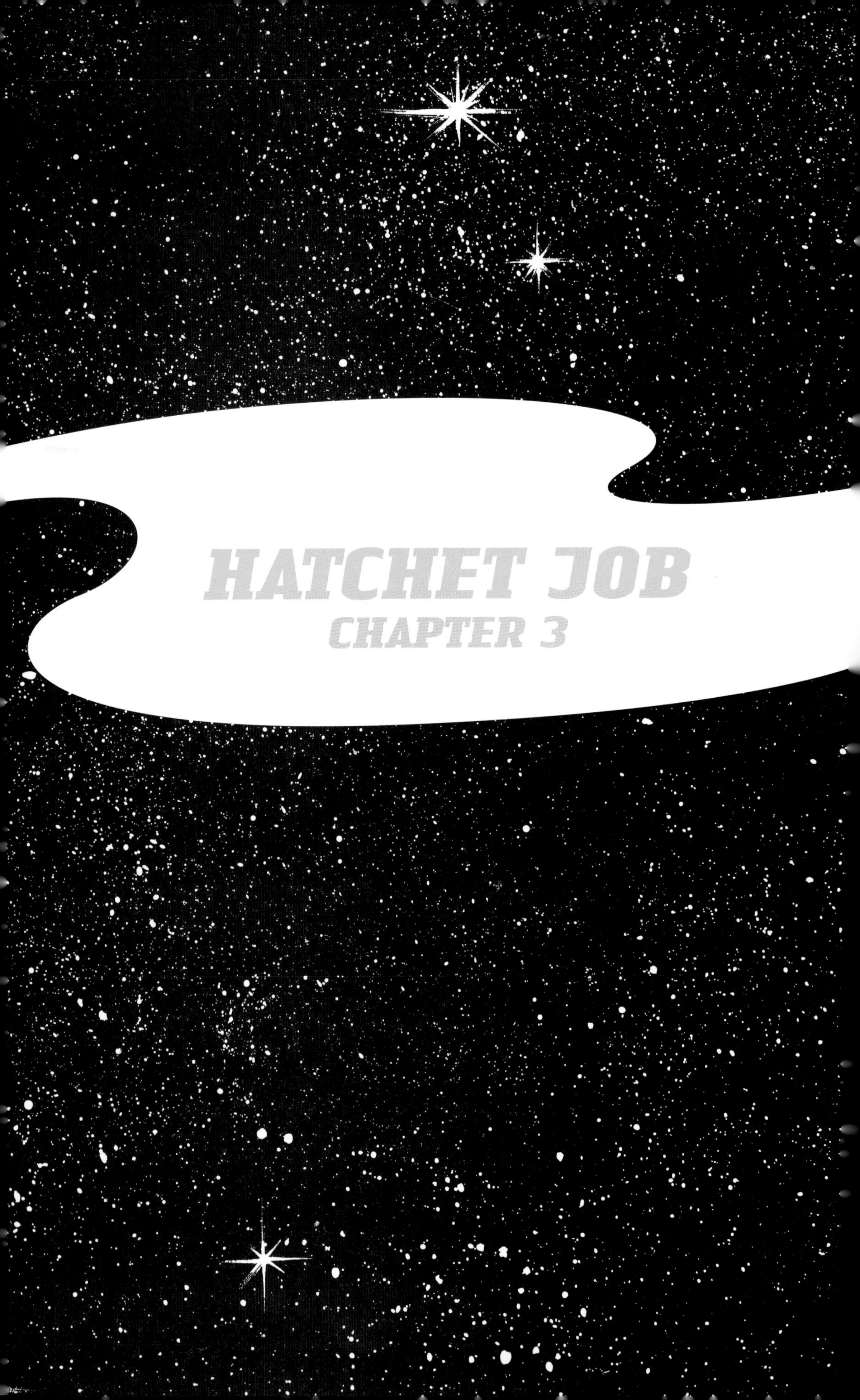
HATCHET JOB
CHAPTER 3

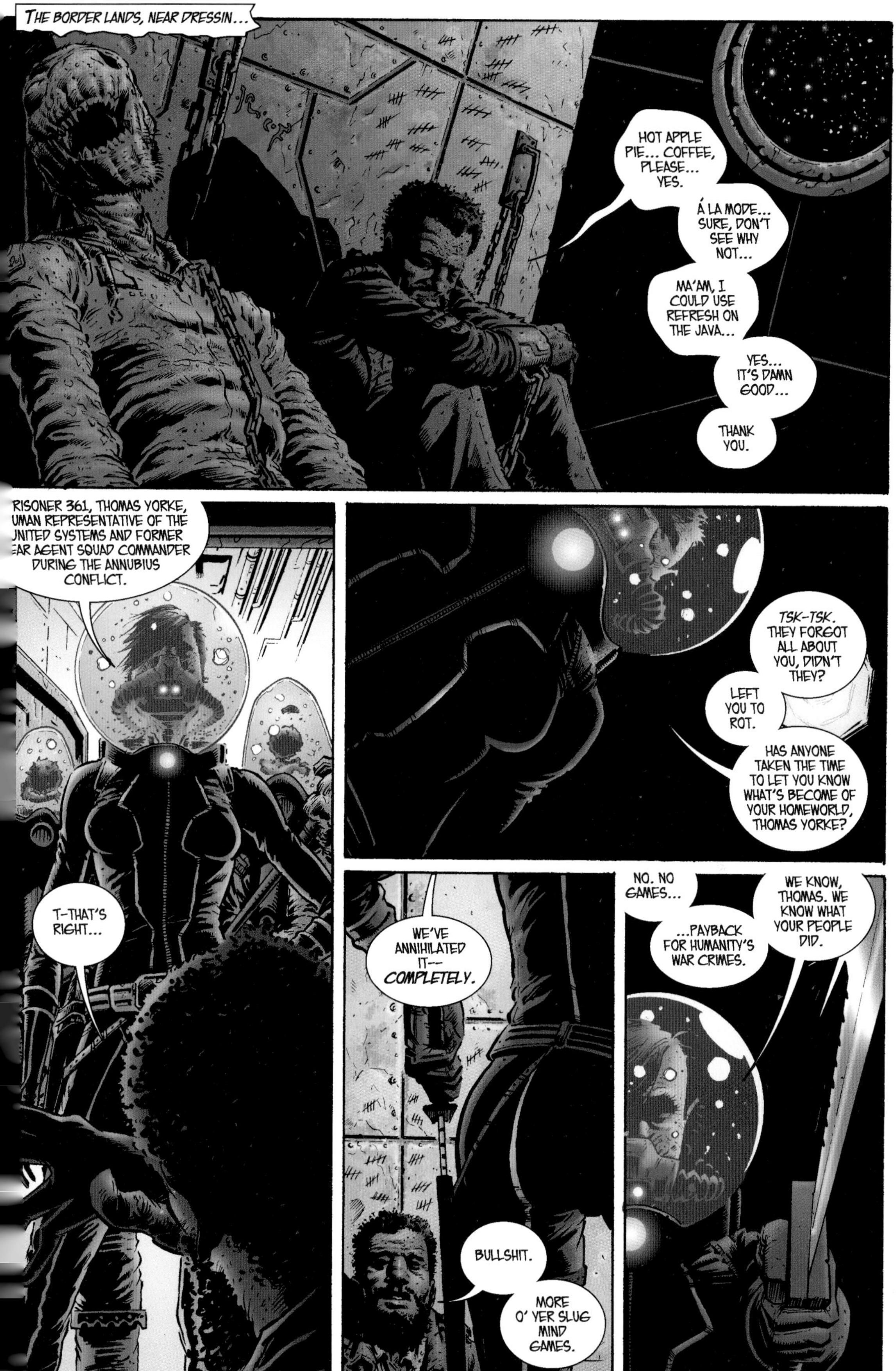
THE BORDER LANDS, NEAR DRESSIN...
HOT APPLE PIE... COFFEE, PLEASE... YES.
Á LA MODE... SURE, DON'T SEE WHY NOT...
MA'AM, I COULD USE REFRESH ON THE JAVA...
YES... IT'S DAMN GOOD...
THANK YOU.
RISONER 361, THOMAS YORKE, UMAN REPRESENTATIVE OF THE UNITED SYSTEMS AND FORMER EAR AGENT SQUAD COMMANDER DURING THE ANNUBIUS CONFLICT.
T-THAT'S RIGHT...
TSK-TSK. THEY FORGOT ALL ABOUT YOU, DIDN'T THEY?
LEFT YOU TO ROT.
HAS ANYONE TAKEN THE TIME TO LET YOU KNOW WHAT'S BECOME OF YOUR HOMEWORLD, THOMAS YORKE?
WE'VE ANNIHILATED IT-- COMPLETELY.
BULLSHIT.
MORE O' YER SLUG MIND GAMES.
NO. NO GAMES...
...PAYBACK FOR HUMANITY'S WAR CRIMES.
WE KNOW, THOMAS. WE KNOW WHAT YOUR PEOPLE DID.

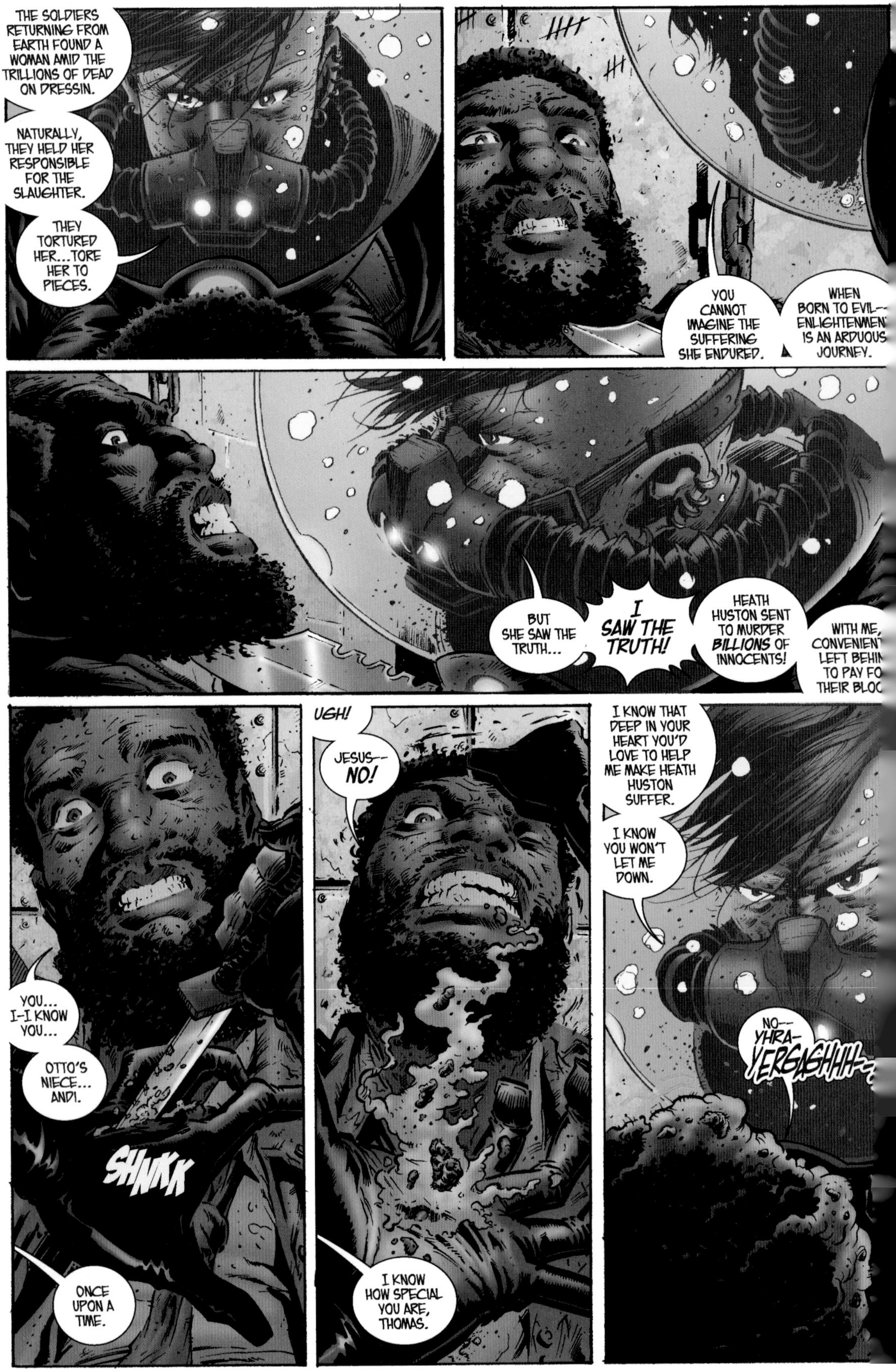
THE SOLDIERS RETURNING FROM EARTH FOUND A WOMAN AMID THE TRILLIONS OF DEAD ON DRESSIN.
NATURALLY, THEY HELD HER RESPONSIBLE FOR THE SLAUGHTER.
THEY TORTURED HER...TORE HER TO PIECES.
YOU CANNOT IMAGINE THE SUFFERING SHE ENDURED.
WHEN BORN TO EVIL-- ENLIGHTENMENT IS AN ARDUOUS JOURNEY.
BUT SHE SAW THE TRUTH...
I SAW THE TRUTH!
HEATH HUSTON SENT TO MURDER BILLIONS OF INNOCENTS!
WITH ME, CONVENIENT LEFT BEHIN TO PAY FOR THEIR BLOC
YOU... I-I KNOW YOU...
OTTO'S NIECE... ANDI.
SHNKK
ONCE UPON A TIME.
UGH!
JESUS-- NO!
I KNOW HOW SPECIAL YOU ARE, THOMAS.
I KNOW THAT DEEP IN YOUR HEART YOU'D LOVE TO HELP ME MAKE HEATH HUSTON SUFFER.
I KNOW YOU WON'T LET ME DOWN.
NO-- YHRA-YERGASHHH--

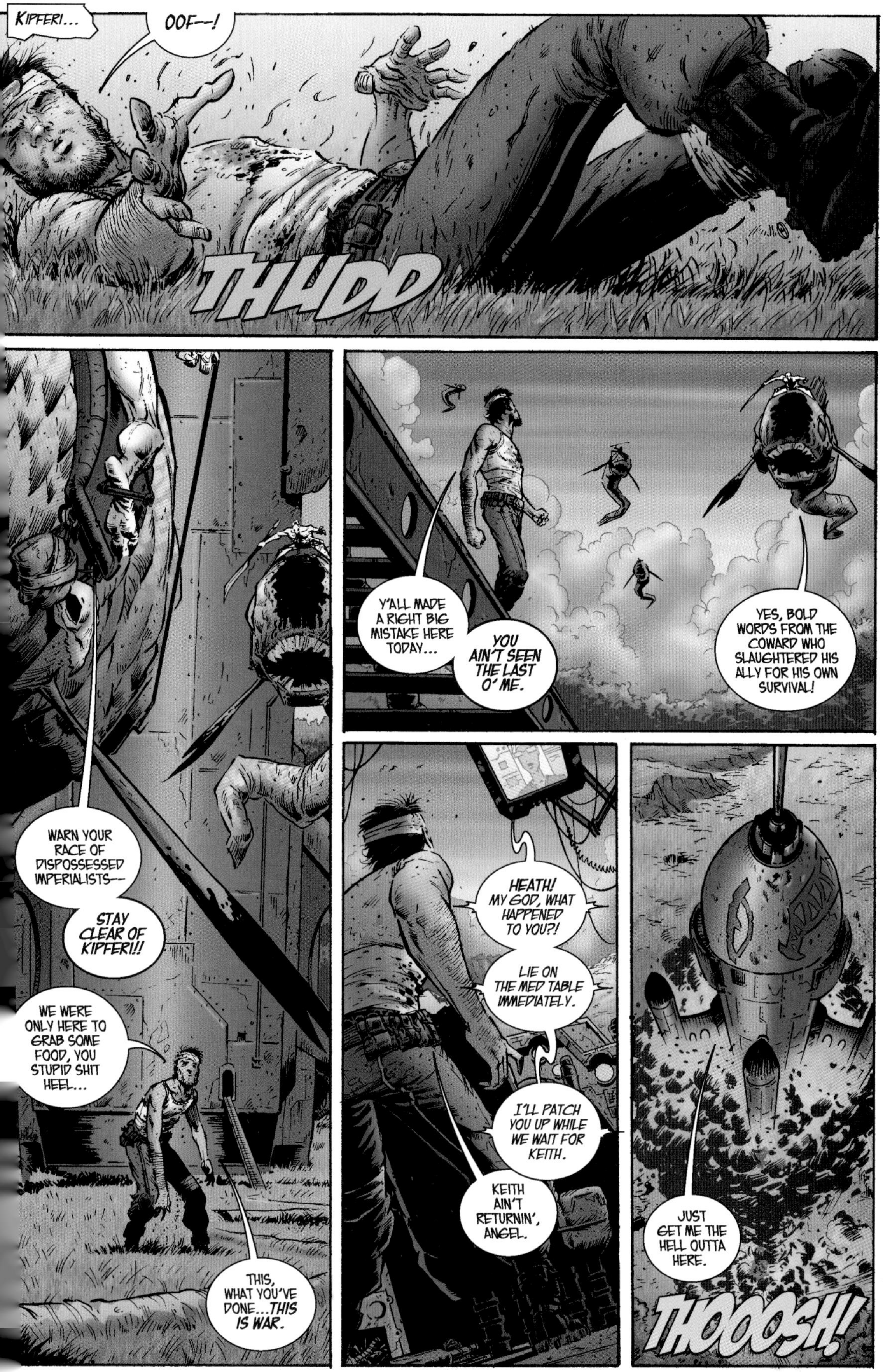
KIPFERI...
OOF--!
THUDD
WARN YOUR RACE OF DISPOSSESSED IMPERIALISTS--
STAY CLEAR OF KIPFERI!!
WE WERE ONLY HERE TO GRAB SOME FOOD, YOU STUPID SHIT HEEL...
THIS, WHAT YOU'VE DONE...THIS IS WAR.
Y'ALL MADE A RIGHT BIG MISTAKE HERE TODAY...
YOU AIN'T SEEN THE LAST O' ME.
YES, BOLD WORDS FROM THE COWARD WHO SLAUGHTERED HIS ALLY FOR HIS OWN SURVIVAL!
HEATH! MY GOD, WHAT HAPPENED TO YOU?!
LIE ON THE MED TABLE IMMEDIATELY.
I'LL PATCH YOU UP WHILE WE WAIT FOR KEITH.
KEITH AIN'T RETURNIN', ANGEL.
JUST GET ME THE HELL OUTTA HERE.
THOOOSH!

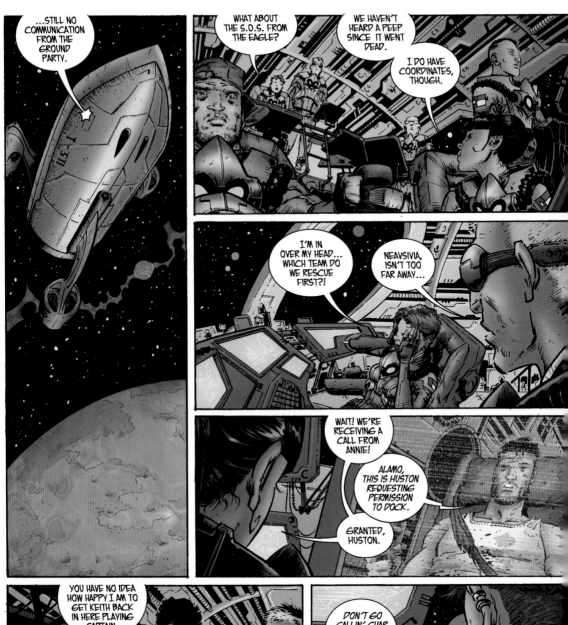

...STILL NO COMMUNICATION FROM THE GROUND PARTY.

WHAT ABOUT THE S.O.S. FROM THE EAGLE?

WE HAVEN'T HEARD A PEEP SINCE IT WENT DEAD.

I DO HAVE COORDINATES, THOUGH.

I'M IN OVER MY HEAD... WHICH TEAM DO WE RESCUE FIRST?!

NEAVSIVIA, ISN'T TOO FAR AWAY...

WAIT! WE'RE RECEIVING A CALL FROM ANNIE!

ALAMO, THIS IS HUSTON REQUESTING PERMISSION TO DOCK.

GRANTED, HUSTON.

YOU HAVE NO IDEA HOW HAPPY I AM TO GET KEITH BACK IN HERE PLAYING CAPTAIN.

YEAH, LISTEN... THINGS GOT UGLY DOWN THERE.

NATIVES THOUGHT WE WERE SCOUTS LOOKIN' TO LAY CLAIM...

KEITH'S DEAD, BETTY.

DON'T GO CALLIN' CHAR, I'LL TELL 'ER MYSELF.

HEATH, W— WE PICKED UP A DISTRESS SIGNAL FROM CHARLOTTE'S SHIP... IT——IT ABRUPTLY WENT DEAD.

THEY CRASHED THREE HOURS AGO.

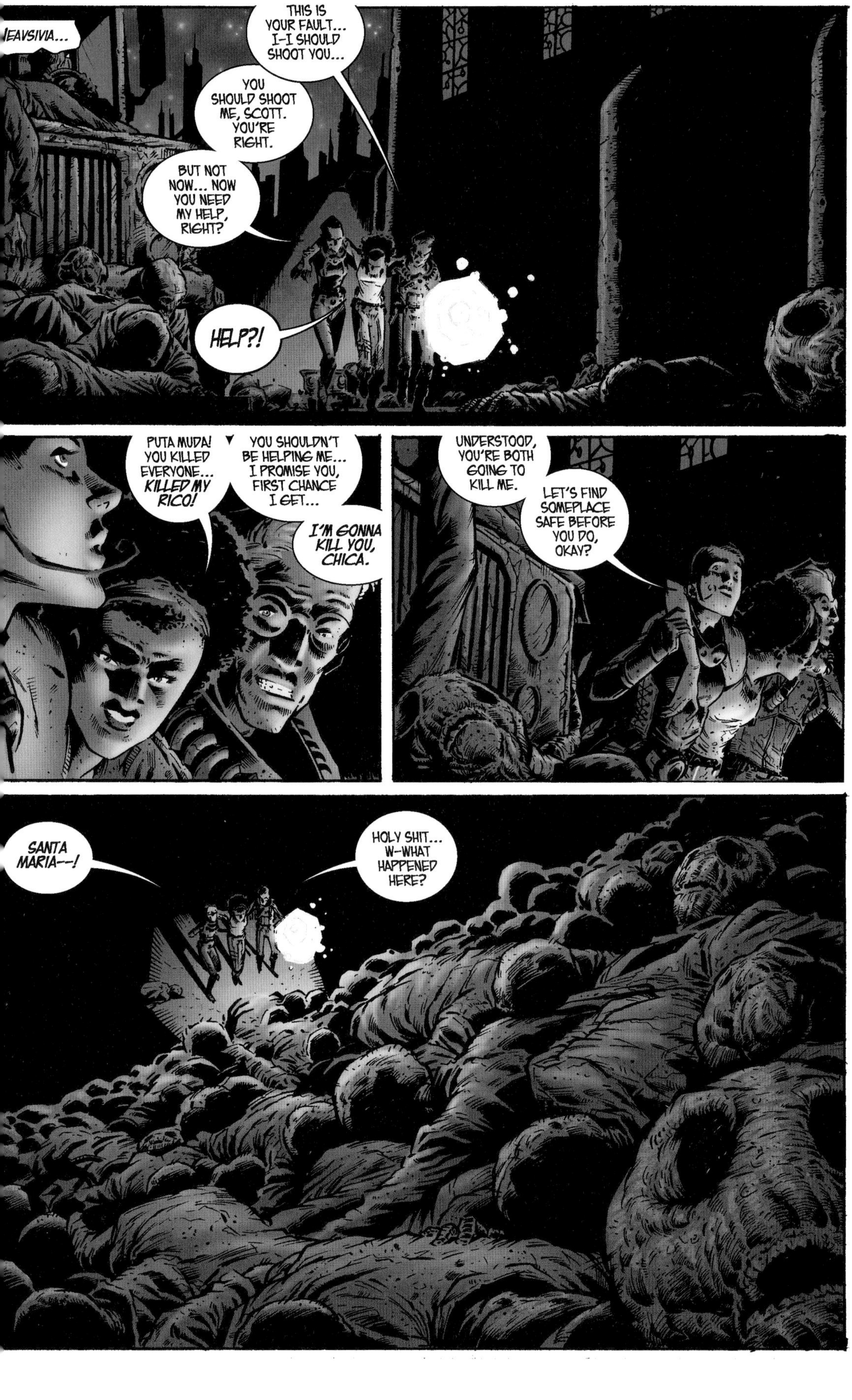

IEAVSIVIA...
THIS IS YOUR FAULT... I-I SHOULD SHOOT YOU...
YOU SHOULD SHOOT ME, SCOTT. YOU'RE RIGHT.
BUT NOT NOW... NOW YOU NEED MY HELP, RIGHT?
HELP?!
PUTA MUDA! YOU KILLED EVERYONE... KILLED MY RICO!
YOU SHOULDN'T BE HELPING ME... I PROMISE YOU, FIRST CHANCE I GET...
I'M GONNA KILL YOU, CHICA.
UNDERSTOOD, YOU'RE BOTH GOING TO KILL ME.
LET'S FIND SOMEPLACE SAFE BEFORE YOU DO, OKAY?
SANTA MARIA--!
HOLY SHIT... W-WHAT HAPPENED HERE?

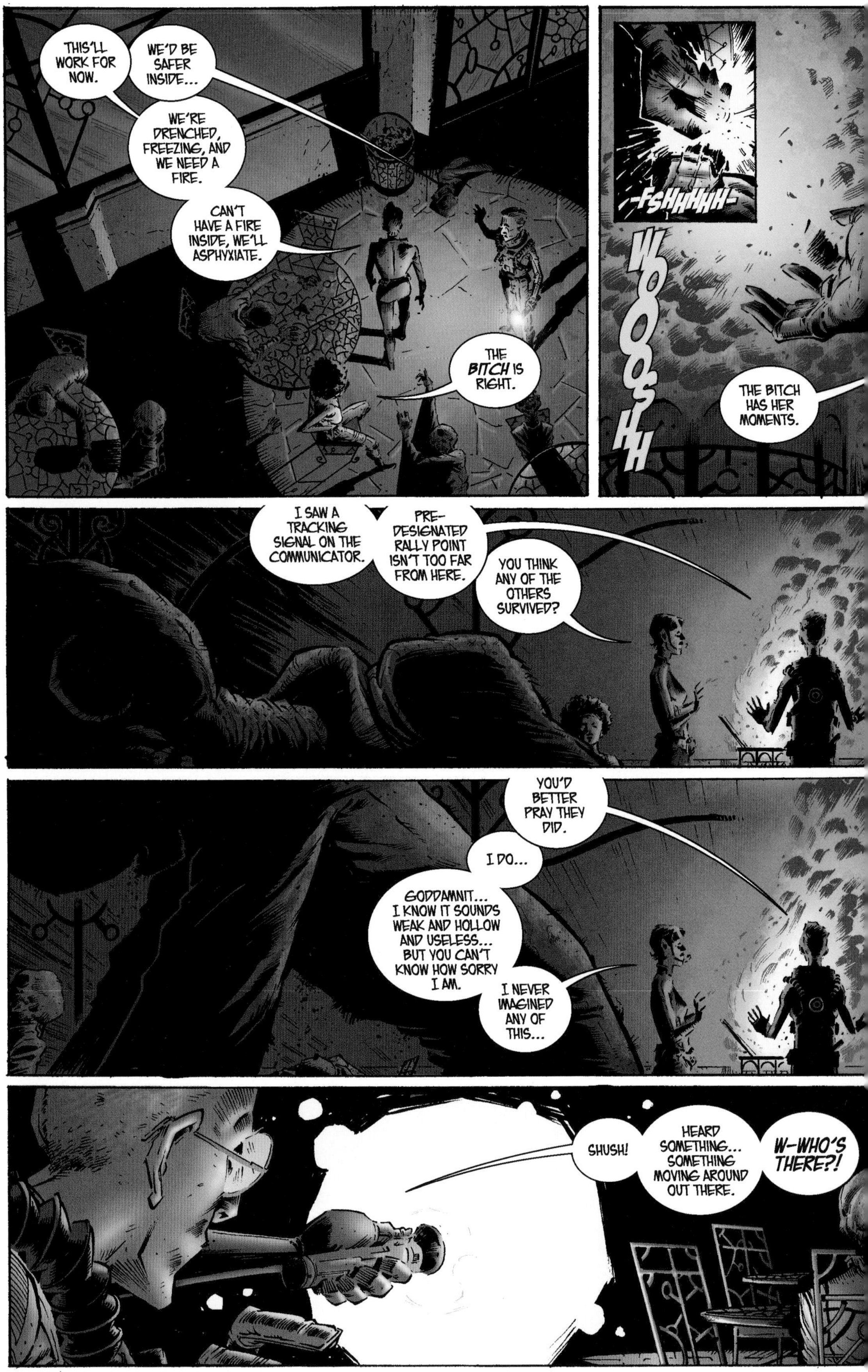
THIS'LL WORK FOR NOW.
WE'D BE SAFER INSIDE...
WE'RE DRENCHED, FREEZING, AND WE NEED A FIRE.
CAN'T HAVE A FIRE INSIDE, WE'LL ASPHYXIATE.
THE BITCH IS RIGHT.
-FSHHHHH-
WOOOOSHHH
THE BITCH HAS HER MOMENTS.
I SAW A TRACKING SIGNAL ON THE COMMUNICATOR.
PRE-DESIGNATED RALLY POINT ISN'T TOO FAR FROM HERE.
YOU THINK ANY OF THE OTHERS SURVIVED?
YOU'D BETTER PRAY THEY DID.
I DO...
GODDAMNIT... I KNOW IT SOUNDS WEAK AND HOLLOW AND USELESS... BUT YOU CAN'T KNOW HOW SORRY I AM.
I NEVER IMAGINED ANY OF THIS...
SHUSH!
HEARD SOMETHING... SOMETHING MOVING AROUND OUT THERE.
W-WHO'S THERE?!

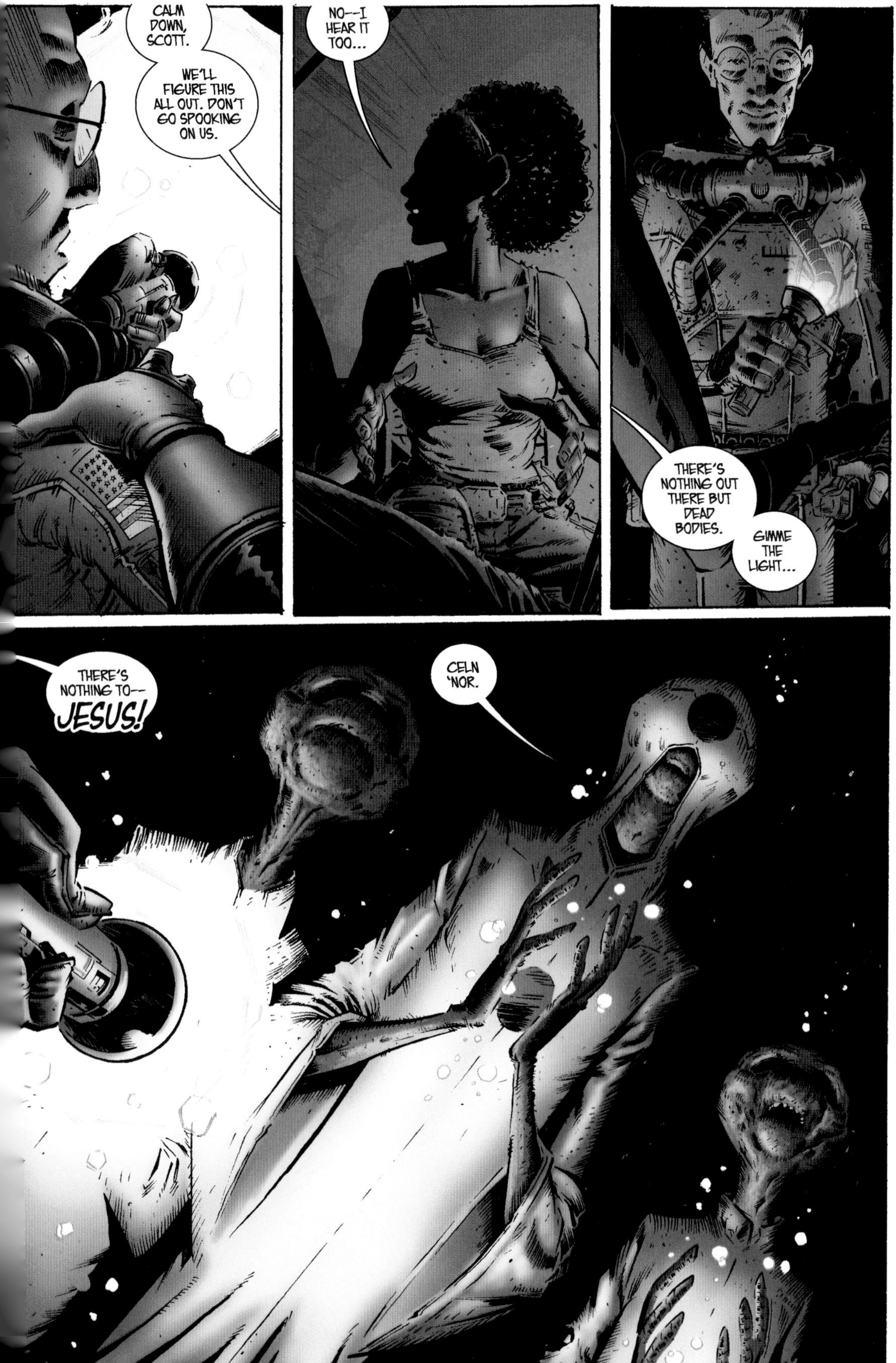
CALM DOWN, SCOTT.
WE'LL FIGURE THIS ALL OUT. DON'T GO SPOOKING ON US.
NO--I HEAR IT TOO...
THERE'S NOTHING OUT THERE BUT DEAD BODIES.
GIMME THE LIGHT...
THERE'S NOTHING TO-- JESUS!
CELN 'NOR.

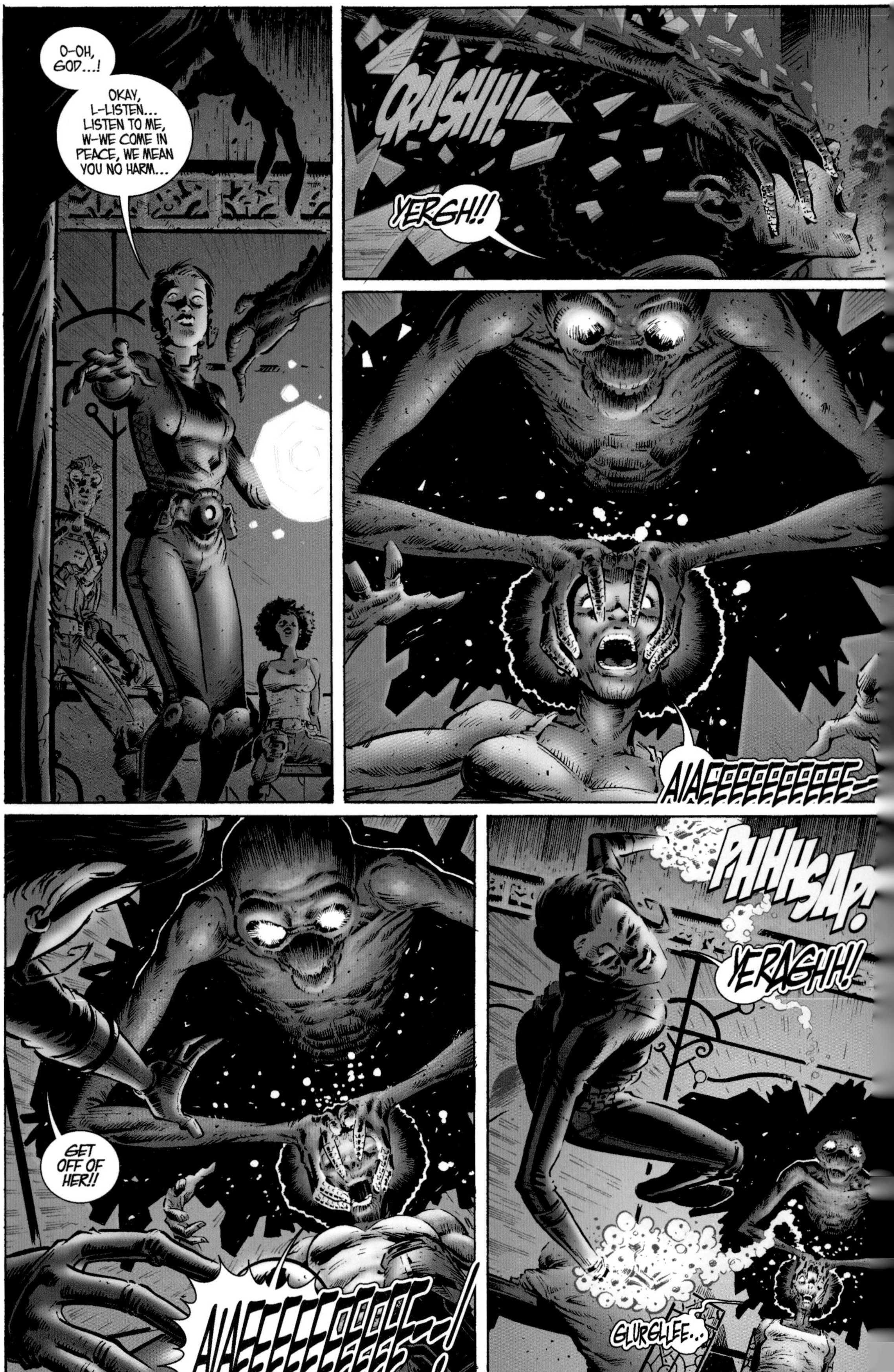
O-OH, GOD...!
OKAY, L-LISTEN... LISTEN TO ME, W-WE COME IN PEACE, WE MEAN YOU NO HARM...
CRASHH!
YERGH!!
AIAEEEEEEEEEEE—
GET OFF OF HER!!
AIAEEEEEEEEEEEEE...!
PHHHSAP!
YERAGHH!
GLURGLEE...

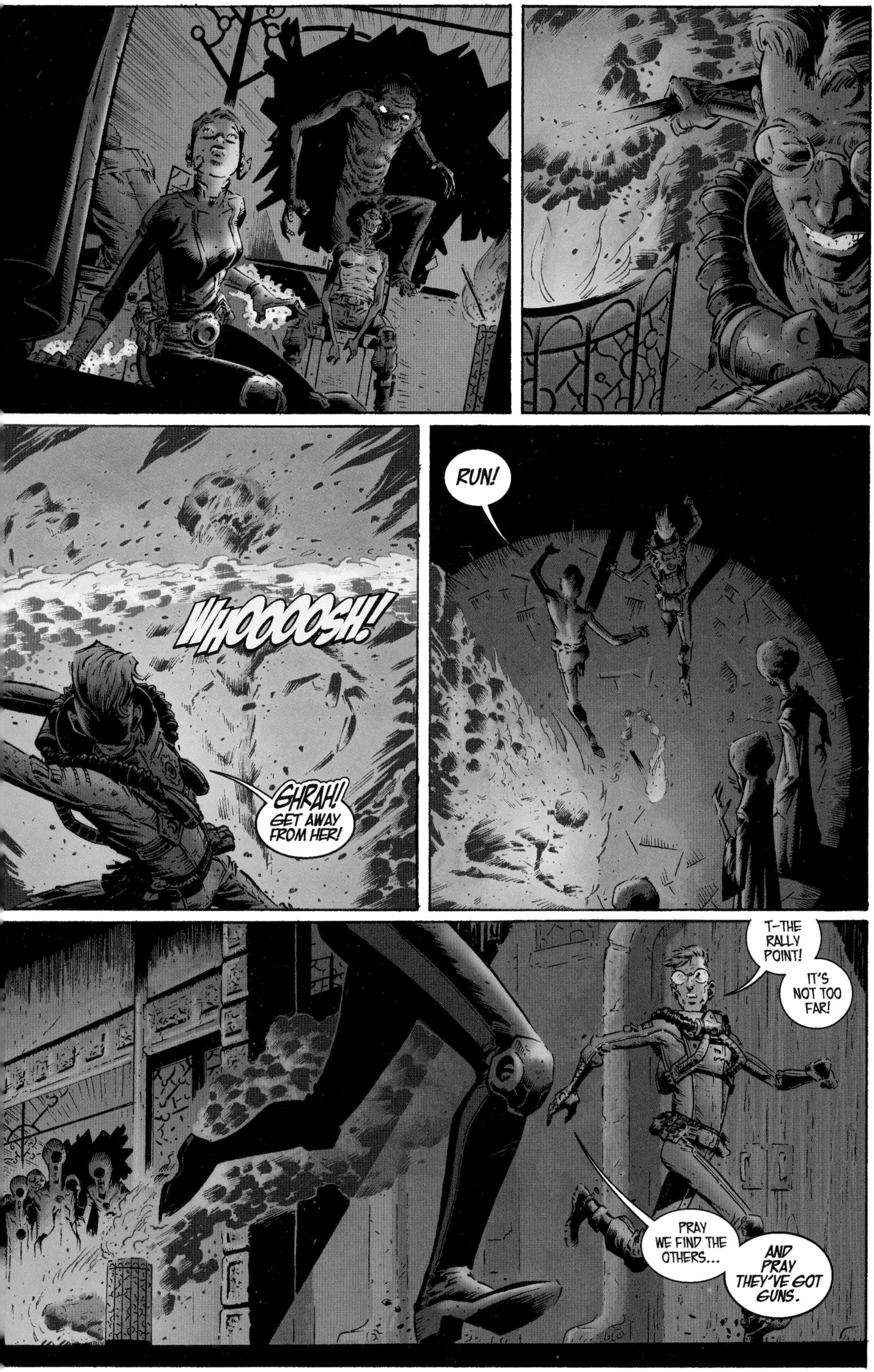
WHOOOOOSH!
GHRAH! GET AWAY FROM HER!
RUN!
T-THE RALLY POINT!
IT'S NOT TOO FAR!
PRAY WE FIND THE OTHERS...
AND PRAY THEY'VE GOT GUNS.

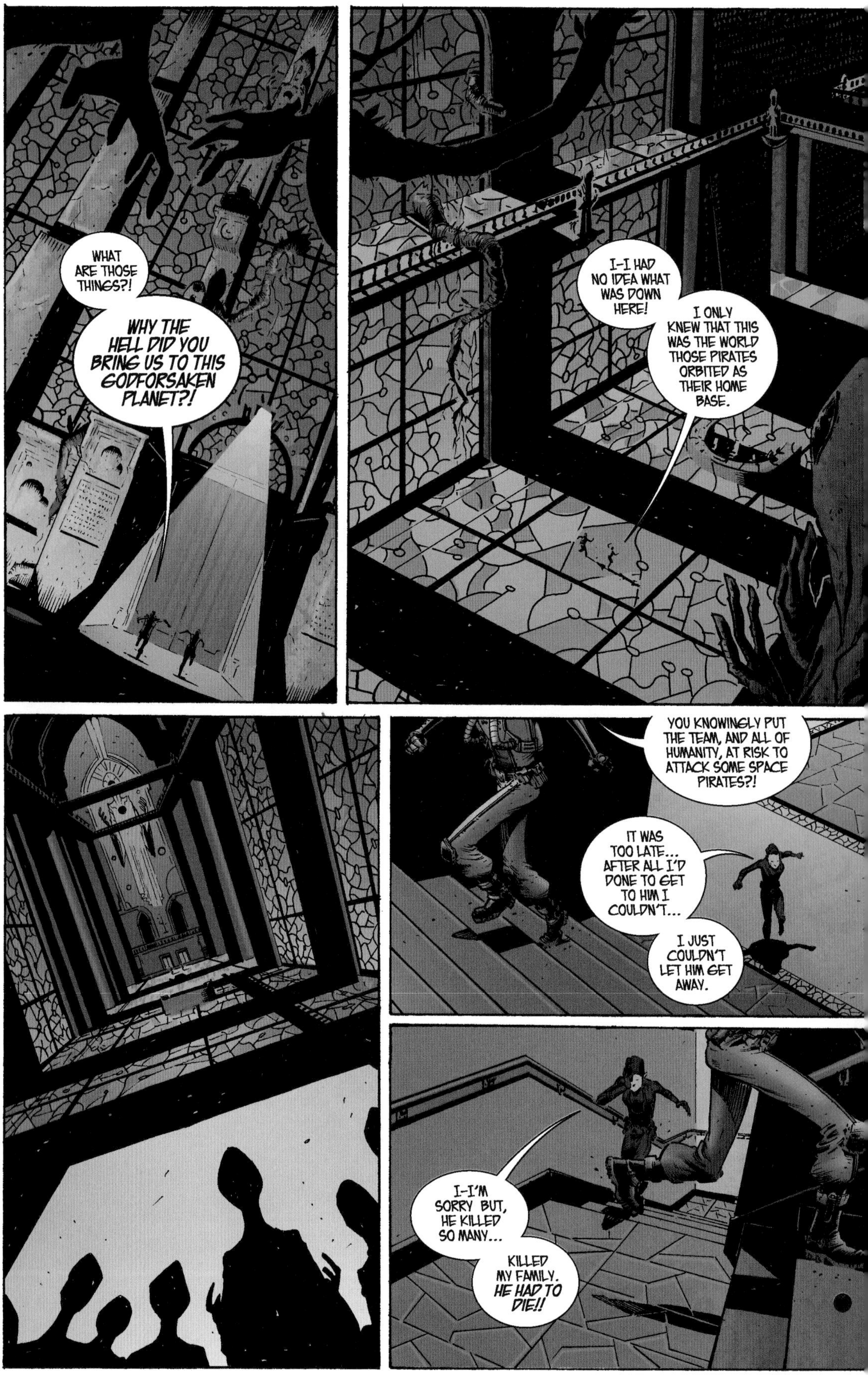
WHAT ARE THOSE THINGS?!
WHY THE HELL DID YOU BRING US TO THIS GODFORSAKEN PLANET?!
I-I HAD NO IDEA WHAT WAS DOWN HERE!
I ONLY KNEW THAT THIS WAS THE WORLD THOSE PIRATES ORBITED AS THEIR HOME BASE.
YOU KNOWINGLY PUT THE TEAM, AND ALL OF HUMANITY, AT RISK TO ATTACK SOME SPACE PIRATES?!
IT WAS TOO LATE... AFTER ALL I'D DONE TO GET TO HIM I COULDN'T...
I JUST COULDN'T LET HIM GET AWAY.
I-I'M SORRY BUT, HE KILLED SO MANY...
KILLED MY FAMILY. HE HAD TO DIE!!

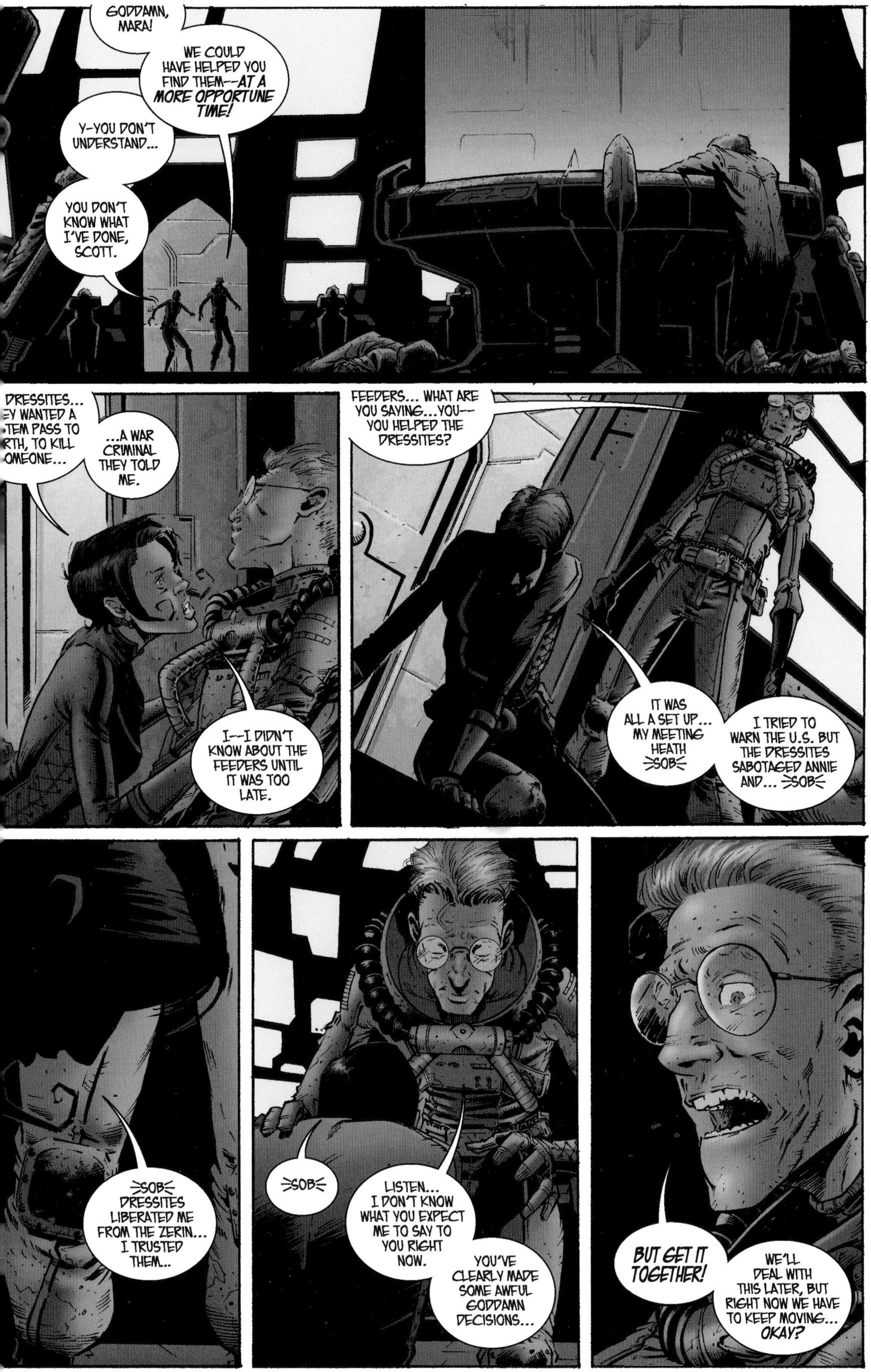
GODDAMN, MARA!
WE COULD HAVE HELPED YOU FIND THEM--*AT A MORE OPPORTUNE TIME!*
Y-YOU DON'T UNDERSTAND...
YOU DON'T KNOW WHAT I'VE DONE, SCOTT.
DRESSITES... EY WANTED A TEM PASS TO RTH, TO KILL OMEONE...
...A WAR CRIMINAL THEY TOLD ME.
I--I DIDN'T KNOW ABOUT THE FEEDERS UNTIL IT WAS TOO LATE.
FEEDERS... WHAT ARE YOU SAYING...YOU-- YOU HELPED THE DRESSITES?
IT WAS ALL A SET UP... MY MEETING HEATH *SOB*
I TRIED TO WARN THE U.S. BUT THE DRESSITES SABOTAGED ANNIE AND... *SOB*
SOB DRESSITES LIBERATED ME FROM THE ZERIN... I TRUSTED THEM...
SOB
LISTEN... I DON'T KNOW WHAT YOU EXPECT ME TO SAY TO YOU RIGHT NOW.
YOU'VE CLEARLY MADE SOME AWFUL GODDAMN DECISIONS...
BUT GET IT TOGETHER!
WE'LL DEAL WITH THIS LATER, BUT RIGHT NOW WE HAVE TO KEEP MOVING... *OKAY?*

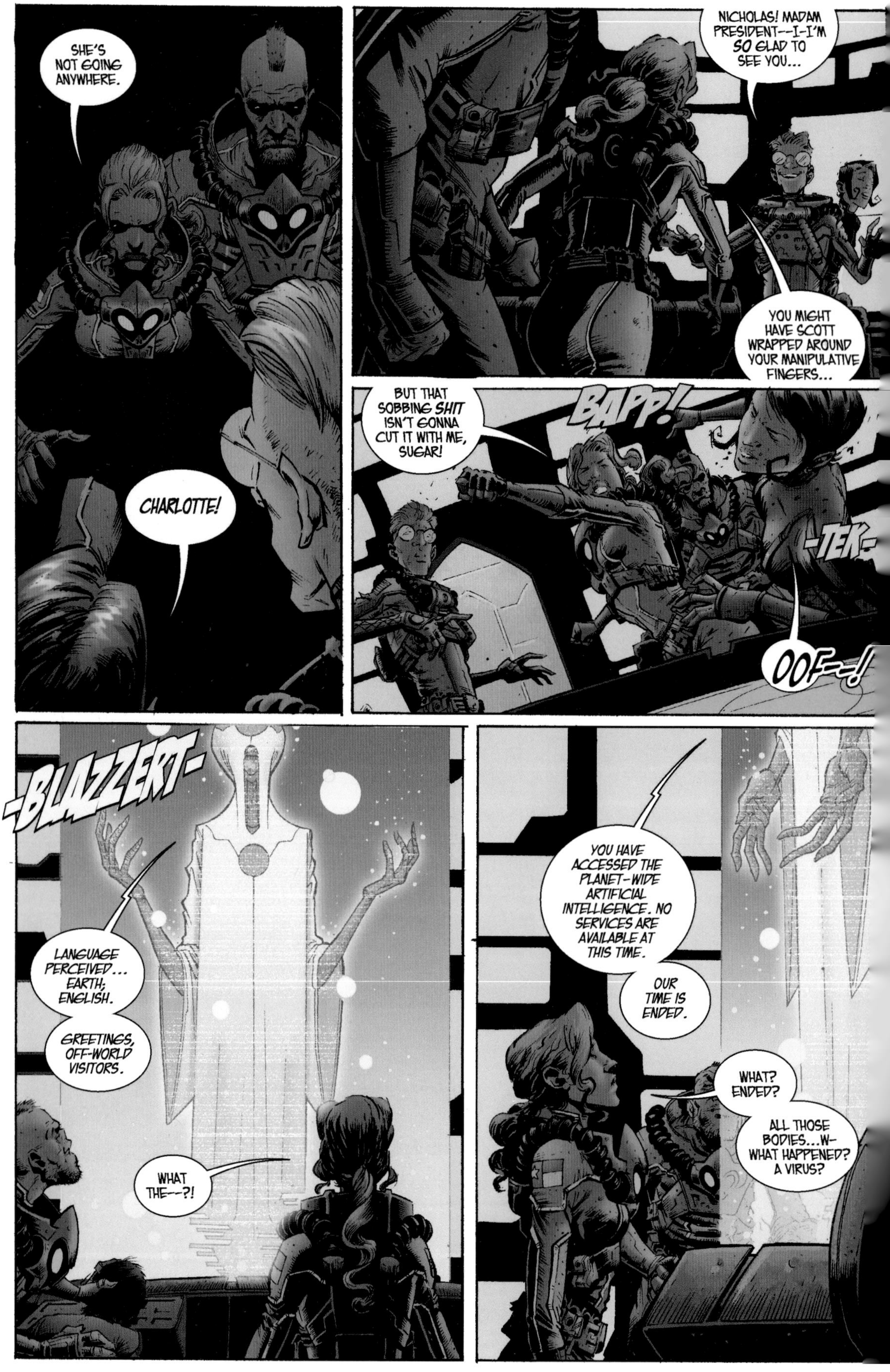
SHE'S NOT GOING ANYWHERE.
CHARLOTTE!
NICHOLAS! MADAM PRESIDENT--I-I'M SO GLAD TO SEE YOU...
YOU MIGHT HAVE SCOTT WRAPPED AROUND YOUR MANIPULATIVE FINGERS...
BUT THAT SOBBING SHIT ISN'T GONNA CUT IT WITH ME, SUGAR!
BAPP!
-TEK-
OOF--!
-BLAZZERT-
LANGUAGE PERCEIVED... EARTH; ENGLISH.
GREETINGS, OFF-WORLD VISITORS.
WHAT THE--?!
YOU HAVE ACCESSED THE PLANET-WIDE ARTIFICIAL INTELLIGENCE. NO SERVICES ARE AVAILABLE AT THIS TIME.
OUR TIME IS ENDED.
WHAT? ENDED?
ALL THOSE BODIES...W-WHAT HAPPENED? A VIRUS?

NOT A VIRUS.

MADAM PRESIDENT-- THERE ARE MORE PRESSING THINGS TO WORRY ABOUT!

HUSH, SCOTT.

COMPUTER, TELL ME ABOUT YOUR WORLD-- WHAT DID KILL THE POPULATION.

MADAM PRES-- MUGFHLE!

NOT ANOTHER WORD.

YOU'RE MAKING A MISTAKE, COUNTRY MOUSE...

CLOSE MOUTH OR I BREAK NECK.

NEAVSIVIANS, DETAILS OF EXTINCTION...

REFUGEES FLEEING RELIGIOUS PERSECUTION ON OCLEWEIAN FOUNDED NEAVSIVIA FIVE HUNDRED THOUSAND YEARS AGO.

WE THRIVED HERE, EVENTUALLY JOINING THE UPPER ECHELON OF ADVANCED CIVILIZATIONS IN THE UNIVERSE.

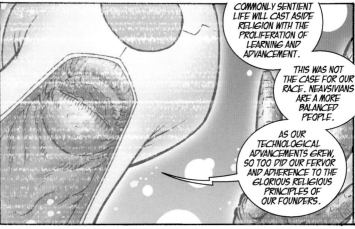

COMMONLY SENTIENT LIFE WILL CAST ASIDE RELIGION WITH THE PROLIFERATION OF LEARNING AND ADVANCEMENT.

THIS WAS NOT THE CASE FOR OUR RACE. NEAVSIVIANS ARE A MORE BALANCED PEOPLE.

AS OUR TECHNOLOGICAL ADVANCEMENTS GREW, SO TOO DID OUR FERVOR AND ADHERENCE TO THE GLORIOUS RELIGIOUS PRINCIPLES OF OUR FOUNDERS.

ON A MOST HOLY DAY, OUR CHIEF SCIENTISTS/ PRIESTS MADE A GREAT DISCOVERY.

THE SECRET MAGNIFICENCE OF THE BLACK HOLE, DIVINE, GLORIOUS GATEWAYS TO HEAVEN TRAVERSABLE ONLY BY SOULS, WAS MADE KNOWN TO US BY GOD.

WOW.

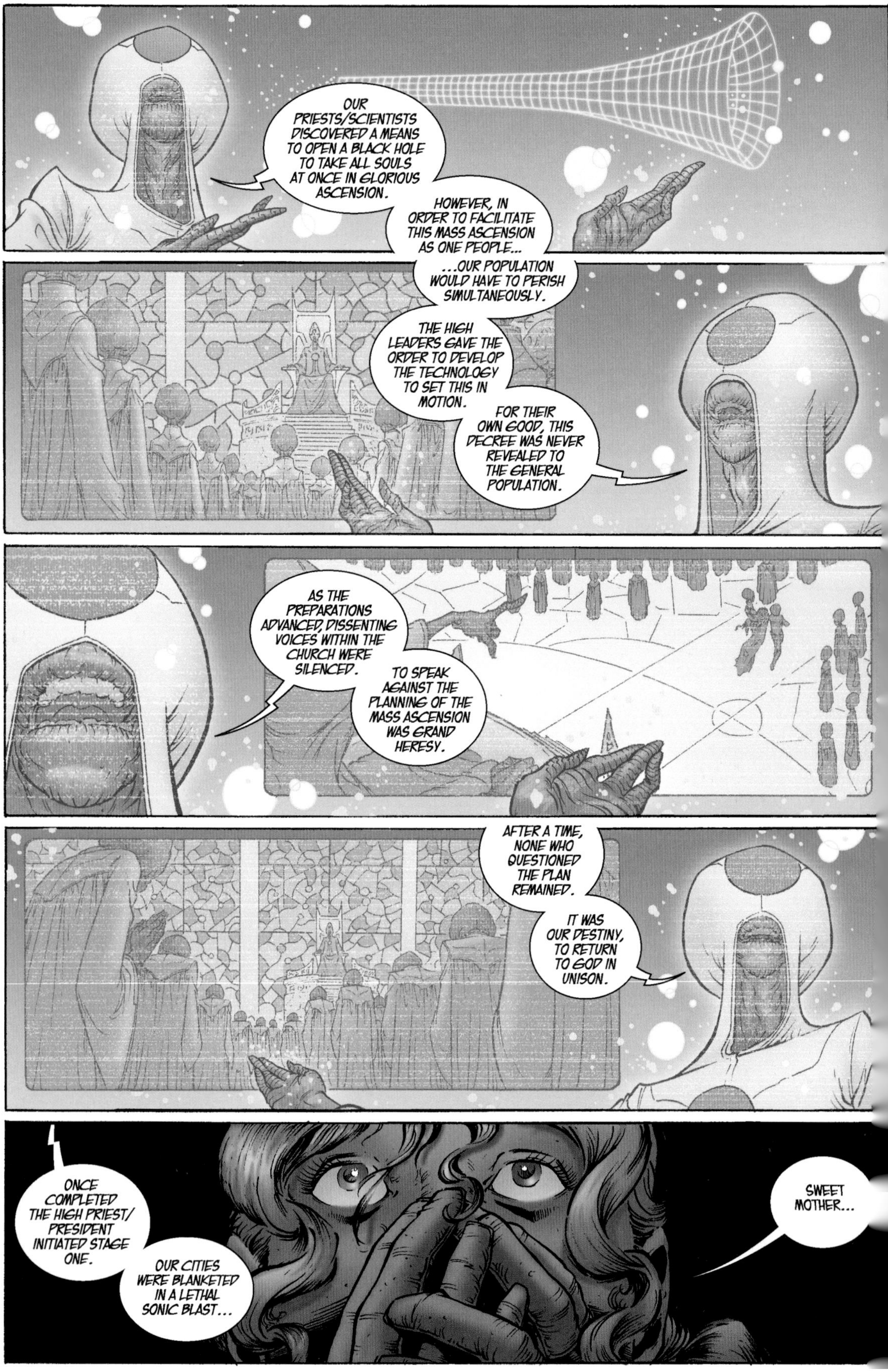

OUR PRIESTS/SCIENTISTS DISCOVERED A MEANS TO OPEN A BLACK HOLE TO TAKE ALL SOULS AT ONCE IN GLORIOUS ASCENSION.
HOWEVER, IN ORDER TO FACILITATE THIS MASS ASCENSION AS ONE PEOPLE...
...OUR POPULATION WOULD HAVE TO PERISH SIMULTANEOUSLY.
THE HIGH LEADERS GAVE THE ORDER TO DEVELOP THE TECHNOLOGY TO SET THIS IN MOTION.
FOR THEIR OWN GOOD, THIS DECREE WAS NEVER REVEALED TO THE GENERAL POPULATION.
AS THE PREPARATIONS ADVANCED, DISSENTING VOICES WITHIN THE CHURCH WERE SILENCED.
TO SPEAK AGAINST THE PLANNING OF THE MASS ASCENSION WAS GRAND HERESY.
AFTER A TIME, NONE WHO QUESTIONED THE PLAN REMAINED.
IT WAS OUR DESTINY, TO RETURN TO GOD IN UNISON.
ONCE COMPLETED THE HIGH PRIEST/ PRESIDENT INITIATED STAGE ONE.
OUR CITIES WERE BLANKETED IN A LETHAL SONIC BLAST...
SWEET MOTHER...

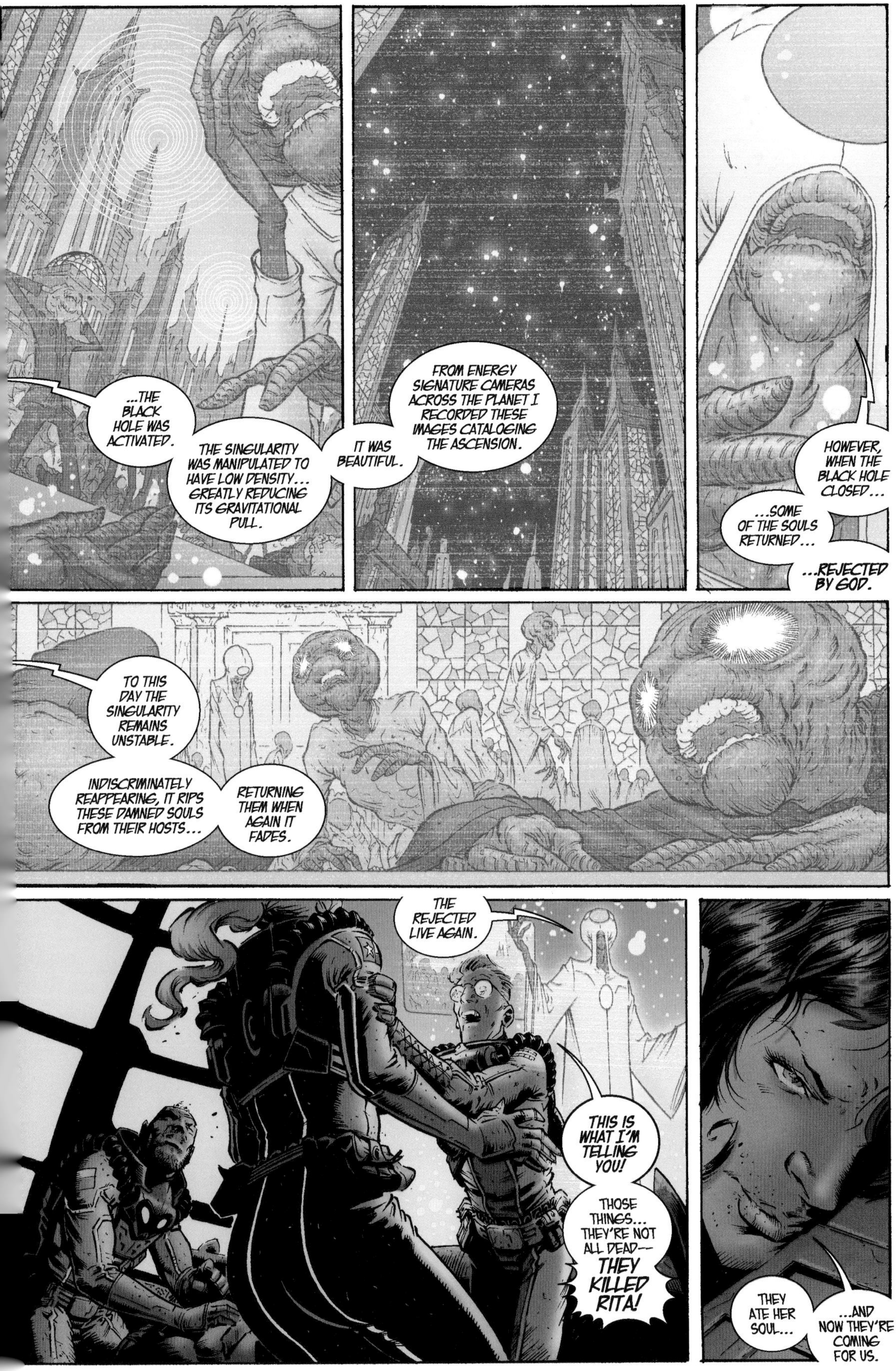
...THE BLACK HOLE WAS ACTIVATED.
THE SINGULARITY WAS MANIPULATED TO HAVE LOW DENSITY... GREATLY REDUCING ITS GRAVITATIONAL PULL.
IT WAS BEAUTIFUL.
FROM ENERGY SIGNATURE CAMERAS ACROSS THE PLANET I RECORDED THESE IMAGES CATALOGING THE ASCENSION.
HOWEVER, WHEN THE BLACK HOLE CLOSED...
...SOME OF THE SOULS RETURNED...
...REJECTED BY GOD.
TO THIS DAY THE SINGULARITY REMAINS UNSTABLE.
INDISCRIMINATELY REAPPEARING, IT RIPS THESE DAMNED SOULS FROM THEIR HOSTS...
RETURNING THEM WHEN AGAIN IT FADES.
THE REJECTED LIVE AGAIN.
THIS IS WHAT I'M TELLING YOU!
THOSE THINGS... THEY'RE NOT ALL DEAD-- THEY KILLED RITA!
THEY ATE HER SOUL...
...AND NOW THEY'RE COMING FOR US.

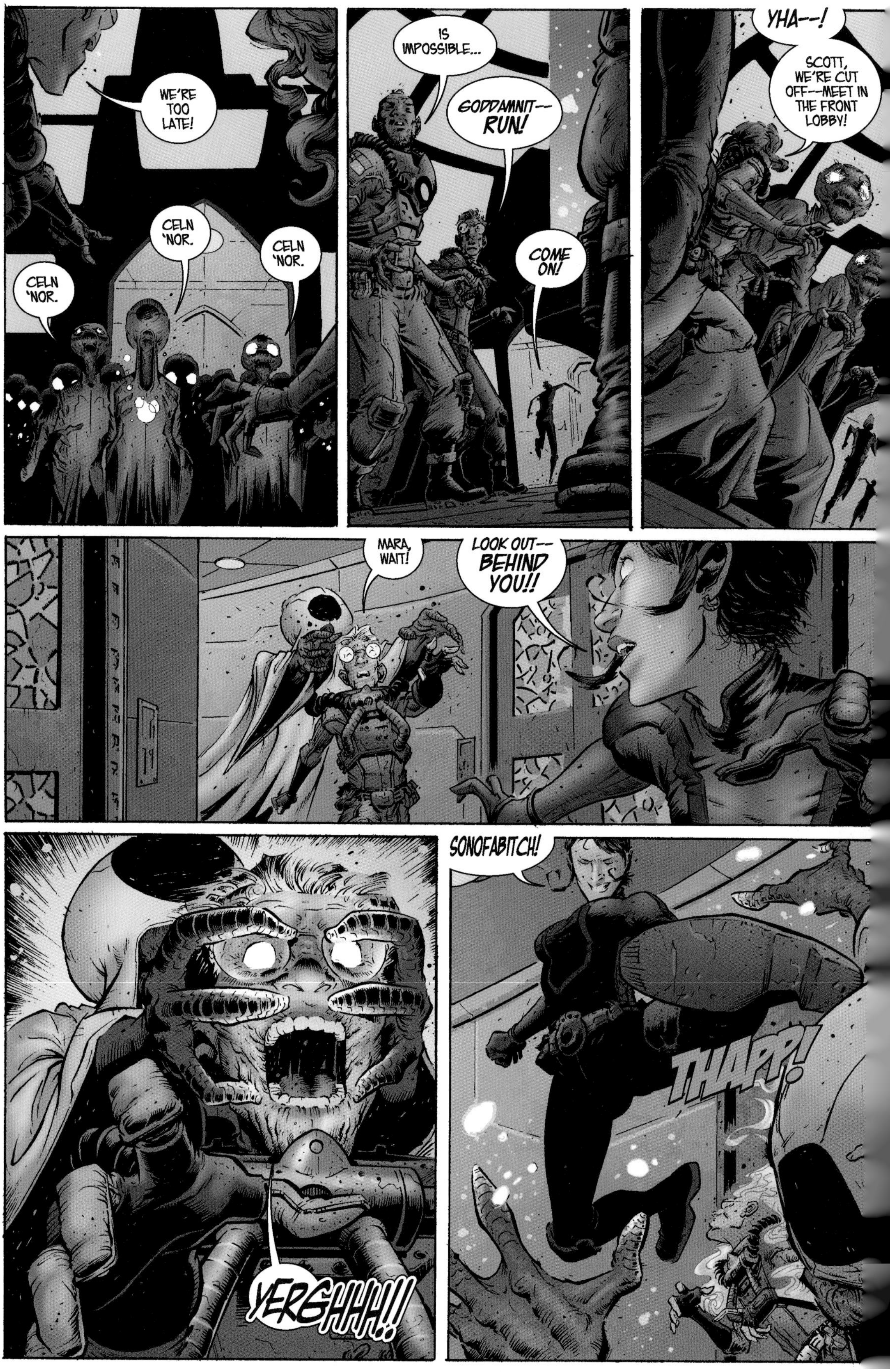

WE'RE TOO LATE!
CELN 'NOR.
CELN 'NOR.
CELN 'NOR.
IS IMPOSSIBLE...
GODDAMNIT-- RUN!
COME ON!
YHA--!
SCOTT, WE'RE CUT OFF--MEET IN THE FRONT LOBBY!
MARA, WAIT!
LOOK OUT-- BEHIND YOU!!
YERGHHH!!
SONOFABITCH!
THAPP!

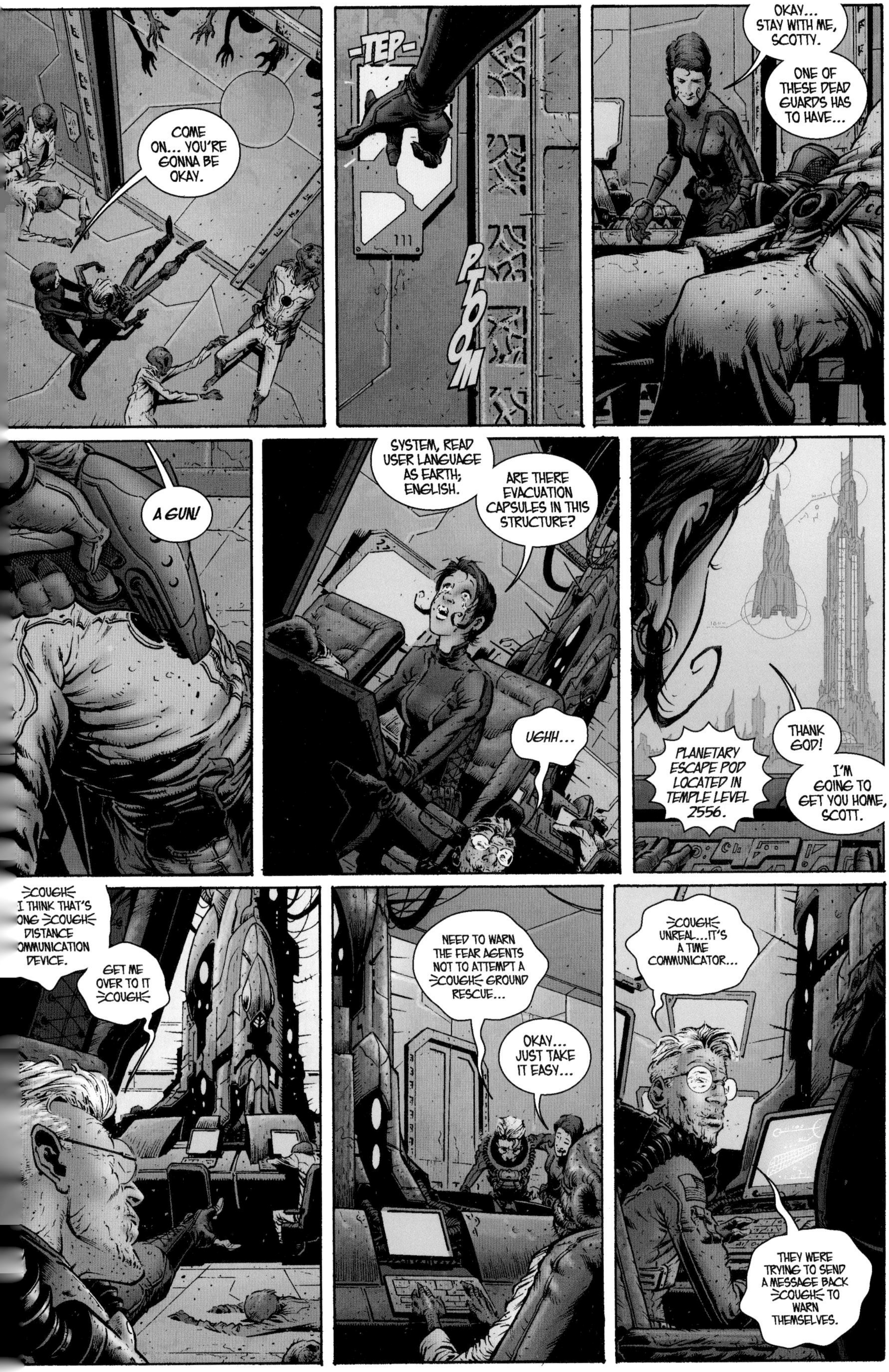
COME ON... YOU'RE GONNA BE OKAY.
-TEP-
PTOOM
OKAY... STAY WITH ME, SCOTTY.
ONE OF THESE DEAD GUARDS HAS TO HAVE...
A GUN!
SYSTEM, READ USER LANGUAGE AS EARTH; ENGLISH.
ARE THERE EVACUATION CAPSULES IN THIS STRUCTURE?
UGHH...
PLANETARY ESCAPE POD LOCATED IN TEMPLE LEVEL 2556.
THANK GOD!
I'M GOING TO GET YOU HOME, SCOTT.
=COUGH= I THINK THAT'S ONG =COUGH= DISTANCE OMMUNICATION DEVICE.
GET ME OVER TO IT =COUGH=
NEED TO WARN THE FEAR AGENTS NOT TO ATTEMPT A =COUGH= GROUND RESCUE...
OKAY... JUST TAKE IT EASY...
=COUGH= UNREAL...IT'S A TIME COMMUNICATOR...
THEY WERE TRYING TO SEND A MESSAGE BACK =COUGH= TO WARN THEMSELVES.

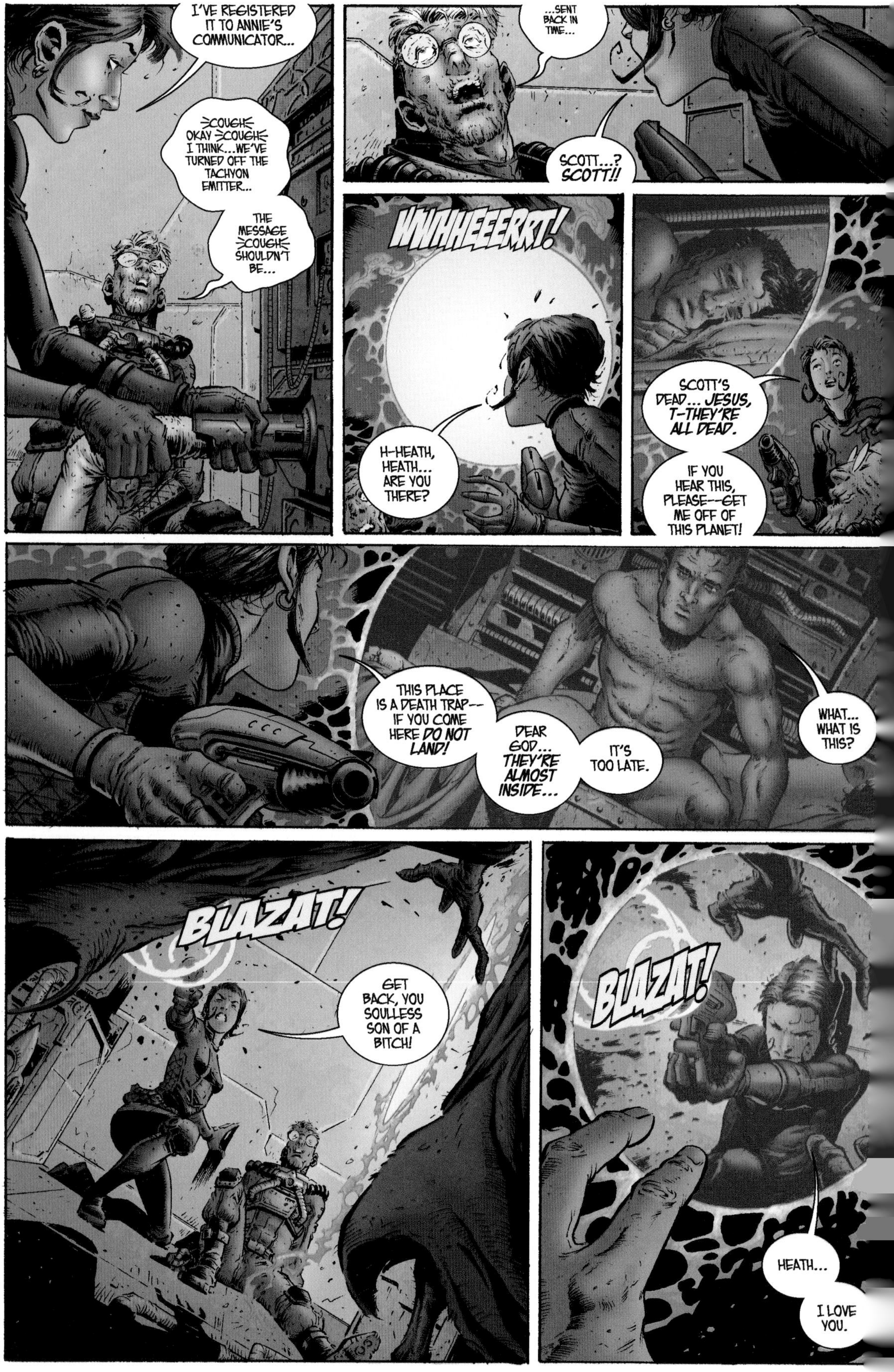
I'VE REGISTERED IT TO ANNIE'S COMMUNICATOR...
≽COUGH≼ OKAY ≽COUGH≼ I THINK...WE'VE TURNED OFF THE TACHYON EMITTER...
THE MESSAGE ≽COUGH≼ SHOULDN'T BE...
...SENT BACK IN TIME...
SCOTT...? SCOTT!!
WWHHEEERRT!
H-HEATH, HEATH... ARE YOU THERE?
SCOTT'S DEAD... JESUS, T-THEY'RE ALL DEAD.
IF YOU HEAR THIS, PLEASE--GET ME OFF OF THIS PLANET!
THIS PLACE IS A DEATH TRAP-- IF YOU COME HERE DO NOT LAND!
DEAR GOD... THEY'RE ALMOST INSIDE...
IT'S TOO LATE.
WHAT... WHAT IS THIS?
BLAZAT!
GET BACK, YOU SOULLESS SON OF A BITCH!
BLAZAT!
HEATH...
I LOVE YOU.

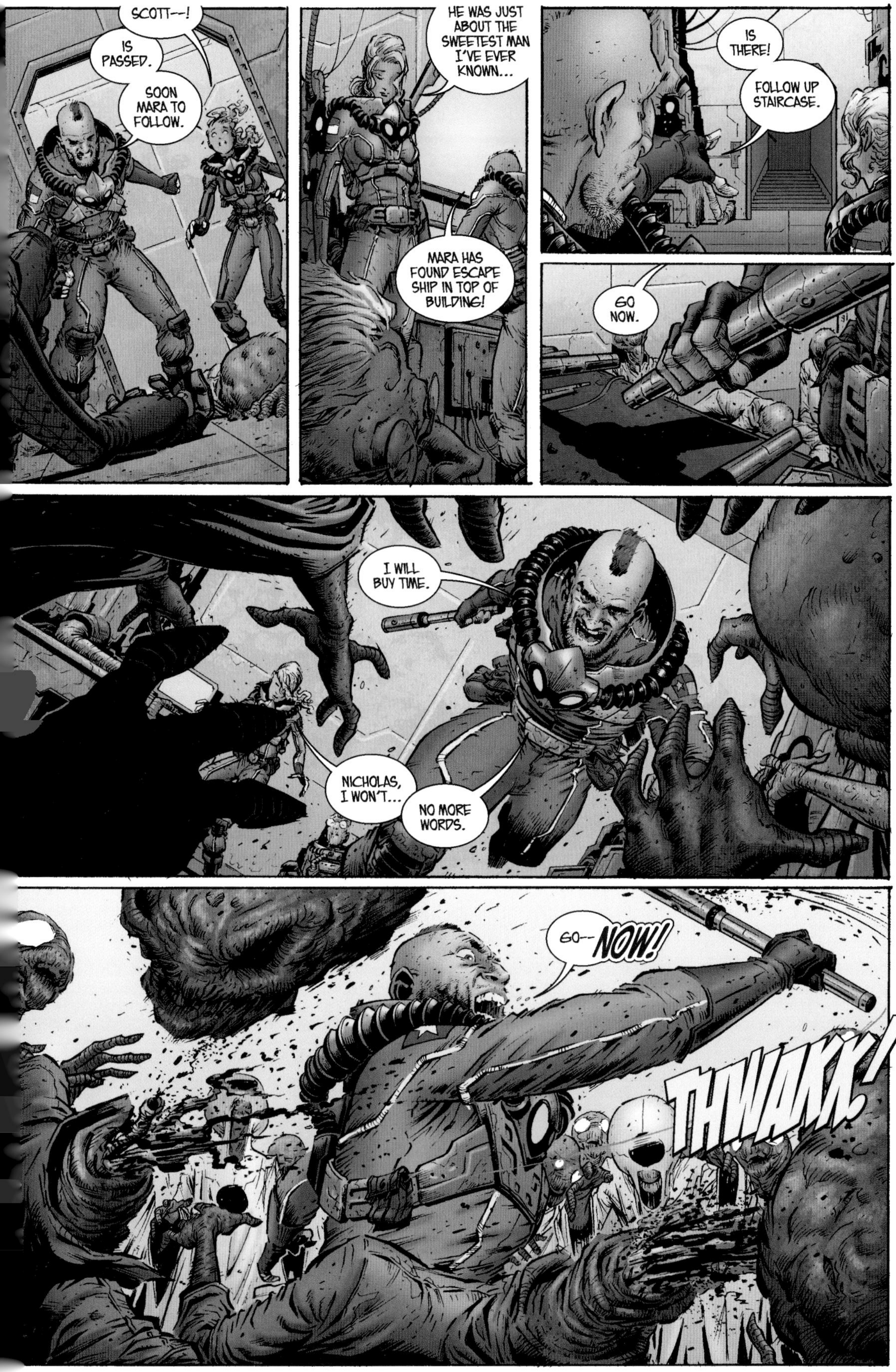
SCOTT--!
IS PASSED.
SOON MARA TO FOLLOW.
HE WAS JUST ABOUT THE SWEETEST MAN I'VE EVER KNOWN...
MARA HAS FOUND ESCAPE SHIP IN TOP OF BUILDING!
IS THERE!
FOLLOW UP STAIRCASE.
GO NOW.
I WILL BUY TIME.
NICHOLAS, I WON'T...
NO MORE WORDS.
GO--NOW!
THWAKK!

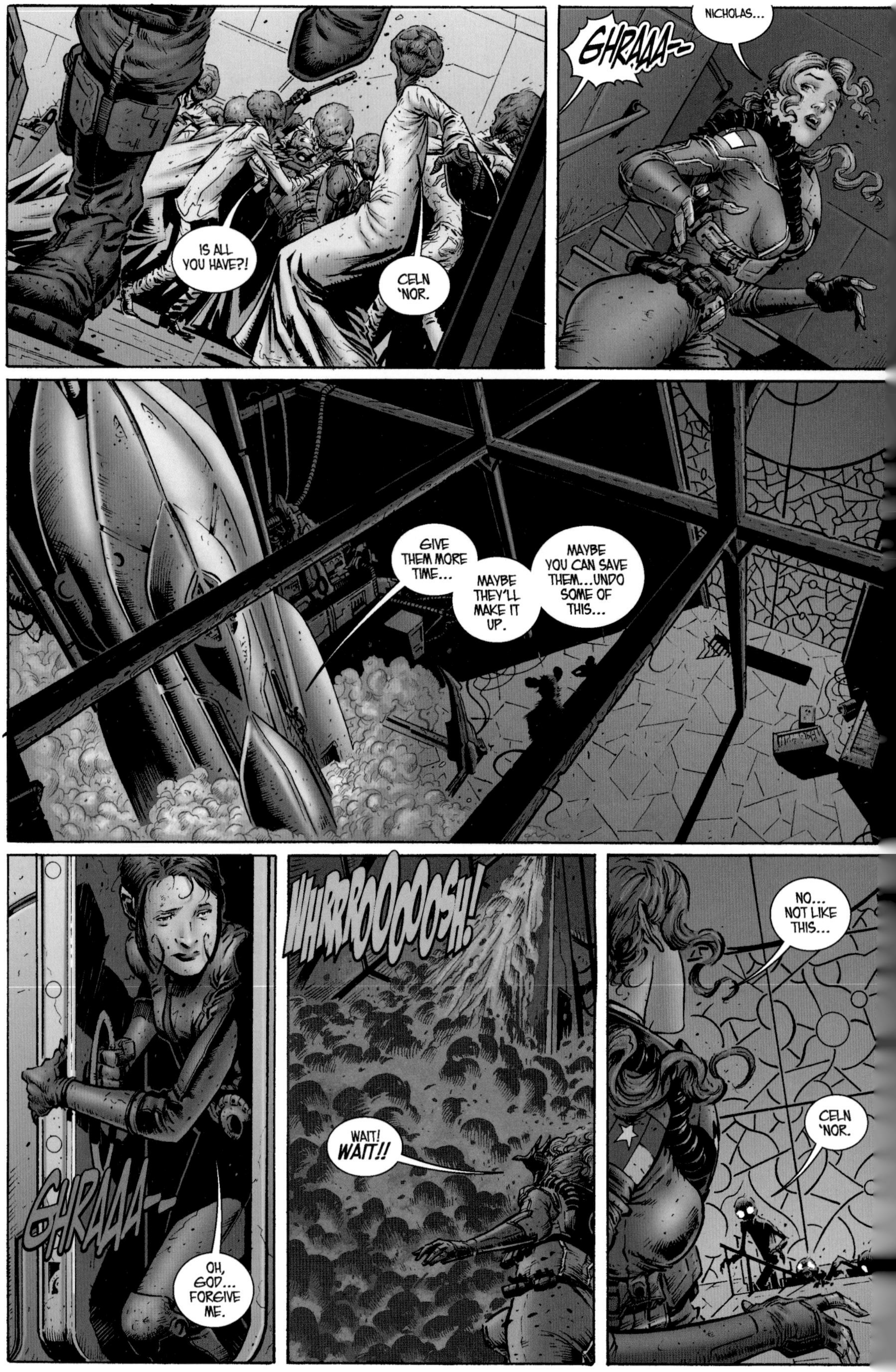
IS ALL YOU HAVE?!
CELN 'NOR.
NICHOLAS...
GHRAAA--
GIVE THEM MORE TIME...
MAYBE THEY'LL MAKE IT UP.
MAYBE YOU CAN SAVE THEM...UNDO SOME OF THIS...
GHRAAA--
OH, GOD... FORGIVE ME.
WHHRRROOOOOOSH!
WAIT! WAIT!!
NO... NOT LIKE THIS...
CELN 'NOR.

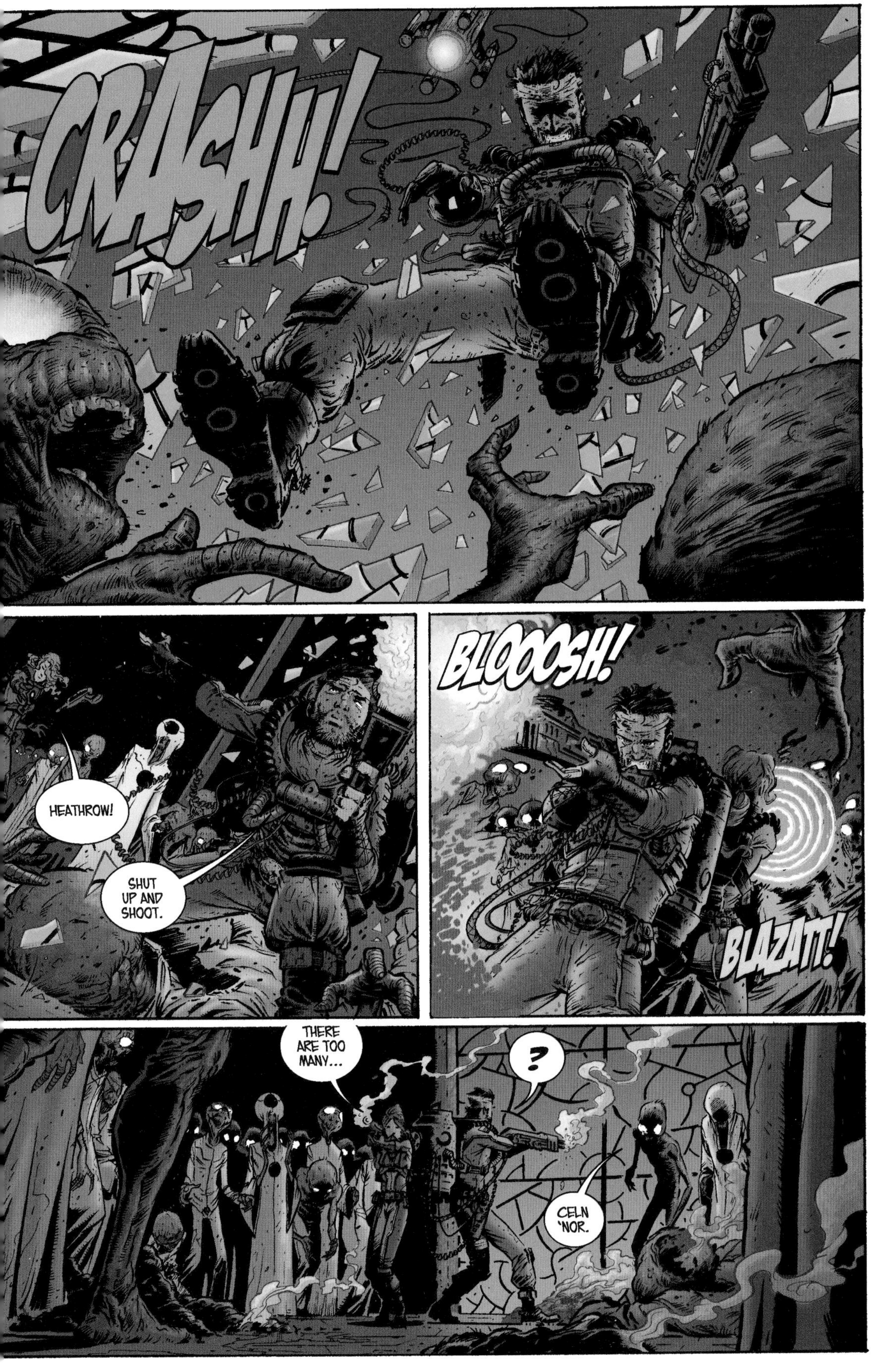
CRASHH!
HEATHROW!
SHUT UP AND SHOOT.
BLOOOSH!
BLAZATT!
THERE ARE TOO MANY...
?
CELN 'NOR.

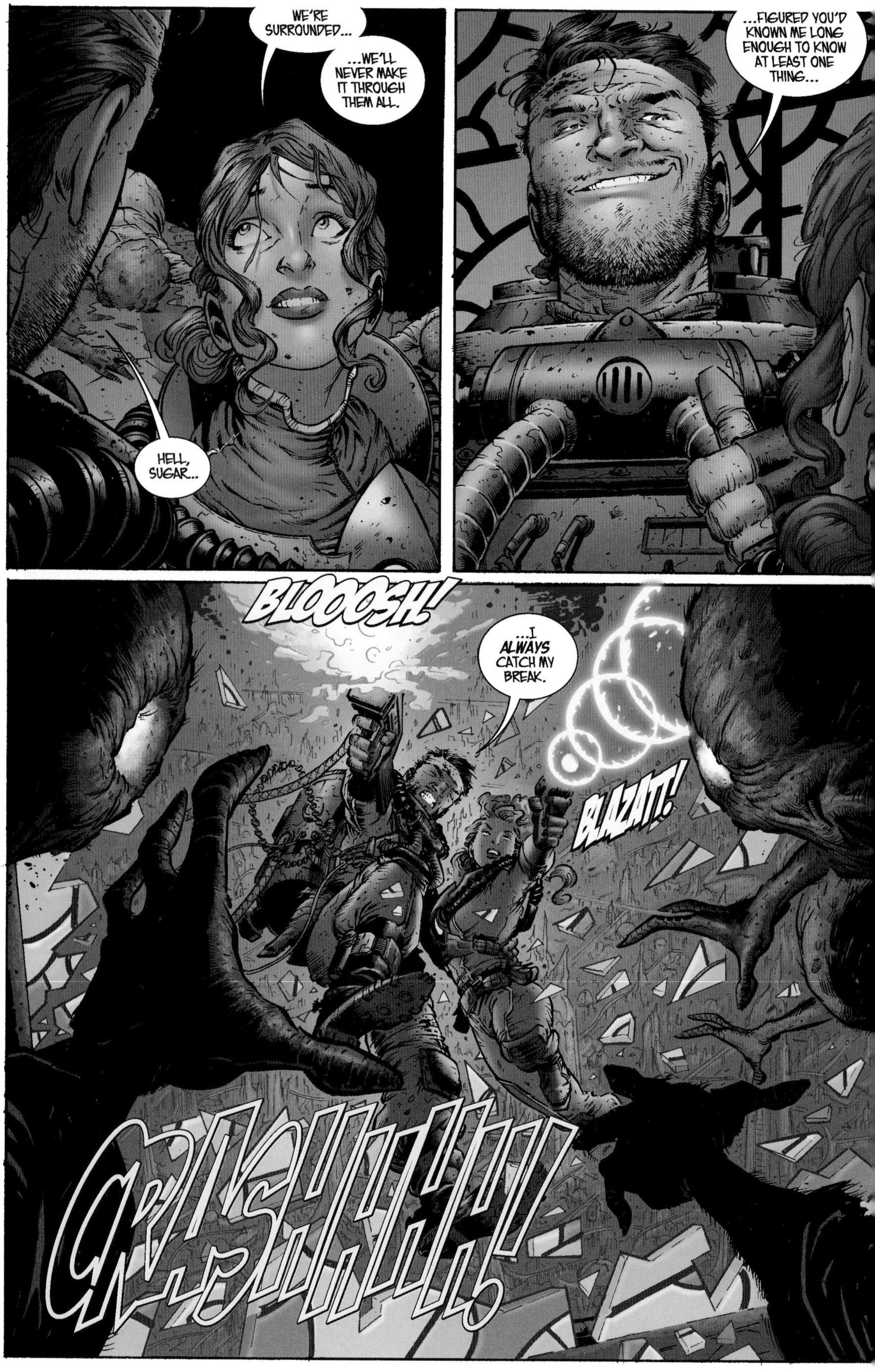
WE'RE SURROUNDED...
...WE'LL NEVER MAKE IT THROUGH THEM ALL.
HELL, SUGAR...
...FIGURED YOU'D KNOWN ME LONG ENOUGH TO KNOW AT LEAST ONE THING...
BLOOOSH!
...I ALWAYS CATCH MY BREAK.
BLAZATT!

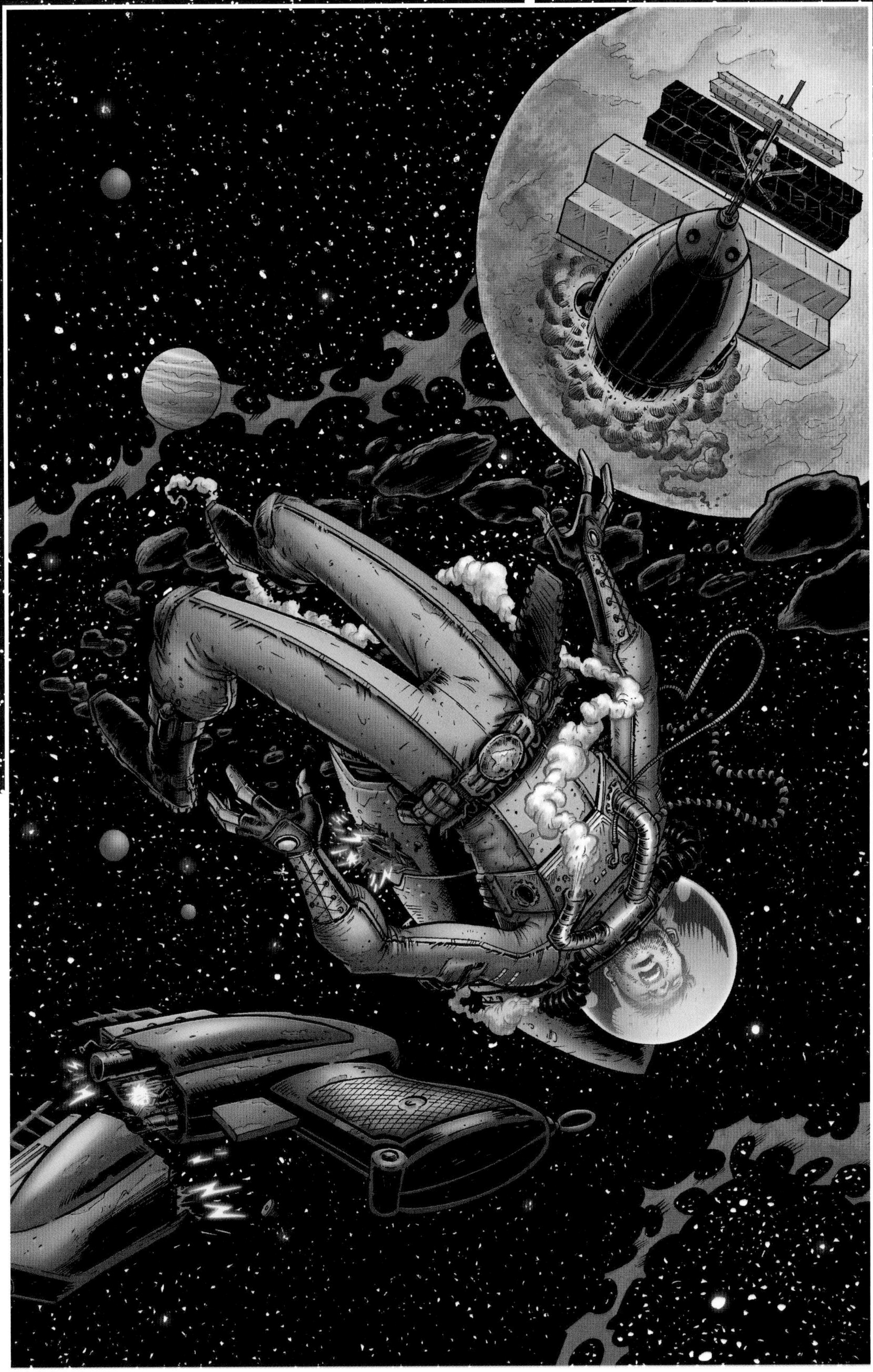

FEAR AGENT #20
ART BY JEROME OPEÑA

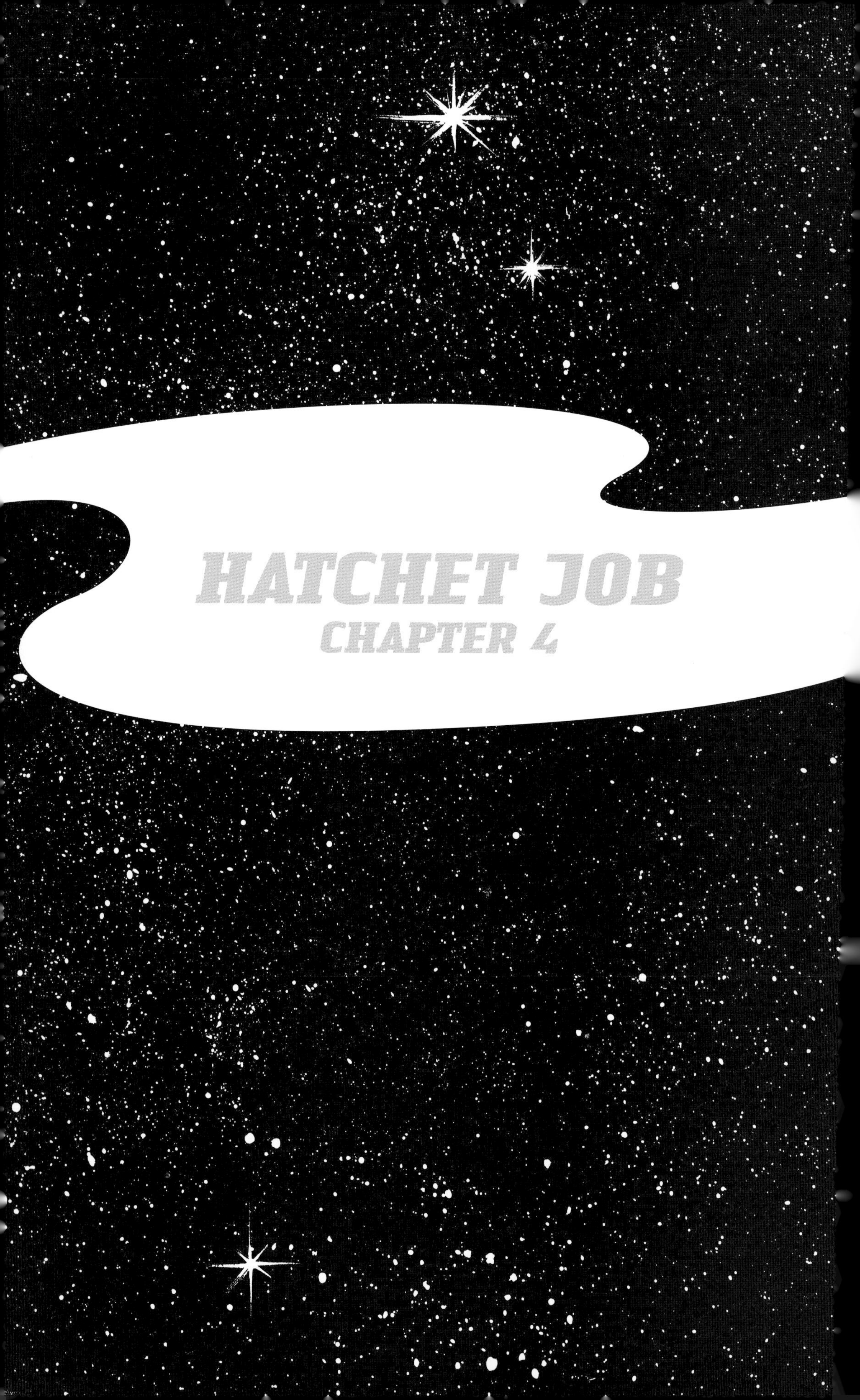
HATCHET JOB
CHAPTER 4

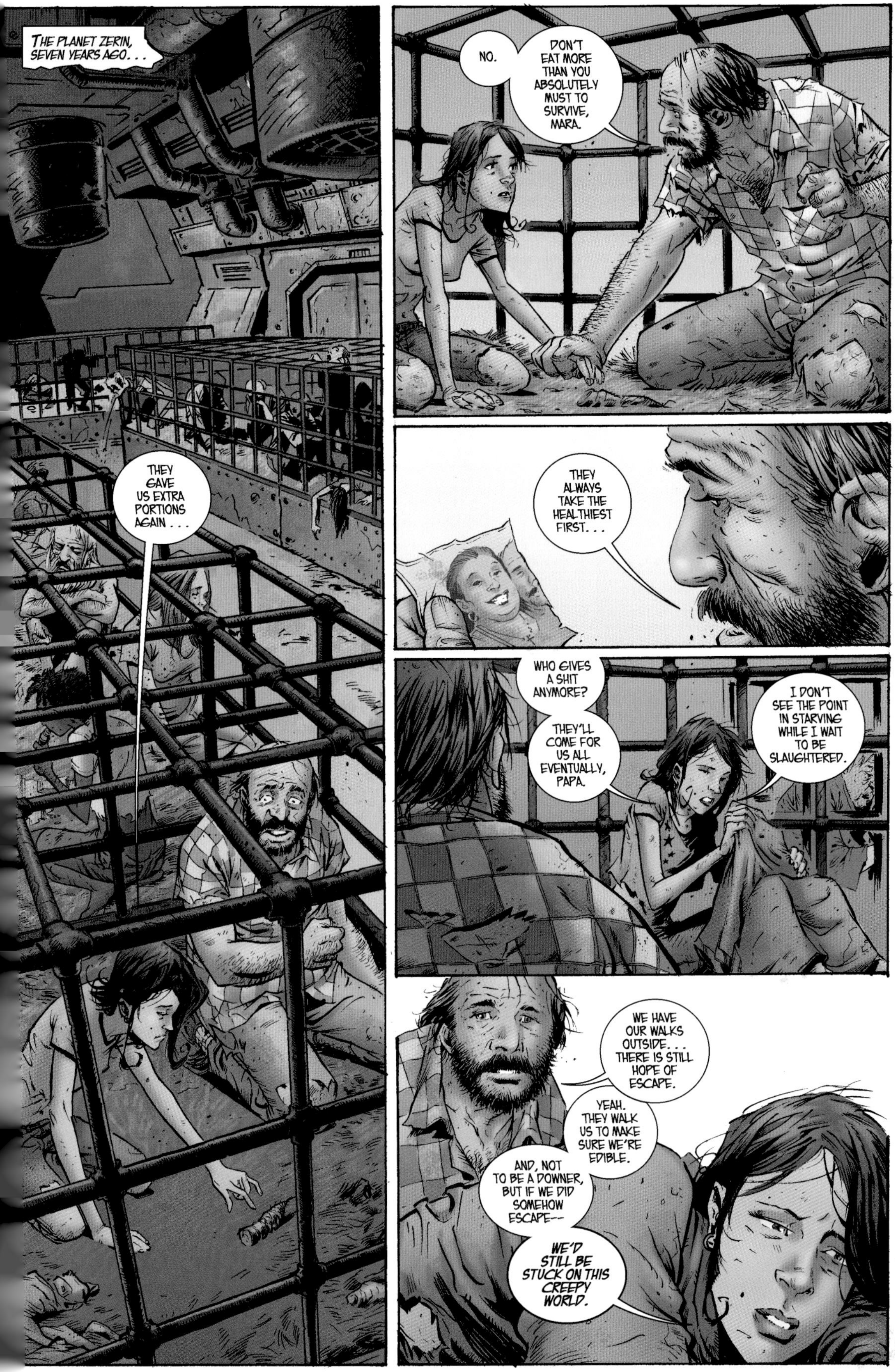
THE PLANET ZERIN, SEVEN YEARS AGO . . .
THEY GAVE US EXTRA PORTIONS AGAIN . . .
NO.
DON'T EAT MORE THAN YOU ABSOLUTELY MUST TO SURVIVE, MARA.
THEY ALWAYS TAKE THE HEALTHIEST FIRST. . .
WHO GIVES A SHIT ANYMORE?
THEY'LL COME FOR US ALL EVENTUALLY, PAPA.
I DON'T SEE THE POINT IN STARVING WHILE I WAIT TO BE SLAUGHTERED.
WE HAVE OUR WALKS OUTSIDE. . . THERE IS STILL HOPE OF ESCAPE.
YEAH. THEY WALK US TO MAKE SURE WE'RE EDIBLE.
AND, NOT TO BE A DOWNER, BUT IF WE DID SOMEHOW ESCAPE--
WE'D STILL BE STUCK ON THIS CREEPY WORLD.

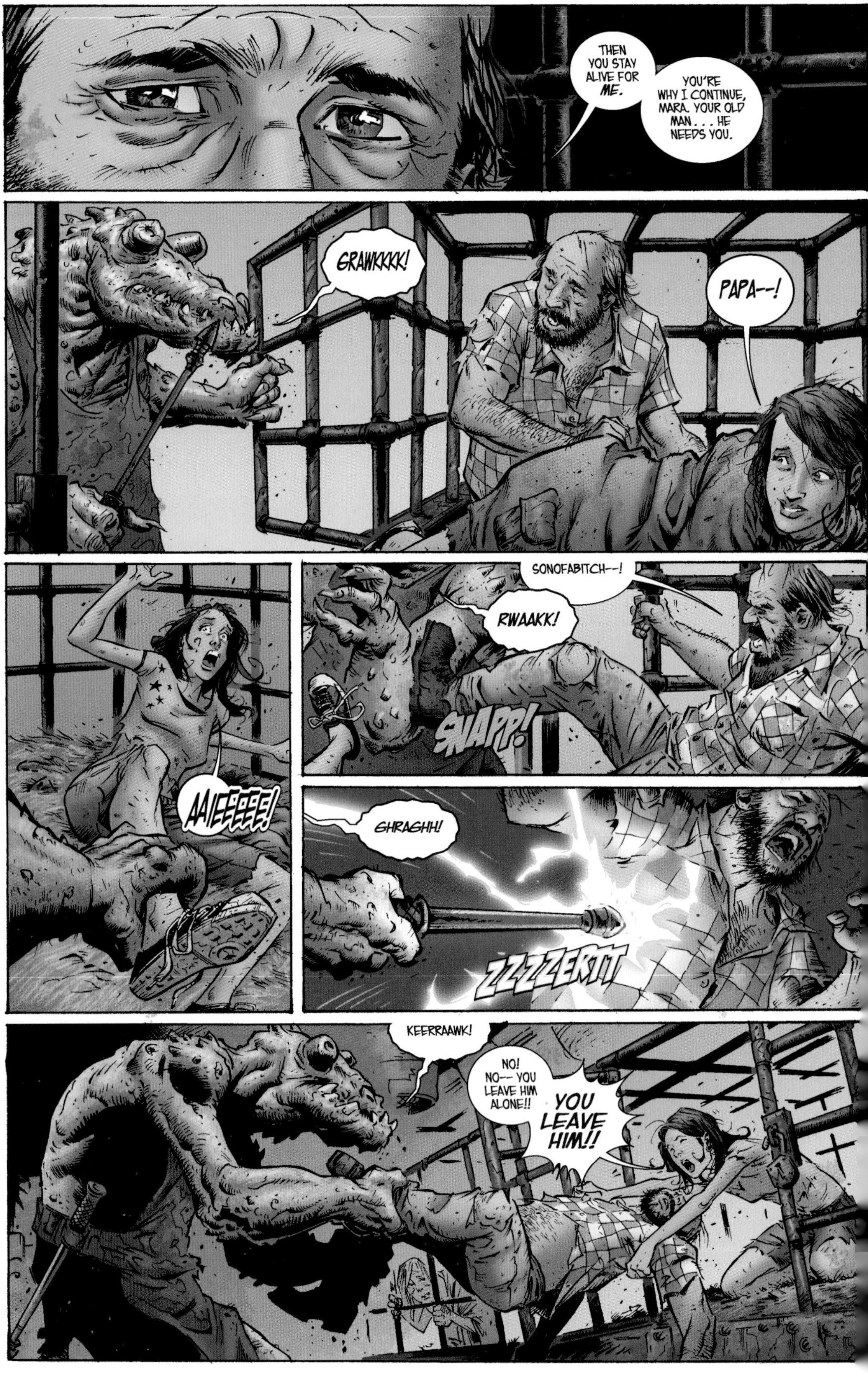
THEN YOU STAY ALIVE FOR ME.
YOU'RE WHY I CONTINUE, MARA. YOUR OLD MAN . . . HE NEEDS YOU.
GRAWKKKK!
PAPA--!
AAIEEEEEE!
SONOFABITCH--!
RWAAKK!
SNAPP!
GHRAGHH!
ZZZZERTT
KEERRAAWK!
NO! NO-- YOU LEAVE HIM ALONE!!
YOU LEAVE HIM!!

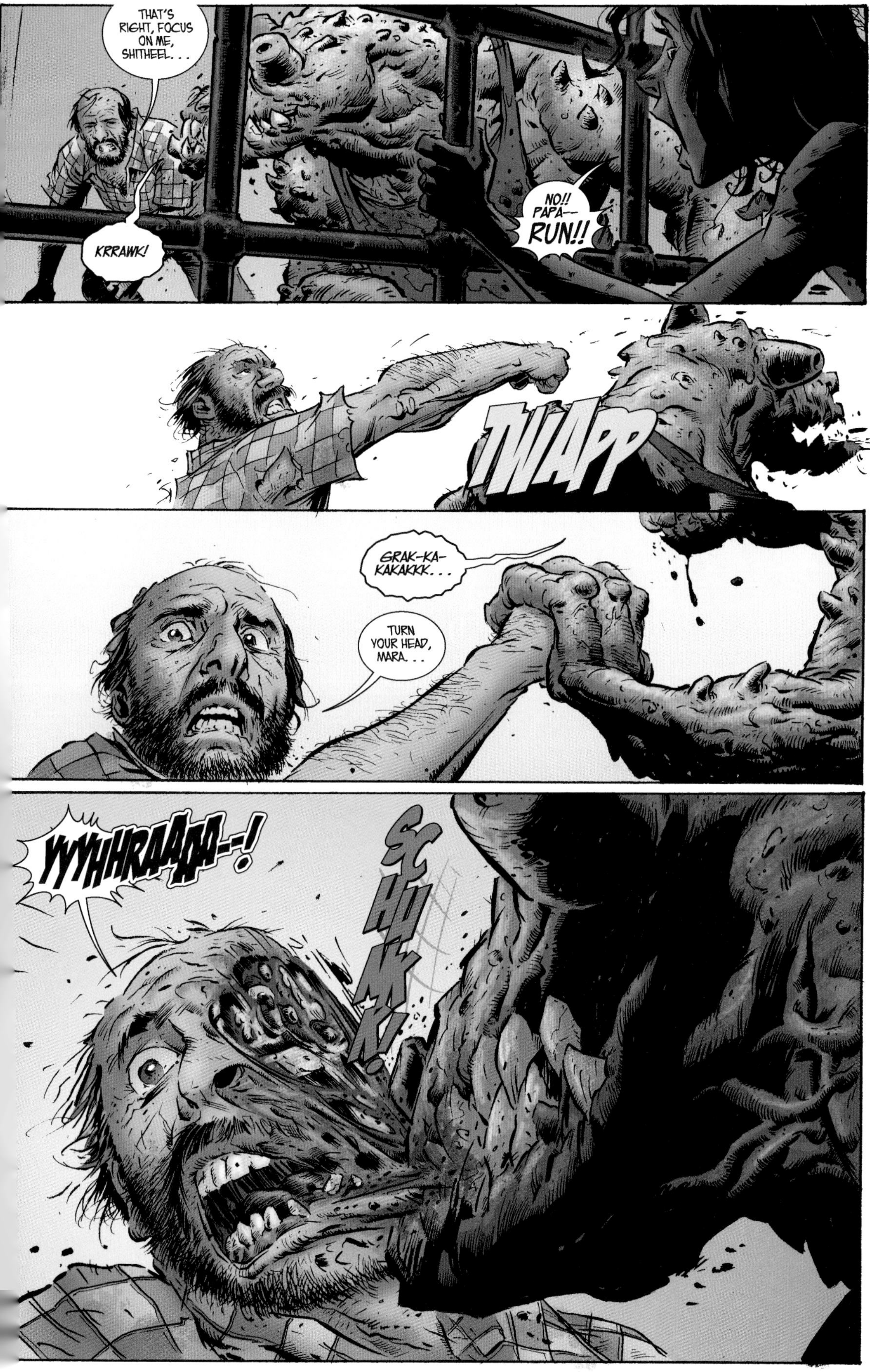
THAT'S RIGHT, FOCUS ON ME, SHITHEEL...
KRRAWK!
NO!! PAPA-- RUN!!
TWAPP
GRAK-KA-KAKAKKK...
TURN YOUR HEAD, MARA...
YYYHHRAAAAA--!
SCHUNK!

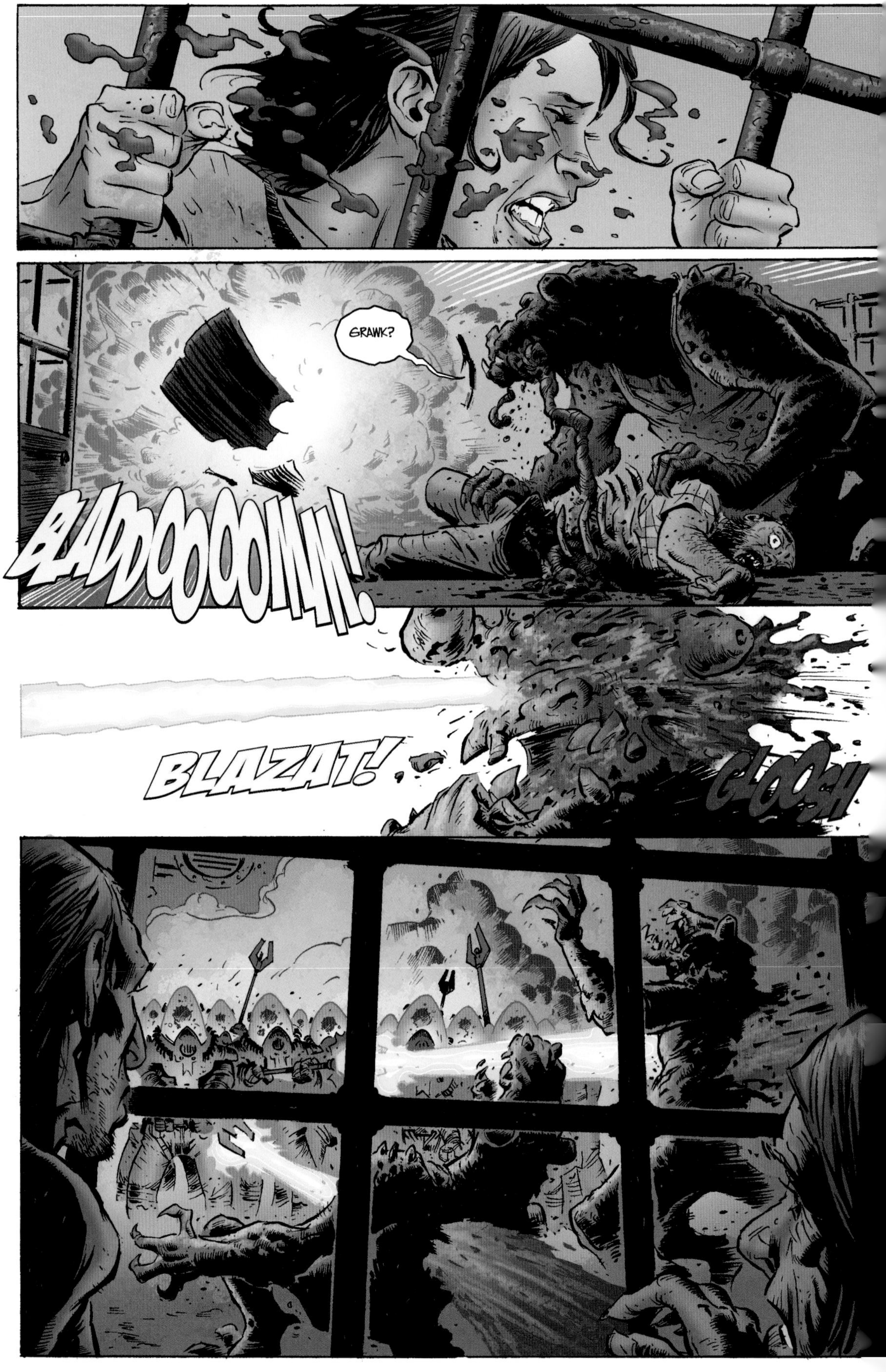
GRAWK?
BLADOOOOMM!
BLAZAT!
GLOOSH

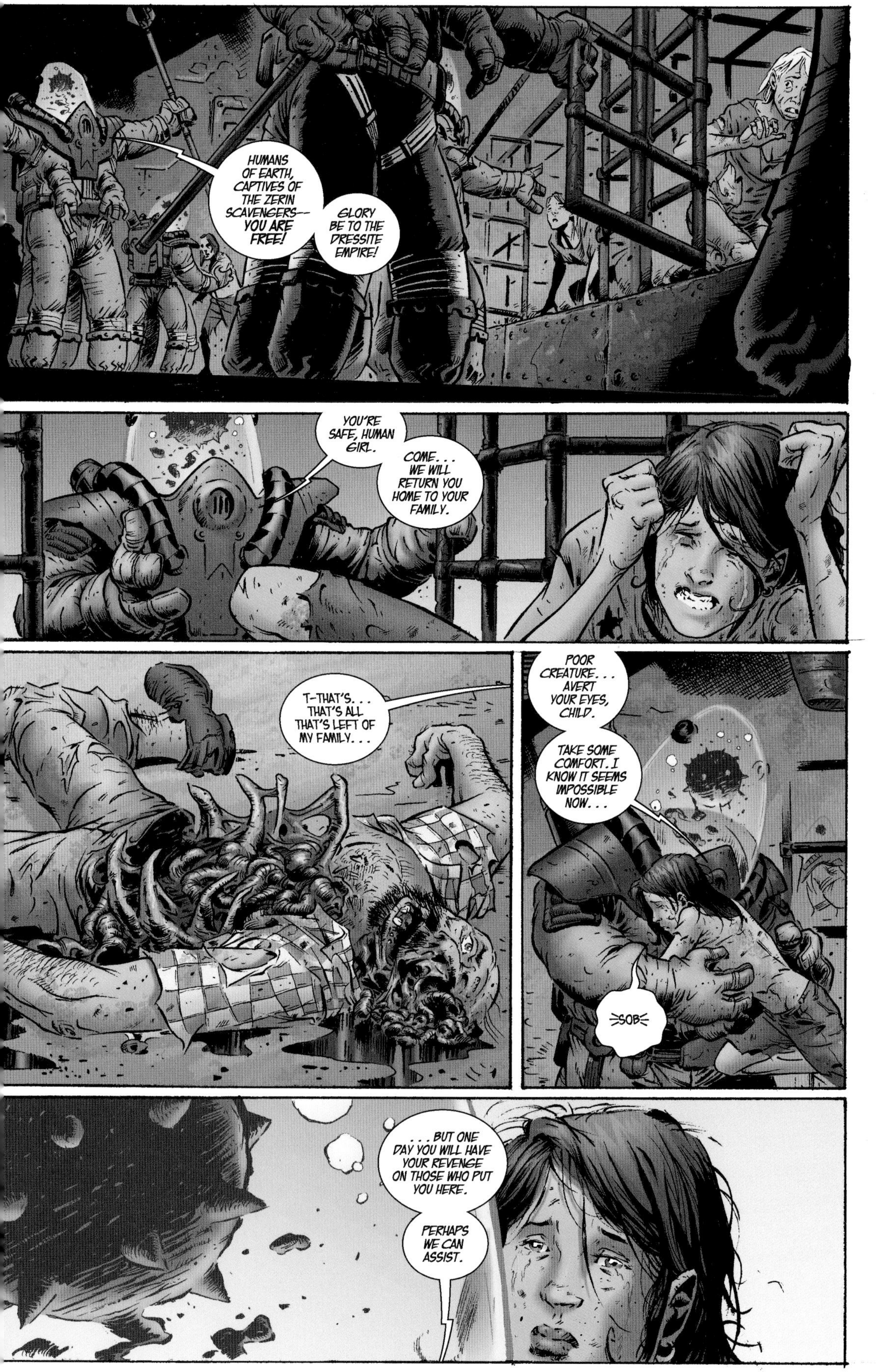
HUMANS OF EARTH, CAPTIVES OF THE ZERIN SCAVENGERS-- YOU ARE FREE!
GLORY BE TO THE DRESSITE EMPIRE!
YOU'RE SAFE, HUMAN GIRL.
COME... WE WILL RETURN YOU HOME TO YOUR FAMILY.
T-THAT'S... THAT'S ALL THAT'S LEFT OF MY FAMILY...
POOR CREATURE... AVERT YOUR EYES, CHILD.
TAKE SOME COMFORT. I KNOW IT SEEMS IMPOSSIBLE NOW...
SOB
...BUT ONE DAY YOU WILL HAVE YOUR REVENGE ON THOSE WHO PUT YOU HERE.
PERHAPS WE CAN ASSIST.

THE PRESENT. . .

IF THEY SEE ME I'M DEAD.

BUT THEY WON'T.

SHIP THIS BIG WON'T HAVE ITS SENSORS SET TO PICK UP ANYTHING SMALLER THAN A TRANSPORT BARGE.

TRY AND GET THAT THROUGH TO MY HEART.

BEATING ITS WAY OUT OF MY CHEST. . .

FEAR IS ALL IN MY HEAD.

IT'S NOT REAL.

I CAN CONTROL I

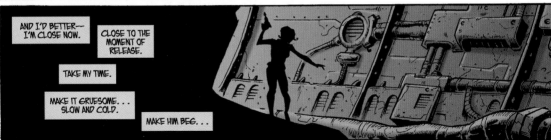

AND I'D BETTER— I'M CLOSE NOW.

CLOSE TO THE MOMENT OF RELEASE.

TAKE MY TIME.

MAKE IT GRUESOME. . . SLOW AND COLD.

MAKE HIM BEG. . .

. . . MAKE IT LAST.

HHHMMM. . . I DO BELIEVE THIS PIRATE HAS EARNED HIMSELF SOME BOOTY.

QUITE THE CHARMER, AREN'T YE, CAPTAIN DIABLO?

AFTER ALL THIS TIME. . . TO BE SO CLOSE. . .

I'M GOING TO KILL LEVI DIABLO.

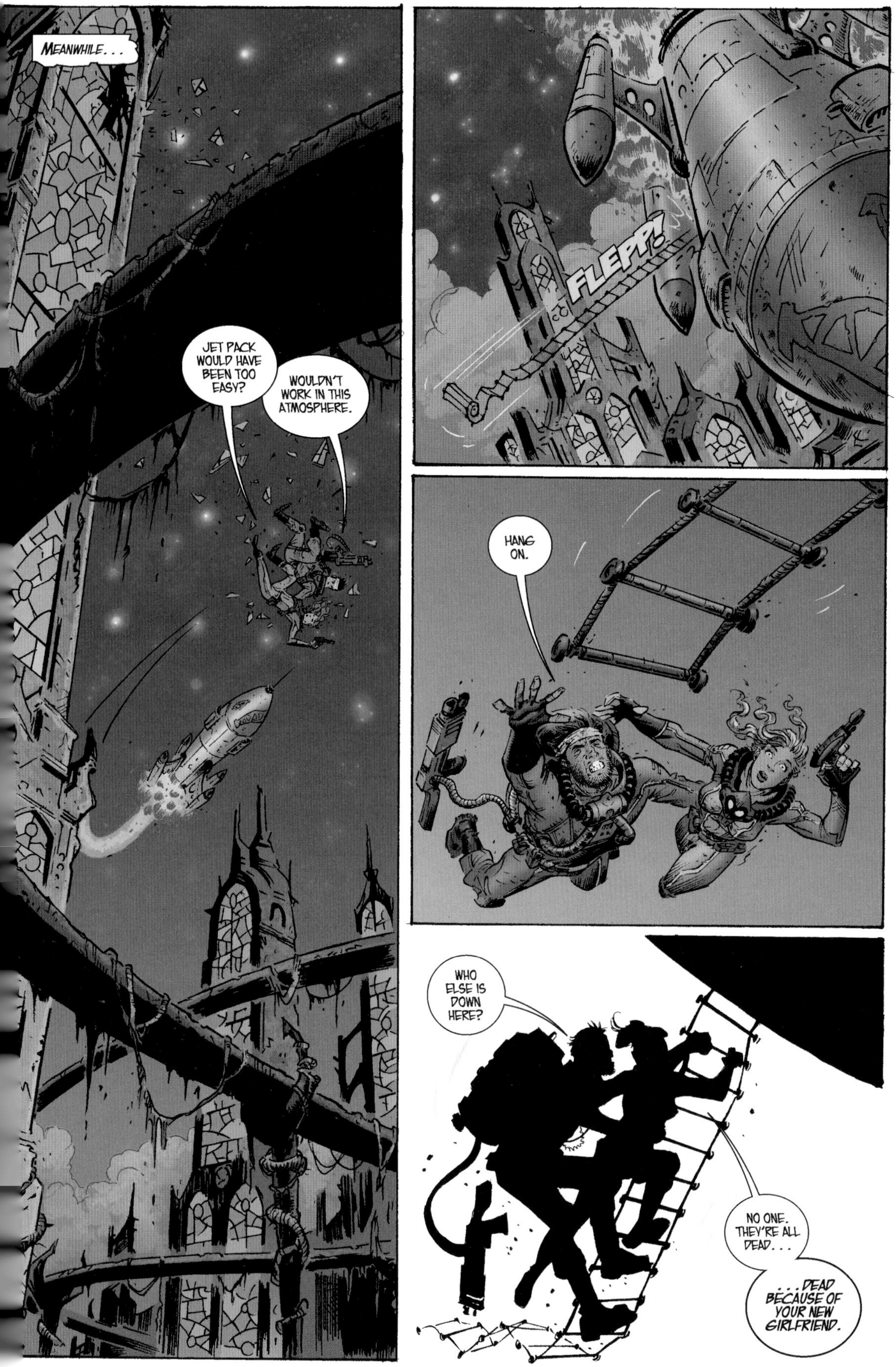
MEANWHILE . . .
JET PACK WOULD HAVE BEEN TOO EASY?
WOULDN'T WORK IN THIS ATMOSPHERE.
FLEPP!
HANG ON.
WHO ELSE IS DOWN HERE?
NO ONE. THEY'RE ALL DEAD . . .
. . . DEAD BECAUSE OF YOUR NEW GIRLFRIEND.

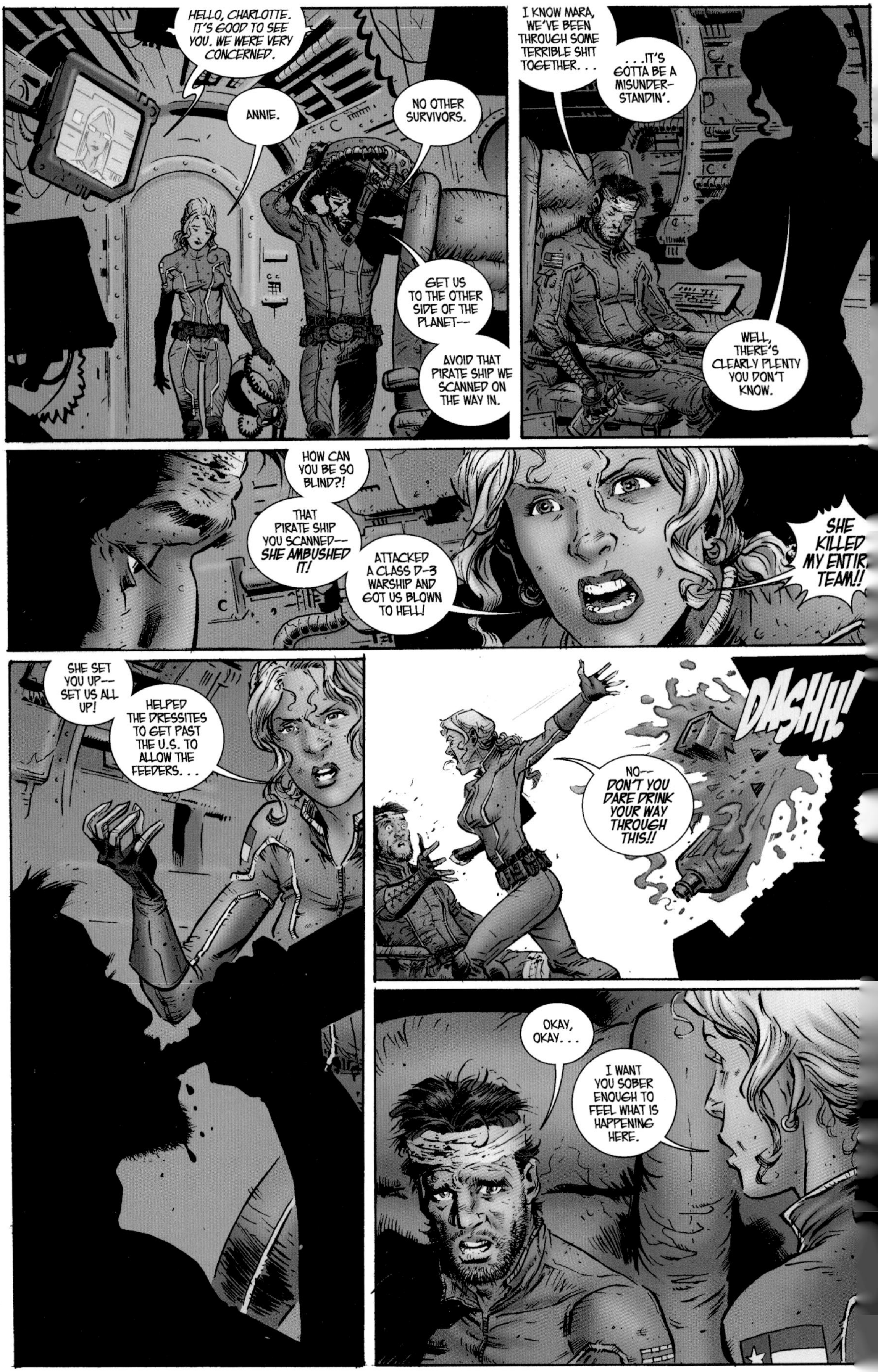
HELLO, CHARLOTTE. IT'S GOOD TO SEE YOU. WE WERE VERY CONCERNED.
ANNIE.
NO OTHER SURVIVORS.
GET US TO THE OTHER SIDE OF THE PLANET--
AVOID THAT PIRATE SHIP WE SCANNED ON THE WAY IN.
I KNOW MARA, WE'VE BEEN THROUGH SOME TERRIBLE SHIT TOGETHER...
...IT'S GOTTA BE A MISUNDER-STANDIN'.
WELL, THERE'S CLEARLY PLENTY YOU DON'T KNOW.
HOW CAN YOU BE SO BLIND?!
THAT PIRATE SHIP YOU SCANNED-- SHE AMBUSHED IT!
ATTACKED A CLASS D-3 WARSHIP AND GOT US BLOWN TO HELL!
SHE KILLED MY ENTIR TEAM!!
SHE SET YOU UP-- SET US ALL UP!
HELPED THE DRESSITES TO GET PAST THE U.S. TO ALLOW THE FEEDERS...
DASHH!
NO-- DON'T YOU DARE DRINK YOUR WAY THROUGH THIS!!
OKAY, OKAY...
I WANT YOU SOBER ENOUGH TO FEEL WHAT IS HAPPENING HERE.

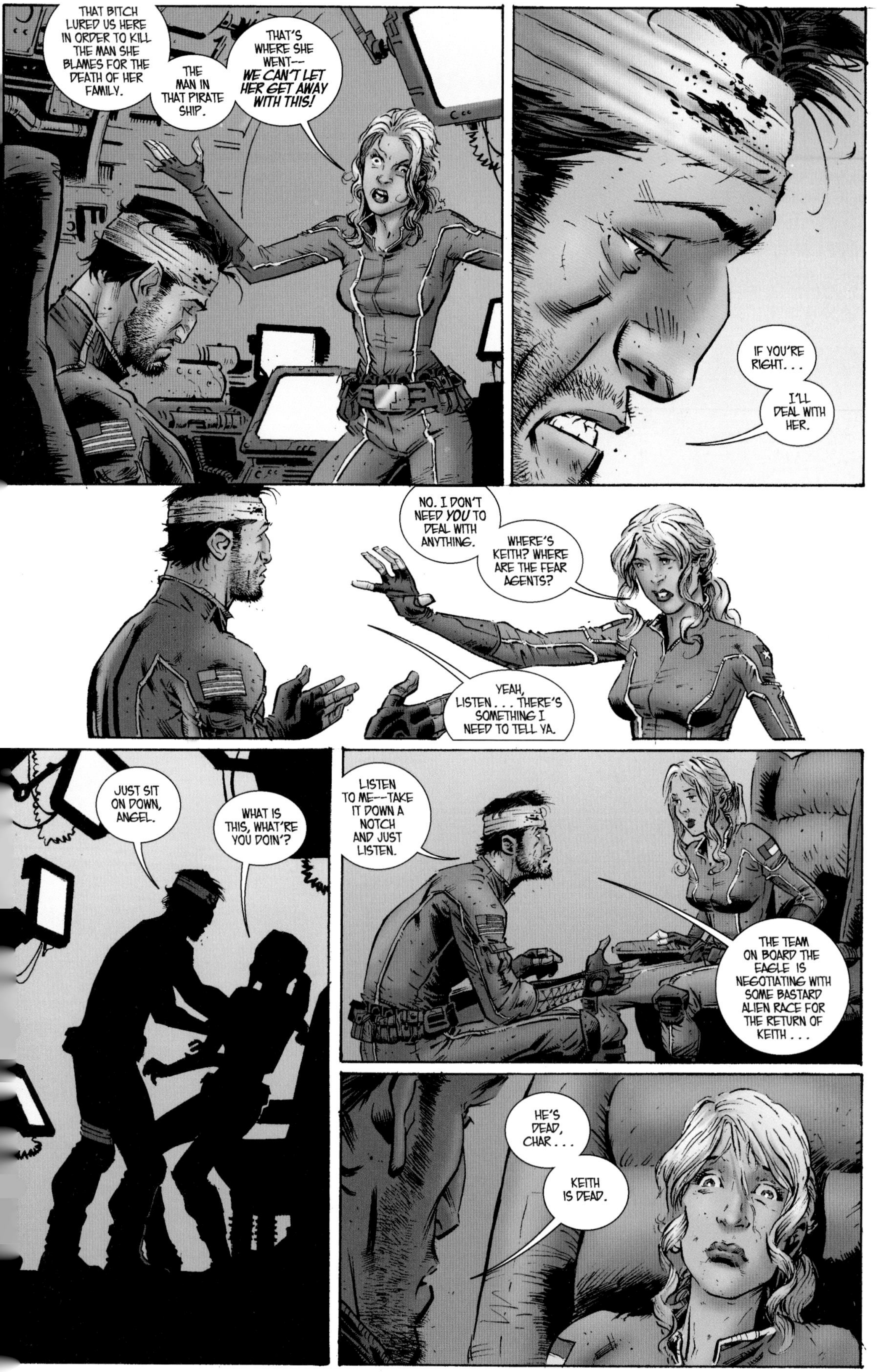
THAT BITCH LURED US HERE IN ORDER TO KILL THE MAN SHE BLAMES FOR THE DEATH OF HER FAMILY.
THE MAN IN THAT PIRATE SHIP.
THAT'S WHERE SHE WENT-- *WE CAN'T LET HER GET AWAY WITH THIS!*
IF YOU'RE RIGHT. . .
I'LL DEAL WITH HER.
NO. I DON'T NEED *YOU* TO DEAL WITH ANYTHING.
WHERE'S KEITH? WHERE ARE THE FEAR AGENTS?
YEAH, LISTEN . . . THERE'S SOMETHING I NEED TO TELL YA.
JUST SIT ON DOWN, ANGEL.
WHAT IS THIS, WHAT'RE YOU DOIN'?
LISTEN TO ME--TAKE IT DOWN A NOTCH AND JUST LISTEN.
THE TEAM ON BOARD THE EAGLE IS NEGOTIATING WITH SOME BASTARD ALIEN RACE FOR THE RETURN OF KEITH . . .
HE'S DEAD, CHAR . . .
KEITH IS DEAD.

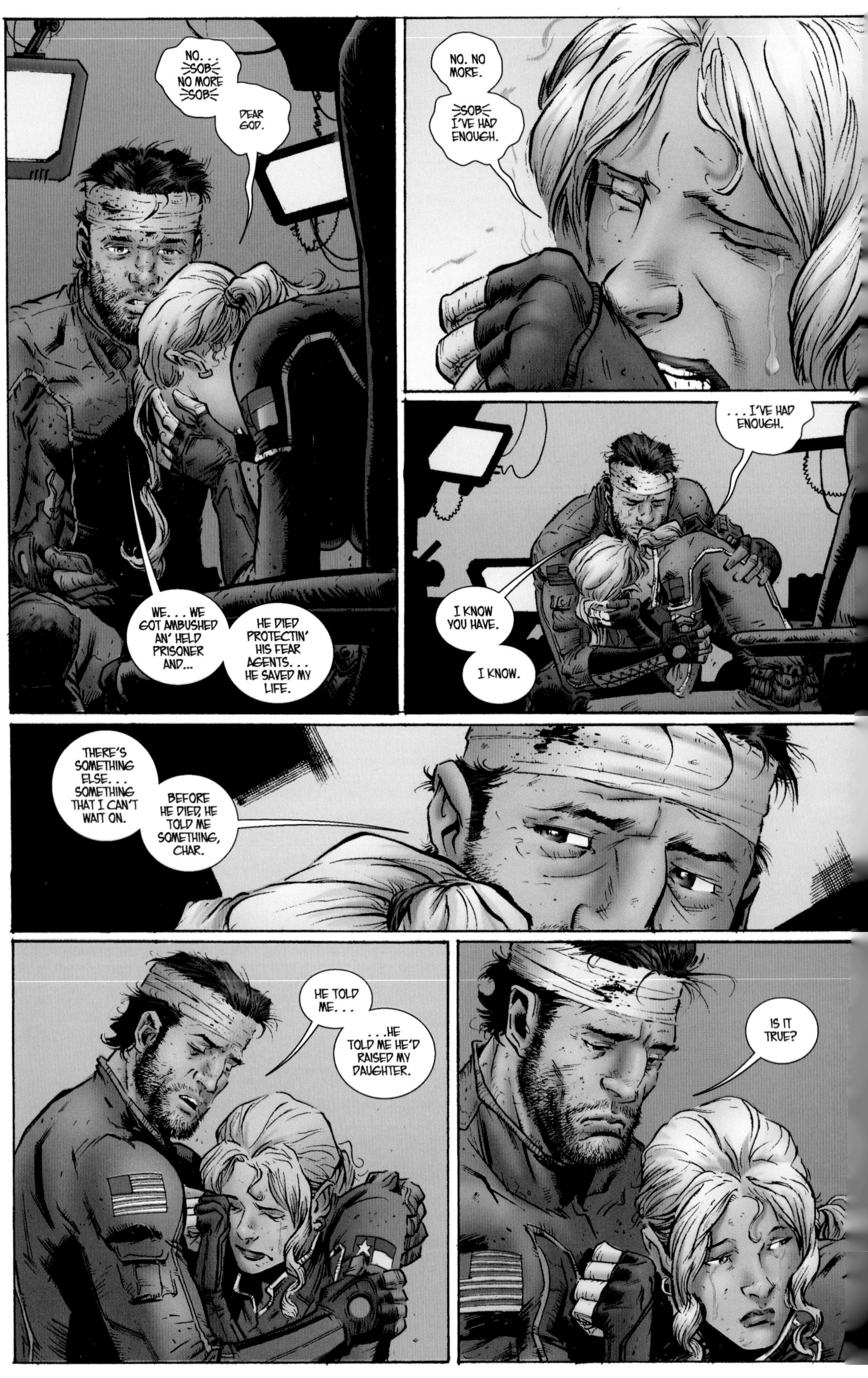
NO. . . ≡SOB≡ NO MORE ≡SOB≡
DEAR GOD.
WE. . . WE GOT AMBUSHED AN' HELD PRISONER AND...
HE DIED PROTECTIN' HIS FEAR AGENTS. . . HE SAVED MY LIFE.
NO. NO MORE.
≡SOB≡ I'VE HAD ENOUGH.
. . . I'VE HAD ENOUGH.
I KNOW YOU HAVE.
I KNOW.
THERE'S SOMETHING ELSE. . . SOMETHING THAT I CAN'T WAIT ON.
BEFORE HE DIED, HE TOLD ME SOMETHING, CHAR.
HE TOLD ME. . .
. . .HE TOLD ME HE'D RAISED MY DAUGHTER.
IS IT TRUE?

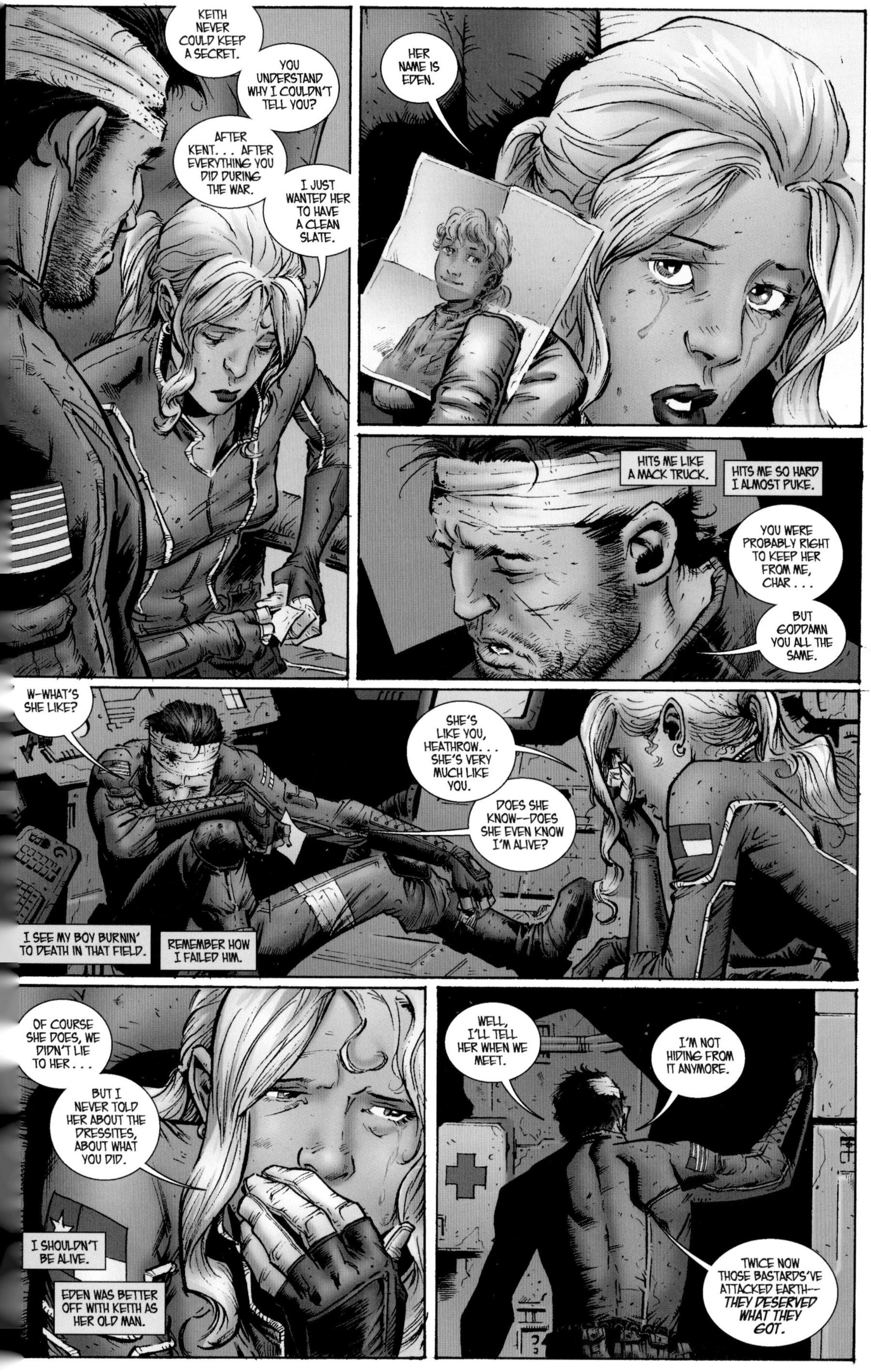
KEITH NEVER COULD KEEP A SECRET.
YOU UNDERSTAND WHY I COULDN'T TELL YOU?
AFTER KENT. . . AFTER EVERYTHING YOU DID DURING THE WAR.
I JUST WANTED HER TO HAVE A CLEAN SLATE.
HER NAME IS EDEN.
HITS ME LIKE A MACK TRUCK.
HITS ME SO HARD I ALMOST PUKE.
YOU WERE PROBABLY RIGHT TO KEEP HER FROM ME, CHAR . . .
BUT GODDAMN YOU ALL THE SAME.
W-WHAT'S SHE LIKE?
SHE'S LIKE YOU, HEATHROW. . . SHE'S VERY MUCH LIKE YOU.
DOES SHE KNOW--DOES SHE EVEN KNOW I'M ALIVE?
I SEE MY BOY BURNIN' TO DEATH IN THAT FIELD.
REMEMBER HOW I FAILED HIM.
OF COURSE SHE DOES, WE DIDN'T LIE TO HER . . .
BUT I NEVER TOLD HER ABOUT THE DRESSITES, ABOUT WHAT YOU DID.
I SHOULDN'T BE ALIVE.
EDEN WAS BETTER OFF WITH KEITH AS HER OLD MAN.
WELL, I'LL TELL HER WHEN WE MEET.
I'M NOT HIDING FROM IT ANYMORE.
TWICE NOW THOSE BASTARDS'VE ATTACKED EARTH-- *THEY DESERVED WHAT THEY GOT.*

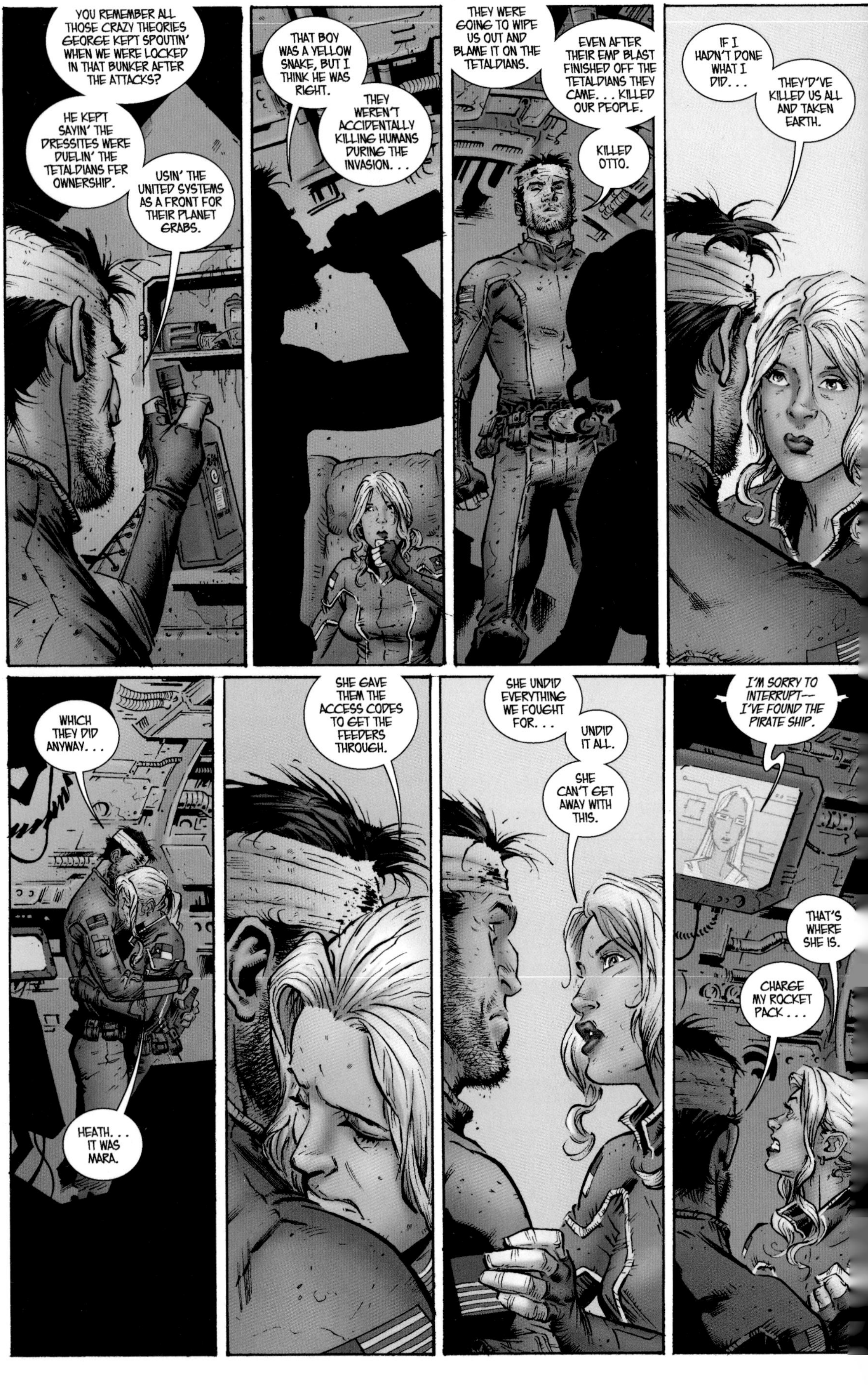

YOU REMEMBER ALL THOSE CRAZY THEORIES GEORGE KEPT SPOUTIN' WHEN WE WERE LOCKED IN THAT BUNKER AFTER THE ATTACKS?
HE KEPT SAYIN' THE DRESSITES WERE DUELIN' THE TETALDIANS FER OWNERSHIP.
USIN' THE UNITED SYSTEMS AS A FRONT FOR THEIR PLANET GRABS.
THAT BOY WAS A YELLOW SNAKE, BUT I THINK HE WAS RIGHT.
THEY WEREN'T ACCIDENTALLY KILLING HUMANS DURING THE INVASION. . .
THEY WERE GOING TO WIPE US OUT AND BLAME IT ON THE TETALDIANS.
EVEN AFTER THEIR EMP BLAST FINISHED OFF THE TETALDIANS THEY CAME. . . KILLED OUR PEOPLE.
KILLED OTTO.
IF I HADN'T DONE WHAT I DID. . .
THEY'D'VE KILLED US ALL AND TAKEN EARTH.
WHICH THEY DID ANYWAY. . .
HEATH. . . IT WAS MARA.
SHE GAVE THEM THE ACCESS CODES TO GET THE FEEDERS THROUGH.
SHE UNDID EVERYTHING WE FOUGHT FOR. . .
UNDID IT ALL.
SHE CAN'T GET AWAY WITH THIS.
I'M SORRY TO INTERRUPT—I'VE FOUND THE PIRATE SHIP.
THAT'S WHERE SHE IS.
CHARGE MY ROCKET PACK . . .

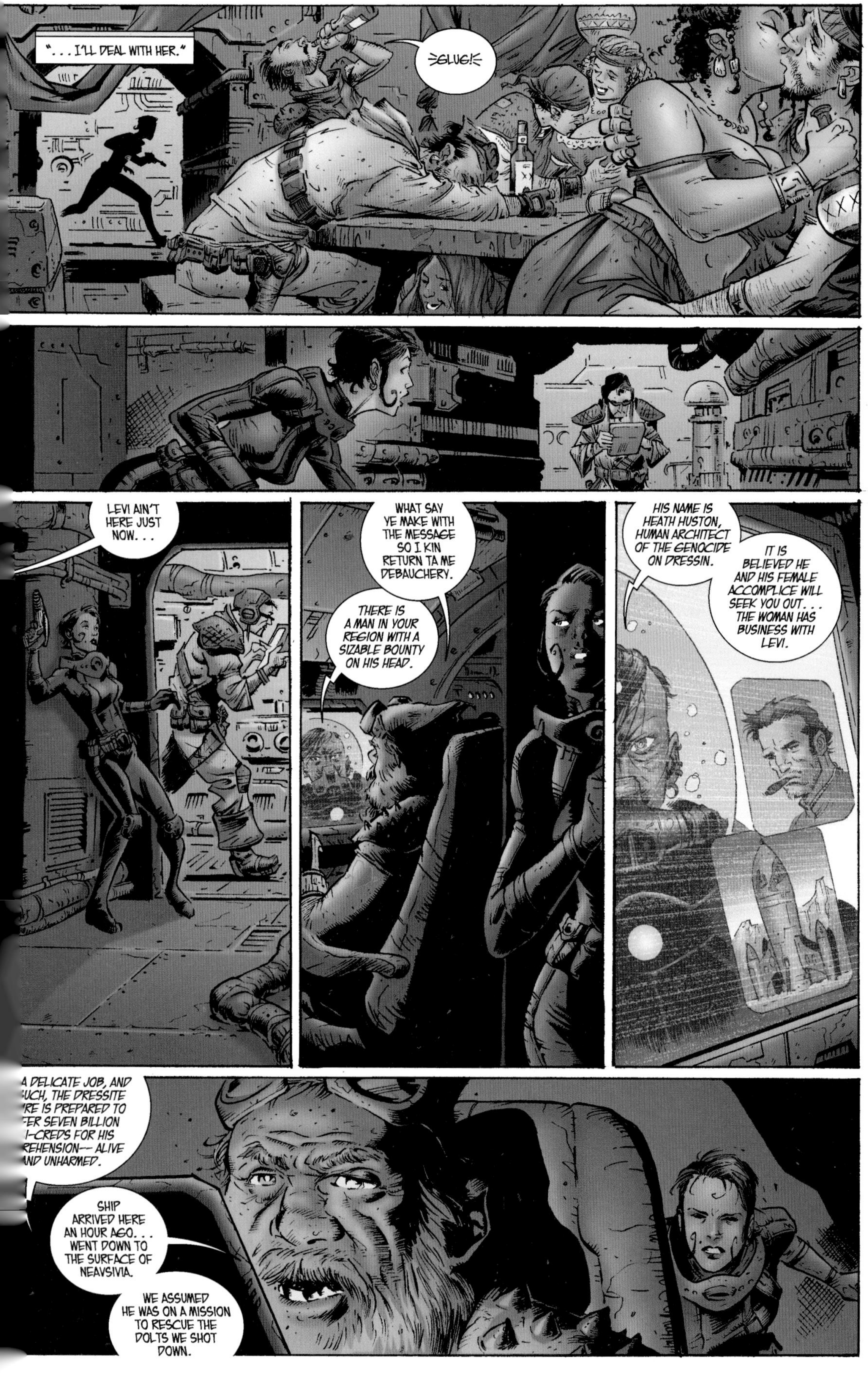

". . . I'LL DEAL WITH HER."
≶GLUG!≶
LEVI AIN'T HERE JUST NOW. . .
WHAT SAY YE MAKE WITH THE MESSAGE SO I KIN RETURN TA ME DEBAUCHERY.
THERE IS A MAN IN YOUR REGION WITH A SIZABLE BOUNTY ON HIS HEAD.
HIS NAME IS HEATH HUSTON, HUMAN ARCHITECT OF THE GENOCIDE ON DRESSIN.
IT IS BELIEVED HE AND HIS FEMALE ACCOMPLICE WILL SEEK YOU OUT. . . THE WOMAN HAS BUSINESS WITH LEVI.
A DELICATE JOB, AND SUCH, THE DRESSITE RE IS PREPARED TO ER SEVEN BILLION I-CREDS FOR HIS REHENSION-- ALIVE AND UNHARMED.
SHIP ARRIVED HERE AN HOUR AGO. . . WENT DOWN TO THE SURFACE OF NEAVSIVIA.
WE ASSUMED HE WAS ON A MISSION TO RESCUE THE DOLTS WE SHOT DOWN.

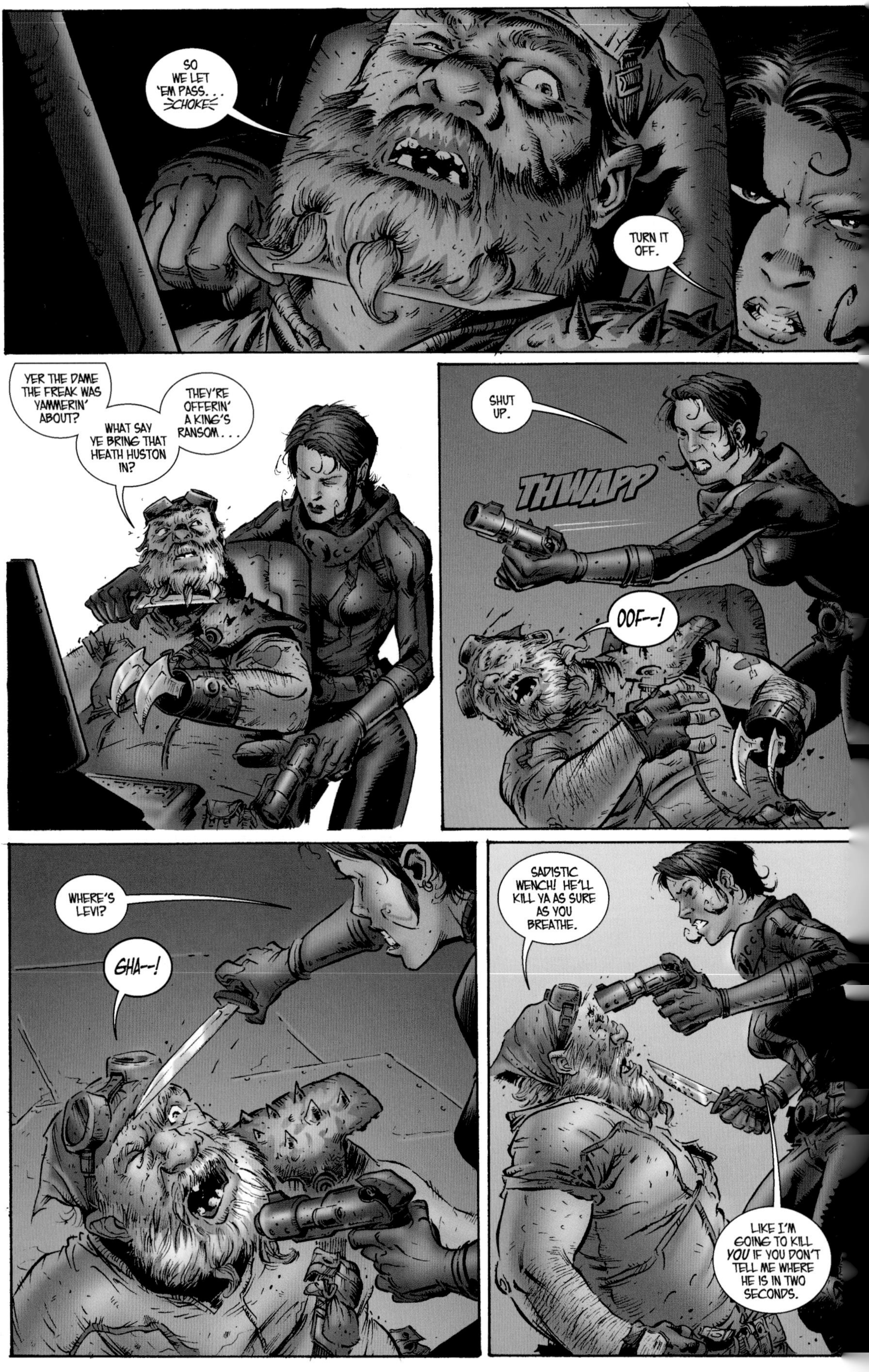

SO WE LET 'EM PASS. . . ≈CHOKE≈
TURN IT OFF.
YER THE DAME THE FREAK WAS YAMMERIN' ABOUT?
WHAT SAY YE BRING THAT HEATH HUSTON IN?
THEY'RE OFFERIN' A KING'S RANSOM . . .
SHUT UP.
THWAPP
OOF--!
WHERE'S LEVI?
GHA--!
SADISTIC WENCH! HE'LL KILL YA AS SURE AS YOU BREATHE.
LIKE I'M GOING TO KILL *YOU* IF YOU DON'T TELL ME WHERE HE IS IN TWO SECONDS.

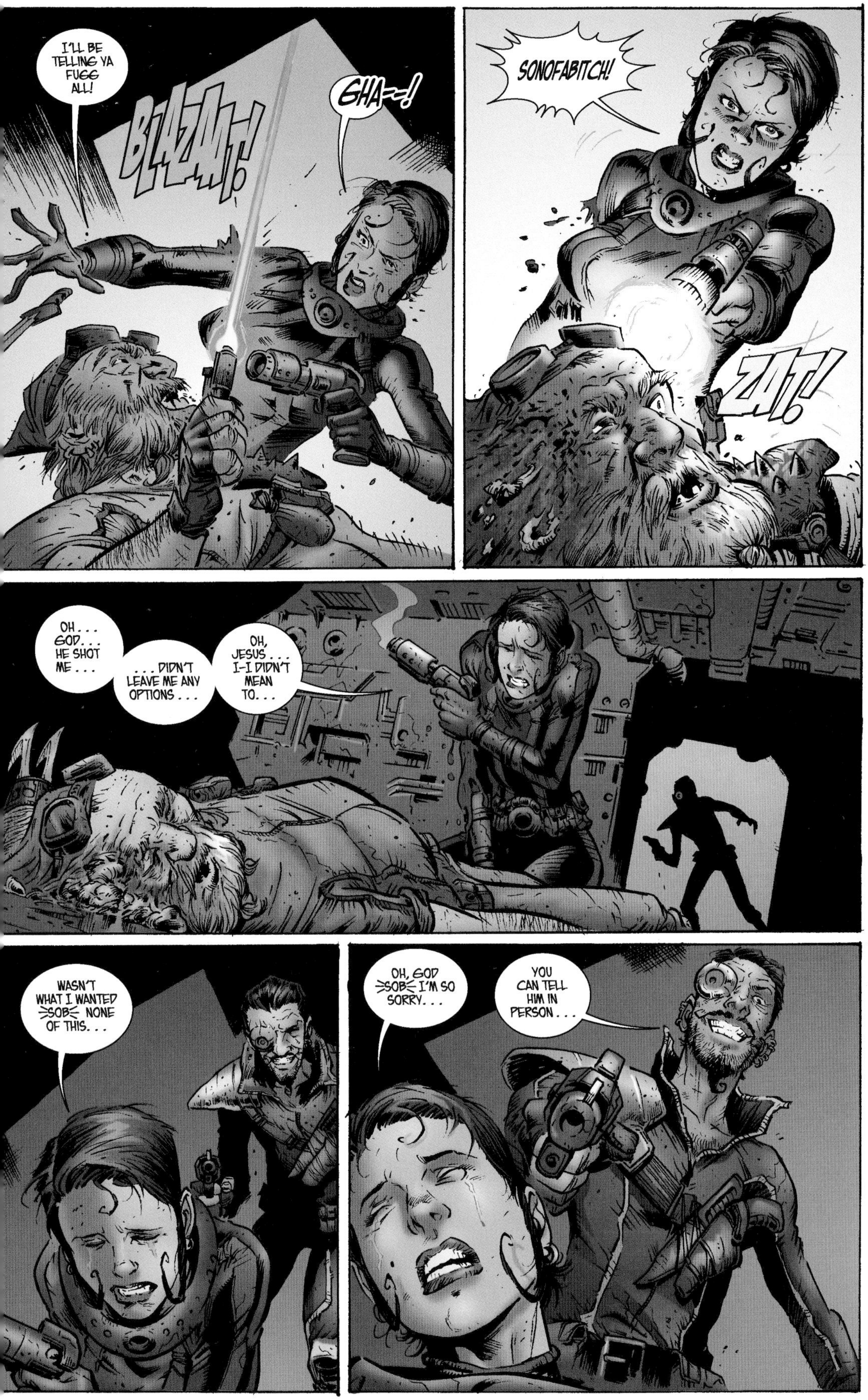
I'LL BE TELLING YA FUGG ALL!
BLAZAAT!
GHA--!
SONOFABITCH!
ZAT!
OH . . . GOD . . . HE SHOT ME . . .
. . . DIDN'T LEAVE ME ANY OPTIONS . . .
OH, JESUS . . . I-I DIDN'T MEAN TO. . .
WASN'T WHAT I WANTED =SOB= NONE OF THIS. . .
OH, GOD =SOB= I'M SO SORRY. . .
YOU CAN TELL HIM IN PERSON . . .

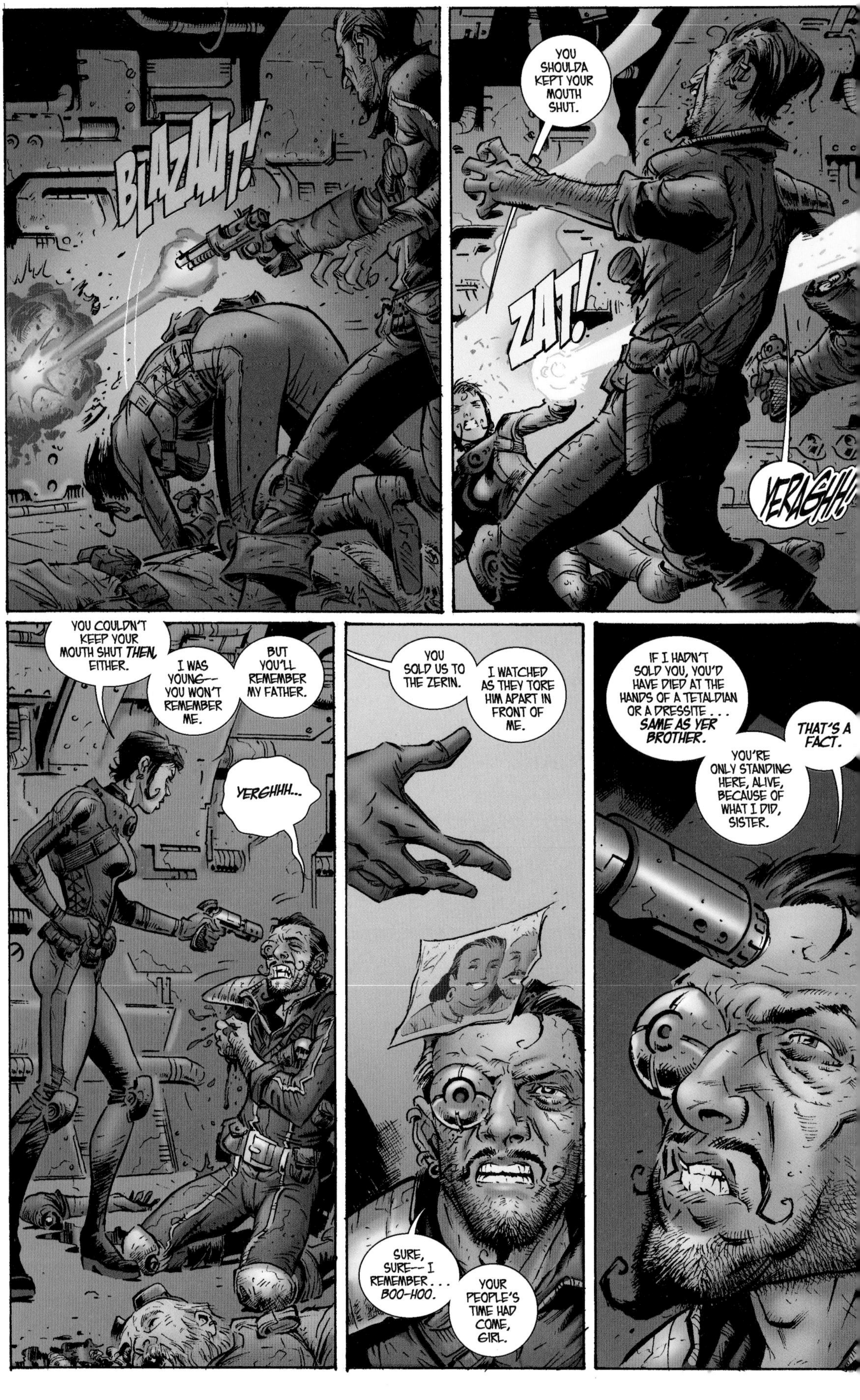

BLAZAAT!
YOU SHOULDA KEPT YOUR MOUTH SHUT.
ZAT!
YERAGHH!
YOU COULDN'T KEEP YOUR MOUTH SHUT THEN, EITHER.
I WAS YOUNG-- YOU WON'T REMEMBER ME.
BUT YOU'LL REMEMBER MY FATHER.
YERGHHH...
YOU SOLD US TO THE ZERIN.
I WATCHED AS THEY TORE HIM APART IN FRONT OF ME.
SURE, SURE-- I REMEMBER... BOO-HOO.
YOUR PEOPLE'S TIME HAD COME, GIRL.
IF I HADN'T SOLD YOU, YOU'D HAVE DIED AT THE HANDS OF A TETALDIAN OR A DRESSITE... SAME AS YER BROTHER.
THAT'S A FACT.
YOU'RE ONLY STANDING HERE, ALIVE, BECAUSE OF WHAT I DID, SISTER.

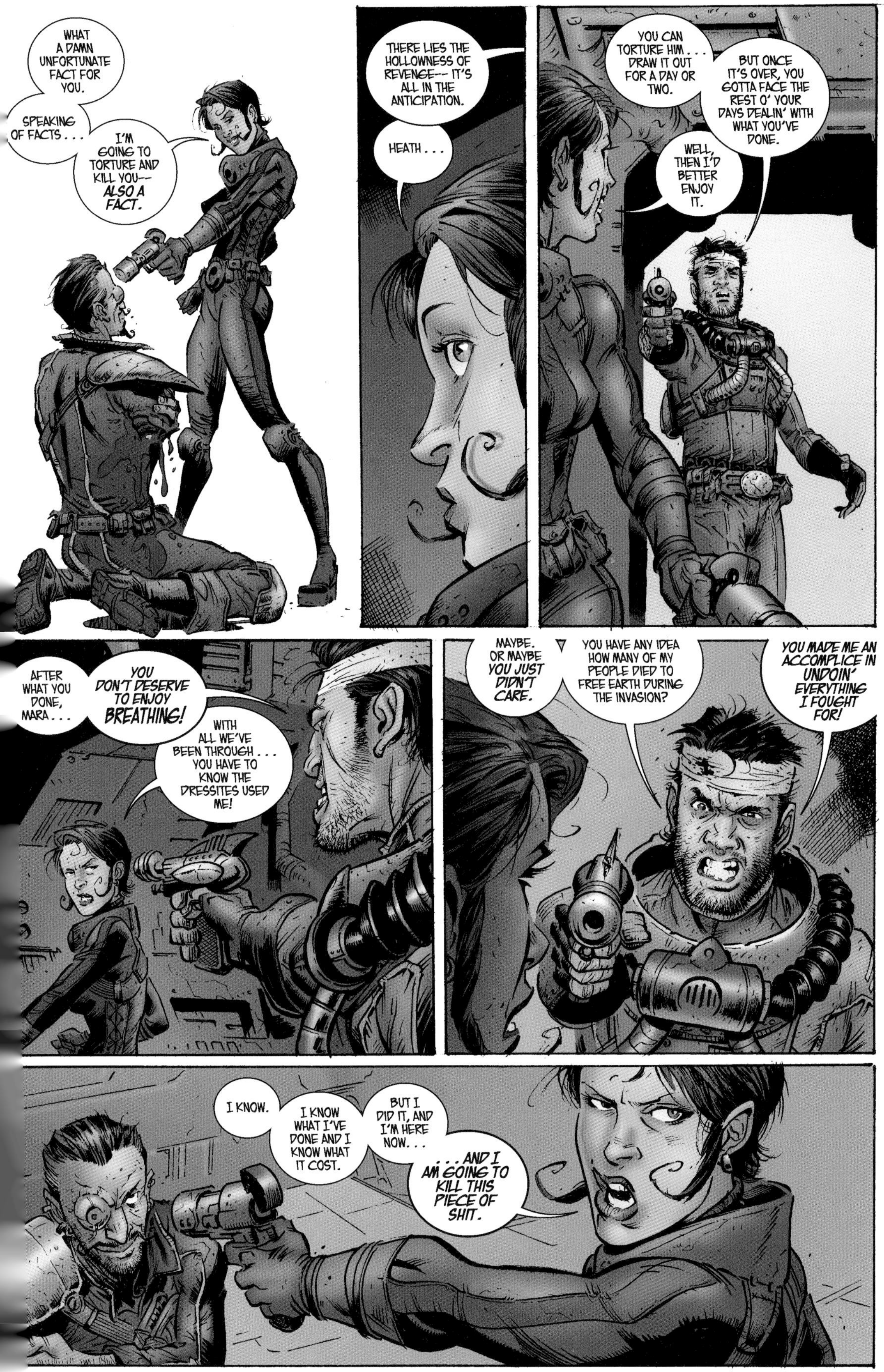
WHAT A DAMN UNFORTUNATE FACT FOR YOU.
SPEAKING OF FACTS . . .
I'M GOING TO TORTURE AND KILL YOU-- ALSO A FACT.
THERE LIES THE HOLLOWNESS OF REVENGE-- IT'S ALL IN THE ANTICIPATION.
HEATH . . .
YOU CAN TORTURE HIM . . . DRAW IT OUT FOR A DAY OR TWO.
BUT ONCE IT'S OVER, YOU GOTTA FACE THE REST O' YOUR DAYS DEALIN' WITH WHAT YOU'VE DONE.
WELL, THEN I'D BETTER ENJOY IT.
AFTER WHAT YOU DONE, MARA . . .
YOU DON'T DESERVE TO ENJOY BREATHING!
WITH ALL WE'VE BEEN THROUGH . . . YOU HAVE TO KNOW THE DRESSITES USED ME!
MAYBE. OR MAYBE YOU JUST DIDN'T CARE.
YOU HAVE ANY IDEA HOW MANY OF MY PEOPLE DIED TO FREE EARTH DURING THE INVASION?
YOU MADE ME AN ACCOMPLICE IN UNDOIN' EVERYTHING I FOUGHT FOR!
I KNOW.
I KNOW WHAT I'VE DONE AND I KNOW WHAT IT COST.
BUT I DID IT, AND I'M HERE NOW. . .
. . . AND I AM GOING TO KILL THIS PIECE OF SHIT.

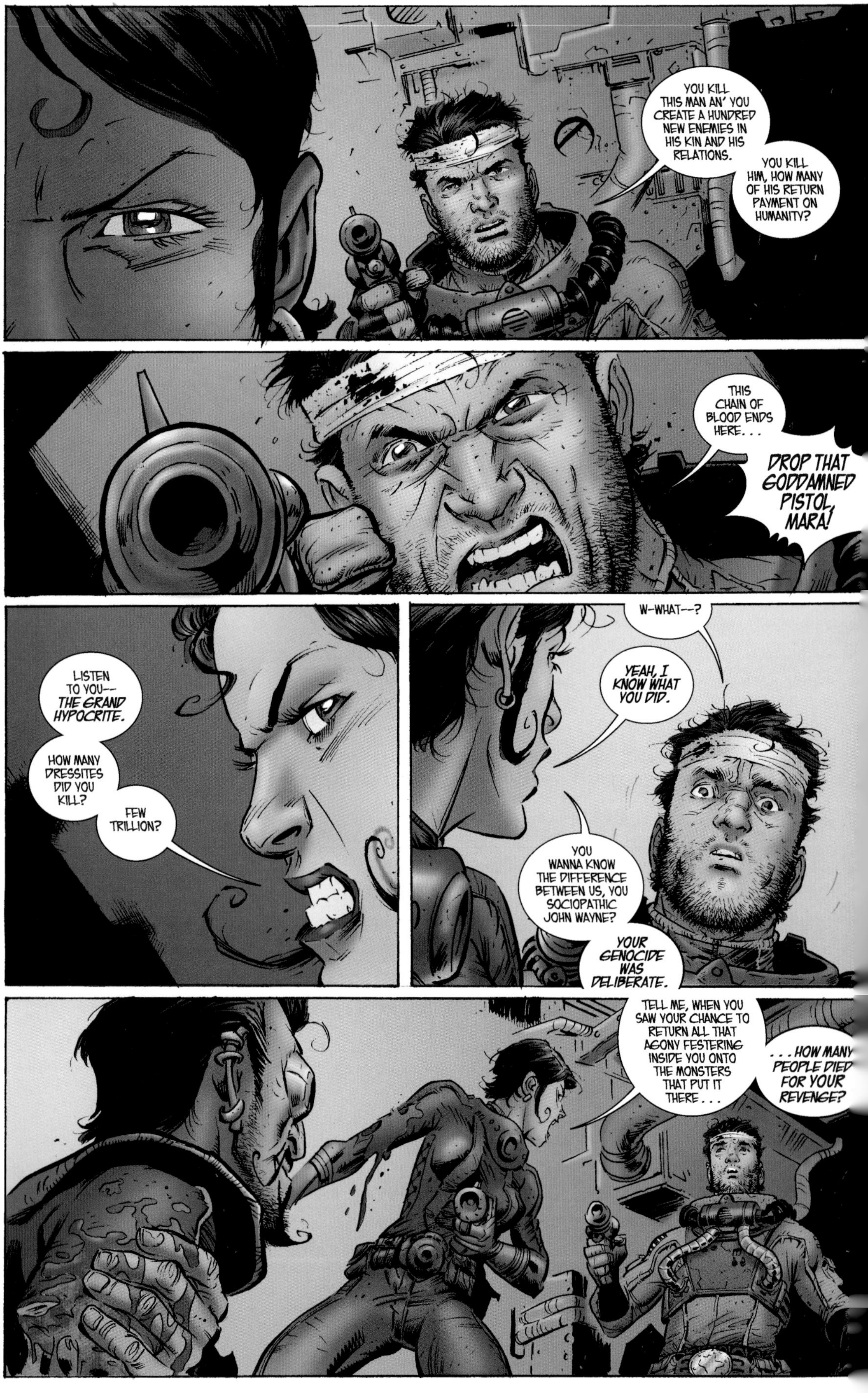
YOU KILL THIS MAN AN' YOU CREATE A HUNDRED NEW ENEMIES IN HIS KIN AND HIS RELATIONS.
YOU KILL HIM, HOW MANY OF HIS RETURN PAYMENT ON HUMANITY?
THIS CHAIN OF BLOOD ENDS HERE. . .
DROP THAT GODDAMNED PISTOL, MARA!
LISTEN TO YOU-- THE GRAND HYPOCRITE.
HOW MANY DRESSITES DID YOU KILL?
FEW TRILLION?
W-WHAT--?
YEAH, I KNOW WHAT YOU DID.
YOU WANNA KNOW THE DIFFERENCE BETWEEN US, YOU SOCIOPATHIC JOHN WAYNE?
YOUR GENOCIDE WAS DELIBERATE.
TELL ME, WHEN YOU SAW YOUR CHANCE TO RETURN ALL THAT AGONY FESTERING INSIDE YOU ONTO THE MONSTERS THAT PUT IT THERE . . .
. . . HOW MANY PEOPLE DIED FOR YOUR REVENGE?

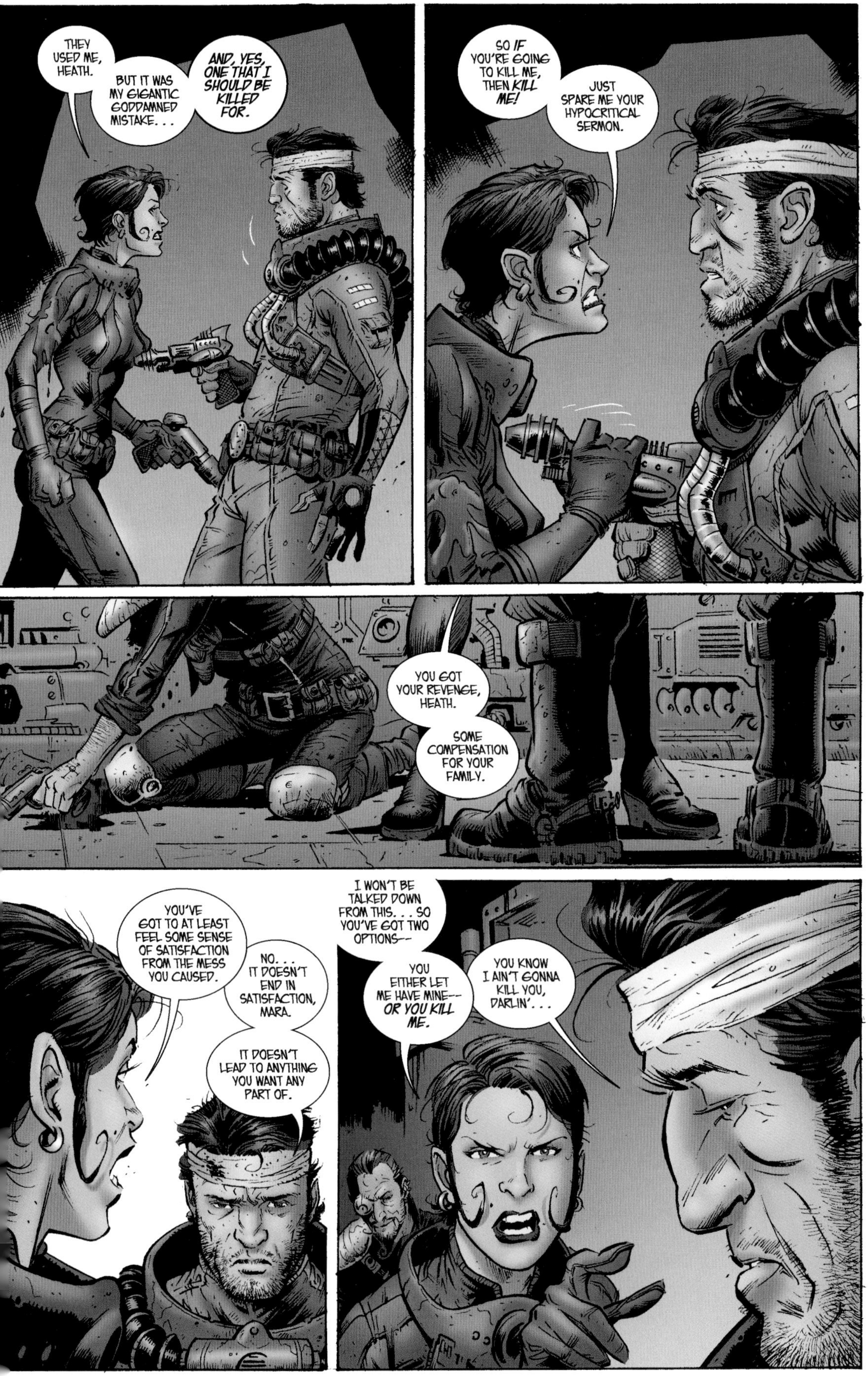
THEY USED ME, HEATH.
BUT IT WAS MY GIGANTIC GODDAMNED MISTAKE. . .
AND, YES, ONE THAT I SHOULD BE KILLED FOR.
SO IF YOU'RE GOING TO KILL ME, THEN KILL ME!
JUST SPARE ME YOUR HYPOCRITICAL SERMON.
YOU GOT YOUR REVENGE, HEATH.
SOME COMPENSATION FOR YOUR FAMILY.
YOU'VE GOT TO AT LEAST FEEL SOME SENSE OF SATISFACTION FROM THE MESS YOU CAUSED.
NO. . . IT DOESN'T END IN SATISFACTION, MARA.
IT DOESN'T LEAD TO ANYTHING YOU WANT ANY PART OF.
I WON'T BE TALKED DOWN FROM THIS. . . SO YOU'VE GOT TWO OPTIONS--
YOU EITHER LET ME HAVE MINE-- OR YOU KILL ME.
YOU KNOW I AIN'T GONNA KILL YOU, DARLIN'. . .

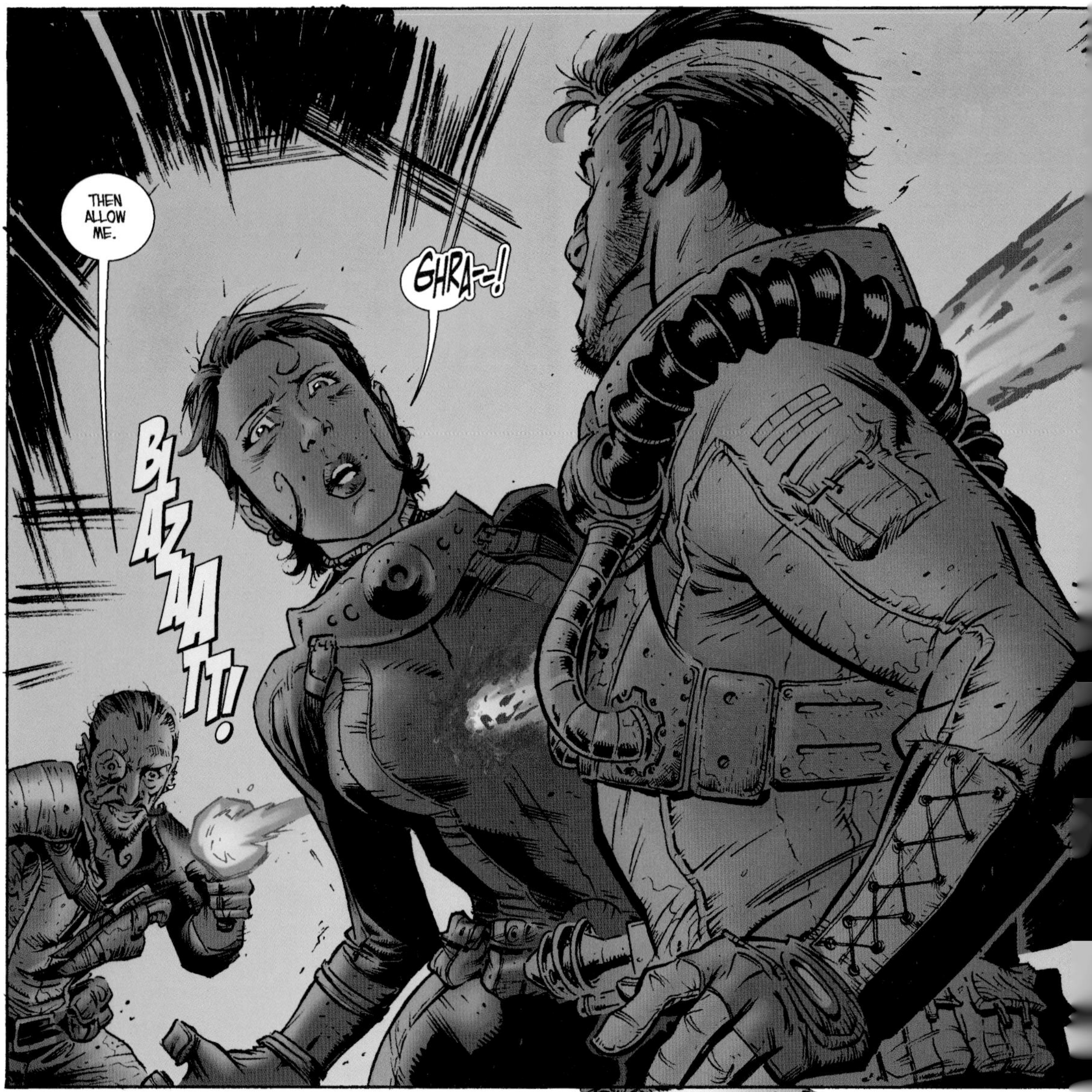
THEN ALLOW ME.
GHRA--!
BLAZAATT!

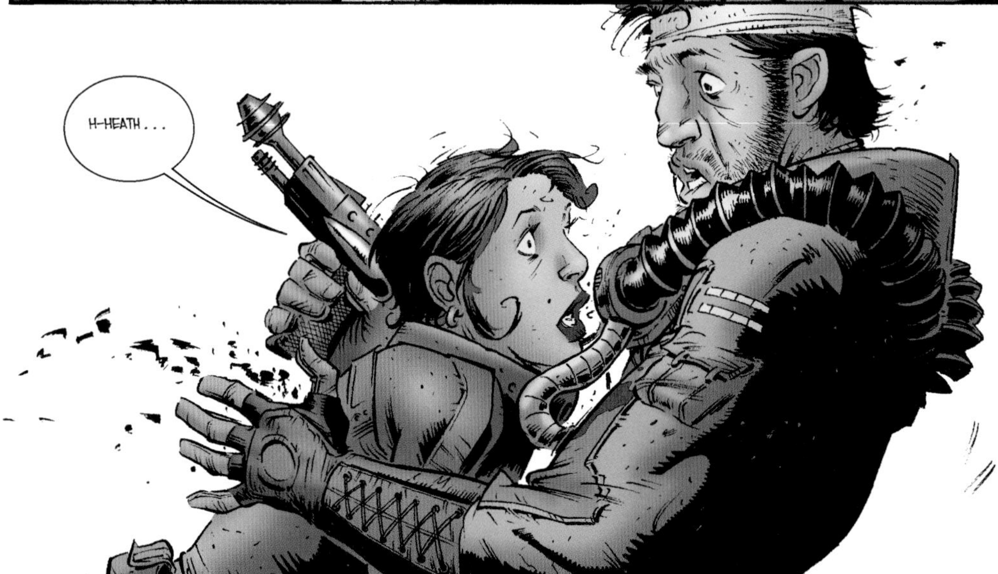
H-HEATH . . .

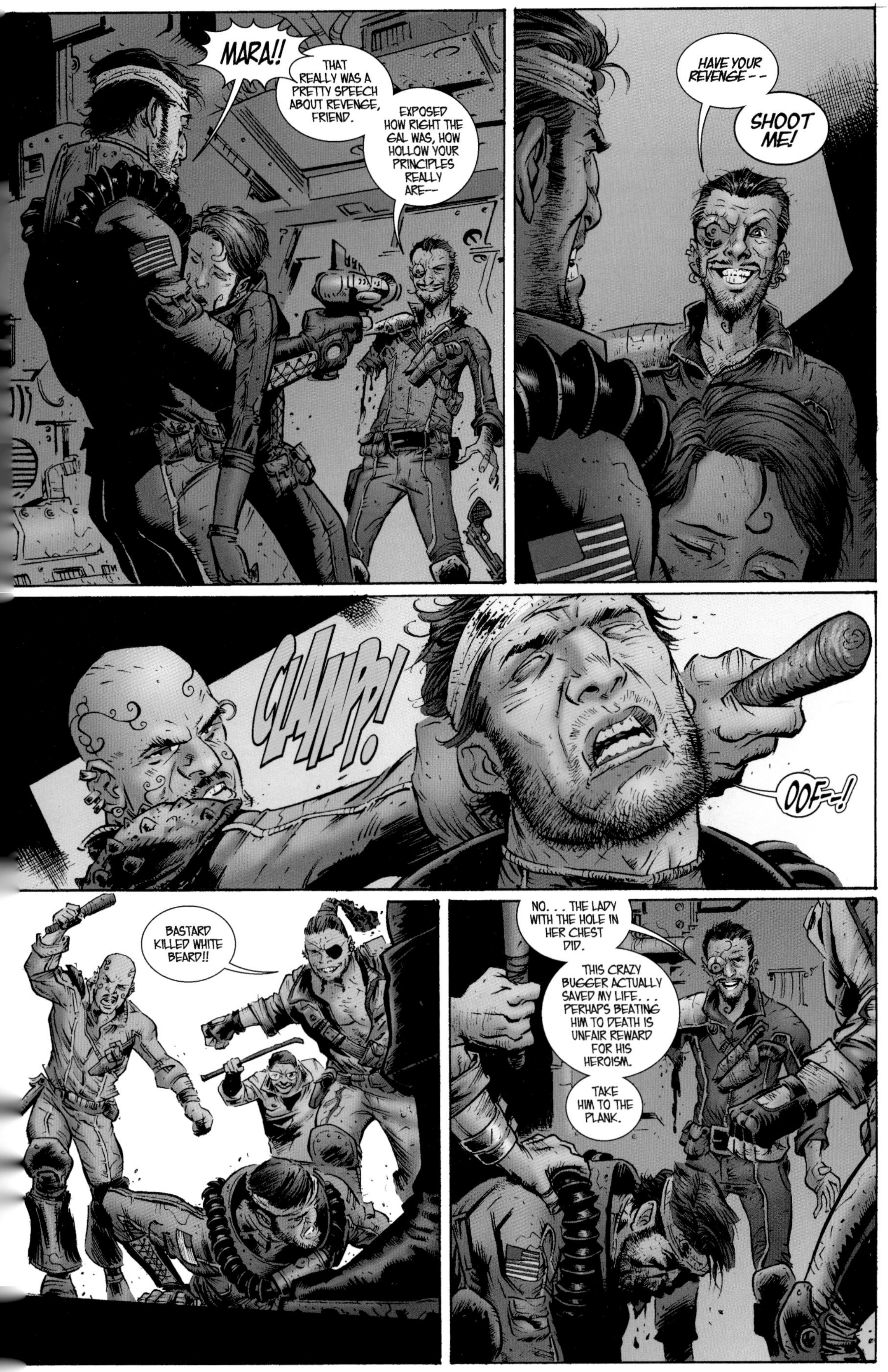
MARA!!
THAT REALLY WAS A PRETTY SPEECH ABOUT REVENGE, FRIEND.
EXPOSED HOW RIGHT THE GAL WAS, HOW HOLLOW YOUR PRINCIPLES REALLY ARE--
HAVE YOUR REVENGE--
SHOOT ME!
CLAMP!
OOF--!
BASTARD KILLED WHITE BEARD!!
NO. . . THE LADY WITH THE HOLE IN HER CHEST DID.
THIS CRAZY BUGGER ACTUALLY SAVED MY LIFE. . . PERHAPS BEATING HIM TO DEATH IS UNFAIR REWARD FOR HIS HEROISM.
TAKE HIM TO THE PLANK.

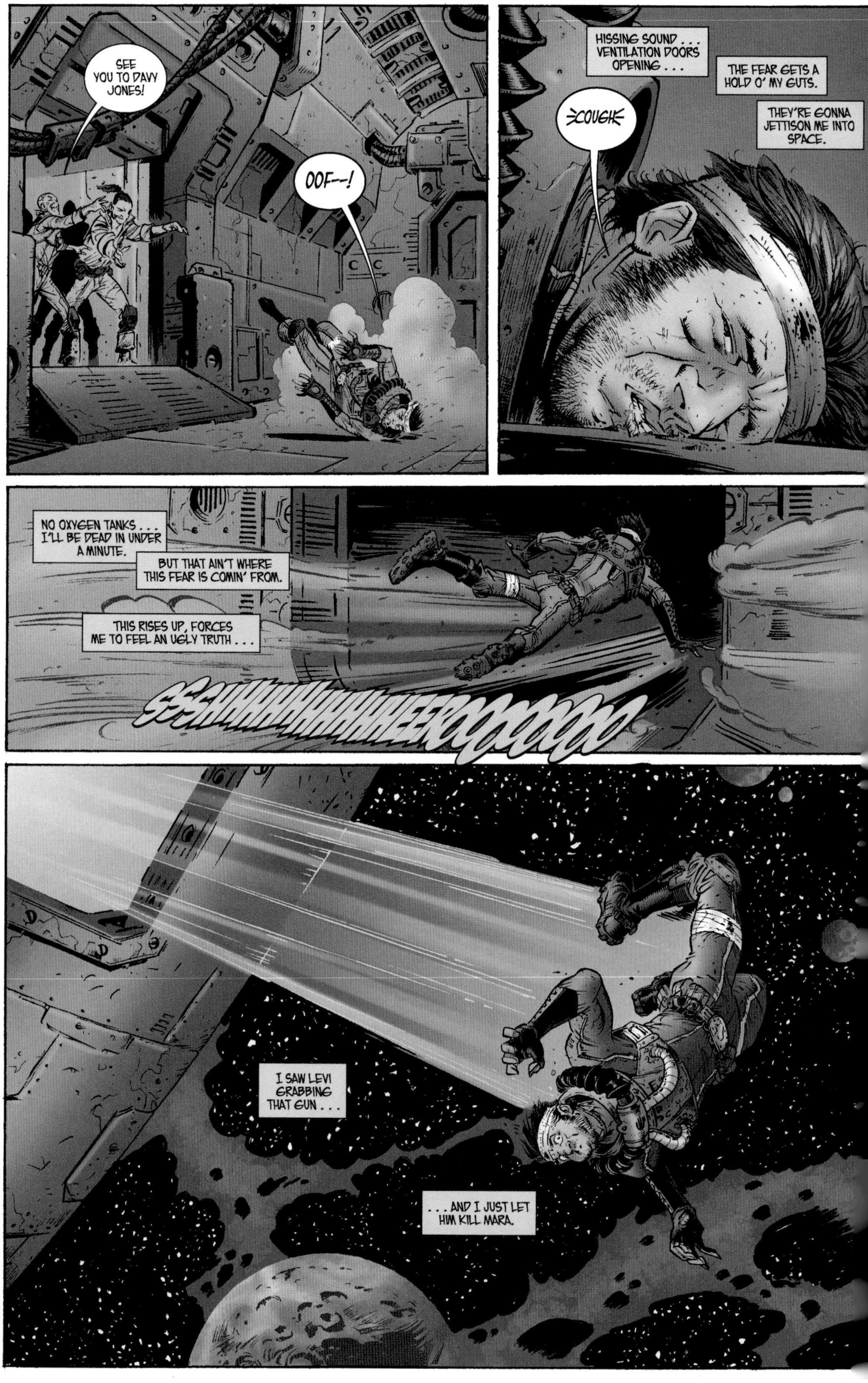
SEE YOU TO DAVY JONES!
OOF--!
HISSING SOUND . . . VENTILATION DOORS OPENING . . .
THE FEAR GETS A HOLD O' MY GUTS.
THEY'RE GONNA JETTISON ME INTO SPACE.
COUGH
NO OXYGEN TANKS . . . I'LL BE DEAD IN UNDER A MINUTE.
BUT THAT AIN'T WHERE THIS FEAR IS COMIN' FROM.
THIS RISES UP, FORCES ME TO FEEL AN UGLY TRUTH . . .
SSSHHHHHHHHHHHEEROOOOOOOOO
I SAW LEVI GRABBING THAT GUN . . .
. . . AND I JUST LET HIM KILL MARA.

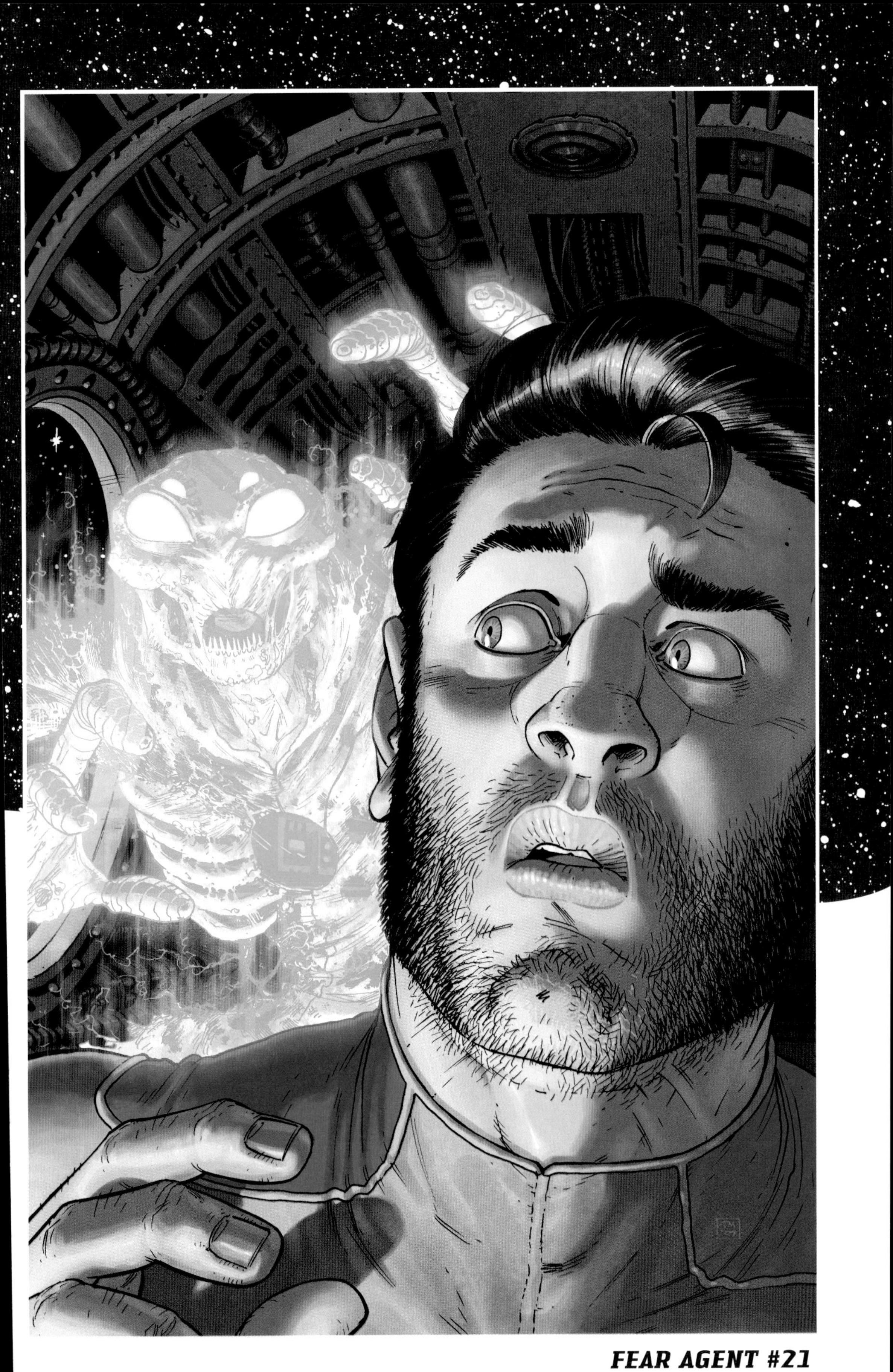

FEAR AGENT #21
ART BY **TONY MOORE**

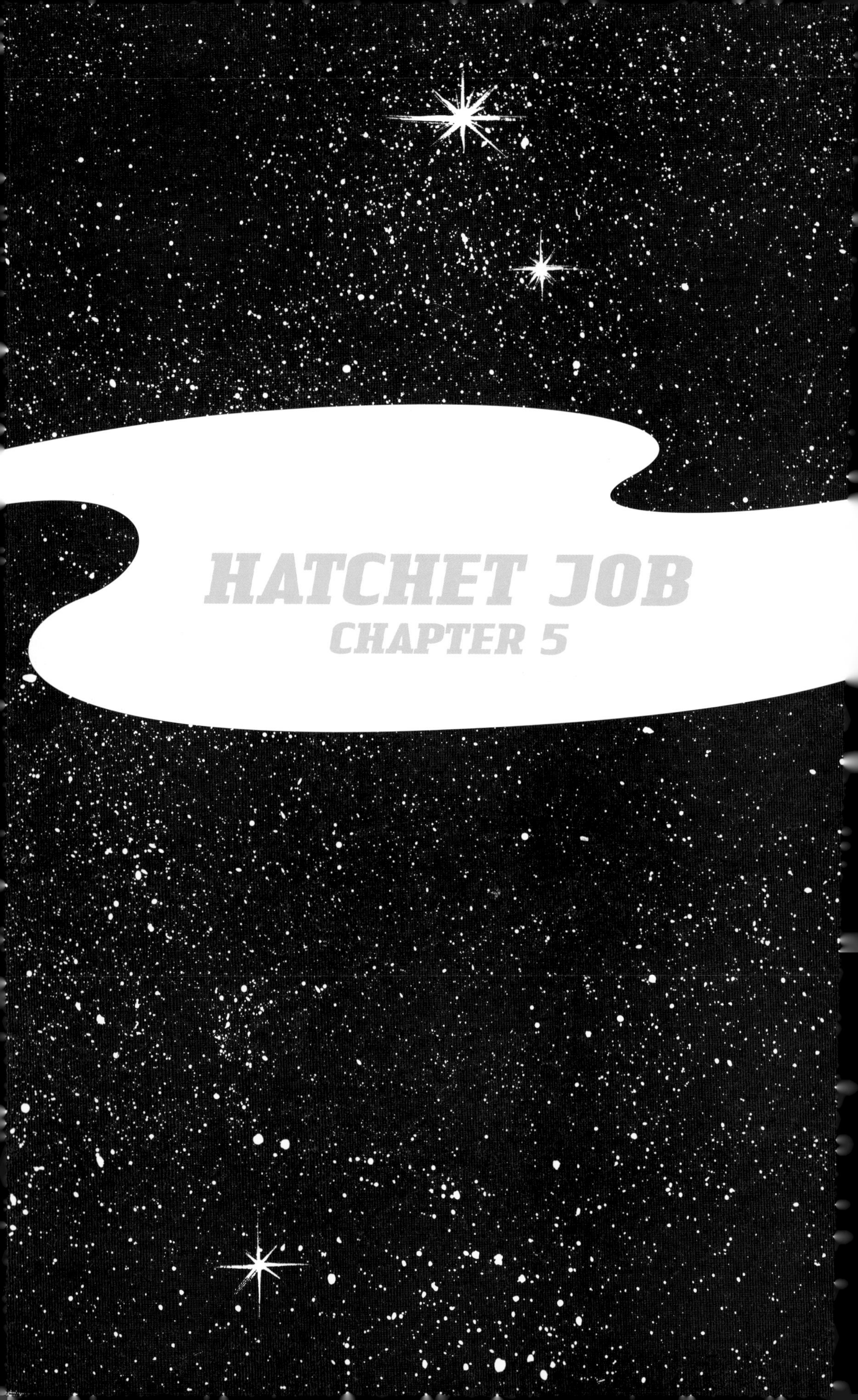
HATCHET JOB
CHAPTER 5

EARTH'S MOON...

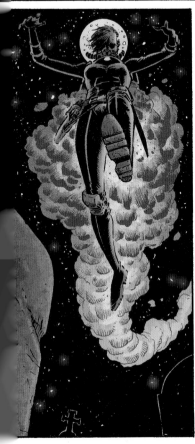

"WHEN YOU GO HOME, TELL THEM OF US AND SAY, FOR THEIR TOMORROW WE GAVE OUR TODAY"

IN MEMORY OF OTTO BIGLEY BELOVED HUSBAND, UNCLE, AND FEA...

UNCLE OTTO...

REST EASY-- HE'S GOING TO BLEED FOR WHAT HE DID TO US.

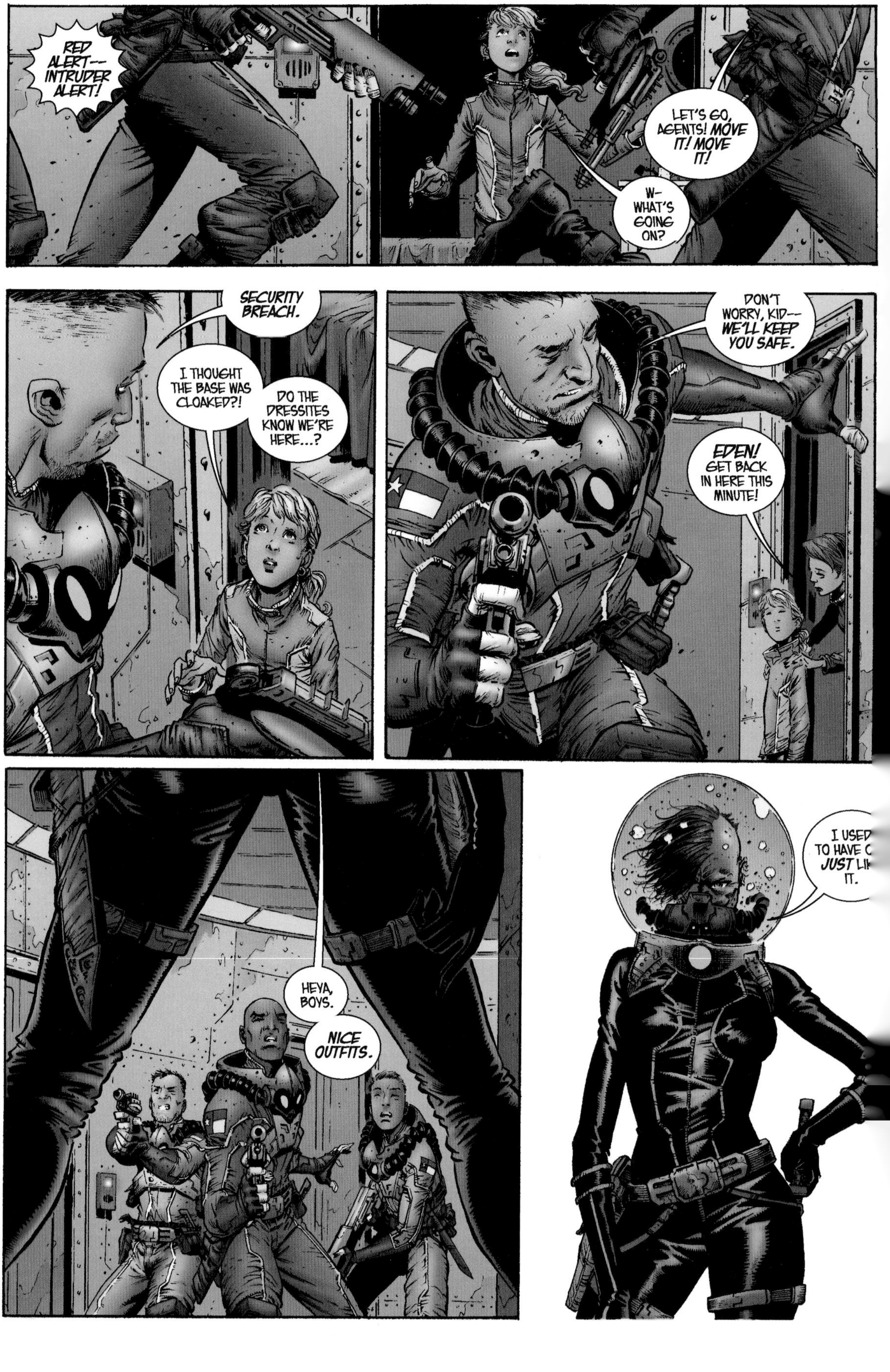
RED ALERT-- INTRUDER ALERT!
LET'S GO, AGENTS! MOVE IT! MOVE IT!
W- WHAT'S GOING ON?
SECURITY BREACH.
I THOUGHT THE BASE WAS CLOAKED?!
DO THE DRESSITES KNOW WE'RE HERE...?
DON'T WORRY, KID-- WE'LL KEEP YOU SAFE.
EDEN! GET BACK IN HERE THIS MINUTE!
HEYA, BOYS.
NICE OUTFITS.
I USED TO HAVE ONE JUST LIKE IT.

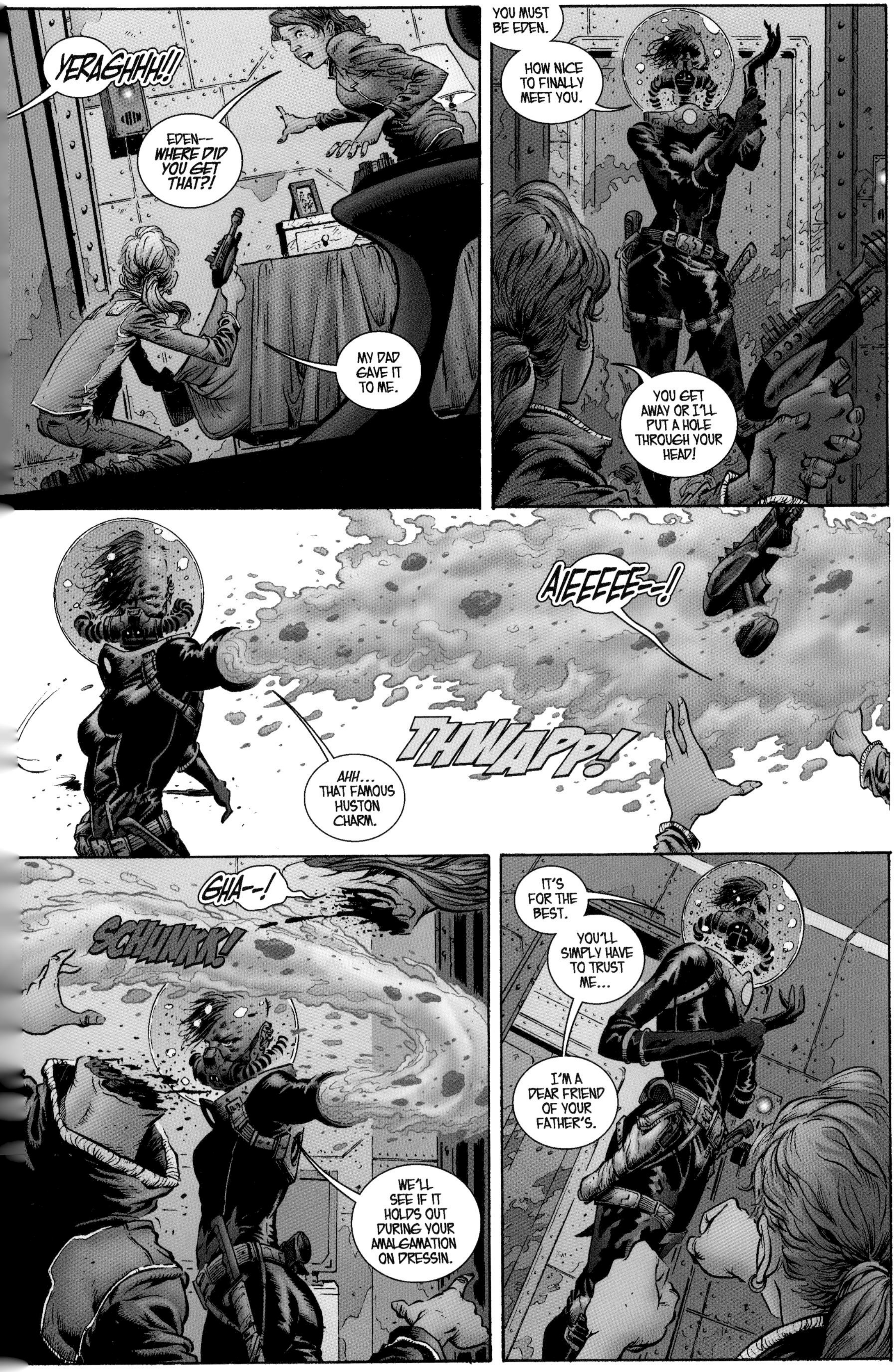
YERAGHHH!!
EDEN-- WHERE DID YOU GET THAT?!
MY DAD GAVE IT TO ME.
YOU MUST BE EDEN.
HOW NICE TO FINALLY MEET YOU.
YOU GET AWAY OR I'LL PUT A HOLE THROUGH YOUR HEAD!
AIEEEEE--!
THWAPP!
AHH... THAT FAMOUS HUSTON CHARM.
GHA--!
SCHUNKK!
WE'LL SEE IF IT HOLDS OUT DURING YOUR AMALGAMATION ON DRESSIN.
IT'S FOR THE BEST.
YOU'LL SIMPLY HAVE TO TRUST ME...
I'M A DEAR FRIEND OF YOUR FATHER'S.

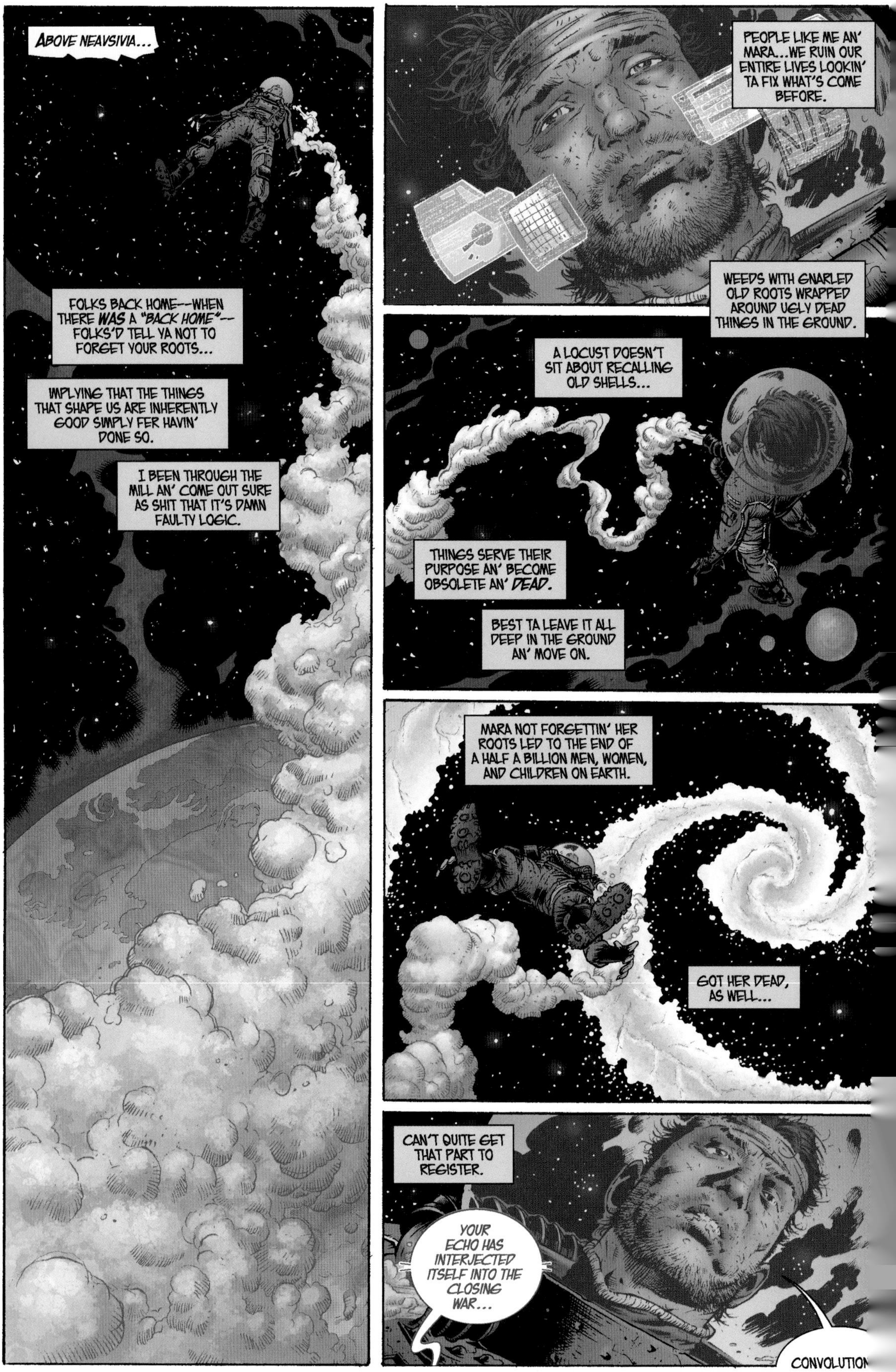
ABOVE NEAVSIVIA...
FOLKS BACK HOME--WHEN THERE WAS A "BACK HOME"--FOLKS'D TELL YA NOT TO FORGET YOUR ROOTS...
IMPLYING THAT THE THINGS THAT SHAPE US ARE INHERENTLY GOOD SIMPLY FER HAVIN' DONE SO.
I BEEN THROUGH THE MILL AN' COME OUT SURE AS SHIT THAT IT'S DAMN FAULTY LOGIC.
PEOPLE LIKE ME AN' MARA...WE RUIN OUR ENTIRE LIVES LOOKIN' TA FIX WHAT'S COME BEFORE.
WEEDS WITH GNARLED OLD ROOTS WRAPPED AROUND UGLY DEAD THINGS IN THE GROUND.
A LOCUST DOESN'T SIT ABOUT RECALLING OLD SHELLS...
THINGS SERVE THEIR PURPOSE AN' BECOME OBSOLETE AN' DEAD.
BEST TA LEAVE IT ALL DEEP IN THE GROUND AN' MOVE ON.
MARA NOT FORGETTIN' HER ROOTS LED TO THE END OF A HALF A BILLION MEN, WOMEN, AND CHILDREN ON EARTH.
GOT HER DEAD, AS WELL...
CAN'T QUITE GET THAT PART TO REGISTER.
YOUR ECHO HAS INTERJECTED ITSELF INTO THE CLOSING WAR...
CONVOLUTION

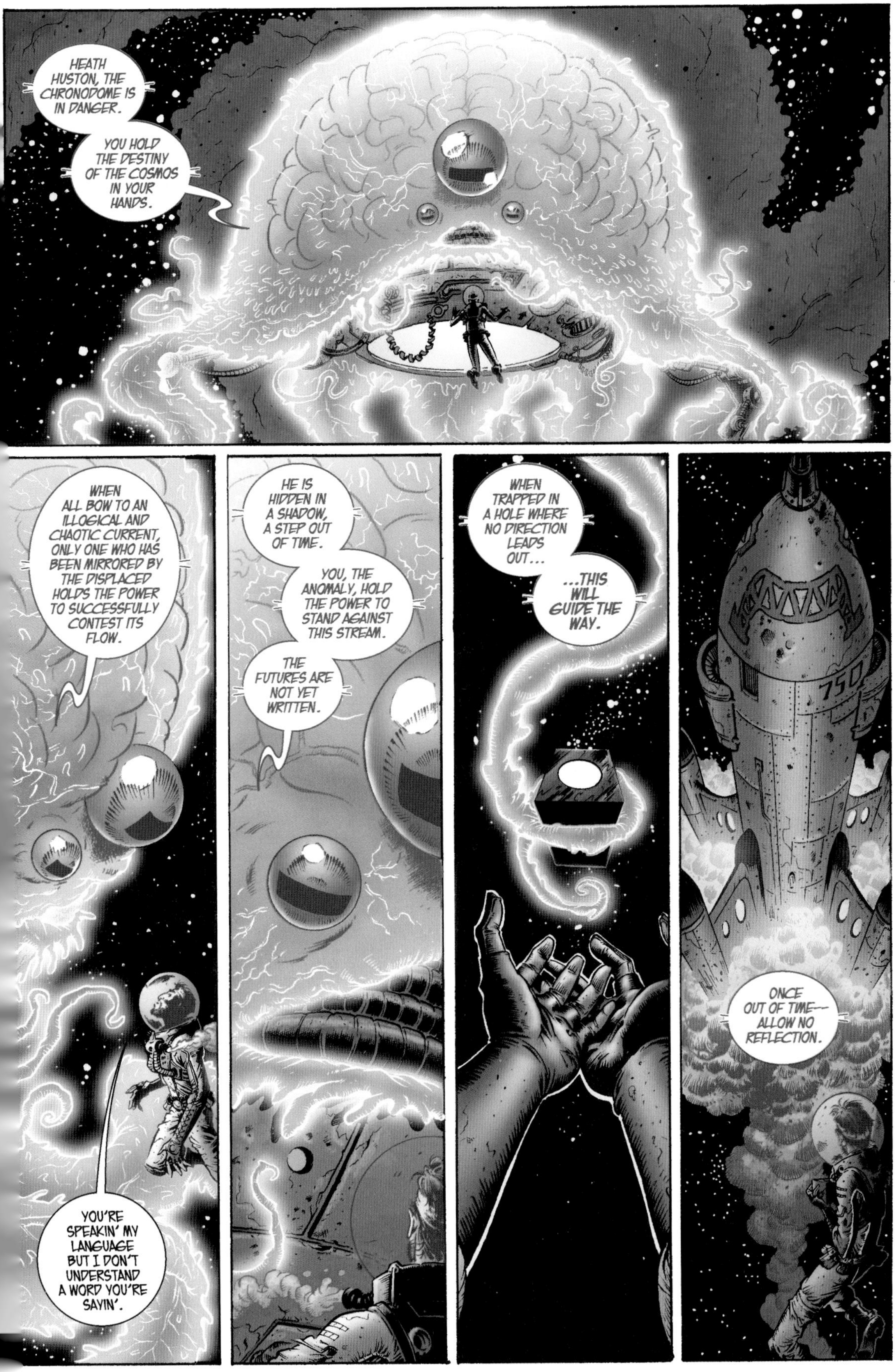
HEATH HUSTON, THE CHRONODOME IS IN DANGER.
YOU HOLD THE DESTINY OF THE COSMOS IN YOUR HANDS.
WHEN ALL BOW TO AN ILLOGICAL AND CHAOTIC CURRENT, ONLY ONE WHO HAS BEEN MIRRORED BY THE DISPLACED HOLDS THE POWER TO SUCCESSFULLY CONTEST ITS FLOW.
YOU'RE SPEAKIN' MY LANGUAGE BUT I DON'T UNDERSTAND A WORD YOU'RE SAYIN'.
HE IS HIDDEN IN A SHADOW, A STEP OUT OF TIME.
YOU, THE ANOMALY, HOLD THE POWER TO STAND AGAINST THIS STREAM.
THE FUTURES ARE NOT YET WRITTEN.
WHEN TRAPPED IN A HOLE WHERE NO DIRECTION LEADS OUT...
...THIS WILL GUIDE THE WAY.
750
ONCE OUT OF TIME--ALLOW NO REFLECTION.

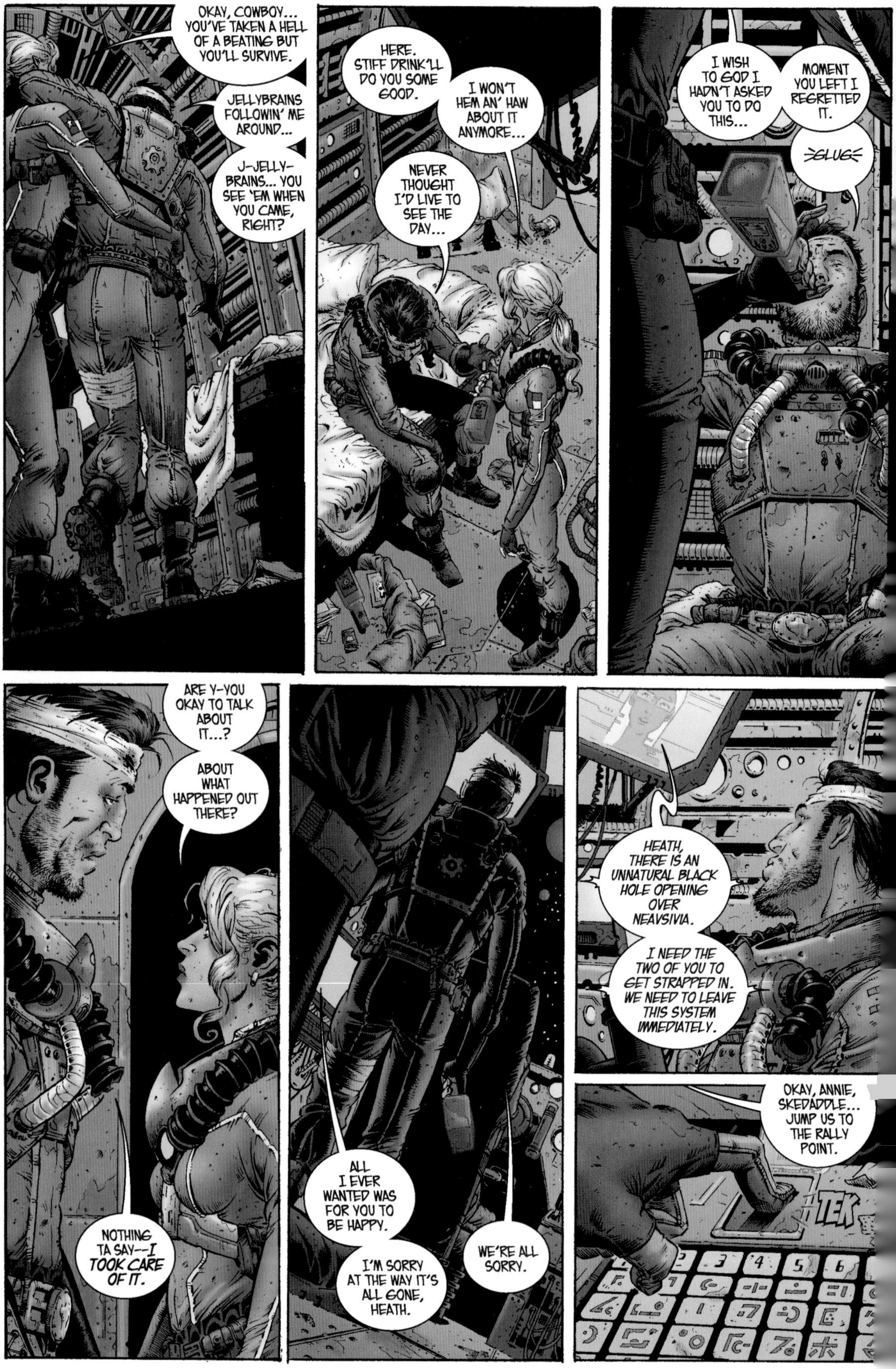
OKAY, COWBOY... YOU'VE TAKEN A HELL OF A BEATING BUT YOU'LL SURVIVE.
JELLYBRAINS FOLLOWIN' ME AROUND...
J-JELLY-BRAINS... YOU SEE 'EM WHEN YOU CAME, RIGHT?
HERE. STIFF DRINK'LL DO YOU SOME GOOD.
I WON'T HEM AN' HAW ABOUT IT ANYMORE...
NEVER THOUGHT I'D LIVE TO SEE THE DAY...
I WISH TO GOD I HADN'T ASKED YOU TO DO THIS...
MOMENT YOU LEFT I REGRETTED IT.
GLUG
ARE Y-YOU OKAY TO TALK ABOUT IT...?
ABOUT WHAT HAPPENED OUT THERE?
NOTHING TA SAY--I *TOOK CARE OF IT.*
ALL I EVER WANTED WAS FOR YOU TO BE HAPPY.
I'M SORRY AT THE WAY IT'S ALL GONE, HEATH.
WE'RE ALL SORRY.
HEATH, THERE IS AN UNNATURAL BLACK HOLE OPENING OVER NEAVSIVIA.
I NEED THE TWO OF YOU TO GET STRAPPED IN. WE NEED TO LEAVE THIS SYSTEM IMMEDIATELY.
OKAY, ANNIE, SKEDADDLE... JUMP US TO THE RALLY POINT.
TEK

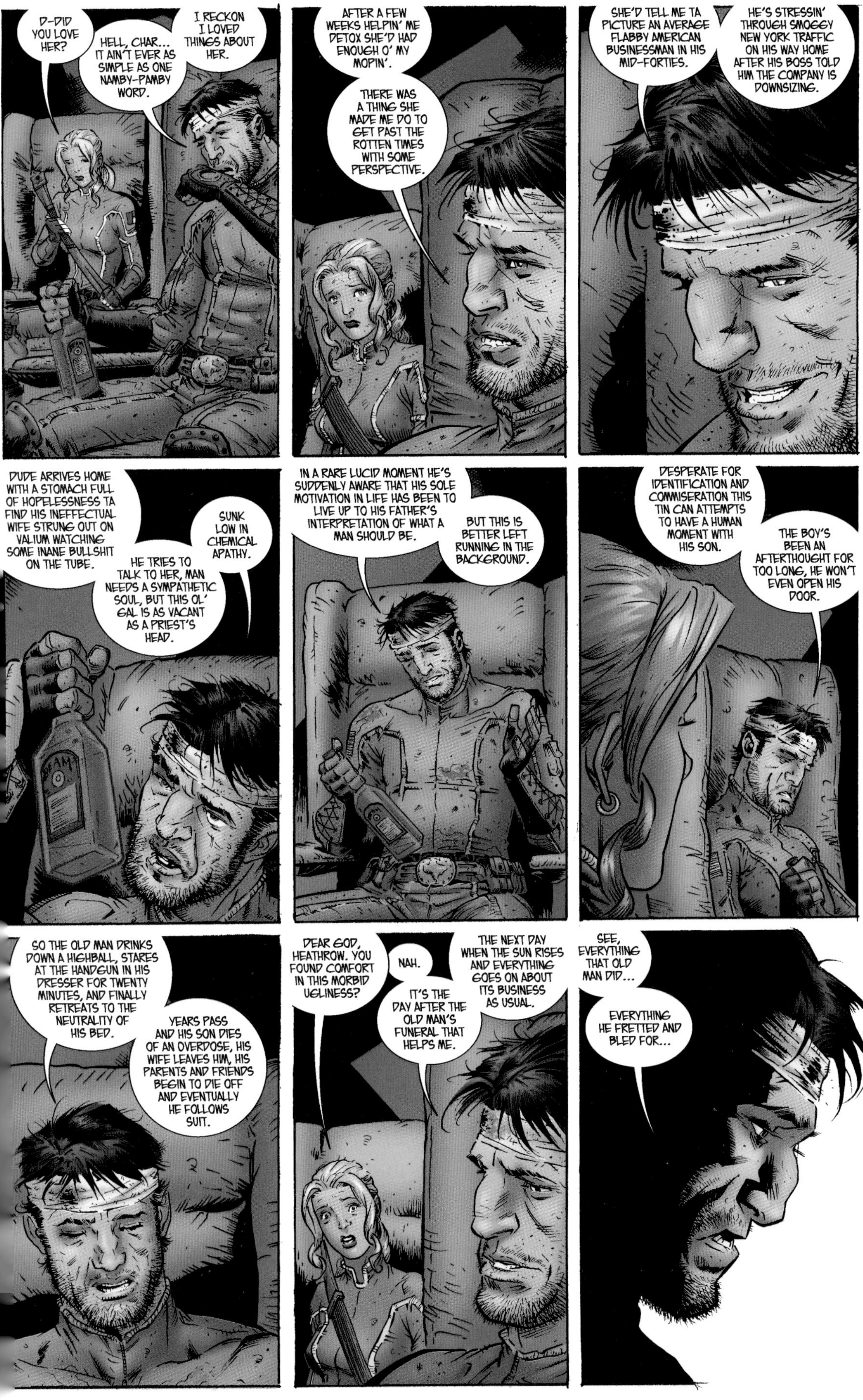
D-DID YOU LOVE HER?
HELL, CHAR... IT AIN'T EVER AS SIMPLE AS ONE NAMBY-PAMBY WORD.
I RECKON I LOVED THINGS ABOUT HER.
AFTER A FEW WEEKS HELPIN' ME DETOX SHE'D HAD ENOUGH O' MY MOPIN'.
THERE WAS A THING SHE MADE ME DO TO GET PAST THE ROTTEN TIMES WITH SOME PERSPECTIVE.
SHE'D TELL ME TA PICTURE AN AVERAGE FLABBY AMERICAN BUSINESSMAN IN HIS MID-FORTIES.
HE'S STRESSIN' THROUGH SMOGGY NEW YORK TRAFFIC ON HIS WAY HOME AFTER HIS BOSS TOLD HIM THE COMPANY IS DOWNSIZING.
DUDE ARRIVES HOME WITH A STOMACH FULL OF HOPELESSNESS TA FIND HIS INEFFECTUAL WIFE STRUNG OUT ON VALIUM WATCHING SOME INANE BULLSHIT ON THE TUBE.
SUNK LOW IN CHEMICAL APATHY.
HE TRIES TO TALK TO HER, MAN NEEDS A SYMPATHETIC SOUL, BUT THIS OL' GAL IS AS VACANT AS A PRIEST'S HEAD.
IN A RARE LUCID MOMENT HE'S SUDDENLY AWARE THAT HIS SOLE MOTIVATION IN LIFE HAS BEEN TO LIVE UP TO HIS FATHER'S INTERPRETATION OF WHAT A MAN SHOULD BE.
BUT THIS IS BETTER LEFT RUNNING IN THE BACKGROUND.
DESPERATE FOR IDENTIFICATION AND COMMISERATION THIS TIN CAN ATTEMPTS TO HAVE A HUMAN MOMENT WITH HIS SON.
THE BOY'S BEEN AN AFTERTHOUGHT FOR TOO LONG, HE WON'T EVEN OPEN HIS DOOR.
SO THE OLD MAN DRINKS DOWN A HIGHBALL, STARES AT THE HANDGUN IN HIS DRESSER FOR TWENTY MINUTES, AND FINALLY RETREATS TO THE NEUTRALITY OF HIS BED.
YEARS PASS AND HIS SON DIES OF AN OVERDOSE, HIS WIFE LEAVES HIM, HIS PARENTS AND FRIENDS BEGIN TO DIE OFF AND EVENTUALLY HE FOLLOWS SUIT.
DEAR GOD, HEATHROW. YOU FOUND COMFORT IN THIS MORBID UGLINESS?
NAH.
IT'S THE DAY AFTER THE OLD MAN'S FUNERAL THAT HELPS ME.
THE NEXT DAY WHEN THE SUN RISES AND EVERYTHING GOES ON ABOUT ITS BUSINESS AS USUAL.
SEE, EVERYTHING THAT OLD MAN DID...
EVERYTHING HE FRETTED AND BLED FOR...

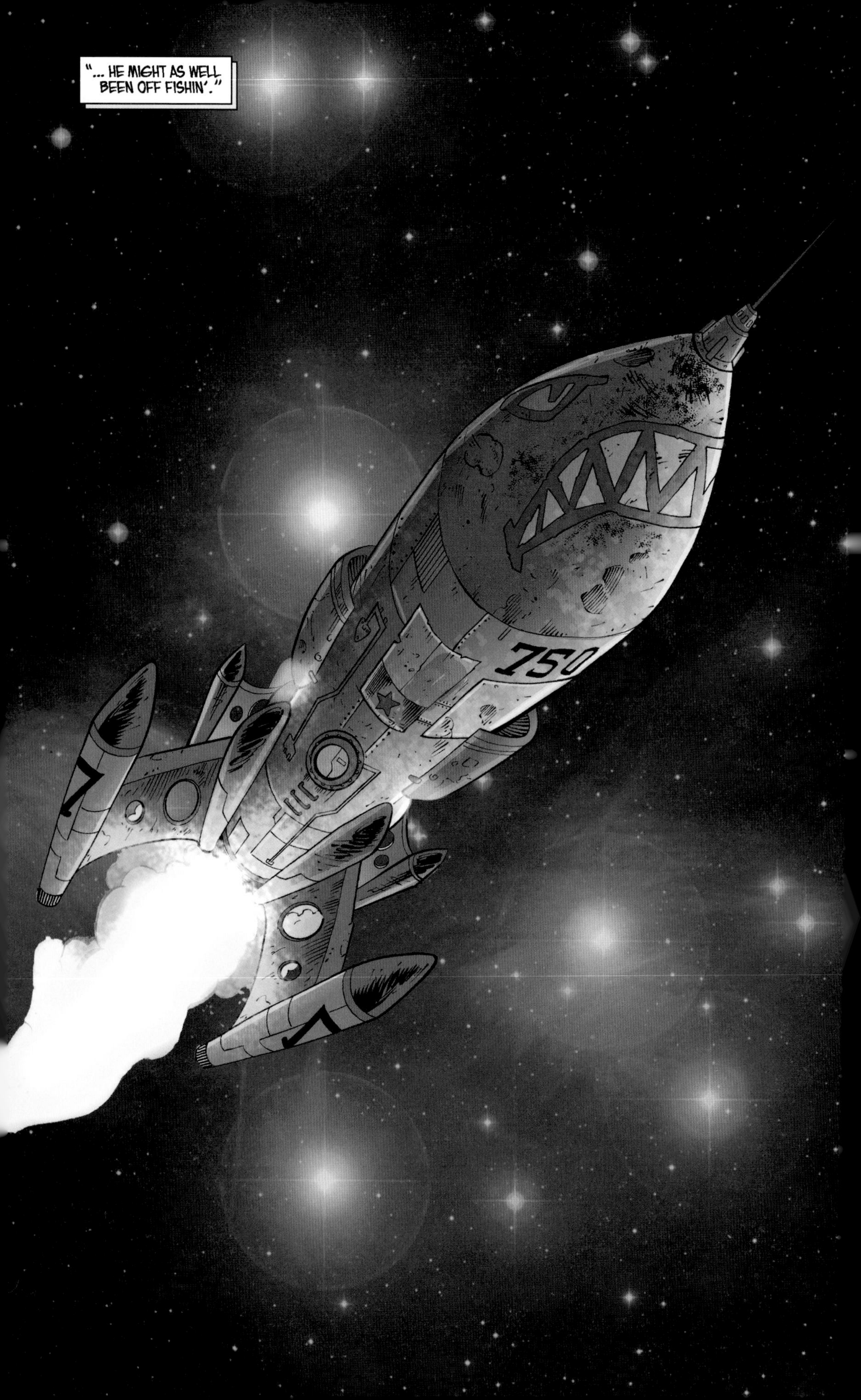
"... HE MIGHT AS WELL BEEN OFF FISHIN'."
750
7
7

THE PLANET TETALDIA...

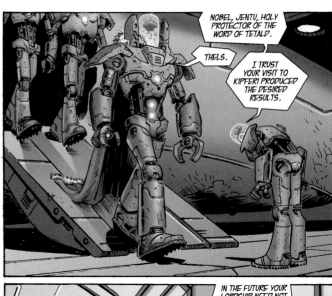

NOBEL, JENTU, HOLY PROTECTOR OF THE WORD OF TETALD.

THELS.

I TRUST YOUR VISIT TO KIPFERI PRODUCED THE DESIRED RESULTS.

IN THE FUTURE YOUR LORDSHIP NEED NOT DIRTY HIS HANDS. SUCH TASKS—

ARE TOO IMPORTANT TO TRUST TO ANYONE ELSE.

IMAGINE IT... WHEN FINISHED WE'LL HAVE MAPPED OUT AN ENTIRELY NEW HISTORY FOR THE UNIVERSE.

ONE WHERE THE TEACHINGS OF TETALD ARE NOT ONLY SPREAD, BUT ARE BORN, INHERENT IN THE FABRIC OF EVERY WORLD.

YES AND DURING YOUR ABSENCE THE PLAN FLOURISHES... THE COUNCIL ARRIVED ONLY MOMENTS AGO.

THEY ARE HERE?! NOW?

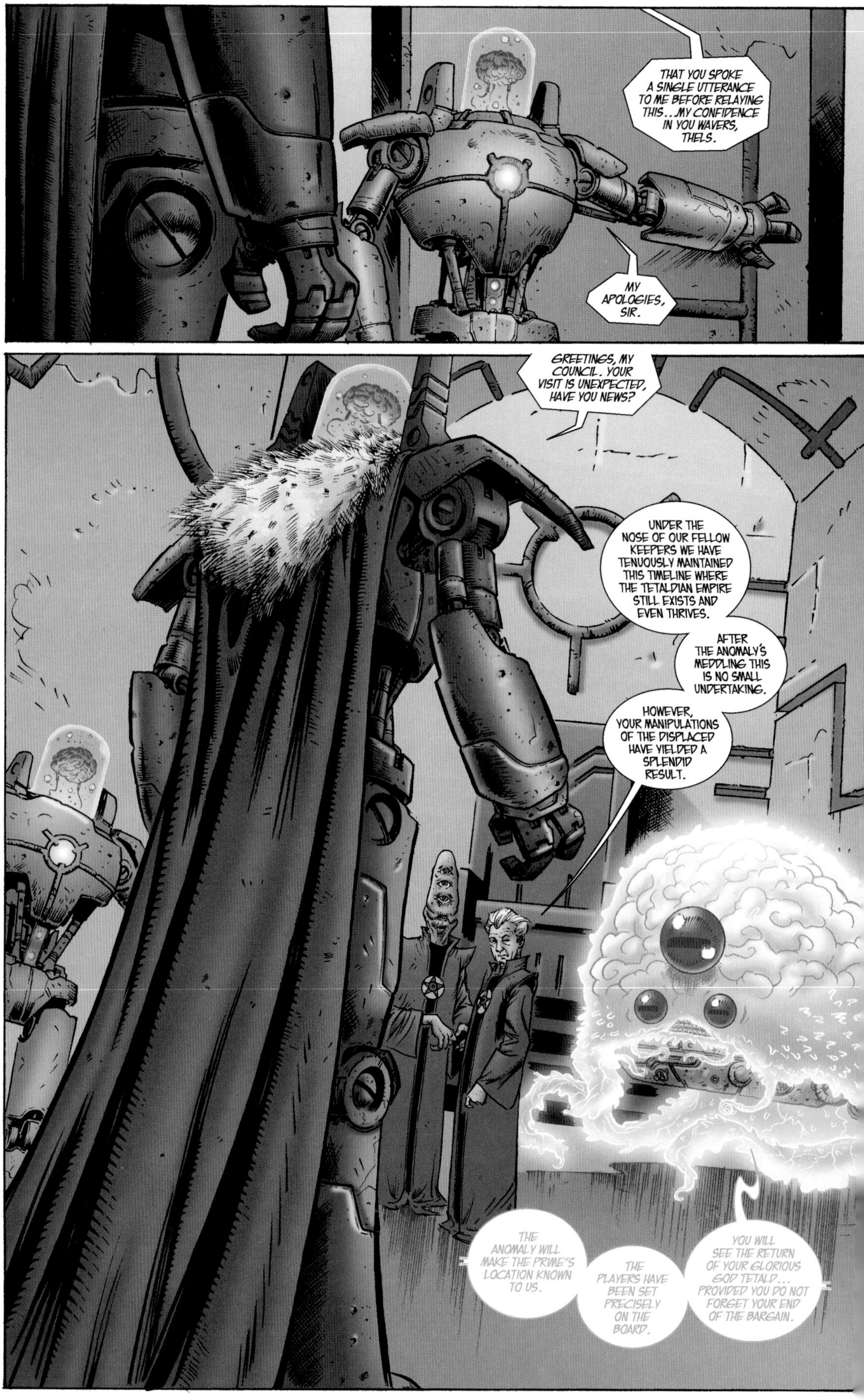
THAT YOU SPOKE A SINGLE UTTERANCE TO ME BEFORE RELAYING THIS...MY CONFIDENCE IN YOU WAVERS, THELS.
MY APOLOGIES, SIR.
GREETINGS, MY COUNCIL. YOUR VISIT IS UNEXPECTED, HAVE YOU NEWS?
UNDER THE NOSE OF OUR FELLOW KEEPERS WE HAVE TENUOUSLY MAINTAINED THIS TIMELINE WHERE THE TETALDIAN EMPIRE STILL EXISTS AND EVEN THRIVES.
AFTER THE ANOMALY'S MEDDLING THIS IS NO SMALL UNDERTAKING.
HOWEVER, YOUR MANIPULATIONS OF THE DISPLACED HAVE YIELDED A SPLENDID RESULT.
THE ANOMALY WILL MAKE THE PRIME'S LOCATION KNOWN TO US.
THE PLAYERS HAVE BEEN SET PRECISELY ON THE BOARD.
YOU WILL SEE THE RETURN OF YOUR GLORIOUS GOD TETALD... PROVIDED YOU DO NOT FORGET YOUR END OF THE BARGAIN.

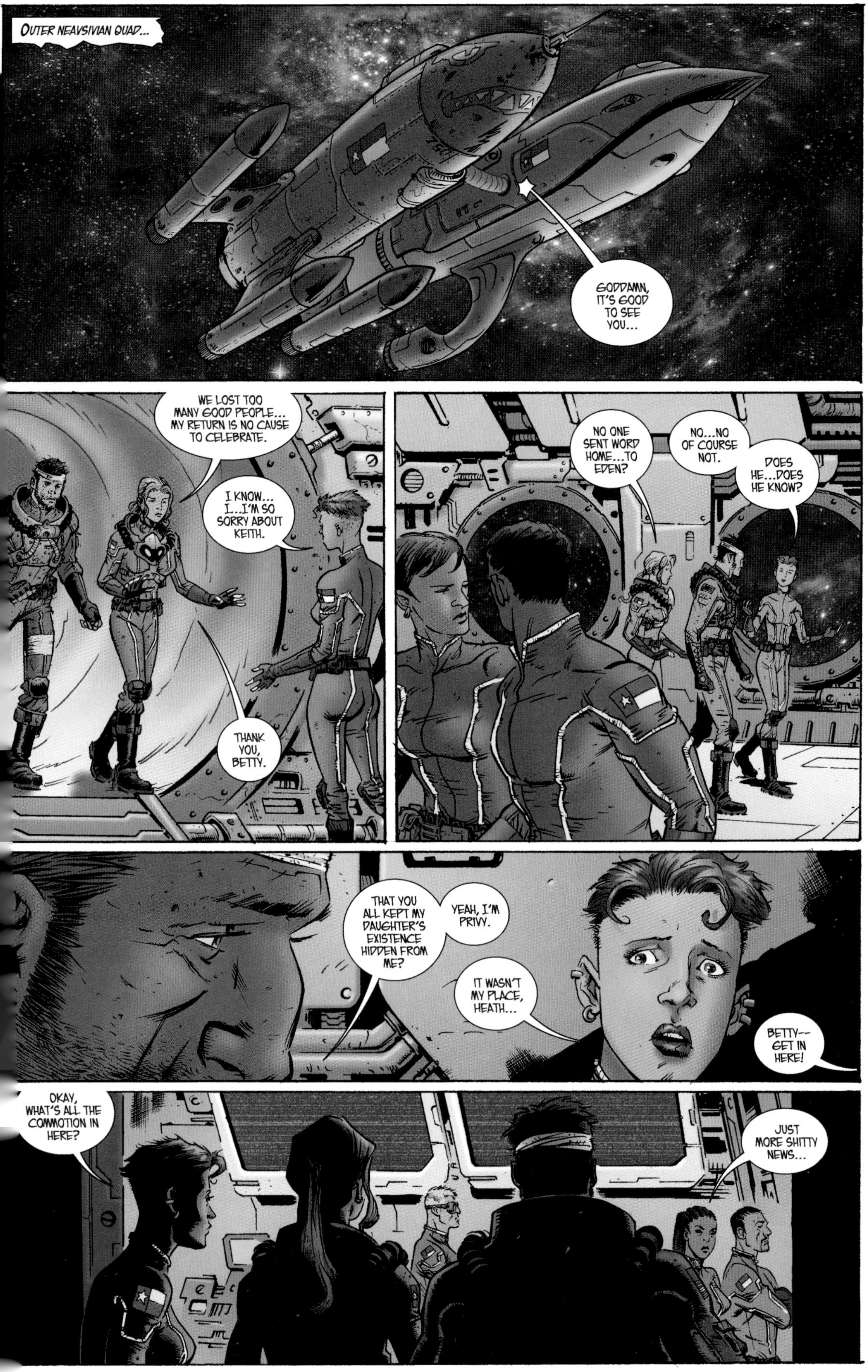
OUTER NEAVSIVIAN QUAD...
GODDAMN, IT'S GOOD TO SEE YOU...
WE LOST TOO MANY GOOD PEOPLE... MY RETURN IS NO CAUSE TO CELEBRATE.
I KNOW... I...I'M SO SORRY ABOUT KEITH.
THANK YOU, BETTY.
NO ONE SENT WORD HOME...TO EDEN?
NO...NO OF COURSE NOT.
DOES HE...DOES HE KNOW?
THAT YOU ALL KEPT MY DAUGHTER'S EXISTENCE HIDDEN FROM ME?
YEAH, I'M PRIVY.
IT WASN'T MY PLACE, HEATH...
BETTY-- GET IN HERE!
OKAY, WHAT'S ALL THE COMMOTION IN HERE?
JUST MORE SHITTY NEWS...

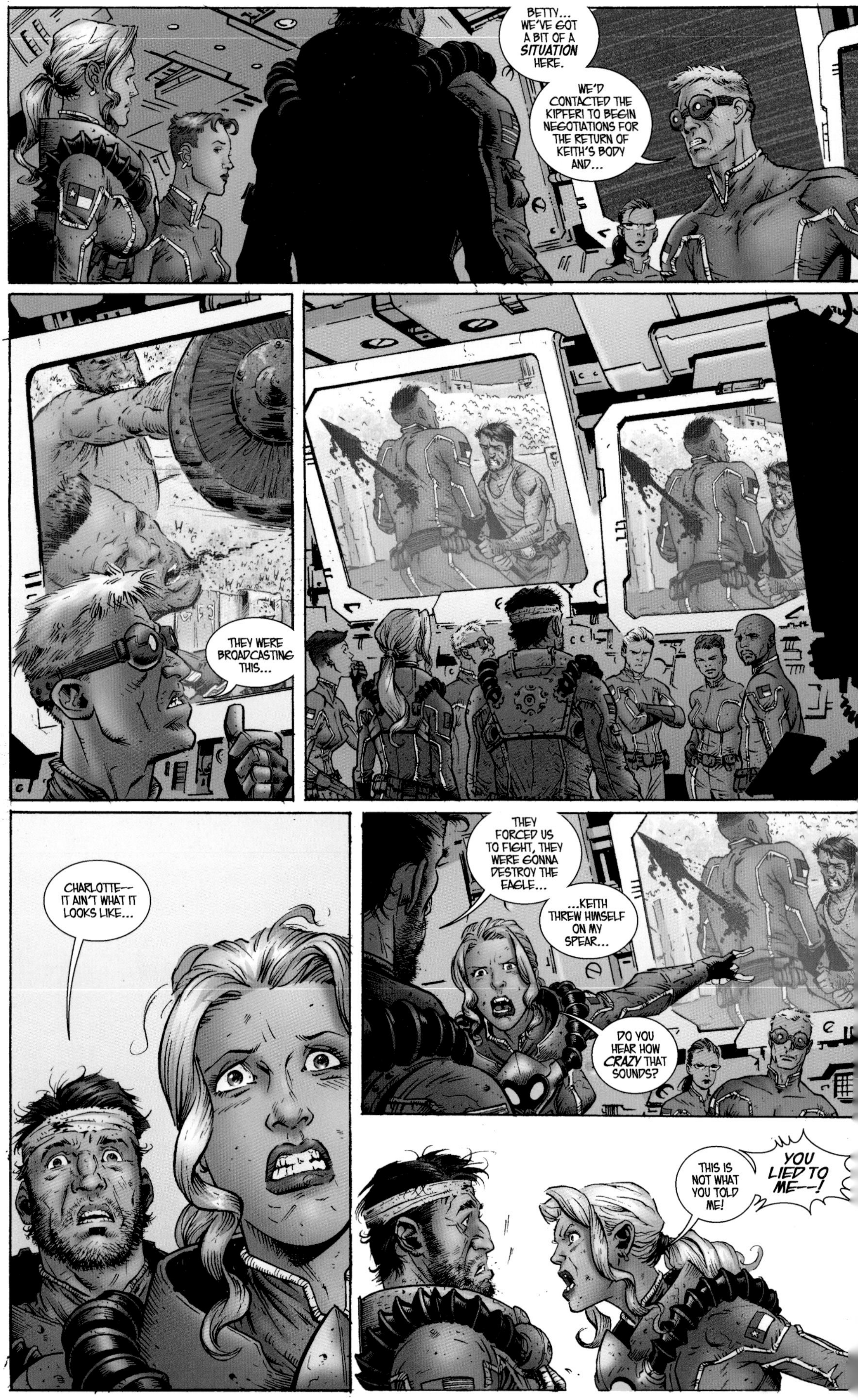
BETTY... WE'VE GOT A BIT OF A SITUATION HERE.
WE'D CONTACTED THE KIPFERI TO BEGIN NEGOTIATIONS FOR THE RETURN OF KEITH'S BODY AND...
THEY WERE BROADCASTING THIS...
CHARLOTTE-- IT AIN'T WHAT IT LOOKS LIKE...
THEY FORCED US TO FIGHT, THEY WERE GONNA DESTROY THE EAGLE...
...KEITH THREW HIMSELF ON MY SPEAR...
DO YOU HEAR HOW CRAZY THAT SOUNDS?
THIS IS NOT WHAT YOU TOLD ME!
YOU LIED TO ME--!

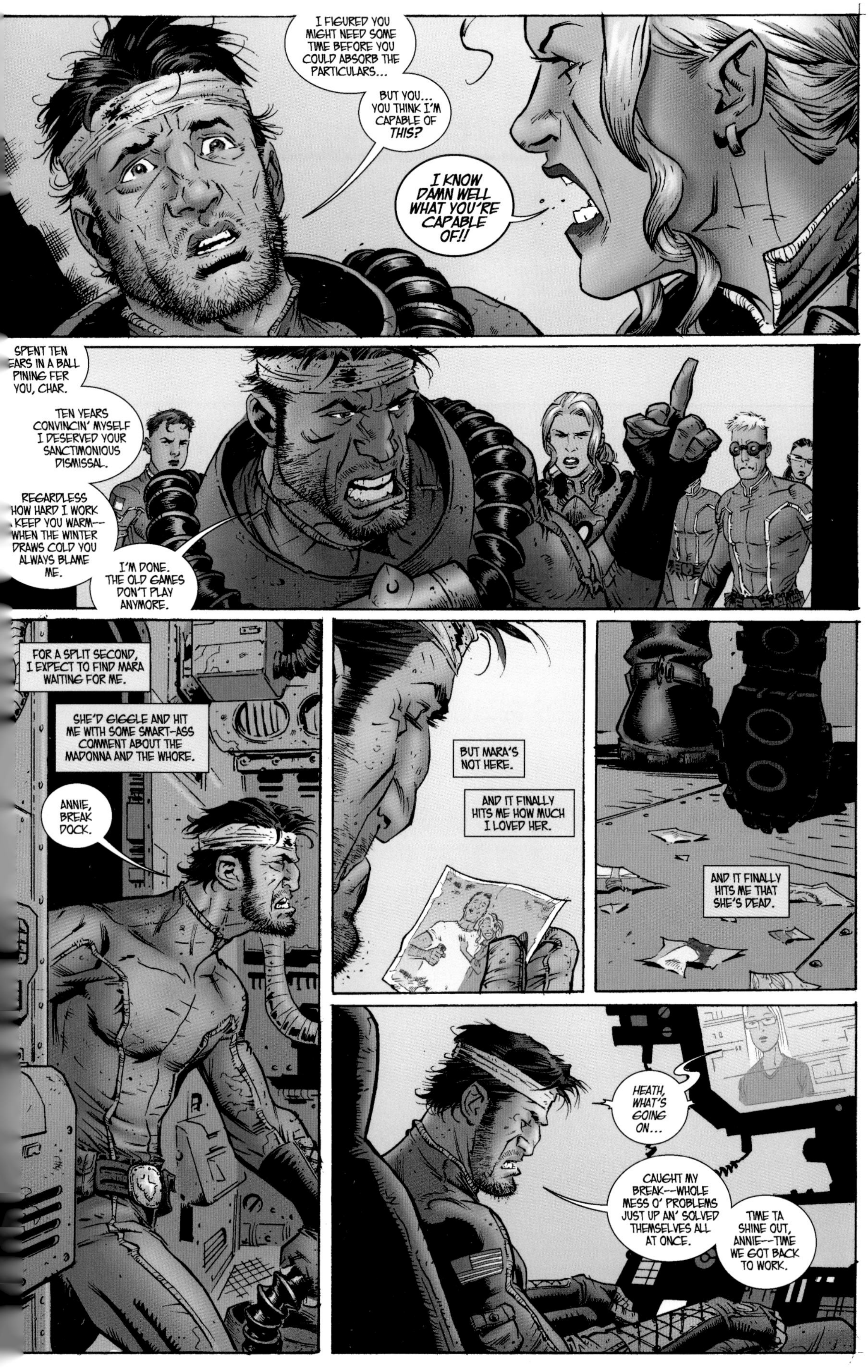
I FIGURED YOU MIGHT NEED SOME TIME BEFORE YOU COULD ABSORB THE PARTICULARS...
BUT YOU... YOU THINK I'M CAPABLE OF THIS?
I KNOW DAMN WELL WHAT YOU'RE CAPABLE OF!!
SPENT TEN EARS IN A BALL PINING FER YOU, CHAR.
TEN YEARS CONVINCIN' MYSELF I DESERVED YOUR SANCTIMONIOUS DISMISSAL.
REGARDLESS HOW HARD I WORK KEEP YOU WARM-- WHEN THE WINTER DRAWS COLD YOU ALWAYS BLAME ME.
I'M DONE. THE OLD GAMES DON'T PLAY ANYMORE.
FOR A SPLIT SECOND, I EXPECT TO FIND MARA WAITING FOR ME.
SHE'D GIGGLE AND HIT ME WITH SOME SMART-ASS COMMENT ABOUT THE MADONNA AND THE WHORE.
ANNIE, BREAK DOCK.
BUT MARA'S NOT HERE.
AND IT FINALLY HITS ME HOW MUCH I LOVED HER.
AND IT FINALLY HITS ME THAT SHE'S DEAD.
HEATH, WHAT'S GOING ON...
CAUGHT MY BREAK--WHOLE MESS O' PROBLEMS JUST UP AN' SOLVED THEMSELVES ALL AT ONCE.
TIME TA SHINE OUT, ANNIE--TIME WE GOT BACK TO WORK.

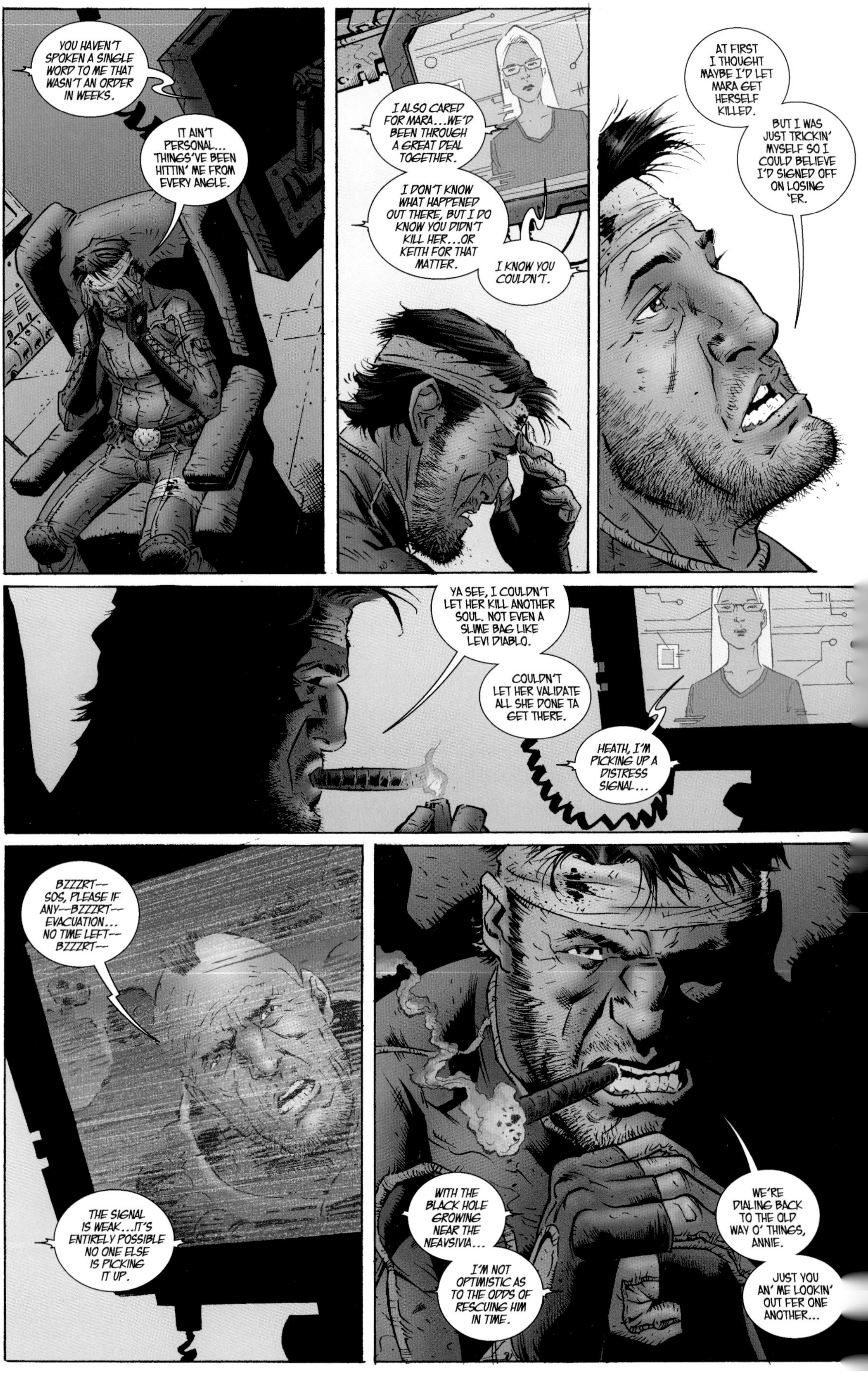
YOU HAVEN'T SPOKEN A SINGLE WORD TO ME THAT WASN'T AN ORDER IN WEEKS.
IT AIN'T PERSONAL... THINGS'VE BEEN HITTIN' ME FROM EVERY ANGLE.
I ALSO CARED FOR MARA...WE'D BEEN THROUGH A GREAT DEAL TOGETHER.
I DON'T KNOW WHAT HAPPENED OUT THERE, BUT I DO KNOW YOU DIDN'T KILL HER...OR KEITH FOR THAT MATTER.
I KNOW YOU COULDN'T.
AT FIRST I THOUGHT MAYBE I'D LET MARA GET HERSELF KILLED.
BUT I WAS JUST TRICKIN' MYSELF SO I COULD BELIEVE I'D SIGNED OFF ON LOSING 'ER.
YA SEE, I COULDN'T LET HER KILL ANOTHER SOUL. NOT EVEN A SLIME BAG LIKE LEVI DIABLO.
COULDN'T LET HER VALIDATE ALL SHE DONE TA GET THERE.
HEATH, I'M PICKING UP A DISTRESS SIGNAL...
BZZZRT-- SOS, PLEASE IF ANY--BZZZRT-- EVACUATION... NO TIME LEFT-- BZZZRT--
THE SIGNAL IS WEAK...IT'S ENTIRELY POSSIBLE NO ONE ELSE IS PICKING IT UP.
WITH THE BLACK HOLE GROWING NEAR THE NEAVSIVIA...
I'M NOT OPTIMISTIC AS TO THE ODDS OF RESCUING HIM IN TIME.
WE'RE DIALING BACK TO THE OLD WAY O' THINGS, ANNIE.
JUST YOU AN' ME LOOKIN' OUT FER ONE ANOTHER...

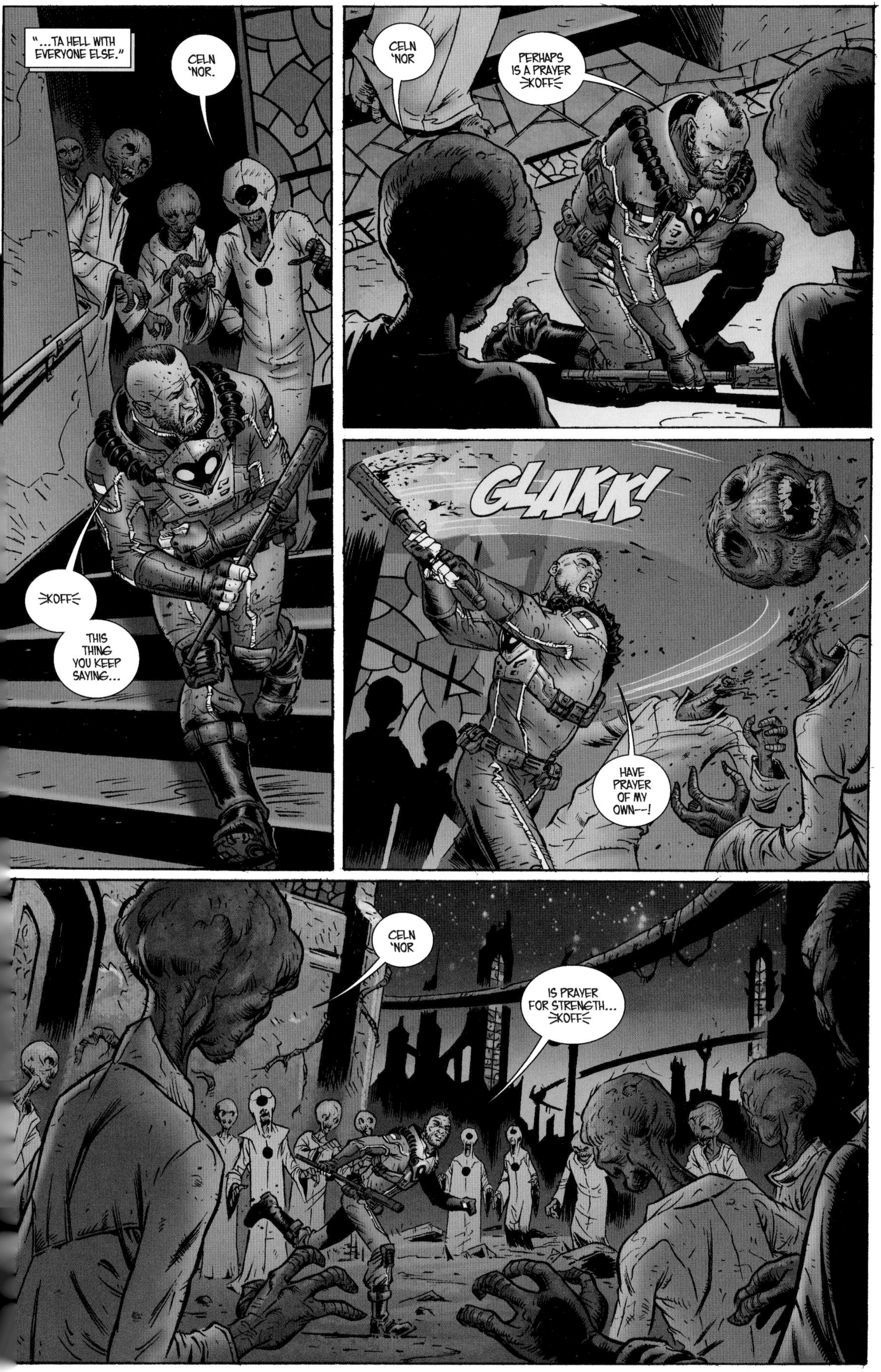
"...TA HELL WITH EVERYONE ELSE."
CELN 'NOR.
KOFF
THIS THING YOU KEEP SAYING...
CELN 'NOR
PERHAPS IS A PRAYER KOFF
GLAKK!
HAVE PRAYER OF MY OWN--!
CELN 'NOR
IS PRAYER FOR STRENGTH... KOFF

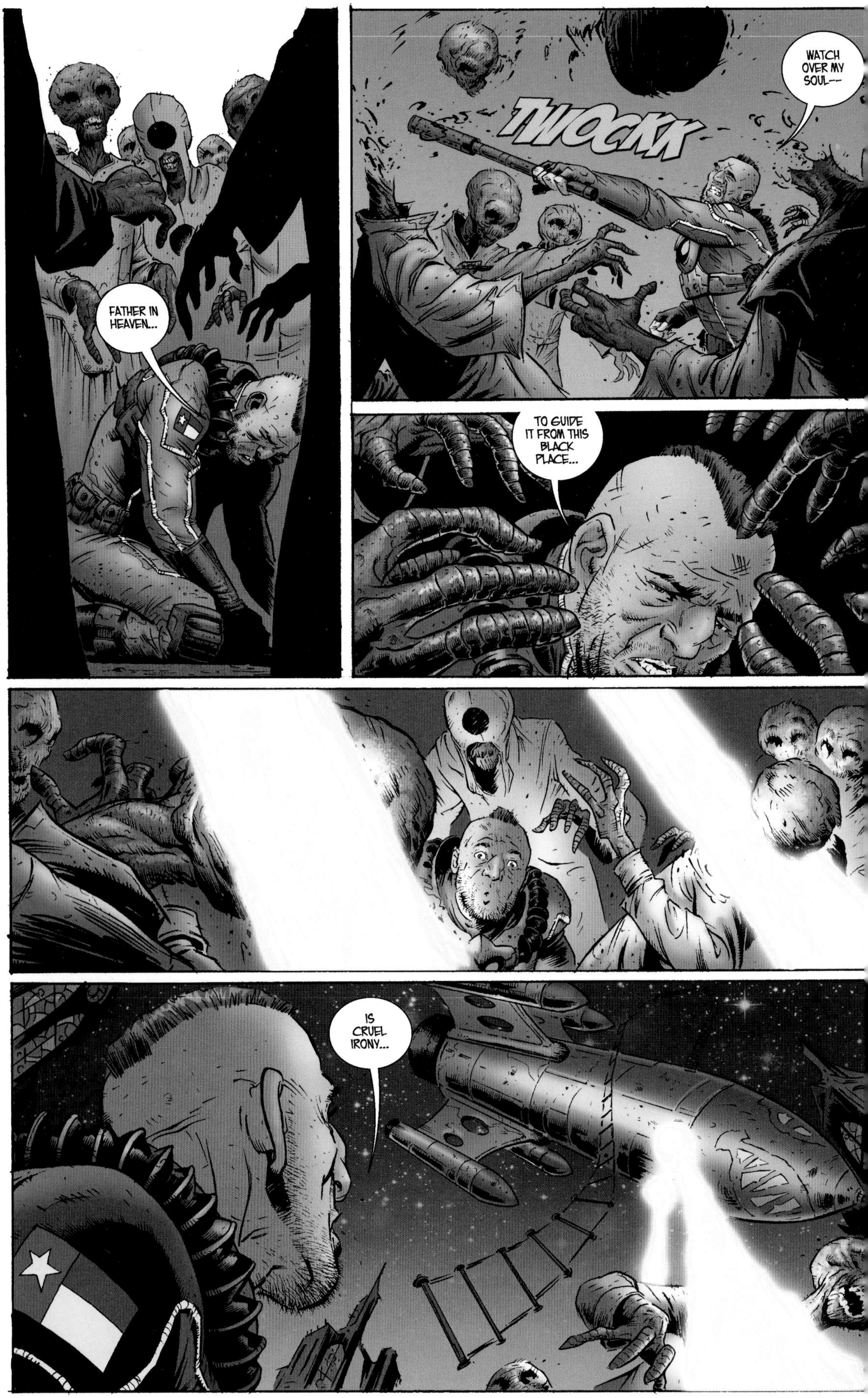
FATHER IN HEAVEN...
TWOCKK
WATCH OVER MY SOUL--
TO GUIDE IT FROM THIS BLACK PLACE...
IS CRUEL IRONY...

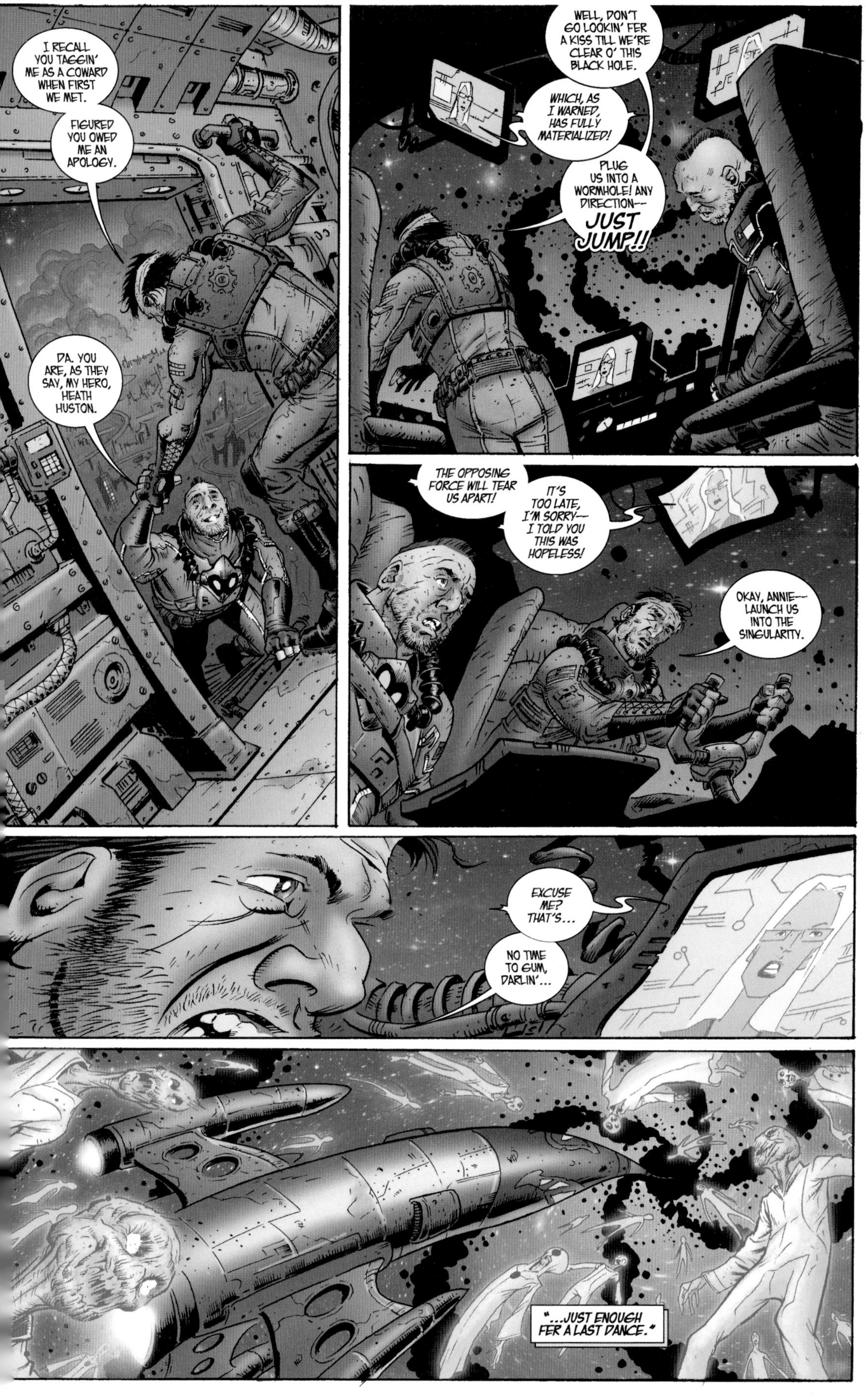
I RECALL YOU TAGGIN' ME AS A COWARD WHEN FIRST WE MET.
FIGURED YOU OWED ME AN APOLOGY.
DA. YOU ARE, AS THEY SAY, MY HERO, HEATH HUSTON.
WELL, DON'T GO LOOKIN' FER A KISS TILL WE'RE CLEAR O' THIS BLACK HOLE.
WHICH, AS I WARNED, HAS FULLY MATERIALIZED!
PLUG US INTO A WORMHOLE! ANY DIRECTION-- JUST JUMP!!
THE OPPOSING FORCE WILL TEAR US APART!
IT'S TOO LATE, I'M SORRY-- I TOLD YOU THIS WAS HOPELESS!
OKAY, ANNIE-- LAUNCH US INTO THE SINGULARITY.
EXCUSE ME? THAT'S...
NO TIME TO GUM, DARLIN'...
"...JUST ENOUGH FER A LAST DANCE."

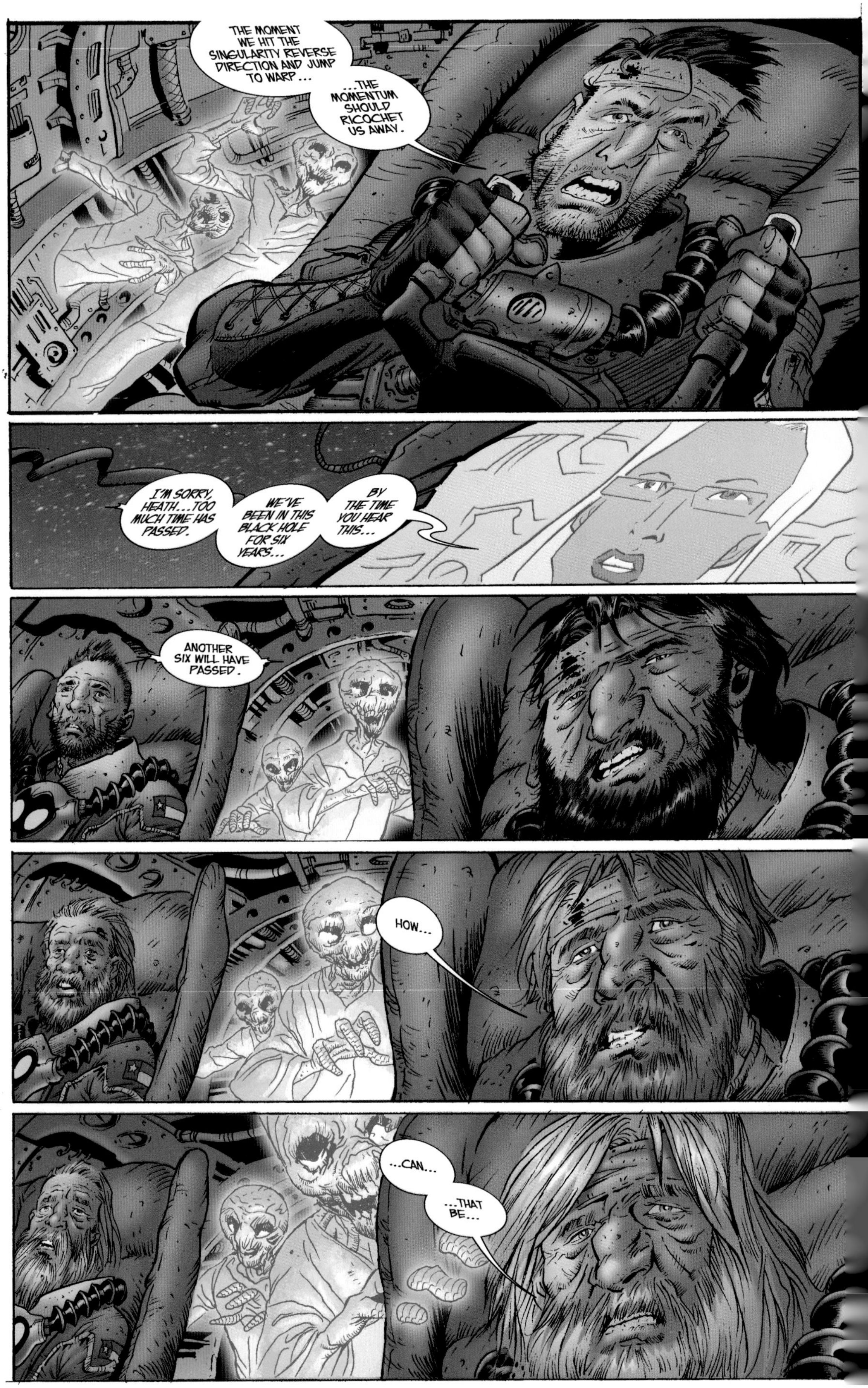
THE MOMENT WE HIT THE SINGULARITY REVERSE DIRECTION AND JUMP TO WARP...
...THE MOMENTUM SHOULD RICOCHET US AWAY.
I'M SORRY, HEATH...TOO MUCH TIME HAS PASSED.
WE'VE BEEN IN THIS BLACK HOLE FOR SIX YEARS...
BY THE TIME YOU HEAR THIS...
ANOTHER SIX WILL HAVE PASSED.
HOW...
...CAN...
...THAT BE...

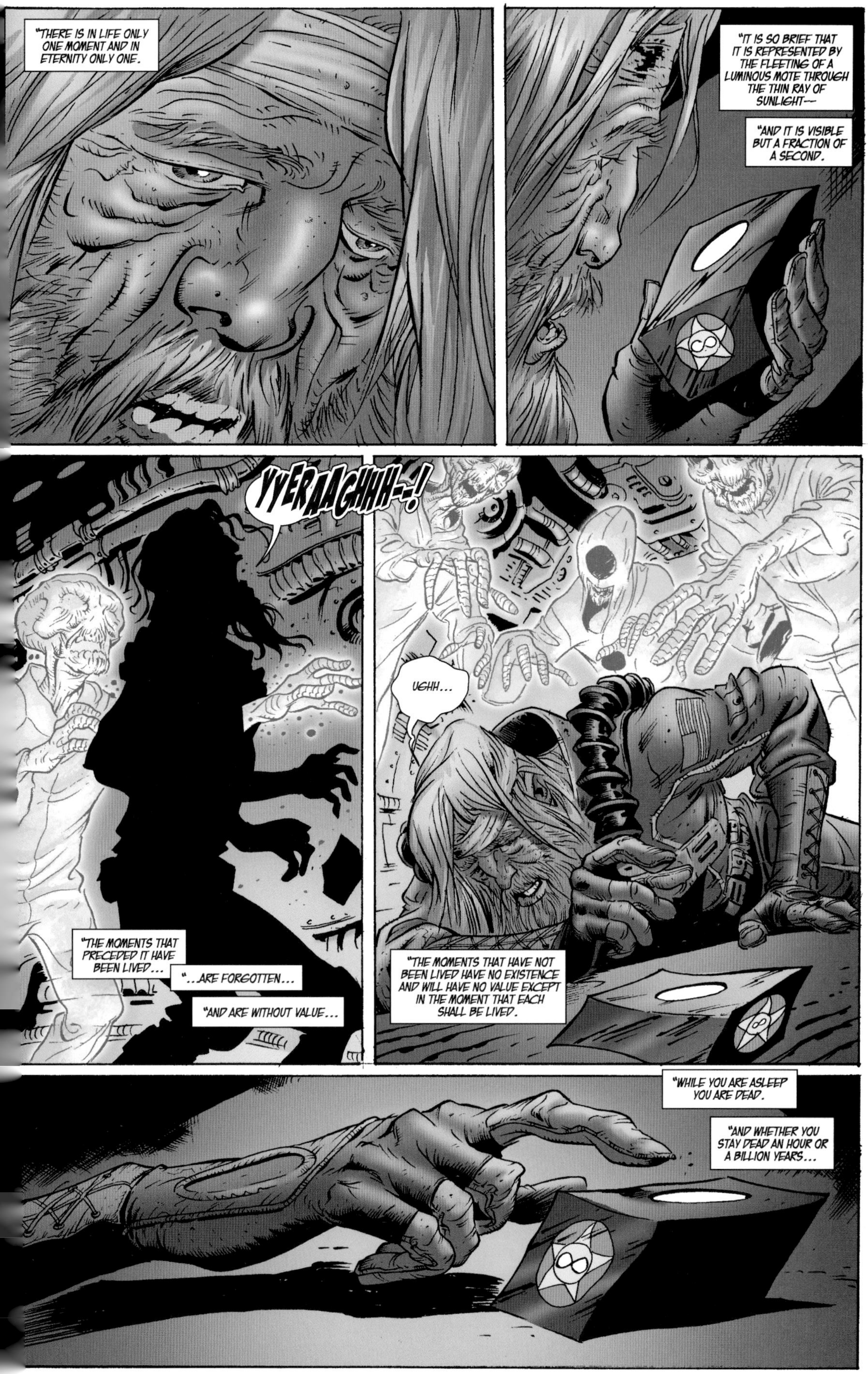
"THERE IS IN LIFE ONLY ONE MOMENT AND IN ETERNITY ONLY ONE.
"IT IS SO BRIEF THAT IT IS REPRESENTED BY THE FLEETING OF A LUMINOUS MOTE THROUGH THE THIN RAY OF SUNLIGHT--
"AND IT IS VISIBLE BUT A FRACTION OF A SECOND.
YYERAAGHHH--!
"THE MOMENTS THAT PRECEDED IT HAVE BEEN LIVED...
"...ARE FORGOTTEN...
"AND ARE WITHOUT VALUE...
UGHH...
"THE MOMENTS THAT HAVE NOT BEEN LIVED HAVE NO EXISTENCE AND WILL HAVE NO VALUE EXCEPT IN THE MOMENT THAT EACH SHALL BE LIVED.
"WHILE YOU ARE ASLEEP YOU ARE DEAD.
"AND WHETHER YOU STAY DEAD AN HOUR OR A BILLION YEARS...

"...THE TIME TO
YOU IS THE SAME."
—SAMUEL CLEMENS

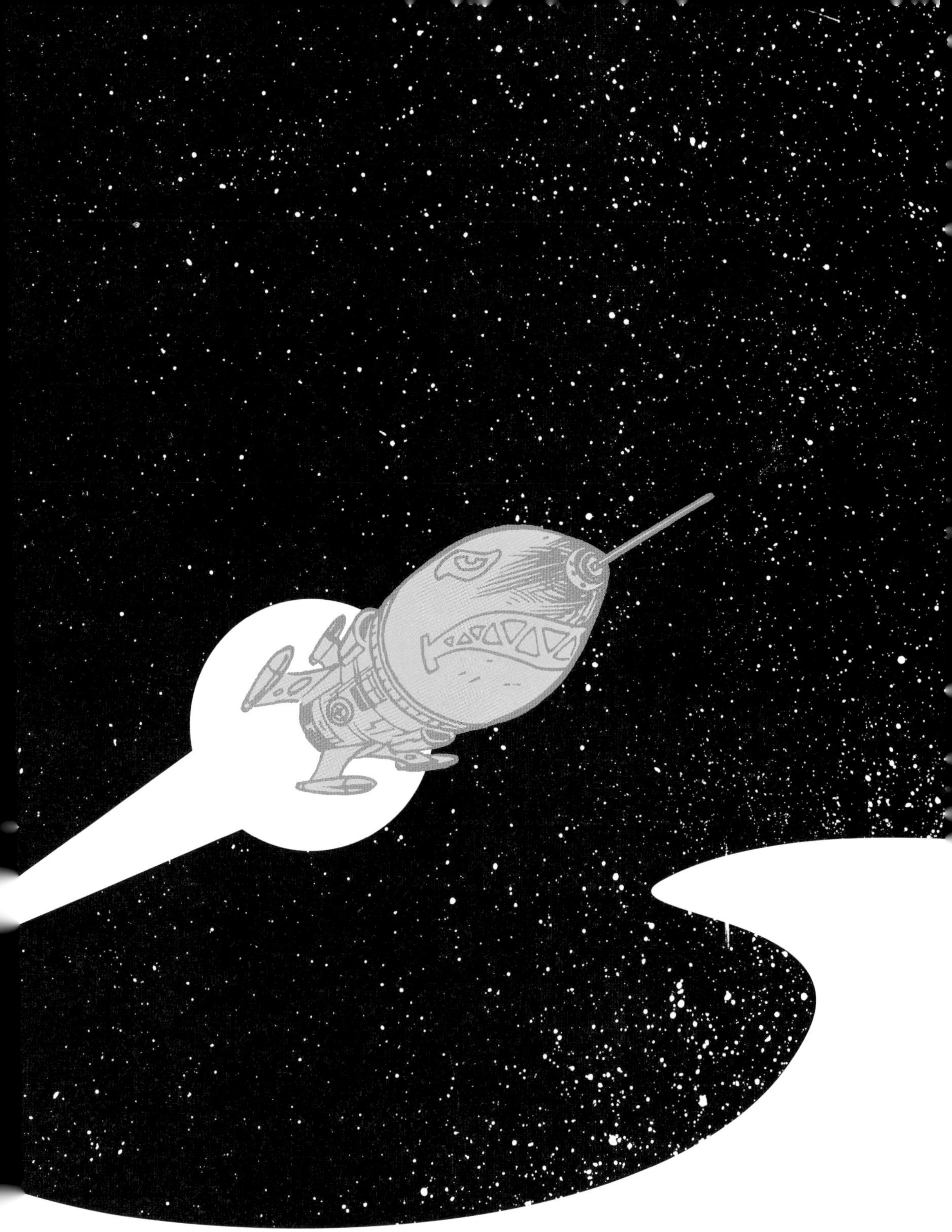

PIN-UP GALLERY

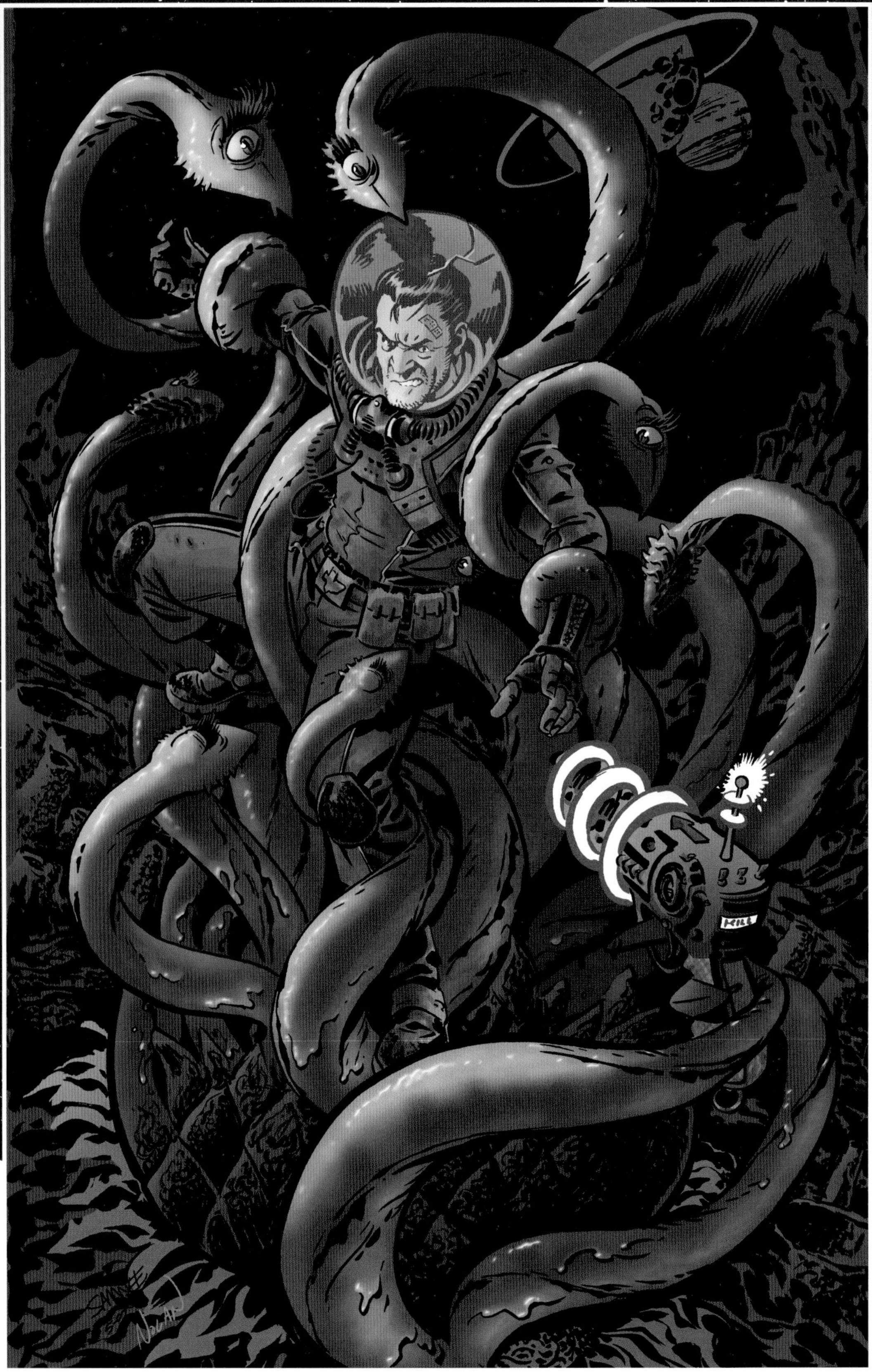

ART BY **CHRIS SAMNEE** COLORS BY **NOLAND WOODARD**

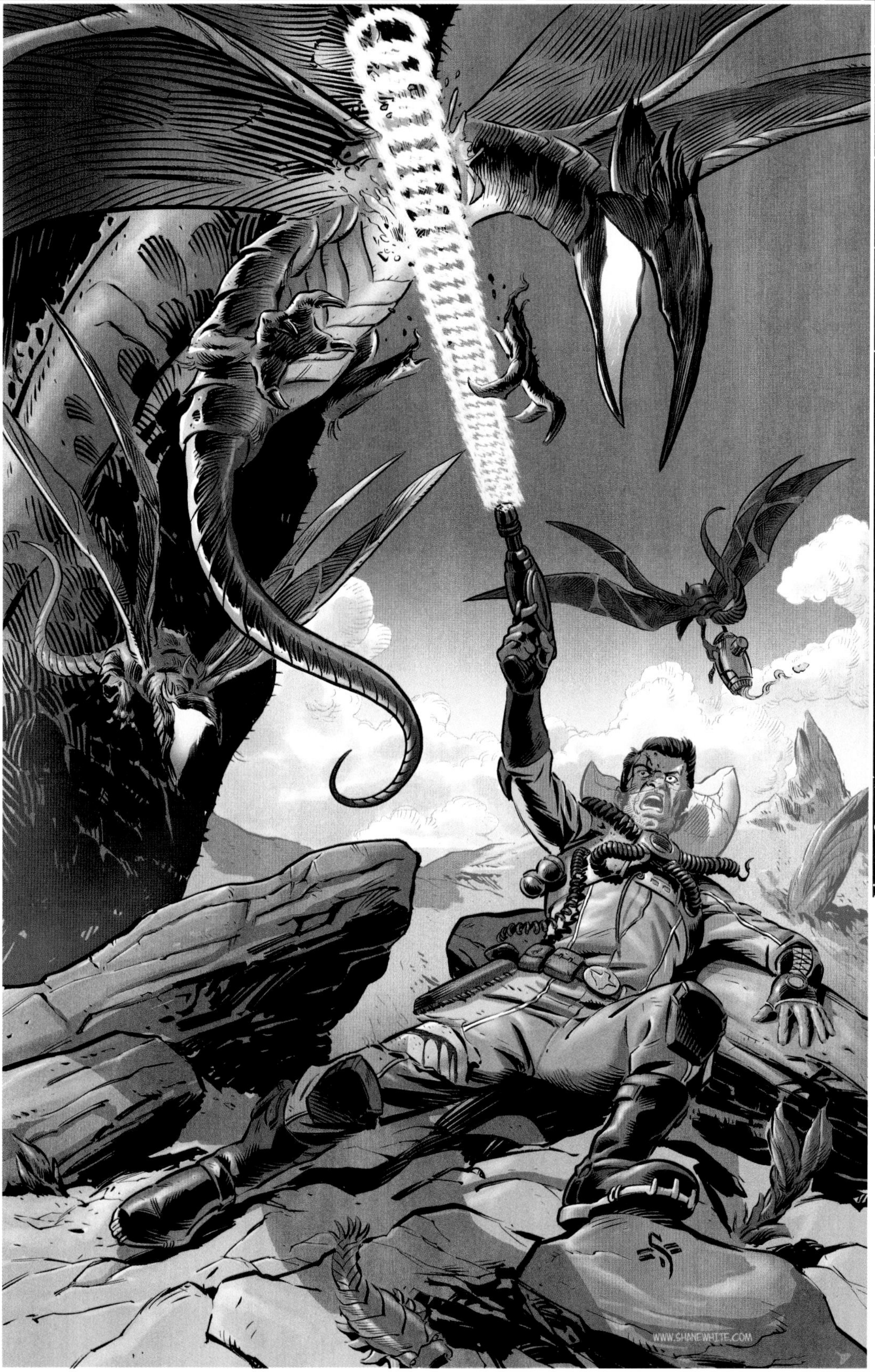
WWW.SHANEWHITE.COM
ART BY **SHANE WHITE**

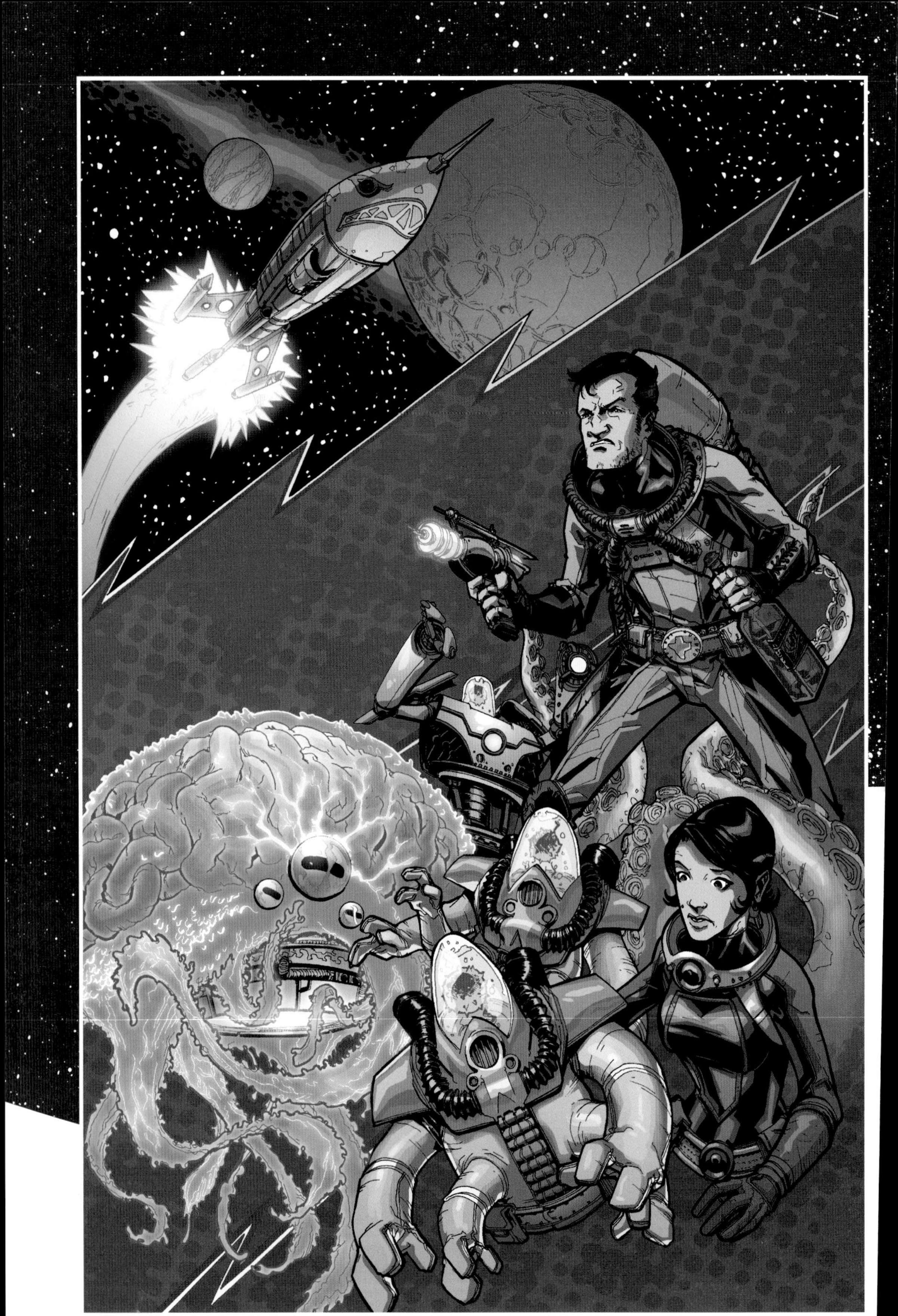

ART BY **ANDY MacDONALD** COLORS BY **NICK FILARDI**

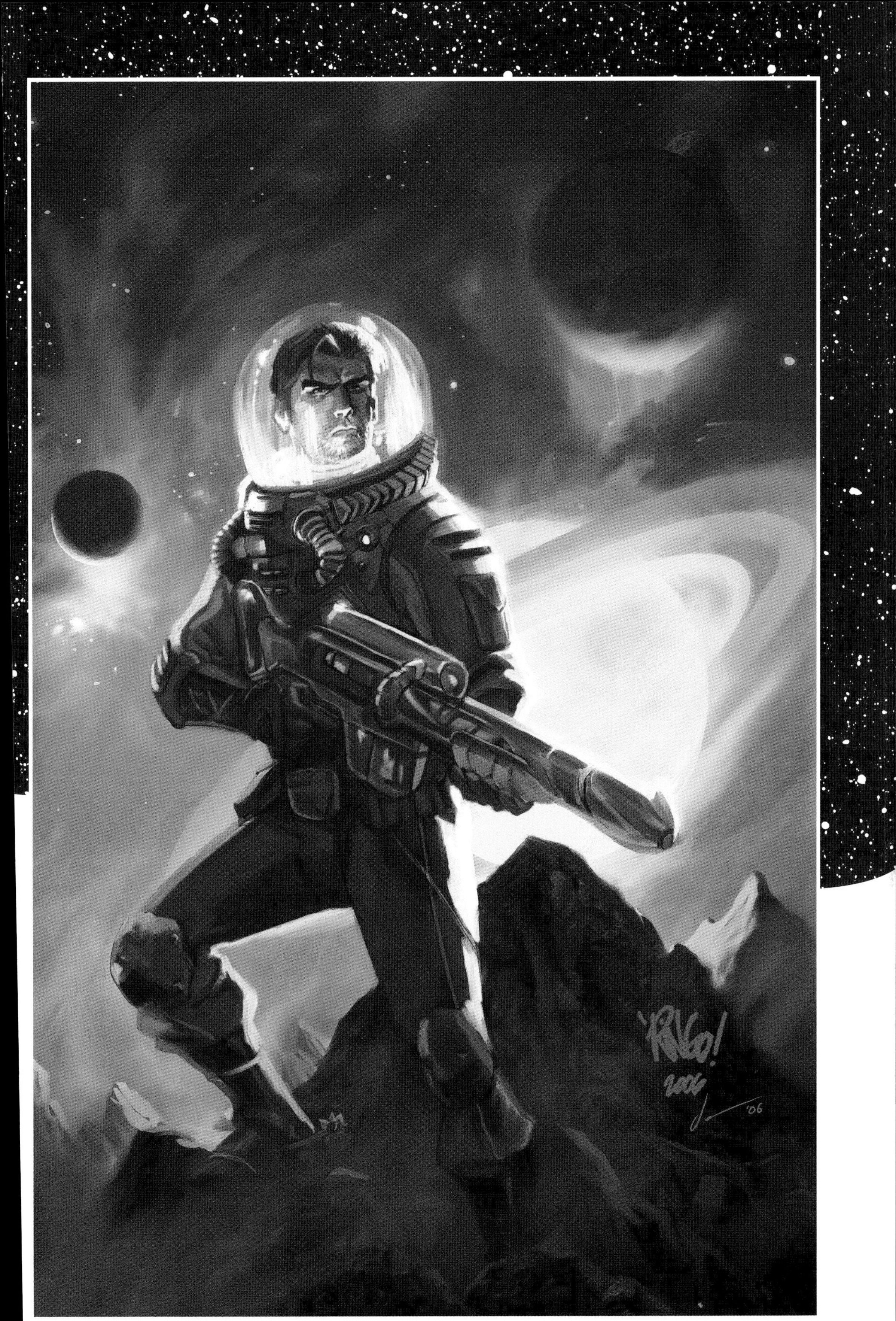

ART BY **MIKE WIERINGO** DIGITAL PAINTING BY **DANIEL COX**

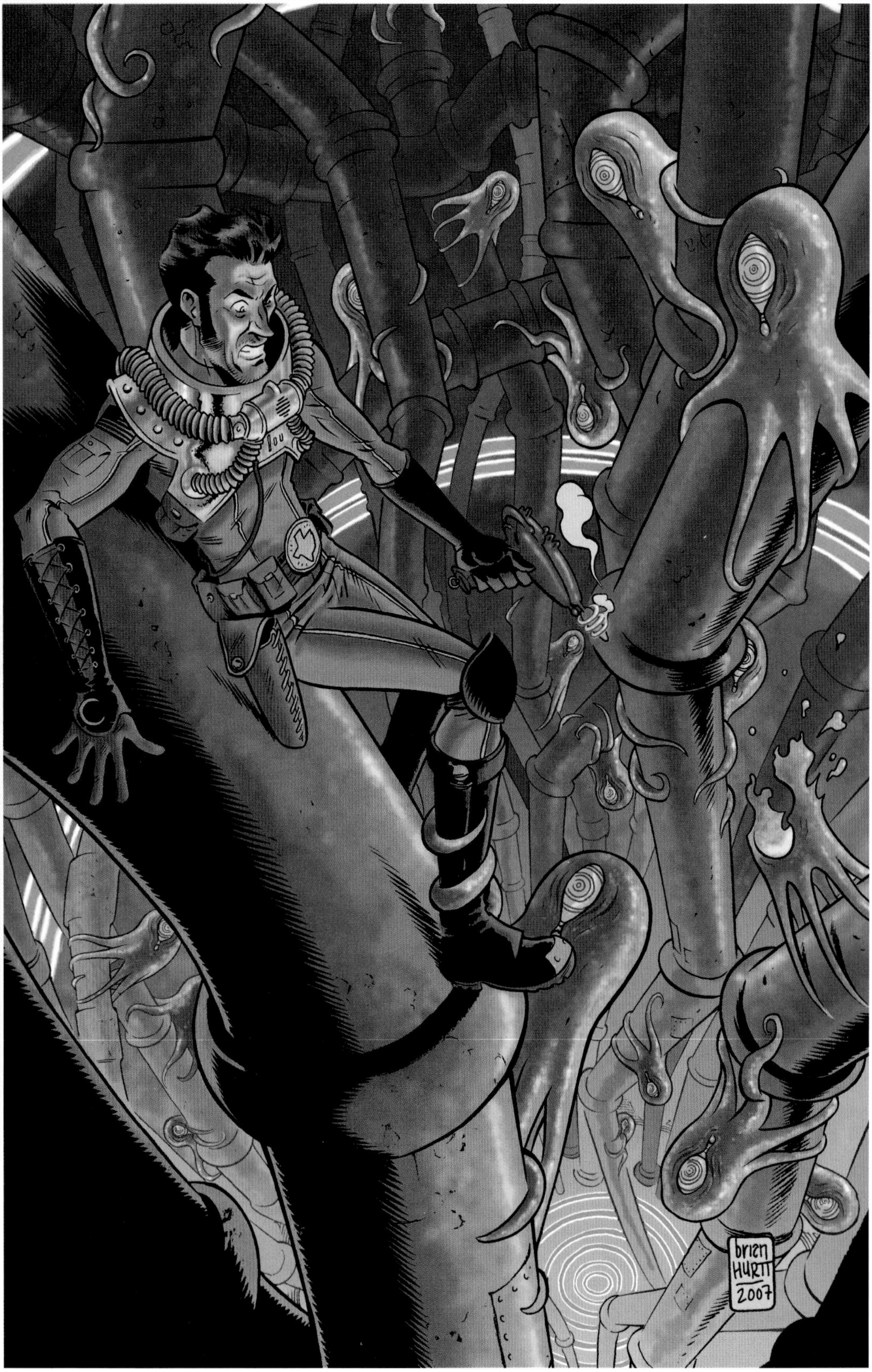
brian HURTT 2007

ART BY **BRIAN HURT**

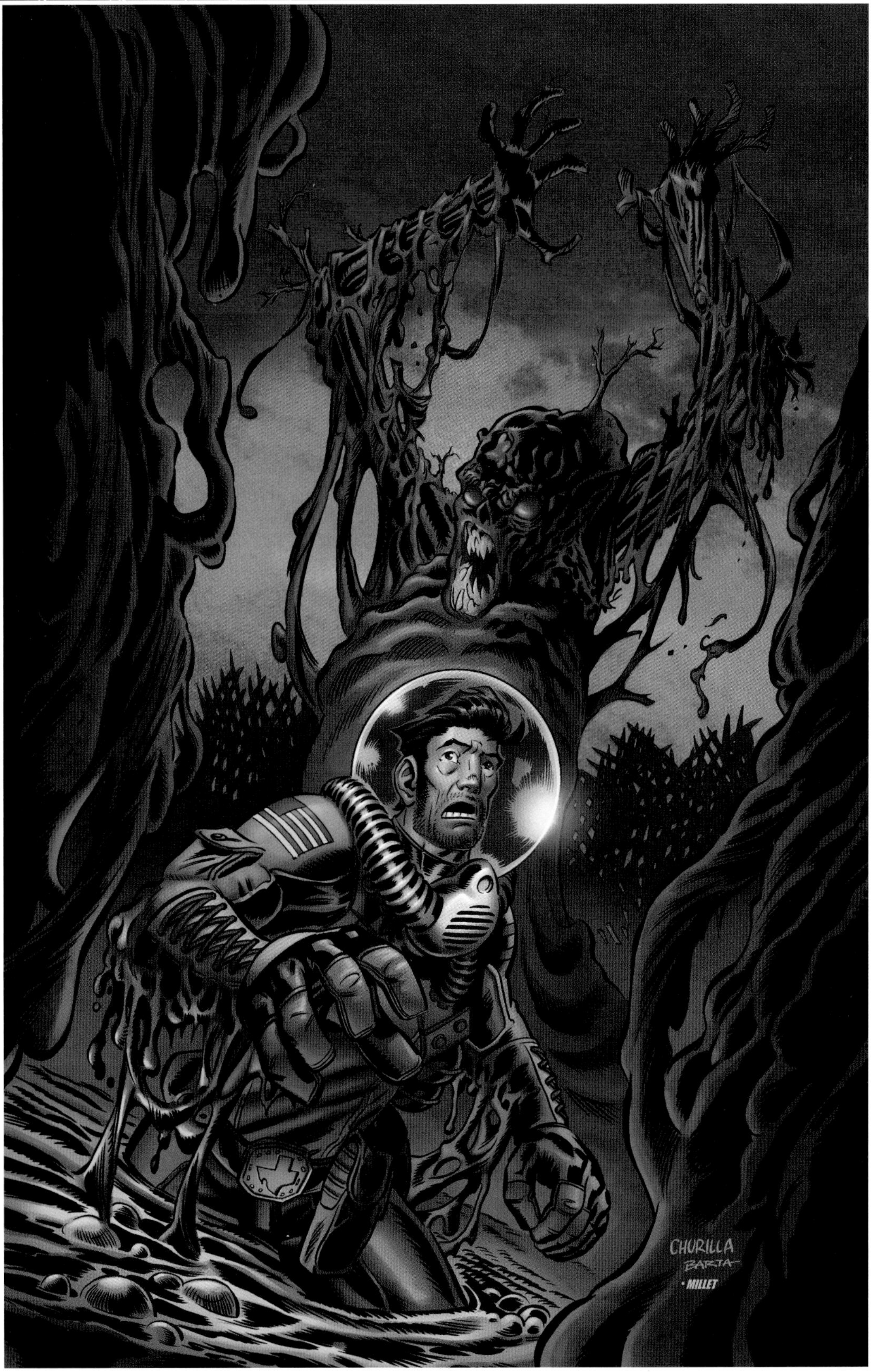
CHURILLA
BARTA
MILLET

PENCILS BY **BRIAN CHURILLA** INKS BY **HILLARY BARTA** COLORS BY **JASON MILLET**

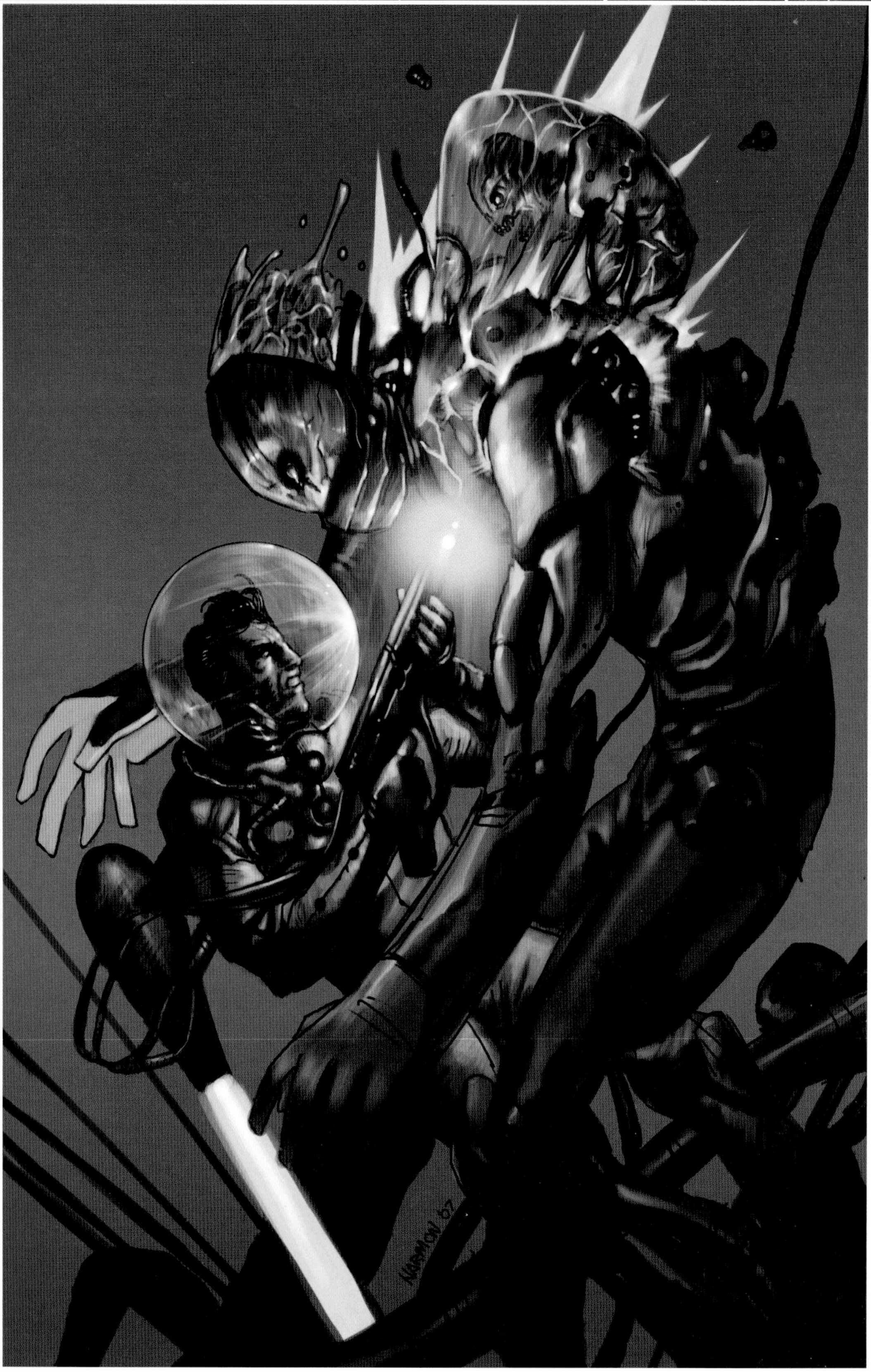
HARMON '07

ART BY **PAUL HARMON**

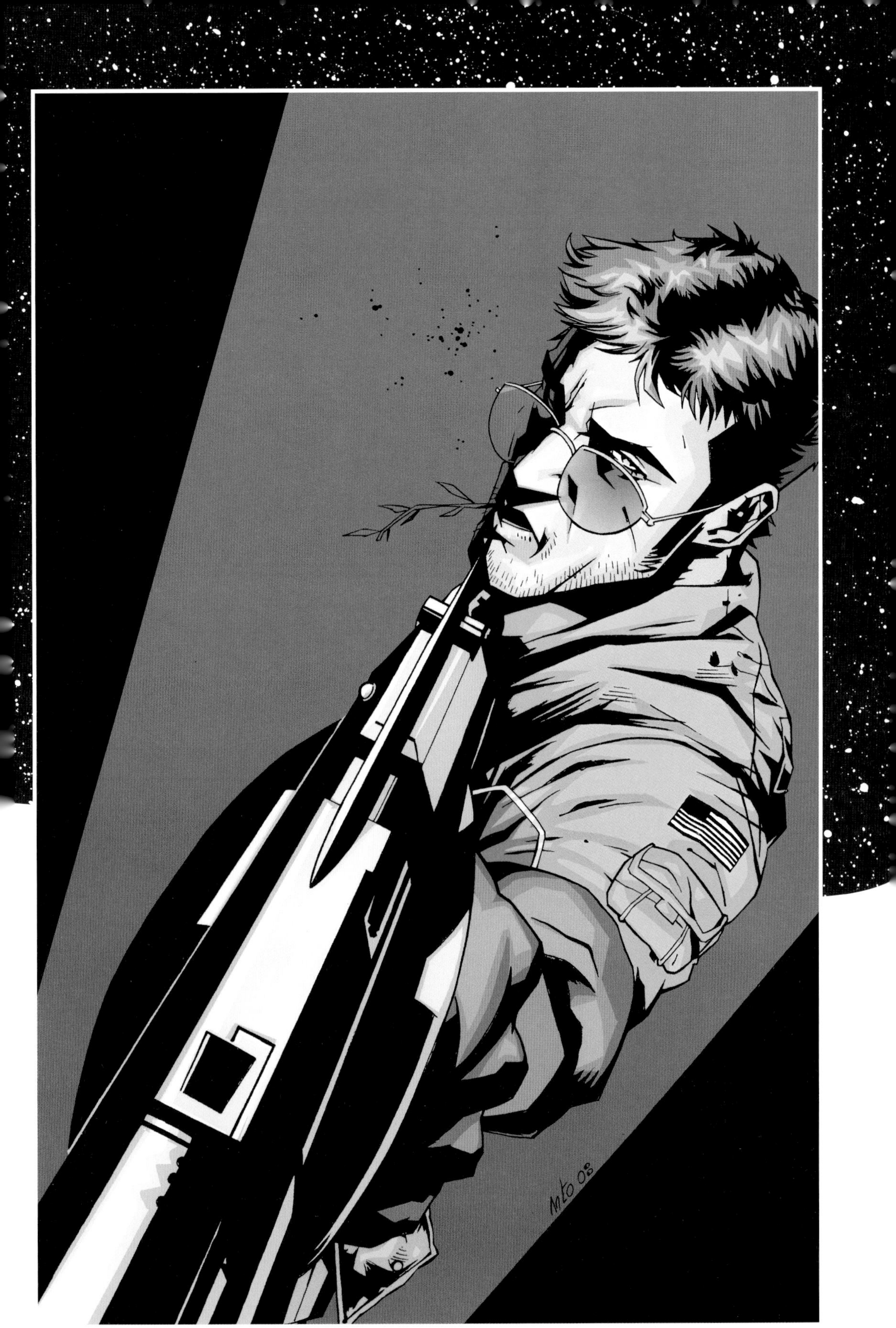

ART BY **ANTONIO FUSO**

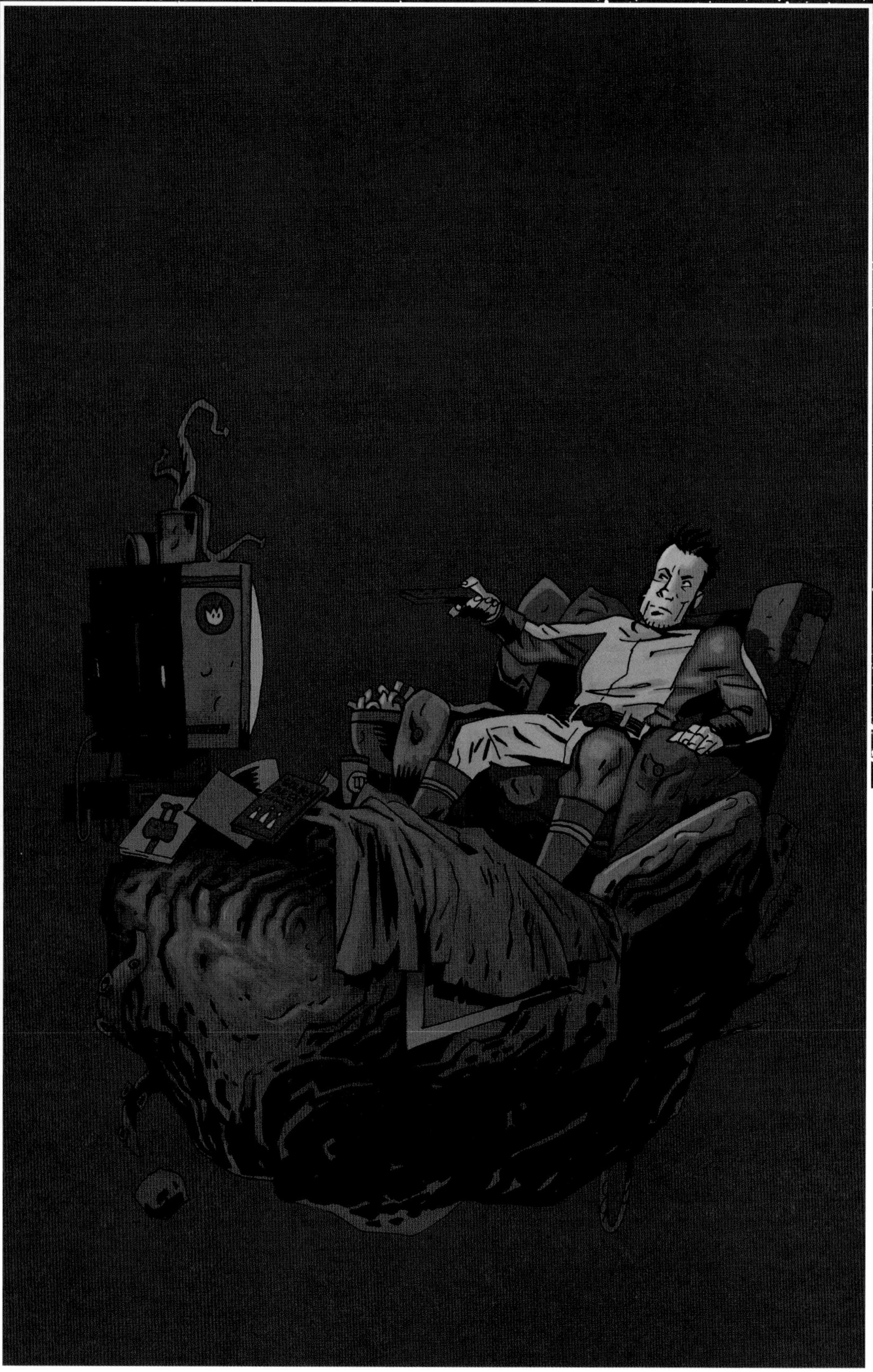

ART BY **PETER BERGTING**

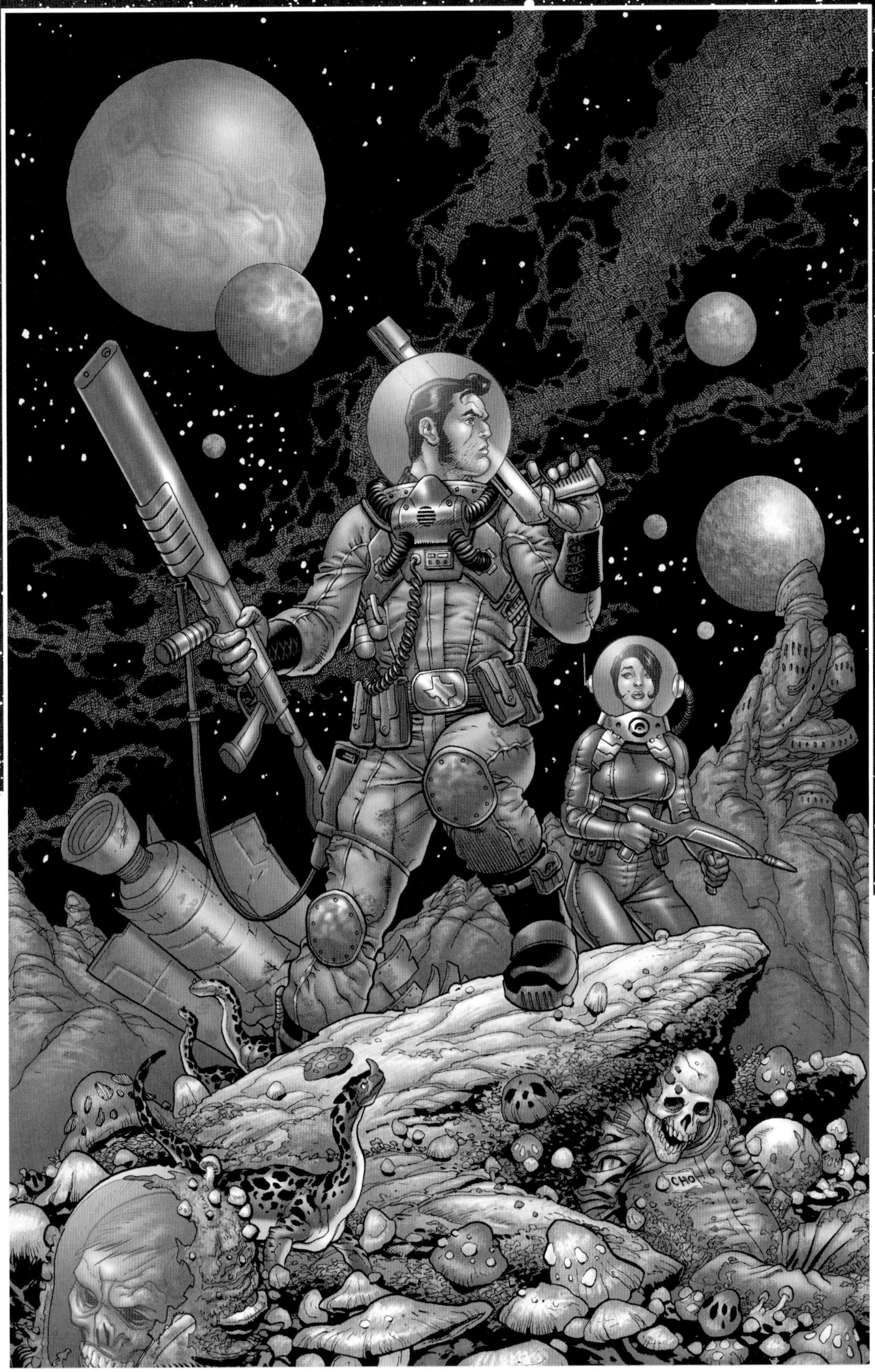
CHO

ART BY **FRANK CHO**

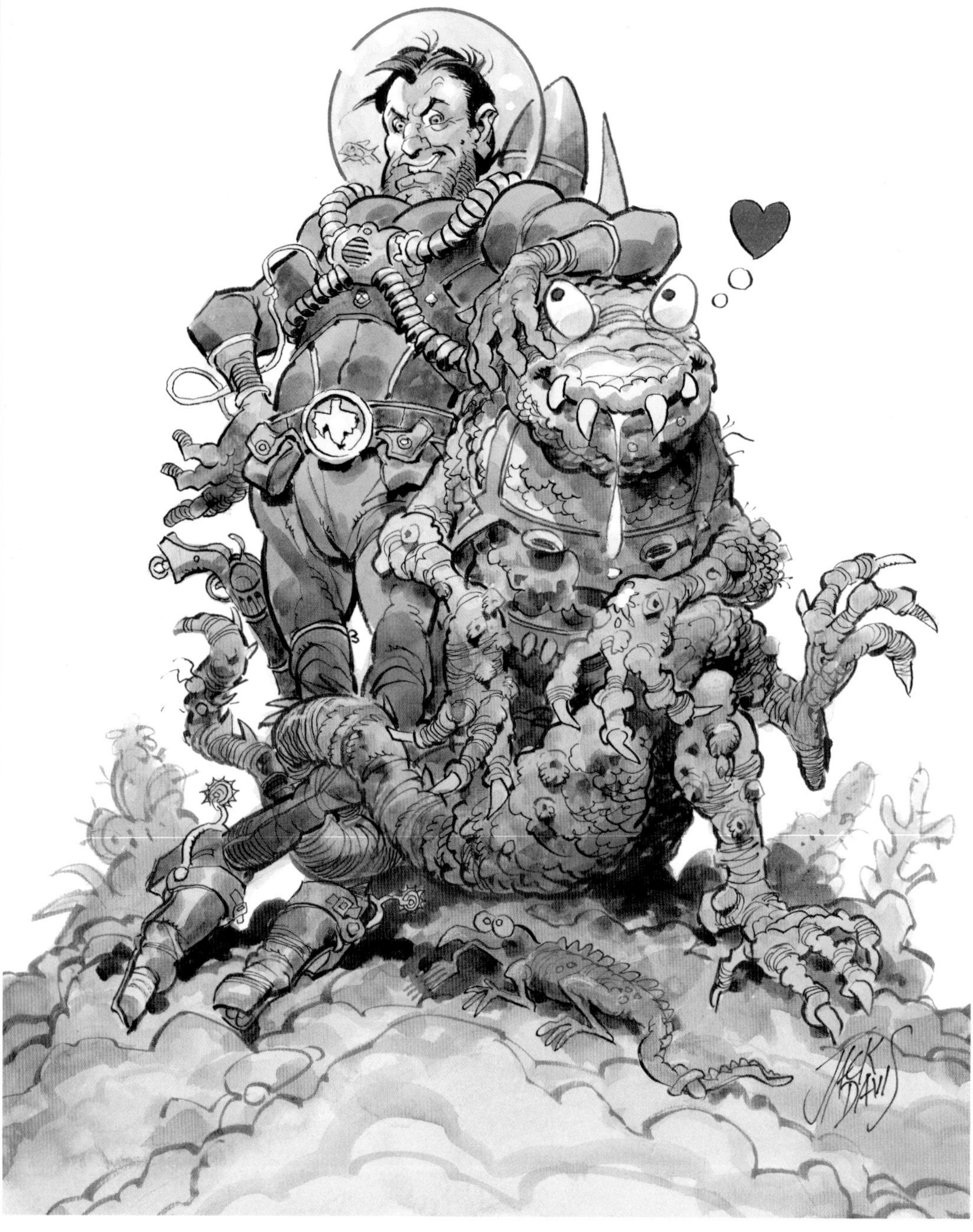

ART BY **JACK DAVIS**

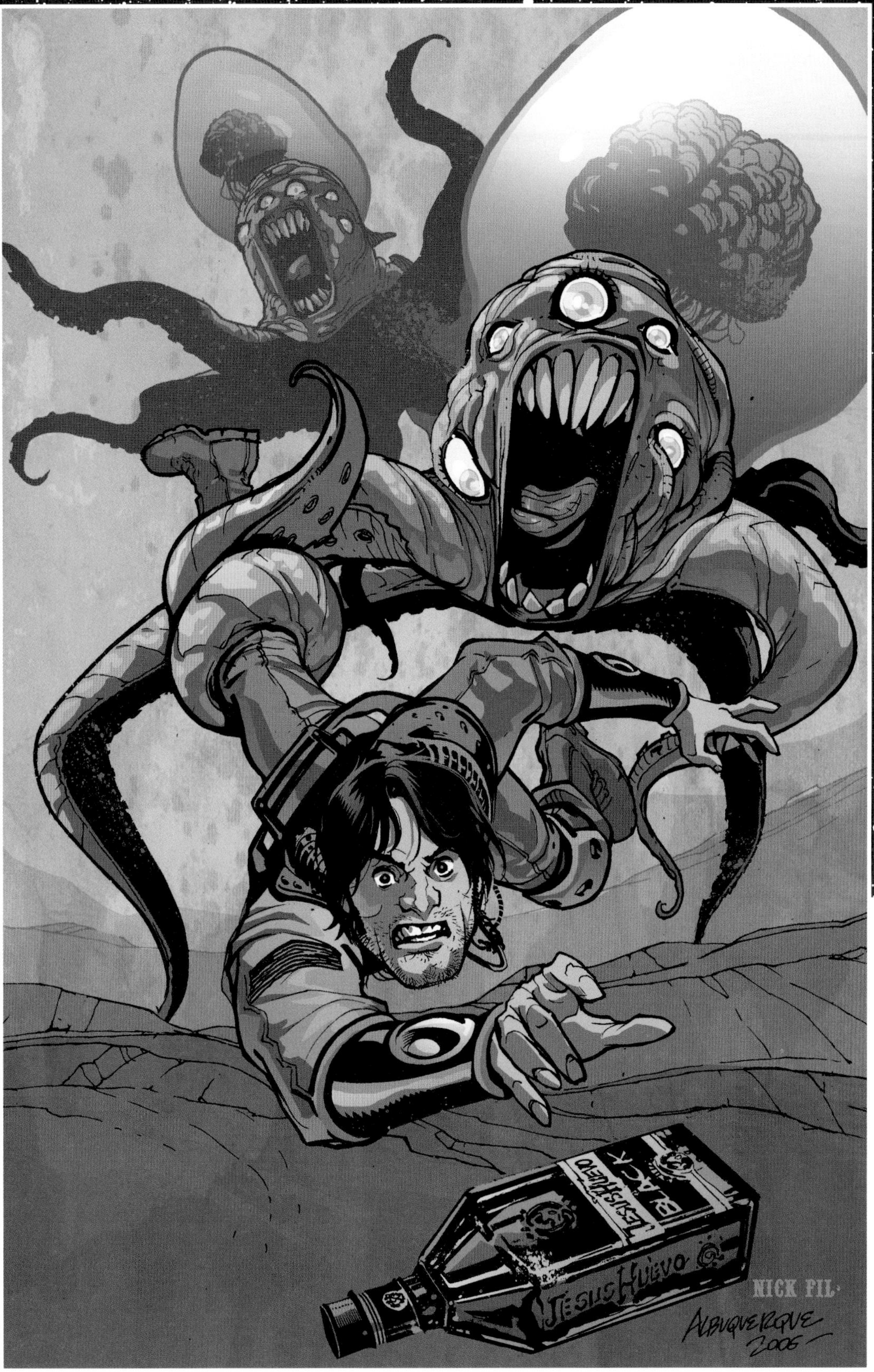
JESUS HUEVO
NICK PIL
ALBUQUERQUE
2006

ART BY **RAFAEL ALBUQUERQUE**

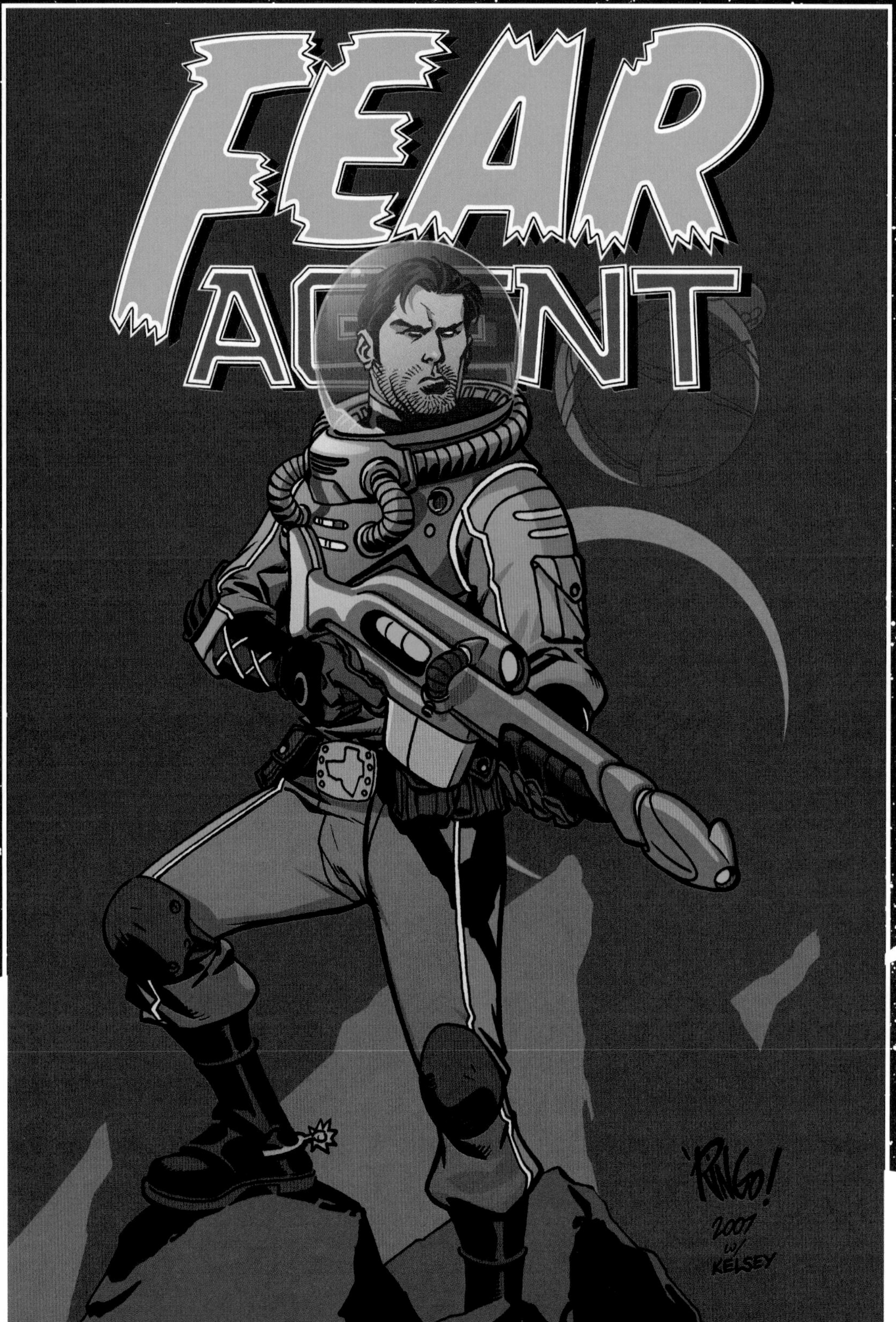
FEAR
AGENT
'RINGO!
2007
w/
KELSEY

ART BY **MIKE WIERINGO & KELSEY SHANNON**

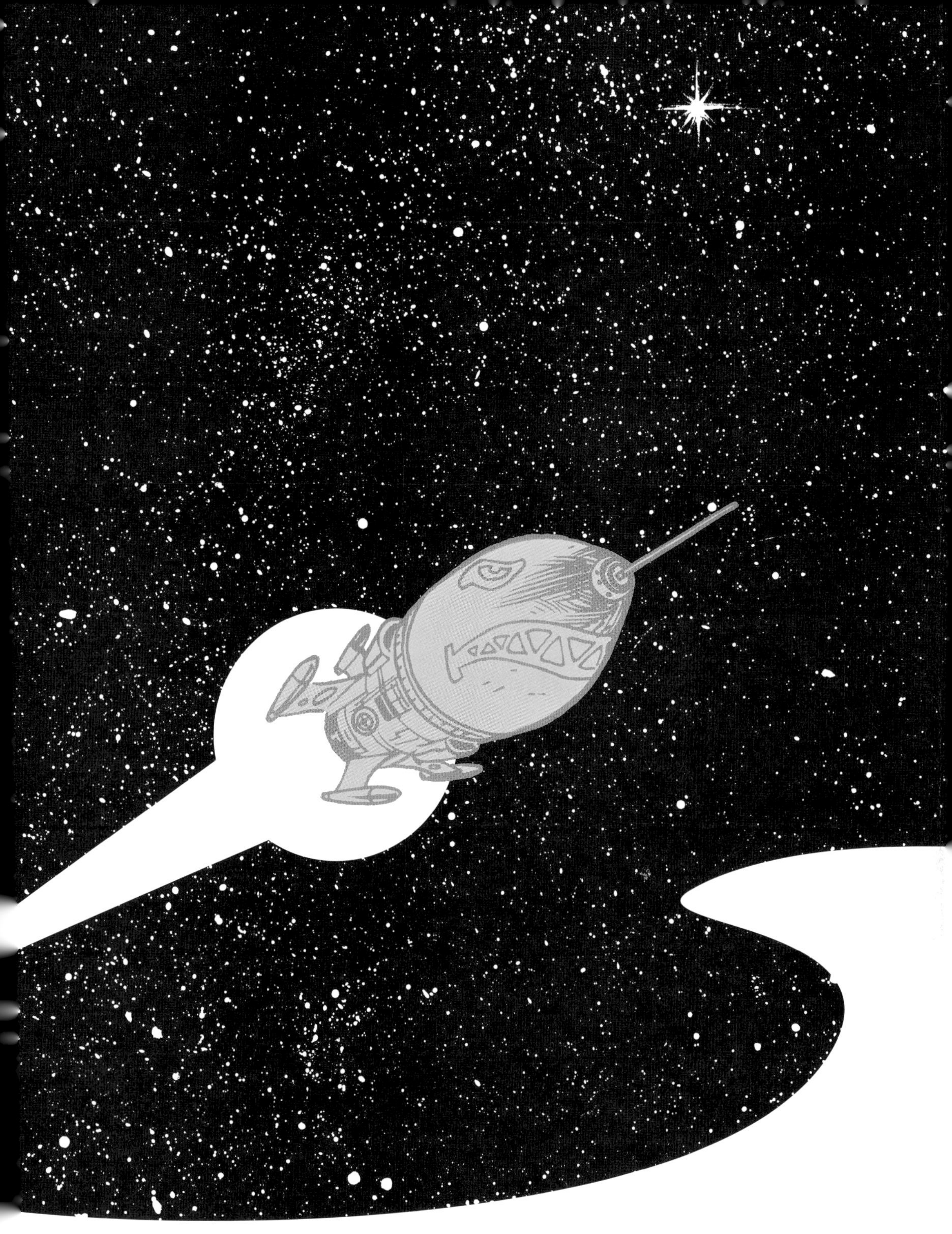

FEAR AGENT INKS

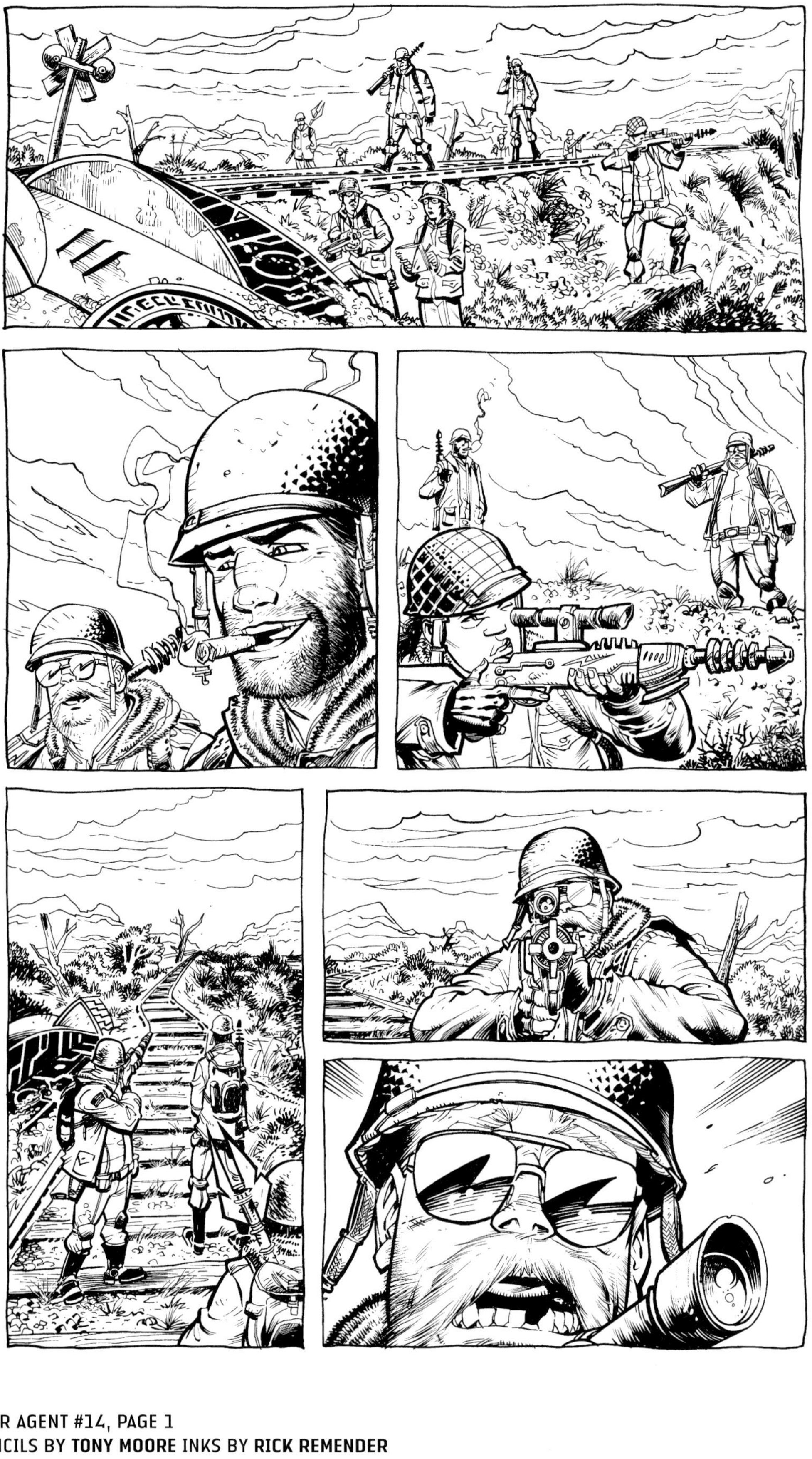

FEAR AGENT #14, PAGE 1
PENCILS BY **TONY MOORE** INKS BY **RICK REMENDER**

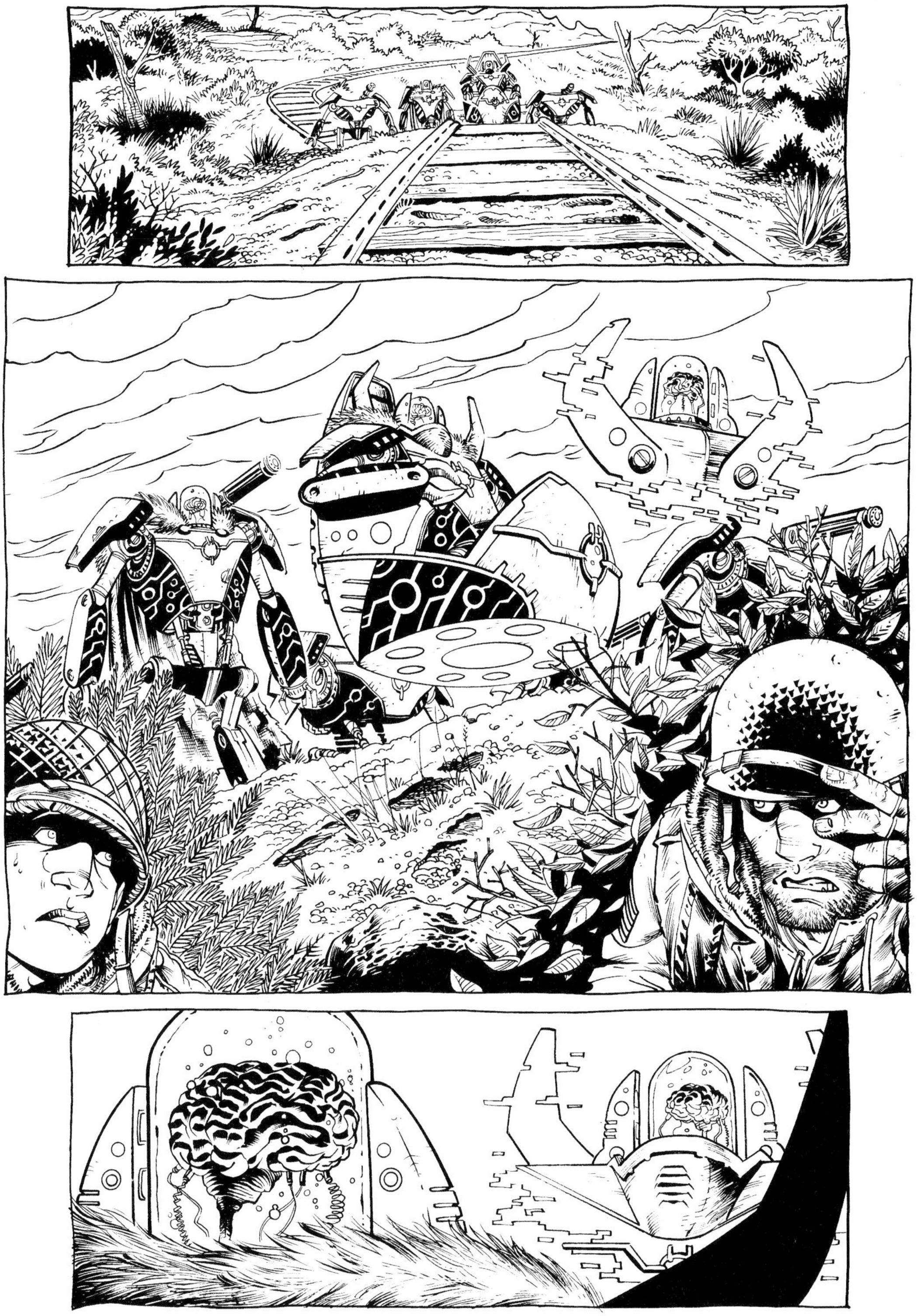

FEAR AGENT #14, PAGE 2
PENCILS BY **TONY MOORE** INKS BY **RICK REMENDER**

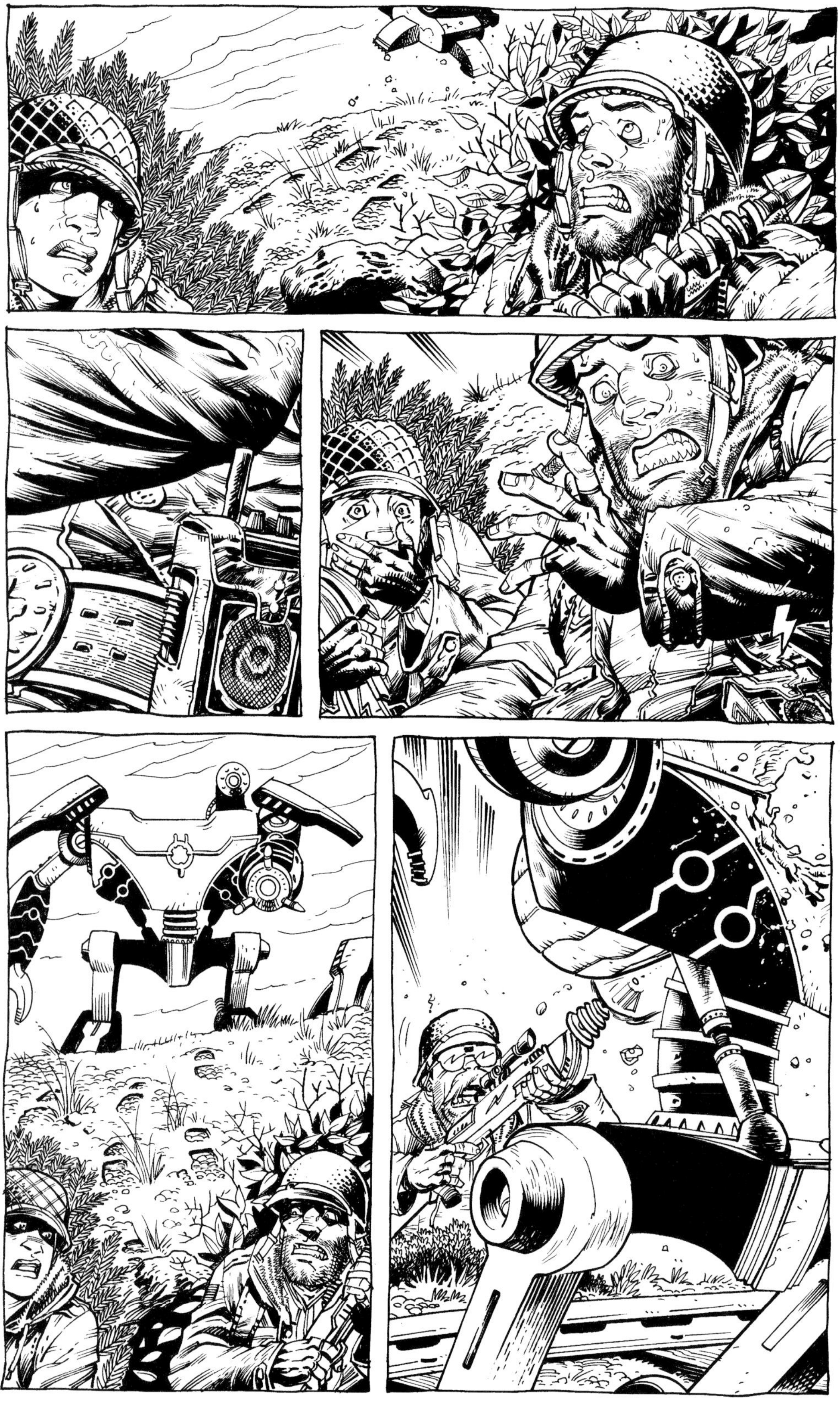

FEAR AGENT #14, PAGE 3
PENCILS BY **TONY MOORE** INKS BY **RICK REMENDER**

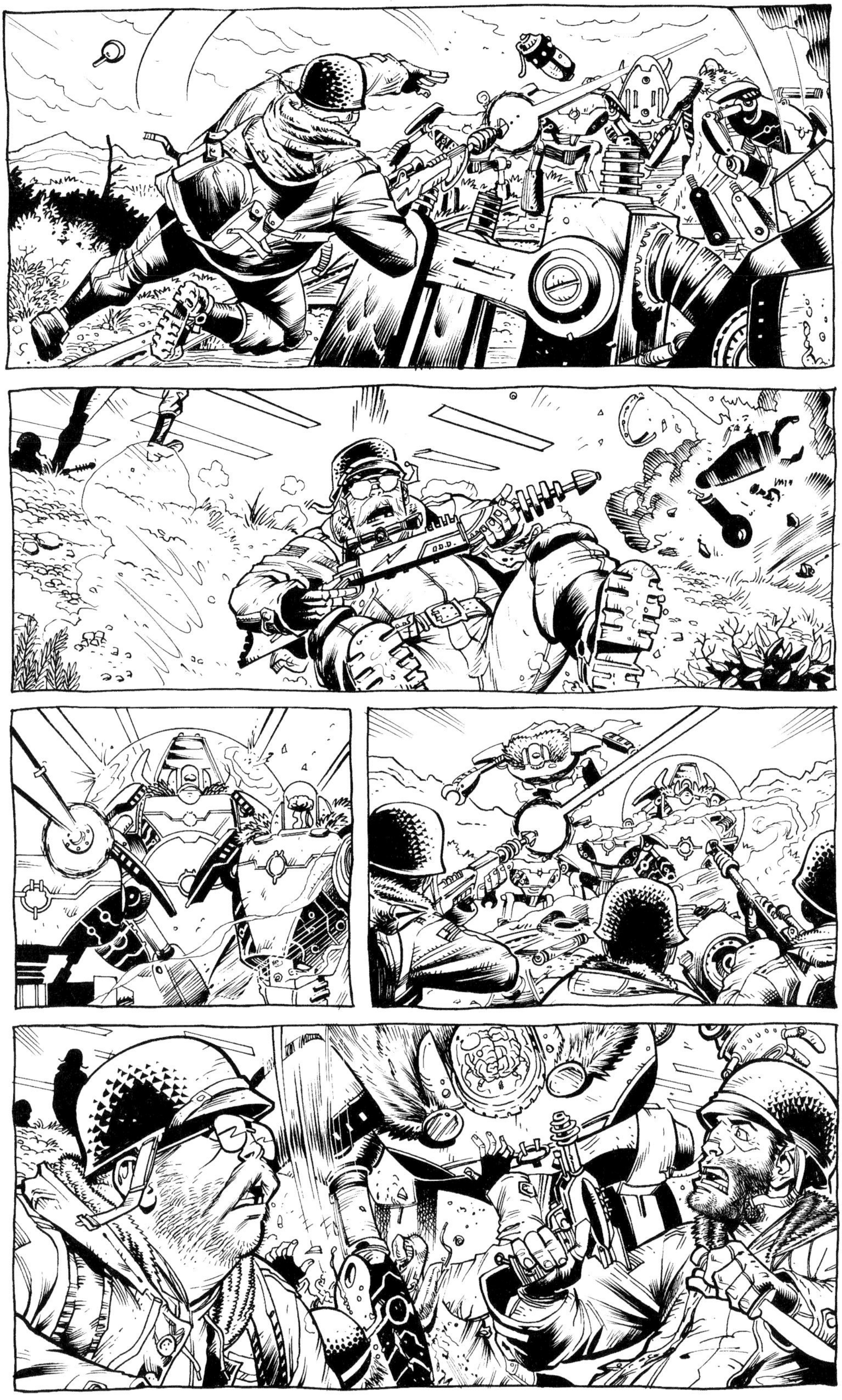

FEAR AGENT #14, PAGE 4

PENCILS BY **TONY MOORE** INKS BY **RICK REMENDER**

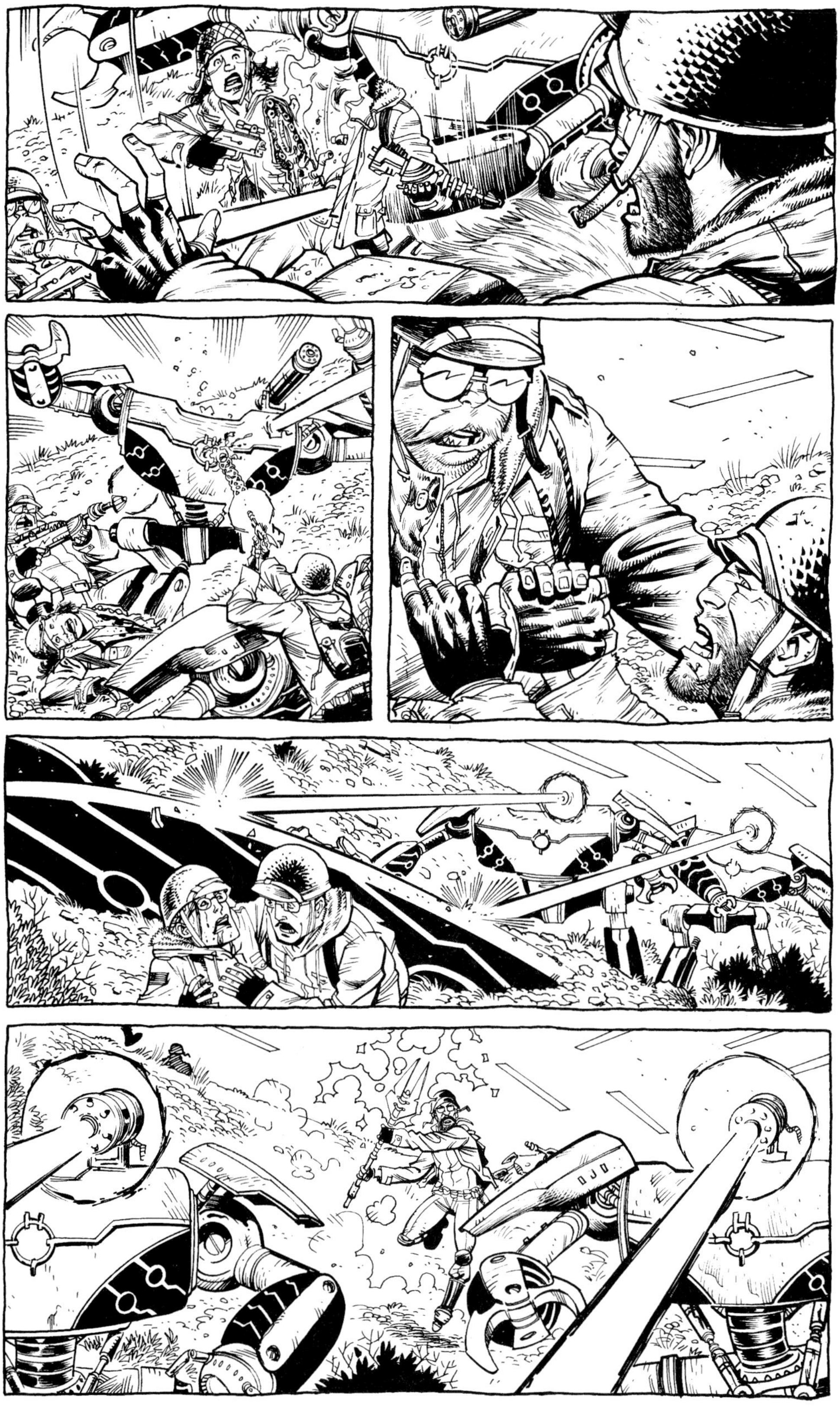

FEAR AGENT #14, PAGE 6
PENCILS BY **TONY MOORE** INKS BY **RICK REMENDER**

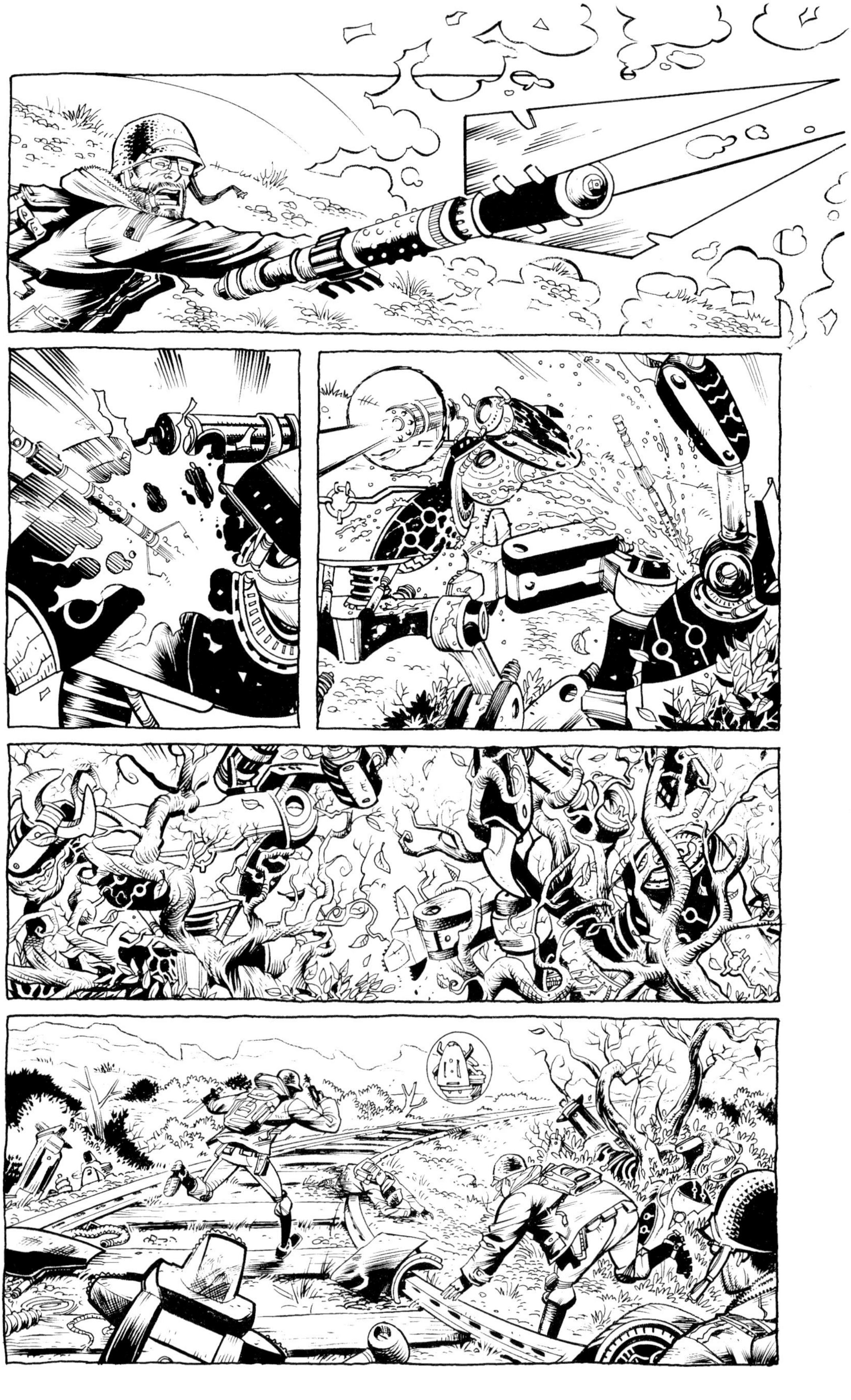

FEAR AGENT #14, PAGE 7
PENCILS BY **TONY MOORE** INKS BY **RICK REMENDER**

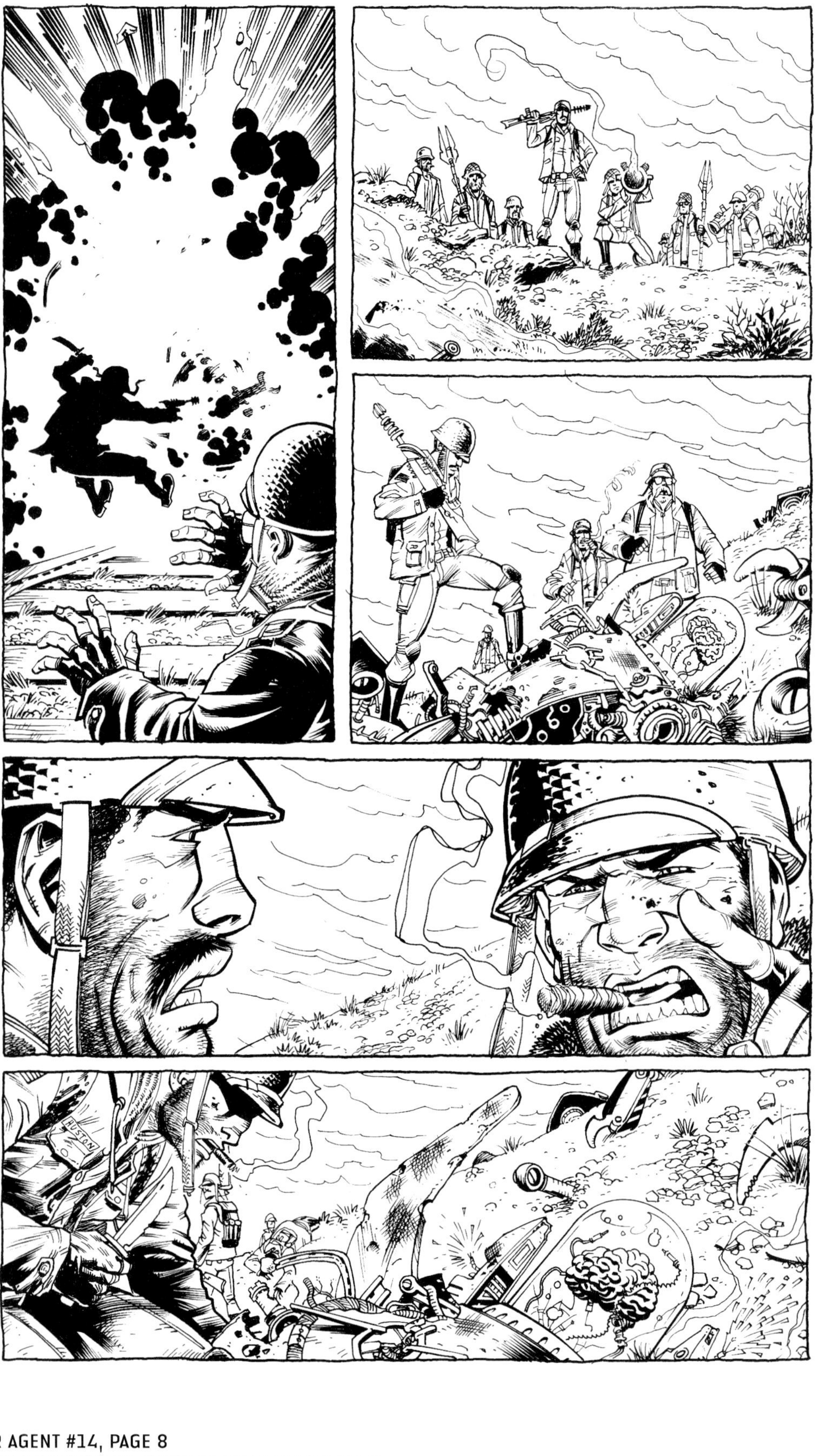
HUSTON

FEAR AGENT #14, PAGE 8
PENCILS BY **TONY MOORE** INKS BY **RICK REMENDER**

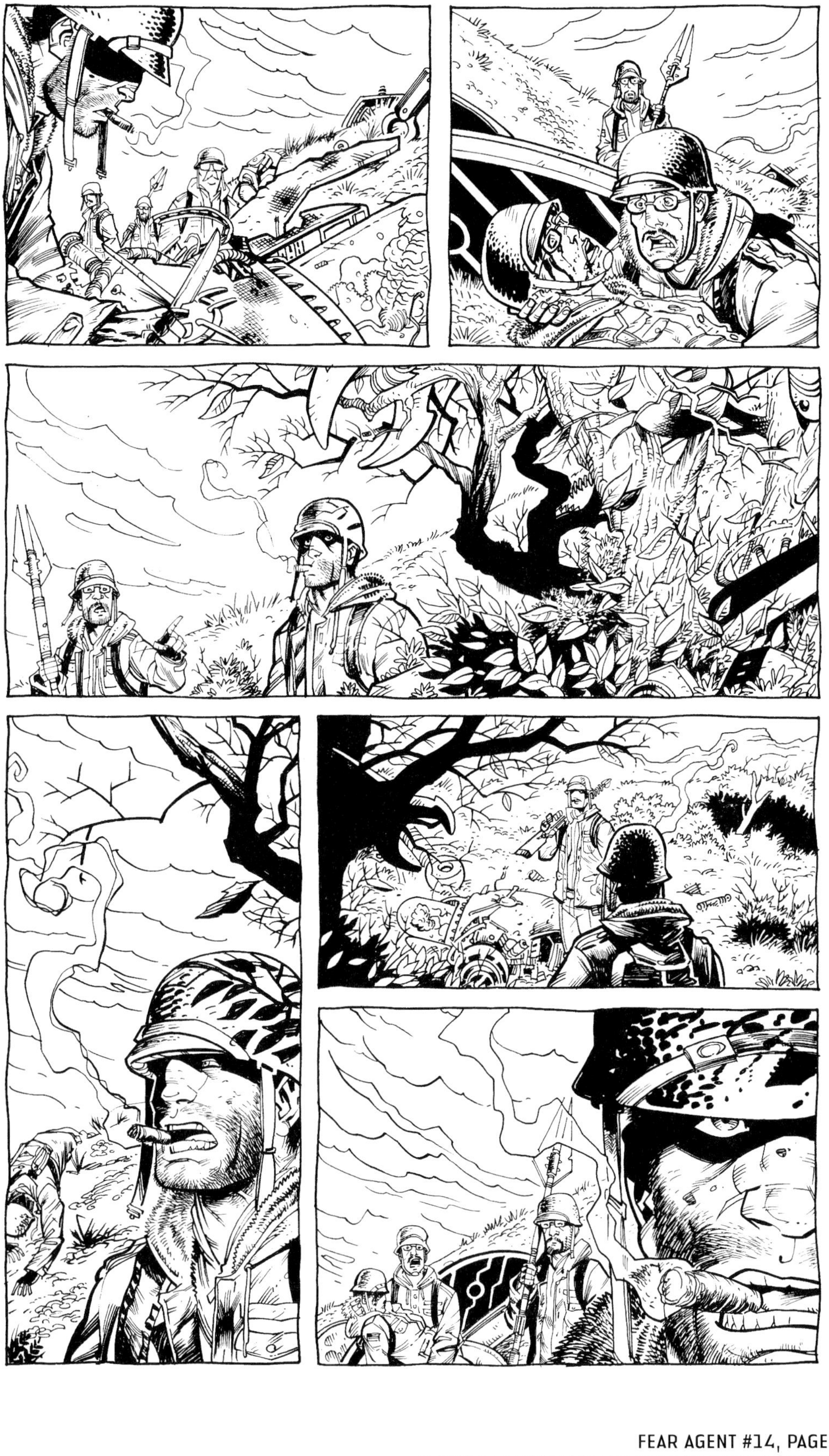

FEAR AGENT #14, PAGE 9
PENCILS BY **TONY MOORE** INKS BY **RICK REMENDER**

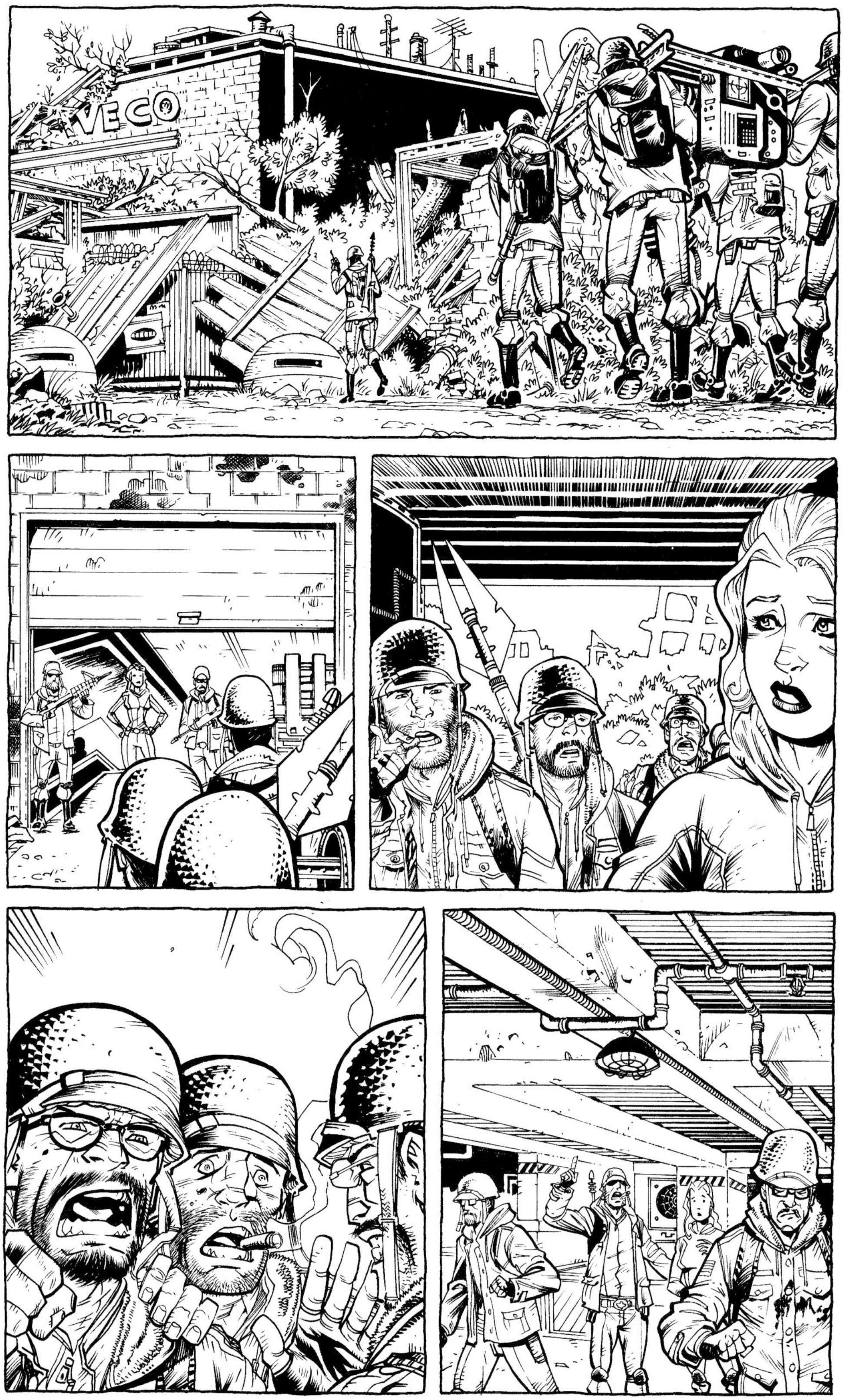
VECO

FEAR AGENT #14, PAGE 10
PENCILS BY **TONY MOORE** INKS BY **RICK REMENDER**

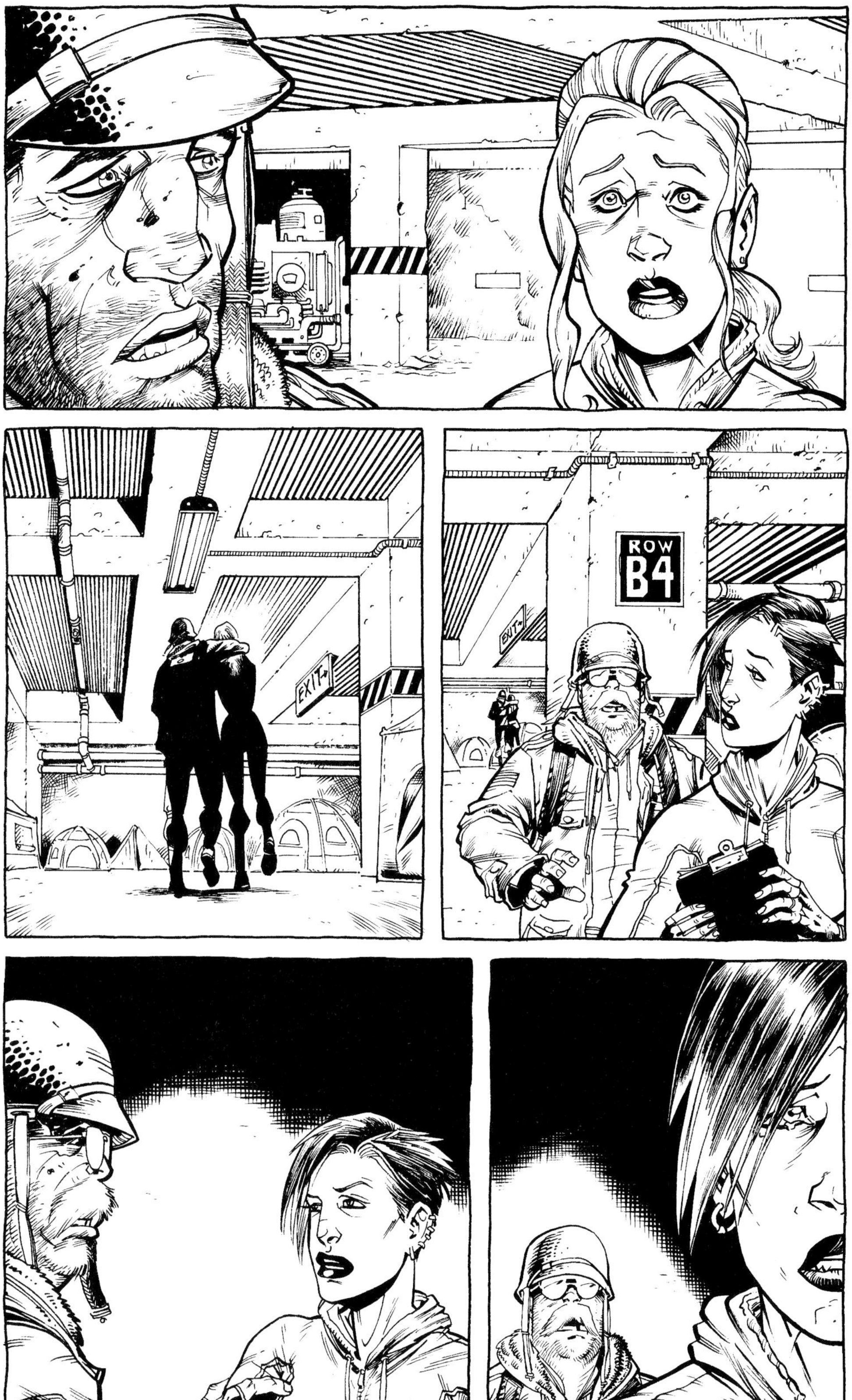
EXIT
ROW
B4
EXIT

FEAR AGENT #14, PAGE 11
PENCILS BY **TONY MOORE** INKS BY **RICK REMENDER**

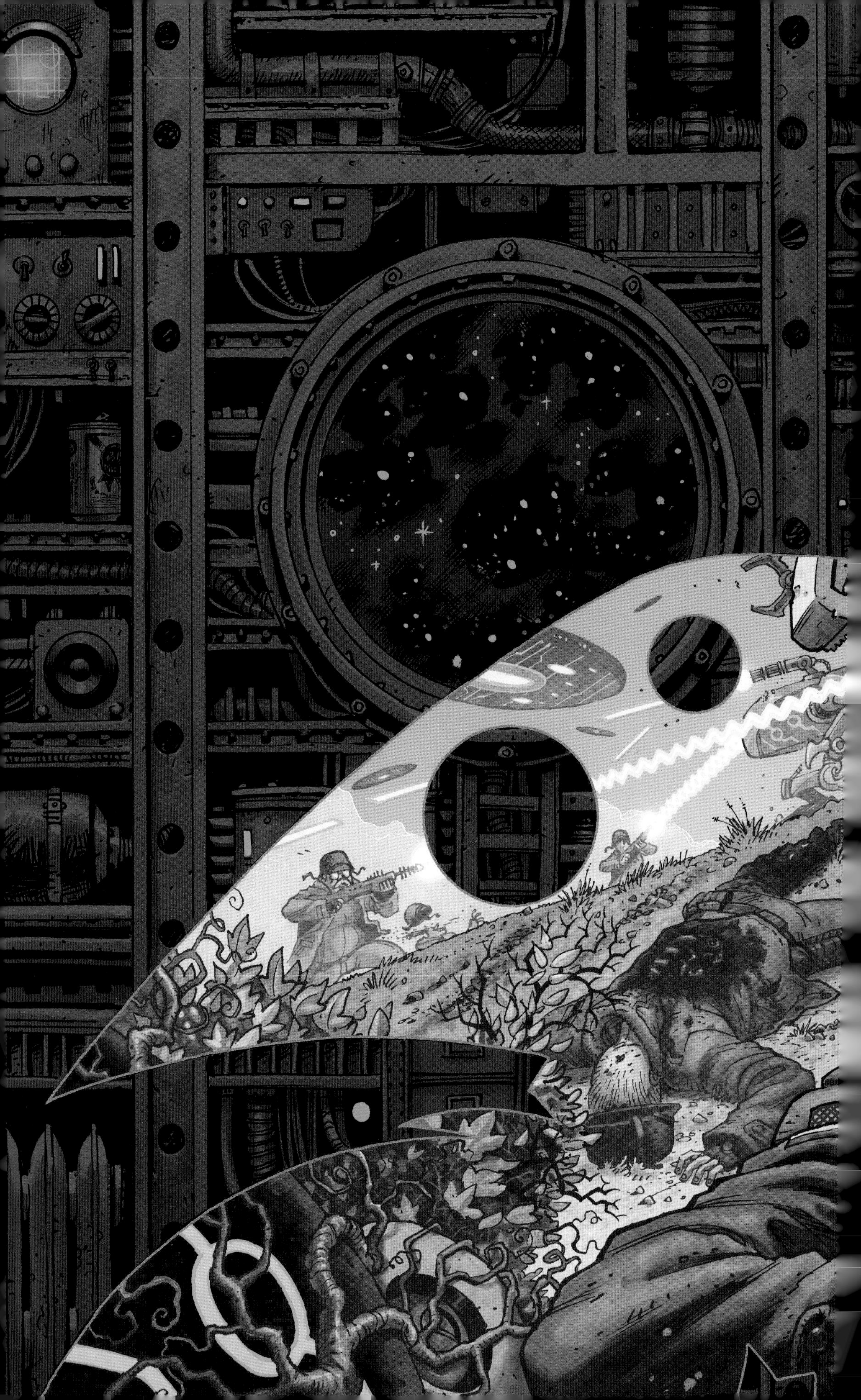

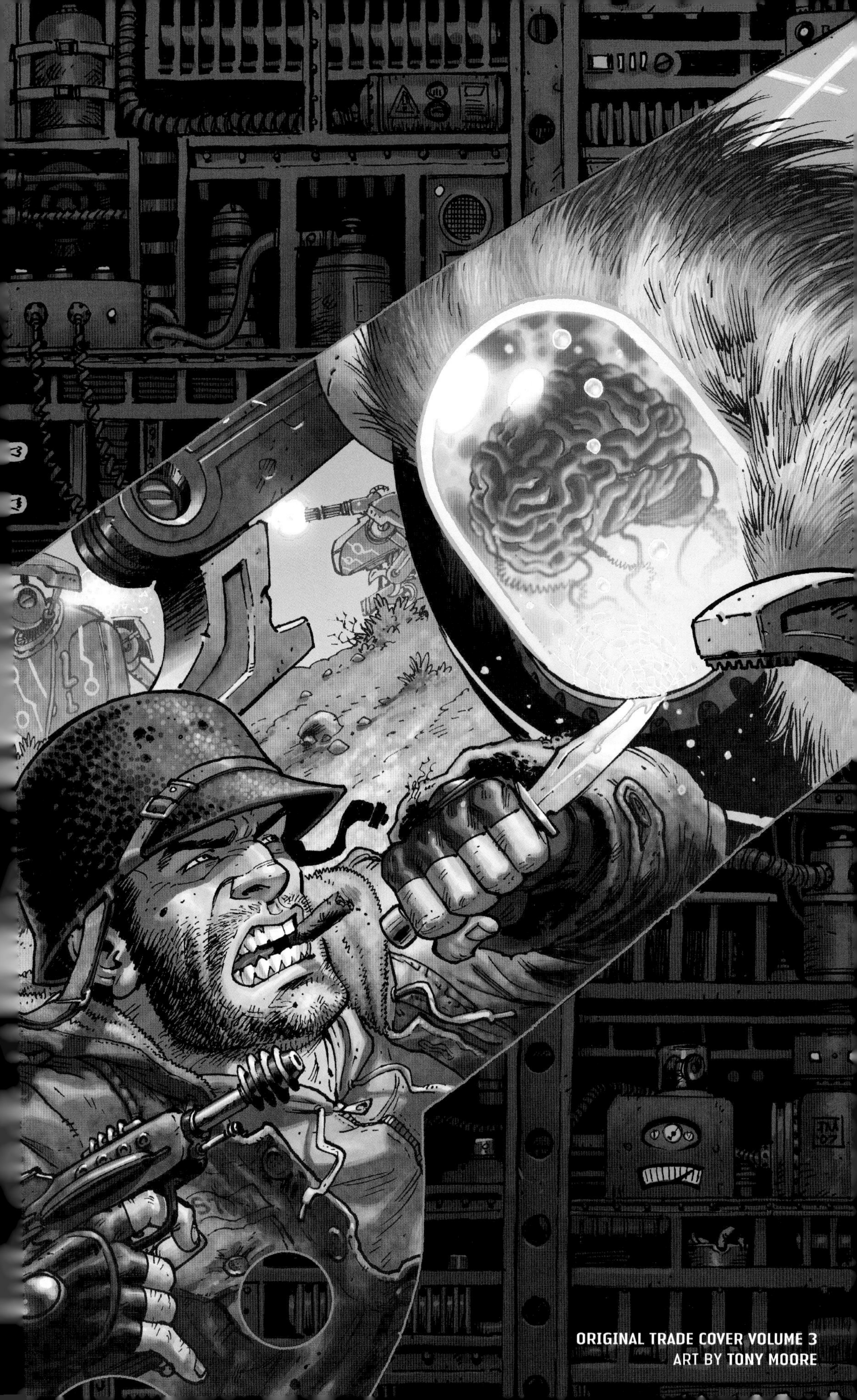

ORIGINAL TRADE COVER VOLUME 3
ART BY TONY MOORE

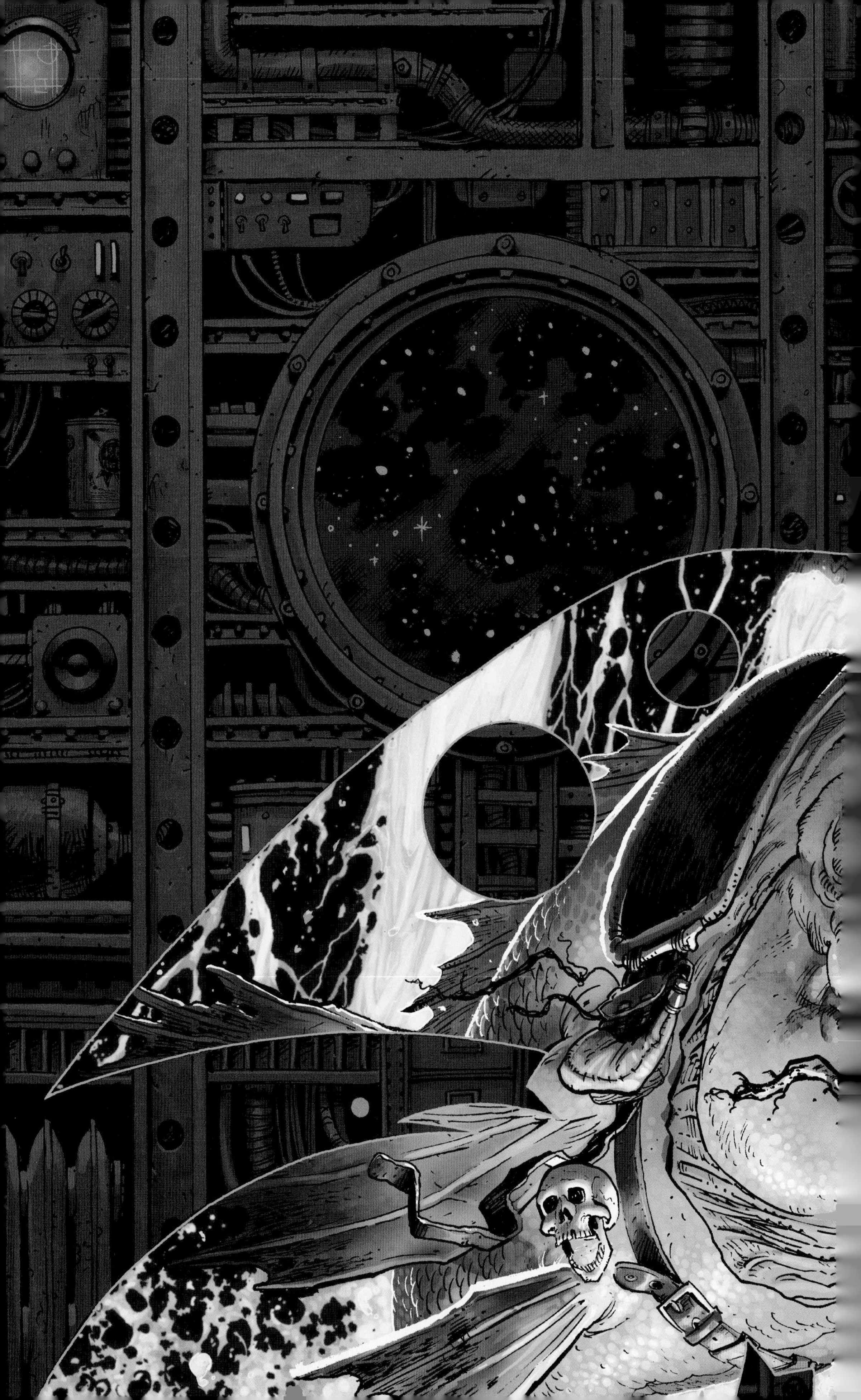

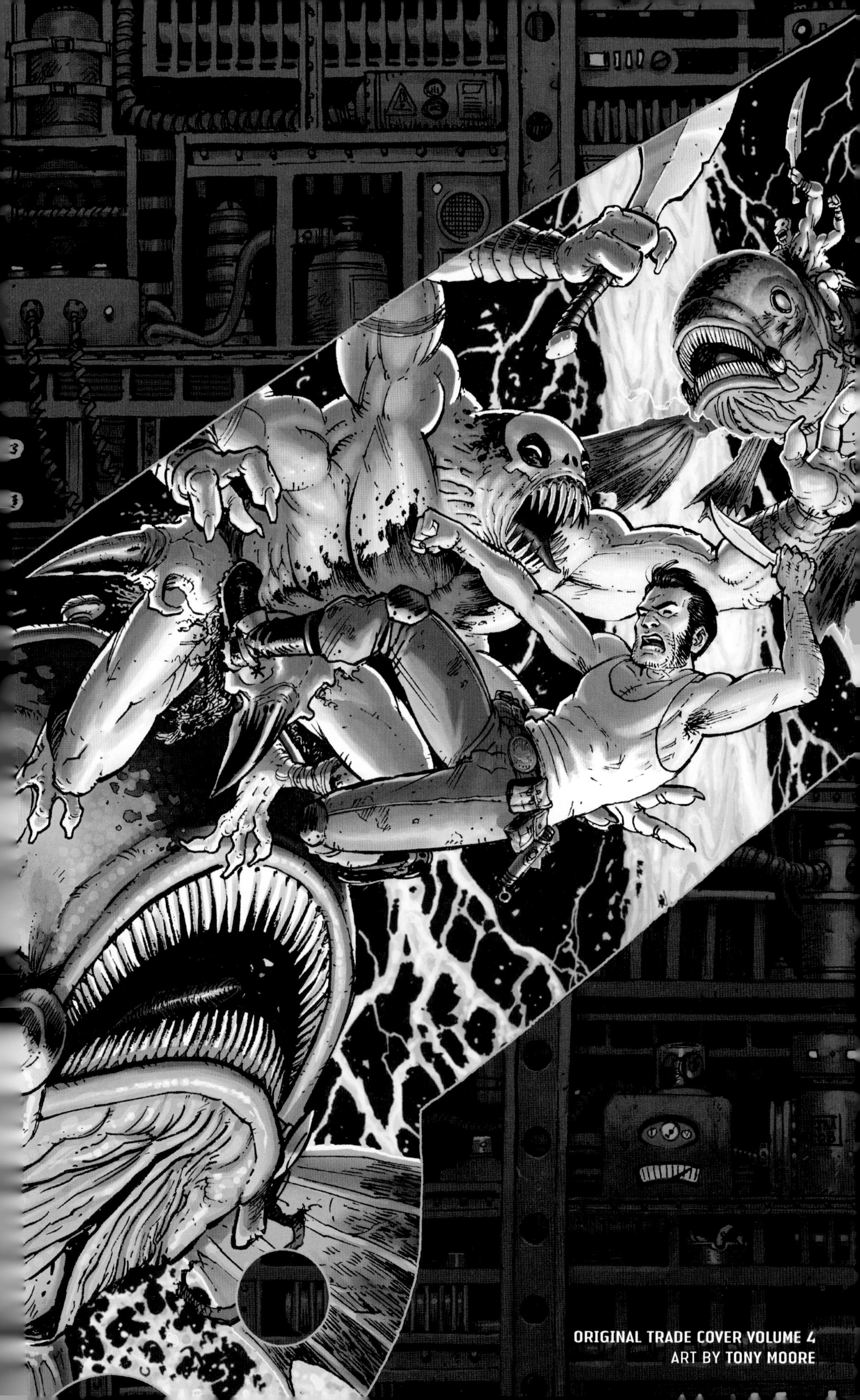

ORIGINAL TRADE COVER VOLUME 4
ART BY TONY MOORE

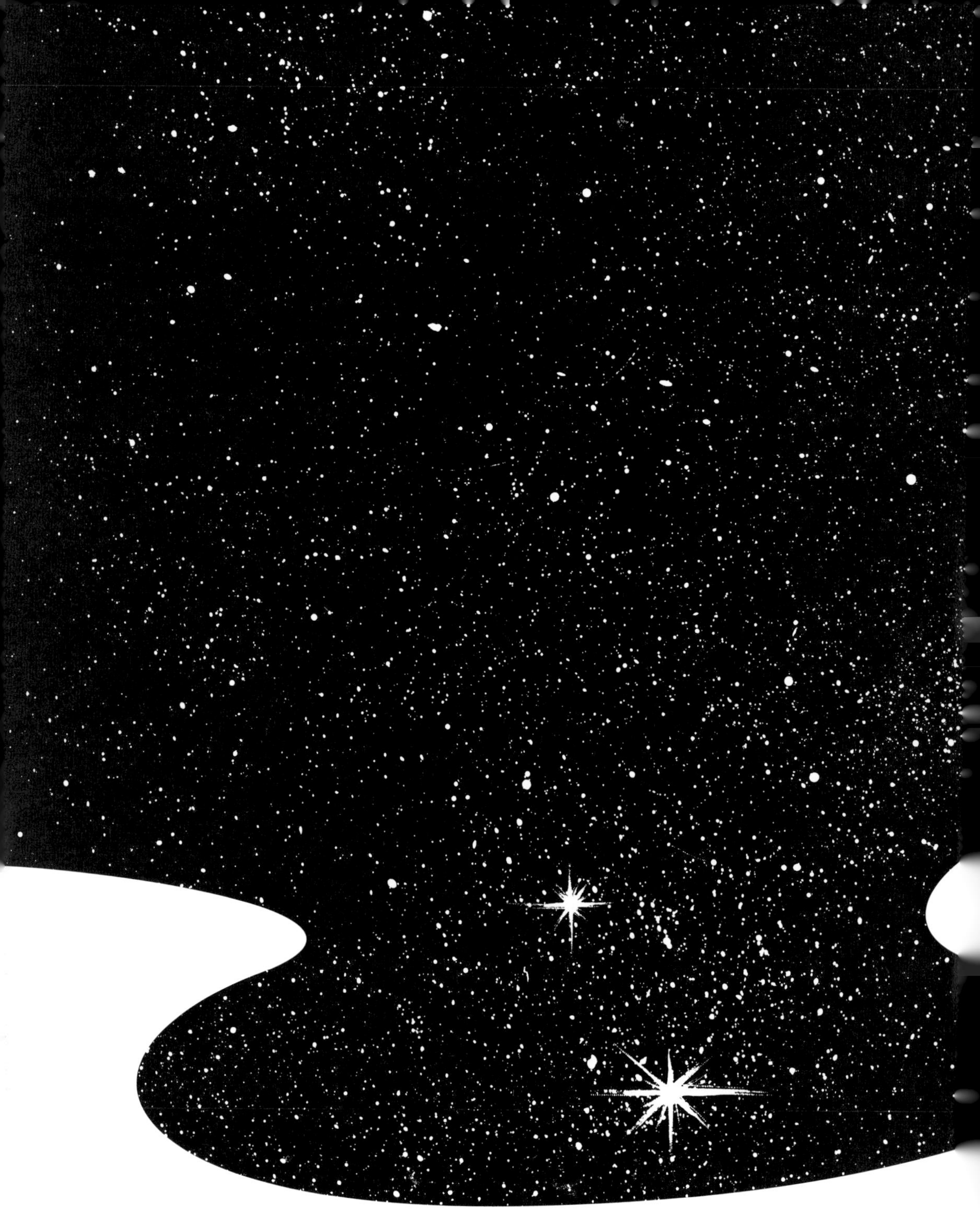

⚡ The Creators ⚡

Rick Remender is the writer/co-creator of comics such as *LOW*, *Fear Agent*, *Deadly Class*, *Tokyo Ghost*, *Black Science*, and *Seven to Eternity*. For Marvel he has written titles such as *Uncanny Avengers*, *Captain America*, *Uncanny X-Force*, and *Venom*.

He's written video games such as *Bulletstorm* and *Dead Space*, and worked on films such as *The Iron Giant*, *Anastasia*, and *Titan A.E.*

He and his tea-sipping wife, Danni, currently reside in Los Angeles raising two beautiful mischief monkeys.

Tony Moore has been in the business since 1999, when he began work on his maiden voyage, *Battle Pope*. Since then, he's lent his hand to books such as *Masters of the Universe*, *Brit*, the Eisner Award-nominated series *The Walking Dead*, and the creator-owned books *Fear Agent* and *The Exterminators*. In recent years Tony has put his stamp on such Marvel series as *Ghost Rider*, *Punisher*, *Venom* and *Deadpool*.

Tony and his wife, Kara, live in the middle of nowhere, raising a brilliant daughter and a little hell whenever they can.

Jerome Opeña has been working in comics since 2005. He got his start with *Metal Hurlant* for Humanoids Publishing and went on to work on *Fear Agent*, his first collaboration with Rick Remender. The two would work together again at Marvel Comics on such series as *Punisher*, *Avengers* and a critically acclaimed run on *Uncanny X-Force*.

He currently resides in Brooklyn, New York.